Born in Chipping [illegible]
nell grew up in [illegible]
Prestwick, Port Eli[illegible]
medicine and then art before going to Sweden to teach English. He married in 1961 and settled in Hertfordshire soon after. He worked in publishing before becoming a freelance hack and graphic designer. Since 1974 he has lived in Ireland (the spiritual home of all writers in English) and has concentrated on historical novels under a number of pen-names. His elder daughter is a molecular biologist; his younger daughter works in publishing.

Also by M. R. O'Donnell

Hell Hath No Fury

A Woman Scorned

M. R. O'Donnell

KNIGHT

First published in 1991
by HEADLINE BOOK PUBLISHING PLC

First published in paperback in 1992
by HEADLINE BOOK PUBLISHING PLC

This edition published 1997 by
Knight an imprint of Brockhampton Press

10 9 8 7 6 5 4 3 2 1

ISBN 1 86019 6241

Phototypeset by Intype, London

Printed and bound in Great Britain by
Mackays of Chatham PLC, Chatham, Kent

Brockhampton Press
20 Bloomsbury Street
London
WC1B 3QA

For
Tom and Caren Farrell

Never short for a word
Never too long with a story

PART ONE

PARTRIDGE IN A PUTTOCK'S NEST

27 August 1881

He sprang out at her from behind a clump of pheasant bower. 'Perdition catch my soul but I do love thee!' he exclaimed.

'Oh, it's you,' Henrietta said.

'Could you ever give us the lend of five shillings?' he added in the same ringing tone – as if that, too, were from Shakespeare.

'Go and see King. He'll give you the lend of some work.'

'He will find me notable cause to work,' the man echoed as he shambled off through the woods in the general direction of the house.

'Who – or what – on earth was that?' Judith asked, eyeing the ragged fellow with a mixture of amusement and distaste.

'Mad McLysaght,' Henrietta replied, slightly surprised.

'Ah! So that's what he looks like.'

'Have you never seen him before?'

Judith shook her head; her long, dark hair rippled down her back, letting in the most pleasant little draughts of air to cool her. She closed her eyes, raised her face to the skies – or, rather, to the canopy of green leaves above them – and repeated the gesture, breathing deeply.

'Did you know,' Henrietta continued, 'that he used to be a schoolmaster? He knows all of Shakespeare by heart. Now he tramps the lanes and sleeps under the ditches and begs for his living. And he's "great gas", as they say, and always ready with a bit of crack.' She sighed the single word: 'Men!' in the tones of her elder sister, Winifred.

Judith, who was doing her best to be grown up now that she had reached the magical age of fifteen – which seemed about ten times older than fourteen – sighed, too. Then, feeling this small token of agreement wasn't enough, she said scornfully: 'A man with education, too!' She envied her friend's decisive manner and firm opinions. Henrietta was sixteen on that very same day – poised now between the schoolroom and the world.

'Crossed in love – or so they say,' Henrietta added. She repeated the word, with a scorn equal to Judith's: 'Love!'

'Quite,' Judith replied severely. Her thoughts dwelled briefly on Rick Bellingham, who was still only fourteen. He was hopelessly and passionately in love with her – which was nice in one way and rather alarming in another. 'You were very firm with him,' she added.

Henrietta, basking in her young acolyte's admiration, tried one of her father's sentiments: 'Firm is it!' she exclaimed. 'If I had my way, they'd bring back the stocks for men like that. Rick adores him, of course.'

'Golly!' Judith was thrilled at her severity. She wondered could you learn to be like that or did you have to be born to it? Henrietta – indeed, all the Bellinghams – seemed born to it; but then Judith remembered overhearing her own parents talking about their rich neighbours once and remarking that they had been nothing but small farmers in the seventeen-forties: 'Which was only four generations back, after all.'

The two girls came out from under the trees and on to the drive. Henrietta ran a critical eye over the gravel, looking for tyre-marks the rakers might have missed, for

Castle Moore was not one of those leaking, impoverished old country seats with buckets and umbrellas in every bedroom; Castle Moore had two groundsmen who did nothing but rake the gravel drives and the paths in the formal gardens all day – and God help them if the marks of a visitor's arrival were still there at his or her departure! Finding all to her satisfaction, she linked arms with Judith. 'Well, young 'un,' she said, 'it hasn't turned into much of a birthday for either of us, has it? Just another tediously hot August day.'

Her reward was immediate. 'Golly, Hen,' Judith gushed. 'Just being let come over here and be with you is better than any old present.'

Henrietta drew a deep draught of satisfaction and hugged her young friend's elbow tight. The drive led beneath two large, sentinel trees, a chestnut and a beech, before widening to form the carriage sweep in front of the castle. Their shade engulfed the two girls, who paused on its farther brink, delaying the plunge back into the harsh light of the sun. Neither mentioned the real reason for the postponement of their joint birthday party – the funeral of Major O'Neill. It wouldn't be right to hold a *proper* birthday party until after the old fellow was decently laid to rest. They had not liked him much, what little they had seen of him. Indeed, very few of his acquaintance would mourn his passing. But the manner of it had spread alarm throughout the entire countryside – or at least among those families who actually *owned* the countryside; for it was said that Land Leaguers had lured him to the lake and drowned him, making it seem like an accident. Henrietta's father, Colonel Bellingham, had gone about saying it was typical of their cowardice; they were afraid to come out and fight in the open like men. His friends in the Property Protection Society considered that a very courageous opinion – though this was not, perhaps, the wisest moment to deliver it.

Relishing the shade, the two girls let their eyes roam across the sunstruck gardens. Laid out almost a century ago, they were now approaching that perfection of colour, line, and tone which their original designers had seen only in their minds' eye. Castle Moore nestled on the westward slope of Mount Argus, one of the highest hills in that great glacial esker which runs across the Bog of Allen – indeed, across the whole of Ireland, from Dublin to Galway. At some unimaginably remote time in the past the Shannon had burst through this barrier and poured on down to where Limerick now stands, at the head of the estuary. In the wake of that geological catastrophe it had left a number of lakes, Lough Derg and Lough Cool among them. But the lake over which Castle Moore presided was man-made from shore to shore, as was the canal that connected it to Lough Cool. It had been started as a measure of relief for the poor in one of the many famines of the previous century; its present size of almost six acres was both a tribute to that charity and a grim commentary on the frequency of such famines.

Today, however, all was serene. Swans did their graceful duty upon its limpid waters, guiding their cygnets along its reedy fringes and sending out ripples to shatter the blinding white reflection of the marble pavilion on its farther bank. The nearer bank was free of reeds; indeed, it was not a bank at all but a stout wall of cut and dressed stone over whose top the lowest lawn grew to the very edge – a sort of watery haha, which drew a sharp line between the silver of the lake and the emerald turf. From there a meandering progression of Italian cypresses and balsam poplars, black by gold, led the eye up over a series of terraced lawns, five in all, to the castle itself.

Fifteen gardeners and five boys kept it all immaculate. Many of them were visible now, toiling in the blistering sun and, no doubt, Henrietta thought, envying the two young ladies their vantage in the shade. She gave another sigh of happiness. 'I do so love watching people work. Don't you?'

Judith shrugged her shoulders up tight to her neck and shivered. 'Yes!' she murmured.

Through the wide-open windows of the castle came the muted sound of the luncheon gong. 'Crikey!' Henrietta exclaimed as she set off at a brisk walk, dragging Judith with her. At the foot of the front steps, however, she caught sight of her mother, coming up from the garden with two maids, laden with baskets of cut flowers. 'Oh, we're safe,' she said and relaxed their pace to a saunter. 'I say,' she added, 'you are going to stay the night, I hope?'

Judith nodded but said nothing, as if to speak might tempt the gods too far.

'And you will sleep in my bed and share your chocolate with me?'

Another nod.

'And d'you know what else?' Henrietta licked her lips and gazed furtively around.

'What?' Judith whispered.

'We'll pull the sheet over our heads and tell each other our deepest, secretest secret. All right?'

Judith nodded, and blinked, and tried to swallow down the lump of gratitude in her throat.

The afternoon passed, as all summer afternoons ought, with a little riding, a game or two with the dogs, a turn on the lake, a desultory stab at a water colour, half a chapter of Sir Walter Scott, tea in the shade of the loggia, arguments, snoozes . . . and all capped with a lively discussion about the best arrangements for dinner. What with it being so hot, they decided to eat alfresco on the upper lawn. Then Henrietta said wouldn't it be fun to carry everything down to the lake and row across to the summer pavilion. Winifred chimed in with, 'Oh yes, let's!' Graham pointed out that the rowing boats weren't yet put away, so it would be easy enough to arrange. Even Philip raised no objection for once; he said they could get *The Star of the Shannon* fired up while they were eating and then go out for a grand cruise on Lough Cool before dark. Rick, the youngest, nodded eagerly. They all looked to the Colonel, daring him to veto the project.

He returned their stares like a bear in a trap. Maude, his wife, smiled at his dilemma. She knew that the notion appealed to him enormously, but she also knew that to 'give in' to his children's demands (as he would see it) would be almost like rewarding a mutiny. It amazed her that after all these years the youngsters still had not learned how to handle him; it would have been better for Winifred and Philip to disagree with the other three – thus putting their father in the seat of Solomon, where he rather liked to be. Still, it was probably more congenial to live in a household where the five of them were incapable of such deviously concerted action. She decided to offer the poor man a way out of his difficulties, and, turning to Judith with a smile, asked, 'What about our *other* birthday girl? Perhaps she should have the final word – seeing the day that's in it.'

Judith's heart skipped a beat. The thought that her preference might be heeded before Henrietta's was bad enough – even though they happened to coincide on this occasion; but that she might lay down the law for the grown-up children, as Winifred and her two older brothers seemed to her, was frightening beyond measure. And she didn't even dare *look* at the Colonel. Nonetheless, in the corner of her eye she saw him nod, which gave her just enough courage to whisper, 'The summer pavilion, please.' Then she closed her eyes and clenched her fists in angry shame, knowing she was as red as a turkey cock and must look worse than a boiled pudding.

Standing a little behind Henrietta and peeping over her shoulder, Rick stared at Judith in anguished sympathy. He would have kill't on the spot any friend who dared tease him for it, but he was so smitten in love with her that he hardly knew where to keep it all; sometimes he felt he would burst with it. She knew of his feelings, of course, but, having no experience of such devotion, was quite unable to respond. She could only be cold and prickly with him – which he accepted as a thoroughly justified reaction to his own knobbly, pimply, awfulness. Until today the only thing they had in common was their age; now she had leaped ahead of him and he would not be fifteen for another six months.

'So be it,' the Colonel declared.

They all cheered and made little jumps on the spot; the older ones exchanged rapid and rather self-conscious smiles – to put their childish behaviour, so to speak, between quotation marks.

It took quite some time for King, the butler, to reorganize the outing. Two footmen and the maids could have managed to haul the feast to the south terrace, but to carry it down to the lake and then across to the pavilion needed reinforcements. Grooms and boys were sent for, and Mad McLysaght was dispatched over the water to sweep out the pavilion and rake the twigs off the grass. 'My lips, that kiss'd the queen, shall sweep the ground,' he said as he dawdled to obey.

At last King was able to report that all was now ready. Then, chattering, laughing, happy, they made their way down the brick paths over the terraced lawns to the waiting boats. 'A brave sight they make,' commented Bridget Dolan, one of the maids already waiting at the pavilion. And a brave sight they made, indeed – the gentlemen all in evening dress, white tie and tails, and the ladies in summery chiffons and tulle and wide-brimmed hats alive with feathers. Kindly Winifred had even found something rather grown-up for Judith, so that she would not feel too out of place. Rick, in his sailor suit, was the only marked child among them. He brought up the rear, between the family and King, who was most imposing of all in his black tie and tails.

An urge to *do* something seized Rick. He ran a few paces, closing the gap between him and Judith, then touched her on the elbow and said, 'Race you to the water.'

After twenty yards or so he turned. She was the picture of indecision, caught between the adult dignity borrowed from her dress and the child who still ruled her desires. 'Ha ha!' he called triumphantly. 'Can't take the challenge, eh?'

She grabbed up her skirts and soon was level with him, racing for the lake. They flew like the wind, laughing, panting, gasping for breath, taunting each other.

'Rick!' the Colonel boomed.

But Rick did not even hear him.

Maude laid a gentle hand on her husband's arm.

'It isn't right,' he grumbled. 'Birthday or no birthday.'

'What's not right?' Winifred asked her mother, making it a matter of interpretation; a direct question to her father might seem pert.

'That little gel is too ready to take up a challenge,' the Colonel told her. 'She's starting to be a woman now. She must learn to curb her ambitions.'

'I shall speak to her about it,' Maude promised. 'Henrietta, dear, do have a word with her, won't you?'

Henrietta gave her promise she would and, rarely for her, intended to keep it, too. She had been rather pleased at the way she had been able to monopolize Judith most of the day, especially when she remembered that this time last year everyone had called the two young ones 'The Siamese Twins'. But Rick, of course, for all his shyness, had spotted the one chink in Judith's new armour: her inability to leave a thrown-down gauntlet where it lay.

The two youngsters arrived at the lakeside with barely a whisker between them. Judith teetered on the stone-walled rim and would have fallen in had Rick not grasped her wrist and pulled her back. 'That proves I beat you,' she panted.

'Or,' he riposted between gasps of his own, 'I got here first and was well set to stop you.'

'Didn't.' She had no breath for more.

'Did.'

'Didn't!'

'You're right,' he conceded.

She shot him a disappointed glance and he realized she wanted an argument. But then he went and picked the wrong topic on which to give her the satisfaction. 'It's that silly dress thing they found for you,' he said.

She turned a chilly profile to him and stared across the lake.

He glanced around and saw that the grown-ups were still satisfyingly far off. 'Actually,' he murmured, 'I think it's jolly pretty.'

She heard the distress in his voice, knew what he really wanted to tell her, and, as always, felt herself pulled in two contrary directions at once. Half of her basked in his admiration, half of her prickled with alarm and sought wildly for an exit. 'Make up your mind,' she said.

'I did,' he insisted.

She waited for him to repeat the flattery but he, remembering that Graham had once said, 'A compliment a day should be enough for any woman, or she'll have the balls off you,' held his tongue.

They were still thus, side by awkward side, when the others arrived. With a single vexed glance the Colonel managed to convey to the pair of them that he would not welcome any further indiscipline of that sort.

They required three boats. King rowed the first, Graham the second, and Rick and Judith, each to an oar, brought up the rear with Henrietta as their sole passenger. Halfway across the lake they entered a pocket of much cooler air, a welcome change from the enervating humidity at the water's edge. As if it were a signal they all began to chatter and laugh again. The wild garden, as the area around the pavilion was called, had always been a free and easy sort of place where, by unstated consent, the strict formality of life at the castle could be relaxed without threatening the entire fabric of family and nation. Judith, infected by it already, turned to Rick and smiled slightly. He smiled back and said, 'We both won.'

'Look!' Henrietta squeezed Judith's arm. 'A kingfisher.' She pointed to an iridescent dart of colour at the head of the lake, where the feeder canal entered it.

'I found his nest this afternoon.' Rick cut himself neatly back into the conversation. 'It's quite near the boathouse. I'll show you when we go for our cruise.'

Henrietta shot him an exasperated glance but it passed him by for he had suddenly remembered seeing a poacher there, in the woodland to the north of the pavilion, just before he found the kingfisher's nest. He meant to tell his father of it when they arrived at the jetty on the wild-garden shore, but a cry from Mad McLysaght put it out of his mind: 'Loud applause and aves vehement!' The fellow bowed and swept off his battered hat with such aplomb that, unless you looked at it closely, you'd swear it was plumed with feathers like a cavalier's. '*Ave et valete*!'

This latter sentiment displeased King, who snapped, 'Less tongue, you! Have you firing enough to keep off the midges?'

'Oh God, I have,' he replied.

'Well, set to then,' the Colonel told him tartly.

A dense belt of trees formed a dramatic backdrop to

the white marble pavilion; from where they stood the sun was just starting to disappear over the tops, so they faced a large pool of shade, hushed and inviting. The diners sauntered up the terraced path and clustered in loose order of precedence around the buffet, birthday girls first. There they pointed out the viands that took their fancy, leaving the maids to compile each plate and bring it to them at the table. The service was of fine English Spode, the cutlery of Sheffield steel, the silver bore the hallmarks of London, the glass was best English Derby flint. The ham, however, was Irish and the rest of the food more local still, since it all came off their own estate – even the cold pheasant, the first of the season.

They sent Mad McLysaght to the boathouse at the head of the lake, to kindle the fire in the steamer's boilers.

There was cheerful crack around the table as stomachs that had endured the extra half-hour's delay took their reward.

'Oh, I'm so glad we decided to eat in the pav!' Maude spoke for them all. 'We've never had a disappointing meal down here, have we? I can't remember one.'

'It's just such a perfect spot,' Winifred put in; her eye lingered lovingly on the landscape all about them. Next week she was going to stay with Aunt Bill and Uncle Arthur in Winchester, until she'd caught a husband, and was already feeling nostalgic at having to leave Ireland.

Watching her, and listening to the bright chatter all around – so unruffled, so confident – Judith suddenly realized what it was about that place, its precise quality of perfection.

The trees behind them obscured what would otherwise be a view across Lough Cool to the hills of County Clare; thus the eye was forced to look east, across the lake to the terraced lawns that rose to their visual crowning in the classical solidity of Castle Moore, with Mount Argus, blue and gold in the gathering dusk, behind it. At this particular hour of the evening the westering sun struck almost horizontal upon tree and grass and stone, making the whole scene resonate with a lambent fire. *And it was all theirs*! That was the unspoken, unmentionable cause of their delight: every twig the eye might discern, every boulder, every blade of grass, had the Bellingham name upon it. What member of that family would not relish sitting here on such an evening as this, monarchs of all they surveyed?

Judith caught Bridget Dolan's eye; the maid smiled cheerfully. *To her*, the young girl thought, *I probably seem one of them*.

King bent over her. 'A little more pheasant, Miss Judith?' he asked. Beads of light perspiration stood out on his lips; his hand trembled as he carried away her plate for a second helping. He was solicitous rather than deferential; he, of course, would never confuse a mere Carty with one of the Bellinghams.

Their pudding was the standard birthday treat – home-made lemon ice cream brought down in a haybox; it was just starting to melt and made a perfect accompaniment to the strawberries, which were rather warm and sweet enough to need no sugar.

Graham, who was to accompany Winifred over the sea and then go on to visit the Holy Land, started a conversation on the sights he hoped to see there.

Rick, soon growing bored with talk of the Dead Sea and Bethlehem, kicked idly at the table leg and caught Philip by mistake. To cut short the ensuing altercation their mother gave the two youngsters permission to get down. 'Go and see how long a daisy chain you can make,' she cooed.

'First show us this kingfisher's nest,' Henrietta said, slipping from the table as if she assumed the permission included her. 'I don't believe you found it at all.'

King followed them a short way. 'If ye'll slip into the plantation there,' he murmured, 'I'll see ye all right. I'll send in another helping of the ices, the way it won't be noticed.'

The two younger ones were tempted but Henrietta said, 'On our way back thank you, King.'

Still he seemed reluctant for them to go. 'It might have melted by then,' he warned.

'Of course it won't!' Henrietta said curtly.

At that the butler had no choice but to return to his duties.

It was four hundred slow, sauntering paces to the boathouse, beyond which lay the nest, or so Rick maintained. But they never found it. As they passed the boathouse door Mad McLysaght came out to greet them and to ask what was afoot. When they told him he replied, 'Who finds the partridge in the puttock's nest?'

And at that moment the first shots rang out.

Rick's immediate thought was that they must have had the guns brought down, unseen, or at least unnoticed, by him, and were enjoying some sport, shooting at leaves and bottles floating in the lake; it would not be the first time.

But then they heard the two maids screaming.

Mad McLysaght sprang toward them from the boathouse door and knocked all three to the ground. 'For the love of God and all His angels,' he hissed, 'bide where ye are now.'

The firing continued, but there was no further screaming.

Rick stood up. The scene that met his eyes was one he never forgot: a crowd of men, ill kempt and roughly dressed, was ranged in a loose semicircle around the pavilion. Two had rifles, the rest carried pistols, and they were all firing calmly and methodically into the party. Before anyone could stop him Rick was on his feet and racing toward them, shouting: 'No! No!' From the corner of his eye he saw the two maids running off into the trees. King, who had been standing helplessly by, came running to intercept him. Rick tried to slip by but the butler put out a foot and tripped him.

'They'll kill you, too, you little fool!' he shouted as he pounced on the boy. 'Get behind me! D'ye hear? Get behind me and stay behind me, no matter what!'

Shocked and winded as he was, Rick would still have charged at the gunmen if the butler had not held him in so tight a grip.

The firing stopped. His nostrils filled with the sickly aroma of cordite, which hung like wraiths on the breezeless air. One of the riflemen looked around with a cold, satisfied smile. He had a red moustache and flaming red hair and his face was vaguely familiar but Rick could put no name to it. His eye fell on the boy and the smile vanished.

'That wan, too,' he shouted.

'You'll have to take me first,' King told him.

'Don't be thinking I wouldn't,' the fellow warned. 'Stand aside.'

The butler's grip on Rick's arm tightened. 'Don't you move, lad,' he murmured.

'One!' cried the man.

'Ye'll not have him,' King said.

'Two!' He raised his rifle to his shoulder again.

'Go back to hell where you came from!'

'Three!'

King folded his arms and watched the knuckle of the man's index finger whiten as it took first pressure on the trigger.

At that moment Judith broke free of Mad McLysaght's clutch and came racing toward the murderers.

'No, Rick, no!' she shouted. And: 'Don't shoot him!'

The gunman turned his rifle on her and fired when she

had covered no more than half the ground. The bullet caught her in the side, somewhere below her left arm, but she kept on running.

'That's no Bellingham girl,' called a voice from the back of the gang. It, too, was familiar to Rick, though again he couldn't place it.

Back by the boathouse, held fast in McLysaght's hands, Henrietta could think of nothing but the Lord's Prayer, which she began to intone in a voice she hardly recognized as her own. She got as far as 'Thy will be done . . .' and found she could remember no more. She just kept repeating the words, over and over.

The gunman recocked his rifle, took a more deliberate aim, and squeezed the trigger again. And again nothing happened. The bolt shot forward with a click like a fat electrical spark, but no report followed. 'Shite!' he cried and cocked one more time. By now Judith was almost on him. He aimed from the hip and pulled the trigger. For the third time it refused to fire.

She fell upon him with twenty-eight teeth and all ten fingernails. He stumbled beneath her onslaught but his superior size and strength soon told. A few moments later he rose again, leaving her senseless and bleeding on the grass.

People were running down the lawns now – footmen, gardeners, grooms, and, most menacing of all, gamekeepers, armed as always against poachers. Though they were still on the far side of the lake, they could spread through the woodland to the south of it and cut off any escape that way.

'Come on, now,' shouted one of the gang. 'This is gettin' too shaky altogether.'

'The boy!' roared the gunman, who seemed to be their leader. 'Give us the lend of your pistol while I finish off the boy.'

A shot rang out from the farther shore. One of the

gang fell dead, cleanly dropped with a bullet convenient to his left ear. The rest took to their heels and fled. When they were well clear of the butler and the boy, the shots from the farther shore came thick and fast. Another man fell, not dead but wounded; there were roars of pain from several others but they kept on running until they passed out of sight over the ridge. They were in their boat and well down the canal toward Lough Cool before the gamekeepers managed to reach the wild garden.

'Thy will be done . . . Thy will be done . . .' Henrietta kept repeating. But her voice tailed off as she heard Mad McLysaght repeat his earlier remark: 'Who finds the partridge in the puttock's nest . . .' This time, however, he completed the quotation: 'But may imagine how the bird was dead, Although the kite soar with unbloodied beak? Even so suspicious is this tragedy.'

From the four corners of the world – their world – they came. From Castle Bellingham in Norfolk, Uncle Hereward, the head of the family, took the first available train and ferry. Philip Montgomery required even longer to come by road from Freke in County Cork; he was Maude Bellingham's older brother, reputed to have a great head for business. Old Harry Bellingham, the colonel's younger brother, also turned up – a pretty useless sort of fellow but they couldn't go taking decisions without him. Had King not shielded Rick from the murderers, Harry would have inherited Castle Moore. O'Farrelly was there, of course, the solicitor from Simonstown – a Roman Catholic, but a sound man for all that, and very shrewd.

But first of all to arrive was Wilhelmina Montgomery, or Aunt Bill to the family – the aunt with whom Winifred had been going to stay near Winchester. She came principally to comfort Henrietta and Rick – and, to be sure, to help nurse the brave little girl who had tackled the murderers barehanded. However, her husband Arthur's parting words had been, 'If those howling asses make the sort of decision I think they're capable of making, you jolly well step in and put a stop to it, old girl, eh?'

'What sort of decision would that be, dear?' she had replied.

'How do I know?' was the helpful rejoinder. 'They're capable of absolutely anything.'

How typical of Arthur! When she'd suggested that he should accompany her and take a first-hand interest in the matter, he said he didn't see how adding one more fool to the party would improve the situation; what he meant was that Fruity Morgan had invited him down to Ashburton for some rough shooting and he didn't see why the murder of his sister, whom he had never particularly liked, and his brother-in-law, whom he detested, and his nieces and nephews, who were just a blur to him, should be allowed to get in the way of the serious business of life.

As the dog cart brought her up the long drive to Castle Moore, Aunt Bill wondered what decisions were, in fact, open to this gathering of the tribe. Surely it boiled down to one quite simple choice: they either sold up, or they didn't. If they sold up, she'd take Henrietta and Rick back to Winchester. Rick could go to Eton. If they didn't sell up . . . well, there'd be a lot of arranging to be done. She thought she might take Henrietta back to England, no matter what. Another couple of years and she'd come out; and it had always been Maude's intention for the two girls to have English husbands.

So there was the choice; good arguments abounded on both sides; how could anyone make a mess of it?

King met her at the door. 'What a terrible business, ma'am,' he said as footmen and maids edged past to gather up her bags. She told them that most of her luggage was following on behind with her maid. Then she turned to the butler.

'I want to shake your hand, King,' she announced.

He balked but she held out her own very firmly. 'This is also on my husband's behalf and, I'm sure, on behalf of the whole family, too.'

She could never have imagined so magisterial a man as King doing anything shyly, but that was his manner as he took her proffered hand and shook it; his grasp was limp, as if he thought it would be disrespectful to show his real strength. 'People make too much of it, ma'am.'

'You risked your life.'

'It didn't seem like it at the time, that's all I can say. People talk as if I weighed up all the pros and cons and made a deliberate choice. The truth is, I didn't even stop to think.'

'Then you have the right instincts, King – which is much more important than mere thinking. We can leave all the world's thinking to the clever people.'

Clever and *thinking* were fairly uncharitable words in Aunt Bill's vocabulary.

'You are very kind to say so, ma'am.' The ghost of a smile passed over his normally imperturbable features. 'Mrs King has placed you in the Holbein bedroom, if that is acceptable? It has a connecting door to the sick room.'

'Ah, where Miss . . . whatshername?'

'Carty.'

'Oh!' Aunt Bill's face fell. '*Those* Cartys?' she asked, hoping against hope.

King nodded. 'I'm afraid so, ma'am.'

'Ah, well.' She squared her shoulders to the distressing news. 'And how is Mrs King?'

'Bearing up very well, thank you, ma'am. The entire house, as you may imagine, is . . .' He sought for words that would be strong without being intrusive.

'I can, indeed, imagine,' she assured him. 'And Miss,

ah, Carty? I'd better go to her at once, I suppose. Bite the bullet. The fellow who brought me from the station said she was not as badly . . .' The gestures of pulling out her hatpin, taking off her hat, and restabbing it completed the statement.

'Indeed, Mrs Montgomery, she lost a great deal of blood and her lung was collapsed, but Dr Wheelehan says time will cure both with little need for intervention.'

'Poor child. And tell me about Master Rick? I've been wondering how he . . . ?' Another gesture – a wave of the hand this time – made substitute for the words.

King hesitated. They had reached the turn at the half-landing. He, being on the inside, had got ahead of her. He paused for her to catch up but she could not tell if that was what had made him hesitate in answering. 'He's not . . . ?' she prompted.

'Still waters run deep, ma'am,' he replied. 'He's a deep little man at the best of times.'

'Deep?' The opinion took her aback. Married to Arthur, and with three sons patterned after him, she could not equate the word 'deep' with anything in trousers; and Rick had always seemed to her a perfectly ordinary little boy – furtive, devious, ugly, and vexatious, even if he was not downright wicked. 'Deep, eh?' she repeated. 'D'you mean he shows no grief at all?'

'He *shows* none,' King agreed as they reached the stairhead. 'Yet I believe he's the one the family should watch. If I may . . .' Like her he left the thought unspoken.

'Well, I've never known your judgement to be at fault, King, especially not your judgement of people. We shall certainly keep an eye on him.'

King inclined his head, gave a light tap on the sick-room door, opened it without waiting for a reply, and inclined his head the other way to usher Aunt Bill within. He returned to his duties, which were heavy that day.

Aunt Bill recognized Judith at once, though she had not seen her for two years and the girl had grown considerably in that time. She also remembered – now – that she rather liked the little thing, despite her unfortunate parentage. 'My dear! Oh, my poor dear!' She sailed across the enormous bedroom, arms high, tears already forming. As she covered the last few paces she was surprised to discover that her grief was quite genuine. Her heart melted at the sight of Judith, pale as a beautiful ghost and with great bruised rings around her eyes.

'Oh, Mrs Montgomery,' she said wanly.

'My poor dear!' Aunt Bill repeated, somewhat at a loss. As she sank to the bed and gingerly clutched the girl's arm to her breast she was vaguely aware of a female figure withdrawing to the far end of the chamber. 'Your mother?' she asked Judith quietly, arching her brows and inclining her head toward this other person.

Judith shook her head, wincing slightly. 'That's Miss Flavell, the nurse. My mother went home to prepare my room. The doctor says I can . . .' She winced again.

The tears brimmed over in Aunt Bill's eyes. Judith stared up in sympathy but had none left to add.

The older woman took a grip on herself. 'Well, dear.' She sat upright on the edge of the bed and dabbed her cheeks. 'You are quite the heroine of the hour. The newspapers are full of it. Have you seen them? Everyone is coming, of course. The whole family. You'll be quite sick of our praises before long, I'm sure. So you'd better practise not-showing-it on *me*!' She heard the unfortunate ambiguity in her earlier words and modified them: 'The whole *remaining* family. My husband is devastated of course but . . .' She waved a vague hand at the world out there, hoping to suggest that things had to go on somehow.

'He had ginger eyebrows,' Judith said. 'And his hair was bright red.'

Aunt Bill's first thought was that she was referring to Uncle Arthur – who had hardly any hair on his head at all. Then she realized who the girl was talking about. 'Ah,' she said.

'King doesn't agree. He says the man was dark. Just plain dark. But I'm sure I'm right.'

After a pause the other said, 'You must try to forget it, dear. I know that's utterly impossible at the moment but as time goes by you'll find yourself able to do it. And the sooner you start, the better, don't you think?'

'One of the others had a very big nose. King says he was a Jew-man, but I don't think so.'

'A Fenian Jew?' Aunt Bill echoed dubiously. 'It certainly sounds unlikely.'

'The funeral is tomorrow. The coroner has . . . agreed.' The correct term was 'released the bodies' but she could not say it.

Aunt Bill wondered whether the girl was hinting that she should be allowed to attend; missing a funeral in Ireland is worse than missing a wedding. Best to say nothing, though, unless she actually came out with it. Best to talk of other things – but what? 'Are you comfortable, darling? Or as comfortable as can be expected? Is there anything I can get you?'

'Is Rick's Uncle Hereward coming? I heard them say he was. Will he take Rick away with him?'

Aunt Bill smiled firmly. 'I don't think you ought to bother your head about such matters at all, my dear. I'm sure you've always been taught not to think of yourself, to forget your own troubles and woes, but that's just for ordinary everyday silly little things. When a person is as seriously ill as you, it becomes a positive duty to forget everything else and just concentrate on your own recovery. Has Reverend Waring called? Perhaps they didn't let him see you?'

'I think I saw him.'

'Then I'm sure he told you to devote all your thoughts and energies to getting well again.'

Judith nodded but with little conviction; then a feeble smile twitched the corners of her lips. She reached out a pale, skinny hand and touched the other. 'They mustn't sell up the estate, Mrs Montgomery. They must stand up for what's right. Make them see that.'

'My dear!' She laughed nervously. 'What an intense little woman you are! But such matters will be decided by far wiser heads than ours.'

A vague rogues' gallery of senior gentlemen in the family flitted disconcertingly past her mind's eye. *Far wiser heads*? She shrugged it off. Why did one tell children such things? Because they had eyes in their heads and could see the truth for themselves. And if they couldn't? Well, it was better to live with a comforting fiction than an uncomfortable truth.

'Tell me about Rick,' Aunt Bill suggested. 'Is he . . . ? Well, *how* is he?'

There was a faint cough from across the room. Aunt Bill glanced up and saw the nurse, standing at the window. She had quite forgotten her. Now the woman pointed at something outside. Aunt Bill rose and went to join her, thinking she might be wanting to draw attention to a new arrival but without saying the name aloud in front of her patient.

However, the carriage sweep was empty. She glanced at the nurse, who pointed again. Now, following that finger more carefully, she saw what had provoked the gesture. It was an answer to her question about Rick – for there he stood, a small, lone figure down by the water's edge, staring across the lake. 'Oh, that's bad!' she exclaimed.

The nurse stared at her in surprise.

'I don't mean naughty-boy bad,' Aunt Bill responded,

vexed at her careless outburst. 'I mean surely that can't be good for him.'

'What?' Judith asked. 'Is it Rick? Is he down by the lake again?'

Aunt Bill turned to her. 'Does he stand there often?'

From the corner of her eye she saw the nurse nod; Judith nodded, too. 'I'll go down to him,' she said; then, turning to the nurse, 'I'm sorry, I should have introduced myself. I'm Mrs Montgomery, Rick's aunt.'

The nurse introduced herself; she seemed well spoken but they did not shake hands.

While Aunt Bill had been seeing Judith, her maid had arrived with the main baggage – fourteen trunks and cases in all. The girl paused in her supervision of their removal to the Holbein room long enough to help her mistress into her hat and cape. Aunt Bill, feeling those deft fingers at work on the intricacies of her hat and pin, was greatly comforted. Normality was being restored to her world. She hated travel – or, rather, she hated the dislocation of travel, having to do things for herself that were normally done by others. She always felt clumsy when pinning up her own hat, for instance; not that she *was* clumsy, but she had been brought up to *feel* so.

'I'm just going down to the lake,' she said.

The sun came out as Aunt Bill went down over the lawns. It had rained heavily overnight – and for several days previously, judging by the proliferation of worm casts among the grass and the sticky, bubbling noises that followed wherever she trod. The breeze was westerly and Rick heard nothing of his aunt's approach until she was almost upon him.

All the way down she wondered what on earth she was going to say to him. What could one tell a child to whom such an appalling thing had happened? The obvious phrases rose to mind – the happy memories he must always cherish . . . the splendid example his two elder brothers had set him . . . the courage with which they had all faced those wicked, wicked murderers . . .

How *correct* it all sounded – and yet how trite and inadequate!

She had never had any fondness for boys, not even her own, but the sight of Rick standing there at the water's edge, staring across at an emptied place, touched something quite elemental within her. He looked so young and vulnerable it provoked her to a sudden and overwhelming love – and with it came a rage of towering proportions. All at once she found herself wanting to tell him never to forget those evil faces, to grow up nursing always his hatred of the murderers and what they had done, to dedicate his life to hunting them down and making them pay for their crime, to wreak upon each and every one the most horrible vengeance his fury could devise.

She was so taken aback by these sentiments she had to pause and try to recollect who she was and what she really believed in. She was, she reminded herself, Wilhelmina Montgomery, respectable and respected wife these last thirty years to 'Wonky' Montgomery of Witney Hall, near Winchester. And she was mother of three grown-up sons – a captain in the Irish Guards, a barrister of the Inner Temple, and a curate at St George's Chapel, Windsor . . .

It achieved nothing; that world seemed so far away, so . . . she could hardly believe it but the only word that occurred to her was *superficial*.

And suddenly she realized who she *really* was, even after all these years: she was still young 'Bill' O'Hara, the terror of Letterfrack in the wilds of Connemara. And then she remembered what she believed in. She believed the winds that howled off the Atlantic at night were the voices of the unquiet dead, calling out their wrongs to the quick, and keening for vengeance; Mrs Joyce, her old nanny, had taught her that. She believed, too, in blood – the kind that ran thicker than water; she believed 'family' was a clan that went far beyond the pathetic little huddle of brother and sister, mammy and daddy. She believed its demands transcended country and state to vie with those of God himself. And in that chilling moment of self-revelation she believed these things with a passion that almost rent her in two.

'What can I do?' she murmured aloud, trying not to surrender to her panic.

'Aunt Bill!'

She spun round to see young Rick flying at her, all knees and elbows. 'Oh, my darling!' she cried, scooping him up and hugging him to her with a strength she did not know she possessed. For he was now the only welcome element in her entire universe – his grief, his pain, his need for her comfort. She buried herself in it to blot out . . . she would not even name it, whatever it was that had come over her like that. Her ancient blood.

She felt a tremor pass through him and, glad of the chance to ask a question that would nudge her back toward a more familiar world, said, 'Are you cold, my lamb? You're shivering. Surely you're not cold?'

The accustomed cosseting of an adult released him. He laughed and slipped from her embrace; she did not resist. 'D'you want me to show you where it happened?' he asked.

The Aunt Bill who had set off from the house a mere five minutes ago stared at him in horror; but the earlier incarnation she had met upon the way now impelled her to answer a simple, 'Very well.'

'Oh!' He was surprised at her ready acceptance; everyone else had told him not to be so macabre. Until this week he hadn't known the meaning of the word. 'This way, then,' he said, holding out a hand to her.

Ageless suddenly, no older than he, yet older than his most ancient ancestor – adrift in time, one could more accurately say – she followed a half-pace behind him, letting him pull her gently, letting this re-enactment be part of his will, not hers. They walked around the northern shore of the lake.

'Did you have a good crossing?' he asked. It was what people always asked visitors from over the water.

'They say it rained heavily, but I slept through it all. Have you been sleeping well?'

'Perfectly, thank you. I haven't had bad dreams about it or anything.'

Was he fishing for compliments? It didn't feel like that. She suspected that his mood and hers were in complete accord. The two creatures walking hand in hand and talking so politely were mere shells, masks of politeness worn to deceive the spirits of this numinous place; by contrast, the two creatures walking flesh in flesh, listening in disbelief to that trivial chatter, were engaged in primitive business that was far less easily named.

'There's the kingfisher's nest,' he said as they crossed the little wooden bridge above the boathouse. 'He's never returned since that night.'

They had to let go hands to cross in single file; they did not resume their clasp when they reached the other side. Instead Rick waved at the wild garden and said, 'There!' He finished the gesture by pointing at the boathouse. 'The roof blew off when *The Star of the Shannon* exploded. Mad McLysaght lit the boiler. He saved my life as much as King, you know. And Judith's and Hen's.'

'Tell me,' she said.

He described the events of that evening, up to the moment when he had broken free of Mad McLysaght's protective grip and raced up over the wild garden toward the carnage. Now, too, he took to his heels and sprinted up over the well-trampled grass toward the pavilion. 'Come on!' he shouted over his shoulder. 'It was like this.'

And Aunt Bill, who could not remember the last time she had run (but whose muscles could suddenly remember, as if it were yesterday, running free in the Connemara winds), picked up her hems and sprang after him. The distance was not enough to wind her but when she arrived at his side she drew several deep breaths nonetheless. His lips were smiling but not his eyes; they shone with something wilder than mere humour, something more compelling, too. He raised his arm level with his shoulder and pointed: 'They just stood there, firing into the pavilion, over and over again. And the man was smiling . . .'

'Which man?'

'The one with the red moustache. The one who wanted to shoot me, too. He was smiling all the time.'

She grasped him by both arms and turned him toward her, giving him a little shake. 'Can you see the face on him?' she asked, spittle flying off her lips. 'Would you know the divil again, a hundred years from now?'

Her words, her phraseology, took him by surprise, though they would be common enough on the lips of any servant at Castle Moore. 'I would so,' he breathed in the same idiom. 'By God I would.'

'See you do,' she told him, still staring into his eyes, trying to impress upon him all those things that could never be said – at least, not in the genteel language they had both grown up with.

He nodded slowly, not taking his eyes off hers, not flinching, though her grip was turning painful.

'See you do,' she repeated, and let him go at last.

He rubbed his arms, not as one who rubs to ease a minor hurt, but favouring the red marks of her hands – as if they were the source of some new power within him.

'Will you take supper with us tonight, Aunt Bill?' he asked. 'Hen and me.'

'Aunt Bill', as she gradually became once more, smiled to realize it was the new owner of Castle Moore who spoke, making it an invitation rather than a mere request. 'I'll certainly sit with you. But Uncle Hereward is expected, too, you know. Someone will have to act as hostess.'

He nodded and took her hand. Now there was no urgency in the gesture; his need to relive, to re-enact that terrible drama was, for the moment, sated.

'Poor little Judith Carty,' she said as they retraced their steps past the ruined boathouse.

The sudden change of subject broke his stride but not for long. 'Yes.' It was a clipped, expressionless monosyllable.

'What possessed her to do such a thing?'

'Possessed,' he echoed.

'When I told King how grateful we all are, he said he did it without even thinking. Perhaps it was the same with Judith. She has the right instincts.'

He nodded. 'Hen would have done the same except that Mad McLysaght had her pinned tight after Ju wriggled free.'

'Yes, I'm sure. I've not seen Henrietta yet.' After a pause she added, 'I'll probably be taking her back to Winchester with me. We'll bring her out in due course – as we intended doing with Winnie.'

'Yes,' he replied. 'It's very good of you and Uncle Arthur.'

'I was wondering about this friend of hers, Judith Carty? Would she care to come too – just to convalesce. What d'you think?'

The sudden grip of his hand was electric. 'Friend of *hers*?' he echoed.

'Isn't she? That's what I assumed.'

He made no reply. She glanced at him and saw he was staring up at the house, his jaw set, the muscles rippling on his temples. 'Whose friend is she then?' she asked.

The tips of his ears flushed but still he said nothing. Again her heart overflowed with tenderness for him. She wondered how it was that she, who had no very warm feelings toward her own sons – and certainly not at the pimply age of fourteen – should feel like this for one who was not even a blood relation. But even as the thought entered her mind she knew it was false. They might not be blood relations, yet somehow there *was* a relationship between them now – and blood was of its very essence.

Uncle Hereward, hatless and without gloves, was standing at the edge of the carriage sweep. He was staring down over the lawns toward the lake and the wild garden. Aunt Bill, having at last changed out of her travelling costume, came down for tea and, noticing him there, went out to join him. 'I saw you and the boy,' he said with a nod at the pavilion. 'D'you think that was wise?'

'Yes,' she said without hesitation.

He looked at her sharply, making her realize she was being unusually positive. 'Really?' he murmured and stared again at the pavilion, as if it might tell him more. 'This bloody country!' he added. 'Fifty years of concessions and where has it got us?'

Uncle Hereward had never sworn in her presence before; he had always considered her too middle class to deserve the privilege – though with Maude his tongue had been very free. She realized she was being promoted. Dead lady's shoes.

'They know who did it,' he went on. 'They have the names of every last one.'

'How?' she asked.

'They caught the injured fellow, the one the gamekeeper shot. Darcy – good Protestant family, too. He sang like a linnet. We'll get them all now.'

'Including the man with the red moustache, I hope.'

'Say?' He frowned at her.

'He would appear to be the ringleader, according to Rick – and the Carty gel. He made a great impression on them both.'

'Ah, well, their identification will be helpful no doubt, but the other man's confession is enough.' He chuckled at the word. 'Confession! Yes, by golly! The best thing we ever did was to emancipate the opposition. Their bishops are tumbling over each other to appear respectable now.' He clapped his hands and rubbed them in rhythmic circles; the dry skin hissed like a steam engine. Old skin, she thought. 'Here comes Philip,' he added, proving that his hearing, old or not, was as acute as ever. He chuckled. 'He won't be pleased to see we've both got here before him.'

'I wonder if he's brought Felicity this time?' Wilhelmina mused aloud.

The old man chuckled again. 'I always rather thought it was a case of Felicity bringing him. She's the one who wears the trousers in that household.'

There it was again. Until now he would never have used the word *trousers* in her presence, either.

Over the next few hours the party assembled in ones and twos; they were fourteen in all who sat around the dinner table that night – the family, the lawyers, the agents, and friends. Wilhelmina was hostess by unspoken consent – the aunt who would now foster the two orphans. The sentiments Uncle Hereward had voiced to her that afternoon were repeated in a hundred different forms: the murderers were known, they would be caught, they would be hanged . . . and one day, God willing, this country would be pacified at last. But their talk went no deeper than that. They all knew each other's views; they knew how divided they were on the vexed subject of what to 'do' about Ireland; and though at any other time they would have enjoyed a little cut and thrust, some gentle bloodletting, this was hardly the occasion.

It might be different, of course, once the ladies left. There were only three of them: Felicity Montgomery, Teresa Bellingham, Harry's wife, and Wilhelmina herself. Since none of them had any stomach for the pudding – a very stodgy spotted dick, served in honour of Uncle Hereward – they withdrew early.

'I wonder what they'll decide?' Teresa said as they settled themselves in the drawing room.

Felicity shivered and pulled her wrap round her more tightly. 'D'you think we might have a fire?' she asked.

Teresa was shocked, not only because she considered the night rather warm but also because it was well known among them that the Colonel had never allowed a fire at Castle Moore before the middle of October.

Wilhelmina glanced up at the footman and nodded. He went to find matches and kindling.

Bridget Dolan, one of the maids, passed him in the door, bearing a tray of coffee. 'Cook said you wouldn't be out the dining room this quick and I said you would,' she told them.

Wilhelmina smiled and said, 'We fled before the spotted dick.'

Bridget nodded. 'Isn't it what I'm after telling her. She's a great cook for the men.'

Teresa was leafing through *Punch* while Felicity tried to peek over her shoulder, but they both looked up when Wilhelmina said to the maid, 'You were actually down there that night, weren't you, Dolan?'

'I was indeed, ma'am,' she said with a reserved sort of pride; but Wilhelmina was quick to notice the wary glint that had crept into her eye.

'Why did they do it, d'you think?' she asked. 'What's the local opinion on that?'

'Mr King says . . .'

'I don't mean Mr King,' she interrupted. 'I mean local opinion. I'll bet they've talked about nothing else since it happened.'

'Indeed they have, ma'am. Sure there's enough air expended on that particular topic to dry all the thatch in Ireland.'

'So what are they saying?'

The woman turned the frankest, bluest pair of eyes upon her. 'Well, I want to tell you about that, ma'am. For the truth of it is, you could listen all year and not hear a whisper as to why.'

'Not a single word?' Felicity, being English, put the question that Teresa, being Irish, knew better than to ask.

'Divil a one, ma'am.'

'But there must be *some* opinion as to the cause,' Felicity pointed out.

'I'll be round with the cream in a hack,' the maid said as she handed out the coffee cups.

'You yourself, now,' Felicity persisted. 'What do you think?'

'Ah well,' Bridget replied easily, 'with fellas like that, ma'am, sure who'd know *what* to be thinking?'

'Are the Castle Moore rents notoriously more oppressive than any others around?'

'There was never a tenant born who didn't complain of the rents, ma'am,' Bridget told her. 'Will I bring you another pot in fifteen minutes or what?'

'No thank you, Dolan,' Wilhelmina replied. 'You may go off now. What's the footman's name, by the way?'

'King, ma'am.' Her face was devoid of expression. 'Tommy King.'

'Oh, really!' Wilhelmina's eyebrows shot up. 'Is he . . . ?'

'A second cousin once removed, ma'am.'

'When did he start here, may I ask?' Teresa put in.

'Yesterday, ma'am.' The woman curtsied and left.

Felicity rose and went to the curtains. Wilhelmina, shocked, thought she was going to draw them and was about to ring for a servant when she saw that her sister-in-law just wanted something to grip and shake in her frustration. 'Why can one *never* get a straight answer to anything in this bloody country!' she exclaimed.

Wilhelmina and her other sister-in-law exchanged amused glances. 'It seemed pretty straight to me,' Teresa said.

'I fail to see that,' Felicity challenged. ' "Sure and begorrah, missiz, wid fellas like dem, a poor colleen the likes of meself wouldn't be knawin' what to be t'inkin' at all at all!" Call that a straight answer?'

'It requires a little judicious unpacking, I agree,' Wilhelmina replied consolingly. 'It needs to be taken in context. But I think we can safely assume these were no ordinary Land League rebels. There was something personal – or *other*, anyway – behind it. Personal or political.'

'How can you possibly infer all that?' Felicity returned to the sofa, sipped her coffee, and pulled a face.

'From her demeanour.' She turned to Teresa. 'Don't you agree, dear?'

Teresa nodded. 'King hasn't wasted much time, has he!' she remarked. 'We must see to it that our hero doesn't start getting ideas above his station, I think.'

At that moment Tommy King returned with an armful of logs and tinder. They were very dry and within moments he had a grand blaze going.

'You're new here, aren't you,' Teresa said as he stood and surveyed his handiwork.

He had a good figure and broad shoulders, which his

livery showed off well. None of the women particularly wanted him to go. And he, aware of it, turned and smiled like a gentleman at his own hearth. 'I started yesterday, ma'am, but I have a certain pull with the quare fella.'

Wilhelmina laughed. 'So we heard.'

''Twould have been a shame to waste it,' he added. 'The iron being so hot and all. Now, is there any other service you ladies might be requiring?' He gave each a brief, roguish smile.

'Yes,' Felicity snapped. 'You can tell us your honest opinion of this dreadful business. Why d'you think those men did it?'

The other two groaned inwardly but kept an impassive exterior.

The man was solemn at once. 'Sure, there's no mystery there,' he said firmly. 'Isn't this county only alive with Fenians and Land Leaguers?'

Wilhelmina exchanged a puzzled glance with Teresa, which the footman, being so eager to impress his words on Felicity, did not notice.

'Is it now?' Teresa asked.

In fact, Keelity enjoyed a reputation as one of the most pacified of Irish counties. It had been cleared out very successfully during and after the famine and was now rather noted for the prosperity of its tenant farmers, most of whom held rather more than the traditional four acres, which was still a mere dream for the majority of Irish peasants.

'Oh, it is, ma'am,' he said with a confidential shake of his curly locks. 'Indeed, it is. There's Major Ferguson after saving his hay with a squad of fusiliers in every headland. And there's no trader this side of Dublin would sell him a penny candle for fear his shop would burn down about his ears. You wouldn't want to set your nose out of doors, now, not one of ye, without a good pistol in your pocket and a good man, a good cudgel, and a good dog at your command.'

He strode to the door while they absorbed this intelligence. 'I'll be by the bell if ye want that fire building,' he said as he left.

'Well!' Felicity was even more exasperated now. 'Who on earth *are* we to believe?'

'I had no idea it was so grave,' Wilhelmina said thoughtfully. 'Maude said nothing in her letters.'

'Dog and cudgel,' Teresa exclaimed. 'In Keelity, too! Why, at one time you could walk the length and breadth of it with a five pound note in your open hand, and not even the *wind* would take it off you.'

'I give up,' Felicity said shrilly. 'I simply give up.'

'I certainly think we should sell up and get out,' Teresa added.

Wilhelmina stared at them with something close to contempt in her eye. 'Isn't that the very thing they want of us?' she said.

Shortly after that King himself came to the drawing room. Wilhelmina noticed he did not raise an eyebrow at the sight of the fire, so he must have had a word with his kinsman before coming in. In fact, she wondered, why *had* he come in. If they had sent the maid off, it was a clear sign they wanted no further service that night. Yet there he was, standing awkwardly by the fire, asking them if there was anything they required.

She took a chance. 'How are things going with the gentlemen, King?' she said.

The other two stared at her in astonishment; it was not the sort of thing one asked – certainly not in such direct terms. But to their surprise, instead of the embarrassment they felt sure the poor man must be suffering, they saw relief written all over his countenance.

'I didn't wish to bring it up, ma'am,' he replied, 'but, seeing as you ask it, I'll tell you they're talking of getting up some sort of a testimonial to me, and I wish you'd talk them out of it.'

'I will not!' Wilhelmina was as emphatic as could be. 'I would consider it a scandal if they did not make some such arrangement for you. I'm only surprised to hear they're discussing it at all. I would have thought it an open and shut argument.'

'But . . . d'you mean they're discussing it with you actually in the room?' Felicity asked.

'Not just with me in the room, ma'am, but with me in person. They want to know what form I'd like it to take.'

'And what did you tell them?' Teresa put in.

'Sure I said I wouldn't presume, ma'am.'

Wilhelmina sensed he hadn't told the half of it. 'How would it be presumptuous?' she asked. 'Especially as they put the question directly to you.'

He stared at her like a caged animal and she knew she had touched a nerve. 'You mean,' she continued, 'it wouldn't have been presumptuous in general – but the particular thing you desire to ask for would be presumptuous?'

His awkward nod conceded the shot had landed convenient to the bullseye, but all he said was, 'I'd sooner not talk of it, ma'am.'

She had half a mind to let him stew in his own juice, with an answer like that, for she was quite sure he *did* wish to talk of it – indeed, had come in here for no other purpose. However, she herself was also avid to learn what it might be so she pressed on with, 'You needn't be talking to *them* about it, King. There's ways and there's ways, you know.'

He bit his lip. His face creased at the effort of some titanic moral struggle within. Then at last he blurted out, 'It concerns the main purpose of this gathering, ma'am, so it's not for me to say anything.'

'Just a moment!' Felicity frowned at him in bewilderment. 'You're saying they asked you what form you would like this testimonial to take – and you can't tell them because it has something to do with the decisions they're taking about Castle Moore and the children?'

The man just shook his head again. 'I'd rather say no more, ma'am.' He even took a pace or two toward the door.

Don't fret, you have no need. You've said enough. Wilhelmina tried to project the thoughts at him.

Teresa was more blunt. 'For God's sake!' she exclaimed. 'You're not worried about your position here, are you? *We'd* take you like a shot.' She glanced at the other two ladies to make sure they noted she'd got her claim in first.

Understanding dawned in Felicity's eyes then. 'So would we,' she assured him.

He shook his head. 'It isn't that, ladies – though I thank you both for the kindly thought. No, it isn't that.'

'But . . . ?' Wilhelmina prompted when he fell again to silence.

He sighed. 'I can't break a confidence, ma'am. I can't repeat what it is they're after deciding back there. But I'll content myself with saying this much – had I the choosing of it, the last thing I'd do in the face of cowards and bullies like that is sell up and flee over the water "like a cod my doubled-up head and tail", as the song says.'

'Is that what they're at?' Teresa murmured.

'They are so, ma'am. And which landlord family in Ireland will be safe when the shutters go up at Castle Moore and the estate is sold off piecemeal to the tenants, for whatever they're obliging enough to offer?'

'Are they suggesting that?' Felicity asked. 'Surely not.'

King shook his head as if he, too, could hardly believe it. 'To see the Bellinghams turn and flee! Well, if that's all it takes, there'll be fresh murders every week in all thirty-three counties of Ireland, that's all I can say. Not that it's my place to pass such comments, mind.'

'But there's no family left, only the children.' Teresa began to grow excited at the suggestion (which she could just sense in the offing) that she and Harry should move in here to show the flag.

King dashed such hopes with his next remark. 'Leave the *boy* here, ma'am. Don't send him away to school – engage tutors for him. Let him be *here* to take the rents and give out the orders – and thumb the Bellingham nose at those blackguards.'

'And if we're boycotted?' Wilhelmina asked. The butler's suggestion was, to be sure, close to her own dearest wish, but she wanted to know how strong the man's resolve might be. She had met too many drawing-room heroes to leave such matters to chance.

'Sure, we're big enough to weather out that storm, ma'am,' he assured her. 'Couldn't we open our own store and serve the whole of the Keelity Property Protection Society – *and* buy cheaper in Dublin or England?' The satisfaction behind this boast suggested he had a score or two to settle with the local traders – especially when he added, 'They'd come to us on bended knees!'

'But Rick's only fourteen,' Felicity protested.

When the butler turned to her the combative glint in his eye was harder still. 'And wouldn't that just double the spit in the eye, ma'am, if you'll pardon the phrase.' Then he remembered who and where he was, for he added, 'And if you'll pardon my boldness in stating an opinion at all.'

'Leave the boy here!' Wilhelmina murmured, as if the notion might never have occurred to her on her own. 'I wonder. I wonder . . .'

PART TWO

PERDITION CATCH MY SOUL

1887

Rick stood on the front steps of Castle Moore, hands in pockets, whistling a jig that had annoyed him all morning by refusing to go away. He didn't even know its name; it was probably called 'Kelly's Kitchen' or something equally uninformative. He couldn't think why it was on his mind at all, but he hoped that by whistling it – fetching it out of him, as it were – he might get rid of it altogether.

It annoyed King, too, who was standing, arms akimbo, on the step above and a little to one side of his young master. The lad knew he was there; he must have heard him come out, but he was stubbornly refusing to turn round and acknowledge him. There had been several such incidents lately. Nothing you could call open insurrection; it was more like testing. The young 'master' was testing his precise degree of mastery in lots of little ways – just like this.

King cleared his throat and said, 'I've laid out your tennis things, sir.'

Rick whistled a few more notes, stopping just the right side of downright rudeness, and said, 'I don't think I'll go over to the McIvers' after all, thank you, King.'

'They were expecting you, sir.'

'Only half-and-half.'

'I think not, sir. I believe it was a firm arrangement.'

Still Rick did not turn round. 'I think you're mistaken there, King. I seem to remember quite distinctly saying to Miss McIver that I'd come if estate business permitted it.'

'Exactly so, sir.'

'Well, I'm afraid estate business doesn't permit it, you see.'

'Indeed, sir?' The man's tone acquired a sour, rather cutting edge.

'Yes, indeed,' Rick echoed. His neck was stiff with the tension of opposing the man like this. How far could he go? he wondered.

There was a silence before the butler spoke again. Now his tone was chill. 'May I ask, sir . . . ?' he said, leaving the rest deliberately unspoken – not out of deference but in the spirit of one who steps out in large strides, forcing a weaker companion to keep pace.

Be specific? Rick wondered. *Or be vague?* He opted for the latter. 'You've been very good all these years, King,' he said in a conciliatory tone. 'No one else could have done what you've done. You have them beaten, coming and going. But it's time I started to pull my own weight, don't you know.'

'In particular, sir?' The prompt held a waspish menace.

'Have you smelled the lake lately?' Rick asked.

'I fail to see . . .'

'It stinks. There's hardly any fresh water coming into it at all.'

'I'll have Donovan look at the drains.'

'It's not drains, it's the brook beyond there.' He nodded away to the north, where a little troutbeck, known rather grandly on the map as the River More, came bubbling out of Mount Argus to become the main feeder of the canal that ran into the northern end of the castle lake. 'Have you seen it lately?'

'I'll get Donovan to look into it,' King promised.

'I'm sure those Robertsons down at the mill have been

diverting it. They still think it's some ancient right of theirs.'

'I'll look into that myself, sir.'

Rick, thinking he'd carried his little rebellion far enough for one day, said, 'Good egg. Perhaps I will go to the McIvers' after all.'

'Excellent, sir!' The relief in the other's voice was almost palpable. 'I'll see that your luncheon is served immediately.'

'Yes,' the lad mused as he turned and went indoors, looking the butler in the eye at last. 'Or perhaps I can kill two birds with one stone – leave half an hour early and ride over the mountain by way of the brook. Yes!' He walked on into the hall and up the staircase to change for luncheon. 'I haven't been that way for a year or more.' He turned and smiled. 'Shockin' altogether!' he added in the local idiom.

King stood in the hallway, biting his lip and staring after the young master. He was getting harder and harder to handle these days. O'Brien, the head stable lad, was behind it somewhere, he felt sure of that. He should have got rid of that man long ago.

Rick dressed for riding and put his tennis things in a bag before he went down to the stables. O'Brien had the horse already harnessed in the gig; his eyebrows shot up when he saw the young master's outfit. 'Mr King sent word you'd be taking the gig, sir,' he said.

'I've changed my mind. Just slip a saddle on him, will you? And a saddlebag to hold these togs, eh?'

O'Brien whistled up one of the stable boys to make the changes; at least the gig would be all nicely polished now for church tomorrow. He stuck his hands in his pockets and whistled again, a brief, formless phrase. An envelope nudged his fingers, reminding him; he must make a chance to slip it to the young fellow. 'Er . . . was there any special sort of a reason, boss?' he asked. 'For riding the horse, I mean?'

Rick grinned at him. 'You know bloody well there is. Who put the idea into my head, eh? The water . . . and those blackguards down at the mill? We'll sort them out once and for all.'

'Ah, is that the way of it, now?'

'It is. King doesn't approve – which is another good reason. But why shouldn't I kill two birds with the one stone? I can ride over the mountain *and* play tennis at the McIvers', easily.'

O'Brien smiled contentedly. 'Well, boss, haven't you a grand day for it.'

They stood in silence awhile, watching the lad lead the horse out from between the shafts. Rick had the feeling they were being watched – not an unusual feeling at Castle Moore. King was somewhere up there in the house, lurking behind one of the windows. But you'd never catch him at it. He'd know just where the shadow was to hide him. 'I'm surprised we haven't seen Mad McLysaght yet,' he remarked. 'He's always here around this time of year.'

They both knew he meant the anniversary of the Castle Moore Murders; and indeed, ever since that dreadful day, the old fellow had never missed being here around the third or fourth week in August.

'He'll be here, right enough,' O'Brien commented. 'At least, I hope so. I have chores in plenty set aside for him. He'll give out that there's not another house in Keelity where he wouldn't be shown an aisier welcome, yet 'tis always here he does be coming.'

The lad waited for the horse to breathe out before he tightened the girth; then he handed the reins to O'Brien while he went off to get the saddlebag. Rick gathered up his tennis togs and refolded them. 'Don't want these to get creased,' he said drily. 'Mrs McIver was quite scathing last time.'

'Did I hear Mrs Henrietta's coming over the water soon?' O'Brien asked.

Rick smiled. 'Did you? I wonder where. I only got her letter this morning and I didn't even tell Mrs King yet.'

'Ah well, it could be yourself is not the only one who's after getting a letter, sir.'

'You?' Rick asked in surprise as the lad came back with the saddlebag. He slipped his togs neatly into it.

'Lord, no.' O'Brien laughed at the very idea. 'A certain party, shall we say?' Deftly he slipped the envelope from his pocket and packed it into the saddlebag under the pretence of straightening out Rick's packing. 'A certain party,' he repeated with a wink. ''Twill all be set down in that, I'm sure.'

Rick's eyebrows lifted briefly but he gave no other sign of comprehension. 'I'll away, then,' he said as he swung himself into the saddle.

The horse, eager to be going, moved off before he was seated; just for that piece of impertinence he forced it to back a dozen paces up the yard, watched by an approving O'Brien. Then, for swank, he asked the beast for a half-pass, diagonally across the yard all the way to the gate. He let it walk more naturally down the back drive, past the walled garden, and out into the woodland. At least one creature knew who was master hereabouts, he thought wryly.

Within quarter of a mile the trees, sparse as they were, had closed in around him. He thought of the mysterious letter O'Brien had slipped into the bag but was reluctant to take it out just yet. He knew it was impossible for King to see him here, but it was not a matter of such nice calculation; the man had a pervasive presence that defied such apparent obstacles as walls and trees. It was a mile at least before that brooding feeling began to wane.

A wind devil came spiralling down among the trees, bending their tops; it almost removed his hat before it went soughing on down into the valley, leaving the air behind it unnaturally still, like air in a museum.

Mount Argus had the minimal attributes of a mountain. It rose to just three feet over the qualifying thousand – and only because Richard, the first Bellingham to own Castle Moore, had carried enough rock up there to raise the crown of it from the nine hundred and ninety-nine feet that nature had originally provided. He wasn't going to have the Lyndon-Furys, who lived down the lake at Coolderg, boasting that they had the only mountain in the county. It also possessed a mountainous-looking ravine, which was, in fact, the quarry from which the stone for the house had been cut, almost two hundred years earlier, in the days when the Seymour-Kanes had owned the place. Now, overgrown and mellowed with moss and lichens, it was hard to tell from the natural article. Rick waited until he was behind those sheltering ramparts before he felt quite safe in opening the bag and extracting the letter.

It was addressed to him but he did not recognize the hand. A very firm, decisive hand it was, too. He tore open the cover. It began 'Dear Rick', but there were no directions at the head of the paper. It must be from someone who knew him on terms of familiarity, but he still could not identify the hand. He decided to play a game with himself: rather than cheat and look at the signature, he would read on and see how far he got before the penny dropped.

It dropped before the end of the opening sentence: 'Did you hear we're going to move back into the Old Glebe?'

Judith!

His hand fell to the saddle, clasping the letter tight enough to tear it.

Judith!

He closed his eyes, wondering if he dared read on – and knowing that not all the powder and shot in Ireland would stop him.

Did you hear we're going to move back into the Old Glebe? Isn't it exciting – at least, I hope you're excited to hear it. I don't care much what anyone else thinks at all. How many years has it been? I don't even want to count.

It seems that one of Papa's inventions has at last 'taken' – that and another little legacy. What should we have done without 'little legacies' all these years! Anyway, he and Mama feel sufficiently confident to take a long lease on the old place (which is to say Mama feels confident, for when did dear Papa not!) and, guess what? Best of all – we're to be moving in on my birthday!

I know it's a sad day for all of us, too, and one whose scars we shall always carry, but it will never be anything other than sad if we don't also try and give it some happy associations, too, will it? And d'you know what would give me the happiest association of all? To see you there, dear Rick, on the day we move in!

I've been a dreadful correspondent to you, I know, and I burn with shame at my dilatory ways. It was very sweet of you to write and say that one letter from me was worth ten from you, but I know it's not true. Actually, I did write letters to you, lots of them, but they were all in my head while listening to the band on Stephen's Green or stifling yawns at the winter subscription concerts and times like that. And then, of course, I'd think: Oh, good, now I've written to Rick – and so I'd never actually put pen to paper.

Heavens, what a flimsy excuse! Nonetheless, it's true. Hen wrote to tell me she might come over this summer with the baby but without Harold, who's got to go out to India on some wretched commission of inquiry, poor chap, in this heat, too. She didn't sound too terribly upset at their enforced separation. I hope that's just my scandalous imagination burrowing away between the lines and making two and two = forty again as usual! But what do you think? Has she written to you?

D'you think we'll recognize each other? You and me, I mean. I'd recognize Hen, of course, because she sent me that photograph of her holding up Yolande, just after her christening. (Does she really call her Yuk?) I think I never saw a portrait in which distaste and suspicion were more frankly delineated – and in the faces of both parties, too!

Oh dear, with every line I write I feel more keenly my guilt at not having written more often. There is so much to catch up on, so much to tell you and so much to ask. And so much one would not dare set down in a letter. For instance, about those men they hanged for the Castle Moore Murders. There are lots of questions to ask about that but I wouldn't dare put even a hint in a letter. Nor my reasons for sending this through O'Brien rather than direct to the castle. Hen warned me about that – Mrs K. and her ever-busy kettle!

Or is my mind poisoned against that couple by O'Brien? I usually see him at the agricultural shows, when I go with Papa, and that's another way I've kept up with the Castle Moore news. I met him at the ploughing competition at Maynooth, too, when Papa's Patent Reversible won the Gold Diploma and not a single order! What a day that was. They sent me to train for a nurse the next week – under strict orders to find a rich doctor to marry. But now, with this latest windfall, they've taken me away again to bring me back to the Old Glebe. They think I may do Rather Better for myself than just marrying any old doctor, but I cannot imagine what they may mean by that, can you?

With all fondness, dear Rick,
Your dilatory and penitent,
Judith.

He read it, and read it again, and read it yet again. Certain of her phrases stuck in his mind. She didn't care much what anyone else thought about her family's return to the Old Glebe; *his* was the only opinion that mattered. And she *had* written to him, often, in her mind. Whenever she was bored – he didn't much care for that bit. And the thing that would make her happiest of all would be to see him there on the day they moved in!

And then that bit at the end about making a better match than any old doctor. What a tease she was! But then, like all teasing, it had a double edge. Was she saying that he and she were such good friends, and such old friends, that they could laugh at her parents' machinations and ignore their ambitions for her?

He stared at the page as if the answer might emerge in some as yet unnoticed cryptographic form. He began reading again and then realized he could go on at it all day. Reluctantly he folded the paper and put it away. He hunted for the envelope but could not find it. Another wind devil? He hadn't noticed one. Probably in an inside pocket. He hunted there, too, and found his watch – one glance at which brought a cry of horror and set the spurs to his horse's side in a headlong dash down to the McIvers'.

Shortly after Rick had made his hasty departure from the

old quarry, King came that way on his regular afternoon constitutional with his two cocker spaniels, Topsy and Turvey. He had the swagger of a landowner though his dress was every stitch that of an off-duty butler – hounds-tooth tweeds, brown bowler hat, blackthorn shillelagh and all. At the start of the winding path that led up to the abandoned quarry he noticed Turvey sniffing at something near the root of a furze bush. Something pale. He thrust the prickles aside with his stick and retrieved it.

An envelope. Empty. *Rick Bellingham Esq. By Hand.* And a very firm, strong hand, too. He sniffed it but could smell only saddle leather. By hand . . . saddle leather . . . he didn't have to cudgel his brains too long to see whose hand it was by.

He thought at once of the Carty girl – except that the writing did not seem to be a woman's. Flynn, the village storekeeper, had told him old man Carty had renewed the lease on the Old Glebe and that his credit was apparently good again – though the country was full of half-gentry in that category: credit *apparently* good.

He tucked the envelope in his pocket, whistled up the spaniels, and continued his promenade. Yes, he'd get Flynn to compare the writing with any notes that might come down from the Old Glebe; Flynn would go through fire and brimstone for him now, rather than see the Property Protection Society Store revived.

At the crest of the mountain the butler stood awhile, staring down at Belivor, the McIvers' place. In among the trees, where the tennis court stood, he could just make out four white dots, prancing this way and that. Mister Rick, young Fergal McIver, his sister Sally . . . and who would be the fourth? He'd have to ask.

When he'd first heard that the Carty girl was returning to Keelity, he'd been pleased, for he remembered her as a rather leggy, pigtaily sort of a thing who wouldn't say boo to a goose and was permanently overawed by anything to do with the castle. But now he recalled her ferocious behaviour on the night of the Murders – and began to have his doubts. Which was she, he wondered, lamb or spitfire?

Probably lamb. He was worrying over nothing. The letter couldn't be from Judith Carty; the writing was much too firm. He decided he was, indeed, pleased she was returning to the district. She'd be another card in his hand, a trump of low value but not to be sneezed at. Now that he came to consider the matter, he realized how risky it was that the only eligible female within easy reach for Mister Rick was Sally McIver. Not that he had anything against her, but he always liked to play one possibility off against another, and to keep a third one simmering away in the background, too, if it were feasible.

Yes – the more he thought about it the more pleased he was that the Carty girl was returning here. The Cartys must be invited over sometime in September. That would put their credit up with old Flynn at the store! He inhaled a deep breath of satisfaction.

The dogs fretted as a squall of wind stirred in the valley to the north of Mount Argus. He set off in that direction, meaning to return along the banks of the stream to discover whether the Robertson brothers had heeded his warning. The water trilled invitingly in his ears as he drew near. He bent and scooped up a handful of the cold, crystal liquid, which he supped noisily. Oh, how good it tasted! He thought of all the poor beggars out on the bog, working on the roads, down in sawyers' pits, turning hay, binding sheaves, pressing clothes in steam laundries . . . all over Ireland at that very moment. What would they not give to be able to be here at his side, sauntering along like a lord, drinking this icy spring water. He supped another handful and relished it even more. 'A long, cool drink from a fresh-running stream.' How often had he tantalized himself with such words when, as a child, he had chased the jackdaws in the fields. That was before he was sent into service, of course; even after then there had been days when he would have killed to be able to do this.

He stood and waved his open hand in the warm air to dry it. He removed his bowler and wiped its sweat-dank band with his kerchief. He replaced it and firmed it up with a dapper little pat on the crown. The crown of a hat. The crown of a head. He thought of the word and smiled. It was, indeed, a crown, and by God, wasn't he the king here! He ran a satisfied eye over the Bellingham acres and thought, What man needs to own land who has the unfettered use of it? And what was money when you could have power instead!

Swinging his stick with carefree mien, he followed the stream down the mountainside, a series of gurgling pools and splashing waterfalls. In the first half mile it was supplemented by the upwellings of three other springs, which turned it from a mere brook to something you could almost think of calling a river. He was now approaching the place where the Robertsons had diverted the waters to their mill. He was glad to see that they had now diverted it back again.

Actually, looking at the matter properly, it was the Bellinghams who had diverted the river – when they needed it for the lake back in old Richard Bellingham's day. All the Robertsons had done was to let it flow once more along its ancient and natural bed. Topsy pointed toward the bushes on the farther bank; Turvey stopped sniffing around at random and agreed with her mate. A moment later the sallies parted and out came the two brothers.

'There's a grand day, Mr King,' called out Tony, the elder one. He was in shirt sleeves, rolled up to his elbows.

King noticed the fellow had a slight graze, weeping blood, on his left forearm. 'It is indeed, Mr Robertson,' he commented. 'Especially if you're a swan down there on the lake. Ye'd best leave it so for a day or two. I'll bring the fella up here meself and show him all's well. The old river bed'll be dry by tomorrow, I daresay.'

'And after that?' asked Francy, the younger and more belligerent of the two.

King grinned. 'I suppose you might say he'll be having other matters on his mind before too long.'

''Tis all very well,' Francy went on, 'but we paid you good money for that water.'

'And good water ye had for it,' King reminded them. 'It's that or close it off for ever. You may choose for yourselves. If ye want my help, I'll see ye all right. Haven't I always seen ye all right?'

'Ah, you're a grand sort of a man altogether, Mr King, sir,' Tony interposed in a more conciliatory tone. 'Sure what's a day? What's two days? We have water enough without this. We might even shut down for a day and go fishing ourselves – if you'd kindly have a wee word with Mister McGrath and his bailiffs?'

'I will if I see him,' the butler promised, and then added grandly, 'and if he sees you first, you may refer him to me. Stick by me, lads, and ye'll come to no harm.'

As he resumed his stroll, Tony stooped to bathe his grazed arm in the pool. Francy gazed malevolently after the departing King. 'I still say now,' he muttered, 'that if we were to approach Mister Rick ourselves, we could come to an amicable arrangement to take the water by day and let the lake have it at night. All aboveboard.'

'Weren't we only greedy,' his brother chided him. 'Sure an hour a day would have kept that lake sweet and himself in blissful ignorance. Greedy or lazy.' He tested the graze gingerly for pain and was agreeably surprised to find little. 'I wonder now, what will be the "other matters" the young fella will be having on his mind by this time next week? Lord, wouldn't you hate to be in that oul' fella's power!' He nodded after the butler, now a mere blur among the trees.

'D'you suppose we aren't then?' his brother asked sarcastically.

'Indeed we are not,' Tony protested. 'Didn't we pay the man fair and square. We owe him no favours.'

'Paid him is it?'

'You were there yourself. You saw me hand him the money.'

'Oh, I saw you well enough,' Francy agreed. 'But who else did, eh? And have we a receipt to prove it? I tell you, that man could hand us in charge to the peelers any day he wants, and divil a word could either of us prove against him. I say we go to himself, young Bellingham, and make a proper arrangement.'

Tony rolled his sleeve down over the graze and tested it yet again. 'That's grand. Listen while I tell you, we'll not cross Mr King, no matter what. Didn't all the storekeepers in Keelity try to boycott him?'

'With a Land League pistol at their necks!'

'And where did it get them, for all their brave words? On their knees! Sure he'd cut the scalp out of the pair of us, so he would.'

Francy spat viciously into the water. 'Isn't that what we all say! There's not one of us with the guts to face him down. But one day we'll have to. One of us will have to.'

'Well, it won't be me.' Tony spoke easily, lightly, being well used to his younger brother's spleen. 'And I'll tell you who else it won't be. It won't be that young Bellingham fella, either. So let's remember which side our bread's buttered. We may laugh at oul' King behind his back, but to his face it's yes-sir, no-sir, three-bags-full-sir.'

* * *

It was Rick and Sally versus her brother Fergal, who was also Rick's best friend; Fergal's partner – the white dot King had been unable to identify from Mount Argus – was Netty O'Farrelly, the solicitor's daughter. They were playing a rather sedate game, the girls being hampered by their wide-brimmed hats, long skirts, and full-sleeved blouses. For their part the lads were none too free in their long white flannels, either. And it all took place under the watchful gaze of the two mothers, Betty McIver and Meg O'Farrelly – to say nothing of the merciless glare of the sun.

Betty had two chief aims: to prevent Fergal from falling seriously for the O'Farrelly girl, who, as a Roman Catholic, would hardly do; and to encourage Rick to fall as seriously as possible for Sally, who had been intended for him almost from birth. Maude Bellingham had often spoken of it as her dearest wish . . . well, perhaps not her *dearest* wish, but something close to her heart, anyway.

Meg O'Farrelly had only one aim: to get Fergal and Netty decently engaged and as soon as possible. She knew Betty would disapprove strongly, but she also knew that Betty was rather dim – certainly no match for her.

Side by side they sat on a vast sofa of bamboo and wickerwork, which creaked like cheap stays every time one of them moved; above them the white and yellow striped awning, which had looked so perfect in the Alps last summer, struck an incongruously frivolous note in that dour garden, whose inspiration was more Scottish than Irish. It was planted almost entirely with yews and junipers, laurels, berberis, and the less flamboyant species of viburnum. The tennis court was completely hemmed in with half-grown Scots pine; the only view from its centre was of the chimneys of Baliver House and of the very crest of Mount Argus beyond.

'What an agreeable sight they make,' Meg commented,

waving a gloved hand vaguely at the tennis court, lingering just slightly on Fergal and her own daughter.

'Yes,' Betty acknowledged in a voice equally vague. 'I'm so glad Netty has struck up a *friendship* with Sally and Fergal. It's especially good for Fergal, I think.'

Meg turned to her with interest.

'Yes,' Betty went on. 'You know how it was in our day – or it certainly was in my part of Scotland. The only fellows one's own age one really got to know were one's own brothers. One developed a faint acquaintance, perhaps, with one or two of their cronies. But nothing like this.' She stretched a hand horizontally toward the youngsters and played a little glissando on the air with her fingers. 'They don't know how lucky they are.'

'Mmm,' Meg put in – and waited for more.

After a brief silence it came: 'The friendships we develop in our youth are the ones that truly endure, don't you find?'

'Mmm.'

'And friendships between men and women – associations that fall far short of romantic love, I mean – true *friendships* – you know the sort of thing I'm talking about, Mrs O'Farrelly?'

'Indeed, Mrs McIver.' Meg felt that yet another *Mmm* would hardly do.

'Unfeigned friendships of that kind are so . . . important.'

'Ah!' Meg nodded a hint that she had never heard a truer word.

The brevity of the reply made Betty feel she had not truly got her point home; she racked her brains for another way to express it. 'It is possible,' she said, 'even across those barriers that normally divide us from one another.'

Meg, thinking she meant the barriers of religion,

agreed even more fervently, though still in a monosyllable.

'With Mr King, for instance,' Betty went on – causing Meg to sit several degrees closer to the vertical. 'Oh yes! Of course, he and I hardly meet on social terms. Hardly!' She emphasized the fact with a little laugh – which she instantly regretted. 'Yes . . . well, what I was going to say is that I nonetheless feel that a distinct friendship has sprung up between us. A long-standing friendship, too.'

Meg, pausing briefly to wonder how something 'long-standing' could 'spring up', replied, 'You and he were acquainted in your childhood, then? I didn't know that.'

'No, no!' Betty responded crossly. 'I'm not talking about childhood. I'm not saying that *all* such friendships absolutely *have* to begin in one's youth. They can develop at any time – as, indeed, between Mr King and . . . oneself. I feel that over these past half-dozen years, ever since . . . well, the awful events whose anniversary falls next week . . . ever since then, a friendship of such a kind has developed between him and me.'

'Indeed?'

Mrs O'Farrelly's tone was so carefully neutral it goaded Betty to explain further. 'Yes, indeed. Despite the *enormous* social gulf that separates us – and that's what I was talking about – despite all that, I feel that when he has come to me for advice on this or that aspect of young Rick's upbringing, it has been very much as a *friend*. D'you see?'

'I do, I do,' Meg agreed eagerly. 'I think that is so *good* to hear, Mrs McIver. And I presume, of course, that *you* often turn to *him* for advice in just the same spirit?'

'That I . . . er.' Betty's voice strayed when she saw where her persiflage had led her. Heavens, all she'd wanted to make clear was that she and King were very thick together when it came to questions of Rick's upbringing and future – so if smart Mrs O'Farrelly had any notion of pairing either of these two young men with her own daughter, she'd jolly well better forget them.

'Yes,' Meg said encouragingly. 'Friendship cuts both ways, after all. You and he give and take advice as between friends?'

'Ah, well, it's not quite as . . . as . . . as . . . what's the wretched word?'

'Mutual? The friendship isn't mutual. Or *tested*! The friendship hasn't been tested in that direction yet?' She chuckled. 'Oh, isn't it all just endlessly fascinating! The ins and outs of everything!'

Betty relapsed into silence, letting her mind wander back through the conversation to discover where it had taken this disastrously wrong turning, and looking for some other avenue she might more profitably have followed. Her fingers played another trill on the wicker of the seat.

But Meg was off on some other tack at once. 'That anniversary you mentioned, Mrs McIver – isn't it also Henrietta Austin's birthday? Henrietta Bellingham, as was?'

'I believe it is,' Betty responded absently.

'*And* little Judith Carty's, too, then. Not so little now, I dare say.'

'Yes. I wonder what became of them?' Betty mused, still with most of her mind elsewhere.

'We shall find out soon enough,' Meg said, delighted to realize that the other knew nothing of recent developments.

'Shall we?' Betty asked; alarm tinged the question.

'But surely you've heard, Mrs McIver? They've taken the Old Glebe again. I'm told they're moving in a week today.'

'Hah!' Betty gave a single laugh of scorn. 'Gossip! As

if that man would dare show his face here again after the debts he left behind him!'

'Oh, but they've all been paid. Even ours – and solicitors, as you know yourself' – she couldn't resist getting that barb in – 'are always the very last in the line. We've been paid with interest, what's more!'

Betty sat bolt upright. Her right hand gripped the arm of the seat but played no five-finger exercise upon it. 'Coming back here?' she echoed.

'To the Old Glebe. O'Farrelly drew up the new lease himself – for ten years. One year paid in advance. I'm giving away no secrets here. In fact, Carty himself asked my husband to give it the widest circulation – considering the cloud he was under when he left five years ago. One of his patents is at last earning him the sort of royalties he always expected them *all* to earn. This one's on a machine for rolling cigarettes, I believe.'

'And the daughter?' Betty asked. 'I thought she had gone into service.'

'Nursing.'

Betty waved a hand as if to suggest that the correction was pedantic. 'I mean, the *best* she could ever have hoped for there was to marry some doctor.'

'Quite,' Meg said. 'Whereas now . . . !'

Her eyes strayed toward the four young folk and lingered on Rick. She did not need to look back to see how Betty McIver was taking to the new situation. That old saying about killing the bringer of bad tidings was quite true. If looks could kill . . .

The tennis reached a mutually agreeable conclusion. The four young people came gratefully up into the shade where the two mothers were seated; the young ladies glowed and the young gentlemen perspired – all in the prescribed manner. They laughed and chided one another over this or that brilliant stroke, or losing stroke.

Their vivacity overwhelmed the two older ones, who were left feeling uncomfortable without knowing precisely why.

Fergal flung himself between them, causing the bamboo to protest in a series of sharp cracks like nearby rifle fire. 'Sit here, Miss O'Farrelly, old thing,' he said to his erstwhile partner, patting the sofa at his side. 'There's bags of room.'

'You should speak more respectfully – and not seat yourself before the ladies,' his mother admonished, while Netty complied eagerly.

'Quite right,' Fergal boomed, as if his mother had been discussing someone else's bad behaviour.

Fergal's manner in general was strange, as indeed was his appearance. He would be twenty in a couple of months but seemed quite grown-up already. He was of average height and his hair was halfway between fair and dark, yet his eyes were a pale blue-grey where one would have expected brown. He had been called skinny at school; now, having put on some muscle, he was wiry and lithe. His face looked like a sketch by an energetic sculptor, someone like Rodin, say – a fluid, bravura piece using very wet clay. His eyes, despite their pale colouring, were deep-set and restless. His cheekbones and chin were his most prominent features, and the flesh between them was taut and vigorous. Yet he hardly ever smiled. That is not to say he lacked a sense of humour. Far from it. But he delivered his jokes without an invoice. His manner was the most peculiar feature of all. He spoke always as if there were a small, invisible crowd about two yards in front of him – with a voice slightly louder than others would use in ordinary conversation, and with a slightly hectoring or cajoling sort of tone. Even after all these years it still drove his mother to fury – otherwise, perhaps, he would have stopped it long ago.

So when he barked, 'Quite right!' – as if he were

intruding his own mature judgement into his mother's conversation – she stiffened and gripped the armrest to contain her anger. 'I think we shall go up to the terrace for tea now,' she said firmly, meaning all of them, of course. She rose as one accustomed to instant obedience.

Fergal and Netty, newly seated, rose in courtesy, as did Meg O'Farrelly. Fergal stared hard at the court; one who did not know him would even say his gaze was furious. 'I'm jolly well going to mark those tramlines myself,' he drawled to his invisible crowd. 'Murphy hasn't the foggiest notion how to do it.' He glanced around as if he were slightly surprised to find them all still there, looking at him. 'You go on up,' he told his three friends. As the merest afterthought he added, 'Or stay and mock.'

Rick, noticing a couple of pine needles caught in Sally's hair, reached up and delicately tweaked them off her. Betty, who had been on the point of insisting that they all come up to the house, saw the gesture and thought better of her words. 'Don't be long,' she said firmly. 'Ten minutes! I shall expect you up there in ten minutes.'

As the two women walked back up the lawns to the house, Meg said, 'I suppose there's little enough harm in it.' Secretly she was delighted that Netty would now have an unchaperoned ten minutes with Fergal but she felt she had a public position to maintain as well.

'One never knows, does one,' Betty replied. 'If one is utterly, utterly strict – as one should be, I know – one drives them to climbing out of windows at night . . . and they start telling each other they might as well be hanged for a sheep as for a lamb.' She glanced back toward the court, though the young people were out of view from that part of the lawn. 'Ten minutes,' she mused. 'And four of them. There can be no real harm in it.'

'And one of them marking the court,' Meg pointed out.

Betty looked at her pityingly and smiled. 'You believed that, did you?'

Meg suddenly felt one down; but, she told herself, it was no less than she deserved for being so smug about Betty McIver's dimness earlier. Intelligence, she reflected, did not necessarily go hand in hand with worldly wisdom.

At that moment they both distinctly heard Sally doing an imitation of a sheep, followed by guffaws from the others. The coincidence with Betty's earlier remark about being hanged for a sheep made them look at each other in a mixture of consternation and amusement. 'They can't possibly have overheard us,' Meg asserted, followed by a more hesitant, 'can they?'

'Impossible!' Betty was quite decided about it.

There was more laughter from the tennis court.

As the two mothers passed out of sight, Rick exclaimed, apropos nothing, 'Ten minutes.'

'Say twenty,' Fergal remarked over his shoulder as he walked to his jacket, which he had hung over a branch. He returned with a packet of cigarettes and offered them nonchalantly round.

'Aren't you going to mark the tramlines?' Rick asked.

The two girls looked at him with kindly amusement. Netty was, in fact, as surprised as Rick at Fergal's smooth duplicity, but she was swifter on the uptake.

'Dare we?' Sally glanced nervously toward the house, her fingers hesitating a few inches from the tempting little cylinders.

'Just take a few puffs of mine, if you'd prefer,' Rick suggested.

'I'd still reek of it,' she objected.

'As well be hanged for a sheep as a lamb,' Netty told her, brushing her hand aside and taking one boldly.

'Ba-a-ah!' Sally imitated a sheep as she followed suit.

They all laughed. Soon the still air about them was

wreathed in pale blue smoke.

'Look, I can blow rings,' Sally said, putting two perfect ones into play among them.

Rick leaned forward and blew a third, which went spiralling through the centre of one of them.

'Oh, through the heart!' Sally dramatized her distress, laying her hand across her own heart as actors do in the melodramas. 'Pierced to the quick!'

Netty tried to blow a ring and failed. 'Botheration!' She tried to rub out the result as if it were a mark on a blackboard. 'How d'you do it?'

Sally lifted her nose high, blew a fourth ring through the middle of Rick's, and said, 'It calls for a certain maturity, don't you know. It's more a question of attitude than mere skill.'

'Like this.' Fergal turned to her. 'Fill your mouth with smoke and make an O with your lips.'

When she obeyed he tapped her cheek gently, one, two, three, producing a perfect little ring each time. Then, before she could react, he ducked his head forward and kissed her briefly on the lips. They – her lips – were already arranged for astonishment; her eyes now reinforced the message. She gasped, choked on the smoke, and coughed until her eyes watered. He patted her solicitously on the back, making each pat more tender than the last until it turned into a caress.

'I say!' His sister eyed him askance.

'What are you two waiting for?' he challenged her. 'The cat's away.'

'But we're all hot and . . . and glowing,' she protested. 'And anyway it's only midafternoon.' She smiled at Rick, feeling sure he'd be able to answer her feeble objections.

But Rick had other things on his mind. 'By the way,' he exclaimed, 'have you people heard the news about the Old Glebe?'

'Oh yes!' Netty turned to him with relief. 'I meant to

say that earlier – about the Cartys, you mean?'

He nodded. 'How did you hear?'

'Daddy did the lease.'

'The Cartys?' Sally – like her mother before her – was suddenly on the edge of her seat. 'Are they coming back to Keelity?'

'Yes, isn't it splendid?' Rick seemed unaware of her dismay. 'What with the Whytes returning from India and the Seymours for the cubbing, we'll be quite a crowd. And my sister may be coming over from England, too.'

The cigarette fell from Sally's fingers. Netty picked it up and returned it to her, which she appeared not to notice. 'When you say we'll be quite a crowd,' she remarked to Rick, 'd'you mean . . . I mean to say, is . . .'

He nodded. 'Judith? Yes, she's coming back, too.' Then, realizing they might ask how he knew, he turned to Netty and added, 'Or so I assume. Isn't she?'

'But I thought the Cartys were absolutely on their uppers,' Sally said.

'Didn't they send Judith into service?' Fergal drawled.

Netty glanced at him sharply. Her mother had warned her that Fergal had once had a soft spot for Judith Carty. In fact, his rivalry with Rick Bellingham for Judith's affections was what had drawn the two boys so close together in the first place. One great trouble with Fergal was that you could never tell when he was joking; indeed, you could never tell what he was thinking at all.

Rick knew Fergal well enough to realize he was being drawn. But in what way? How was he to respond to that last comment? Of course, he was supposed to leap to Judith's defence, to point out that nursing wasn't at all like going into service. He was supposed to nail his colours to the mast. He inhaled deeply and just managed not to cough. 'Yes,' he drawled in imitation of Fergal. 'I suppose it is a *kind* of service, nursing.' The way the smoke dribbled out as he spoke looked very grown-up, he thought. 'Though the Hon. Pamela Stokes is a nurse, isn't she?' he added.

'Honorary,' Sally snapped angrily. 'She's never drawn a penny of her salary.'

Netty stepped in quickly. 'Did you say your sister was coming, Mr Bellingham? She's married, isn't she?'

Rick grinned at her. 'Yes, and she's still only twenty-two.'

Netty bit her lip in excitement. 'D'you think they'll trust her to chaperone us?'

'She has a baby daughter called Yolande, whom she calls Yuk,' he replied, not entirely to the point.

'Of course they'll trust her,' Fergal said.

His sister, excited at the prospect of a sympathetic chaperone of almost their own age, asked why.

'Haven't you caught on yet?'

Sally frowned. 'What d'you mean?'

'I mean Mama knows jolly well I'm not marking the tramlines. She didn't believe me for one moment.'

'Really?' Rick asked in surprise. He was looking at Sally and thinking how 'fast' she looked when she smoked; he wondered would he dare steal a kiss from her – just jokingly the way Fergal had done with Netty. A further tiny thought flitted obliquely through his mind: if he did, it would help misdirect Fergal about his feelings for Judith. He was savvy enough by now to know that any renewal of his former interest in Judith Carty would not be welcome to the rest of the Bellingham family – and most certainly not to the McIvers.

'And yet she left us alone?' Netty said. She wondered at the fine distinction between leaving two young ladies alone with two young men and leaving two young ladies in the care of *one* young man while the three of them watched a second young man do a job of work.

'*They* left us,' he corrected. 'Your mother knows it, too.'

'I can't believe it,' Netty replied, though she could feel her mind preparing to accept the almost unthinkable. 'But why?'

'The jailer is often far more bored than the prisoner, I'm told,' Fergal explained. 'They're only interested in preserving the form of the thing. It's not at all the same as it was in grandpapa's day. Although, mind you, if what he told me is true, there was a fair difference between form and substance in *his* day, too.'

'In what way?' Netty asked ingenuously – or was it disingenuously? She was learning a thing or two from Fergal this afternoon.

Without the ghost of a smile Fergal pointed his cigarette toward Rick and said, 'Ask that one. He was there, too.'

'Oh yes, *do* tell us, Rick,' Sally teased, showing she knew very well what her brother was talking about.

He decided to take a chance with her. 'It's so silly,' he said, as if he were answering her question. 'It's not as if we *couldn't* get up to all sorts of mischief in twenty minutes, but it's the suggestion that we're incapable of acting responsibly. I mean, here we are – four utterly responsible young people, aren't we?' He looked rapidly at each. 'Aren't we?'

Fergal remained poker-faced but the two girls stared at him, wondering how this 'explanation' in any way answered Sally's question.

'I mean,' Rick went on. 'I could do this, for instance.' He leaned forward and kissed Sally swiftly on the cheek, withdrawing before she could become alarmed.

'Or this.' He kissed her again, nearer the lips and not so briefly.

When he withdrew he saw her staring at him, perfectly

poised between passing it off with a laugh and . . . what? Slapping his face, probably.

'Or this.' He kissed her full on the lips. He was so amazed at their softness and the sweetness of their touch that he broke contact almost at once and hastily resumed his original line. 'I could do all of that,' he said. 'Yet do I? Of course I don't! Because I can be trusted, see?'

They all laughed.

Fergal flicked his cigarette end out into the centre of the court. 'Time we were going,' he said. 'Tell you what, Miss O'Farrelly and I will race you up through the woods. You start from this end of the court, we'll start from that.' They rose and drifted to their starting points.

'The form of the thing!' Netty chided when she and Fergal were alone at their end of the court.

'Precisely,' he agreed. 'The form is all that matters.' To the other two he called out, in a rather bored, perfunctory voice, 'Readysteadygo!' all as one monotonous word; then he linked his arm with Netty's and sauntered up among the trees.

For Rick, left alone with Sally, the whole day turned rather serious. His lips still felt that brief touch of hers. He both longed to renew the sensation and dreaded it, knowing it would subtly yet profoundly change their friendship for ever. And on the very day he had received Judith's letter, too – with the most wonderful news ever. Was he going to be the sort of man who broke women's hearts? Something within him thrilled at the thought; the rest of him was ashamed at it.

The moment they were safely lost among the trees, Sally stopped and turned to him. Her eyes sparkled; her skin, still faintly glowing, was fair as fair; the perfume of her body rose all around him, making him shiver – as that particular perfume always did.

Their lips touched and her sweet softness overwhelmed him again, this time for a long, long minute.

A voice within told him he was being a cad. He tried to think of Judith but now she was just a name.

The Cartys travelled from the station to the Old Glebe in an open landau, an extravagance that later caused some headshaking in the community, when word of it spread. Some fools never learned, people assured one another smugly, *that* family would be back in Carey Street before you could say 'Glad I am to see ye home.'

No such thoughts crossed Rick's mind, however, as his horse drew level with them, about half a mile from the gates of their old-new home. He greeted Judith's parents with all the easy grace of his upbringing; but his eyes were for her alone. She was even lovelier than his most fevered imaginings, prompted by the easy intimacy of her letter, had dared him to envision. Her eyes, pale grey and luminous, seemed to brim over with a private merriment, shared with him and only him.

'Well!' she said.

He breathed out forcefully, unaware until then that he had been holding his breath at all. 'Now, indeed, I realize it has been six years, Miss Carty,' he told her.

'Rick!' she chided. 'Less of your Miss Carty, if you please.'

Her smile almost stopped his heart. And she, too, was delighted to see how handsome he had become during her long exile (as she considered it) in Dublin. For a magical moment they were locked thus, each in happy, full-scale audit of the other – liking, and more than liking, everything they saw.

At last the steadiness of her gaze began to discomfit him. He said, 'I don't know why I'm so surprised that you've . . . well – you've grown.'

'The man who pays her milliner will confirm that!' Carty put in.

'Edward!' her mother exclaimed crossly; then, turning

to Rick with a smile, 'I'm sure there's not another girl in Ireland with a keener sense of economy than Judith, Mr Bellingham.'

'She means I wouldn't give you the steam off my porridge,' Judith translated mischievously.

Her mother only just managed not to slap her hand. Carty gazed up into the canopy of the beech beneath whose shade they happened to be passing and whistled a silent ditty; his wife, still trying to smile her reassurances at Rick, did not notice the gesture. She, too, was delighted to see what a good-looking young man he had turned into; it would make Judith's duty a real pleasure for her.

'Everyone's jolly pleased about your success, sir,' Rick told him.

'Everyone?' Judith asked in amused surprise. Her wide, generous lips were always alive with some slight movement, as if gathering for a laugh or an amusing remark.

'Of course they are, dear,' her mother insisted. 'The people of County Keelity are the most magnanimous and warm-hearted in the whole of Ireland. They'll be delighted that your father's untiring efforts have at last reaped their just reward.'

Judith winked at Rick, the eye her mother couldn't see. 'I'm sure that's true of the McIvers,' she said. 'D'you see much of them, Rick?'

'We've been playing quite a bit of tennis lately. Fergal won the scratch under-twenty-ones in Simonstown last month.'

'Fergal!' she exclaimed, as if it were a name from long, long ago. 'Good heavens, little Fergal, eh?'

'Not so little now,' he told her impatiently. He did not wish to speak of Fergal at all, only of her and how *she* had grown. But her figure had become so feminine, and in the motion of the carriage imparted such restless grace to her silhouette, he was afraid of what the incandescence of his feelings might lead him to say.

'Talk of the devil,' Carty exclaimed. 'Or am I deceived?'

They were turning in at the drive of the Old Glebe; he nodded towards the house, where, indeed, Fergal McIver was standing waiting – and not at the foot of the steps, either, but on the broad stone landing at their head, like the lord of the manor.

'What's *he* doing here?' Rick asked, unable to keep the annoyance out of his voice. But it was nothing compared with the rage that stirred his innards as his eyes fixed on the hated intruder – his best friend. That was a blind, shapeless fury, a force from somewhere outside him, far larger than his own cramped soul – as large, it seemed, as mankind itself, and certainly as ancient. It subsided, but not into oblivion.

'You answered that question yourself, just now, my boy,' Carty told him. 'Surely he's come to express the delight of the entire county that my cigarette-paper gumming machine is whirring away in factories from Virginia to Vladivostock – as a curious result of which no trout in Lough Cool will be safe from this moment forth.' He smiled at Rick. 'Isn't that the general idea?'

Rick smiled back rather thinly. He was pleased to note how annoyed Judith's mother was to see Fergal standing there. Judith's response, however, was less comforting.

They were approaching the house. She leaned over the edge of the landau and pointed at Fergal, who now began to saunter down the steps as if he owned them. 'Fergal?' she cried in delighted amazement. 'Is that really you? I can't believe it.'

The young man, who had prepared himself to be all suave and cool, saw her now at close quarters and lost his tongue entirely. His jaw hung slack, if not quite vulgarly agape, while he just stood there and stared at her, thinking he had never seen anyone quite so lovely in all his life. And when, in the last few yards, she stood up, opened the door, and leaped lightly down, he almost turned and ran, so much did her beauty frighten him.

She grasped his arm to steady herself and murmured, 'Oh, thank you!' as if he had saved her from a fall.

'Judith, my dear!' her mother cried out. 'Please remember you are no longer in the nursery. Leaping down like that – such antics! What must these two gentlemen think of you?'

One of those gentlemen, Fergal, hardly heard her. He was transfixed – staring into Judith's eyes, astonished at the message he was reading in their depths. Yet he was no more astonished than the young lady herself. The momentum of her little leap had brought her face rather close to his. Fergal's immediate response was to glance away, as from a lamp too brilliant to stare at directly. But she had gone on looking at him, trying to provoke him to smile and laugh.

And then he had turned to her, and she found herself staring into those amazingly pale eyes, so like her own in colour, but deep-set and seeming to burn with their intensity, and in that moment she – or a part of her at least – was freed from whatever promise she might have made, or implied, to Rick.

It was not expected, not wanted, not welcome, not in the least bit comforting – which made it all the more powerful, of course, since, with every count against it, it thrived. *No!* her eyes pleaded with his. *Make it stop. Say something trivial, hurtful even. Shatter this moment into so many bits it can never come back.*

'I say, McIver, hand Mrs Carty down, won't you!' It was Rick who broke the spell, though he shattered nothing for her.

The servants all came out on to the top step at that

moment – cook and a scullery maid, McGinnis, the butler, two upstairs maids, and a tweeny; there were introductions all round.

'Oh, I want to see the house – dear, dear Old Glebe,' Judith cried, all animation again. 'Rick, do come with me. Let's see how many old places we can remember.' She held out her hands invitingly, almost pleadingly, to him, still on his horse.

Mollified, he slipped from the saddle and handed the reins to Fogarty before he trotted to join her. She took his arm and clutched it tight, in a manner that combined both innocence and intimacy, as she led him indoors.

The family's baggage had come down the day before, and the furniture had arrived a week before that, so the place had already acquired a lived-in feeling. 'It's almost as if we'd never left, isn't it? Not for you, of course, but I never saw the place empty. Has anyone lived in it since? Oh, and what about Hen? Have you heard from her? Is she coming over? The summer's almost gone now. I know, let's start at the attics and work down.'

She gave a little skip as she let go of his arm, bringing her to the foot of the stairs ahead of him. She still had a slender waist but her hips were now those of a woman; they did not need the flattery of a bustle beneath her dress but fashion had placed one there, anyway. The effect, as she walked upstairs ahead of him, made him catch his breath and try desperately to think of . . . well, almost *anything* else. After a few steps she turned and called out, 'You, too, Fergal. What are you hanging back like that for?'

Gladly he rejoined them upon the stairs and together they completed their climb to the attics. 'D'you remember a gurking competition up here one terribly wet winter afternoon?' she asked with a laugh as they went into the first of the poky little rooms. 'Gurking' had been their word for belching.

'And you won,' Fergal reminded her. 'It wasn't fair, because . . .'

'I never won,' she protested. 'It was Sally. Actually, it should have been Rick but he let Sally win because he had a little bit of a pash on her in those days, didn't you?'

She turned her bright eyes on Rick, who cringed with embarrassment at the memory.

'Not just in those days, either!' Fergal said meaningfully.

She was quick to catch the nuance. 'Oh?' she asked, looking from one to the other, waiting to see who would tell her first.

'Me?' Rick asked with hollow scorn. 'Me and Sally?' He laughed, none too convincingly, before, desperate to make up lost ground, he added, 'There's no more between me and Sally than between you and Netty. In fact . . .' He paused, smiled condescendingly, and concluded, 'No, I won't say it.'

'Say what?' Fergal challenged. 'There's nothing you could say.' He turned to Judith. 'There's nothing he could say, honestly.'

Rick saw the smile twitch at the corners of her lips, saw her prepare to tease Fergal for his earnest denials. Tease me, instead! he thought angrily. Why waste your time on him?

As she drew breath to speak she thought better of it and turned to Rick. 'Oh Faithlessness, thy name is Man!' she declaimed, and then broke into laughter.

Immediately Rick's mood swung the other way. She can't bring herself to make light of it with him, he thought. Her feelings are too serious. But she can jest all right with me. I don't count, obviously.

'Is that from Shakespeare?' she asked when only Fergal laughed. 'If not, it jolly well ought to be. Is Mad McLysaght still alive? Does he still come round each summer?'

Rick, realizing that his solemnity was unwelcome to her, saw his chance to escape with dignity. 'Perdition catch my soul but I do love thee!' he said, staring at her and challenging her to disbelieve he meant it, every word – yet smiling broadly all the time.

'That's right!' She was delighted to see him back in a more familiar mood. 'That's what he said . . .' Her face grew solemn when she remembered the precise occasion. '. . . on that day,' she concluded flatly. 'That dreadful day.'

She reached forward and touched Rick's arm. 'I suppose people try not to talk about it with you, too. My parents will never discuss it with me at all. I think it's wrong, don't you? We shouldn't bottle it up.'

He nodded tersely, amazed at her ability to change their mood so suddenly and so totally, and to carry both of them so firmly with her.

She took a backward pace or two and sat down in the window seat, oblivious of the dust upon it. 'I remember it almost every day,' she said, 'but there's no one to talk about it with.' She looked sharply up at Rick. 'Does it feel like that with you?'

Again he nodded. 'I can still see you running up over the wild garden like that – all ankles and elbows. And I was so afraid.'

She smiled briefly at this picture of herself. 'The most awful thing of all is that I don't think I could do it now. When you're a child, things are so wonderfully absolute, aren't they? You just *do* things because . . . well, you just do! I can't say what would stop me now, but I don't think I'd have it in me to fly at those fellows like I did.' She tried a little laugh. 'I don't have the right ankles and elbows any more.'

Fergal, aware that his father had been counsel for the defence of the murderers, maintained an unhappy silence and distance now. Then Judith turned to him, or, rather, to include him in her next question, which was more rhetorical than actual. 'Those men they hanged – they *were* the wrong ones, weren't they?'

Fergal nodded solemnly, but only just perceptibly; Rick gazed uncomfortably at his feet.

'Why were none of us called to give evidence?' she continued. 'I wrote to your father' – she nodded at Fergal – 'offering to identify them – I mean as *not* being the right ones. And I said Hen and Rick could confirm it.' To Rick she added, 'Didn't he ask you, too?'

Rick nodded.

She turned back to Fergal. 'Then why didn't he call us?'

'King was so positive. You were just children at the time.'

'We're not now, though.' She turned to Rick and asked him sharply. 'Didn't you talk to him about it? King, I mean? Didn't you tell him you were sure he'd got the wrong ones?'

'Of course I did.'

'And?'

'The trouble was, the ones he identified – the ones they hanged – were all named at the time by the fellow they caught – Ciaran Darcy – the one the gamekeeper dropped in the woods.'

'But they couldn't produce his signed confession, could they!' she challenged. Then, to Fergal, 'Why was that?'

He shrugged uncomfortably. 'The police mislaid it. But the sergeant who actually took the confession on the night was there to testify.'

'But not the man himself,' she said grimly. 'He was safely hanged by then.'

'What d'you mean, *safely* hanged?' Rick asked.

'I mean . . .' she appeared to mull over several possibilities in her mind before saying '. . . it's all jolly convenient. However!' She clapped her hands and made an effort at a smile. 'That's quite enough for one day. Good lord, I never imagined we'd get round to that so swiftly. You didn't answer about Mad McLysaght. Has he turned up yet?'

'No.' Rick, though still shaken by the intensity of her feelings on the subject, was also determinedly jovial. 'You have that treat in store.'

'Among a thousand others, I'm sure. Oh!' She rose with a vast sigh of happiness and put an arm around each of them. 'It's wonderful, wonderful to be back! How I've missed you all!'

'I've missed *me*,' Rick replied. And when they turned to him in amused puzzlement, he added, 'I'm beginning to remember all sorts of things I'd forgotten.'

They each slipped an arm around her, each felt the other's unwelcome presence, and each simultaneously gave the other a light pinch and a punch.

'Boys, boys!' She unpeeled their arms from her waist and hugged them tight to her, each on its own side.

A gong called them to luncheon. They walked to the stairhead as if tied in a double three-legged race. As they let go of each other, to negotiate the stairs, she said, 'It is a most odd phrase, isn't it – when you think of it: "Perdition catch my soul but I do love thee!" Why *perdition*? Is it a man who says it or a woman? Not that it matters, really. But why should the fact that he or she is in love arouse thoughts of damnation and purgatory? Don't you think it's odd?'

'Not if your name's Othello,' Rick said.

He remembered the intensity of his jealousy and rage earlier that morning, on seeing Fergal waiting at the house. Somehow this accidental linkage with the Shakespeare play made that rage more acceptable, giving it a context and diminishing its shock, which had been the shock of strangeness as much as anything.

'The Great Tragedies!' Fergal added, giving the words

the importance of a quotation.

'Why "great", I wonder?' Judith asked.

'Because they're all over and done with inside two and a half hours, I suppose.'

'And,' Rick added, not to be outdone, 'you can call for the author and pelt him with rotten eggs if you didn't like it.'

After Henrietta's arrival at Castle Moore the young people tended to congregate there rather than at Baliver; as a married woman, even though she was only a year or two older than they, she made an acceptable chaperone. And the tennis court was better. Those, at least, were their ostensible reasons for coming to the castle; the real reason was that King wished it so. Now that a new and unknown quantity had been added to the complex human equation upon whose resolution all his ambitions were based, he wanted the young folk where he could keep his eyes and ears – all forty of them – on them. No maid took a tray of lemonade out to them without reporting back on what she had overheard – but that was a mere supplement to the full budget of eavesdropping from the footman Tommy King, the wily butler's kinsman, who was thoughtfully sent out to act as ball boy.

It was almost always the same six young people: Rick and Fergal, Sally and Netty – the original foursome augmented now by Judith and Netty's brother Percy, an easygoing youth of twenty, slightly plump, like his sister, and a brilliant if erratic student of the law. He was articled to Cathcart and Cathcart in Parsonstown and ought to have been there now; but he had decided to take the week off and see if old Cathcart (the only one now extant – and him only just) noticed.

On this particular September morning, with the dew just off the grass, Percy lay on a groundsheet at Henrietta's feet, stripping the seeds off a selection of grasses and husbanding them in small piles near his elbow. 'I do so adore tennis,' he commented absently, being completely absorbed in his stripping and sorting.

'You're not even watching it,' Judith complained. She was sitting, rather peeved, at Henrietta's side for she had been enjoying their conversation until Percy had turned up with an armful of ripened grasses.

'I don't need to with these particular champions,' he replied. 'I could tell you exactly what's happening blindfold. Rick is playing to the limit of his skill and poaching half the shots Sally ought to take, under the impression he's being chivalrous. She's fuming about it underneath because she's actually a far better player . . .'

'But she doesn't look at all angry,' Henrietta objected.

'I know,' he said admiringly. 'Good, isn't she! But then girls can afford to let men carry off the frivolous trophies – as long as they themselves win at the much more important game of life.'

Henrietta laughed; she had discovered over the last few days that her mind and Percy's were strangely attuned – that is, she often knew what he was talking about, especially when he was at his most oblique or obscure. It made Judith angrier still. 'What are you babbling about?' she snapped. 'Win *what* game of life?'

He looked up at her. 'She must practise giving way to men in trivial things, of course.' His tone suggested that was Rule One of the game. His thumb evenly stripped another ear of grass, gathering the harvest in the crook of his index finger. Then, turning to Henrietta, he added suddenly, 'And she must practise hiding her true feelings – until it becomes important to reveal them.'

Henrietta, made uncomfortable by his intensity, said, 'What are you going to do with all those seeds?'

'Eat them,' he replied, as if that, too, were pretty obvious.

'You are a very annoying young man,' Judith complained.

'I've been reading about the Hottentots,' he replied.

She clenched her fists and tried to recruit some sympathy from Henrietta, who merely laughed and said to Percy, 'You didn't tell us about the other two champions out there.'

'Fergal's playing left-handed,' he said, as if nothing had intervened since his verbal dismissal of Rick and Sally, 'because he's still young enough to believe that sportsmanship is more praiseworthy than winning. He's taking a lot of Netty's shots because she's too fat to get to them herself.'

'You can talk!' Judith sneered.

He stripped another seed head and lifted it straight to his mouth.

'Euurgh!' Judith turned away in synthetic disgust.

'You *are* eating them!' Henrietta exclaimed. 'What do they taste like?'

'Me learn plenty water two arrow-shots that way,' he replied in imitation Hottentot; he pointed north, across the court. Then he ate another small mouthful, of different seeds. 'Kudu and rhino pass this way two suns ago,' he added.

His utter solemnity made Henrietta laugh, almost hysterically; even Judith reluctantly gave in. She informed him he was impossible.

Then, still solemn, he turned and held her in a steady gaze. 'Shall I tell you *why* both Rick and Fergal are being so gentlemanly?' he asked quietly.

'No thank you,' she replied with an amused primness that at last made him smile.

Henrietta saw the softening in her attitude and remarked, 'He grows on one, don't you find?'

She was spared from answering directly by a call from Fergal: 'What's the joke? What's he said now?'

'He's telling us about the Hottentots,' Henrietta explained.

Sally laughed. 'There now,' she remarked to her brother. 'I'll bet you're glad you asked.'

Netty gave out an exhausted sigh. 'D'you want to come and take my place, Judith?' she asked.

Judith leaped to comply. 'Anything to get away from this herbivore brother of yours.'

Percy turned to Henrietta and murmured, 'Frumentivore, actually,' as if she, but not Judith, would understand the subtlety of his correction.

She smiled back at him, mainly for the implied compliment; in fact, she *had* been rather good at Latin – good enough to know that the word for *seed* was not *frumentum*, either. When the actual word occurred to her, she flushed slightly, for it was not one to be used – or even thought of – in mixed company. Their eyes met again and she realized he knew just what she was thinking, or determinedly trying *not* to think, at the moment. His slow, lazy smile was the first indication she had that he was dallying with her – or would like to dally with her. A small squirt of panic hollowed out a space in her midriff. Actually, the surprising thing about it was that it was only small.

The energetic swish of Netty's skirts as she flopped into the chair Judith had vacated scattered his carefully hoarded seeds.

'My *semen*arium!' he cried, parodying anguish – and winking at Henrietta in case the word had not occurred to her.

'You'll have to go and gather up some more,' she told him.

Percy, eh? As a dallier, a trifler with her affections? She had never considered him in that light before – indeed, she had never considered any man in that light before. Nor, she assured herself hastily, did she mean to do so now.

'He ought not to be here at all,' Netty said. 'Cathcart'll go mad.'

'If he ever finds out,' Percy added. 'Actually, I'll just sprinkle some dust over myself before I *do* go back and he'll never notice.'

'I don't follow,' Henrietta put in.

Percy chuckled. 'That's his system for knowing how long things have been around the office. We had a query last week on a case he settled back in eighteen-eighty. And he just looked over the floor of his office – have you ever been in his inner sanctum?'

Henrietta shook her head.

'Everything just stands there in piles on the floor – deeds, files, wills, everything. And he just looks at the thickness of dust on a pile and he can tell you its age in a twinkling. Anyway, when this query came in last week he just ran his eye over the piles and pointed to one about six feet away and said to me, "It's in that one, about fourteen inches down." And he was dead on.'

As his two companions laughed he added, 'One day Mrs Trimble will be able to restrain herself no longer. She'll go mad and dust the lot – and that will be the death of the firm. We'll never find a thing after that.'

Netty, suddenly restless, rose to her feet again. 'I'm going to collect some grasses for myself,' she said.

'They don't taste all that wonderful,' he warned her.

'For pressing, oaf!' she rejoined. 'In my herbarium. Are you coming, Hen?'

Henrietta, who, indeed, intended joining her, caught Percy's eye. 'In a mo perhaps,' she replied, not really knowing why she had changed her mind so suddenly.

Instinct, she assured herself. If she ran away from him, it would endow him and his impertinence with a significance it did not possess.

'I'll keep your place warm,' Percy promised his sister as she strolled away. He sat in the chair and leaned back, making the wickerwork creak; he ended up almost at attention, except that he was more horizontal than vertical. 'How is Mr Austin?' he asked casually.

'Good heavens, Percy! I've only been here a week – and he's gone to India. How should I know how he is?'

'Ah!' There was an odd note of sadness in his tone.

'Did you really think I'd have received a letter from him already?'

'The romanticism of the young bachelor!' he mused.

'In what way?' She cast around for something to add that would snatch the conversational initiative back from him – and then realized she did not actually want it for herself. Let him babble on – what did it matter? It would fill some of the tedium until luncheon.

'Well, if I were only a few years married – to a girl as splendid as you, I mean – and I were off to India for Lord alone knows how long . . .'

'Almost a year.'

'Really?' His head jerked in her direction and his repetition of the word carried a smile upon it: 'Really! Anyway, if I were to be absent for so long, I should have left a whole treasury of letters with a friend, to be portioned out at one a day until the regular correspondence from India could take over.'

'Did you say *incurable* romanticism?' she asked.

'No.'

'Well, you should have.'

'Ah!'

There was such a weight of forced sadness in his sigh that she was tempted to laugh. 'Perhaps it's not incurable,' she told him soothingly. 'But it certainly is romanticism.'

'Not all it's cracked up to be, eh?'

'What isn't?'

'Marriage.'

'How old are you, Percy?'

'Old enough to refrain from saying "jolly nearly twenty-one". Why?'

'And you're already pondering the state of matrimony?'

There was a significant pause before he replied, 'All the time.'

He was suddenly quite serious. And all the flippant, casual remarks she had been vaguely mustering in her mind, ready to be trotted out as they seemed appropriate, were rendered out of place. 'Why?' she asked.

He glanced rapidly at the players, at his sister, plucking grasses beyond the eastern edge of the court, at Tommy King, the footman, and then turned to her with an awkward smile. 'It's the great divide, isn't it – much greater than between rich and poor, or English and Irish.'

'What?' she asked, though she knew very well what he was driving at.

'It's almost greater than the divide between man and woman – which is odd, when you think about it. I'm talking about marriage – the difference between those who are in it and those of us who are still on the outside.'

She knew that this sudden serious turn in the conversation ought to leave her disquieted, but it didn't; indeed, it made her feel oddly relaxed. Instinct advised her to trust it – that sense of relaxation. 'For some people,' she pointed out, 'it's not a question of *still* being outside. I mean, they've already made up their minds that's where they want to be, and that's where they'll quite happily stay.'

'Forget them.'

'That group doesn't include you, obviously. Have you any particular young lady in view, may I ask?'

He sat properly in the chair and crossed his legs, smoothing out the creases in his trousers.

'And would she be very much in view at this

particular moment?' Henrietta pressed.

He linked his fingers in an arch and rested his chin upon them. 'It's more abstract than that,' he said solemnly. 'It comes from working in a solicitor's office, I suppose. I mean, we all grow up filled with romantic notions about finding a soul-mate . . . happily ever after, and all that sort of thing. And then one sees the other side of the coin – the squabbles, the backbiting . . . the last wills and testaments filled with revenge – designed for no other purpose than to hurt and exclude. D'you know what I mean?'

After a pause she said, 'I do.' She drew a deep breath. 'Oh, Percy – indeed I do!'

That afternoon they went for a swim in the lake – an operation that required a great deal of cooperative delicacy and tact on the part of all concerned. The young ladies changed into their ankle-length, wrist-length, high-necked bathing costumes in the boathouse and entered the water fully before they put so much as their noses out beyond the door that opened on to the lake. The young gentlemen changed into their half-sleeved, calf-length bathing suits behind the summer pavilion, a furlong distant, and entered the water among the rushes to the south of the landing jetty on that shore. Thus it was no more than the floating heads of the young ladies that met the floating heads of the young gentlemen – an event that took place about fifty-two inches above the gravel-bottomed patch near the centre of the lake.

The ever-attentive Tommy King gathered the ladies' dressing gowns and towels and brought them up to the jetty in case one of them wished to get out without swimming all the way up to the head of the lake again.

For a while the youngsters circled one another in wary fashion, laughing nervously, splashing and retaliating with sedate boldness. It was Henrietta who broke the ice, socially speaking. She stood up. And though the water and her bathing suit, between them, revealed nothing of what the average respectable ballgown would have laid bare, it was nonetheless an audacious move. The eyes of the others met uncertainly, still mere inches above the water line.

'Hallo, hippo!' Percy greeted his sister, squirting a mouthful of water that carefully missed her.

'Just for that!' she shouted and, leaping half out of the water, swamped him in her descent.

'Don't you dare!' Sally warned her brother.

But she was too late, for he had already launched himself at her in a precautionary attack. 'Best line of defence,' he told her as she surfaced in a green fury of bubbles and set about splashing him with her cupped hands and a needle-point precision.

'Arise, Sir Henrietta!' Rick cried then, diving beneath his sister and lifting her in piggyback, her arms round his neck, her limbs around his waist. 'I hope you realize this means war!' he challenged the others.

Neither of his fellows needed second bidding; each raised his sister to knight-errant status and entered the lists in a joust whose object was to haul one of the other girls off her brother's back.

Judith watched them awhile, thinking that perhaps it would soon be her turn to play knight errant on one of the boys' backs. Both Rick and Fergal cast many a glance in her direction, wondering would they dare, daring each other; their very hesitation made her realize it was too late for that – a year too late at least. She turned and swam across the lake to the jetty, where young King, eyes already averted, held forth her dressing gown – or, rather, the one she had borrowed off Hen.

Up through the uncut meadow of the wild garden she meandered, swiping at seed heads with the tassels of her gown. Then it struck her that she had not stood upon this ground since the evening of the Murders. The hair prickled on the nape of her neck and the afternoon felt suddenly chill.

She forced herself to look at the marble pavilion, but it was an anticlimax. Her mind had replayed the scene so often that the place had lost its power to sicken. Indeed, a curious reversal now occurred: the pavilion acquired the deceptive super-reality of a scene viewed in a stereoscope. She felt she could walk toward it for ever and still not arrive; she could reach toward it and beyond, but never touch its stone or breathe its air.

A sense of loss overcame her; she realized she had been counting on this place to recharge, as it were, the reservoir of her anger – not simply at what had happened that night but at the injustice that had followed, a year or so later. Then, glancing again at the pavilion, serene and white in the sun, she was struck by the thought that something of the spirit of that evening had, after all, survived. Not the frenzy, not the hatred, not the blood, but all that serene and sunlit happiness which had gone before it. She remembered a moment when she had seen one of the Bellinghams gazing up with languid satisfaction at the scene across the lake: the lawns and gardens, the modern castle and the old tower, the mountain beyond; and it had struck her that they owned every twig of it, every leaf, every stone. The pavilion owed its very existence to that fact. It was where they could come to celebrate their good fortune.

Now her mind pursued the thought further. People like the Bellinghams had no need to invent cigarette-gumming machines, like her father, or go into court to plead the cause of others, like Mr McIver, or draft wills and convey titles to land, like Mr O'Farrelly; all they had to do was sit tight and collect the rents. Wouldn't *anyone* who possessed such a perfect little kingdom build a pavilion of marble in a wilderness of wild flowers at its very heart, where they could sit on a summer's evening and relish it all – and all without a single, vulgar word spoken!

It was the first time such a distinction had occurred to her, setting Rick apart from the rest of them; but then she felt that was unfair. Actually, something Rick had said the other day kept coming back to her – his joke about being able to pelt the author with rotten eggs if you didn't like his tragedy. It set her thinking, first about the difference between the tragedies of real life and those of the stage. The biggest difference, of course, was that life's tragedies had no single author, unless you wanted to blame God for everything; life's tragedies rose out of a conspiracy among the entire cast.

That notion crossed her mind again, now, as she lay in the wild garden, only yards from the spot where one particular conspiracy had almost killed her in its random trawl for victims, six years ago.

It would not do, she realized. You could not scatter responsibility casually among the entire cast like that. You had to pin it on someone in the end.

Even the innocent?

There it was again.

Lying at full length in the grass, with the lake water drying silkily on her skin, she became aware that she was stretched rather too comfortably for such uncomfortable, Puritan thoughts. She rose on one elbow and dug her left hip into the sun-hardened ground as a kind of mortification. She gazed down at the brothers and sisters, still at their horseplay. When would they tire of it and come out?

Suddenly she realized it was no longer brother and sister as horse and knight. That was Sally on Rick's back and Hen on Percy's . . . and plump little Netty was all on her own, splashing both couples with impartial vigour.

So where was Fergal?

'Boo!' He stuck his head up above the long grass, about ten feet away.

She laughed and feigned a small heart attack to show he hadn't frightened her at all. 'How long have you been there?' she asked.

'You looked so severe I didn't dare approach,' he replied – not exactly answering her question. 'I hope you didn't feel excluded?'

'No. We were an odd number. Someone had to wait in the wings.'

His eye gauged the distance between them and the middle of the lake. 'That's a big stage if these are the wings,' he commented.

'Now Netty's the odd one out.'

He smiled. 'I left them to it as a kindness to poor Percy, really. He's a stout fellow in many ways but he's not up to playing horse to Netty's knight, I'm afraid. And she's more devastating on her own two feet.'

Judith nodded and drew the dressing gown around her – a kind of unconscious permission for him to advance those last few feet. It was humid and sticky inside the towelling folds and she had to fight an impulse to throw it off; she envied him the slightly greater freedom to show the skin of his forearms and calves.

'What were you thinking?' he asked as he seated himself a yard or so to her left. He hugged his knees to his chin and stared at the five who were still in the water. 'You did have a most disapproving look.'

'I was thinking about the night of the Murders,' she said.

'Ah!' Somehow his tone conveyed that he had suspected as much but did not think she would be so frank as to admit it.

'This is the first time I've been back here since then.'

'Of course.' He glanced at her briefly, and in slight

surprise. 'I hadn't realized that. We've been here so often since then that it's lost something of its . . . you know.'

She smiled wanly. 'I'm afraid it's lost that sort of power for me, too, Fergal.'

He saw where her eyes were resting. 'It's just a pavilion, you mean? Like any other pavilion?'

'Not quite. But my memories of the hour or so immediately before the Murders is stronger. I remember sitting there among them thinking if I were a Bellingham, then every last inch of the view from here would be mine. And then, of course, I realized that's exactly why they built it there in the first place.'

'A vantage from which to gloat!' He chuckled. 'I never thought of that.'

'I don't suppose they did, either. Not deliberately.'

'And what birthday was that for you? Your fifteenth?'

She nodded, wondering why he asked.

'Did you really think such profound thoughts at that age?'

'Profound?' She chortled scornfully.

'Not for a grand old dame of twenty-one,' he allowed. 'But for one who had only just turned fifteen – I'd call it pretty profound.'

She made no reply, not thinking the compliment worth dismissing a second time. Instead, she told him what thoughts had been prompted by Rick's throwaway remark about authors and rotten eggs; this time Fergal paid her no joking compliments about her profundity.

'D'you think we absolutely must pin responsibility on *someone*?' he asked. 'Not just for obvious tragedies or great wrongs but for everything? There's an author for everything? Is that where your idea leads?'

How like a man! she thought. He couldn't leave an idea to grow where it was, in the middle of some half-defined area, shadowy and fertile; he had to dig it up and carry it to the edge, to the strong light where nothing could remain hidden.

She said, 'I was just thinking – that's why they hanged those four who were innocent. The prospect of hanging no one – except Ciaran Darcy, who was shot over there and who was half dead anyway – that prospect was too awful to contemplate. They had to blame someone, if only a scapegoat.'

'Otherwise?'

She still felt hugely reluctant to pull her ideas out into the open, exposing them to the glare of his scrutiny; but his question forced her to say the first thing that came into her head: 'Otherwise they'd have to blame themselves. No, not they – *we*! We'd have to blame ourselves. We are the real authors of everything that happens to us.'

He breathed out a long, silent whistle and, lying back in the long grass, paid her the highest compliment of all: silence.

To fill it she asked why he'd left the others.

'I was afraid you might have felt left out.' He nodded at the lake, where the game seemed to be petering out in a general collapsing of horses. 'Down there. It was pretty thoughtless of us.'

'You make too much of it,' she told him. 'As for feeling left out, I'm only amazed at how quickly I feel I'm one of the old crowd again. I suppose it's because I never left in spirit. I never thought of Dublin as anything but an exile.'

Rick and Sally dog-paddled away from the other three. Was there collusion between the two McIvers? Judith wondered.

'Did you make no friends while you were there?' he asked.

'Not like us.' In case he should take it too personally she waved a hand to include the others down in the water. 'There were girls I went to play with, and walked on the North Strand with, or went to Howth . . .'

'And young cavaliers who escorted you to dances?' His tongue lingered teasingly on his lip but she could feel a serious edge to the question, too.

An imp prompted her to start an entire new fiction. 'Oh, Fergal!' she gushed, as if she could no longer contain her secret and had only been waiting for someone to ask her. 'There was a young fellow who lived in the house across the road from us in Drumcondra – Tarquin D'Annunzio – he was so handsome . . . you wouldn't believe it!'

'An Eyetie?' Fergal said coolly.

'You know how handsome they are. All the girls fell for him, of course, but there was something . . .' She shrugged at the impossibility of conveying anything so wonderful and huge. 'Between him and me. It was very special. And I miss him *so* much. I think about him all the time, you know. *Do* you know? D'you know that *special* feeling?'

He cleared his throat uncomfortably. 'I suppose I might. What did he do, this . . . paragon?' He made the word sound like a synonym for scoundrel.

She shook her head sadly. 'Oh, he didn't *do* anything – and I'm sorry to say he was very far from being a paragon. I have to admit he wasn't the brightest young fellow I ever met. In fact, to be quite honest, he was fairly dim-witted. Excruciatingly dull – no conversation at all. And he drank far too much. And kept the most disreputable company . . .'

Looking into his eyes, so full of shock and disappointment, she wondered how much longer she could keep it up – how much longer it would be fair to keep it up. But she was enjoying her invention so hugely, not to mention his gullible discomfiture – and after all, he did start this line of conversation – that she decided to harry him just a little further.

'But . . . but you said . . .' he protested, almost incoherently.

'I know,' she agreed sadly. 'Aren't we women hopeless! No wonder you won't let us vote. But I only had to look into Tarquin's eyes and I absolutely melted to a jelly. Even now I feel my insides going all hollow. I'll bet you don't even know the feeling I'm talking about.'

'I do!' he protested. And suddenly she saw such anguish in his eyes that her teasing humour shrivelled at once.

He drew breath to say more, and some instinct within her – far quicker than thought – knew that he must not be allowed to say it, not in response to such merciless teasing as this. 'Fergal!' she chided. Leaning toward him she put the flat of her hand on his chest and pushed vigorously, making him roll one complete circle down the slope.

It came just in time to save him; a fraction of a second later and he would have committed himself. 'You!' he roared, leaping to his feet and standing astride her while she pretended to cringe in his shadow.

'What made you say such horrid things?' he cried, relieved that he had been allowed to step back from a brink whose danger he was just beginning to comprehend; even now, at the core of his good humour, he felt a bristling anger.

'What made you *believe* them!' she countered. 'It doesn't say much for your opinion of me, does it!'

Having no answer to that, and yet not wishing to concede her point, he moved his toe into the pit of her right arm and tickled her there.

'No!' she begged urgently, grabbing his calf in both hands.

It was a futile gesture for it merely exposed those ticklish sites even more openly; a moment later his right toe had joined in the fun.

'No, please no!' she begged, laughing between staccato shrieks and writhing desperately. She reached a foot up to kick him but when he saw where it was aimed, an instinct he could not oppose forced him to drop to his knees and straddle her wriggling form, trapping her at the waist between his knees with all the ferocity of a rider who has lost his stirrups at full gallop.

Fergal was an excellent horseman so the power of his grip took her breath away in every sense of the phrase. 'Pax!' she gasped, grabbing his wrists as she felt his hands moving to complete the work his toes had begun.

'I'm not sure that pax applies to mere tickling,' he told her, struggling not very hard to continue. Sobriety was beginning to return and he was a little afraid of where their horseplay had brought them.

'Well, it does,' she assured him. 'So there!'

He relaxed his grip but found himself shamefully reluctant to move to a less compromising position away from her – not least because, by some strange paradox, such a move would be like admitting that their position *was* compromising, while to stay as they were would pooh-pooh the notion. It helped that she still clung to his wrists, though now her touch was gentle.

'*Did* you believe me?' she asked.

He nodded ruefully. 'I'm a pessimist, I suppose.'

She put the remark to one side, to dissect later. 'In fact, there *was* such a fellow,' she admitted. 'Not called Tarquin, mind, but very handsome. And *very* dim. And several of the girls did rather get a pash on him.'

'But not Judith Carty!'

Her eyes narrowed. 'You're doing it again, Fergal. If you sat over there, I could start learning to breathe once more.'

Now it was easy to move away from her. 'D'you want another dip?' he suggested.

She rose on her elbows, far enough to see the water over the long grass. Henrietta must have sent Netty to join Rick and Sally, for form's sake. She smiled. 'No. Let's just lie in the grass here and talk, eh?' Her ribcage and hipbones still remembered the ferocity of his grip – still savoured his touch. She put that aside to dissect later, too.

'What about?' he asked, stretching himself out quickly in case she changed her mind. He was on her left again, with the sun full upon him; his body was a careful six inches from hers. He lay on his side, with his head on the prop of his right arm.

'Tell me what you're going to do,' she suggested. 'I suppose this summer will be the last long holiday of your life? The last childhood type of holiday, anyway.'

He nodded glumly and echoed her thought in other words, 'Childhood's end.'

She knew he was referring, obscurely, to the horseplay they had just abandoned. 'So what now?' she asked.

His eye was taken by a sparrowhawk, hovering briefly over the woodland below the lake. 'I'm attracted to the law, but not to the business of advocacy. And nor do I want to spend my life doing conveyances and wills and the like. Yet the idea of an academic career in the law doesn't exactly thrill me either.'

'It must be wonderful,' she said solemnly, 'knowing exactly what you *don't* want to do in life.'

He narrowed his eyes. 'Are you just going to mock me all day?'

The smile faded from her face. 'It's myself I'm after mocking, Fergal, if truth were told. I don't even know what I *do* want to do. Anyway, if you can't be an advocate or a solicitor or a professor – what does it leave?'

He shrugged. 'Precious little. The diplomatic and politics.' He spoke the two words with no enthusiasm. 'Anyway, the pater's being very decent. He has chambers in Dublin, of course, but an office in Parsonstown, too – because he has quite a practice in the Midlands circuit. So he's allowing me to work beside his clerk there, looking up precedents and doing general dogsbody work, just to get a feel for things. It's quite a slog.'

'And what are you now? Twenty-one?'

He nodded. 'Not too late. Five years from now I could be third secretary in quite an attractive embassy – assuming I go for the diplomatic at all, of course.'

So there it was – a small claim, tactfully staked, waiting for the assay. She smiled up at him through half-closed eyes and wondered whether her future might not, after all, lie with him rather than Rick. In a curious way, the answer seemed to have nothing to do with her, or with any deliberate choice she might make. She remembered when they moved to Dublin, driving up the street where their new home stood, and her father had jokingly challenged her to pick it out from its near-identical neighbours. And of course she couldn't. It had struck her as odd that a house which was to be her home for the Lord-knows-how-many years, a house that would soon seem special and different from all the others, should reveal not the smallest, meanest clue in advance. She remembered staring up and down the street, close to panic, mentally shouting at the houses: 'Come on, come on! I know it's one of you! Just give me a little sign!'

But, whatever the stars or tealeaves or cards might be capable of foretelling, the house had been unable to oblige. And now, gazing into Fergal's eyes as he stared at the lake below, she could read no hint as to whether she might one day find them the most compelling and attractive eyes in the world.

All she knew was that she did not find them so now, for all that she liked him as a friend.

Down in the water the random paddling of the five swimmers brought them close together, near the head of the jetty. They stood in the muddy ooze and splashed each other once again, but with little of their earlier vigour.

'We fairies, that do run from the presence of the sun, following darkness like a dream, now are frolic!' The words, in the booming delivery of a Henry Irving, rolled across the water and halted them in their play.

'McLysaght!' Henrietta called out delightedly. 'You're welcome indeed! But why so late this year?'

'It was a good year, mistress,' he called back. 'The season that's in it.'

'Would you ever go round to the summer pavilion,' she shouted across to him, 'and gather kindling for a fire.'

'I willingly obey your command.' He drew off his hat and waved it with a courtly flourish.

As he set off, Henrietta said to the others, 'We can put some sausages and mutton chops on a spit and eat them down here.'

'And no servants and no tablecloths and no napkins and no silver,' Rick added. 'Let's have a really savage feast.'

His sister looked dubiously at Sally and Netty, mutely canvassing their opinion. The excitement of the game was still upon them and the words 'savage feast' struck precisely the right chord – and so it was agreed.

It was evening before all the elements of even a 'savage' feast could be assembled – a golden autumnal evening at Castle Moore, though dirtier weather was already assembling low down on the horizon over south County Clare. It was still just light enough for them to see each other's faces, but dark enough to make the flames seem bright. A sense of borrowed time descended upon them; their festivity, which had been to celebrate no more than the fleeting moment, was suddenly hemmed in by other concerns – memories of yesterday, anxieties of tomorrow.

Henrietta thought of committee meetings back in England, meetings that would be held without her – though her absence would make not the slightest difference to the conclusions they reached. She was, she realized, just a bit of life's ballast, dead weight that allowed other vessels to buffet their way through the great sea of life. Only here at Castle Moore did she feel she had any importance.

Percy silently rehearsed a bouquet of excuses for his absence from the office that week; equally silently he wondered what was happening to him, and what he really hoped to achieve with Henrietta. And why did Sally appear to be taking a sudden interest in him?

Fergal reached his hands toward the flames and remembered that afternoon's conversation with Judith, especially her remark that each individual is the true author of everything that happens to her – or him. That was the uncomfortable part – the idea that he had had no one but himself to blame for all the shortcomings and disappointments of his life. He wished she hadn't said that. It was all right for schoolmasters and parsons to come out with notions like that, you could tell they didn't mean it – 'Not only with their lips but in their lives!' It's what they were paid to tell the populace. But Judith had really meant it.

He wondered how long it would *really* be before he was 'in a position' to offer any young lady the security and prospects she would expect. A stony ground it was that stretched ahead of him; nothing would grow there but impossible daydreams. How rich was Judith's old man? he wondered. It was hard to believe that something so trivial – a device for rolling cigarettes or whatever it was – could transform anyone's life so swiftly. But if the old boy was *very* rich, perhaps he'd put his daughter's happiness above all other considerations and give her a whopping dowry. Then she could marry whoever she liked, whenever it suited her, even if that lucky fellow hadn't yet finished his legal studies. Or perhaps there was something that he, Fergal, could invent, too? Some simple, everyday device that all the world had been waiting for without even knowing it. He could start building it in his bedroom, then move up to a shed, then a barn . . . and finally his own proper factory. And at last he'd be inside that magic circle of gentlemen rich in security and prospects.

Pleasant as these fancies were, they glossed over one awkward little fact: they all required Judith to be in love with him – which she plainly was not. But how do you *make* a girl be in love with you? He stared at her, bathing her in wave after silent wave of his infinite yearning, and wondering why she did not even glance his way.

Judith, despite her brave words to Fergal that she hadn't felt excluded earlier that afternoon, now felt that she was, indeed, set apart from them all in some indefinable way. When her father had to give up the Old Glebe six years ago, the loss of friends she had known from childhood had gone hard with her – and not just the loss of friends, but of all their haunts, as well – their secrets, their fierce, fleeting loves and hates. She had expected her return would magically restore those lost treasures to her, though a moment's thought would have shown the absurdity of such hopes. The words she had blurted out to Fergal on the spur of the moment that afternoon now haunted her. Those absurd hopes were, indeed, the cause of her present unhappiness, and she had only herself to blame.

Now, to her annoyance, she found herself attracted by the prospect of escaping into an even earlier daydream – one so absurd that it was beyond the reach of scorn. She gazed into the trees behind the summer house and thought of a forest somewhere, a fairytale forest with a gingerbread house in a clearing where she could live at peace with the birds and the little forest animals and let the rest of the world go its own dreary way. It had been her favourite daydream ten years ago; why it came back to her now, she could not think – did not even *want* to think. Also, there was Rick, a new and disturbing element who had to be accommodated somewhere in the phantasy. She wanted him to be there, too. Not all the time. Not even most of the time. But, for instance, they would eat together . . . venison and trenchers and things, with the juices running down their chins just like now – and tasty morsels gathered in the forest. And they'd sit by the fire afterward, gazing fondly at each other, just like now, with the twinkle of the flames in their eyes, just like now, and then he'd rise and kiss her and . . . walk out into the forest, or disappear . . . anyway, just not *be* there any more. The empty childishness of this daydream annoyed her immensely, even as its sentimental smoothness wooed and lulled her disappointed spirit. There should be something more worthy in her life than such idiotic scribble. A sense of emptiness, an awareness of profound unfulfilment, depressed her yet further.

Netty sat beside her, wondering why Fergal couldn't see that his hopes of Judith were utterly vain. And even if they weren't, Judith was obviously going to turn into one of those sweet, selfish, vain, tyrannical women who would lead him a fierce old dance and never give him true peace or happiness. And why couldn't he see that if he wanted true peace and happiness, he ought to start with a wife who adored him to distraction and would rather die than cause him pain? And why couldn't humans communicate by telepathy any longer? And had he been quite honest with her in the pine grove above the tennis court at Baliver that day, when he said he thought skinny girls were a fright? Judith Carty was as skinny as a scallion.

To be sure, the seven young people did not each sit or sprawl in their own little cocoon of ruminative silence while these thoughts and fancies flickered in their minds. They talked ten to the dozen, laughed immoderately, chewed on a delicious mixture of blood-raw and cinder-crisp mutton, wiped their lips and chins on the backs of their fingers and licked them clean again, teased, reminisced, complained, exchanged mock insults and even more mocking compliments . . . in short, behaved like any such crowd of privileged youngsters who had known one another almost from the moment they could crawl – and who now enjoyed the supreme stroke of luck that one of them had crossed the magical Rubicon into wedlock, which gave them licence to consort thus dangerously together. But behind that lighthearted façade, the tormented thoughts and mocking daydreams played on, and endlessly on.

Sally listened to Rick reciting some humorous episodes from last season's hunting field. She noted how his eyes roved around from hearer to hearer, auditing their responses, cutting his tale to the cloth of their interest and patience; he was always a grand man with a story. A week or two ago he would have looked in her direction twice as often as in anyone else's; but no longer. Now it was Judith, Judith, Judith at the centre of his field. Sally remembered the strange excitement of riding piggyback on his shoulders in the lake that afternoon, and then the triumph of her brief swim alone with him – which would have been a very ordinary achievement in the days before Judith Carty reappeared among them; she had spoiled everything. Sally, like her brother, wondered how you could *make* someone be in love with you – not quite against their will but when they were as yet undecided; how did you tip the balance in your favour?

Unlike her brother, she had arrived at a tentative answer: you didn't throw yourself at his head; far from it – you made him think he might lose you to another if he wasn't pretty smart. So now, whenever Rick happened to glance her way, he found her looking at Percy, staring at Percy, smiling at Percy, admiring Percy. But it was no coldly laid-out strategy – it was an ancient urge, deeper than thought and reason.

And Rick, telling his tale with the ease of the born raconteur, wondered why his two favourite listeners were suddenly so remote with him. Judith just sat there, staring off into the trees, and Sally was ogling Percy O'Farrelly, of all people. He recalled, with a shameful kind of glee, how it had felt to carry her on his shoulders in the lake that afternoon, screaming with the pleasures of horseplay, her thighs clenched tight around his neck and cheeks. Yet, even as the skin of his neck tingled at the luxuriant memory, he found himself wishing it had been Judith, not Sally. Or Judith as well as Sally? Yes, he reluctantly allowed, that would have been most pleasant of all. He began to wonder if any one woman would ever content him.

And King, who had come down to inquire if the young ladies and gentlemen would like a fire set up in the music room, in case they might wish to dance before the evening broke up, paused and surveyed them keenly, waiting for an appropriate moment to intervene. He halted near Mad McLysaght, who lay in the dewy grass a couple of dozen paces off, ready with more firewood as it might be required. 'They've finished eating, so,' he commented.

' "Go to the feast, revel and domineer!" ' was the almost inevitable reply.

'Save it for them,' the butler growled. 'I'll thank you to speak plain with me. What are they talking about?'

''Tis hunting, your honour. The young master is after recalling a livelier hunt than he enjoyed on the day itself, I'm thinking.'

Over his words King caught Rick's mention of a covert, a horse, a rider or two. He relaxed. The young master should follow the hounds more this season, he decided. It was an all-absorbing occupation – or it had that potential. It would keep his mind off . . . all sorts of other things.

' "A solemn hunting is in hand," ' McLysaght added under his breath.

'What's that?' King asked. Then, nodding at the group round the fire, added, 'There, d'you mean?'

The other merely grunted.

'Who'll get the fox then?' King pressed.

'Fox, ape, *and* humblebee,' McLysaght cackled. 'Was your honour ever aware that the humblebee can sting?'

'You're a lighthouse in a bog,' King commented in disgust as he went on toward the group.

'And was your honour ever aware,' the other called after him, 'there's a species of humblebee here in old Erin that's unknown over the water?'

'Brilliant but useless,' King rejoined as he stooped over the young gentry and put his question.

It was Sally who answered for them. She pointed to the darkling sky over the lough and said they all ought to be getting on home.

They rose and sauntered down to the jetty, leaving a small battlefield of discarded bones and napkins for other hands to tidy.

While they bickered over who was to go in what boat, Judith stood knee-deep in the autumn grass and gazed back at the trees on the brow of the rise, behind the summer pavilion. Henrietta's voice, soft at her side, said, 'There were dark clouds over the lough on that evening, too. Remember?'

Judith gave a wistful nod. 'I was thinking about that evening . . .'

'I'm sure everyone was. I don't suppose we'll ever be able to picnic down here, any of us, without . . .'

'Yes, but I wasn't thinking of that.' She turned and stared intently at Henrietta. 'D'you know what I remembered?'

Henrietta, mesmerized by the pale fire in those wide eyes, just shook her head.

'They carried me up, if you recall, to the sickroom. I was going to sleep in your bed and we were each going to share our deepest secret with the other. But they took me to the sickroom.'

'Of course. You lost a lot of blood.'

'I cried and cried.'

'We all did.'

'Yes, but I cried because I wasn't with you.' She laughed then, as one does at a childish memory.

Henrietta grasped her arm and said, 'Stay tonight then! Let's say it was only a postponement.' Then, a little embarrassed at her own impulsiveness, she began to add reasons: 'We've so much to catch up on . . . we can send the dogcart round for your things . . .' The one reason she did not give was that their 'deepest secrets' were now infinitely deeper.

'Your man was singularly *un*delighted,' Judith commented as she slipped into bed, well before Henrietta was ready; her tongue still tingled from the strange minty toothpowder they used at Castle Moore.

'My man?' Henrietta, only half listening, was holding up her dress and wondering whether it would do for morning wear tomorrow. In London she changed dresses four times each day.

'King.'

'Oh, him!'

'Yes, what d'you make of him?' Judith continued.

'In what way?' The question was wary.

'Well, he's always perfectly deferential, always the perfect butler, and yet . . . D'you know what I mean?'

'And yet what?'

'You *do* know what I mean. He should be carrying a big placard like in those cartoons in Punch, where it says *John Bull* or *Ireland*. He should carry a placard saying, *And yet . . .*'

When Henrietta made no reply she added, 'Surely you've noticed how he orders Rick around.'

'Have you spoken to Rick about it?'

Judith pulled a glum face. 'It's hardly the sort of thing, is it? By the way, I'm getting this half of the bed warm for *you*, I hope you realize. Papa calls me a furnace. He says he should pay me to slip between their sheets an hour before bedtime every night.'

The word *pay* jarred slightly with Henrietta but it was several moments before she pinned it down. The use of it, even in jest, revealed that, although the Bellinghams and the Cartys were on terms of social intimacy, a considerable gulf nonetheless divided them; the notion that a lady might receive *pay* for anything, even in jest, was distasteful. It was something no Bellingham would ever have said. If Harold, her husband, overheard Judith making such a remark he would insist on dropping her at once.

That thought alone was enough to revive her spirit. Harold would strongly disapprove of Judith, so she, in her husband's absence – and ignorance – would go out of her way to cultivate their old friendship. 'Jolly kind of you!' She smiled triumphantly. 'How much d'you want me to pay? At Eton, you know, they send the fags to go and warm the bog seats. No pay there, of course. Actually, come to think of it, I've always wanted someone to go ahead and warm up the whole world for me.'

Judith giggled. 'Oh, you can pay me in secrets.'

'Ah!' Henrietta was wistful again. 'I've been thinking about that.' She began brushing her teeth vigorously, speaking in staccato bursts between times. 'When we were that age we used to think the whole world depended on secrets, didn't we? Don't you remember thinking that?' Brush brush. 'The green baize door didn't just close off the nursery . . .'

'There never was a green baize door at the Old Glebe,' Judith put in smugly.

'Oh yes there was! I was about to say, before I was so rudely interrupted – we all had a green baize door in our minds as well.' Brush brush. 'It opened into chambers that were just waiting to be filled with all those grown-up secrets.' She put down her toothbrush carelessly and it fell to the carpet; she left it there for her maid in the morning.

'I suppose so,' Judith conceded reluctantly. She was rather proud of the fact that she had never been confined to the nursery in the same formal way as the Bellingham children.

'Move over!' Henrietta became a jocular sergeant major. A moment later, as she slipped between the pre-warmed sheets, she said, 'Oh, bliss! You *are* a furnace, aren't you.'

Over in the chill half of the vast bed Judith forced herself not to shiver or show any reaction to the cold into which her own suggestion had now banished her. She lay on her side, facing Henrietta, her head nonchalantly resting on the prop of her hand, and said, 'Now pay me.'

Henrietta smiled. 'And that was the next thing I was going to say. When we do finally push open that green baize door, the one in our minds, we find to our disappointment that the rooms are empty.'

'Empty?'

'Well, perhaps not absolutely bare, but just full of

tawdry – all knick-knacks and gewgaws. It wasn't worth all that yearning and aspiring and . . . being good.'

'Really?' Disappointment in Judith contended with an odd sort of excitement that Henrietta could be so positive and so utterly damning about the grown-up world, which still intimidated her more than somewhat.

'Haven't you found it so?' The question was slightly surprised.

'I think I've only pushed the door open a little crack with my toe and peeped round it. So far I haven't really, you know, explored it or anything.'

'I shouldn't bother if I were you. It's not worth it.'

She didn't, Judith noticed, say, 'Stay happy in your little nursery.' Not quite. But the implication was clear. A fleeting glimpse of her favourite nursery daydream – the gingerbread house in the sylvan glade – occurred to her. Before she could think about it she heard herself saying, 'D'you know what was going through my mind down there by the lake this evening?'

'You told me.'

'No, apart from that. I was looking at the trees behind the summer pavilion and trying to pretend they went on for ever. Well, not for ever – but like a forest in a fairy tale. And I thought if I could have a little charcoal burner's tiggeen somewhere in a clearing in that forest . . . I mean, I could be truly happy there. Living all alone, you know, very simply.'

'Happy ever after!'

'I know.' Judith let out a brief, irritable sigh. 'I know it's childish but I often think about it. I don't really want to but I can't stop it – the picture of that darling little tiggeen, and me living in it. Like when you get a tune on your brain and it won't go away. I get so angry with myself. Don't things like that happen to you?'

Henrietta had to think. She held her breath without realizing it. Then she let it out in a rush, making it sound as if Judith had almost hit her with the hardness of her question. 'I suppose they do,' she said reluctantly. 'Not that particular daydream. But I do think of . . . oh, I don't know – the way life might have turned out differently for me.'

'If . . . ?' Judith prompted when she volunteered nothing more.

'If I hadn't . . .' she hesitated a long while before she added, '. . . married Harold. There, I've said it!'

Judith gasped. When she had spoken of secrets, she hadn't meant anything so dire as that. The silence began to burn. 'Isn't he . . . I mean, hasn't it turned out the way you . . . ?' She gave up trying to find some nice way of putting it.

Henrietta said it for her. 'The way I hoped? I don't know what I hoped, Judith. I seem to be . . . I don't know – cut off – yes, I seem to be cut off from the girl I was here. The girl you used to know. I can't remember what I once hoped for, or even if I ever hoped for anything! Do *you* remember? Did we ever talk about it? What *did* I want in those days?'

'We used to talk about "when we are married" at lot.'

'Did we?'

'Surely you remember? It wasn't serious – or maybe it was. A serious sort of game, perhaps?'

'And what did we think it'd be like?'

'We used to talk about dinner parties . . . the sort of carriages we'd keep . . . dresses, maids . . . where we'd like to live. You always wanted to live in Belgravia – and now you do. So wishes can come true, you see. You can't have forgotten all that, Hen, surely?'

There was silence in the other half of the bed – silence and a curious little convulsion.

'Hen?' she prompted.

Again, only silence.

'Shall I put out the lamp or just turn it down?'

There was another small convulsion; to her horror Judith realized that Henrietta was weeping. 'I'll just turn it down, so,' she said to cover her embarrassment. When she lay back on the pillow, with her fingers linked behind her head, Henrietta flung herself on the nearer arm, buried her face in the crook of the elbow, and wept without restraint.

Compassion and tenderness overcame Judith's embarrassment and she all at once felt quite calm. 'There, darling,' she murmured, folding her arms around her and cuddling her head into the pit of her neck. 'Go on! You'll feel better for it.'

'I'm so miserable,' Henrietta blurted out between her sobs. 'Ever since the baby, I've been so utterly . . . rotten.'

'Don't talk about it unless it helps. I'll listen if it'll help but I don't want you to tell me things you might later regret. When I said secrets, I didn't mean anything as big as this, you know.'

'Don't ever get married,' Henrietta said. 'That's the most important secret anyone could ever tell you. Do anything rather than marry! Those things we used to talk about, all those dreams – *they're* the tawdry and the gewgaws I mentioned just now.' Her animation began to overcome her sorrow. She lifted her head and sniffed back a glutinous blockage of tears from her nose, at the same time wiping her eyes on the frilly epaulettes of her nightdress. She even managed a wan smile and the dim lamplight made her wet eyes sparkle. 'It's an awful tale to be telling a young slip of a thing the likes of you – with all your hopes of marrying Rick and all his hopes of you, too . . .' Her voice tailed off as her eyes became accustomed to the gloom and she saw Judith's expression. 'You're shocked, of course,' she said.

'No!' Judith managed a light laugh. 'Quite the contrary. It's what I've hinted to Rick once or twice since we came back to Keelity. The only reason we've moved back to the Old Glebe, you know – well, two reasons, actually. The first is so my mother can show all those who used to sneer at us behind our backs . . .'

'Oh, I say!' Henrietta objected.

'They did!' Judith patted her arm. 'It doesn't matter now. In fact, Mama's rather glad of it because she can now rub everyone's noses in it. And the other reason, of course, is for me to set my cap at Rick and become the mistress of Castle Moore.'

Henrietta corrected her a little archly. 'Mistress is rather an ambiguous phrase, don't you know! Say Queen of Castle Moore, instead.'

'Instead of King!' Judith responded darkly. 'That's who rules the place now, isn't it!'

Henrietta closed her eyes and slumped into the division between Judith's pillow and her own.

'Isn't it!' Judith insisted.

'Not tonight, eh?' the other murmured. She opened her eyes and begged. 'I know what you mean. I know why you worry. And I know I ought to be more concerned about it than I can bring myself to feel. But it's just that I'm so . . . I have so much else to think about.'

'Of course, darling.' Judith reached out gently and began stroking her hair. 'I'm a brute.'

'No you're not,' Henrietta assured her with more spirit. 'You're an utterly determined and tenacious young lady – as you know full well. But you admit it, which is your saving grace. It's what stops you being a brute. Because the brutes of this world are those who simply have no idea how awful, how utterly awful, they are.'

Judith just went on stroking her hair and wishing there were some more significant comfort she might offer.

'He has a calendar on the table in his dressing room,' Henrietta said. 'All the year on a single page. You know the sort of thing. And Yuk was born in May – May the seventh.'

'Was it ghastly for you?' Judith asked. She knew at once that Henrietta was talking about Harold, her husband. 'The actual birth, I mean?'

'No. I suppose everyone warned me so much – and you always think of dying and things like that – and all my dearest, kindest friends had told me how *horrible* it was going to be – and actually, in comparison with all that, it was one of the easiest things ever.' She chuckled. 'They hate it when I tell them that. And now they all say, just wait till next time!' The humour faded as she resumed her former line of thought. 'I actually rose from my bed the very next day. I was so *bored* and miserable. And I drifted into his dressing room and almost the first thing I saw was that calendar – and d'you know what he'd done? He'd drawn a neat circle round . . . guess which date?'

'May the seventh?'

'No! Can't you guess what that calendar's for? He'd circled *June* the seventh. And the eighth, of course. Monday and Tuesday. It's always two nights in a row with him. And then July the seventh and eighth – Thursday and Friday. And then August the seventh and eighth – Sunday and Monday. I couldn't believe it – well, I could, because I'd been married to him over three years by then. But it means that on the very night of our daughter's birth, probably while I was actually pushing her out into the world, he was sitting there in his dressing room drawing those perfect circles of his round the seventh and eighth of each successive month of the year. And he really thinks he's being so kind and considerate – that's the truly appalling thing. He knew how I felt, how miserable I was. I just lay there night after night, dreading the approach of that fateful Monday in June. And when it came, I whispered, "Not tonight, eh?" – just like I said it to you a few moments ago – which is what made me remember all this: "Not tonight, eh?" And he said, with the kindliest smile and the gentlest manner, "Yes, my dear, tonight. It has been exactly one month, you know?" As if I could forget it! "So, from now on, instead of the thirtieth and thirty-first, or the twenty-ninth and thirtieth in April, June, September, and November" – I'm not making this up, you know, he really does go on like this . . . "instead of those days – or the last two days of February, it will now be the seventh and eighth of each month until Providence sees fit to grant us another dear scion." Actually, d'you understand what I'm talking about, Ju? Have they told you the most overrated secret in the world, yet?'

Judith, who had more of an intimation than a proper understanding of the matter, assured her that no explanation was necessary.

'And the thing is, you see,' Henrietta concluded in a voice both weak and forlorn, 'I'm tied to this kindly, decent, thoughtful, patient *monster* until one of us dies. Perhaps he'll get one of those vile tropical maladies out in India and *never* come back. Oh, bliss!'

The conventional protest died unuttered in Judith's throat. Her friend's confession had been so desperate, so piteous, she could not sully it with words that were merely trite.

Henrietta let out her breath as if she had steeled herself for the banal commonplaces Judith now withheld. 'Bless you,' she whispered.

Judith, realizing she ought to say something, could only think to ask what Henrietta and Percy had talked about during their time together in the lake that afternoon. To her surprise, Henrietta reached out, grasped her hand, and clutched it to her bosom. 'Thank God for you, my dearest, dearest friend. Where did you acquire such wisdom?'

'What?' a bemused Judith asked.

'Don't turn all coy, not now. You know very well that Percy is now my biggest . . . I was going to say problem, but he's so much more than that. He's also the biggest happiness in my life at this moment. And the way I feel – he's probably my only chance of happiness ever.' She managed a little laugh. 'Poor boy – it's not at all what he bargained for!' She clasped Judith's arm even more tightly to her. 'But the reason I'm so grateful to you is that you already *know* all this – obviously, or you wouldn't have asked.'

She was so effusive that, just for a moment, Judith caught herself thinking yes, she was pretty perceptive and wise.

Henrietta went on. 'He probably thought – a few stolen kisses, some hasty fumbling after dark in the old orangery . . . that was probably the limit of his ambition. He can have had no idea what I was going to suggest – what I have, in fact, suggested.'

'What is that?' Judith withdrew her arm from the other's grasp and resumed stroking her hair.

'He'll go out bughunting tomorrow afternoon, and I, quite independently, shall be taking a ride. And, quite accidentally, you understand, we shall meet at the old quarry on Mount Argus.'

'And then?' Judith asked, though an answer of sorts hovered vaguely at the edge of her perception.

Henrietta giggled and said, 'I'm not going to use the only word I know for it.' Then, more coolly, she added, 'Harold has no word for it at all.' After a further little pause she concluded, 'In fact, what's *really* going to happen is that I'll discover at last whether the man I married is especially ghastly or whether they're all just as bad.'

King did not sleep well that night; he did not sleep well on any night in early September, for, on the fifteenth of that month each year – or, actually, on whatever Friday fell most convenient to it – he had to face the Bellingham Inquisition, otherwise known as the annual audit. And this year, six years on from the murders that led to his present elevation, it promised to be more rigorous than ever. Usually the man in the chair was Harry Bellingham, the late Colonel's brother – a fairly easy-going oul' fellow, though you had to keep a travelling eye on Teresa, his wife. This year, however, Uncle Hereward, the head of the family, was coming over from Castle Bellingham in Norfolk and bringing that Wilhelmina Montgomery woman with him. King could remember her as Miss O'Hara, when she was only engaged to 'Wonky' Montgomery and used to come visiting Castle Moore to stay with her future sister-in-law, Rick's mother.

In fact, King knew a fair bit about all the O'Haras of Letterfrack, because a cousin of his kept the inn at Leenane and that was their country. They were an unprincipled and unreliable lot, in his opinion, like most of those families who turned coat in the seventeenth century. If people were going to be unprincipled – again in his opinion – they should at least have the decency to be consistent about it. Like himself, now.

The acid of those thoughts etched away at his peace of mind as he set out on his usual afternoon constitutional, taking Topsey and Turvey to fret over the hares; he went a different path each day, to keep the world on its toes. Today it was to be upon the slopes of Mount Argus. As he made his dyspeptic way along the lane between the walled garden and tennis courts he noted with mild surprise that the youngsters were not, as he had expected, playing upon the court. In fact, they were nowhere to be seen.

A moment later he heard a shout from the woodland beyond the court: 'Judith! Come and look at this one. Is it edible?' The voice was young Fergal McIver's.

King relaxed; they were obviously gathering mushrooms. It had rained overnight, so the pastime would keep them busy for a good few hours. Last year they had found a huge puffball, with flesh as firm as a young pullet. Sliced and fried with a coating of egg and breadcrumbs it had served a whole week of breakfasts. His mouth filled with saliva even at the memory.

His surprise was renewed when the Carty girl herself stepped out on to the lane behind him, just as he was about to take the path up the mountain. 'Miss Judith,' he murmured.

She noticed that he merely lifted his hat and replaced it; for Henrietta and Sally he removed it and waited to be told to put it back on again. She did not mind, however, for his lack of deference enabled her to make a suggestion that would have been impossible for either of the other women. 'Are you out for a stroll?' she asked blithely, skipping to his side. 'May I go with you?'

'And what of Mr McIver, Miss?' he asked. 'Isn't he after calling you beyond?'

'Oh, he will either live or he will die,' she replied lightly. 'I'm weary of stooping, and these mushrooms make my fingers smell quite musty.'

'Lemon is a most effective antidote, Miss,' he replied, moving to one side of the path to give her room.

'Dear King!' she exclaimed. 'You know everything, don't you? Everything useful, anyway, I should think. Where *did* you learn it all?'

While she spoke these compliments his mind was automatically thinking of ways he could put this unexpected turn of events to his advantage. He glanced casually at her and was transfixed by those astonishing eyes, large and pale – and, it now seemed, so eager to discover where he had acquired his encyclopaedic knowledge. He averted his gaze at once and swiftly gathered himself.

When he turned to her again he was quite prepared. The fire curtain of his misogyny was safely in place and through its cracks he could calmly explore and appreciate her beauty – but as a third party now, a connoisseur, perhaps even a dealer.

'One picks things up as one goes along, Miss,' he replied. 'As the man says, the old and the ugly do be needing their compensations, too.'

While she hesitated, wondering whether he was fishing for compliments, he added a gallant afterthought: 'Not that you'll ever be in want of such compensations yourself, now.'

'Ah, g'wan!' she chuckled. 'Are we going up all the way to the old quarry?'

'Sure we might and then again we mightn't. It's a grand enough day for it. You'd see all five counties today.'

The thought that he might have been fishing for compliments made her consider him in that light. She wondered would she call him handsome? He had one of those faces that could be anything. He should have been on the stage. He could have saved a fortune in make-up. If he was angry, she thought, or in a bullying or overbearing mood, he'd be as ugly as Old Nick himself; you'd notice how his eyebrows met and how fleshy and self-satisfied his lips were and how sleek his skin. But in a good humour – or even in a calm, slightly wary mood, like now – his eyes were large and dark and dancing, and his lips generous. It was the same with his physique; neither one thing nor the other. You'd call him 'comfortable' if you were well disposed to him and 'portly' if you weren't.

'Oh, *do* let's go up there,' she begged. It was the first part of her plan to lead him away from the place. The second part would come when the quarry was almost in view and the path divided; then she'd look at the lower branch, which led to the beck, and discover she was only dying of thirst. 'Can we see the Old Glebe from up there?'

'I don't think so,' he told her. 'I believe it's hid behind Kildowney Hill and the trees.' With a mischievous glance, which she failed to notice, he added, 'You may see Baliver from there, though, plain as a white horse on the bog.'

'Do the McIvers own the eastern slope of Mount Argus?' she asked, more for the sake of making conversation than out of real interest.

'Indeed and they do not,' he informed her, wondering what prompted her interest in property and ownership. 'The Bellinghams own every blade of grass down to the back gate of Baliver.'

By 'the Bellinghams' he meant Rick, of course. She was about to say so when a small voice within warned her he'd make more of it than she intended; a moment later, another little voice asked where would be the harm in misdirecting him a little like that. So she said it: 'Not so much the Bellingham*s*, actually, King. Not in the plural, I think.'

He chuckled. 'Sure you're right enough there, Miss Carty. The ownership is very singular indeed.'

The unsleeping predator within him settled to an interesting vigil. He had known from the beginning that she had had some ulterior motive for this oh-so-casual stroll, but he was still cautious enough to wonder whether she'd revealed it yet. In his estimation, based on long experience of nubile spinsters, it could be only one thing: the prospect of wedding bells. It was all they ever thought about – if they knew what was good for them. He decided to give the boat a little push. 'Will I show you the bounds of the whole estate?' he asked. 'You may see it all from above. Did none of the Bellinghams ever show you?'

'I don't recall,' she lied, for in fact Henrietta had never tired of showing off their lands. Her own mother, too, had brought her to the top of Mount Argus only last Sunday, the day after their return to the Old Glebe, and pointed out the bounds by way of subtle encouragement.

'That's surprising now.' His voice was larded with scepticism. 'Miss Henrietta was very partial to showing it off in the old days – all twenty-five thousand acres of it. A lot of it is water and bog, mind, and scree like this. But there's enough of the other to keep body and soul together. I'll show you when we get there, so I will.'

Judith had had no time to plan this little walk; she had merely caught sight of the butler setting out on his constitutional and realized that he intended going up Mount Argus. And today of all days! It was just like him to do the most inconvenient thing. Usually he took the opposite direction, down the long drive to the gate lodge, along the lane to the lake shore at Coolnahinch, then home again by way of the woodland and front lawns. She was desperately thinking of something inconsequential to talk about when he said, 'That's another birthday come and gone, then, Miss Carty. Another anniversary.'

'Yes.' She sighed. 'It's a little less upsetting each year. I don't know whether one should be ashamed of that – or grateful? But it's the case.'

'It's only natural,' he responded soothingly. 'It's not a thing I'd talk to Master Rick about, you understand, yet I ought to be knowing. Mr Hereward is sure to ask it – and Mrs Montgomery. Would you have a notion yourself now how the wounds have healed with him? Were you after talking to him about it since ye came back?'

'Not . . . well, we've mentioned it, but not what you might call a discussion, exactly. He's very calm about it – but then he always was, even at the time, I don't know if you recall? Everyone thought him a bit *too* cool.'

'Not I,' he replied fervently.

'Nor I. I believe he was more affected by it than anyone.'

'Did he say nothing particular about it though, on the anniversary itself, maybe, when ye met?'

'Not really.' She screwed up her features, as if scraping the barrel for something to give him. Her tone was apologetic when all she could come up with was: 'He said he'd never forget their faces, those murderers. He'd know them till his dying day. But sure, isn't that true of all of us? Miss Henrietta says the same – or Mrs Austin, I suppose I must start calling her. I can't get used to that, can you?'

King whistled the dogs to heel as they were about a hundred yards from the fork in the path. 'Well, those blackguards are all safely in their boxes now, Miss,' he said smoothly.

'Let's hope so, King,' she agreed.

'No doubt of it.'

'Wouldn't it be a fearful thing, now, to meet one of them still alive and well?'

The man laughed. 'No fear of that, Miss Carty. Come to think of it, of course, they're not in their boxes. They bury them straight in a pit of quicklime, inside Mountjoy, don't they.'

Judith shivered. She had been able to see the jail from their house in Drumcondra, and had even stood at the window, staring at its wet slate roofscape, at the hour appointed for the hanging of the 'Castle Moore Murderers'. She stared away at the horizon and said, 'I didn't know that.'

'Sure they do. And the lime has them consumed in hours, like the vermin they are.'

'Please, King!' she insisted.

He smiled smugly and offered no apology.

They reached the fork in the path. 'Lord!' she exclaimed, 'But that's a thirsty climb, that hill. Isn't there water down this path somewhere?' She took a step in the direction of the stream, hoping to lead him away from the quarry and . . . whatever might be going on there.

'Ah,' he said easily. 'You may come upon the same water higher up beyond. The very source of it, where it comes bursting and bubbling out of the hillside. *Uisce vár*. And you may still have the view from the mountain-top.' Very firmly he took half a dozen strides toward the quarry, turned, and waited for her to catch up.

He knows! she thought. Of course, King knew everything.

'I have a thorn in this foot,' she said, catching hold of a salley and lifting her left shoe. She was wearing galoshes, too, which made the tale unlikely. 'Just under the ankle,' she added. 'Topsey!' she called at the top of her voice. 'Leave it!' The dog was pointing at the quarry. She just hoped its occupants had heard her cry.

King's patience was almost exhausted by the time she'd hunted the thorn down. It proved too small to be visible. 'Isn't it only amazing,' she said, holding up nothing, 'how a tiny wee thing the size of that can make life a misery!' She chuckled at his annoyance. 'Like the princess and the pea.'

'Very like the princess and the pea, Miss,' he said coldly.

And glory be! At that very moment Percy himself came sauntering down the path, his butterfly net over his shoulder and a killing bottle hanging by its thong from his wrist. It was empty. 'I had the blighter!' he said disgustedly. 'I chased him right up to the quarry then that thundering great horse came along.'

'What horse?' Judith asked.

'Hen's,' he replied with a sort of deprecating tolerance. 'She's up there now, pretending she can still remember how to ride.'

'Oh, I must see that!' Judith hitched her skirts just

above her ankle and trotted away up the last furlong of the path.

'A grand day for the race, King,' Percy said.

Judith's movements were so graceful neither man could take his eyes off her.

'A grand week ye've had of it altogether, Mister O'Farrelly.'

Judith passed out of sight.

'I'll stick to woodland moths, I think,' Percy said as he resumed his downhill walk.

Judith found Henrietta desperately struggling to hook up her bodice at the back; the horse was grazing contentedly among the rocks nearby. 'Goodness, Hen, what's happened?' she asked.

'What d'you think!' Henrietta replied angrily.

'Why didn't Percy stay and help?'

'Because I heard a very clever girl shouting a warning, so I sent him away as fast as possible. God, it's so easy for men to dress!'

'But what were you doing?' She wanted to hear it had been no more than a call of nature.

Henrietta turned and stared deep into her eyes, first one, then the other. 'Was that clever girl you?' she asked.

'Of course it was.' Judith laughed as she skipped round her again to do up the last hook. 'You know it was.'

'I thought it was, but now I'm beginning to wonder. These questions you're asking – they're not at all clever.'

'There!' Judith closed the last hook and launched her back into the respectable world with a gentle pat.

Henrietta turned and faced her again; now there was a kindlier light in her eyes. 'If you want to know, darling – what I've *really* been doing – I've been discovering it's Harold who's . . . I mean that I'm not . . . that it isn't my . . .' Again she was peering hard into Judith's eyes;

something she saw there made her conclude: 'Well, it doesn't really matter.'

Halfway down the path Percy met Rick coming up. They acknowledged each other with a wave when they were still separated by a hundred yards or more; in snatched glances, each tried to assess the other's mood as they drew steadily nearer.

'Any luck?' Rick asked when they came within conversational distance.

'Got away from me at the last minute.' Percy gave a lopsided smile. 'Thanks to your sister on her bloody horse.'

'Steady the buffs! What was she doing up there?'

They met and halted. Rick seemed out of breath. Yet he was in pretty good condition – he must have been running earlier, Percy decided. 'Pretending she hasn't forgotten how to ride. You ought to take her in hand, man. Or O'Brien. She's not safe. I thought it was like riding a bicycle – something you never forgot once you've learned it.'

All the while Percy spoke Rick was searching his face for clues as to what had really been going on up there. He had his suspicions, of course, ever since he'd seen the pair of them at the side of the tennis court yesterday, and then swimming round the lake together. And there was the change in Hen's demeanour last night and today; from being rather jumpy and ever-ready with a dismissive opinion or slighting remark, she'd gone all placid and tolerant. Most disquieting of all, when *he'd* suggested Judith might stay the night at Castle Moore, Hen had said it was utterly out of the question; but suddenly, during the 'savage feast', she'd changed her mind, as long as Judith did not occupy a room alone.

The condition was perfectly reasonable, of course; in

fact, he himself would have insisted on it if Hen had said nothing – for the sake of Judith's reputation. But the way she had put it suggested something more than mere precaution; there had been some positive element in it, too. Rick felt sure it had a connection with . . . whatever was going on between his sister and Percy. It might just be what they called a tennis-court flirtation – except that she had never been that kind of girl. She either fell heavily for someone or she kept a proper distance. Perhaps marriage had changed her? No matter – Rick felt he should take no chances.

'Where are you off to?' Percy asked. 'So out of breath and all.'

'I am not out of breath,' Rick asserted, annoyed that Percy had somehow wrong-footed him . . . put him on the defensive. To be precise, he was annoyed he had allowed Percy that petty success. Unthinkingly he added, 'Actually, I thought I heard Judith calling out.'

'Aha!' Percy's gleeful exclamation, accompanied by a suggestive lift of his eyebrows, put Rick even more on the defensive.

'No, you howling cad!' he exclaimed. 'I thought . . . she sounded as if she was having difficulty with those two dogs.'

'King's dogs.'

'Yes.' Rick frowned. 'Well, to be exact, they're not King's dogs. They belong to the castle – to me if anyone. Jesus, what does it matter who they belong to? I just thought she'd got into trouble with them. And what business is it of yours, anyway?'

'None at all, old boy.' He grinned. 'But then I didn't raise the subject in the first place, did I? She's out walking with King, if you're interested.' A mischievous possibility occurred to him. He gazed at the sky and repeated the words to himself: 'Out walking with King? Walking out with King? Yes, there is a difference, I suppose.' He grinned saucily at Rick, as if expecting him to share the jest.

Rick smiled awkwardly. 'Look,' he said, 'I don't understand any of this. I mean, I don't want to fall out with you.'

'Nor I with you, old chap.' Percy pulled a punch on his shoulder. 'So why are you following me around?'

'I am not following you around.'

'If not me, then who?' Percy made the question seem genuine. He glanced rapidly over his shoulder and then fixed Rick with an accusing but incredulous smile. 'Not . . . surely not . . .'

'Did you talk to Judith at all?' Rick asked impatiently.

'Obliquely, I suppose.'

'What in God's name does that mean? Obliquely?'

'I mean there I was, explaining how Henrietta's horse put paid to my bughunting, when the dear girl ran off to talk with her. You'll find them up by the old quarry, I'm sure. And you'll not find King, either. I'm sure of that as well.'

'Why d'you say it in that tone?'

'Because King is avoiding Henrietta like the plague. Surely you've noticed?'

'Where are you off to now?' Rick asked, not knowing what else to say.

'Back to the fungi, I suppose.' Percy took a token pace or two down the hill.

Rick, unable to leave his worries unresolved, called after him, 'See here, O'Farrelly, I don't want to blackguard you if this business is quite innocent, but if it's not – I'm giving you due warning – if it's not, I'll horsewhip you all round the parish.'

Percy threw back his head and roared with laughter.

'I fail to see what's so funny,' Rick told him coldly.

'Of course you do,' Percy assured him. 'Of course you do.'

'Perhaps you'll enlighten me, then?'

Percy sighed. 'Well, just for a start now, you have the quarest notion of defending a lady's honour that ever I heard. Advertising it "all round the parish" with a horse-whip is not a form of defence that most women would welcome. People notice these things, you know. One young man whipping another – they notice things like that and it *whips* their curiosity to a fair oul' lather, as I'm bound to enlighten ye.'

'You take me too literally,' Rick warned.

'And you take me too seriously, old chap. In any case, the honour of a married lady is a matter for her husband, don't you think?'

'While he is present, yes. In his absence it passes back to her family.'

Percy squinched up his eyes and peered at Rick as if he had never examined him closely before. 'God but you're priceless,' he murmured at last as, turning on his heel, he strode away.

Rick felt like flying after him and giving him the pasting he so thoroughly deserved; what stopped him was the apprehension that Percy would, even so, have triumphed.

Angrily he stamped up the path. The horse was hitched to a furze bush at the mouth of the quarry; Henrietta was seated on a boulder, a little way in. Percy was right in one thing: there was no sign of King. But he was wrong in another: there was no sign of Judith, either – which made it easy for Rick to come straight out with it. 'What's going on between you and O'Farrelly?' he asked testily.

'M. Y. O. B.,' she responded equably. 'I'm not your unmarried sister any longer.'

'God! You . . .' He was momentarily at a loss for words.

'What?' she asked with a steely smile.

'That's what Percy said, too. Have you been talking about it with him? I mean, do you discuss the business so coldly with him?'

'The nerve of the fella!' Henrietta exclaimed to a passing cloud. 'Have *I* been talking about it with him? The real question is have *you* been talking about it with him? How dare you? It's nothing to do with you.'

'I dare because I'm your brother – because a woman's honour belongs to her husband and her brother – her brothers, if she has them, and her father, if she . . .'

'You are my *little* brother, may I remind you – a fact that was never more apparent than at this very moment. And may I also inform you that a woman's honour is first and foremost her own. And also . . .'

'*If* she has the sense to defend it.'

'Oh God, Rick, would you ever go and take a long walk off a short jetty! You're my little brother. You're wet behind the ears still. You've hardly stuck your nose outside the gates of Castle Moore yet, and you think you know the world well enough to hand out the orders to me.'

'Lord, there *is* something going on!' Rick stared at her wildly, running distracted fingers through his hair. 'I didn't dare suppose it till now. How *can* you, Hen? How will you ever be able to look poor Harold in the eye again?'

She gave him a pitying smile and shook her head. 'There's no point,' she murmured, more to herself than him.

'Hah! You can't answer me, see,' he taunted.

Wearily she repeated his question: 'How shall I ever be able to look him in the eye again? Nothing will be easier! I'll just take pattern from the way he looks *me* in the eye when he comes home with the gluepot stink of debauchery on him – not to mention the long, fair hairs that he can't even be bothered to remove.'

Rick just stood there, staring at her in horror, repeating her words in his mind, ransacking them against all hope for some other possible meaning. To add to his anguish, Judith reappeared at that moment from behind the rock where a call of nature had taken her.

'Well, well,' she said drily. 'We live and learn.'

Sally looked across the clearing to where her brother and Netty were picking mushrooms side by side. She smiled to herself at the way Netty clung to him like a burr. Earlier he had behaved in the same way toward Judith, until she had suddenly exclaimed, 'Oh, there goes King – I want a word with him.' And off she went, just like that.

With Percy away somewhere, too – hunting bugs, he said – it all looked dreadfully dubious of course, especially in the absence of Henrietta. If Fergal had any sense, he'd have offered to escort Judith; but clever little Netty had anticipated that and had drawn Rick's attention to what was going on – or looked as if it was going on – or was about to go on.

Actually, Sally had her own suspicions, especially after watching Percy and Henrietta yesterday. The fact that he was 'off somewhere', innocently hunting bugs, while she was 'off somewhere', innocently riding . . . well, that was pretty dubious, too. Especially as she'd chosen Gertie, the laziest and most placid mare in the stables and not at all the sort of horse you'd take for an enjoyable ride. Sally knew that Rick had been uneasy about it; so Netty's warning had been all he needed to make him don his shining armour and go charging up the mountain.

And now there was poor Fergal, having to honour the half-proclaimed promises he had made to Netty among the pines near the tennis court, two weeks ago – since merely to walk alone with her there was an unspoken pledge of *some* kind – never mind the kissing they had enjoyed. Sally realized it would be a sisterly kindness to rescue him; besides, she didn't want him to yield any more hostages to fortune with Netty O'Farrelly. He'd made a very good job of spoiling Rick's unimpeded courtship of Judith – starting with that brilliant opening gambit of being there on the front steps of the Old Glebe to welcome her on her return to County Keelity. That, of course, had been Sally's advice; her brother, she had learned over the years, needed the constant benefit of sisterly advice.

She straightened up and stretched her back. 'Oh, I'm getting a bit sick of this,' she called out as she crossed the clearing to join them. 'Got any gaspers, Fergal? I'm dying for a puff.'

'Oh yes!' Netty took off her shawl and spread it on a fallen tree for the three of them to sit on. She hated that shawl because it made her look like a tinker woman; but her mother insisted that young girls were peculiarly susceptible to kidney complaints (meaning she herself had had that susceptibility when young) and should always cover their backs well. Netty, knowing that extravagance was another of her mother's *bêtes noires*, tried to run through as many shawls in a year as possible.

Fergal took out his gaspers and offered them round; his sister took one but Netty said she'd share his. He stared uncomfortably off into the distance, up the hill, the way Judith had gone. She followed his eyes and said, 'What *is* going on up there, I wonder? Everybody vanishing all the time.'

He blew a perfect ring and then destroyed it with a disorderly cloud of smoke.

Sally, who had learned to inhale, spoke and let the smoke out of her mouth at the same time – like the Comtesse de Cretonne, the femme fatale in *Laura the Forsaken*, whose voice was 'gravelly and interesting'. Disappointingly, Sally continued to sound like Sally, speaking under a slight strain. 'The real question,' she said, 'is what does Judith want with King?'

'Why should she want anything with King?' Her brother's tone was prickly.

'Because she said so. "I want a word with him." That's what she said. Besides, King is hardly the walking companion one would *choose*, is he!'

'He's always plotting something,' Netty added. 'And even when he isn't, he looks as if he is. Can you understand the Bellinghams trusting him the way they have? I mean, really, he's had the run of his teeth with this place, hasn't he?'

'Teeth and fingers,' Fergal boomed like a judge.

Sally sat up and began to take notice. Until now she had seen King as nothing but 'the butler at Castle Moore' – an unusual butler, to be sure, after his heroism on the night of the Murders; but Netty's gloss on the man was a new element in her estimation of him. 'D'you mean he's taken advantage of it?' she asked.

Netty leaned forward to see if the question was serious before she replied: 'Sure he'd be a saint not to, don't you think?' She glanced up at Fergal, who was looking at her with a puzzled frown. 'Don't you think?' she repeated.

'No.' He shook his head. 'I mean I never thought of it. D'you think he does take advantage that way?' He glanced at Sally to include her. 'Fingers in the till?'

'I'm sure of it,' Netty said stoutly.

'Could be libellous,' he warned.

She smiled sweetly and said, 'Slanderous, actually. Libels are written.'

He blew an amused cloud of smoke at her and proffered the cigarette. She drew in a puff and returned the compliment. 'You'll thank me one day,' she assured him. 'You'll sit some exam where the distinction's important and you'll remember I told you. So there! But to get back to King, have you never heard your parents talking about it? Mine do. I thought it was common gossip.'

'Sure it would get back to the Bellinghams in no time. Harry Bellingham would hear of it for certain.'

Netty chuckled. 'If Harry Bellingham was set on fire he wouldn't know it until he read it in the *Irish Times*. Teresa might, but you know their opinion of women in that family!' After a moment's pause she added more gently, 'Or in that older generation, anyway.'

This qualification puzzled Sally. Why would Netty bother to make it – unless she, too, had a little bit of a soft spot for Rick? She was certainly no stickler for abstract justice and fairness all round. It was a possibility she'd have to bear in mind. Until now she'd thought she and Netty were 'enemies' in the sense that their interests were diametrically opposed: she, Sally, wanted her brother to set his cap at Judith and win, leaving Rick to revive his former affections for her – whereas Netty wanted Fergal never to look at Judith again. But the idea that she might be entertaining vague hopes of Rick as well could not now be discounted. 'Rick's not much different, alas,' she said by way of a test.

'How can you say that?' Netty asked at once.

Now surely a girl who had no interest in a fellow would, on hearing such an opinion upon him, simply turn and say, 'Really?' or something equally neutral and encouraging of further revelation? Sally grew more wary yet. 'It's not his fault,' she conceded. 'And I don't think it's anything deeply ingrained. It's King's influence, actually. I think he's got no time for women at all. Have you ever seen the way he orders that little mousey wife of his around?'

'He's always been quite charming to me,' Netty said.

'Rick or King?' Fergal asked.

The two females looked at him wearily.

'Well,' he protested. 'You switch from one to the other with each new breath. It's jolly hard for a fellow to know which one you're tearing to shreds at any given moment.'

'Well, we know perfectly well,' his sister assured him.

'Perfectly,' Netty confirmed. 'And anyway, we aren't tearing them to shreds, we're just discussing them in a calm and ordinary manner.'

'I was going to say,' Sally added, 'charm doesn't come into it. A lot of men who dislike women are perfectly charming to us. I think it's the most objectionable thing about them.'

'Yes . . .' Netty drew breath to speak at length in support of this opinion but Fergal said, 'Do you women always go on like this?'

Netty took the cigarette from him for another puff but said nothing. His sister ignored him, too, as, speaking past him, she said to Netty: 'It's as if we're not even significant enough to be rude to. They'll only be rude to us if we really get in the way. Otherwise they'll just be perfectly charming to us, like to little pets.'

'The kind that bite,' Fergal muttered.

'The pets that bite are the best kind to be charming to,' Sally assured him. 'Anyway, that's King's sort of charm.'

'D'you really think he has so much influence over Rick?' Fergal asked. 'I've seen the dear boy being quite rebellious lately. When he rode over to play tennis with us the week before last, for instance, King said he was to go in the dogcart, not to ride over Mount Argus. But he rode all the same.'

Netty blew a shred of tobacco off her lip. 'I didn't know that,' she said.

'So there.'

'It's not a very *big* rebellion, is it?' Netty objected on further reflection. 'A clever man like King might even encourage such trivial rebellions – to allow Rick an illusion of independence.'

Fergal took the stub of the cigarette from her and blew three good rings. 'Why have all you women got it in for poor old King? I think he's just a butler, doing his job – plus a bit extra because of . . . well, circumstances.'

'What d'you mean *all* us women?' Sally asked – taking the words out of Netty's mouth.

'Well, Judith's got no time for him, either. That day she came back, almost the first thing she said to Rick and me – well, to Rick, really, because I never saw them – but almost the first thing she said was that they hanged the wrong people for the murders and that King was mainly to blame for it.'

'What did Rick say?' his sister asked.

'He pooh-poohed it. He didn't seem to like it – for King to be accused like that.'

'Of course he didn't!' Netty said, as if her entire thesis were now vindicated.

Sally leaned forward and peered at her. 'D'you really think that's true?' she asked.

'About the murderers?'

'No. About Rick being completely under King's thumb?'

Netty shrugged. 'Don't take my word for it. You watch when they're together. You'll see it for yourself.'

'Yes,' Sally murmured thoughtfully. 'I rather think I'd better.'

For two years after the Murders, Henrietta had been fostered by Aunt Bill, though she had only seen her – and briefly at that – during school holidays. No great intimacy had ever developed between them. In fact, since her marriage and removal to London four years ago, she had seen nothing of her aunt at all, though they lived less than a hundred miles apart. She was therefore rather shocked at the change in her. It was not that she was less sprightly or had a duller mind, but when they had last met one had still been able to glimpse the few remaining vestiges of the girl she once had been; now, at forty-eight, one could already discern the first signs of the old lady she would grow into.

Aunt Bill saw the momentary hesitation in her niece's eyes, wondered whether to make some amused remark, and decided on the whole not to. However, she did put a more than usual vigour into the way she negotiated the stairs, giving a little spring at each step – nothing indecorous, of course, but enough to make the servants (who watch such things very closely) spread the word that 'the oul' wan' was as bouncy as ever.

She was as alert as ever, too. She hadn't been in Henrietta's company for five minutes before she realized that the young woman was a great deal happier with life than family gossip had led one to expect. Her skin seemed to glow and there was a merriment in her eyes that was almost improper after four years of marriage – especially marriage to a dullard like Harold, whom she, Wilhelmina, had known since he was about ten. So either the family was wrong – a conclusion she found hard to contemplate – or *something* had happened. 'My, you have been enjoying yourselves,' she exclaimed when Henrietta paused for breath. 'I hope you've all been *behaving* yourselves, too – which is not always the same thing. Indeed, in my experience, the two rarely coincide.'

'Of course we have.' Henrietta laughed effusively. 'How could we not? Safety in numbers, you know.'

All the while she had rattled off her news she had been impeding Aunt Bill's maid in her unpacking – intercepting each new dress and enthusing over its beauty and splendour. Now she held up one that was quite unsuitably old for her and said she'd just love to own it if Aunt Bill would pass it on when she was tired of it.

Aunt Bill, who had by now discreetly repaired the ravages of the journey, came to her, took the dress, held it up against her, pinning it with a pinch at the shoulders, and surveyed the result critically. Then, fixing her niece with a penetrating gaze, said, 'Really?' Not waiting for a reply, she passed it to the maid and went to the door. 'Let's go for a little walk,' she commanded. 'I think it's only showers. What are all your young charges doing at this moment?'

'Playing billiards. I'd love to go for a walk.' The latter sentiment was spoken with something of a sinking feeling. The way Aunt Bill had said 'Really?' made her feel that her every little secret was already known. 'They're also supposed to be getting up some sort of charade to amuse the clan gathering.'

'Good. We can happily leave them to that, I think. There *is* safety in numbers in such a case. And there's no danger of their overhearing *us*.'

'That sounds ominous,' Henrietta said as she followed her aunt out.

'Ominous? Dear me, no. I simply want you to tell me about them, especially the Carty gel and the McIver gel. Decisions will have to be made soon about your young brother.'

'Oh dear!' Henrietta laughed as she tripped down the stairs. 'Do we arrange the *boys'* marriages in our family, too?'

At the half-landing Aunt Bill turned and stared briefly at her. 'Too?' she echoed before turning and continuing her way to the front hall.

'I thought marriages were supposed to be made in heaven,' Henrietta added.

'When did you think like *that*?' Aunt Bill asked sarcastically. 'Not recently, I'm sure.'

Outside, suitably coated and galoshed, they paused a moment on the front steps and drew deep draughts of air, as if the interior of the house had been stifling and foul. Aunt Bill said, 'We'll go down the brick path and along the lakeshore, then up through the woods to the drive, I think.'

'King's usual route,' Henrietta commented. 'Except he goes clockwise.'

Aunt Bill made no remark until they reached the start of the path; then she said, 'You may begin with Judith Carty. She was a great chum of yours in the old days, wasn't she?'

'She still is. She sometimes stays the night here with me, and we talk and talk.'

The brick path, which divided the terraced lawns from the flower beds and shrubberies, was wide enough for several to walk abreast, even two ladies in fashionably hooped and bustled dresses. Aunt Bill took her niece's arm; the jocular suggestion was that she, so frail and elderly, now needed that support; the truth, as both of them knew, was that she would thus be able to feel the slightest tic of surprise or alarm.

'Does she show much interest in marriage?' Aunt Bill asked. 'I don't mean the usual prurient curiosity common to all gels of that age. I mean a serious interest.'

Henrietta sighed. How could one tell? When marriage was really the only prospect open to girls of their class, how could you separate genuine, heartfelt interest from the dutiful 'I suppose I'd better start thinking about it' kind? 'She's not prurient, anyway,' she replied.

'Because she's shy . . . or immature?' The riposte was immediate.

'Are those the only alternatives?'

'The only ones that matter.' Aunt Bill laughed. 'Of course, she may already know more than you and me put together – and be twice as bored by it all. Who can say what sort of company they kept in Dublin, before this windfall stroke of luck brought them back to the Old Glebe. I suppose it *is* a little more permanent this time?'

'Carty himself seems very confident. The patent has years and years to run and factories all over the world are installing the machine.'

'Yes, I know. Bernard got one of those awful, grubby men who work for solicitors – inquiry agents, they call themselves – to look into it.' Bernard was Aunt Bill's middle son, the barrister. 'Their reports were *very* encouraging. Isn't it an astonishing world at times! One would expect the men who invented railway trains or the telegraph to be millionaires, but they aren't. It's the inventor of some obscure cigarette-rolling machine who makes the real fortune.'

'Is that what they said?'

Aunt Bill nodded emphatically. 'Perhaps not a million, but well up toward it. Still, that isn't really our concern. We're not desperate for a big, fat dowry. We just don't want any new liability, such as a bankrupt father-in-law. The Bellingham estate is extremely healthy, in fact. It must be one of the few in Ireland that is. King seems to have done well by us. The Good Steward himself.'

Henrietta said nothing.

Aunt Bill commented on her silence.

'I've always had my doubts about King,' her niece replied, and even though they were several hundred yards from the castle by now, she could not stop herself from glancing briefly over her shoulder to make sure they were not overheard.

'Ah!' Aunt Bill waited. 'So you also have your doubts about that man!'

'You mean *you* do, too?' Henrietta tried. 'Tell me.'

'You first, dear. I've only just arrived.'

'The trouble is I've never *liked* him. I mean, he's not the sort of man anybody *likes*, is he?'

'He's a Roman Catholic,' Aunt Bill pointed out, as if the thought followed on. 'Everyone in the county shook their heads and tut-tutted when your father appointed a butler who was *Irish*, never mind Roman Catholic.'

'Well, they don't do that any more,' Henrietta asserted. 'Not since he turned the tables on the Land

League and boycotted *them*. However, I didn't mean anything about him being Roman Catholic, nor the darling of the Property Protection Society. I mean his character – his nature. He wasn't put into this world to *be* liked, and he knows it, and he doesn't try to change it. He just gets on with his task. So if you ask me to point to this or that failing, I can't. It's just a generally uneasy feeling one has about him – which is so hard to disentangle from simple aversion. One might be being wretchedly unfair to the poor fellow.'

'And wretchedly uninformative to one's elderly aunt,' Wilhelmina said with a mincing preciseness of diction, giving Henrietta's elbow a friendly squeeze at the same time. 'You're not in a court of law, dear. Inside the family you may say anything, even if it's outrageously untrue. We eventually sift it all down and get whatever nuggets we can. You should hear my Bernard on the subject of your Harold! Or perhaps you shouldn't.' She smiled. 'Another time, anyway. So do tell me about King.'

Henrietta stored away her aunt's little aside, knowing full well it was an invitation to unburden herself on the subject of Harold at some later time. 'Actually,' she said, picking her way over the brick path with sudden care – to emphasize the care she was taking with her words, too – 'actually, I'm not the only one to have my doubts. Judith's also got her eye on him. She thinks his influence over Rick is . . . well, not of the best. He's more or less had the rearing of Rick since that night.'

'The boy's had his tutors,' Aunt Bill pointed out.

'King ran circles round them.'

'What a quaint expression! Do you mean he saw them off?'

'I mean, in anything Rick did, or was permitted to do, King had the last word.'

They reached the lakeside and paused a moment in

silence, staring across at the white pavilion, whose brilliance intensified the autumn tints on the trees beyond.

'We'll visit the graves this Sunday,' Aunt Bill murmured.

'I've been going every week, of course,' Henrietta told her. 'So does Rick. King insists on that.'

After a further silence Aunt Bill said, 'Leave King aside for the moment. Tell me more about the Carty.'

They resumed their stroll along the stone walk. In her mind's eye Henrietta saw her own head and Percy O'Farrelly's down there in the water, making one slow, life-shattering circuit of the lake. That had been just a week ago today. A powerful urge to tell her aunt all about it seized her. She even drew breath to speak, but then it deserted her as swiftly as it had come. All her aunt knew of it was a sudden twitch in her arm, about five seconds after her request to be told more about Judith Carty. She noted the fact and said, 'Well?'

'I suppose it's the effect of having an unconventional father and an extremely conventional mother,' her niece began.

An opening remark of that kind always annoyed Aunt Bill – the use of a word like 'it', which could refer to anything, or nothing at all; however, she bided her time, knowing how reluctant the girl was to say even a single word about her friend Judith Carty. Her trouble was she hadn't yet joined the grown-up world – not in her emotions; she still thought of herself as one of the young crowd. And the trouble with me, she thought to herself, is that I, too, know the same feeling. But her mind recoiled from pursuit of that notion. She had to forget herself and concentrate on her niece. More than ever now she was convinced that the girl's difficulties lay in her marriage to Harold; if that were as unhappy as the talk in the family suggested, then it was no wonder she'd hanker after the old, carefree, single days, and no wonder she'd feel more kinship with those still in that joyous condition. '*Is* Mrs Carty so very conventional?' she prompted. 'I hardly remember the woman. It's a warning to us all, perhaps. We are far too restrictive in our social relations. We forget we live in a world where today's outcast may be tomorrow's Lord of Lower Egypt.'

'She is *painfully* conventional,' Henrietta replied. 'Which wouldn't matter so much if she were also intelligent. But she has a brain the size of a pea. It's a dreadful embarrassment to poor Judith, I can tell you.'

The judgement amazed Aunt Bill, though she was careful not to show it. How could the girl be so incisive about the mother and so reluctant and wishy-washy about the daughter? 'In what way does she reveal this pea-sized brain of hers?' she asked.

'Oh, every time she sees poor Rick she finds some excuse to praise Judith to the skies – and in such inappropriate ways: how *frugal* Judith is, how good with animals, how fastidious with her clothes, what a good disciplinarian she is with the servants . . . it just never ends.'

'And is it true?'

'Of course not. She's no better and no worse than the rest of us. And in any case, it's the last sort of praise that would commend her to my dear little bro.'

'Ah!' Aunt Bill pounced as if Henrietta had just made a point of some significance. 'Perhaps I'm starting at the wrong end. Tell me what *would* commend a young gel to your dear little bro.'

Henrietta shrugged awkwardly. 'Like any young man, I suppose, he'll fall for a pretty face.'

'Yes. Falling is one thing – and it's not just confined to *young* men, either, let me warn you! But marriage is quite a different kettle of herring. I know we like to mock the men for their superficiality in that respect, but, to be honest, in my experience, they are every bit as shrewd as we like to suppose *we* are in picking a suitable mate – and bugger the looks.'

'Aunt Bill!' her niece exclaimed in horror.

'*Calme toi, ma chère!*' she replied soothingly. 'You're among the grown-ups yourself now. Different rules apply.'

'Even so!' Henrietta exhaled forcefully, a voiceless *whooo!*

'Even so!' the other echoed in a tone of finality. 'So tell me – when you say Rick might well fall for a pretty face, in other words, the Carty gel . . . I take it she is still pretty?'

'Oh yes. Walk down any street with her – we were in Simonstown last Monday, and you could see the eyes following her and the heads turning – men and women both.'

'I see. *That* kind of beauty. Is she herself aware of it?'

'Yes, but not in any vain sort of way. Quite the opposite.'

'I don't understand that, my dear. How can a woman be aware of her own head-turning beauty without being vain?'

'Because it frightens her. If she could give it away, she would.'

'Her beauty?' Aunt Bill put in quickly.

'Yes.' Henrietta, unaware of any overtones to the phrase 'give it away', was puzzled.

Aunt Bill drew in a deep breath of contentment. At last she had cracked her niece's reserve in talking about her friend – or 'divulging her secrets', as she would doubtless put it. One simple swearword had done the trick; now it was just a matter of keeping up the pressure. 'How do you know this?' she asked.

'Because her favourite daydream is – oh dear! I feel awful talking about her behind her back like this.'

'Why? Is it extremely childish, this daydream? Most daydreams usually are, you know. I'd be quite ashamed to tell you mine!' When this produced no quick response, Aunt Bill went on. 'It wouldn't mean *she* is childish, you know. She doesn't sound it – not if she has the measure of her own mother in the way you described.'

'Oh she's not childish at all,' Henrietta assured her.

It was all the older woman had been waiting to hear. 'In that case, my dear,' she said soothingly, 'if you're quite confident of her maturity, she must already appreciate the fact that, what with the clan gathering here this week, our talk will naturally turn to the subject of matrimony and Rick. She will also realize that one of our chief sources of opinion will be you. Why, I expect that fully half of what's she's told you about herself has been spoken for that very purpose.'

'Oh, but she's not at all calculating like . . .'

'Poppycock! Of course she is! *Any* woman is. Don't try to tell me *you* aren't, for I simply shan't believe you.'

Henrietta made no reply.

In a softer tone Aunt Bill went on, 'Oh, I don't mean she lay awake half the night planning all the things she was going to tell you, so you could pass them on to us. That sort of "calculating woman" only exists in those penny dreadfuls the servants leave lying about the house. I mean "calculating" in the way you and I are calculating, at this very moment – the way we pick and choose what to say to each other, not hours in advance but actually while we're conversing. And the way we choose our exact words, too. Anyway, the top and bottom of it is – if Judith Carty is at all interested in Rick, she must know very well that conversations like this will have to take place – dozens of them. That's just part of life's great obstacle race. So tell me, what is this favourite daydream of hers?'

'She wants to live alone in a sort of fairy-tale cottage deep in the forest and have nothing to do with the world at large.'

'She actually *wants* to?'

'She finds such a prospect very pleasant to contemplate.'

'Ah!' Aunt Bill sighed with relief. 'That, of course, is quite a different matter.'

'Is it?'

'Good heavens, yes. When I was your age I found it very "pleasant to contemplate", as you put it, the idea of being a royal mistress in the age of Charles the Second. But if some little imp had appeared in a flash of fire and brimstone, saying it could all be arranged very easily – well, the idea would soon have lost its rosy hues, I can assure you!'

Henrietta realized she was holding her breath when it began to hurt. 'Did you really, Aunt Bill?' she gasped.

'Of course. D'you mean you've never had such notions?' She leaned forward and peered into the younger woman's face. 'Your cheeks are answering for you, my dear.'

Henrietta smiled – but not, as her aunt supposed, in simple admission of her guilt. She was smiling because she realized she had passed far beyond mere notions of becoming someone's mistress. What a quaint word, anyway, once you actually knew what it involved! 'Lover' was better. She actually *was* another man's lover – and she was quite sure that Aunt Bill had never progressed beyond her daydreams of such bliss (if progress was quite the right word). All at once she felt vastly more mature than Aunt Bill; and part of her maturity lay in realizing that, whereas five minutes ago she was on the verge of blurting out her dreadful, wonderful secret, now all the wolfhounds in Ireland would not drag it out of her. She suddenly felt more grown-up and more self-confident than at any time in her life – though she was not yet grown-up enough to realize how dangerous such elation can be.

Aunt Bill went on: 'As for La Carty's charming little daydream, that is surely very easy to explain. It is a product, and a very understandable product, of a young girl's trepidation as she approaches the mysterious state of matrimony.'

'Perhaps so,' Henrietta allowed.

Aunt Bill gave an exasperated sigh. 'And perhaps I owe you an apology, my dear – if it's the sort of thing a mere apology can atone for.' She felt her niece's arm stiffen with apprehension and went on, 'I mean, I never said a word to *you* on the subject before you married Harold, did I?'

'You told me not to worry about drinking too much champagne at supper on the first night of the honeymoon.' She laughed ruefully. 'Actually, the first night of the honeymoon was spent being violently sick on the Channel ferry – and the second night was spent returning from the dead.'

'And the third?'

'That's when champagne might have helped. But there wasn't any.'

'And would anything *I* might have told you have helped?'

They came to the end of the stone-wall part of the lake shore. Here, at the beginning of the woodland, the path became more natural in appearance, parting company with the water and winding this way and that among the trees. 'I'll go first,' Aunt Bill said quickly, for she had realized that only from in front could she turn at whim and see the girl's face.

'Why are you asking these particular questions now, Aunt Bill?' Henrietta inquired.

'Can't you see? Because your situation vis-à-vis the Carty is similar to mine vis-à-vis you in the period before your marriage. If I'm right about the fears that lie behind this modest daydream of hers, then a kindly word or two from you would be of enormous help to her. Or' – she paused significantly and glanced back at her niece – 'would they? That's the question: Could you tell her anything of value? And would you?'

'If she asked.' Henrietta made her tone deliberately light, as if they were talking about the most trivial matters. A sense of panic was beginning to grow in her at the ease with which her aunt had managed to edge a conversation about Judith toward a heart-searching examination of her, Henrietta, instead.

They resumed their stroll down the woodland path. 'You wouldn't volunteer, though – even if you knew what was troubling her?'

'Perhaps if it was *troubling* her.'

'Tell me about the McIver gel then,' Aunt Bill said suddenly. 'Is she in a similar quandary? How well d'you know her?'

Henrietta, thinking she'd got off the hook at last, breathed a sigh of relief. 'Not nearly so well as I do Judith, of course – but then, I suspect, there's rather less to know.'

Again Aunt Bill was silently amazed at her niece's ability to make neat, crisp, forthright judgements about all the world – except for Judith Carty. 'A bit of an empty-head, eh?' she suggested.

'Oh no! Full! Sally's bright as a button and very sharp, but not nearly so complicated as Judith.'

'If her head is so full, what's it full of?'

'Thoughts – all pointing one way. Sally is consumed with thoughts of being mistress of Castle Moore. She and her mother, both. Mrs McIver is also very single-minded.'

'Aha! This is like bicycling downhill, suddenly. How does Rick feel toward La McIver, then?'

Henrietta pondered the question – for so long, indeed, that her aunt was moved to say, 'Well, at least it's not a simple for or against!'

The younger woman chuckled. 'It certainly isn't. You see, Rick is really very young, I mean for his age. I don't wish to appear to criticize you and Uncle Hereward and all the others who were party to that decision, but leaving Rick all on his own here with tutors and King hasn't exactly helped him grow up.' She reached forward and placed an arm on her aunt's shoulder, taking her a little by surprise. 'Sorry – have I offended you?'

'No, go on. I can't say I disagree with you – though we did it for all the best reasons.'

'I mean, if he'd had to fight his own corner in that savage hyena pack called "Eton", he'd be a very different fellow by now. He looks like a grown-up. He can talk like a grown-up. But inside him . . . he isn't.'

Aunt Bill glanced briefly over her shoulder. 'Are you saying he's flattered by the McIver girl's interest and equally flattered by that of the Carty, and so, in racing parlance, is happy to play the field?'

'In a nutshell.'

'And if we pushed him to the wall? No more shilly-shallying, young fellow my lad – make up your mind?'

'I'm pretty sure he'd plump for Judith.'

'Good. Then we'll be careful not to push him unless that's what we want. And talking of plump' – her voice brightened several degrees – 'there is one more filly in the stakes, I believe? A gel called Netty O'Farrelly?'

Henrietta realized how industrious her aunt had been that morning. True, the O'Farrellys had been on the fringe of the castle circle for years now, ever since the father's legal skills had proved so great as to outweigh his disadvantages as a Roman Catholic; but it was only in the last few months that Netty and Percy had become regular visitors. Some spy here might just have had time to write to Aunt Bill about it, but it was far more likely she had 'discovered' the fact in her conversation with O'Brien on the way from the station this morning.

A further thought struck her: O'Brien couldn't stand King. So what else had Aunt Bill been told on her obviously fruitful twelve-mile drive from the railhead at Simonstown?

'The O'Farrellys are Roman Catholics, of course,' she replied.

Aunt Bill made an ambiguous noise and said, 'Well, we'll concentrate our attention on the Carty and the McIver.'

It occurred to Henrietta that her aunt wilfully referred to them in that way because it made it easier to overlook their femininity, their essential sisterhood. *The* Carty and *the* McIver made much easier pawns than Judith and Sally. 'There is a tiny little complication,' she said hesitantly.

'Oh dear. Whenever I hear those words "tiny little complication" I turn quite pale. One woman's "tiny little complication" is another woman's death knell. Go on.'

'Sally's brother, Fergal, is also head over heels in love with Judith.'

'That's the Fergal who was always Rick's best friend?'

'And still is. Though how long *that* will survive, I have my doubts.'

They had reached the road. Aunt Bill made a nimble leap over the lowest part of the ditch and turned to assist her niece. She saw the brief surprise in the younger woman's eyes and said, 'Plenty of life in these old bones yet!'

'I never doubted it,' Henrietta replied.

Her aunt laughed and, throwing an arm around her shoulders, gave her a warm hug. 'Oh, Hen, I'm so glad we took this walk together. I've learned so much – not least about you, my dear.'

'Me?' the other echoed in alarm.

'Yes. To be quite candid, I never had much feeling for you either way when you were younger, but now I think you've grown up into an absolutely splendid young woman – one I find I'm quite thrilled to know.'

Henrietta felt the wind knocked out of her at this revelation. 'Really?' she gasped.

Aunt Bill cleared her throat delicately.

Henrietta persisted: 'Did you really not like me all that much, Aunt Bill?'

'No, I was just thinking about that,' the other admitted reluctantly. 'It didn't sound quite true, even as I said it. The fact is, I think I was a little *reluctant* to get to know you. Perhaps I had an intuition that benign neglect was all you needed to turn into the rather splendid person you are.' She laughed effusively. 'Well, I certainly gave it you in full measure! Anyway – we were talking about something much more important than this. Ah yes – I remember: young Fergal McIver and his passion for the Carty gel.'

'Also – another complication – Netty O'Farrelly has a bit of a pash for Fergal.'

'Oh, the pain of it all!' Aunt Bill cried with gay insincerity. 'I remember it so well. And I'm sure you do, too – even if neither of us can remember the young men's names now. Aren't you glad it's all behind you at last?'

Henrietta made a noncommittal gesture with her hands and a noncommittal noise that might have been a small laugh.

Aunt Bill said, 'The one to be sorry for is poor Fergal, of course. I'll bet his mother and his sister give him no peace. His rôle is quite obviously to bear down on the Carty gel and cut her out, leaving his best friend Rick to turn all his attentions on the sister. And men make such a *thing* about friendship, don't they? We women know it's all very well in its place, but they make an absolute idol of it. Yes . . . poor old Fergal!'

'Apparently Fergal kissed Netty quite recently – before the Cartys came back to the Old Glebe, mind you. But still . . .'

'Yes, as you say – but still! They're lucky they don't live in Vienna. Sylvia Mainwaring was telling me that the *instant* a dance is over the young ladies have to return to the chaperones. I mean *immediately*. If they linger with their partner for even a few seconds, then they have to announce their engagement before the ball is over or the young lady's reputation is in ruins and she'll never be invited anywhere again.'

'How absurd!' Henrietta sneered.

'Yes, but a kiss is *almost* the same with us, don't you feel? Or is it all very different nowadays?'

Henrietta chuckled. 'I can't see any girl suing for breach of promise and offering as her only evidence a single kiss on a brief stroll between the tennis court and the house.'

'Ah.'

'You sound rather sad about it.'

'Well, it would have been nice to have something to hold over the young man in an emergency. It's always nice to have things to hold over people, don't you find? It smoothes one's path through life. Oh dear, my head's beginning to ache with all these revelations. I think that's quite enough for one morning.' She grasped her niece's arm again and started propelling her up the incline toward the castle gates. 'Actually,' she said blithely, 'quite the nicest discovery I've made today is *you!* What a very nice young person you are. I do hope Harold appreciates you properly?'

Henrietta found herself poised so exactly between the alternatives – passing it all off with some light reassurance and telling the older woman everything – that no words emerged from her at all.

'I hope *someone* appreciates you properly, then,' Aunt Bill added, leaning forward, as she had done back by the lake, and peering intently at her.

And, just as had happened at the lake, her niece's cheeks and ears answered for her – only this time Aunt Bill made no comment on the fact.

All she did was smile the most satisfied smile of all – and there had been many others during their walk.

The Saturday morning of the clan gathering was devoted to accounts. It was dull, manly stuff – or so the men assured the women as they closeted themselves with McGrath, the agent, and Maurice O'Farrelly, the solicitor, who was also Percy's father. Aunt Wilhelmina and Henrietta wandered from room to room, making a desultory check on Agnes King's diligence as supervisor of the upper servants. They found little to criticize, even in the dimmest corner. Both agreed it was extraordinary that a woman who was hardly ever seen – or hardly ever noticed, anyway, for she flitted about the house like a quiet ghost – could exert such discipline on so many servants.

Henrietta remarked that the numbers did seem a little disproportionate – eight maids, four footmen, and a butler-housekeeper couple, all to look after one twenty-year-old youth; not to mention the below-stairs household, which added a further seven to the tally. Then, with the mathematical bit between her teeth, she went on to number the outdoor servants in the stables, gardens, and game coverts – producing a grand total of fifty-two. 'And all to look after Rick!' she exclaimed. 'We manage in London with a mere twelve.'

'They're hardly just to look after Rick, dear.' Her aunt laughed. 'Two or three suffice for that. The rest are here to maintain the house and estate.'

'To flaunt the flag in the face of the rebels, you mean.'

'Oh, that's in the past, surely? The rebels are all hanged – the ones who provoked us to that gesture, anyway. Nowadays . . .'

'Are they?' Henrietta interrupted.

Her aunt, catching her tone, stared sharply at her. 'What d'you mean? Of course they are.'

'Judith doesn't think so.'

'What does *she* know . . .' Aunt Bill began scornfully before changing it to: 'Oh, yes, of course.' After a brief silence she added, 'Has the gel talked to you about it?'

'Several times. She wonders that she and I – and Rick – were never called to give evidence at the trial. It wasn't much of a trial, either, was it?'

The older woman ignored this last remark. 'But you were mere children – not you, perhaps, dear, but the other two. And King was so positive.'

'Yes, wasn't he!'

'And there was the confession of the man they shot at the time, Ciaran Darcy.'

'The "lost" confession.'

'Technically, yes. But the sergeant who took it down originally was there to give evidence.'

Henrietta made no reply to that.

Aunt Bill went on, 'I trust the three of you aren't going about fomenting a suspicion that a sergeant in the Royal Irish Constabulary would do anything so awful as to fabricate evidence! Especially in a hanging affair.'

'Why? D'you think it impossible?'

Her aunt stared at her in consternation. 'Whether it's possible or not is quite beside the point. The point is that people in our position simply cannot go about the locality pouring doubt upon the RIC. They are all that stands between us and the next boat to England.'

Now it was the niece's turn for astonishment. 'Aunt Bill! I've never heard you say such things before! D'you really believe that?'

'I thought everyone did. Why? D'you fondly suppose we are loved and cherished to distraction?'

'Well – I see nothing but friendly faces and smiles wherever I go. And cheerful inquiries after my health and Rick and so on.'

Aunt Bill let out a single laugh of contempt; but, as they were drawing within earshot of two maids, busy at their dusting, she dropped the subject for the moment. It continued to bite its way through her mind, though – the strongest acid being, not the suggestion that the RIC might be something less than perfect, but that Rick, Henrietta, and the Carty girl might all be of the opinion that those murderers were still at large. It touched something ancient and elemental within her – as it had in the immediate aftermath of that dreadful day.

Actually, now she came to think of it, Henrietta had said nothing as to Rick's opinion on the matter. She was about to broach the subject – the maids being safely out of earshot again – when she saw the lad himself, strolling toward the front door with Fergal. She then had a better idea. 'Good morning, young man!' she called out. 'And what are your plans for today?'

Rick, who had formed no plans at all, quizzed his friend.

Fergal immediately turned to that invisible audience who followed him everywhere at a respectful distance and told it they had vaguely discussed the possibility of a little coarse fishing on Lough Cool.

In fact, no such discussion had taken place but he hoped the idea of cold, choppy water in mid-September would be enough to give the chaperones, young and old, a pause.

But Aunt Bill was the veteran of many a frozen trawl over Killary Harbour, Ireland's only fjord. 'Capital!' she cried. 'Where's the third young man – Percy, isn't it?'

Rick put a finger to his lips and looked fearfully about.

'O'Farrelly senior is in the library with the others,' he explained.

'And?'

'Well, the fact is, dear Aunt, O'Farrelly junior is supposed to be sharpening his quill – or whatever they do in lawyers' offices – in Parsonstown at this very hour. So he's closeted somewhere with an improving book – hiding from the old man.'

'An improving hiding is just what he deserves by the sound of it,' she replied severely, to a small chorus of dutiful laughs. 'Still, that leaves two of you. What are the three gels doing? Are they here today?'

Fergal's invisible gathering levitated several feet in the air; doggedly he continued to address it: 'Netty's caught a sniffle, and her mother makes her wear such outlandish things when she shows the slightest sign of a chill that she has preferred to remain at home and press things in her herbarium. The other two are patching some of the theatrical clothing for tonight's dumb crambo.'

But when Sally and Judith heard of the fishing trip on the lake, they decided that the costumes would do. They were by now such habituées of the castle that they kept several changes of clothes in one of the dressing rooms – whither they now raced to select those best suited to a bright September morning on the lake.

'I think the sun is about to break through,' Aunt Bill warned them as they reached the halfway landing. Then, turning to Henrietta, 'Aren't you going, too, dear?'

Her niece gave a sad little smile and produced the parental trump: 'Unfortunately, dear Aunt, Netty O'Farrelly isn't the only one with a sniffle. Poor little Yuk has a distinct chest this morning.'

'I think you'd *better* come, nonetheless,' the older woman insisted. 'Betty or . . .' Other maids' names escaped her for the moment; she waved a hand vaguely in the direction of the nursery door. 'One of them is perfectly capable of looking after her.'

But Henrietta insisted humbly: 'I should never forgive myself if . . .' Following a long-established family tradition she left the rest hanging.

'Henrietta!' Aunt Bill called peremptorily after her departing back.

'Shall I get a packed lunch put up for you all?' was the firm reply. 'Five, is it? Two with hearty appetites.'

Judith came downstairs in excited leaps and bounds. 'Three!' she corrected jovially. A froth of white lace set off her flashing, black-booted ankles to perfection, holding the two young men entranced in guilty voyeurism. Aunt Bill went at once to the foot of the stairs to interpose herself between them. But to her despair Sally appeared at the half-landing at that moment, and, with a cry of 'Four!' put on her own unwitting exhibition for the two young men, who, each in his own way, felt even guiltier at their brief enjoyment of the offering – until Aunt Bill turned her icy features toward them and shamed their gaze groundward.

After they had gone, leaving a sprinting footman to bring their packed lunch down to the boathouse, Henrietta offered a sop to the Recording Angel by paying a brief visit to the nursery and holding Yuk even more briefly in her arms. Her only reward for this rare act of tenderness was a sneeze; disgusted, she passed the bundle back to Bridget Dolan, the maid who was acting as assistant nanny during their visit to the castle.

Halfway down the nursery stair, the gloomiest in the entire castle, she noticed something glittering on her breast. Her disgusted finger discovered it to be a relic of the baby's sneeze. She whipped a handkerchief from her sleeve and began carefully to gather it up. After no more than two dabs a gentle hand reached out of the deep twilight, which never deserted that landing, and continued the action with consummate delicacy – long after the necessity for it had passed.

She had no need to say his name. She knew every little disorder of his breathing by now. She heard the hammer of his heart as it disrupted the flow of air through his nose and throat, turning it into a whispered petition more eloquent than sonnets. She spun herself slightly, bringing the fullness of her breast into the path of that caressing hand, whose fingers no longer held her kerchief; at once they found her nipple and, through it, spun a magic web of well-nigh unbearable pleasure along every sinew of her body.

'Not here,' she whispered.

The gentle pressure of finger and thumb almost felled her; his other hand rose to her left breast and played the bass clef in a music more ancient than mankind itself. She hugged her body to his, trying to escape the sweetness of his tormenting caress. 'In the old schoolroom,' she gasped. 'Down on the next landing.'

They achieved its sanctuary without discovery, though the nursery door opened noisily as they closed the schoolroom door behind them. 'No, nobody,' Betty Dolan's voice called out in confirmatory tones. The door slammed above them and silence fell – a silence as thick as the dust on the four old schooldesks, which were still expectantly facing the long-untenanted lectern by the window.

Henrietta remembered how much she had hated that arrangement, for it turned their tutor into an unreadable silhouette, while it rendered his pupils vulnerable to the merciless glare of daylight.

She heard the key turn in the lock as she pushed between the desks to the chaise longue that still stood beneath the window sill.

'What's *that* doing in a schoolroom?' Percy asked as he joined her.

'We're not the first here,' she murmured, caressing its

velvet covering. 'Someone's dusted it recently. I wonder who?' Now they were safe, she enjoyed the idea that time stretched infinite before them; she relished the thought that they could wring the last drop of pleasure out of every little caress, every fleeting kiss, before passing, unhurried, to the next.

'Yes, but what's it doing here?' he repeated.

'Monsieur Beruchet, our old French tutor, used to admire himself, posing in it. Like this.' She seated herself in manly fashion, one leg straight along the chaise longue, the other bent at the knee with the foot on the ground. 'He held his book like this – always some dry old tome with a name like *Merveilles de la peinture*, and not a single painting in it. And he always wore one of those soft velvet kepis, with a tassel, you know?'

Deftly Percy seated himself between her spreadeagled thighs, managing to insinuate his knees beneath the hem of her skirt and petticoats and slide himself nearer her. 'I've already heard ten more things about Monsieur Beruchet than I ever wished to know,' he said, 'though I'll gladly second any vote of thanks to him for this bequest.' He patted the headrest of the chaise and then took her adorable head between his hands. 'I've been on fire since that day up on the mountain,' he murmured, staring first into one eye and then the other as if he knew he would never decide which was the more adorable. Her eyelids drooped and fell shut.

Between him and her there arose a perfume peculiar to desire, hot and muskladen. Her hands drooped into her lap, accidentally touched him there, where importunate flesh strained at the clench of his fly. Her nimble fingers made short work of his release, and the heat within her grasp was that of a furnace. Even then, in the melting, all-consuming passion of that instant, some small part of her mind remained aloof enough to marvel that what she found so grotesque and repulsive in her husband was, in this young fellow, the most desirable possession in the world. Certainly the desire to possess it, totally within herself, was now overwhelming.

'Then finish what you started up there,' she whispered, lifting her skirts and forking herself wide upon him.

Her familiarity with Harold's slow, well-meaning rapes of her person had not prepared her for a man 'on fire', a man with a hair trigger, who began to cry at once in angry ecstasy . . . a man who, a minute or so later, joined her in a little grunt of delighted surprise, when they both discovered that his premature crowning of the occasion had taken none of the starch out of him.

'What a man is my own darling boy!' she whispered in his ear as she eased herself on to her back, and her heels on top of him – and all slowly enough to maintain their communion every inch of the way. 'Now there's no hurry at all,' she added.

Just beyond the stout oak door Agnes King turned to her husband and nodded grimly.

'Good,' he whispered, and they tiptoed away below the stairs, avoiding the treads that creaked. They knew every such tread in the house, of course.

The pleasure of sitting in a small open boat in a cold breeze on choppy waters, watching two rather sullen young men whose eyes were glued to a pair of painted wooden bobbins floating a short way off – two young men whose only conversation concerned the heading of the boat and the differing characters of tench, bream, and dace . . . such pleasure soon palled on the two younger women. They made the fact so plain that they were gladly set ashore to prepare luncheon on the island. Aunt Bill, still smarting from Henrietta's insubordination, stayed aboard and grimly assumed the ghillie's rôle with the oars. She had a far better idea than either Rick or Fergal where the fish would bite and she soon had them in such good humour they were more than reconciled to the lie that had brought them here in the first place.

Sally and Judith, marooned unhappily together, but happy at least to be dry and out of the wind, set about kindling a fire for a brew of tea and some potatoes baked in their jackets.

'I don't believe those poor boys wanted to fish at all,' Judith commented. 'They never for one moment believed Mrs Montgomery would take the suggestion up like that.'

Sally, red-faced from puffing up the fire, straightened herself and tucked wisps of fallen hair back into her bonnet. 'Whoo! Why does forced breathing always make one giddy?' Her eyes sought and found the boat, which was now a good half-mile away. 'Never mind what *they* wanted,' she replied. 'This is what *she* had in mind all along – you and me safely out of the way. She has a bone to pick with those two – or with Rick, anyway. She was absolutely furious at Hen for staying behind. Did you see the look on her? It would have served in place of mustard.'

'I didn't notice,' Judith responded offhandedly. 'What does she want to tell Rick, d'you think?'

Sally ignored this diversionary question; Judith's casualness had been far too casual. 'Didn't you think Hen's staying behind just a bit . . . you know, blatant? Poor little Yuk's got a sniffle, indeed! When has she ever concerned herself about such things?'

Judith, realizing that an offhand dismissal of the topic wasn't going to work, replied, 'Perhaps she had a twinge of conscience at last. Or perhaps she has a better memory of what utter boors men turn into once they get rod and line in their grasp.'

'Or perhaps she, too, wanted to read an improving book!'

‘Yes, that’s also possible,’ Judith agreed.

Sally gripped her elbow and shook it with comic petulance. ‘You know jolly well what I mean!’

‘What?’

‘Don’t pretend. You know jolly well there’s something going on between Hen and Percy.’

‘Is there?’

‘Of course there is. D’you remember last Saturday, when we were all picking mushrooms? And you saw King going for a walk up Mount Argus? And you said, “Oh, I want a word with him!”?’ Her sing-song tone was gently mocking. ‘And then you shout a warning and hey presto, down the mountain comes Percy! And who comes tumbling after? Why, it’s Mrs Austin on her horse! What a surprise!’

Judith gave a weary shrug. ‘And who else came tumbling down? King, of course. And Rick. And me! Work away, Sal! A desperate tailor can make a shirt of any old rag!’

Sally, smiling at the flames, which were now quite merry, began to sing, idly, as if to herself.

‘ “Per-ci-v’l went up the hill, but not to fetch some water . . .” ’ Her manner became crisp again as she broke back into speech. ‘We saw King go up. And we saw Rick. And we saw you. But Hen told us she was going hacking down by the lake shore. And Percy said he was going bughunting over at Robertsons’ mill. That’s the difference.’

Judith realized that her pretended detachment was doing Henrietta more harm than good; she came about on the other tack at once. A slow smile spread over her face. ‘Yes, I remember now. I never thought of that. What d’you suppose *could* be going on between them?’

‘We-ell,’ Sally replied judiciously, ‘I expect she tells him how blissfully happy she is in her marriage to Harold

Austin, while he lies back and stares at the sky, running his mind idly over all he's learned on the indissolubility of the marriage bond.'

Judith laughed despite herself. 'Sally!' she remonstrated. 'You're quite dreadful!'

'Well what do *you* suppose they do, then?'

Judith became serious again. 'I should think one of the nicest things about being married is that you're free at last to cultivate proper, sincere friendships with men. Without' – she smiled acidly – 'the rest of the world jumping to the vilest conclusions.'

'Vile.' Sally echoed the word with some surprise; her tone suggested it was the very last one she would have chosen.

'What would you call it, then? I mean, supposing you were married and you began to cultivate a quite proper but also quite deep affection for one of your husband's friends, and . . .'

'I didn't know Percy and Mr Austin were even on speaking acquaintance.'

'Very well, then,' was the petulant response. 'A young man who would most certainly be one of your husband's friends *if* your husband were there. All right? Is that precise enough for your pedantic taste?'

Sally raised her hands in a pacifying form of apology, but her grin said: Why so touchy?

Judith reined in her impatience and forced herself to smile back. 'In those circumstances, wouldn't you call it "vile" if all your friends immediately assumed you were . . .' An awkward gesture completed the thought.

'Were what?' Sally insisted.

'Whatever *you* were insinuating. Falling down and breaking your crown? I don't know.'

'We still have to explain why they each told us they were going in opposite directions and yet both chose the same one in the end . . . ah, well!' She abandoned the inquiry. 'You're right, really, Ju. What does it matter? I say, aren't I good at getting a fire to go! Let's gather some wood and start up a really topping blaze. They'll love us for it.'

Judith swallowed her exasperation and they went off in search of wood to carry back to the fire. Though the island was small enough to walk its entire shore in five minutes, it boasted a good stand of pine at its centre. They made their way to it first.

'What you said just now was jolly interesting,' Sally continued. 'About being able to make proper friendships with men once you're married. Don't you think *we* can have proper friendships – us and the boys, for instance?'

'Not really.'

'You surprise me. I'd have said we do. What d'you think is lacking, then?'

'Well, we enjoy a sort of *group* friendship and we have jolly good laughs and games together and we all feel comfortable and we can tease each other without awkwardness . . . and all that. But . . . well, for instance . . .' She drew a deep breath and plunged in. 'If it wasn't you and *me* walking here but you and . . . I don't know – Rick, say! If it was you and Rick. I mean, it's impossible, I know, but wouldn't it be nice to . . .'

'It *is* nice!' Sally interrupted.

'What d'you mean?'

'I mean it's not impossible. I've been alone with Rick. Lots of times.'

'Lots?' Judith fought desperately to keep her dismay from showing.

'Only last month, for instance. Just before you returned to the Old Glebe. He came over to play tennis and we went for a walk in the pinewood, just the two of us.'

'Oh.' Judith relaxed somewhat. 'You mean just walking back from the court to the house.'

'We were still quite alone.'

'For three or four minutes! What can you talk about in that time!'

Sally grinned mischievously. 'We didn't do much talking, dear.'

Judith turned and faced her, gripping her arm fiercely. 'But don't you see! *That's* what I'm driving at, Sal. We can all of us snatch four or five minutes alone together. But what do we do with them? Kiss and canoodle! Murmur sweet nothings! You don't get to *know* people like that. Kissing and canoodling get in the way. Wouldn't it be nice to walk around this island for an hour with a young man you rather liked, and *not* kiss! Not even hold hands. But just *talk*! Don't you see what I mean? Just talk.'

Sally, to whom such an idea was quite foreign, began to get the first glimmering of what Judith meant. Even that much alarmed her. 'Talk about what?' she asked nervously.

'Anything. Everything. His interests. Your interests. What *are* Rick's interests? Do you know?'

Sally tried to think of some subtle way of asserting that his chief interest was herself – but it was rather like trying to find a subtle way of killing someone with an axe. 'Castle Moore, I suppose,' she said lamely when the silence forced her to speak. 'I mean, he'll have to run the estate himself, some day.'

'D'you suppose he ever will? Can you see him doing it?'

'Of course he will!' Sally stared back in amazement. 'And indeed I can.'

Judith shrugged and returned to their search for firewood. Soon they had assembled enough fallen branches and driftwood to make a respectable blaze. They began dragging it down to the lee shore, where the initial fire was beginning to die.

'We'll get the lads to break this for us,' Sally said.

'We will not!' Judith asserted. 'Our boots are as stout as theirs, I daresay. And together we'd outweigh either of them. Come on!' She canted a branch up on a low boulder, about a foot high, and put her arm loosely about Sally's waist. 'One, two, three – jump!'

Laughing, Sally complied. The log snapped cleanly.

'What we can do *together*, eh?' Judith said laconically.

Thanks to Aunt Bill's superior knowledge of the ways of Irish fish, the two lads soon had a respectable little hoard for their luncheon. The breeze had slackened over the past hour, and veered to north-east, carrying to them the seductive aroma of woodsmoke. 'Feeling peckish, Aunt Bill?' Rick asked hopefully.

'Why not?' she responded, giving a few light touches to the left oar to bring her head-up to Turk Island.

'Here, we'll row now,' her nephew said guiltily. 'You've done splendidly but you jolly well deserve a rest.'

'Stay where you are, you mutinous dog!' Her smile was jovial. 'I can row the pair of you out of the water any day. You should have seen me at the Killary Harbour gala when I was your age. I could race the porpoises, so I could. Tell me, Fergal,' she went on as if it was all part of the same train of thought, 'was there ever any suggestion in your family that they hanged the wrong people for the Castle Moore Murders?'

Fergal just stared at her, open mouthed. His personal public-meeting crowd seemed to have deserted him.

She frowned, as if she now suspected she had made a mistake. 'It *was* your father who defended them, wasn't it?'

He exchanged an awkward glance with Rick. 'Somebody had to,' he pointed out diffidently.

'Yes, yes. We all realize that. The glories of British

justice and so on. Nothing personal. But it does mean your family must take more than the ordinary sort of passing interest in the case – or so I'd have thought. Which is why I'm asking you . . . have you heard anything to that effect?'

Her insistence on staying at the oars was canny. Fergal now had nothing with which to distract himself, to occupy time; the imperative to answer was thus more urgent. She did him the courtesy of looking away, of sparing him the sight of those merciless dark beads, her eyes, for a moment or two. But when she aimed them at him once more he capitulated. 'Not really,' he said.

'Not . . . really.' She repeated the two words with a slow, judicial gravity and then smiled at him. 'I never *quite* know what that means. Does it mean you've heard nothing at all? Or that you've heard the odd remark that might or might not be construed as a comment of some kind?'

He nodded. 'I might have, Mrs Montgomery – and then again I mightn't.'

She chuckled. 'Ah yes. That's the third possibility. Dear old Ireland! Well, tell me – what might you or might you not have heard?'

Greatly daring, he responded with, 'Might I ask whether you have any particular reason for making this inquiry, Mrs Montgomery?'

She noticed he no longer consulted Rick by means of little sidelong glances; after the initial shock of her question he had rapidly regained control of himself. He added, 'Has anyone mentioned the possibility of error to *you*, for instance?'

She rested oars a moment and gave him a cautious little nod. 'One of the witnesses on that evening – one who was not called to give evidence.'

'Miss Carty!' Rick said at once.

'*Not* Miss Carty, as it happens,' she assured him.

'Hen?' he asked as if he could hardly believe it. Then understanding dawned. 'Judith's been getting at her!' He stared hard at his aunt and said, 'But why are you taking such an interest, after all this time?'

All this time? She thought – and then realized she had forgotten how long the six years between fourteen and twenty were. To her, the same number of calendar pages had come and gone in a twinkling. Rather than give an immediate answer she addressed herself once more to Fergal – in case he should think he was off the hook. She resumed her rowing again, too. 'Did you happen to go to court at all, young man?' she asked. 'Do you follow your father's forensic triumphs so closely? What I really mean is, did you *see* the prisoners?'

He nodded, wary once more. 'I saw them being led away to the station after the verdict. They paraded them through the town in chains.'

'And did any of them have red hair? A red moustache?'

'You couldn't tell, I'm afraid. They were all close-cropped. Their own families said they hardly knew them.'

'Ah. Pity.'

'Why d'you ask, Aunt Bill?' Rick put in.

He meant why was she asking these questions in general, as she very well realized; but she chose a narrower interpretation. 'Well, dear boy, my memory of such dismal occasions does tend to grow mercifully faint – but one thing I do recall. I was here only a day or two after it all happened, if you remember? And the one thing both you and Miss Carty remarked upon was the bright red hair one of them had. She mentioned his hair, I think, and you said moustache or eyebrows. But you were unanimous that it was red.'

'The one who winged her and tried to kill me,' Rick said, as if it had slipped his memory over the years.

She stopped rowing suddenly and her eyes flashed with some personal lightning. 'You can see his face still!' It was not a question.

In that instant he recalled their meeting down by the lake – not as he had often recollected it since that day, and just as often dismissed it as one of those strange, emotional scenes that people create at moments of crisis. Now he recalled it with a great surge of primitive feeling – all those passions she had managed to awaken within him (or, he was now mature enough to wonder, *implant* within him?) on that suddenly unforgettable day.

Fergal, the merest bystander now, felt shrivelled in the blast of vengeful wrath that seemed to pour out of the old lady (as she appeared to him). It was like an aura in the boat between them, aunt and nephew.

It began to fade the moment she plied the oars once more. 'Did *you* attend the trial?' she asked Rick in a tone that, coming so hard on the heels of her earlier passion, seemed laughably conversational.

'King thought it best not to,' he replied.

She pursed her lips grimly, as if she had expected some such answer, and said no more.

The jollity of the two girls soon changed their mood for the better. It began when the boat was still a hundred yards or so offshore. Having discovered how easily they could break the dry old branches, they had saved most of them to give a small exhibition of their prowess. And now, like a pair of country dancers, they yoked an arm around each other's necks and, on the count of three, made a leap in the air and brought all four boots crashing down on the sacrificial branch.

'Bravo!' The two youths egged them on from the lake, partly in relief, but also in genuine enthusiasm.

Aunt Bill glanced briefly over her shoulder, shuddered at the indecorous scene which met her eye, and began to row with enough vigour to create a bow wave.

'Look at her!' Judith exclaimed between leaps. 'How old is she?'

'She must be getting on for fifty,' Sally replied.

'Lord, I hope I'm as agile at that age – if I even reach it.'

To all four youngsters anyone over thirty was entering a state of advanced decrepitude.

There was a low, sheer-sided rock about four yards from the shore; long ago – perhaps even thousands of years ago – someone had built out the land to join it. So it was a dry-shod party who came ashore and gathered eagerly round the blaze. Aunt Bill gave it an approving nod and vanished among the shrubbery for a moment. The two girls went to join her.

Fergal and Rick stooped to gut the fish. 'Bloody sheep – women,' Fergal commented.

'Keep your voice down for Christ's sake!' Rick warned anxiously. 'There's only me here.'

'Sorry. But don't you agree? One has to go, so they all have to go. I've often noticed that. And the way they laugh, too. Like a flock of turkeys. One goes *golla-golla-golla-golla-golla* and then they all start!'

'Actually, I could do with a piss myself.'

'Well, hold it back or they'll just think you're a copycat.'

Rick giggled. 'I saw three servant lassies squatting by a ditch at Simonstown Races last month. Oh, what a vision of beauty! I could see everything. The quantities of hair they have down there is only amazing!'

Fergal let a small silence grow before he asked, 'What was all that in the boat just now?'

'Oh!' Rick took up a handful of guts and flung them out into the lake. 'She's an odd old stick at times.'

'I believe you!' After a pause he added in a more speculative tone, 'She didn't press me on that question she asked. I wonder why not?'

'Perhaps she saw the answer in your eyes. Perhaps your expression gave it away. She's great guns at that.'

Fergal threw away his collection of guts, too. A seagull plummeted down from nowhere and plucked a beakful off the face of the lough. 'What expression?' he asked belatedly.

Four or five more gulls joined the first and a squabble broke out. 'There's going to be a storm,' Rick observed.

'What expression?'

'I don't know,' Rick snapped. 'I wasn't exactly hanging on every line of your ugly mug, you know.'

Fergal made an elaborate parody of pacifying him with buckets of water and imaginary fans. Then, slyly, he asked, 'Aren't you at all curious to know the answer yourself?'

To his surprise, Rick's eyes were suddenly filled with fear. 'Christ, no!' he exclaimed fervently.

The women returned at that moment, allowing no time to probe this unexpected response; they bore fresh armfuls of wood to 'explain' their absence.

Rick said he thought there was a bit of an old griddle on the other shore, where they'd cooked some rashers and sausages once last summer; he wandered off in search of it.

Fergal, after holding back a while, ran to join him. 'I wish you hadn't bloody said that – about wanting a piss,' he grumbled. 'I was all right until then.'

There was now enough hot ash to rake out over the potatoes, and enough in the way of glowing embers to cover the ash and bake them. Sally and Judith argued over the best way to manage it and then appealed to Aunt Bill. She told them to take four potatoes each and see whose came out best. 'Let Nature be our Instructor and Guide,' she pontificated. But as soon as the sentiment was out, it jarred with her finer instincts and she regretted it.

With a great effort that left him purple-faced, Rick managed to souse a small boulder about eight feet out in the water; Fergal said he could easily have done the same if Rick had challenged him earlier. Honour satisfied, and the pressure gratefully relieved, they wandered in search of the previous summer's griddle. They found it covered in rust but Rick carried it down to a gravelly part of the shore and managed to get most of it off by vigorous rubbing in the shingle.

'When I said my aunt's a queer old stick,' he remarked as he worked away, 'and you said you believed me . . . what did you mean?'

Fergal cleared his throat awkwardly. 'Same as you, I suppose.'

'Tell me all the same.' He rose and they set off to rejoin the ladies.

Fergal drew a deep breath and took the plunge. His invisible audience returned. 'I mean . . .' he boomed.

'Shite, man! I said tell *me*! Not the whole bally island.'

'Sorry. Anyway, I mean I can never make my mind up about her. Even when we were very young – when your people were still alive. You'd think she was one of *them* . . . very English, if you take my meaning?' He glanced nervously at his friend.

'Go on.'

'And then suddenly she'd do something or say something and you'd realize she wasn't at all English. Like, when I said just now that I might have heard something at home – and then again I mightn't. And she laughed and said "dear old Ireland" or something. I thought, By God, old girl, never mind Ireland that's you to a T! Don't you agree? You can never make up your mind about her, one way or another.'

Rick halted. They were approaching the stand of pines; in a moment or two they'd be within easy earshot of the woman. There he composed his answer carefully.

Fergal misunderstood his silence. 'I'm sorry if I said anything amiss now . . .' he began.

'Not at all.' Rick nudged his arm reassuringly. 'I know just what you mean. I often think there's an almighty war going on inside that woman. She could have a face on her like Edinburgh granite and you'd never see a twitch of a muscle – and yet inside her they could be refighting the Battle of the Boyne.'

'Clontarf!' Fergal said at once.

'What d'you mean?' Rick asked with a puzzled laugh.

'I mean it's much older than Jamesites and Williamites.' He took a step toward the fire, to force an end to their conversation. 'A woman at war with herself?' he mused. 'That's the truth of it, all right.'

The fish tasted so good they ate the lot. The two young men then had a vision of themselves returning home empty-handed, able to say no more than, 'You should have seen them!' to anyone who'd listen. So, despite the mauling she had given them, Rick said, 'Aunt Bill, you brought us such luck this morning, you wouldn't care to come out and share your superior craft with us yet again, I suppose?'

Fergal, who had been about to suggest the same, saw the disappointment in Judith's eye and changed his mind. 'Sufficient unto the day,' he said. 'I think it's still warm enough for a dip in the castle lake, don't you? I vote we go back and have a jolly good plunge. I'll race you half a mile and the girls can referee.'

'Oh, thank you very much!' Judith protested. 'Just my idea of a perfect afternoon – watching men being clever!'

Aunt Bill rose to her feet with an agile ease that was slightly assumed; she was still proving to the absent Henrietta that she was not yet in her dotage. 'While you make your minds up,' she told them, 'I shall take a brief constitutional around the island. Miss Carty, would you care to join me?'

Judith leapt to her feet at once and declared that nothing would give her more pleasure – though her backward glance at the other three spoke a different truth. Aunt Bill's first words, however, put her on her mettle: 'I was so surprised, my dear, to find you living down here in the country again. How do you feel about leaving the grand metropolis and returning to a dull little backwater like County Keelity? I expect you're most dreadfully disappointed.'

'Oh, but not at all, Mrs Montgomery,' the girl protested. 'Quite the reverse, in fact. Dublin was no fun at all. We lived in very straitened circumstances there – while my father perfected his machine, you understand.'

'Yes. Of course, we're all *so* pleased about his success.'

'You're too kind to say so. But Dublin wasn't at all a "grand metropolis" to me, I can assure you.'

'And yet, in that case, I should have thought your present situation even worse.' Aunt Bill halted and stared across the lough; her eye automatically began to single out good fishing spots. 'At the very moment when your people *do* have the means to enjoy Dublin society, they bring you down here. Of all places!'

Judith frowned. 'Why "of all places"? Oh, I see what you mean – the Murders.'

Instinctively they turned to face the castle; but the grove of pines, which dominated the island from every inch of its shoreline, was in the way. Memories crept in to fill the vacuum. In Judith's case, memories of the day in question; they had no power to disturb her now. 'I think it affected Henrietta slightly worse than it did Rick, for instance – though she was shielded by Mad McLysaght while he was much closer to danger.'

'How interesting,' Aunt Bill murmured as she resumed

her stroll. 'D'you think that might be what is affecting her present behaviour?'

The question threw poor Judith into a quandary. If she took it up, she might be led into treachery, for she regarded Hen as her closest friend; if she pretended she didn't know what was being implied, Mrs Montgomery might take her for a simpleton; and if she made some remark that showed she knew precisely what the older woman meant, but did not consider it a fitting topic of conversation – well, that would be almost like a snub. 'Perhaps,' she replied cautiously. 'But then again I don't think you can explain anything we do by pointing at this or that *single* cause, do you?'

She had spoken off the top of her head, merely to obscure the issue, and had therefore tossed the remark out in a light and casual fashion. But to Aunt Bill it seemed quite a profound observation, especially from one so young and (she hoped) inexperienced – and even more especially since it was delivered in such a nonchalant manner. Judith, taking silence for incomprehension, added, 'I'm sure I don't know why I do half the things I do. And if I can't be sure of my own reasons . . . well, it makes me even less sure about other people's.'

Aunt Bill, who had merely wished to discover what the girl knew, or could remember, of that fateful evening, was sufficiently interested by this remark to allow her aim to be diverted; if there was ever a moment when she began to think of Judith Carty as a serious candidate for the position of the next Mrs Bellingham of Castle Moore, that was it. Of course, there was a long way to go yet, but the girl was no longer utterly beyond the pale. 'What a very true and thoughtful sentiment,' she murmured. 'Tell me, has it just this moment occurred to you, or do you often think of such matters?'

'I suppose I think about them quite a bit,' Judith admitted reluctantly. 'But no, *think* is altogether too grand a word.' Her laughter lightened the mood between them. 'We all of us spend a lot of time thinking about *why* we do this or that.' She gestured briefly toward the other three to show what she meant by 'all of us', and then concluded, 'My father, I'm sure, would laugh me to scorn if I dared call it *thinking*.'

'All the same, such notions . . . may I call them notions without inviting your father's contumely?'

Judith laughed. Why did people say Mrs Montgomery was so formidable? she wondered. She was quite human when you got close to her.

'I'm sure such notions never crossed my mind until after I was married. *Long* after, in fact. There's nothing like marriage to bring you up with a jolt, you know.'

'I suppose not,' Judith replied uneasily. Just when she had steered the conversation so successfully away from the topic of Hen and her 'behaviour', Mrs Montgomery seemed to have given the reins an effortless twitch and brought them back to it.

'The greatest shock is when you suddenly wake up to the fact that this stranger in your house is going to go on living there until death do you part. *That's* when most of us begin to ponder such questions as *why* do we do certain things; that's when we begin to realize that we may have no reason at all – no single, big reason, I mean. Just many tiny little reasons whose combined power is sufficient. D'you remember how Gulliver was held down by the Lilliputians? Their mighty cables were no more than button thread to him – but there was enough of it to hold him captive nonetheless.'

'Yes. And you can't point to any one strand and say, "There's the one that's holding him!" That's what I mean about our reasons for doing things, too. You can't pick out one and say, "That's the fellow who's causing all the trouble." Can you?'

Aunt Bill cleared her throat delicately. 'When I speak

of the shocks that follow in the wake of marriage, my dear, please understand that I speak with no *particular* reference. Nothing uniquely personal, I mean. Indeed, it was an almost universal discovery among all my acquaintance.'

Judith felt emboldened to take her arm. 'And was anybody ever kind enough to warn *you*, Mrs Montgomery, before the event?' She glanced sharply at the older women but her eyes twinkled as she added, 'You are trying to warn me, I believe?'

Aunt Bill was beginning to realize how grossly she had underestimated this young lady; she made a quick mental note to trust Henrietta's judgement of people more strongly in future – which she quickly corrected to Henrietta's judgement of other women. She also decided to be more direct with Miss Carty than would have been her usual habit. 'To be quite candid, my dear,' she replied, 'I had no intention of raising the matter at all. Perhaps we can return to it on another occasion? We shall very soon run out of foreshore and what I really wish to know is how much you recall of that dreadful day, six years ago? Your earlier words encourage me to press the question now.'

They had covered about two-thirds of the entire shoreline, for the island was little more than a pocket handkerchief. 'I'll tell you something I've never told anyone before,' Judith replied.

She felt the other twitch at once and knew she had riveted her attention.

'If you're quite sure . . .' Aunt Bill murmured.

'Quite. The one person everyone's forgotten is Mad McLysaght. He was there, too – not simply there, either. I mean, he saved Hen's life in all probability, and mine, by holding me back as long as he did. But also we forget that he was there *before* any of us, gathering kindling for a little bonfire. And I'm sure he saw something.'

'Did he say as much? Is that what you've never told anyone else?'

'I'm just coming to it. In a way, he *did* say as much – he told us all. As we got off the boat, he swept off his hat and cried, "Loud applause and aves vehement!" – which is from Shakespeare.'

'Now there's a surprise!' Aunt Bill commented.

Judith chuckled. 'It's from *Measure for Measure*. The next bit wasn't though. It was his own. He added the greeting, "*Ave et valete!*" – hail and farewell. And King got very angry at that and sent him off with a flea in his ear.'

Aunt Bill, who had begun to despair that the girl would have anything of significance to reveal – despite her earlier promises – pricked up her ears at the mention of King. On the surface, however, she remained sceptical. 'How would King know that *valete* means farewell?' she asked.

'From the death notices, I imagine. You see it in lots of them.'

'Oh yes, of course. Here, but not over the water.'

'But the point I'm coming to,' Judith went on, 'is what he said later, after I'd escaped. Perhaps I should explain that the three of us youngsters were down at the boathouse when the firing started. And Mad McLysaght, who was steaming up *The Star of the Shannon*, knocked us to the ground and almost smothered us to keep our heads down. But Rick struggled free and then I followed, so Henrietta was the only one who remained. She told me all this only recently and it's been on my mind ever since. He clung to her like a limpet, of course. And when it was all over, when the murderers ran away, he said, "Who finds the partridge in the puttock's nest?" Actually it wasn't simply out of the blue like that. He said it just a few minutes earlier, before the shooting, you see. When we first went down to the boathouse, Rick said something to him about looking for a partridge's nest. He said it then, too: "Who finds the partridge in the puttock's nest?" But when he said it the second time . . .'

'To Henrietta alone?'

'Well, not really to her, she says. More to himself – speaking aloud to himself. But she's sure he meant her to overhear. The second time he completed the quotation. D'you know how it ends? It's from *Henry the* . . . something. Part Two.'

'It doesn't matter, dear,' Aunt Bill cut in impatiently.

'Sorry. Anyway, it goes: "Who finds the partridge in the puttock's nest, but may imagine how the bird was dead, although the kite soar with unbloodied beak? *Even so suspicious is this tragedy*." So he must have known *something*, you see – even before there was any shooting at all . . .'

'D'you mind saying it again?' Aunt Bill interrupted.

Judith said it several times before she could complete her own train of thought: 'It means that even before the first shot was fired, he must have known something was afoot – because that's when he said about finding the partridge in the puttock's nest, d'you see?'

'What *is* a puttock, by the way?'

'A bird of prey. Some dictionaries say it's a buzzard. Other say it's a kite.'

Aunt Bill smiled. 'You *have* been looking things up!'

Judith nodded. 'As soon as Hen told me.'

They had now drawn very near the other three. Aunt Bill stopped and stared across the lough, as if she wanted one final drink at the view. 'For any particular reason?' she asked.

'Yes, I thought I might tackle Mad McLysaght directly – ask him straight out if he really did see anything that day.'

'And have you done so, may I ask?'

Judith shook her head. 'I'm afraid to. Not afraid of

him but afraid of . . . what he might tell me. He might say things that I couldn't just leave . . . things I might have to do something about.'

Aunt Bill continued to stare across the water.

'D'you know what I mean?' Judith prompted.

The older woman nodded slowly. 'More than you may suppose, my dear. It isn't that *you* might have to do something about it, is it?' Her eyes swept past Judith, catching her briefly before they settled on Rick. 'The partridge,' she mused. Then, turning to look at Castle Moore, which was just visible over the woodland from here, she added, 'And there's the kite's nest . . . the kite with the unbloodied beak, eh?'

Judith nodded.

Aunt Bill drew a deep breath, as people do when they reach some important decision. 'Well, it's quite clear that *one* of us has to tackle Mad McLysaght. I have the advantage of years. On the other hand, you have the shared memory – which might be the necessary starting point. But we'll have to be quick. The fellow will be moving on soon.'

They neither returned to their fishing nor swam in the lake; in fact, they spent the afternoon rehearsing their dumb crambo. The choice of phrase was Rick's – *King, our Hero* – which they broke into four scenes. The first, 'King', was straight from Shakespeare, from *Hamlet*, in fact, where the Gloomy Dane coaches the strolling players in the art of acting, concluding with the line, 'The play's the thing with which to catch the conscience of the king!'

The second scene, 'Our', was loosely based on a melodrama Percy had attended in Limerick last spring – in particular on a scene in the graveyard where the conscience-stricken murderer, played now by Percy himself, was apprehended in the very act of exhuming his fair victim's corpse so that he might hold her in his arms once more and, by swallowing poison, 'die upon the midnight *hour*'.

The third was a simple mime that allowed Henrietta, Judith, Sally and Netty (recovered already from her little chill) to show off their prowess at Greek dancing. While doing so they strewed rose petals upon the ground, leading up to the climax in which Tomás King himself, the egregious butler, clad in a tablecloth-toga and crowned with a wreath of genuine laurel, entered stage left, walked majestically across the scene, and exited stage right. The rose petals were actually scraps of crepe paper which two of the maids spent part of the afternoon cutting out – just as they would spend part of the following morning gathering them up again.

The fourth and final part, which introduced the phrase in its entirety, was a solo performance by Henrietta. It took the form of a lecture to a Ladies' Finishing School on prizegiving day, all about the virtuous bliss to be discovered by the Good Wife in her daily domestic round 'in the little empire of the hearth' – the king and hero of which was, naturally, the Good Husband. She had written it herself, as a parody of those quaint homilies on *Knowing Your Place* and *Pleasing Your Masters* that had been popular in reading primers for the servant classes earlier in the century.

That evening they all dined well, the party being augmented by the parents of the cast – Betty and Frank McIver, Norman and Thelma Carty, and Maurice and Meg O'Farrelly. It was the first time the O'Farrellys had been invited inside the castle for an occasion that was purely social; indeed, as far as anyone could recall, it was the first time any Roman Catholics had ever dined there at all. There were jokes about the Seymour-Kanes, the original builders of the present castle – how they must be turning in their graves. But, as the jokers immediately pointed out, the very fact that they could now laugh about the whole silly business showed what enormous strides the country had been making lately. Meg O'Farrelly almost made a further joke about mixed marriages but stopped herself just in time; the tide of present laughter was not yet running quite that high.

So it was in a jovial mood that they all trooped through to the drawing room, where the footmen had rigged an impromptu stage at the end opposite the fire.

The first scene, from *Hamlet*, went down very well. Fergal took the title rôle, which made it especially comical – for all the tricks and gestures he warned the strolling players to avoid, 'sawing the air with their hands', and so on, were gestures he commonly used in real life. Yet he was so earnest and solemn in handing out the advice, no one could tell whether he was aware of it or not; and, of course, there was never a flicker of a smile from him to let them know his tongue was in his cheek. The laughter was almost out of control by the time he had finished – and no one had the slightest idea what the word of the buried phrase might be; the betting was on 'saw', because it had two meanings, and words with multiple meanings were always popular in dumb crambos.

In the second scene, Percy made a surprisingly convincing villain. The flesh crawled at the moment he exhumed the corpse of the lover he had so infamously betrayed (played by his sister Netty). When he held her in his arms, staring up at a gibbous moon, and gave his most moving speech – 'Ah ye gods, come strike me dead . . .' there was a lump in many a manly throat and a tear in many a gentle eye. The sudden and startling irruption of Rick, the gallant and honourable squire whose betrothed the fair victim had been, at the head of a trusty band of labourers and police – 'Now stay your vile hand, you double-dyed villainous dog . . .' – brought the audience to its feet in a flush of virtuous wrath.

The Greek dancing raised an eyebrow or two. It was, in fact, a repeat performance of one given by Sally and Netty and two other girls at the benefit gala to buy new cornets for the Simonstown Silver Band last summer; Mrs McIver played the identical music, note for note. They had taught Henrietta and Judith the steps that afternoon. But a vision of dancing maidens in loose-fitting costumes, viewed by flattening and unflattering sunlight across a distant lawn upon a crowded summer's afternoon, is one thing; the identical performance, viewed at much closer quarters, bathed in the warm radiance of stage lighting, which both flatters and models the loosely clad female form, is quite another. And had it not been for the delightful innocence of the four performers, and the reassuringly classical trappings, and the strictly pastoral references in the music, Aunt Bill, who was turning Betty McIver's pages, might have acted upon her initial inclination, which was to whisper briefly in the pianist's ear and 'accidentally' turn two pages in one. Even so, it was touch and go. The appearance of King at the climax of the dance, so exalted and stately, produced a cheer – of relief, it must be said – that almost fetched down the plaster.

After that, it was plain sailing for Henrietta and her solo *tour de force* – or it should have been. At the rehearsal that afternoon the others had gradually ceased their gossip and petty bickering as the sheer comedy of her performance compelled them to watch, to smile, to chuckle, to laugh, to guffaw, and finally to collapse in a heap of helpless mirth. But that had been by daylight with everyone just standing around informally in their everyday clothes. Now, as with the Greek dancing, the atmosphere, the lighting, and the costume created an entirely different mood.

On top of it all, people were still a little nervous after the doubts occasioned by the dancing; they no longer knew whether they were being invited to watch comedy or tragedy.

They had also been thrown off the scent by the deliberate confusion between *hour* and *our*; so the guesses were as wild as they were improbable.

It began to go wrong from the very first sentence: 'I address my remarks today to the very flower of the nation's womanhood.'

Judith, knowing what was coming, burst into a giggle.

Aunt Bill – mainly because she did not wish to miss the hidden phrase when it appeared, but also, to some small degree, because she did not think Henrietta's fine sentiment merited such levity – turned upon the poor girl with a peremptory: 'Sshhh!'

Henrietta darted a brief, distressed glance at her aunt but, as she was wearing a rather severe pair of halfmoon glasses, which reflected the light brilliantly, the subtlety of the message from the eyes behind them failed to get across. Thus, in turn, her opening rhythm was lost.

The comedy of an ostensibly serious talk like that relies so absolutely on the timing of each phrase, on the precise rise and fall of each syllable, that, once those elements start to fall apart, the speaker loses touch with the audience and the whole thing falls flat. It had never happened to Henrietta before, so she had no experience on which to draw to help her get back on the rails.

In attempting to come to her assistance, the young people only made matters worse. The lines were no longer funny and yet they laughed. The older generation, now taking the parody as a serious contribution, were scandalized at what they could only interpret as cynical mockery and, taking cue from Aunt Bill, shushed them angrily to silence.

There came a point where it was not even possible for Henrietta to break off and simply inform them that her performance was, indeed, supposed to be comical; they had now invested too much of their judgement and authority in the belief that hers was a serious – though, in the context, perhaps, slightly misplaced – contribution. She had no choice but to plough helplessly on.

Yet the space intended for laughter demanded to be filled by *something*. For her, the actual meaning of the words – words no longer funny – flooded in to fill it. Laughter would have served another purpose, too – as an anaesthetic to dull the pain of her own wretched marriage; without it, the irony of her words was bitter indeed. Until then she had not realized how much of her own experience of matrimony she had poured into her parody – by opposites, of course. And now, as that realization seized her, the contrast was too stark to bear. Her voice continually broke throughout her final paragraph and only an indomitable will carried her to the end.

'Remember, then, my dear little sisters, that the province of our sex, though subordinate, is one of inestimable privilege in our miniature realm. Our duty to submit is imposed upon us both by our own sweet natures and by our very frailty. From it flows that natural disposition to humility which is the very essence of our feminine being. Our physical weakness, the trials of our nature, our defencelessness in this vicious world – these all prompt a profound trust in our lord and master. It is an instinctual readiness to lean upon his all-powerful, all protecting arm and declare him our king, our hero, which . . .'

The speech should have ended: '. . . indeed, is a woman's most enduring strength – her chiefest jewel.' But the tears were by now streaming down her face. She got no farther than 'a woman's most . . .' when her voice and spirit gave out entirely.

'I'm sorry,' she whispered. 'I'm sorry.' And she just stood there, head bowed, eyes closed, sobbing in utter silence, repeating, every now and then, a feeble whisper of, 'Sorry.'

Percy at last could stand it no more. He emerged from the wings and put an arm around her.

'Mister O'Farrelly!' Aunt Bill's cry of outrage electrified the entire gathering; but for that, no one would have taken the gesture amiss or suspected that there might lie behind it something more than an offer of solace from a sympathetic bystander.

That, in turn, scandalized his mother into calling out his name, too. But he ignored her, as well, and started to help Henrietta to the safety of the wings.

'*Do* something!' Judith said frantically to Rick.

'I will indeed,' he rejoined angrily.

In fact, it was he who saved the day. For, as the pair of them came off, he grabbed his sister's wrist, jerked her roughly to him, and slapped her face hard; the hubbub of 'did-you-evers' that now gripped the audience prevented their hearing any of it. He thrust his face close to hers and hissed, 'Come back on stage now and *smile*! Make it look as if that was part of the act. *Smile*, damn your hide!' He gripped her cheeks and pulled her lips into a ghastly rictus of sham merriment.

Percy drew back his one free arm and lunged out at Rick with his fist. But Henrietta caught him just in time and the blow glanced almost painlessly off Rick's shoulder. 'No, he's right,' she said. 'Come on! We'll all go on.'

'Let's sing,' Judith suggested. 'What can we sing?'

Fergal slipped an arm round her waist – which forced Rick to do the same on the other side.

'There is a tavern in the town, in the town . . .' Fergal began.

They were already stamping in time with the words as all seven of them took up the second line: 'And there my true love sits him down, sits him down . . .' Before the end of that line they were doing a sort of dancing march on to the stage, grinning like gargoyles, and throwing the audience into a confusion of 'oh-I-say' and 'here's-a-how'd'ee'do'!

But, since the instinct to join an audience is as strong as the instinct to perform for one, they resumed their seats and swallowed their misgivings and – by the end of the second chorus, 'And on my breast carve a turtle dove . . .' – they found themselves genuinely back in the right spirit.

Rick drove the final nail in the coffin of the audience's misgivings by laughing and pointing at them and shouting 'Caught you, caught you!' all the while they applauded. And they, having by now twigged that their failure to laugh at Henrietta's turn had caused her to break down, were happy to accept the impeachment.

But what really crowned the moment for Rick was the firm but gentle squeeze of Judith's arm about him and the 'Well done, darling!' that she whispered in his ear. She had never called him darling before; no girl ever had.

And after all that, such was their emotionally battered state, no one could guess the dumb crambo. The youngsters had to drag King back on stage – now in his butler's tailcoat again – and point to him in silent mime and put the genuine laurel wreath back on his brow before Betty McIver remembered the penultimate phrase of Henrietta's speech and cried out: 'King, our hero!' – which won her a box of bonbons from Kelly of Grafton Street, while the butler got an extra special round of applause and hear-hears.

By that time Henrietta's smile was quite genuine once more; everyone congratulated her on the power of her acting, assuring her she had deceived them completely.

Aunt Bill, implacable still, added, 'Oh, yes, dear. You are a *mistress* of deception!'

There was no curtain to ring down on the performance;

actors and audience gradually mingled, laughing, repeating favourite bits, dishing out the reassurances in true Anglo-Irish fashion – the typical Anglo form being: 'Well, old chap, at least you didn't disgrace yourself', and the Irish: 'You looked only gorgeous, my dear!' Both forms carried precisely the same weight of commendation.

Judith worked her way gradually toward Henrietta and waited a quiet moment before she murmured, 'Do you wish me to stay tonight?'

Henrietta's glance was so desperately grateful that Judith was moved to dampen its intensity. 'Only if it would help,' she added nonchalantly, as if her friend's emotion had not been apparent to her.

Henrietta took the hint and, visibly reining herself in, said in a more casual tone, 'D'you want that? Yes, it would be rather nice.'

Judith, now filled with foreboding, went off to inform her parents of the arrangement.

Uncle Hereward was meanwhile talking to Aunt Bill. 'That was an extraordinary performance,' he remarked. 'What possessed her to put on such an act?'

'I can't imagine,' Aunt Bill replied, waiting to hear more of his opinion before she put in her own pennyworth.

'Was it a joke of some kind? A joke that fell flat? Is that why she broke down? Sometimes I think the world's gone mad.'

She took a gamble. 'D'you know what I could do with, Hereward? A good stiff whiskey. Care to join me?'

Henrietta's eyes followed them out of the room. Comfortless again she sought Judith and saw that she had been watching them, too. They gave each other a wan little grin.

Rick, who never took his gaze off Judith for long, observed this exchange and murmured to Percy, 'I wonder what my sister and Judith are up to? She had quite a little chat with Aunt Bill today but she won't tell me what they said. D'you have any notion?'

Poor Percy thought that by 'she' he meant Henrietta. And since he had been sure he had guilt written all over him even before Henrietta's performance this evening, he was now quite convinced the whole world knew their secret. Therefore Rick must be testing him. 'No-o,' he said with uneasy nonchalance. 'Not a sausage.' The news that his dearest darling Henrietta had probably blurted everything out to that old dragon, Mrs Montgomery, set his thoughts racing. She must be in quite a turmoil, poor dear; no wonder she had broken down like that. 'You did jolly well to save the day,' he told Rick gratefully.

'Yes. What a bloody enigma they are, don't you think? What came over her?'

Sally never took her eye off Rick for long, either; when she did, it was usually to glance at Judith. Now she saw him staring at her rival and talking in a worried undertone to Percy O'Farrelly. How that fellow had the nerve to show his face here after going out on stage to that idiot Henrietta and more or less telling the world what was going on between the pair of them, she couldn't imagine. Still, he'd get his comeuppance soon enough! That comment from Mrs Montgomery about her being a mistress of deception was just a ranging shot; she'd get the full broadside soon enough. However, her sharp eye had noted an earlier exchange between Judith and Henrietta, which made her sure they were hatching something. Look at the evidence; there was Percy talking to Rick, and Percy's paramour Henrietta talking to Judith . . . and Mrs Montgomery taking Judith aside so blatantly that afternoon . . . Oh yes, *something* was undoubtedly being hatched behind her back.

She needed an ally. By rights it ought to be her own brother, Fergal. He was so besotted with the Carty girl he ought to be here at her side, now, happy to join forces in an enterprise that would put his ring on Judith's finger and Rick's on hers. Instead, he was across the room, buttering up that absurd Mrs Carty, who had no more control over Judith than a kite has over the wind – and who was, in any case, hell-bent on seeing her daughter installed as the next Mrs Bellingham of Castle Moore. Where then could she, Sally, turn?

King, supervising the clearing up of the room, kept a sharply covert eye upon the family and guests. By some miracle he had come unscathed through the morning's audit, despite the poison that O'Brien had been pouring into O'Farrelly's ear for months. Fortunately McGrath, the agent, couldn't stand the solicitor, and the tussle between them had left King looking like the peacemaker – a man with an unfair share of the burdens of the estate. But wasn't the proof of any pudding to be found in the eating? And you'd only need one look of the young master to see that whoever had had the rearing of him since the Murders surely knew his onions.

What it boiled down to was this: the battle had been to convince the family they'd done right six years ago and had no cause for regrets since. That battle was won. Now it was just a rearguard action to keep them in that happy frame of mind. You could never stop the steady seepage of poison, of course – not in this damn country, where one man only needed to rise an inch above his fellows before the knives were out. But you could always be convenient with a little dropeen of an antidote.

The Carty girl was his big affliction of the moment. When she'd first come back to Keelity, he'd welcomed it, remembering only the credulous, overawed little filly-foal she'd been. The wild beauty who'd turned up last month, however, was a mare of a different kidney. Nothing would put a sense of awe upon her now, and credulity wasn't in it at all. The little birds of Castle Moore had whispered in his ear that she'd been 'saying things' about the Murders, casting doubt on the polis, and things like that. He'd watched her through his glasses that very afternoon, taking Mrs Montgomery aside for a little stroll around the island, and a profound unease settled upon his soul. Now his unsleeping eyes quartered the room like a hawk his territory; and as a hawk's eye can detect the movement of fur caused by the beating heart of a mouse, so his was keen for every little nuance in the intimate to-and-fro of these alien people.

Take Sally McIver, now. Standing there alone, and going the wrong way about everything. He'd overheard the Carty girl offer to stay the night. That was all wrong. It should have been Sally to butter up Judith, to only *drown* her in friendship. It should be Sally saying to Judith, 'Would you not stop the night with us, darling?' She should be throwing out those girlish confidences like grappling irons – giving her brother a chance.

And as for that jackass, Fergal – what in the name of God did he think he was doing, smarming himself all over Mrs Carty like that? Sure the Emperor of China had more influence over the girl than that woman!

He began to despair of both young McIvers – not least because they were his best bet as allies in the struggle now looming.

At last the furniture was all back where it belonged; the dents the feet made in the rugs and the scratches on the floorboards were put in context once more. The butler gave his gloves a masterful little tweak and made for the door – taking a slight dog-leg of a route that brought him past Sally McIver.

'The victor's laurel becomes you, Mr King,' she told him as he drew near.

He replied with a modest smile that it was kind of her to think so. 'Though I doubt there's such a thing as victory in real life, Miss,' he added solemnly.

'Just an endless battle, eh,' she commented.

'So it would seem.' He paused at her side and treated the assembly to a butlerian survey.

'I suppose you count everything, all the time,' she said – a little desperately.

It struck him that she *wanted* to talk to him but didn't know how to keep up the conversation . . . what lines to pursue. He laughed. 'Did it look like that?' he asked ruefully.

She became a little easier. 'You know well it did. So tell me – who's missing?'

'The quare fella and Mrs Montgomery,' he said at once.

Normally he would never have called Uncle Hereward 'the quare fella'. But it seemed appropriate to the occasion, somehow – the ultimate ice-breaker.

And so it proved. Sally gave a surprised little laugh and then said, 'Well, *I* know where they are! Didn't I hear herself tell him she could just be doing with a nice ball of malt.'

He took another risk. Dipping his head in acknowledgement of her information, he said, 'That's not like her.'

They both knew that in the normal run of things he would never talk of a senior member of the family like that with a very junior guest. She swallowed her unease and replied, 'No. Didn't I think so at the time. I wonder what made her say it?'

King, who had been ready to pull in his horns after a mild reprimand from her, relaxed even more. 'The young master tells me that Miss Carty had something very particular to tell Mrs Montgomery this afternoon.'

It surprised Sally that Rick would tell King about things like that. His usual references to the butler were couched in the same tone and language as schoolboys use in talking of some stern and remote old master. It pleased her, too, however. She had sometimes thought of cultivating King as an ally but had always fought shy of it, believing that his influence over Rick was waning fast. Rick spoke only of disobeying, circumventing, foiling the man – never with anything like affection or respect. Perhaps what Rick said and what Rick did were two different things? And, after all, he had chosen the phrase for the dumb crambo.

She took a chance on it, anyway. 'Actually,' she said, 'it was the other way round: Mrs Montgomery insisted that Miss Carty accompany her – though whether to tell her something or seek some information, I couldn't say.'

'That's a pity,' King said evenly.

Gratuitously Sally was moved to add, 'It was to seek information, I would think. She only arrived on Thursday and Miss Carty's been here a month or so already. That would be the likely way of it, wouldn't you say.'

There was no pretence now that they were butler and guest; it alarmed her a little – wondering how they had reached this point in so short a while.

And King, sensitive as ever to the slightest change of mood in those around him, decided he had shown the hound enough of the hare for one meeting, and said, 'Well, I expect it was about arrangements for visiting the graves tomorrow, Miss McIver. I know she's keen for Miss Carty to accompany her – the one person who was there that dreadful night who never yet took part in the family ceremony.'

'Wasn't Mad McLysaght there, too?' Sally asked.

'Aye!' King laughed and made to move on about his duties. 'And all the other chirping crickets.'

'Don't turn the lamp right off, eh?' Henrietta said. 'D'you mind if we talk a bit?'

Judith, lying in the left half of the huge bed, nearer the light, turned the wick down to a glow that was dim enough to encourage the little secrets to come out of hiding, though it would no doubt soon seem bright enough to make their eyes smart. 'I'd not have offered to stay if all I'd wished to do was sleep,' she replied. 'I suppose there's not much point in beating about the bush, is there?'

'Why? What d'you mean?' Henrietta asked nervously.

'Well, what d'you imagine your Aunt Bill took Uncle Hereward aside and told him – that shorn hoggets were up twopence at Nenagh mart last week?'

Henrietta lay back and pummelled a trough in the pillow with the back of her head. 'You're right,' she said grimly, between blows. 'The goose is cooked, I daresay.'

'They'll not allow you to stay on here, I suppose you realize – or if they do, they'll get Cathcart and Cathcart to send Percy off to the wilds of Connemara on some goose-chase errand that'll keep him there till you're gone.'

Henrietta stared at the ceiling.

'Mmm?' Judith prompted.

'If they try any such tricks . . .' she said slowly and then, thinking better of it, merely turned to Judith and smiled. But her friend's face, coal black against the tiny, guttering wick, was unreadable. The smile wavered. She made a conscious effort to maintain it. The corners of her mouth twitched in response to the struggle. But at last her wretchedness won; she flung her head upon Judith's shoulder and yielded to bitter tears.

Judith reached her arms around her and hugged her tight, not too far from tears herself.

Eventually the worst of the storm passed and Henrietta whispered, 'I'm sorry, darling. That's the very last thing I intended to happen.'

'Why?' Judith asked in surprise.

Henrietta gave a little shrug and began to ease herself away again. 'Because it's just so easy, isn't it! Just to wallow like that in misery and . . . and . . .'

'Shame?' Judith offered hesitantly.

'No!' Henrietta sat up defiantly. 'Never! Never!'

'All right! All right!' Judith gave the sleeve of her nightdress an urgent, pacifying tug or two.

'Sorry.' Henrietta smiled a self-deprecatory little smile and lay down again, inches from but no longer touching her friend. 'Give me your hand,' she invited.

Judith turned on one side, facing her, and laid her free arm on her nearer shoulder. Henrietta brought her right hand across and clasped it tight, as if its mere touch was insufficient reassurance. 'Shame is the one thing I'll never, ever feel about all this,' she said.

'Yes, I had already twigged that,' Judith affirmed heavily.

Henrietta stared at the ceiling again, marshalling her thoughts, allowing time for the passion to subside. 'I need to talk, just talk about it,' she said, almost to herself. 'I need to tell someone.'

When she did not follow it up, however, Judith said, 'Your last word on the subject was – well, you were hoping to discover whether Harold is uniquely awful or whether all men are . . .'

'He's uniquely awful!' Henrietta asserted. 'Or perhaps Percy O'Farrelly is uniquely . . . wonderful!' She shook her head at the monstrous inadequacy of any superlative to describe that superlative young man; her voice shivered again. 'Oh God, Ju, I love him so! D'you know how it feels to love a man like that? To think about him *all* the time? To feel his existence . . . no, to feel that the world has suddenly become a different place, *because* of his existence? Just to think of him, when he's not there, is to feel a great yawning emptiness open up in front of me – a space that should be filled with him. And I imagine my arms reaching out to enfold him – and oh, the sweetness of that embrace! And the pain, too, because I know he *isn't* there! How grey my day becomes, how comfortless my soul!'

'I know,' Judith said.

'Every time I think of him it's like . . . you know in the Roman Catholic chapels, how they light candles in front of the Virgin and the saints? I feel it's like that. Every time I think of him, it's like . . . as if I was lighting a little candle inside me. And they burn and burn and burn. And every time I look back over the day, I see it ablaze with little candles, all for him. For *him*!'

'I know,' Judith assured her.

'I'm so in love with him, I don't know what to do or where to turn. There's no one I can tell, only you. You say, "I know." Do you *really* know? Can you imagine an obsession like this that gives you no peace?'

'I don't need to imagine it,' Judith said. 'Everything you say about Percy, I could say about Rick.'

Henrietta clutched the hand tighter to her. 'Oh, my darling! I didn't know. I never even guessed . . . I had no idea. You certainly don't show it! Does Rick know?'

'No!' Judith's hand, which had until now been a passive repository for Henrietta's feelings, turned and grasped hers vehemently. 'And he is not to learn of it, either. Promise?'

Henrietta, too startled to reply at once, just stared at her.

'Promise!'

'Yes, yes – of course I do. Why have you said nothing? It'd be so easy for you. I mean there's no bar to . . . you wouldn't be forbidden to . . .' She faltered when she saw that Judith's other hand was tapping her forehead.

'Here,' Judith said. 'The bar is here. The forbidding – or foreboding – is here. We'll talk about it later, if you want. I didn't mean to talk about it at all, as a matter of fact. It was just when you challenged me like that. Anyway – to go back to where we were – the point is, I *do* know how it feels to love someone to distraction like that. The next point is, what to do about it? What are you going to do about it?'

Henrietta relaxed once again and let out her breath with a sigh. 'Exactly!' she glanced sidelong at her friend and added, 'you are so strong. D'you know that? You must be strong – to feel like that and yet to be able to say you didn't mean to talk about it at all. I want to talk about it all the time! I do, in fact.' She let go of Judith's hand briefly to mimic her earlier gesture, tapping her brow. 'Up here, I sometimes think I'm turning into two people, completely at war with each other. I mean two people with different ideas, different values' – she gave a bitter laugh – 'two religions, even.'

'What? Like Roman Catholic and Protestant?'

'Christian and Pagan, more likely. You see, I know perfectly well all the things a wise Christian would tell me. I tell them to myself all the time. The sanctity of the matrimonial vow. The deadly sin of adultery, for which I shall almost certainly rot in hell – worst of all, Harold will be there beside me, for he commits the same sin every week, I should think.'

'Harold?' Judith was aghast at the accusation. 'I thought you said he was a tender, loving, patient, understanding monster, or something like that.'

Henrietta nodded wearily at the ceiling and turned a bleak smile upon her friend. 'He believes – he has been brought up to believe – that a tender-loving-etcetera husband is one who does *not* burden his wife with his own base desires, which he sees as squalid and ignoble. Except, to be sure, when they are used after the Creator's Purpose – which is for the procreation of children. So, his doctor chum tells him the best dates for that purpose and he rings them in his diary . . . and that takes care of those days . . . and in between times, like the loving monster he is, he spends *his* money – which was once my dowry – and risks *our* health, finding relief for his squalid, ignoble desires among his squalid, ignoble women.' The clutch on Judith's hand grew tighter. 'And I don't *care*!' she added in a fierce whisper. 'I wish he'd go away and live with them for ever, and squander everything – just as long as I never had to look him in the face again and hear the echo of those vile words, *till death us do part*! Why don't they make the parson put on a black cap at that point in the ceremony?'

'But Hen,' Judith murmured, 'if he deceives you all the time . . .' She abandoned the sentence, however, when she realized it involved a comparison between Henrietta and her Percy, on the one hand, and, on the other, Harold and his 'hoors' (for, although no one had ever *fully* explained the institution to Judith, Henrietta's words had closed a small, open loop in her mind, leaving her in no doubt at last).

Henrietta saw where the question would have led, however, and smiled. 'That small voice of sanity within me would never let me off so easily as that,' she said. 'An eye for an eye . . . an adultery for an adultery? Too easy by half! Don't you agree?'

Judith gave an unhappy nod.

'No,' Henrietta went on, 'when you stand up there on Judgement Day and they throw your soul into the balance, it doesn't matter what anyone else may have done – to you, for you, against you . . . It's you and you alone they're weighing. So I *know* that what Percy and I have done – and will do again as often as circumstance allows, let me say – is a deadly sin. I know that if Harold finds us out, it will be the end of everything. He'd divorce me. My own family would disown me. Even Percy would probably finish with me.'

'No!' Judith protested.

'Oh yes, my dear. Perhaps he wouldn't, but I daren't let myself sink into that pleasant phantasy! What? Me, the outcast Magdalene – or the Woman Taken in Adultery, surrounded by all those righteous sisters who, of course, have never, *never* sinned, all casting as many stones as they can lay hands on! – me come creeping back here to Castle Moore, the Veiled Lady in the West Wing whom nobody ever talks about in public – me being rescued by brave, wonderful Percy O'Farrelly, regardless of the ruin of his own career as a rising young solicitor! I don't think! My behaviour may be childish in the extreme – I can hardly deny that! But my observation of mankind, and especially of *man*kind, is not affected by it.'

'Golly!' Judith murmured.

'So! I have no illusions as to what folly I am engaged in. I warn myself of it a hundred times a day. My head is full of voices totting up each and every consequence. I'll lose my home, my inheritance, my family . . .'

'Even little Yolande. You'd never see her again,' Judith put in.

Henrietta fell silent, then shook with some emotion. Judith, thinking she might be weeping again, moved so that her shadow no longer obscured her – and saw that she was, in fact, trembling with silent mirth. 'Call it a measure of my depravity, if you like,' she said, taking a grip on herself, 'but I was about to tell you how very *like* you it was to find the *one* ray of comfort in this bleak and desolate scene!'

Judith, too choked with sadness to speak, merely gave her shoulder a squeeze.

Henrietta, serious again, lay back, closed her eyes, and breathed deeply once, twice. 'So, there are all these voices yapping away inside me like a pack of headmistresses in full cry . . . and then there's *me*. The innermost me, which has no voice at all. I see myself like some solid little fortress of stone, set in the middle of a tidal rip. And the waters flow this way and that, hither and thither and all about me, buffeting away – and they have no effect at all. Comes the lull between tides, and there I am, just where I was before. They say water will eventually wear away stone, but I'll be dead long before *that* stone is worn away. D'you see what I mean about feeling like two different people at war with each other? Do *you* think I'm going mad?'

'I don't know,' Judith had the honesty to reply.

'It's enough to *drive* one over the edge.'

'But I don't think it'll drive *you* – any more than it will me.'

'Oh yes,' Henrietta said bleakly. 'I'd forgotten you're in the same boat – though I don't see how that can possibly be.'

Judith gave a single, unhumorous laugh. 'If I am, then I'm rowing in the opposite direction! All *my* sensible voices are telling me to marry Rick . . . or "let him press his suit for my hand", or whatever the next proper step may be. But when they run out of breath, *I'm* still there, like your stone fort, resisting it for all I'm worth.'

'But why? If you love him so much? If you love him the way I told you I love Percy, surely . . .' She left the obvious conclusion unspoken.

'Fear?' Judith offered.

'About . . .' Henrietta cleared her throat delicately '. . . men? Marriage? You know what I mean. Is it that?'

Judith shook her head. 'It's not knowing him. Is the Rick I *think* I love anything like the real Rick? Did you love Harold when you married him? I mean, did you think you did? Was the feeling anything like this feeling you now have for Percy?'

Henrietta gave a tight, reluctant little nod. 'I was such a ninny.'

Judith thought the admission good enough to allow her to rest her case; to press it all the way home would be to rub salt into a wound she was supposed to be helping to heal.

But Henrietta, taking her silence as a partial concession that their two cases were, indeed, very different, went on, 'I didn't know him at all. You're right there. He was charming, attentive – obviously smitten with me . . . all the things, in fact, which he still *is*! He still loves me to distraction in his own way. He's still so charming and attentive in those few hours he can spare me each week. He hasn't the faintest idea how much I loathe and detest him. If my maid told him I did a cartwheel in the bedroom when I heard he was being sent to India for months and months, it'd break his heart. He *thinks* he's an absolutely model husband!' She laughed bitterly and then choked on whatever further thoughts this last comment provoked.

'What?' Judith asked.

'Model husband! God, I *was* a ninny! I had no idea about marriage at all, I thought of our house in Belgravia like some gigantic dollshouse that I was going to be allowed to play with every day. And Harold would be a little model man with me as his little model wife . . .' The irony at last overcame her and, rather than cry again, she fell silent, inhaling deeply once more but this time with a shiver on her breath.

And this time the silence between them was prolonged; so much so that Henrietta was on the verge of exhausted slumber when Judith said, 'In fact, I'm beginning to suspect that my interest in whether or not they hanged the right men for the Murders is actually part of it.'

'Eh?' Henrietta's throat was choked and she had to clear it several times before she could do more than croak saltily, 'Part of what?'

'I see Rick looking at me with the devotion in his eyes – that hunger – and it's as if something inside me panics, and the first thing I think is, "Quick! Distract him! Point those terrible eyes in some other direction!" Don't you ever get that feeling when a man looks at you with such intensity?' She shivered. 'Surely you do?'

'No,' Henrietta murmured fondly. 'When I see that look in Percy's eyes, the very last thing on my mind is how to *dis*tract him!'

Judith realized at last that there was, indeed, a difference between her case and Henrietta's. For poor Henrietta was now so lost *inside* her love for Percy she could no longer feel more than a token sympathy and sisterhood for others who might be similarly distressed. Her blood ran chill at the thought that a similar fate might yet overtake her if she did not make an effort to avoid it – an effort ten times greater than anything she had yet expended.

Tomás and Agnes King tiptoed to the very end of the passage before they dared even whisper. 'See, old lady?' he said at last. 'You have to get that close if you really want to know what's what.'

'I don't see we've learned anything we didn't already know,' she grumbled. It was well enough for him, with the good layer of fat on his bones, but she, who hadn't a pick of flesh about her, was chilled to the marrow.

'We've learned that which we could not possibly guess – only that we heard it fall from her own two lips.'

She drew her dressing gown tighter about her and said, 'Well it is for you, then!'

'We know why the Carty girl is poking about like that into things that don't concern her. It's an ill wind that blows *no* one any good. And now we know the quarter it's blowing from, sure we can trim our sails to it better than any!'

They were back in their bedroom by now. When she slipped off her dressing gown his hands were at her, quick as two ferrets. 'And haven't we the darling way of keeping warm, my love,' he whispered in her ear as he pulled her down and drew the cold sheets over them.

And she kissed him and sighed and told him he was a marvel, as ever. And she lay there, between sheets that would never be warm for her again. And she thought over all that poor Mrs Henrietta had said. Such thoughts and ideas had never once crossed her mind; yet as each confession had followed the other, they fell, as it were, into a ready-made hollow in her mind. They were new thoughts, yet they were not alien to her. Something within her had wished to murmur *yes*! to each and every one.

She said it now, though: 'Yes!' Out loud. 'Oh yes!'

And her man clamped himself to her all the tighter and chuckled. 'And aren't I only the living marvel!' he whispered in her ear.

Judith was wrong about Connemara; in fact, the very next day, Sunday, The Allied Powers of the two families packed the wretched Percy off to the Kingdom of Kerry – 'for experience of rural-court practice and general assistance'. As he said in his farewell note to Henrietta, smuggled later in the week by a conscience-troubled Netty, what on earth did they imagine he'd been gaining and providing in Parsonstown? The O'Farrellys were very understanding; indeed, it was hard to say which family was the more embarrassed by the 'episode', as they decided to call it. A most comforting word, in Aunt Bill's opinion. From then on she was at her niece's side, day and night.

After Matins that morning, at the church of St Kieran in Kilgivern, the vicar, the Reverend Waring, returned with the family for luncheon at the castle. The private memorial service in the family mausoleum was to take place immediately afterward.

This year Judith, too, was present. They were ten in all. The table, with all its spare leaves inserted, could comfortably seat thirty. With all but two leaves removed, however, the clutter of hefty mahogany legs created three loose groupings: Uncle Hereward at its head had Felicity Montgomery and Teresa Bellingham for company; Aunt Bill, playing hostess at the other end, in place of the demoted Henrietta, had the vicar and Rick; and in between, occupying the two spare leaves, were Harry Bellingham and Philip Montgomery (Aunt Bill's brother and, of course, brother to the murdered Maude Bellingham), and Judith and Henrietta. Sometimes, depending on the ebb and flow of conversation, the middle group would divide – the two women leaning to Aunt Bill's group, the two men joining their wives and Uncle Hereward.

The vicar spent the first few minutes establishing his credentials. He was, in fact, Reverend the Honourable Aloysius Waring, the youngest son of the Marquis of Clancarty, which was the courtesy title borne by the heir to the Duke of Connaught. He didn't insist upon his own title of Honourable, he explained to Judith, seated at his right, because, well, he had rather advanced views on that sort of thing.

No one was spiteful enough to point out that it was an easy enough attitude for him to take since the ducal demesne was now reduced to one fifty-acre farm in Mayo, plus a few thousand useless acres of mountainside on the shores of Lough Mask and some rather more valuable fishing rights in the lough itself; the thought did cross the mind of everyone who heard him, though.

He then spent the next few minutes enumerating the times he had dined recently with the Earl of Rosse in Parsonstown and the Marquis of Clanricarde in Portumna.

Aunt Bill decided that, in view of the occasion and the man's obvious nervousness at being invited to table at Castle Moore, he should be allowed one more minute of this persiflage; then, if he did not stop of his own accord, she would intervene. Henrietta, however, smarting from her demotion, had a shorter fuze. 'I'm so glad to hear you saying all this, Vicar,' she told him, smiling her warmest smile and leaning forward across the table. 'Since going to live in London I've come to realize that Society in Ireland is vastly in advance of its counterpart over the water. As far as I can tell, the English are frozen solid somewhere in the Thirties. Before the repeal of the Corn Laws, anyway. It is quite disgraceful!'

'Frozen, er, Mrs Austin?'

'Quite glacial, I do assure you. Not one of my friends in Belgravia includes a single gentleman of the cloth on her guest list. Not one! Well, there is the Bishop of London, of course – but he's a baron in his own right.'

'Henrietta, my dear,' Aunt Bill interrupted in a sweetly cautionary tone.

Henrietta turned to her: 'And it's just the same with barristers,' she said, mindful that, of Aunt Bill's three sons – her cousins – one was in the church and another at the bar. 'And doctors, too,' she threw in, to show that nothing personal was intended. 'I think it is *so* absurd. I should like to break ranks on the matter and invite the lot to dine, but I'm afraid I lack the courage. That's why I admire you so much, Vicar – to have a courtesy title and yet not to use it. That is *so* brave.'

'Oh, well . . . I don't know, you know . . .' he stammered in his delight.

Both Aunt Bill and her niece were astonished to see that he took her remarks quite seriously. Aunt Bill nodded severely at Henrietta to show her enough was enough, but the younger woman could not resist adding, 'And you are so right, too, to make everybody *aware* that you do, in fact, possess a title – even a courtesy title – otherwise, of course, they'd have no idea you're taking a deliberate stand on the matter. I mean, it's no good nailing your colours to the mast if the ship itself has sunk, is it!'

During this speech Aunt Bill had been trying vainly to reach past Rick with her foot to give her niece a good kick. It was just beginning to dawn on the Rev. Waring that the honey pouring toward him across the tablecloth was rather copious and much too sweet, even for honey. But Rick, alerted by his aunt's gymnastics beneath that same cloth, leaped in with a more genuine offering: 'If you'll forgive me for saying something rather presumptuous, Vicar, I found your sermon this morning extremely thought-provoking.'

'Ah!' he exclaimed happily. 'Well, Mr Bellingham, such indeed was my intention, don't you know. Er, which bit in particular, may I ask?'

Rick, who had, in fact, occupied his time staring at Judith, three pews in front of him and on the opposite side of the aisle, said, 'Oh . . . the middle bit, you know. Where you developed the theme of . . . er . . .'

'Stewardship,' Judith put in helpfully.

'Yes,' Rick said with relief. Then, thinking the man could hardly have spoken on such a theme without mentioning the parable, added, 'The need to, you know, be the Good Steward.'

'Ah!' The man's eyes kindled dangerously. 'You twigged, though, didn't you, that I told only half the story! There was so much more one could have said on that topic – though it would seem rather seditious from a pulpit in the Irish Midlands, I fear. The Good Steward, to be utterly candid, took a great risk with his master's money. Our Lord quite obviously lived in simpler times, when money was easier to multiply and the risk of doing so much smaller. He lived before the South Sea Bubble and the Canal Bubble and the Railway Mania and Gold Swindles – and so on. My own grandfather, the Duke of

Connaught, would be a rich man today if he *hadn't* sought to emulate the Good Steward of Our Lord's Parable and multiply the estate to which it pleased Providence to call him. But, of course, to utter such thoughts before *hoi polloi* – the Great Unwashed, ha ha – would hardly do!'

'But they are certainly apposite at *this* table, Vicar,' Henrietta said solemnly. 'The stewardship with which this young gentleman at my right is soon to be burdened is quite awe-inspiring.' She smiled amiably at her brother.

These enthusiastic words made the vicar decide that his embryonic suspicion of Henrietta had been unworthy. He, too, smiled amiably at Rick. 'I'm sure Mr Bellingham needs no sermon from me, or anyone else, on the nature of stewardship,' he said. 'My purpose this morning was to introduce the notion to those unfortunates who have *not* acquired that happy instinct along with their mother's milk.'

Aunt Bill, seeing the light of battle in Henrietta's eyes, begged Judith mutely for support. And Judith, because she could see how close to some kind of crisis her friend was (and having blamed herself for missing those identical signs during last night's dumb crambo), decided to step in. 'You are right when you say there is so much more you could have told us, Vicar,' she said. 'For instance, what of our stewardship of all those other things, besides money and investment, that Providence has given us?'

'Ah, yes, Miss Carty! The beauties of Creation! How we acquisitive and avaricious men rely upon you ladies to remind us of their existence – with your modesty and self-denial and unassuming devotion to your little domestic duties! Your minds are ever on the Higher Things, God bless you!'

'I was thinking,' Judith replied, 'of our stewardship of

that wider society in which we all are members. Not the . . .'

'Our Protestant faith,' he interrupted. 'True, very true.'

'Even wider than that,' she said, resuming a line she was now determined to follow. She stared at Henrietta as if her remarks were intended as a mild reprimand of her earlier comments – though a fleeting wink tipped the real game. 'I do not mean that Society which frets itself to death over whether to invite a doctor or a parson to dinner, but . . .'

'You are right again, Miss Carty,' he assured her. 'It is absurd.'

'. . . but,' she insisted, 'our wider society, many of whose members spend the day worrying about eating a dinner *of any sort at all* – never mind whom they might or might not invite to share in it. They are surely part of our stewardship, too?'

'Quite,' he muttered uncomfortably. 'Ah yes, quite!'

'The pheasant are holding up very well this year, I hear,' Aunt Bill remarked, then, turning to Rick, 'will there be the usual shoot in October?'

She had hoped to change the subject, or at least to end the merciless game being pursued by the two young ladies. But Rick, who had been enjoying it as a spectator, was delighted to be offered a place on the field. 'Of course,' he assured her. Then, turning to the Rev. Waring, 'Perhaps you'd like to join in this year, Vicar?'

Aunt Bill beamed with delight at her success.

'Or,' Rick added, 'are your views on blood sports as implacable as ever?'

Aunt Bill kicked him under the table; she had not known that the man had any views at all on country sports.

Predictably, the poor man's hackles rose. He had once, on an unguarded Sunday, remarked during a sermon that the removal of large tracts of countryside from productive agriculture – as rabbit warren, pheasant manor, and fox covert – at a time when starvation stalked the land, might call for some very special pleading on Judgement Day. It had, of course, taken months for the scandal to subside and for every ruffled feather to be preened back into place. No one had mentioned the unfortunate lapse for more than a year, so it was doubly annoying for it to arise just now, at this particular occasion.

He smiled thinly. 'I should feel honoured to receive such an invitation, Mr Bellingham,' he said, 'and delighted to accept it – if *only* to set that canard to rest once and for all. I have no *contrary* views on blood sports . . .'

'Eh? Say? Contrary views on blood sports?' called Uncle Hereward from the far end of the table.

'Yes, Mr Bellingham. I was explaining to your nephew – who has been kind enough to invite me to join the guns next month – I was saying, I have no views *against* such sports. It is a canard put about the parish by people who do not wish me well – all because of one rather carelessly phrased remark I made in a sermon.'

The old man, who had been willing to let it go at the earlier assurance, now cocked an eyebrow and said, 'What? You don't say!' in a manner that did not allow a smile and a shrug for an answer.

'I merely commented – and I do most earnestly assure everyone present . . .' He looked around like a rabbit at bay, for 'everyone present' now had eyes and ears only for him. 'I do most solemnly assure you that it was the merest aside to, ah, quite another topic. I simply commented that the growing tendency to convert entire estates into hunting preserves was not one that should be allowed to proceed without thought. This casual aside was wrenched from its context and, used, as I say, to . . . ah . . .' He became aware that his words were by now wrapped in a silence as profound as any that swallowed up his sermons in church. 'Ah well,' he concluded with a nervous little laugh. 'So much for that.'

Aunt Bill, aware that any remark on blood sports, whether pro or con, could launch Uncle Hereward on a verbal odyssey that would occupy the rest of the meal, turned desperately to Henrietta and said, 'I was interested in your earlier remark, my dear, about the stiffness of Society in England. I must say that, even after thirty years' experience of it, I still cannot bring myself to like it. They are still an alien people to me – stiff, priggish, petty-minded, mean-spirited, and snobbish to a quite disgraceful degree. I never step off the boat at Kingstown without drawing a deep breath of gratitude to be home again, don't you?'

She had chosen her subject aptly. Henrietta knew well enough how unhinged Uncle Hereward was on the subject of blood sports; her heart had given a little leap of joy when Rick stepped in with both feet like that, for she knew that the meal over which her aunt had insisted on presiding was headed at full steam for disaster. In the normal course she would not have uttered a syllable to deflect it. But the sheer ghastliness of English Society was a topic even dearer to her heart than foxhuntin' was to Uncle Hereward's and she could not resist the offer to expand upon it now.

'I was thinking that only the other day,' she said, 'when we called on the Lyndon-Furys at Coolderg. You know that vast oak table they have in the entrance hall – all covered with riding boots, novels, invitations, bills, postcards, rabbit traps . . . I even saw a fox's brush that Trapper must have brought in and forgotten after a hunt – and not a very recent hunt by the smell of it! And I just stood there thinking, well, isn't this marvellous! I'm sure there must be houses in England where you could walk in and see something like it, but I don't know of any. I felt so homesick, I almost wept.'

'*Home*sick?' her aunt echoed, flicking a nervous eye toward King, who was imperturbable as ever. '*This* home has never been like that, I'm sure.'

Henrietta chuckled. 'It would be if Rick had his way, and if there were half a dozen like him living here.'

'The Lyndon-Furys are a disgrace,' Harry said suddenly. 'If you ask me, it's that sort of casualness will spell their ruin. Trapper will inherit nothing if they don't pull their socks up.'

'What can they do?' Philip asked gloomily. 'It's hardly their fault if there's a general depression in agriculture.'

'It's their fault for not anticipating it. We all knew that the years after the famines were too good to last . . .'

And so the conversation sailed into the safe home waters of self-congratulation: how wise the Bellinghams had been to spread their risks, to buy into coal mines in Wales, into the coachbuilding trade in London, into South American railways and Canadian telegraphs . . . and all the other profitable enterprises whose dividends now supported the estate whose income had once made the investment possible.

As the smug tide rose to bathe the table in its rosy shimmer, Aunt Bill smiled gratefully at her niece, who knew that the worst of her punishment was now, so soon, over; the truth was that neither woman could afford to fall out with the other for very long.

The Bellingham mausoleum was almost lost in the heart of a damp grove of laurels beyond the stables and a little way up the slopes of Mount Argus. It was a stiff walk and Uncle Hereward and old Harry Bellingham were both out of breath by the time they arrived. Rain had fallen steadily while the family sat to luncheon but now the sky was blue again, filled with fleecy white clouds that scudded low, almost brushing the top of the mountain.

The service ran its predictable course; the prayers, impeccably chosen, were spoken with a nasally dying fall that made it almost impossible for the mind to stay listening for long. Rick posted a little sentinel at his ear, to catch the usual perorations of Anglican prayer and alert him of the cues for his amens. Then he let his mind wander back to that evening whose events were at the root of this grim ceremony. The joint presence of Judith and Henrietta – for the first time at such a commemoration – exerted a powerful influence upon him, and he found himself remembering it with a clarity that had eluded him in the past.

The first thing that struck him was the enormous contrast in mood and tone between the occasion itself and this, its memorial. The service was solemn, measured, grave – almost portentous; the actual event had been casual, disjointed, haphazard. In his mind's eye he saw the half-circle of murderers standing around the pavilion, emptying their handguns into it, and now, as then, he found himself unable to relate that ragged scene with the awful and permanent consequences that followed it. They were so like a harvest gang, standing with their shotguns around the last island of barley, waiting for the reaper to scare out the rabbits and hares . . . it had seemed then, and still seemed now, as casual as that.

His memory roamed wider, backwards and forwards in time from that dire moment. Details he had forgotten, or not bothered to remember, suddenly returned to him. His sailor suit; he remembered the very texture and feel of it now. And the petty argument over whether or not to get *The Star of the Shannon* in steam. His mother's skilful handling of his father – suggesting they leave the decision to Judith . . . Now, for the first time, he saw how adroit her manipulation had been. And his desperate jealousy of Judith's friendship with Hen. And how he'd challenged her to a race, just to get her away. And how his mother had spoken for them all when she had said they'd never had a disappointing party down at the summer pavilion. And how Winifred had gazed so lovingly and long at the sundrenched landscape – knowing that soon she'd be leaving it all behind. And Graham, in the same nostalgic mood, talking of his forthcoming tour of the Holy Land . . .

Yet it was not so much these mere events he remembered now – the sequence in which these things happened . . . the words that people spoke. It was something far deeper. Something to do with their characters, with the way they actually were. It was the *feel* of them all there, all together, a family at peace – or as much at peace as any family can ever be. He remembered how they fitted together, belonged one to another, made up one complete whole.

Suddenly, more than at any other time since that moment of shattering, he felt the loss of that completeness. There were great holes in the emptiness surrounding him – one where his father ought to be, another for his mother, for Winifred, for Graham, for Philip – aching voids that neither prayers nor tears could fill. He felt like a caged animal, one that has been caged so long that it no longer has any hope of escape. All at once he realized that tears were streaming down his face. He was not crying, and yet the tears fell like raindrops into the neckband of his shirt.

Judith, two paces away, closed the distance between them and took his arm. For some reason, neither looked at the other; but those voids in the emptiness all around him ceased to ache. There was no spiritual balance sheet within him where her sudden presence at his side was totted off against his loss, but he knew that this moment, like that one, was already marked down as never to be forgotten, too.

A strange dizziness overcame him, just for a second or

two. No one noticed except Judith, who felt the sudden slackness in his arm and whose suppressed alarm jolted him back to full awareness. But in that brief, disjointed instant, he had an intimation of himself as an old man, standing by the pavilion – and the Bellingham flag still flying over Castle Moore. And Judith was beside him, an old woman, too, holding his arm just as she held it now. And for a moment even more brief he seemed to pass out of the realm of space and into the strange dimension of time, so that he *saw* the intervening years as a kind of flowing thread, uniting him-and-Judith-now with him-and-Judith-to-be.

When it passed, when Judith's worried clutch hauled him back to the world of rheumy throats and shuffling feet and ragged amens, that pisgah sight – the actual vision of time as a thread linking the present with its promise – dissolved. Only the promise remained; but it was strong; it was now his greatest comfort. So that when he turned at last to Henrietta and saw the concern in her eyes, he was able to smile and reassure her. And when his eyes strayed onward to his Aunt Bill, and there met a different concern – something altogether harder and more savage – he was able to accept it, too.

For in that brief sojourn inside the mind and body of himself, unguessable years into the future, he had felt a peace and an assurance that was denied him now. He knew that *that* was a Rick Bellingham who had long since settled a score with history.

The ceremony was over at last; the celebrants stood for a minute's silence before they left. Judith, side by side with Rick, ran her eye for the hundredth time over the stilted curlicues with which the rural mason had embellished the family motto: *Quod Habeo Teneo* – What I Have I Hold. He had copied the style from the memorials for the first Bellinghams to be interred in these vaults, a hundred years earlier, but that fine, italic tradition had died, the flourish had gone out of it. Though she had never in her life held mallet and chisel in her hands, it made her want to take up such tools and add that missing flair. She knew she'd make an even more hamfisted job of it than the carver whose work displeased her, but that was beside the point. She could *see* it was wrong. Her frustration simmered into anger.

It was such a trivial thing to notice, she wondered why she made so much of it – standing there, fuming at the mild incompetence of some nameless village stonemason. Reluctantly she admitted to herself that she was merely using the poor man as a kind of lightning conductor for a rage that had no other outlet. Her desire to improve the bungled inscription, even though she hadn't the first idea how to go about it, was somehow mirrored by her desire to overturn a far greater transgression in the world at large – and she hadn't the first notion of how to set about that, either.

Time, though it had increased her outrage at that injustice, had dimmed her memories of the event itself – the very memories that should be spurring her to *do* something, to right the wrong and bring the wrongdoer to rights. Ten days ago she had stood in the long grass of the wild garden, staring at the pavilion . . . and it had failed to restore that sharp and bitter scene to her; now the glorious solemnity of this Anglican service was further thickening the mist before her eyes.

She felt the beginnings of panic rising within her, along with an intimation that nothing would ever be done. She remembered lying in the grass in her wet bathing costume, in Henrietta's dressing gown – not far from the very site where the red-headed man had dropped her with a badly-aimed shot – and staring down at her companions as they laughed and splashed in the lake. To her surprise she now found herself wishing she had not left the water, had not gone alone to the summer pavilion to renew her unwitting promise to the dead, a promise she was not aware of making until then.

She should have stayed. She should have played.

But no sooner had those words popped into her mind than her whole spirit rose to reject them. Without moving her head, or drawing attention to herself in the smallest way, she glanced around at the company, seeing them in a new light. It suddenly occurred to her that they were all in some way flawed. The ancestors commemorated here in this building, had been ruthless enough, and single-minded enough, to acquire what their descendants now enjoyed. And they had passed it down intact, every brick and stone, every last acre – everything, indeed, except that essential ruthlessness, the single-minded determination without which the family motto was just one more fragment of historical bric-a-brac.

And she, poised at the edge of that charmed family circle, felt the ground yielding beneath her feet, felt herself being drawn into a graceful slide down that oh-so-gentle slope. How pleasant not to resist! How amiable to slide all the way down and join them at their privileged games in the cool waters of their private lake!

Their meditations over, they bestirred themselves and shuffled out to their daily preoccupations. A symbolic pheasant rose in clattery alarm as Uncle Hereward emerged. Rick and Judith alone remained.

His hand found hers but the gesture failed to revive her spirit, for she knew well enough what was going through his mind at that moment. His adoration of her, his need for her to be *there*, the new centre of his world – these only burdened her more and increased her sense of guilt. 'Despise me,' she wanted to tell him. 'How else can I respect your judgement? How can I take you for anything but a fool when you insist on adoring me so?'

'These tablets of stone,' he said, 'these prayers, these

ceremonies . . . they do nothing, do they?'

His bitterness surprised her out of her self-absorption. She looked up at him sharply.

'In the middle of it,' he explained, 'when old Waring was droning on and on . . . "Forasmuch as without Thee we are not able to please Thee . . ." What does that *mean*? It's like saying that without red paint we can't paint anything red. Anyway, I suddenly got the feeling we were like those savages who light fires and make smoke signals and do ritual dances to bring rain. Prayers! And bits of carved stone! What's the difference between them and smoke signals, eh?'

'Rick?' she murmured, squeezing his hand.

He raised hers to his lips, kissed it briefly, then clutched it to his breast. 'Thank God you've come back, Ju,' he said. 'Without you . . . I don't know.'

A lump in her throat prevented her reply – which would have been to tell him she was not worthy of such adoration.

'The worst thing about death . . .' he began, and then paused.

'Yes?' she prompted.

He closed his eyes. 'It's not the coffin, the burial, the darkness, the cold earth – all those usual things. It's just the fact that they're not *there* any longer – not *doing* things. Winnie would probably have had two or three babies by now, for instance. I could be reading bedtime stories to them, or flying their kites – generally being an uncle, you know? And it would be Graham's job to worry about the Castle Moore estate, not mine. And Philip would be a curate somewhere and we'd go on cycle tours of Kerry together or something like that. Death stops all those stories being written. D'you know what I mean? It takes all those possibilities away.'

Silently she put her arms around him and buried her face in the crook between his shoulder and his neck.

'We have a *right*,' he said bitterly, 'to see our parents grow old, to see how their powers slowly fade – their power over us among other things. We have a *right* to our own slow decline.' Then, unable to bear the misery into which his own words had led them, he gave a brief, laconic chuckle. 'I invent it for them, you know. I've never told anyone this before, not even Hen. So don't you tell her, will you?'

'I'm not sure . . .' she croaked before her voice broke. But she managed to gather it together again and continue: '. . . not sure what you mean.'

Another brief laugh, this time embarrassed. 'Oh, I continue their lives in my mind. Invent things for them – almost as if I owe it to them, you know. I sometimes feel I was spared that night in order to be able to do it for them.'

He eased himself apart from her and stared at the ground. Someone had carried in a bit of gravel on their boot; he moved it with his foot until it fell into a crack between two slabs. 'The trouble is, I'm not consistent. I should think they're thoroughly fed up with me!' Now he laughed more heartily. 'Last month the Pater was made Governor of the Cape, but the month before that he had a stroke – which shattered all our lives.' He smiled at her. 'I don't just wallow in sentimental what-iffery, you see. One of Winnie's babies died, too, once. Twice, actually. It has to be realistic, you see.'

She took his hand and squeezed gently. 'I had no idea,' she murmured.

'I started it that same week, the week it happened. Of course, at that age you have no idea why you do things, have you? You just do them.'

'And d'you know why you do it now?'

He nodded and gave her an almost guilty smile. 'Habit,' he replied. 'Actually, d'you believe in second sight?'

She stared at him in amazement: his ability to set a mood, and then to change it in the twinkling of an eye, was, indeed, amazing.

'I had a sort of . . . vision or something just now,' he explained. 'Me as an old man. I didn't see my *self* – not that sort of vision. I actually *was* myself. I mean, I was sort of staring out from inside my own head. Except I was old.' His hand gestured vaguely toward the door. 'I was standing, or that old man was standing, down by the summer pavilion . . .' The words petered out. They seemed so inadequate. They described the situation well enough – at least, they stated baldly what had happened. But they utterly failed to convey his true experience, the certainty, the conviction . . .

'How did you feel?' she asked.

He smiled at her and clutched her hand even tighter to his chest. 'You understand me, anyway,' he said. 'Even though I can't begin to describe it. I felt . . . at peace. That's all I can say. It's not like I feel now. I felt at peace. I could face these memorials and feel at peace.'

'Rick?' She swivelled round to face him. He was taller by a bare inch; when she drew herself up, as now, she could meet his gaze, eye to eye, level.

'Mmm?' His tongue darted out and moistened his lips; nervously he watched her face for clues.

'What are we going to do?'

Why had he not told her that in his premonition of the future she was at his side, an old woman, too – and that was the essence of his peace? It was too late now. It would come as a mere afterthought. It would sound like a bit of charming embroidery.

He meant to reply, 'Never leave each other.' But the words that came out were: 'Never let each other down.'

She gave the smallest tilt of her chin, not really meaning it as an invitation. A moment later his lips were on hers and his arms about her, and the sweetness of the moment was enough to drown all her misgivings. It was, she felt, the moment on which their two lives pivoted and swung into one single line.

When at last they broke contact and she laid her head beside his and pressed herself tight to him and gasped for air, he said, 'Actually, I felt at peace because you were there, as well.'

'And was I also old?' she asked, making her tone jovially petulant, for she could recognize a bit of charming embroidery when it stood up and winked at her like that.

Rick chuckled. '*He* didn't think so – the old man who was me.'

'And what would he think of us?' She went on clinging to him, relishing the touch of his body against hers and wanting to prolong it.

'We shall have to wait and see,' he answered. Then, solemn once again, 'I don't suppose he'll have forgotten this present moment. He won't forget this, even in the hour of his dying. So all we have to do is stay together and wait.'

She shivered and held him even more tightly. Yet not all her present happiness could hold back the words: 'I'm afraid we'll have to do a great deal more than that, my darling.'

Rick and Judith made a little detour on the walk back from the mausoleum, taking them through a grove of false nutmeg or pheasant bower. As they entered it, meaning to stop and kiss again, away from the prying eyes of ancestors and the unavenged dead, someone began playing a tin whistle on the far side of the ragged clearing – an Irish jig that darted like a nervy butterfly, never settling anywhere for long.

'Mad McLysaght, I'll bet you anything,' Rick said.

'No takers,' she replied.

They found him easily enough, though he was well

sheltered from the damp breeze by the thickets of shrubs around him. He broke off as they approached.

'You'd charm the linnets from the trees, McLysaght,' Rick assured him.

He grinned and replied, 'Did you know the word *linnet* does not appear once in the works of the Immortal Bard? The name of Ireland he gives us thirty-two times, but on the subject of our sweetest bird the Swan of Avon is mute. I don't think he ever came here, you know.'

'D'you still read Shakespeare yourself, Mr McLysaght?' Judith asked. 'Or have you it all in your head by now? If they burned every last copy of his writings, could you set it all down again with no trouble?'

'I could not,' he assured them. 'Sure there's no man alive nor ever lived could do that, nor woman neither. Are you partial to him yourself now, Miss Carty?' He eyed her critically. 'I'd say you were.'

She laughed. 'Can you tell as much just by the look of a girl then?' she asked.

'I can of course.' He did not even smile. ''Tis in the eyes mostly. You have the look of it in your eyes. And what's your favourite?'

'Oh?' She teased him archly. 'Can you not tell that in my eyes too?'

'Let me see,' he murmured, fixing her with a stare that soon made her uncomfortable. 'It must be there. It will be there. The eyes have it. *All's Well* would it be? "Where thou wast shot at with fair eyes"? Perhaps not! The *Dream*, maybe. "Love looks not with the eyes, but with the mind"? Sure, ye know that already, the pair of ye. But I have it now. The *Shrew*! "Aren't you bold to show yourself the forward guest within *your* house" – this *your* he directed at Rick – "to make your eye the witness of that report which you so oft have heard"? 'Tis *The Taming of the Shrew*! Amn't I right now?' – he laughed genially.

She laughed also, but not so easily, and with an uncertain glance or two at Rick. 'You have the right of it,' she admitted. 'I don't know how you guessed.'

'Sure there's no guessing in it at all.' He tapped his cheekbone below his left eye. "Tis all in there. D'ye understand what I mean now? All in there.' He winked.

'Is there any way of getting it out?' Rick asked bluntly. 'We understand what you mean very well.'

'The shortest distance between two points is . . . ?' The old fellow lifted his eyebrows to reinforce the question.

'A straight line,' Rick answered.

He shook his head. 'If I may say so, Mr Bellingham – and no offence intended – that's a very English sort of an answer, so it is.'

'And what's the Irish answer, then?'

Judith, sensing he needed something to launch him, repeated the question: 'The shortest distance between two points . . . ?'

'. . . is never long enough to be interesting,' he told them.

'Hmph!' Rick snorted testily. 'You mean you're never going to come out with it straight.'

The fellow grinned once more. 'I have seen the day of wrongs through the little hole of discretion.' He tapped his cheekbone again, too.

'Well, in that case, I'm sorry we interrupted you,' Rick told him. 'I preferred the jig you were playing.'

He dipped his head in a courteous nod and put the penny whistle back to his lips.

Rick and Judith continued their homeward stroll, harried by the butterfly notes. 'Damnation!' he said. 'I didn't handle that too well. I'm sure he knows far more than he's ever admitted. He's afraid of King, of course. If ever we wanted more out of him, we'd have to let him see what side his bread is buttered – or that we can butter it thicker than King.'

Judith said nothing.

'Eh?' He jogged her arm. 'Don't you agree?'

'I was thinking.'

'Annoyed at me for muffing our chances?'

'No,' she replied abstractedly. Then she hugged his arm and repeated the assurance in a more fervent tone. 'There's something familiar about that last quotation. That oul' wan only ever says half of what he means. I've heard that last quotation somewhere – and recently. "The little hole of discretion" – I've heard that. It must be in *Love's Labours Lost*. That was at Sheridan's Theatre in July and Papa took us to see it. You must have a complete Shakespeare somewhere in the library, haven't you?'

'Yes!' He sighed with playful grimness. 'Despite my best efforts to lose it!'

It took them almost half an hour of frustrating reading-at-the-gallop but eventually they pinned it down.

'Act Five, of course!' Rick said. 'Wouldn't it be!'

But Judith was triumphant. 'See!' she cried. 'I said there'd be more, didn't I!' Her finger pinned the page at Armado's speech:

> For my own part, I breathe free breath. I have
> seen the day of wrongs through the little hole of
> discretion, and I will right myself like a soldier.

'I will right myself like a soldier!' she repeated happily. 'That's a promise.'

After a short silence Rick said, 'Not much of one, though, is it?'

'It's a start, at least.'

Aunt Bill took almost a week to arrive at her decision,

but then, having considered every alternative from all possible angles, she would countenance no objection. It was her decision and it was final. There were so many considerations to balance; and so much depended on getting the *right* balance between them.

The most immediate problem was, of course, the shocking affair of Henrietta and Percy O'Farrelly – though, in the long run, it was the least important. It was dwarfed, in fact, by the towering problem posed by King. The power he had acquired since becoming what, in earlier days, would have been called the High Steward of the Castle Moore estate was positively medieval and could not be allowed to continue. Unfortunately, none of the menfolk in the clan could be persuaded to see matters in that light, so, being a mere woman, she had to tread a devious path to attain her ends.

Some instinct impelled her to seek out Mad McLysaght, which she did on the morning after the memorial service in the mausoleum. And lucky for her that she did, too, for she found the old Familiar packing his bags (or, in his case, a large, spotted bandanna) and preparing to move on to his winter quarters near Athenry – a walk of some forty-five miles, if you could fly like a crow, or eighty-five, as the man himself would make it.

'I'll go the first mile with you, so,' she offered.

Wiser than her nephew and Judith, and more in tune with the ways of Irish country folk of her own generation, she made no reference to the Murders, even though yesterday's ceremony would have given her an easy enough introduction to it. For the first half-mile or so they spoke only of inconsequential things, until the sound of their voices together was no longer strange to them. By then they were within sight of the main gate.

There had been a dry gale overnight, which brought down the first heavy fall of leaves that autumn, some of them prematurely; they were disappointingly soft underfoot. But the sun was high and bright as it dappled the drive, and the wind had dropped to the merest zephyr. The groundsmen made a brave sight as they raked last night's fall into piles, which they were now kindling in the first burn of the season.

'Who'd not envy you to be setting forth on such a bright day, Mr McLysaght!' she remarked. 'And you so well shod again.'

'Indeed, ma'am,' he agreed, halting briefly to stretch one of his new boots into the sunlight for all the world to admire. 'But for them fellows, I'd have been gone a week since. But 't'has tooken me all those days to soften them.'

'I'm doubly glad, so, for we never had a chat this year, and if you were gone before I had come, it would have been desperate. You're keeping well by the looks of you. Are you writing much poetry this year?'

'Divil a verse, ma'am,' he replied at once, 'except the one I'll speak for you now, by your leave? 'Tis in Irish, but I can speak it in English, too. 'Tis called *The Young Girl's Lament*.'

And with no more preamble than that he launched into his composition:

'Twas five years ago in the woods of Coolnahinch
My love appeared to me by a weeping tree
And all the birds flew up
They were flying, they were flying
And I knew my love was dying
On the gallows tree

After a respectful silence Aunt Bill said, 'A lament indeed.'

'There's more to it, of course,' he told her. 'I wrote it for Miss Kitty Rohane of Flaxmills, the poor girl – to lighten the road she had to tread, those years.'

'And where is Coolnahinch?'

He paused and stretched an arm toward the woodland on the downhill side of the drive. ''Tis all that land between here and Lough Cool, ma'am.'

'And Miss Kitty Rohane,' Aunt Bill said, committing the name to memory, 'does she live in Flaxmills still?'

'Sure what else is there?' McLysaght replied laconically.

They were hard by the main gate now. Aunt Bill paused and commented that it had been a grand little stroll. He halted, too, a little way beyond her and turned. With the sun aslant his gaunt, weatherbeaten face he had the magnificence of an ancient seer; she watched his eyes quarter the landscape, shooting past her on the first sweep, resting on hers on the return. 'That was all O'Laughlin land once,' he said.

'And who did they steal it from in their turn?' she asked evenly.

His eyes twinkled as he conceded her point with the merest nod. 'The holding of land is a quare oul' thing. Ye Bellinghams hold it the Norman way, in fee simple. But when the O'Laughlin held it, didn't he hold it for *all* the clan. Any man o' that name could set his foot here and say 'twas his. There's a fierce difference in that, now.'

'The old order passeth . . .' Aunt Bill replied in the same unflustered manner.

He shook his head, more in sadness than dissent. 'With difficulty, ma'am. It yields with difficulty. It strives for resurrection. It changes colour and finds a new seat. Ye could look it in the face and never know it for what it once was.'

She smiled at his fancies, but not, she hoped, in a hurtful way. 'It all sounds mildly seditious to me, Mr McLysaght. Are you going about the countryside, alarming the populace with such notions?'

'Arrah, 'tis all play, ma'am,' he assured her. ''Tis the

things Mr King and meself do be talking about when we've nothing better to do. "The play's the thing!" as the man said.' He turned to leave her, but she, caught up in this new line of conversation, said, 'King? Really?'

He half-turned back again to indicate he really had to be pressing on. 'And there's a quare thing about that fellow, ma'am. His mother is an O'Laughlin, like all that side of his family.'

With a cheery wave he passed through the gate and was gone. The cloying reek of woodsmoke, damp and eyewatering, enveloped her.

Hereward proved an easier nut to crack than Aunt Bill had dared to hope; she tackled him on the Tuesday afternoon, the day after her meeting with McLysaght. In fact, he fell in with her plans so readily (for Hereward) that she wondered if his mind had not already started to move along similar lines to her own. She dared not probe too far, though, for fear of showing him she'd got there first – in which case, he'd just dig in his heels and stubbornly refuse to move another inch.

To ensure that neither King nor any of his minions overheard, she wrapped the old man up well and took him out for a walk, straight down over the lawns to the lake. She began with the least important of her concerns. 'That wretch Percy O'Farrelly,' she said, 'can hardly be kept down in the wilds of Kerry for more than a month or two. And the alternative – sending Henrietta back to London – is out of the question.'

'O'Farrelly,' he barked. 'I told the father to get the lad's barnacles scraped while he was down there.'

'Really?' Aunt Bill replied. The phrase meant nothing to her – and to query it might lead to a long and fruitless diversion of *her* chosen line of conversation. 'Anyway. To get back to Henrietta . . .'

'Blunt the edge of his ardour, see?'

'Yes, of course. I was saying that we can't possibly allow Henrietta to return alone to London.'

'Can't?' he asked.

'Of course not, Hereward! Lord, if she can misbehave so brazenly here, where every Tom, Dick, and Seamus knows who she is, just think what she'd get up to in London, where anonymity flows like water!'

'Have her to stay with you, then,' he suggested.

It was, to be sure, a perfectly reasonable suggestion, but it suffered one fatal drawback: it did not suit the rest of Aunt Bill's scheme at all.

'Wonky would have her head on a charger before the week was out,' she responded, dismissing the thought entirely.

To have a husband who cordially detested his wife and all her family was, in many ways, an uncomfortable cross to bear; but it had one undeniable advantage – you could paint him any colour you liked and he'd never get to hear of it. In sober truth, Wonky would completely ignore Henrietta, even if she deliberately kicked his shins.

'Hmph, see your point,' Hereward muttered, going several paces out of his way to crush a slug beneath his boot. 'Hard to know what to do. Say?'

'If the mountain won't come to Mahomet . . .' she replied, watching him struggle to dislodge the clinging gobbet of slug-flesh from his heel. 'The answer would seem to be for me to remain on here. Percy O'Farrelly could camp on the lawn then, for all the good it would do him.'

'God!' he exclaimed, shaking his boot vigorously, 'I wish we could get glue as good as this over the counter. What is it?'

'It's called life,' she told him.

'Say?'

'I'm just a little worried about Rick, though.'

He found an obligingly cocked brick in the path and at

last stripped away the remains of the dead gastropod. 'Rick, eh? In what way?'

She took his arm to forestall any more death-dealing sorties on the Castle Moore fauna. A lone swan flew overhead, honking on each beat of its wings. 'Isn't she a beauty!' he exclaimed in delight. 'Just look at her glide through the air! Better than that awful ballet Frieda dragged us to see.' He risked a totter by raising his stick to his shoulder and saying, 'Pschw! Gotcha!' Lovingly his eye followed the arc of its imaginary fall.

Aunt Bill took advantage of his distraction to say, 'I fear that something of the O'Farrelly-Henrietta situation may be developing between Rick and the Carty gel, too.'

Hereward came back to the here-and-now with a jolt. 'Rick?' he asked. 'Surely not. Too much sense. I mean, women are all very well in their place – nothing personal, m'dear. You know what I mean. Rick would never leave the huntin' field early just to get home and moon over a bit of skirt, what?'

Of course! Why had she not seen it before? She had defined her strategy well enough but the tactics had remained obscure to her – until now. The way to most men's hearts was allegedly through their bellies but Hereward was made of different stuff; the way to his heart lay by way of fox covert, salmon leap, and deer park.

'I'd never have believed it until now, Hereward,' she replied. 'But I'm afraid it's come pretty close to that. The boy has taken to reading rather a lot.'

'Solitary vice,' Hereward murmured.

'No, *reading*!' she shouted, wondering what word he had misheard. Then, glancing into his eyes, she realized he had not misheard at all.

'He's not the robust little Nimrod we all remember,' she added. 'Or, rather, he is but he's also become quite a thinking young man, in his way.'

'Needs his barnacles scraped, too. They all do.

Anyway, what's this to do with Miss Carty?'

Aunt Bill remembered her tactics; somehow she must make poor Judith seem like a threat to Rick-as-a-sporting-man. 'Well,' she replied, 'if Miss Carty were ill, say, the lad might go hunting nonetheless, but his mind wouldn't be on it, d'you see. It'd be with her. He'd be a danger to himself and every living thing in sight. Except the fox.'

The old man received this appalling news in shocked silence. 'Can't send *her* away, I suppose,' he suggested. 'Say?'

'Hardly. As she is excluded from the economic world both by her sex and her father's position, its harsh but effective levers cannot be applied to her. Besides, there is a wider point to be made in all this.'

He looked blankly at her and then beyond, hunting with his eyes among the shrubbery as if he might discover this allegedly wider point lurking there like some game-bird, begging to be shot down. She decided to risk all. 'Wonky is of the opinion that land is becoming a bit of a millstone round the necks of those unfortunate enough to possess it – farming land, I mean. I suppose if you owned a few acres round any town, you'd get by. But with the cheap food that's now flooding in from the Empire – including America, of course – well, he thinks there's no possible improvement in sight.'

'The wider point . . . ?' he interjected, preferring to take lessons in economics from people who did not wear skirts.

'. . . is that good management of landed estates has never been so important as now. And Rick will never learn it all just by staying here and picking McGrath's brains. He should go to England for a year or two. I imagine he could profitably spend a few months with you at Castle Bellingham? Castle Moore is well enough managed, I dare say, but I'll bet Castle Bellingham could knock it into a cocked hat! Then we must think of the *other* part of his inheritance – the investments and the funds, you know. After a stint with you in Norfolk he could drift down into the City . . . learn a thing or two about stocks and shares, stuff you won't find in any old book. Don't you think?'

'Work for money?' Hereward was aghast.

'Of course not! Honorary work. He could also sit in the Inner Temple with Bernard – make himself useful copying things, or whatever barristers' clerks do with their time. In short, he could get to learn how the world works. You'd be astonished to realize how much of the world and its ways just pours across a barrister's table in a year.'

'Hmph!' Hereward snorted. He could see the point well enough. Even worse, he could see no good argument against it. His instincts told him that a country landowner belonged on his land, keeping down vermin, showing the flag (especially in Ireland), and reaping all the pleasures he could with rod, horse, and gun. But even deeper instincts told him that the winds weren't blowing that way any more – and probably wouldn't do so for the rest of the century, which, after all, had only a dozen or so years to run. 'How long d'you think the young 'un should be away?' he asked cautiously.

The minute the words were out he knew they were a mistake, for they conceded the very point he was trying to defend by way of his rearguard skirmish with her.

'Certainly until around this time next year. He'll probably have got over his childish infatuation for Miss Carty by then. You see, part of the problem is that they are both survivors of the Murders. It provides them with a ready-made intimacy of spirit from which, ahem, intimacies of a less spiritual nature may flow.'

'Ah well, leave that to me,' Hereward said.

'Yet if we try breaking them up by frontal assault,'

Aunt Bill went on (not quite grasping Hereward's meaning, anyway), 'the sort of thing your parents or mine would have done without a qualm, we'll simply drive them together more strongly. That's the way of young people these days.'

'Leave him to me,' Hereward repeated. 'I'll get the barnacles scraped off him.' Mentally he aimed-off-for-wind on a couple of squirrels he had just spotted on the far side of the lawn.

'We must achieve our ends without once using the words *no* and *don't* and *never*,' she assured him.

'And meanwhile there won't be a Bellingham here at Castle Moore to fly the flag.'

'There will be Henrietta and there will be me,' she said grimly. 'I don't think anyone will mistake Castle Moore for the estate of an absentee!'

'Of course – but King would see to that, anyway, God bless the man!'

'And he will have every assistance from me, I do assure you!'

He broke off their conversation to complain to one of the gardeners that there weren't enough shrubs and herbaceous plants of the kind that provided good seed fodder for the game. Only when this important grievance had been aired did he return to their conversation. 'What's Wonky going to say?' he asked. 'Losing your services?'

'Oh, he'll survive. You just invite him down to Norfolk for a shoot or two and he won't even notice,' she assured him. 'Besides,' she added in tones of unassailable virtue, 'we must all make some sacrifice, mustn't we.'

No one could remember the last time a person from Castle Moore had called, in the social sense, at the Old Glebe; to call unannounced was certainly without precedent. Aunt Bill did both on the day after her successful brush with Uncle Hereward. A fox in a dovecote could not have caused a greater stir.

The moment her carriage was espied turning in at the gate, Norman Carty was summoned from his workshop to wash the grease and copper filings from his pores. He was occupied that day in trying to modify a ball valve to make it indifferent to the thick scale that formed upon anything and everything to do with the local water, which was so full of limestone that a tumbler of it, left on the bedside table overnight, had a clouded film on the glass by morning.

Judith and her mother were going through the agency lists of houses to rent in Merrion Square for the Dublin Season, which, though still many months away, was already the most pressing matter in their calendar. Prosperity had come too late to get Judith presented last year; they could not afford to let another twelve months go by. In scrabbling the papers together, Thelma Carty overturned the inkwell, most of whose contents were absorbed by Judith's costly new dress before it could damage the old and slightly threadbare carpet. The Castle Moore carriage was at the door by then and maids were running about like headless chickens, putting their mob caps on awry and tying their pinafores askew.

Carty himself, wiping his hands in a great wad of cotton shoddy, took in the scene at a glance before he strode through the mêlée and, to his wife's undying chagrin, opened the door himself.

'Why, Mrs Montgomery,' he cried. 'What a sight for sore eyes you are. Is that a touch of frost on the grass? Come away in with you and get yourself warm by the fire. I won't shake hands.' He advanced the greasy shoddy by way of explanation.

Thelma, in a fit of ultra-politeness designed to compensate for her husband's rather cavalier greeting, curtsied – as if their visitor were royalty. The three half-dressed maids, taking cue from their mistress, curtsied too. Carty, seeing how bravely Aunt Bill was struggling to retain her composure, said, 'Pay them no heed, Mrs Montgomery. They're after practising for next February's Drawing Room till it's gone to their heads.'

Aunt Bill went through the rituals of a more everyday greeting while she wiped her boots free of damp sand from the drive. They led her to the fire in the drawing room. Thelma had recovered something of her equanimity by then and launched herself into the usual commonplaces of such a visitation.

'As a matter of fact,' Aunt Bill said when she had drunk her fill of the weather, the prospects for the hunt, and the shockingly poor turnout at Mrs O'Riordan's funeral last week, 'I was rather hoping to have a word with Judith. I trust I have not called when she is out?'

'No, not at all,' Thelma assured her. 'She's . . . er . . . upstairs but she will be here shortly.' Her heart sank when she saw that this reply had caused their visitor to form the suspicion that Judith had not yet arisen from her bed. 'She was up with the lark this morning,' she added apropos nothing.

Her heart sank further when she saw that her footnote had served only to deepen the lady's suspicion. She was casting around for something further to add when Mrs Montgomery changed the subject by asking Carty what she had interrupted him at.

'Have ye trouble with the water closets at the castle, ma'am?' he asked.

Thelma wished the ground would only open and devour her.

'Water closets?' Aunt Bill replied. 'We have no water closets.' She saw her hostess quietly dying of shame and some imp made her add, 'We use the dried, crumbled turf in the good old way.' She craned her neck and peered out into the garden. 'And we have better roses for it than you, I may say. Anyway, what has that to do with my question?'

'Ah, well now, had you experience of water closets in a limestone area like this, you'd know the difficulty I'm attempting to solve – a water valve that'll scrape the lime-scale off itself even before it has the chance to form.'

Aunt Bill raised an amused eyebrow. 'And after that, what next? A fire engine that'll dowse fires before they even have a chance to start?'

He chuckled. 'Sure half the roofs in Ireland would do that service for nothing! There'd be no sale for such a machine. But every house in Ireland – every *progressive* house, I mean – would give its eye teeth for such a self-cleaning valve as mine.'

Aunt Bill smiled. She had never had dealings with old Carty in the past; now she found herself taking quite a liking to him – if only his wife would stop cracking her knuckles and biting her lips red-raw.

Judith arrived downstairs at that moment; she came into the drawing room bearing the ink-stained dress before her. 'Oh hallo, Mrs Montgomery,' she said by way of greeting. 'Fancy seeing you here. D'you know any way of getting ink out of linen? I think we're going to have to take the whole panel out and let in a new one.'

Aunt Bill cut short a discussion of the two dozen best ways of coping with inkstains by saying that she hadn't a great deal of time and was anxious to have a word with Judith, if her parents would permit it.

Her parents almost fell over themselves to permit it; Carty left them alone with a promise to show their visitor the present state of his invention before she left – if she were interested.

Judith smiled a vague apology as soon as they were alone – vague enough to cover both her parents.

'You have a most interesting father, Miss Carty,' Aunt Bill told her.

Judith smiled wanly. 'After twenty-one years, Mrs Montgomery, I suppose I'm rather used to him. He can become very taken up with his work, as I'm sure you've just discovered. Lord knows what he'll say at the Castle next season – Dublin Castle, I mean.'

'Ah! You are to be presented at last?'

Judith nodded. 'That's what we were planning when you arrived. The ink got knocked over in all the excitement. However, I'm sure it's something far more important that brings you here?'

Aunt Bill noted approvingly how swiftly and firmly Judith had moved into the position of hostess – directing the conversation like that, but without dictating its content. 'Indeed,' she said. 'I had an interesting talk with McLysaght the day before yesterday, as he left us for his winter quarters in Athenry.' She chuckled. 'He *is* a bit like a one-man circus, isn't he! Retiring to his winter quarters.'

Judith nodded. 'I hope you got more out of him than Rick and I, then. We met him after the memorial service and it was the usual bouquet of hints and scraps of Shakespeare and nothing bona fide.'

'Not a single word from the Bard did he give me!' Aunt Bill replied triumphantly. 'But I got the plainest hint you ever heard that King sees himself in the noble role of an ancient clan chieftain – holding the Castle Moore estate in trust for "his" people, if you please!'

Judith looked up sharply at this intelligence but a moment later fresh doubt came over her. 'The trouble with McLysaght,' she said, 'is you'd never know was *he* after putting such ideas into King's head in the first place? There's a divil in that man. He'd love to set the country on fire, but only if the matches were to be discovered in other hands.'

It had taken Aunt Bill several hours to arrive at the same conclusion; she admired the mind that could leap to it at once – especially when it had so much less experience on which to draw. She decided to put rather more of her cards on the table than she had intended when she set out for the Old Glebe that morning. Partly it was because of that admiration, but mainly, she had to admit, it was because, if she didn't, this astute young woman would surely notice the gaps – and wouldn't be too backward about filling them in, either.

'Old McLysaght's a bit like us in that respect,' she said. 'Us women, I mean. If we wish to set the country on fire, we jolly well have to make sure the matches are in other hands. Neither you nor I is going to solve the problem of King on our own. Or even acting in concert, together. You know what I mean when I speak of "the problem of King"?'

Judith nodded and waited cautiously for more.

'Without Rick we'll get nowhere. He's the key to it all. I don't know what conclusions, if any, you've reached about my nephew, but I've been watching him closely since my arrival last Thursday . . . was it only last Thursday? Gracious! I believe King has very astutely encouraged him into petty acts of rebellion – which allow him to imagine he enjoys total independence of the man. Or do you think I'm being too harsh?'

Judith gave a dejected little shake of her head. 'I wish I could say otherwise, Mrs Montgomery.'

'Your greatest fear, I imagine, would be that King might use his influence – his considerable influence – to persuade Rick to pay rather more attention to Sally McIver and rather less to you?'

Judith glanced at her sharply. The thought had, of course, occurred to her – often. But Mrs Montgomery had hardly been here a week. What had *she* seen in that time to make her draw such a conclusion?

Aunt Bill, guessing the cause of her alarm, added, 'Not that I have any direct evidence of it, mind, but it would seem to be a natural alliance, don't you think? Certainly from that young lady's point of view. At least, if I were in her boots, that's the way my mind would be inclining at this moment.'

Judith nodded gloomily. 'May I ask how long you intend staying at the castle, Mrs Montgomery?'

Aunt Bill smiled. 'What a pleasure it is, Miss Carty, to deal with a person whose mind not only runs along remarkably similar lines to one's own, but runs so swiftly, too – and without a squeak of rust! May I call you Judith, in future? And you may call me Aunt Bill.'

The suddenness of this thaw took Judith's breath away. She flushed with pleasure and expressed her delight at the suggestion.

'Good,' Aunt Bill said firmly. 'I'm rather glad about that. And so to your question. The truth is, I think I shall be staying over here – for the foreseeable future, at least. And so, too, will Henrietta, by the way. Enough said, I hope! I shall certainly be staying on until after the Dublin Season next year. If your mother wishes me to present you at one of the Drawing Rooms, I shall be most happy to oblige.'

'Really?' Judith asked, too delighted to express her gratitude in more formal terms.

'And don't go renting a house in Merrion Square. My cousin always lends me her house in Stephen's Green.'

Now Judith could only gape her gratitude. But a fresh worry assailed her. 'And will Rick . . . ?' She hardly dared frame the question.

'Ah, yes,' said Aunt Bill. 'Rick. I passed a sleepless night wondering what on earth to do about that young man. Tell me if you disagree, but I believe it would be not just in his best interests but in the best interests of us all – and not least of all yourself – for him to be removed from King's influence for a season.' She pursed her lips and waited.

Judith, as quick to grasp this point as those Aunt Bill had made earlier, sought desperately for any explanation beyond the one most obvious. 'Dismiss King, you mean?' she asked hopefully.

Aunt Bill shook her head. 'But without Rick here to give his actions some cloak of legitimacy, King will be Samson shorn of his locks.'

That, however, was small comfort to Judith, who was still struggling to come to terms with a decision that she had recognized as not merely inevitable but also as right, the moment it had dawned on her. 'A season, you say?' she asked miserably.

'Let's say a year. But you'll see him more often than that, I should think. You could go on to the London Season directly after Dublin, and I'm sure there would be several invitations down to Norfolk.'

'Norfolk? Oh, yes, I see.'

'I shall tell King of these arrangements – or, rather, Uncle Hereward will, after I've had a little talk with him. You see what I mean about our needing to thrust the matchbox into the hands of the men! Uncle Hereward will inform King that, in the opinion of the family, young Rick needs to see how other large estates are managed in this modern age. And, when you consider that the assets of the Castle Moore estate are nowadays scattered about the globe, the lad should have some understanding of finance as well. The best dung is still the master's boot – but the acres it fertilizes are more likely nowadays to be acres of white paper in bank ledgers.' She smiled. 'I rather like that! I must remember to use it in my little talk with Uncle Hereward. It will greatly assist him to clarify his thoughts on the subject.' She leaned forward and patted Judith's arm. 'Cheer up, my dear. You surely never thought it would be a simple matter of returning to

Keelity and fluttering your beautiful eyelids at him once or twice?'

Judith smiled.

It surprised Aunt Bill, who had expected at least one or two tears to fall.

Judith realized she would have to explain. 'I was beginning to fear that nobody cared about the injustice that was done – the wrong men being hanged, I mean.'

'And what has that to do with my visit here this morning?' Aunt Bill asked warily.

Greatly daring, Judith leaned forward and gave her arm a squeeze. 'You needn't hide it from me, Aunt Bill,' she said. 'You're clearing the decks, aren't you? You *are* going to do something about it.'

'Him. I shall certainly do something about King.'

Judith frowned.

'Well, he's the one who was behind it all.' The hesitation in the girl's demeanour made her add, 'Surely?'

Judith shrugged awkwardly.

Aunt Bill saw that she had to press the point to a more definite conclusion than that. 'You don't agree?' she challenged. 'Do you know something I don't? I should have thought it a foregone conclusion.'

'King has the mind of a gombeen man,' Judith ventured. 'I don't think he could plan and execute an outrage like that, but he's exactly the sort who'd step in and take advantage of it. He's quick enough – and cunning enough – to do that.'

Aunt Bill nodded sagely, as if to hint that she would give this opinion some thought; but Judith could see in her eyes that she was never going to be shaken out of her implacable enmity toward King.

In other words, Aunt Bill was going to be an unreliable ally in the struggle ahead. Her spirits began to sink again – until she realized that it was better to know as much from the outset than to discover it at some critical moment in the course of that struggle.

'Sure I'd never be one to go questioning his honour's decision, now,' King said. 'But when all's said and . . .'

'And it *is* his decision, King,' Aunt Bill interrupted sweetly. 'Surely you can see it's for the best – not only in the boy's interest but in that of the whole estate?'

'Well now, ma'am,' he said, struggling to reply in the same conciliatory and reasonable tone, 'you have your finger on the pulse of it there, right enough. The estate, you see. The estate's the thing, now. Master Rick hasn't an enemy in the world, and the Lord knows I'd be the last to wish one upon him. But if he had one, then the worst blackguard of all couldn't say the young fellow's made a hames of running the estate as it is, now.'

'You never spoke a truer word,' Aunt Bill assured him.

'And that's without the benefit of any of your fancy learning from over the water.'

She smiled. 'But you couldn't tell me he's done it *entirely* without help – now could you!'

The butler nodded a small concession. 'McGrath is a good man. I'd blacken the eye of anyone who said different. But . . .'

'I wasn't thinking of McGrath.'

'. . . but an agent's an agent, for all that. 'Tis the *master's* stamp puts the true mark on any estate. Take the Clanricardes now. Haven't they good agents in Portumna. But when the orders come down the wire from London – as they did to evict all those who withheld their rents in the Land War – sure what can any agent do, good, bad, or indifferent? And look at the troubles they've had with their tenantry ever since. And compare it now with those who had the mud of their own estate on their own boots every day, like the Rosses in Parsonstown. There's no comparison at all, ma'am. And I say 'tis courting disaster to send the young master away just at this time.'

Aunt Bill's smile never wavered. 'I can't understand why you're so modest, King. Sure we all *know* who we're indebted to when we look at the smooth running of the Castle Moore estate, and the good relations we enjoy with the tenantry. You can stand there till you're blue in the face, telling me 'twas Master Rick did it all on his own. But can you deny he ever turned to you for advice? There's Mr O'Riordan whose wife died last week, and him a cripple, poor man. How's he going to manage the farm without her? And is it yourself will stand there and tell me the Kings haven't known the O'Riordans this century and more? Wasn't your mother an O'Laughlin, now – the same as poor Mrs O'Riordan, may she rest in peace? And will you tell me Master Rick is that sort of an eejit will make his own decision, and never a word of consultation with the nearest representative of the King clan? And would you be that poor sort of a man who'd withhold his good advice when called upon to give it?' Her laughter toppled this mounting heap of impossibilities. 'Wriggle as you might, you can't escape praise when praise is your due, man,' she assured him.

He wriggled as he might. 'Sure there's consultation in it, ma'am. And I'm not saying as a little local knowledge, such as I may furnish, hasn't come in handy to Master Rick from time to time. But 'twas only an ounce to his ton.'

'Ah!' She waggled a teasing finger at him. 'We all know when a ton is finely balanced, an ounce is enough to send it one way or another. The whole of Keelity knows it. I'm sure O'Riordan knows it. Were you at his wife's funeral? I'm sure you were.'

'Indeed I was, ma'am,' he replied, starting to look very uncomfortable now.

'And I'll make no doubt he took the chance of a word

in your ear – knowing how the minds of country people work. I'm sure he canvassed the possibility of a small abatement in the rent while he hired a man or a good strong woman to help him in his troubles?'

King licked his lips and stared at her desperately, for, of course, she had the right of it to the last syllable. But how much did she know and how much was guesswork? Who else had she talked to? 'Arrah!' He gave a dismissive laugh. 'Half the county believes I have Master Rick by the ear. Did they but know how he'll ignore my advice in the smallest matter, then they wouldn't give me the time of day! If I put out his striped suit, he'll wear the worsted. If I suggest he take the dogcart, he'll tell O'Brien to bring out the carriage – or saddle up the mare!' He flashed a tolerant smile. 'I'm not complaining now, ma'am. I'd not want you to be taking me amiss in that way. Divil a word of complaint is in it now. I admire a spark of liberty in a man that's born to inherit all the independence he could ever want. It becomes him, if you take my meaning.' He lifted his hands in a resigned sort of benediction. 'And sure what can I do anyway, only advise – and suffer gladly the O'Riordans of this world and all those other fools who suppose me to be at the heart of it all!' He studiously avoided looking at *her* when he spoke of 'fools' in that vein.

'Well this modesty becomes *you*, King – if I may say so. And I'd add that it's precisely what I'd expect of you!' She, in her turn, studiously avoided laying any special stress on this latter sentiment.

It left him feeling brave enough to extend the area of their discussion. 'To be sure,' he said in a speculative sort of tone, as if the thoughts were occurring to him on the spur of this particular moment, 'if Master Rick does leave us here for any length of time, there will be need for *someone* to make those decisions that were his until this.'

'McGrath?' she suggested.

King gave a circumspect nod. 'A good enough man in his way.'

Her voice assumed a no-nonsense ring. 'You can speak plain with me, King. Of all the upper servants at Castle Moore you're the oldest and most loyal. The one we all trust without the slightest reserve. Isn't that what I'm after telling you all morning! Anything you say will not go beyond these walls – except, perhaps, to himself in Norfolk and Colonel Montgomery and people of that sort. But I mean it would never get back to the man that was in it. So tell me truly all about McGrath.'

With every show of reluctance King allowed, again, that the agent was a good enough man in his way but that he wasn't the sort you could leave to make decisions all on his own, not for any extended period of time. 'How long, ah, would ye be thinking of Master Rick's apprenticeship to the Old Firm?'

'The Old Firm?' she queried.

He smiled. 'Life, Experience, and Company Unlimited!'

'Ah! Well, a good few months, anyway. A year?'

The man's face was a study in contradictory emotions. There was obvious disappointment there – that his easy catspaw was being removed at one stroke like this. On the other hand . . . 'A year,' he echoed aloud. Yes. Left on his own here, with some kind of authority over McGrath . . . a man could do wonders in a year. It might even be better than having to work through the increasingly independent and assertive young master. He squared himself to a decision. 'I believe McGrath could manage affairs well enough, ma'am – if 'twas no longer than that.' He chuckled. 'And 'twould stop the world and his wife from camping in *my* ear – as if *I* have the say in anything here beyond the proper station of a family butler.'

'D'you mean it?' she asked with interest. 'He could manage the place soundly enough on his own, eh? Well now, isn't that a comfort to us all!'

She noted the alarm in his eyes; obviously he had not expected to be taken so absolutely literally. She relented and fed him a little of what she imagined he had wished her to say in the first place: 'But see here – d'you mean he could manage *entirely* unaided?'

He relaxed and bit his lip. 'Well, if you press me hard to it, ma'am,' he went on judiciously, 'I'd have to allow he'd manage even better – even better – if there was a little consultation in it.'

'With yourself, you mean?'

His shrug was out of a textbook on diffidence. 'If that were the family's wish, ma'am.'

She smiled indulgently. 'But you'd have all the world and his wife camping in your ear again!'

'Well, who knows? I might even feel lonely without them.' He gave a brave laugh, to show what hardships he'd already endured for the sake of the Bellinghams. 'And if they do themselves no good by it, sure they do me no harm – beyond treating me to a free sup of porter once in a blue moon.'

She rose from her seat and rubbed her hands briskly. 'Well, I'm glad we had this chat, King. I think we may take it we understand each other well enough now. And I hope you're happier with the decision than when I first put it to you?'

'Indeed and I am, ma'am. Not that I ever questioned it, of course, but I'm grateful you've explained it so carefully. May I ask one further thing?'

'But of course.'

'Will I dismiss the servants now, and just keep the maintenance staff on board wages?'

'Oh, certainly not.' She laughed at the very idea. 'In fact, that's the next matter I wanted to come to. I'm sure

I don't need to tell you how exercised our minds have been by the . . . ah . . . *situation*, let's call it, that has arisen between Mrs Henrietta and the O'Farrelly boy?'

'Indeed not, ma'am. I feel I and Mrs King are largely to blame for not noticing it earlier and nipping it in the bud.'

'Lord, man, there's not a particle of blame attaches to either of ye! These things rise up like winter storms – dead calm in the morning and trees blowing down by sunset. But to get to the point. After carefully considering all the other possibilities, we have decided that the safest place for her until her husband returns from India, is here.'

'Here!' King almost choked.

'I know. It's a bit of a surprise. But where else is safer? Send her back to London – with her husband out in India – and . . . well, it's less than twenty-four hours away these days. O'Farrelly could be over there before your back was turned. And if she came to stay with us, I'm afraid my husband would eat her a mile off. No, here's the best place.'

He gulped. 'But, begging your pardon, ma'am, you couldn't be asking Mrs King and me to exercise *control* over her. 'Tis hard enough with the young master. But Mrs Henrietta's a married woman and quite beyond the control of the likes of us, humble people as we are.'

'Oh!' She struck herself on the forehead as if to say how could she be so silly as to forget! 'I should have said that first of all. *I* shall be staying here, too, of course. I wouldn't *dream* of asking you and Mrs King to exercise control over Mrs Henrietta. Fear not! I shall be here to keep an eye on . . . everything.'

His expression at that moment reminded her of something she had seen at the Surrey Agricultural Show last spring, at a demonstration of shepherding skills – or shepherdessing skills in this particular case. The sheepdog had cut a single ram out of the flock and driven him through what looked like a wide open lane of hurdles into a wider and even more open pasture – and had kept him pinned there while the shepherdess deftly converted the two-sided lane into a four-sided pen. The look on that ram's face was the mirror of the look King gave her as she swept from the room.

PART THREE

TO SEE THE FLAG UNFURL

January 1888

Uncle Hereward said very little on the train to London, yet something was clearly preying on his mind. He stared at cows in the fields and muttered, 'Cows!' And when Rick said, 'I beg your pardon, sir?' he said, 'What?' And then, no doubt catching a faint echo of his own outburst, said, 'Oh. Ah. Funny to see cows so close to London!' – which wasn't even true. There were plenty of cows actually *in* London, never mind in the fields three miles outside it. 'Especially in February,' he added.

'But it's still January, Uncle,' Rick pointed out.

The *Norfolk Inquirer* on the man's lap confirmed it: Saturday 28th January 1888.

'Even more rum,' was the only reply to that.

His obvious nerviness grew worse when they reached the outlying villages around Epping. By Stratford he was behaving as if he were seated on a nest of red ants. At last he came out with it – or with something. 'Kildare Street Club,' he said.

'Er . . . yes?' Rick responded. They had stayed at the club for two days on their way through Dublin last September.

'You recall that young puppy who made a lascivious remark about a maidservant in the hotel opposite – where members' wives put up?'

'Oh yes!' Rick had forgotten the incident until that moment. The young fellow – Maria La Touche's son, someone said – had remarked that the girl cleaning the window opposite was remarkably good-looking. That was all. It hadn't seemed even faintly lascivious to Rick – just the sort of thing any fellow might say to another. But one gruff old member – an Evangelical, no doubt – had positively torn into the poor chap. 'You're clearly one of those idle young scoundrels who go about seeking the destruction of servant girls . . .' and so on.

'What of it?' Rick asked now.

'And I suppose you remember the conversation you and I had as a result of the, er, contretemps?'

'The facts of life.'

'Quite. Quite.'

Rick wondered why – if the subject made the old boy so very uncomfortable – he insisted on bringing it up again now.

'Did you read that book I left under your pillow?' his uncle went on.

'Oh, was that you, Uncle? I wondered.'

'You didn't suppose it was your aunt, I hope!'

'Of course not.' In fact, he had thought it might have been one of the maidservants – for a jape. The book was called *Some Thoughts for Young Husbands* by Dr Wallace Greerly, DD MA MD.

'What did you think of it?' His uncle stared doggedly out of the window, refusing to engage his nephew's eye.

Rick pulled a dismissive sort of face. 'All a bit vague, wasn't it, sir? May I speak frankly?'

'Yes, yes!' He responded with anguished heartiness. 'That's the whole purpose of this expedition, what. Say?'

Rick had not been aware they were on any kind of expedition.

'Scrape off the barnacles,' the old boy added.

Off what? Rick wondered as he followed up his threat to speak frankly: 'Well then, sir, to be quite candid, I found it very hard to follow in places. I mean, I can see the good doctor's point when he says that savage peoples tend to show all the masculine characteristics and that civilized ones veer more toward the feminine side of things. Fair enough. But, as he points out, it's all on a sort of sliding scale. Nothing's one hundred percent masculine, nor a hundred percent feminine, either. And I can follow his notion that it's the same with people. I mean, men *do* have their feminine side and women have a touch of the masculine about them, too. You've only got to watch the girls playing tennis to see that!' He thought of mentioning his aunt's moustache, too, but decided against it. 'However, when he goes on from that to say it applies to our actual organs, too – I don't follow him there, I'm afraid.'

'Does he?' Hereward asked in amazement. 'I don't remember that.'

'Yes. In the chapter on physical differences.'

'Of course it's *years* since I read it.'

'Ah. Well, it does look to be quite an ancient book. I wondered if things had changed a bit since it was written.'

'Are you sure about this, my boy? What does he actually say?'

'Well' – Rick gulped and plunged headlong in – 'Of course he takes about four pages over it . . . men having nipples and so on . . . but what it boils down to is that if I hadn't read *Fanny Hill*, I wouldn't have had the faintest notion what he was talking about.'

Uncle Hereward appeared to choke. After his fit of coughing subsided he said, 'If you hadn't read *what*?'

'*Fanny Hill*. All the chaps in Keelity have read it. It's a much better book on that sort of thing than your Doctor Greerly's old tome – if you don't mind my pointing it out, sir.'

'How? Who? I mean, where did you get your hands on *that* book?'

'Napier Lyndon-Fury lent me his copy, before he went up to Dublin. Apparently it's true, by the way, that he's the real father of Mrs Stephen O'Lindon's little baby girl. Hen told me so in her last letter.'

'Never mind that! Heaven's above – *Fanny Hill*! Perhaps this expedition's a bit of a waste of time.'

'May I ask what expedition you're referring to, sir?'

Uncle Hereward stared at him in perplexity. 'I told you just now, my boy. To scrape off the barnacles!'

'Oh well, then, if you're quite sure?' she said at last.

'Quite sure,' Rick insisted. 'Absolutely. I know my uncle means well . . . and it's certainly no reflection against you, but . . .'

'In that case, I might as well put my nightie on again.'

She sat up. Rick averted his eyes – but immediately discovered he could see her in the looking glass, anyway. He also discovered that all his willpower had been exhausted in that first noble act of self-denial; a further aversion of his eyes seemed, for the moment, impossible. She really was rather splendid to behold.

She was holding the nightdress over her head, as high as her arms would reach, while she fiddled with some drawstrings that seemed to be giving her trouble. The hem of the flimsy little garment covered no more than the upper half of her face. The lamplight, warm and brilliant, threw her torso into vigorous relief – though relief was not the feeling it stirred in Rick's already unquiet bosom.

At last she sorted out the problem and the nightie fell swiftly down to sheathe that disturbing vision – more or less; he could not help being aware how flimsy the garment was and how curvaceous she was beneath it. Her eyes found his in the looking glass. Her lips parted in a gamine smile. 'Caughtya!' she exclaimed.

'Why not just put on your clothes at once?' he asked.

She stared at him in amazement. 'But your uncle's paid for the whole night.'

He laughed. 'Surely that's beside the point now.'

'Don't you understand? What's he going to say if I walk out of here, and me still a virgin, after only thirty minutes!'

'I could make up the money to you.'

'That's the least of it, my dear! You'd worry him sick. He'd think you were one of the *other* sort, if you know what I mean.' She lay down and smiled sweetly up at him. 'So if you want a quiet life, my darling, you'll just have to – how shall I put it – "sweat it out" until morning.' She wriggled a little under the bedclothes and brought herself an inch or two closer. 'You hadn't bargained on that, had you!'

Rick drew a deep breath and gazed frantically around the room. 'I'll sleep in the chair, then,' he said, without much conviction.

'God love us!' she sighed in an odd mixture of fondness and exasperation. 'Let's try this, instead.' Drawing out the bolster from under their twin pillows, she pulled it down the centreline of the bed between them and plumped it up into quite an impressive barrier.

Relieved at last, Rick lay down, safe on his side of it, and half-turned to face her. He wished she hadn't placed the thing so far down in the bed; for his peace of mind it ought to conceal her head as well. Her lustrous, flaxen hair and sharply pretty features were just as disturbing as any other part of her. He guessed she was in her mid-twenties – yet that was odd. Until now, women of that age had seemed almost to belong to his parental generation; in fact, anyone over twenty-one was grown-up and quite beyond him and his world. Even Tricia, as she was called, had seemed one of that forbidding group at first – which was why his alarmed spirit had found it so easy to decline her suggestions. But now she was . . . well, almost like a friend.

'You're an odd one,' she said. 'How old are you?'

'Twenty-two.' It was a long time since he'd felt an impulse to lie about his age.

'Your uncle said twenty.'

'I'm twenty-one next month, actually – in which case, I'll be in my twenty-second year. But I'm sorry. I shouldn't have lied.'

She reached a hand toward his face and straightened one of his curls. 'I don't mind. The whole of my life is one big lie.' She went on straightening his curls. 'You've got lovely hair,' she said.

'D'you really think I'm odd?'

Her smile was rather wan. 'No, love. Not if you want the truth. It's the other ones who're odd – the ones I meet all the time, who can just jump into bed with any old girl they've never seen before, whose name they don't know, and who they'd never dream of lifting their hats to out in the street. They're the *odd* ones when you think about it – which is something I don't do too often, because where does it place *me*!' She laughed briefly, and with a bitterness that surprised him, for she had been so warm and outgoing up until then.

'I'm sorry,' he mumbled. 'I didn't mean to stir up . . . you know. Things like that.'

She gave another little laugh, much warmer this time. 'No, it's me to apologize.' Her fingers stopped playing with his curls but she rested the backs of her knuckles lightly on his cheek. 'I'm as unfamiliar with *this* situation as you are, you know.'

'Really?'

'Really and truly. I couldn't tell you the last time I just . . . passed the night with a man – just talking. Never, I should think.' When he made no reply she nudged his cheek gently and said, 'Penny for them?'

'Honestly?'

'Yes.' Her reply carried a faint note of surprise.

'Well, pardon me for saying it, Tricia, but you strike me as, er, a lady of quite a good background. Very much the sort of lady *I'd* raise my hat to in the street – if we were acquainted, I mean.'

She laughed and gave his ear a playful tweak. 'You don't call *this* "being acquainted"?'

'You know what I mean.'

The laughter tailed off into a sigh. 'Yes, I know what you mean. Well, I'm sorry if I disappoint you, but my life story is my own affair – and so are the steps that led me to *choose* . . . this way of making a living. All right?'

'Yes, of course. Actually, that wasn't what I meant.'

'Oh. Well, what did you mean?'

'I don't really know. I suppose I meant I could talk to you – I mean really *talk* to you. About anything.'

'Ah!' She withdrew her hand from his cheek and thrust it back toward him, beneath the bolster, to hunt for his, which was advancing in mild alarm to repel her. She linked fingers with it and brought it to rest between them, under the bolster. 'Is there a young lady in your life, then?' She gave his hand an encouraging squeeze.

'Two,' he replied. 'Well, one really, but I often think about the other.'

'D'you mind if I know their names? Only it makes it easier. You needn't tell me their surnames.'

'Judith and Sally. Judith's the one, really, but Sally's the one I sometimes think about.'

'Are they both pretty? Or is one pretty and poor while the other is an heiress but plain? That would be more interesting.'

He was about to ask her if she was going to take the conversation seriously when some little instinct told him she was already doing so; it was just her way of allowing him to escape into a joke if he needed to. It also struck him that, before tonight, such an insight would never have crossed his mind. He warmed still further to her and felt an urge to confide everything. 'Actually,' he said, 'I'm the one with the inheritance.'

'Ah, and they're both after it?'

'Not at all. Well it's more complicated than that. I want to marry Judith. I've sort of asked her, or got near it, anyway. But every time things start to look serious between us, she sort of shies away. Apparently she told my sister, who's already married, by the way, she told her she has this dream of living in a little cottage deep in a forest. A very simple life. Baking bread and gathering berries. I don't know. And me being her dearest friend but not her husband. I just visit her every day and we walk in the forest and talk our heads off and it's all . . . beautifully simple and idyllic.' He chuckled. 'A bit like you and me, here and now, come to think of it.' She said nothing and the lamplight behind her was so strong he could not make out her expression. His humour faded. 'Stupid, isn't it?' he concluded.

'No.' She swallowed heavily and added almost in a whisper, 'Just . . . go on talking, Rick.' After a pause she whispered, 'Please.'

'Well, I mean it's obvious she's frightened of me, isn't it? Frightened of all men, perhaps. And I don't know what to do. I try and be as gentle as I can with her – but then you feel such a milksop and you think she can't possibly respect you. Or d'you think she can? I wish I knew.' After a pause he said, 'What d'you think? Be honest.'

She inhaled deeply, to the very limit of her lungs, and then, turning into her pillow, let it out explosively, as if clearing something from her windpipe. 'I don't know yet,' she said. 'Tell me more. Tell me about Sally. You haven't described either of them yet.'

'Judith's twenty-one, almost my height – well, they

both are, in fact. She's got dark, wavy hair. She's slender. Graceful. Very feminine, somehow. At least, when *I* hear the word "feminine", she's the one I think of. She has the most amazing grey eyes. Pale in colour but very deep and arresting.'

'And Sally?'

'She's a month or two younger than me . . . and fair-haired and . . .'

'Like me.'

'A bit more toward red than you.' He reached shyly across and stroked her hair once. 'Yours is beautifully silvery, especially in this light. Anyway, Sally's more auburn, with eyes of bright blue and lips like a porcelain doll's.'

'And her figure?'

He cleared his throat. 'Hard to talk about it without sounding, you know, crass and all that.' He laughed awkwardly. 'A lot like yours, if you must know.'

She grinned again. 'Describe mine, then,' she challenged.

He relaxed still further and, lying on his back, eyes almost closed, began to intone, 'Curvaceous, voluptuous, provocative . . . stimulating, rousing, excitimmm . . .'

Her fingers sealed his lips and she giggled. 'It sounds like you should marry them both.'

He nodded glumly. 'I can understand why there are laws against it. But seriously?'

'Seriously?' She pulled his hand briefly toward her, from under the bolster, and kissed the back of it warmly. 'You're right when you say Judith's the one for you.'

'How d'you know?'

'It's in your voice. And what you say – the words you choose. You have a way with words, Rick – but then you would, wouldn't you?'

'Mmm?'

'Being Irish, I mean. Oh God!' She closed her eyes

and shook her head. 'Why can one always see the way out of other people's difficulties so clearly, while one's own are like . . . eels in a mudbath!'

'Perhaps it's a good thing I've been brought away from home for a bit – away from both of them. Though we're always writing to one another.'

'All three of you?'

'Each of them to me and me to each of them. They're neighbours, so they see each other every week I should think.'

Tricia gave a light laugh. 'I should love to be hidden behind the curtains when they do! And I'll bet you write lovely letters, too.'

'I enjoy writing, that's true.'

'But it's more than that, love. You've got understanding, too. Like this idyllic daydream your Judith has – not many men I know would even put up with something like that, never mind understand it – which you obviously do.'

He shrugged awkwardly, being unused to such compliments. 'I still don't know what to *do*, though. So what d'you advise? How should I treat this fear that seems to possess her when she contemplates . . . you know?'

'Possession of a different kind! If you want my frank opinion, Rick, I think you should continue exactly as you are. When you talk of being a milksop, you mean compared with other young gentlemen around you? Men you hunt with? The young fellows at your clubs? Young officers from the local regiments?'

'Yes.'

'Well, if you're afraid of seeming a milksop in comparison to *them*, take my word – it's no bad thing. Don't worry.'

'Honestly?'

'Don't you believe me?'

'I'm just thinking of the way they all behave – the girls,

I mean – at a hunt ball, say. I mean the way they flutter and coo about the officers and their uniforms. I mean, at our last fancy-dress ball I got myself up as a Cossack officer and I could *feel* the difference in the way the girls treated me – girls I've known from childhood.'

'Oh!' Tricia replied sarcastically. 'I thought we were talking about marriage and real life.'

Rick said nothing.

She kissed his hand again and whispered, 'Sorry!'

'No.' He smiled ruefully. 'You're right. I did tell you to be honest, after all.'

'Can I give you one more bit of advice – which may be a lot more dangerous if you follow it? Dangerous to you, I mean.'

'What?' He lifted his head off the pillow but she reached out and made him relax again before she linked fingers with his once more. 'Why d'you have to touch me?' he asked in an amused tone.

'I like it,' she said simply. 'I need to. I always have. D'you mind?'

'No, I like it too. What's this dangerous advice?'

'Have you ever tried talking to Judith the way we're talking together now?'

'Good heavens, no!'

'Why say it in that tone? D'you think it's wrong?'

He swallowed heavily. 'No. It's just . . . well, it wouldn't be done, would it?'

'Ah!'

'Well, would it?'

'That's not the question, Rick. The question is *should* it? And my own answer, obviously, is yes! I don't mean rush at it like a bull at a gate. Just take it very slowly, one small step at a time. But you might, in the end, be able to get her to talk about these fears of hers. And then . . .'

'Lord!' he exclaimed.

'Well, what's *your* brilliant idea?' she challenged. 'The usual comedy of errors? Never breathe a word about it? Pretend you're a pair of porcelain dolls, smooth as the side of an egg? Get her tipsy on the wedding night. And blunder away until dawn, wishing you hadn't spent this night with me just talking?' She squeezed his hand hard and gritted her teeth. 'Sorry! Sorry, I didn't mean that last bit. Just call it wounded pride and forget it. I'm sure that a nice, *gentle* gentleman like you isn't going to blunder at all. But I did mean the rest of it. If you gave me a penny for every man who's blurted out to me that the thing they enjoy most about girls like us is just the chance to *talk*. To talk with a woman about intimate things – things that matter to them – things they'd love to discuss with their wives and daren't . . . if you gave me a penny, I say, I could retire tonight! I don't know what's wrong with people.' She moved her other hand up and clutched his tight between both of hers, which shivered with the intensity of her emotion. 'Where have we gone wrong, Rick?'

He had no idea what to say to her. For want of anything better, he reached out his free hand and stroked her hair once again.

A violent fit of shivering overcame him suddenly. He could not fix his eyes on anything and the room kept spinning round. 'I think . . .' he stammered, 'I think I'm ill . . . or something.'

She let go his hand and reached her arms out to him, smiling broadly. 'Well, at least I can cure that,' she murmured. 'Come on.'

And cure him she did – 'with a wide-open smile at each end of the busk', as they say.

Aunt Bill knew she dared not ask too close to Castle Moore for the precise whereabouts of Kitty Rohane, the tragic young woman for whom Mad McLysaght had written his only poem of the year. In the end she entrusted the business to Judith – who asked her maid, who replied that Miss Rohane lived in a row of cottages in Birr Road, Flaxmills. She added that tragedy, having found an easy mark five years ago, had never strayed too far away since then. Eighteen months back, in the autumn of 'eighty-six, Mrs Rohane, aged no more than forty-two, had died while giving birth to her eighteenth child, thirteen of whom had survived her. 'She looked seventy if she was a day,' said the maid. 'Seventy and starving. Sure there wasn't a pick of flesh on her.'

The cottages, she added, were part of the former Sharavogue estate, which had been bought up some decades ago by the Lyndon-Furys of Coolderg; Sharavogue House had stood tenantless since then, but the Lyndon-Furys used the cottages to house workers in their two local enterprises, a distillery and a joinery. James Rohane was a charge hand at the joinery, and his two eldest sons – Kitty's younger brothers – worked there as well.

Aunt Bill also had to rely on Judith to provide the transport and the excuse to use it – an easy enough service for a lively and popular young lady to perform. Judith had moped for about ten days after Rick's departure. Then, fortified by his letters, which were long, frequent, and absorbing, she had perked up enough to start accepting invitations to all the local balls, of which there was at least one each week. Young officers from the garrisons were automatically on every invitation list, so nubile young ladies were greatly in demand – even those like Judith, who were not seriously 'in the market'.

At a ball in Coolderg Castle just before Christmas, she had struck up a particular friendship with Madeleine Lyndon-Fury, who now, in the second week in February, obliged by inviting her and Aunt Bill to tea – and obliged them further by permitting them to leave early, so that their interview with Miss Rohane would not add a suspicious extra hour to their time away.

'What a very *nice* young lady,' Aunt Bill commented as they set off down the castle drive. 'I'm astounded she has never married. What is she now? Twenty-two? Twenty-three? Getting a bit long in the tooth for it, anyway.'

Judith merely smiled.

'Ah!' Aunt Bill rubbed her hands together. 'What do you know that I don't, eh? *Is* there someone in the offing?'

Judith shook her head. 'She's sworn me to secrecy.'

'Oh dear. That sounds ominous – ladders up to windows in the small hours and all that sort of thing, I suppose?'

'I can't say. The whole county will know soon enough, I expect – if not the whole of Ireland. It'll be the talk of . . . or the *whisper* of the Dublin Season, I'm sure.'

Aunt Bill's eyes narrowed. 'Not the footman!' she exclaimed wearily. 'The fellow who brought up our tray?'

Judith's response, though she was quick to mask it, confirmed a bullseye. 'Lord, how hackneyed!' Aunt Bill concluded. Then she grinned. 'Actually, he was rather a darling, wasn't he!'

'But how did you guess?' Judith asked in amazement. 'He was only in the room half a minute – and they didn't even *look* at each other. They're so careful about that.'

Aunt Bill chuckled. 'You said it yourself – they didn't even look at each other. I never saw two people labour so hard *not* to look at each other. But I didn't imagine it was anything so serious. After all, Felicity Montgomery can't look young King the footman in the eye – for much the same reason – but I never thought there was anything going on between them. However, you tell young Madeleine that if she can't do better than that, then young Thomas – was that his name? – ought to look out a ladder rather smartly. If her people weren't so obsessed with betting, whiskey, and hunting, they'd have spotted it long ago. What'll he do? What's he good at? What'll they live on?'

Judith did not immediately answer; instead, she said, 'I thought my cross was hard enough to bear – living between one postman's knock and the next. But I believe hers is worse, living day and night with the temptations of Saint Anthony.'

'What'll they live on?' Aunt Bill repeated.

'She has a small annuity, which can't be stopped. She thinks they'll just about get by.'

'Bread and cheese and kisses! And the whole country will cut her dead – I hope she realizes that. What a malevolent god Cupid is, to be sure!'

'I thought Eros was the god?'

'Yes, well, he's even worse.' Aunt Bill smiled sourly at her. 'How are you managing these days, if it's not impertinent to ask?'

Judith made several awkward gestures before she answered – implying it was all too complicated and difficult to convey in a few words, or even in many words. 'At the beginning it was a sense of physical loss, you know – like a bereavement, I should think, though I've never lost anybody so close to me. Touch wood. But . . . not seeing him, not hearing his voice, not being able to touch him. That was what I missed. But now it's . . . I don't know – it's just *him* I miss. Something happens and I think, Oh, I must tell Rick about that. Or I hear something amusing and want to share it with him. And he's not there. D'you know what I mean? It's not just an emptiness all around me. The want of Rick is like a hole carved out of the emptiness – a *double* emptiness. I can't describe it.'

Aunt Bill reached across the carriage and squeezed her arm. 'I think you have. And very well.'

'I'll tell you another thing that worries me. I didn't

mean to bring this up today, but since you mention Rick . . . I called at Baliver on my way here to return a book I borrowed from Sally – only to learn she's gone.'

'Gone?'

'To London. The odd thing is, I only saw her last week and she didn't say a word about it. Rick's not in London by any chance, is he?'

Aunt Bill smiled. 'No, I can set your mind at rest there. He is quite positively staying at Castle Bellingham, a hundred miles away – until the Dublin Season at least. So if the McIver gel has gone over on the off-chance of seeing him in London, she's got a disappointment coming.'

Judith did not appear as mollified by this news as she might. 'Only Rick mentioned something in a letter about Uncle Hereward planning to take him up to London. Last month that was. And then when I wrote back and asked what they'd done, he didn't say a word. I mean, he replied to everything else but he completely ignored that.'

Aunt Bill shook her head and shrugged; she plainly thought it a matter of little importance. 'I had a letter from Hereward last week. He said nothing of going to London. Did Rick say what for?'

'Is Uncle Hereward getting a new yacht or something?' Judith replied. 'I can't recall the exact words, but Rick said it was something to do with seeing a boatbuilder. Or something to do with boats, anyway.'

This detail was so unexpected, and so uncharacteristic of Hereward, that Aunt Bill started to take a little more interest in the subject. And that, in turn, caused her to remember Hereward's rather strange expression for what, in her day, had simply been called 'making a man of him' – something altogether too unpolished for a mealy-mouthed Evangelical like Hereward, no doubt. 'It makes no sense to me at all,' she said in a rather bored tone.

But Judith had noted that longish pause for thought, and the stiffness that had momentarily seized the woman, and the awkwardness behind the assumed ennui with which she now dismissed the topic. So there *was* some significance in that visit to London, after all. The only question that remained was, did Sally's sudden departure for the capital have any bearing on it? She let the subject drop for the moment and watched Aunt Bill, who was now staring out of the window.

Aunt Bill, lost in her own thoughts, harked back to their earlier conversation about the intensity of Judith's feelings for Rick. Delicately she probed her own emotions, wondering if it was still in her to regret that no such love had ever clouded her days. Then, with a sigh, she turned back to her young companion and said, 'And so to this afternoon's real business. Tell me, did Miss Lyndon-Fury manage to discover anything particular about the Rohanes?'

Judith nodded and became brisk again. 'Something we might use, in fact. Kitty Rohane's next-eldest sister, Josie, is just sixteen and is hoping to go into service. And since my mother happens to be looking for another living-in-maid, we might make that our excuse for calling.' After a pause she added, 'Oh, and her lover – the one in McLysaght's poem – was Peter Deasy, the one they hanged last.'

The cottage was one of ten, all identical in design, but they had no difficulty in picking it out; the laundry of fourteen occupants is hard to hide. It was still only mid-afternoon, so all but the youngest children were at school. The two visitors found the young woman out in the garden, unpegging the washing, though it was not yet dry; a large blue-black cloud almost overhead and seeming to reach right down to the ground, only half a mile away, gave reason enough.

'Miss Rohane?' Judith asked.

'The same, ma'am.' The woman gave a quick curtsy and then glanced apprehensively at the approaching rain.

'Here, let me help.' Judith stepped quickly to her side and took the pegs from her, leaving her free to handle the sheets, which were all she had left to take down.

'God be good to you!' the woman said with a grateful smile.

They made it indoors just as the first outsize drops of rain began to fall; it was as if ten thousand cloud-dwellers had each simultaneously upended an eggcup filled with water. Miss Rohane slammed the door against it and, still cradling a vast bundle of damp washing on her hip, pushed a draught-stopper against the crack with the toe of her boot. 'Or we'll be here in a lake,' she said dourly. 'What man would build a house six inches below the garden?'

'Only a man,' Aunt Bill told her.

'You're right enough there,' the woman replied as she set the washing down on the draining board and straightened it up. 'Mrs Montgomery, isn't it – of Castle Moore?'

Aunt Bill nodded graciously. Judith, determined to be more democratic, held out her hand, 'And I'm Judith Carty of the Old Glebe, Kilgivern.'

'Ah, with the father!' Miss Rohane's eyes said she'd heard of them. 'The inventor.'

'Indeed.'

Shyly she took the proffered hand and shook it. Her three youngest siblings, who were too young for school, sat huddled by the turf fire; the baby was asleep, the other two were carefully washing potatoes in an enamel bowl.

'I have nothing in the house fit to offer,' Miss Rohane said awkwardly as she pulled out chairs for them.

'Ah, we're only after taking tea with Miss Lyndon-Fury,' Judith explained. 'That's really why we've called upon you, Miss Rohane. I happened to mention to her that my mother is on the *qui vive* for a living-in maid and she mentioned your sister Josie. I wonder is she placed at all yet?'

The young woman's eyes danced with hope. 'She's placed this week, Miss Carty, but only for the week – down at O'Lindon's furniture factory, where they have a thousand chairs to lacquer for sending over the water.'

'A thousand!' Aunt Bill echoed.

'Oh, they're going great down there. But I could send Margaret in her place. Will I do it now? She'll be home from school in two shakes. Oh Lord, 'twould be the crowning of Josie, so it would – a good place in a good family like yours, Miss Carty.'

'Ah no,' Judith told her. 'Let her work out the week as agreed. We're not in that sort of a hurry. She may come over to see us on Sunday afternoon. Bring all her things with her, so she might stay if the place suits her.'

'If the place suits *her*!' the woman echoed scornfully. 'Sure she wouldn't give herself such airs, or she'd earn a pandying from me. And I'm sure she'd suit *ye*, Miss Carty. She's quiet, biddable – and quick. She does be picking up the learning as quick as you'd wish. Father Corcoran says 'tis a shame to have tooken her from school, the learning that's in her. And she so neat, too. Ye'll find her no . . .'

'She'll do admirably, Miss Rohane,' Aunt Bill cut in. Her sharp eye had taken the room apart during the conversation. You'd never suppose that this young woman and thirteen others lived in this tiny four-roomed house. Their meagre belongings were all around, crowding every shelf and filling every corner – but neatly; there was not a thing out of place. The bare stone floor was clean enough to eat off. The turf by the fire was stacked like a Chinese puzzle. Not a single dirty crock stood in the sink by the back door. The pegs where the overcoats of those at school would soon hang were each labelled with a name in a clear Roman hand.

'She has no character yet, mind,' Miss Rohane warned. 'Excepting what Father Corcoran wrote down for her.'

'This house is her character,' Aunt Bill assured her. 'If you want to place any of them in service, take my advice and find some way to induce the mistresses to call upon you here. They'll leap at the chance.'

Judith was slightly put out at this interference – until she recalled the true purpose of their visit; of course, Aunt Bill needed some pleasant opening of her own. More could have been arranged about Josie and the Old Glebe but she held her peace and yielded the floor to her companion.

''Tis the kind one you are to be saying it, ma'am,' Miss Rohane said.

'I daresay it's the only way to manage it. Once you let it go . . .'

'Indade, indade.'

After a brief silence Aunt Bill half-rose as if to go. Then, as a new thought seemed to strike her, she settled again. 'Something I intended asking you,' she said, 'the moment Miss Lyndon-Fury mentioned your name. Are you, by any chance, that same Miss Rohane who's acquainted with Mad McLysaght?'

'Sure everyone knows that wan!' she exclaimed with a defensive sort of jocularity.

'You know he stayed at Castle Moore almost two months last summer? He always comes around the anniversary of the Murders.'

Miss Rohane's agitation was too sudden and too marked for them to ignore.

'So you are the person I mean,' Aunt Bill went on.

'McLysaght spoke a poem for me, which I found extremely disturbing.'

The woman swallowed heavily. 'Sure he had no right,' she almost whispered. The two children by the fire sensed her anxiety and froze.

'Right is what's in it,' Aunt Bill replied, never taking her eyes off the other. 'Right and wrong. And righting wrongs also, where it's not too late.'

'I have nothing to say to you, ma'am.'

For a moment the eyes of each dwelled in the other's, making assessments, looking for some truth, however veiled. Then Aunt Bill rose. 'I'll accept that for the moment,' she said as she made for the door. She pulled away the draught stopper and opened it. Bright sunshine flooded inward over the threshold. 'Well, that cleared the air!' she exclaimed, gazing up at the sky. Then, glancing sharply back at Miss Rohane, 'But I meant what I said about righting wrongs.'

The moment she had gone, the woman plucked at Judith's sleeve, halting her in the very doorway. 'About Josie?' she said.

'Oh, that was no pretext,' Judith assured her. 'She may come on Sunday with every expectation of being engaged.'

'But *that*' – Miss Rohane's finger stabbed the air in the presumed direction of Aunt Bill – 'was the true cause of your visit.'

''Twas the other true cause, yes.'

'Why? Are ye not glad *someone* was hanged for it? And yourself kill't in the shooting, Miss Carty.'

Judith shook her head, her eyes clouded with pity. 'The day they hanged those men, Miss Rohane, I wept as bitter a tear as ever I wept in my life before or since, for I knew they'd got the wrong ones.'

'Did you so?' The woman was appalled. 'But why did you say nothing?'

'I did. But they'd no more harken to me than they did to you. What was I? Fourteen or fifteen? And a little touched . . .' She tapped a gloved forefinger against her temple. 'Or so they tried to make out. But I want to tell you this now.' She held all five fingers outstretched before the other's face. 'May this hand wither at its root if, within the years you could count upon it, I have not brought to justice those men who should have hanged that day.'

Kitty Rohane, mesmerized, lifted her own hand and pressed it against Judith's, finger to finger, thumb to thumb, palm to palm. 'We,' she said.

A short while after Judith and Aunt Bill left Castle Moore that afternoon, a sudden whim seized Henrietta to pay a visit to Baliver and take refreshment with Sally. She did not even send for the dogcart but herself went round to the stables and leaped aboard as soon as the cob was spanned in. Donovan, the odd-job man, was at the reins. Not a word passed between them that was not about the weather, the price of cattle, and the crowd they expected at old Phil Whelehan's wake that night; but as they approached Five Lanes, the man grew tense and began to lick his lips between every other sentence. Five Lanes was a crucial junction in both their lives, though for quite different reasons.

For Donovan it was the location of Kelly's bar-sub-post-office-hardware-store-grocery-and-victualler – though only the first item in this commercial cornucopia was of interest to him. For Henrietta it was where she either turned left for the McIvers' or went straight on for Parsonstown.

A few hundred yards short of the place she said casually, 'You have a bit of a frog in your throat this evening, Donovan.' Among the rural folk of Keelity, 'evening' began at around two o'clock of the afternoon.

He relaxed. 'I have, ma'am, now you mention it.' He cleared his throat in an unconvincing demonstration of the fact. 'God send it gets no worse than that.'

'I'd hate to be the cause of it, if it did,' she went on.

'I should be at home, sitting beside a good fire, so I should, and sipping a drop of the oul' cure-all.'

'A fire without and a fire within.'

'There's no better in all the world, ma'am.' He was growing tense again for Kelly's was almost upon them and no precise arrangement was yet mooted.

'They'll have a good fire in there, I expect,' she said, as if she had only just noticed the bar. 'And that's a perilously damp and chill stables at Baliver where you'd be waiting those hours for me, and sure it's but a step or two that's left of the way . . . Couldn't I take the reins myself and no harm in it at all?'

She left a happy man with a shiny new sixpence to burn beside the turf in Kelly's bar; his eyes were so keenly fixed on the black draught of porter as the curate lifted the head off it with his ivory spatula that he didn't even notice she took the wrong road out of that place.

In Parsonstown she left the gig with one of the less reputable farriers in Castle Lane, the opposite end of the town from the Ormonde Club in Cumberland Square; in fact, she avoided the square altogether, for there would surely be someone there who'd recognize her. And so she made her way through the back lanes of the town, an object of mild curiosity among the poor who inhabited them; they came out of their doors to watch the fine lady pass. Sometimes such creatures brought stews and nutritious scraps, but this one simply passed by and finally disappeared through the side door of Lumley's Tea Rooms and Dancing Academy.

Her routine was well-rehearsed by now. In fact, all she had to do was nod to the tea-room waitress as she entered and then go straight upstairs to the dancing academy;

it was, of course, deserted at that hour on a Friday afternoon. She had timed it well; there was only ten minutes to go before the waitress carried the afternoon tea across the road to the partners and seniors at Cathcart and Cathcart. Mrs Lumley, Philomena by name, was related to the Cathcarts, so the arrangement was not as odd as it might seem; she was also a profoundly sentimental woman, convinced that the Law got its way far too often in this life and that True Love needed all the assistance a sensitive soul could offer.

The waitress who carried over the tea nodded, in her turn, at Percy, who seemed to take no notice at all. However, a few minutes later he discovered some documents that needed a revenue stamp, an affidavit to take to the Commissioner for Oaths . . . in short, enough in the way of papers and errands to keep him out of the office and 'somewhere about the town' for a good couple of hours.

Five back alleys later and he, too, slipped in by the side door of Lumley's. Philomena Lumley trotted up the stairs after him and whispered – needlessly, considering the place was deserted – that he could lock the door behind him and she'd see a pitcher of hot water was left at the threshold in half an hour. Flushed with excitement, a borrowed or second-hand passion, she returned below and composed herself to behave with outward calm. The notion of an adulterous love seized her imagination with some force almost every day; and, what with the oft-refreshed population of young officers at Crinkle Barracks, there was no shortage of potential candidates for the position. But she also knew she would never allow it to stray beyond the bounds of her hot and fertile imagination; so Henrietta was something of a heroine in her books – a woman who dared.

The first time Percy and Henrietta had met like this they had both felt rather ashamed of their behaviour. As soon as the key was safely turned in the lock, they raced out of their clothes and into union with each other, and hardly a word spoken, hardly a kiss exchanged. The power of their compulsion was no excuse; they felt they owed some sort of tribute to the very civilization whose code they were so flagrantly violating – a courteous word or two, a few lingering kisses, one or two chaste embraces that could, accidentally almost, shade over into a darker passion. These, they felt, would be appropriate, like small gifts to propitiate a vengeful or jealous god. But their hunger was too great for such finesse.

Twenty-five minutes later Philomena carefully replaced the knot in the panelling of the door and, feeling wonderfully invigorated and refreshed in her own battle with love's decline, went to fetch the promised hot water.

A quarter of an hour later still, two civilized beings were at last able to sit down and face each other without trembling, talk without impatience, and take tea as the cure for what was now their chief hunger and thirst. It was awkward enough, with her sitting athwart his lap on the rather ricketty chaise longue, but much less so than their earlier connection there.

'I no longer feel ashamed,' she said proudly.

'I never did,' he replied.

'I don't mean of our love, silly.' She rubbed noses with him. 'I mean of the way we almost tear the clothes off our backs the moment you lock the door. I used to think Philomena would somehow know what we were doing and we ought to . . . you know, be less animal.'

'Animal?'

'Yes. It *is* animal. Surely you've taken fillies to stud? The way they go at it straightaway. Anyway, what I mean is I no longer think that word – animal – is an accusation. I'm proud of it. Oh God, Percy, I love you. Every minute with you is a little miracle.'

He was too choked for a moment to reply – and too worried about spilling his tea.

'Talk to me.' She drained her cup and set it down so as to snuggle tighter to him.

He finished his tea, too, and, though still thirsty, set the empty cup beside hers and took her into his embrace. 'I'll tell you the strangest thing,' he said. 'The world is full of pretty girls.'

She giggled. 'That's not strange. It's full of handsome young . . .'

'Just wait till I tell you! Before last summer they used to drive me mad. I'd sit in church, *whipped* to utter distraction by half a dozen shapely necks, delicious shoulders, adorable tresses – right, left and dead ahead. I'd go to point-to-points and place the odd small bet, you know. And then they'd be coming up to the finishing line and I'd be yelling my lights out for O'Doherty's mare, or whatever I'd bet on – and then suddenly I'd see the bend of a girl as she'd be getting out of her carriage, or Dark Rosaleen whispering God knows what secrets into the delightful, shell-like ear of Pretty Pol, and I'd just melt on the spot. And I didn't care who won the old race. I'll tell you, I lived in one long delirium over the girls.'

'And now?'

'Pfft!'

'Pfft?'

'Pfft! San fairy ann! I wouldn't stop to tie a bootlace if I saw half the court of Venus herself heading toward me.'

She laughed in delight. 'Is *that* why men's bootlaces always seem to be coming undone! I've noticed it but I'd never have guessed. Tell me more. Tell me all. I want to know all.'

'Well, it's a new delirium now. D'you think of the future much these days?'

'No.' The answer was firm and immediate. 'As long as we can go on meeting, I don't care about the future at all. Do you?'

'Only in a very lunatic way.'

She drew a little apart from him and squinted up in puzzlement.

He gave an embarrassed smile. 'I have lunatic conversations with your husband. "Now see here, Austin," I say . . . and then I tell him everything, man to man. No anger, no fear – all very cold and factual. The way I'd write a resumé of some litigation for the Cathcarts. In my imagination, of course, I'm already a qualified solicitor, living and working in London. Small, select practice. Very rich clients. Not much work. Dashed good income.'

She giggled and hugged herself back into his arms again.

'And so,' he went on, 'I just put it to him straight. We don't want a scandal, do we? You and he will cohabit as man and wife but you'll cease all conjugal relations. I shall become a bosom friend of the family, take lodgings with you, go on holidays abroad with you, and so on.'

'And what does Harold say to all this?'

'We shake hands on it in a most manly fashion. He admires my self-restraint – for of course he knows I only need to ask you to leave him . . . and that would be the ruin of his career. There are tears of gratitude in his eyes as he falls over himself to agree to all our conditions. But I'll tell you the most extraordinary thing of all.'

'What?' She closed her eyes. The boom of his voice inside his chest, to which her ear was fervently pressed, was hypnotic.

'Love is such a tyrant, such an all-devouring monster, it convinces me that this absurd arrangement is entirely possible!'

'Here's a quare thing, Mrs King, my dear! Didn't I tell them they were too quick altogether to bring the O'Farrelly lad back from Kerry?' King entered the bedroom that night with a smirk on his face and his diary opened in his hands; long spills of paper marked several other pages.

'What is that, my dear?' his wife asked offhandedly. 'Oh, I was wondering where the spills had gone. I had to make more.' She took one and rolled a curl of hair around it tight, until it hurt at the roots. Agnes King was one of those who believe that beauty must be paid the tribute of pain.

'Wednesday, October the twenty-sixth last,' he replied, turning to the first of the marked pages, 'Mrs Montgomery on a medical emergency to the tooth puller in Simonstown. Mrs Henrietta on a sudden whim to the Old Glebe. Monday the fourteenth of November last: Mrs Montgomery across the lake to lunch with the Fausse-Delauneys. Mrs Henrietta cries off ill at the last moment, recovers miraculously at the next, and again visits the Old Glebe on the spur of the moment. Tuesday twentieth December . . . similar unexpected chink in prison wall – and Mrs Henrietta once more to the Old Glebe and the obliging Miss Carty. Friday sixth January – same again. Wednesday eighteenth January – again.'

'Yes, yes,' his wife put in impatiently.

'There is a pattern dear – a pattern until today. Today, Friday the tenth of February, the unfailingly entertaining Miss Carty is herself being entertained at Coolderg. So today, for the first time when the cat's away, today Mrs Henrietta takes a sudden whim to call upon Miss McIver instead. I wonder, now, is Sally McIver going to prove quite so obliging as Miss Carty has always been?'

Agnes rolled her elasticated nightcap down over her curlers and turned to him with an intrigued smile. 'D'you mean you don't believe she ever went to see the Carty girl once, all those times?'

'Perhaps not. Perhaps Miss Carty doesn't know to this day how her name has been used. I wonder where Mrs Henrietta and that Percy O'Farrelly meet?'

'What's *your* interest, may I ask?' She rose and carried the lamp to her bedside table, where she took out her teeth and put on her reading glasses. 'I confiscated this off the Dolan girl today. *The Life of Nell Gwynne* – most shocking it is!' She opened it at a page fairly deep into the story and settled happily to continue to be shocked.

'It's our interest, my love,' he said firmly, climbing into bed beside her and laying the flat of his hand across her page. 'Passions like that – passions that lead people into folly . . . passions that will not be brooked nor denied . . . they are gold in the bank to us.'

'Anyway,' Agnes said wearily, 'if 'twas Sally McIver she was after calling on today, she got a disappointment.'

'Oh?'

'Indeed she did. Haven't the two McIvers, mother and daughter, left for London yesterday.'

He laughed. 'Are you sure?'

'I heard Mrs Jellicoe herself speak of it in the post office this morning. And if their own housekeeper isn't to be trusted on a matter like that . . .'

'Good, good. I just wondered was there more than one horse's mouth between you and the fountain, that's all.'

He took up a pencil and added in his diary: 'Does Mrs H know the McIvers went to London yesterday?'

'Will you inform Mrs Montgomery?' Agnes asked.

'Indeed, and I will not!' he exclaimed. 'Mrs Henrietta in *our* power is a great deal more handy than she would be in the power of that oul' wan.'

'Oh, here's a new tune!'

He bridled. 'What d'you mean?'

'I mean when Mrs Montgomery first said she'd stay on here, weren't *you* like a headless chicken with the fright! And making discreet inquiries about a quick passage to Timbuctoo – or the moon?'

He could not deny it. He had seriously thought the game was up then. So he dismissed the memory with a rueful laugh. 'You'll never go wrong if you err on the side of caution,' he pointed out. 'I was wrong about her and I admit it – and I thank the Dear One for it, too. I thought she'd have the estate out of our hands before you could say Botany Bay. I thought she'd start asking questions in every tiggeen in Keelity about the Murders and the trial.'

'And divil a word has she said – divil a finger has she lifted.'

'I know. I know, woman. Amn't I after saying it meself: I was wrong. Thank God!' He closed his diary and reached for the elasticated protector that kept his moustache in place overnight. 'She's as free of suspicion as a new-born babe, God love her!'

There were seven daily sailings between Holyhead and Dublin, five to Dublin port itself and two to Kingstown, just six miles south of the city centre. The Bellinghams always took the *Pride of Hibernia* which steamed out of Holyhead at two-fifteen precisely – except, as it turned out, on that particular Tuesday afternoon in mid-February, when Rick came back to take part in the Dublin Season. The delay was entirely due to Lady Ardilaun – or, rather, to the fussiness of the purser.

Whenever her ladyship crossed the water, one of her coaches preceded her by several days. A footman, riding as a groom, then returned – either to Holyhead or to Kingstown, depending on which direction her ladyship was travelling – and waited to receive the flowers for her stateroom; these were picked on the morning of her voyage, from her gardens in either Howth or London, and sent down to the pier on an early train. But on that particular day they had failed to arrive, or the footman was drunk, or the garlands had been discovered infested with earwigs . . . the rumours were passed around like snuff at a wake and were just as variable in quality; but all agreed that Lady Ardilaun's stateroom was bereft of blooms and so, of course, the purser insisted that Something Had To Be Done before she could be invited to step aboard.

'The poor Captain must be chewing his nails to the quick,' a knowing fellow-passenger told Rick as they waited up forr'ard to watch the ritual chaos of casting off. 'He has a four-hour allowance for the mails and for every minute over that, sure isn't he fined a thousand pounds!'

Rick recalled that in *Through the Looking Glass* the train-driver's time was said to be worth a thousand pounds a minute; he guessed that his informant's tale belonged more to the genre of Lewis Carroll than to reality, but he pulled a solemn face and sucked a lugubrious tooth to show he was duly impressed.

A voice, not instantly familiar in all that din, cried, 'Rick! Good heavens, what a wonderful surprise!'

He turned and found himself face-to-face with Sally McIver, flushed with happiness at this chance encounter.

'Sally! How extraordinary!' He swept off his hat and held out his hand.

'Ah, come on with you!' She grasped his hand but only to pull him closer while she offered her silky smooth cheek, which he, at an awkward angle, kissed awkwardly.

Still holding his hand she pulled him away from the rail, murmuring, 'We'll do better than that later, eh?' Her eyes sparkled and she bit her lip; her manner suggested both that she knew she had proposed something a little forward and that she also knew he wouldn't mind. 'Have you taken a cabin?'

'No,' he told her. 'I never feel the crossing is long enough, do you? Have you taken one? Are you travelling alone?' They went up the companionway to the first-class deck.

'Good heavens, no!'

'Well, I didn't mean utterly alone, of course. But just with a maid.'

'No.' She heaved her shoulders wearily. 'There's Mama and Uncle Sefton and a footman and . . .'

She was interrupted by ironic cheers from the side nearest the jetty. They ran to that rail and were just in time to see two red-faced servants coming aboard with armloads of flowers. Two minutes later – no doubt in response to an elaborate chain of signals invisible to those on the deck above – Lady Ardilaun and her party were ushered aboard with ceremonies usually reserved for royalty.

'What it is to have money, eh?' Sally murmured ruefully.

'D'you think so?' he asked.

She caught the surprise in his tone and said, 'Don't you? Well, you *do*, of course – have it, I mean.'

'Not like them.' He nodded at the last of the party, probably her ladyship's companion or some lesser relation being brought to Dublin for her coming out. 'But even if I did . . . I don't know. The way they carry on seems a bit pointless to me.'

'Why?' She was genuinely puzzled; there was nothing argumentative in her question.

Instead of answering her at once he said, 'I've been in London this past week, living at . . .'

'Have you? So've we! What a pity we didn't know. We could have met.'

In fact, she and her mother, having heard at third hand that he was, indeed, to be in London that week, had come over of a purpose and had passed their time scouring the town for him as discreetly as two well-bred ladies must. Their search had, as it turned out, been fruitless, until this very hour – of which Sally was now compelled to make the most.

'Well, I was to have stayed with my cousin Bernard, you know . . .'

'The one who's a barrister or something?' Bernard's had been the most obvious place, and the first they had tried, but his rooms in Lincoln's Inn Fields had been shuttered and locked.

'Yes.' Rick was both surprised and pleased that she knew.

'He's one of Aunt Bill's sons,' she explained. 'She does speak of them from time to time, you know.'

'Oh yes. Of course you see quite a bit of her at home, I expect.'

'She never speaks with much affection, mind – but that's her way, isn't it? You mean you didn't stay with cousin Bernard? We were eejits not to have thought of looking you up there.'

He glanced at her and then forced himself to avert his eyes – ashamed of the thoughts her presence and nearness were stirring in him. Her face was even prettier than he had remembered, and though her winter overcoat was so thick, it was well enough tailored to leave him in no doubt that her figure was as alluring as ever. 'No,' he replied. 'It wouldn't have been any good. He had a case in Nottingham, called early, and had to go down and stay all week. And for some reason, the powers that be didn't think it altogether wise to leave me all on my ownio in Town for a week. Can't imagine why!' He grinned.

She linked arms with him and squeezed. 'Oh, Rick! If only we'd known, eh? You could have come and stopped with us in Saint James's. Aaargh!' She shook a fist at the overcast sky. 'Wouldn't it have been fun?'

Her lips were as soft and sensuous as Tricia's had been. But, whereas it was all right to have such incandescent feelings about girls like Tricia, it was uncomfortable to feel them welling up with the likes of Sally on his arm. Especially when she talked of 'fun', and with such trusting innocence in her eyes. A light flush of sweat dappled his back.

'I'm desolated,' he answered easily – then, with more feeling: 'Even more than you can imagine, because what Uncle Hereward did, in fact, arrange was for me to put up at the Travellers'. And he got my other cousin, Arthur, to keep an eye on me. Arthur is Bernard's elder bro – thirty years old but answers to two hundred – major in the Irish Guards and all that. Fiercely evangelical – marches with a crozier in his knapsack. Thinks the height of dizzy excitement for a young fellow is a couple of hours of two-handed bezique before turning in at ten. Then up at six for a ride in the Row!'

'And that's what you've been doing all week? You poor darling!'

'That *sort* of thing. It's too dreary to go into all his other *divarsions*, as he called them. He can't pwonounce his r's either. Can you imagine him shouting commands on Horse Guards Pawade at Twooping the Colour? *Fwont wank wight wheel*! Eeuurgh!' He shivered dramatically and they both dissolved in laughter.

'Oh, Rick, we have *missed* you!' she sighed. 'And I'm especially furious to have missed you last week. We must keep in better touch in future, don't you agree? Mama just adores any excuse to go shopping in London, so she'd be a walkover.'

There was a loud blast on the ship's siren and a sudden flurry of activity, both on the quayside and aboard. They strolled aft to watch the bustle there and see the waters boil with the flurry of her screw. Sally renewed her arm-hold in his, bringing herself a few inches behind him so that the side of his arm was pressed against the softness of her breast. He let his pace get slightly out of step with hers so that his arm brushed up and down against her there. To make it appear that he himself was utterly unaware of what he was doing, he pointed out some paintwork that needed retouching, a wet patch on the deck for her to avoid . . . and any other distraction that came to hand.

It was a small enough pleasure, he assured himself, and anyway it would not last long for she would surely pull away when she became aware of it. But she, it seemed, remained utterly unaware; she wandered happily on at his side, answering his prattle with chatter of her own, and even hugging his arm tighter against her bosom when she wished to emphasize certain words.

He remembered some of the things Dr Greerly said in that book Uncle Hereward had 'left lying about' – *Some Thoughts for Young Husbands*. How, for instance, one could always tell a true lady from her coarse sister, no matter how gorgeous her apparel, how refined her speech, how opulent her home, how distinguished her descent. For the true lady is as devoid of sensual passions as the newborn babe and passes through life happily untroubled by their burden from cradle to grave. Quite clearly, Sally had no idea of the feelings those delightful swellings beneath her coat could arouse in a fellow; she hugged his arm to her bosom now as she had hugged her rag doll there in the nursery.

In which case, he reasoned, if he were suddenly to snatch his arm away, it would give his scarlet perception of their embrace a greater weight than her innocent one. Plainly, his arm should stay where it was and Sally should do with it whatever she wished.

They watched the casting off and marvelled, as always, that all those ropes and hawsers eventually managed to end up in such neat coils on deck.

'You were about to say something earlier,' she reminded him. 'I forget what precisely – about being as rich as the Guinnesses.'

'Oh yes. How did I get from there to being forced to stay at the Travellers'? I remember – I'd been looking forward to staying with cousin Bernard. That was it. Not that his idea of amusement is much better than his older bro's, but at least he's still got both feet out of the grave. But what I was really looking forward to was that it would be the first time in my life – d'you realize that, Sal? – the first time in my *life* when I'd be free of servants. Doesn't it ever strike you how little privacy we have? The first thing we do when we train any new servant is teach them not to knock when they come into a room.'

'Except a bedroom.'

'You know what I mean. Drawing room, morning room, et cetera. They don't knock because it would draw our attention to their presence and we're not really supposed to notice that they're there – like furniture. We only notice a piece of furniture when someone takes it away – if that isn't too Irish. And people like the Guinnesses have ten times as many servants as we have. They're probably never, ever alone – except when they're snoring.'

She said nothing.

'Don't you think?' he prompted. 'Just you try and count up the number of times in a year when you're really alone. You'd be surprised how rare they are.'

'Actually,' she replied – and there was a touch of surprise in her voice – 'd'you realize that we are in the middle of one of those rare moments at this very minute?'

He glanced around and saw it was true. She veered off toward the deck housing that contained the first-class cabins, being careful to choose a spot between two portholes, where no one could look out upon them. It was also in the lee of a lifeboat davit, where no one emerging from the door would immediately see them, either. Her eyes darted all about. 'Yes,' she said happily. 'Quite, quite alone!' And, without further ado, she pulled him to her, closed her eyes, and raised her face expectantly for his kiss.

He didn't *want* to kiss her, of course. He was committed, heart and soul, to Judith. But she was excessively pretty, and it would be a dastardly insult to ignore such a heartfelt invitation, which was surely as innocent of polluted motives as was Sally herself . . . and . . . and anyway it was too late now.

The softness of her lips was . . . *crikey*!

The softness of her *tongue* was like . . . warm marshmallow. Actually, it was like the softness of Tricia's tongue when she had taught him that style of kissing.

Sally struggled for breath, broke off their kiss, gasped hugely, hugged him like a bear, shivered with a passion he would never have suspected in her, then returned to their kiss – opening her lips at once and tormenting his tongue with hers – a soft and infinitely pleasing invader, which teased and tickled and flirted with his own tongue, tempting it to follow hers back between her lips and there play this same delightful game.

'Oh, Rick, I have missed you!' she panted as she broke from him for the second time.

'Ah . . . me, too,' he assured her.

'Really?' She drew her head back and stared at him, all merry-eyed, as if she could hardly believe her good fortune. 'Really?' she repeated.

Unfortunately, the act of throwing her upper half backward like that produced, by the simple laws of physics, an equal and opposite forward thrust of her nether half – or would have done if Rick's nether half had not been there to prevent it. The resulting pressure reduced her coat, dress, and several layers of petticoat to something the mere thickness of felt – an appropriate word, in the circumstances. The light sweat that had earlier dappled Rick's back was now more copious. 'Yes, honestly,' he gulped.

'My, oh my!' She fanned her face. 'Perhaps this isn't such a good idea, then!'

'In what way?'

'Well!' Her laugh was an odd mixture of the embarrassed and the amused. 'If we were just two old nursery chums having a bit of amusement . . . sort of pretending grown-up and all that, where would be the harm? But if you're actually feeling quite serious about it, then perhaps we'd better be a little bit wiser, too.' She looked about and saw the bows were clearing the inner breakwater. 'Actually,' she added, 'we'd better go inside, just for ten minutes or so, or they'll think I've come to grief somewhere. But we can slip out again soon.' She wriggled past him and, taking him by the hand, pulled him toward the door of the first class. 'You suggest a walk,' she told him. 'Make it look as if we only just met half a minute ago.'

Rick glanced at the clock over the customs hall and realized it had only been ten minutes in any case. How could so much have happened in so short a time? How could he have got from merely offering his hand to shake hers to . . . *this*?

The first Drawing Room of that Season was held in the Throne Room at Dublin Castle on the Saturday after Rick's return to Ireland. He stayed with Aunt Bill at her cousin Catherine's town house in St Stephen's Green. 'I *adore* both the Dublin Season and the Punchestown Races,' Catherine always said. 'They are the two occasions in the year when I can absolutely guarantee I shall not be plagued by chance visitors. And I can go out into my garden with my trowels, my secateurs, and my raffia, and simply *wallow* in clay.' It was said that more than one such chance visitor to her country house in Kildare was told by a brazen colleen (who bore a remarkable resemblance to the lady of the house, except that she was covered in mud from head to foot and spoke with the most hideous east-midlands accent) that 'de missez izzen't haawwm todeay'.

Rick stood at a window in the borrowed house, staring down upon the Green. He had never attended a Drawing Room, or any of the great functions of the Season, but he had heard they were all a most tedious bore. He could well believe it; he was already bored to death at Aunt Bill's and Judith's endless rehearsals of how to curtsy and manage her train without a trip and all that. And Henrietta had to have her say, too, of course; she had been presented at Buckingham Palace and considered herself quite adept. They had practised for days in Judith's ordinary clothes; and he had overheard them at nights in the bedroom, too, pretending that a spare dressing gown was her train; and now that she was in her ballgown proper, they were at it again in the drawing room next door: 'Kiss right cheek. Kiss left cheek. Don't pull a face. Don't giggle at the powder that's come off on his beard. Move onward to her ladyship. Down till it hurts . . . count three . . . up . . . four paces back – no! Don't kick it, dear. Sli-i-ide it . . . so! Yes! Now try it again. Only more fluency this time.'

Lord, he thought, what fools we mortals be, as Mad McLysaght would say. Still, the old hands had told him there was a dashed good buffet in the Picture Gallery afterwards. And even the most dreadful occasion could be made quite amusing in letters to friends. Ask Jane Austen!

Judith had banished him here to the library because she said she could feel the ennui only radiating out of him in solid waves; also, if he couldn't quite remember that tune, it would be a courtesy to one and all if he'd stop whistling the first four and a half bars of it through his teeth like that. Aunt Bill had ushered him out, telling him under her breath not to mind the poor girl who was distracted with nerves and he should understand what an ordeal it was for her and make due allowance – all of which he thought he had been doing anyway.

And what about *his* nerves, come to that? Sally McIver was a debutante this year, too. Betty, her mother, was a sister-in-law to the Dean of the Chapel Royal, who had wangled a permit for them to use the private entrée at the back of the Castle; no doubt he'd also arrange for Sally to be presented just ahead of Judith – for there was nothing so orderly as an alphabetical arrangement, nor an arrangement by social precedence, nor by any other reasonable criteria whatever. 'Just the usual Castle bun-fight,' someone at the club had sneered last night. The Kildare Street Club had a rule barring anyone who lived within thirty-five miles of Dublin, which kept it free of the liberal and cosmopolitan influences of the city – the influences that were all too distressingly apparent up at the Castle.

Thoughts of Sally McIver troubled him mildly. He still could not understand how it had happened. It had all been so swift. Of course, she had meant nothing serious by it. She was just a giddy young girl who enjoyed a bit of innocent flirtation – more because she knew it broke the rules than because it meant anything serious to her. She could have no idea what havoc it had played with his feelings. He still loved Judith; he and she were bound by ties – spiritual ties – that nothing could sever; but he could not help remembering the sweet softness of Sally's lips, the buxom warmth of her as she snuggled tight against him, the childlike joy in her sparkling eyes as they dwelled on his. To rebuff her would be like rejecting the friendship of a trusting and innocent child – and for the basest of reasons: because *his* response to it all was far from innocent and pure.

A large pantechnicon went rumbling by. Its dark side turned the window into a temporary looking glass in which he saw himself reflected with something of a shock. If there was ever a more stupid and unflattering costume for men than court dress, he had yet to hear of it. He looked like a hired mute at a nouveau-riche funeral; his soul shrivelled at the sight. The only bright thought that came to buoy him up was that every other man there would appear equally stupid. The tight bottoms of his pantaloons itched at his calves. He was in the middle of scratching them when Judith appeared in the doorway. 'You'll ruckle up your hose if you do that,' she said crossly.

'It's driving me mad,' he told her.

'Just learn to grin and bear it, then. And be grateful you're not being squeezed to death inside a mile-high stockade of whalebone and steel. Oh, I have such a *headache!* This is the worst day of my life, I hope you realize.'

He held out his arms to offer what comfort he could but she told him he'd only disturb her powdering. 'Is it time to go?' she asked petulantly. 'Thank God Mama's not here. That would be the last straw.'

Aunt Bill appeared. A dainty notebook hung on a fine gold chain from her wrist and she was ticking off items in it with an ivory propelling pencil. Henrietta followed, making adjustments to Aunt Bill's mantilla. Aunt Bill said, 'Yes . . . yes . . . yes . . .' with each neat tick. When everything was yessed and ticked, they all went down to the carriage which, having been waxed and polished all morning, had stood waiting at the kerb for the past twenty minutes. It took them five more minutes to settle in, what with the need to arrange their gowns to avoid creases, to cover themselves with shawls and travelling rugs, to place the vanity box where they could get at it in the minutes before alighting, to make sure that the smelling salts were handy . . . and the million and one other things that caused Rick to wonder why anyone ever spoke enviously of those who were 'in' Society.

'Oh Lord!' Judith whispered to Henrietta in a voice that Rick understood he was not to overhear, 'I need to . . . you know.'

'It wouldn't do any good, darling,' Henrietta whispered back. 'You'd only feel the same way all over again two minutes later. Just tell yourself it's hysterical and to be utterly ignored.'

'And I hardly drank a sip at luncheon,' Judith complained in a more everyday voice. 'I'm sure I'll faint of thirst if nothing else.'

Rick wished he had, indeed, not overheard this conversation, for now he desperately wanted to go, too. *Just hysteria*, he told himself. *Ignore it*.

It didn't work. He smiled sympathetically at Judith.

'Oh, Rick!' She reached an apologetic hand across the carriage. 'Have I been utterly beastly to you? I'm sorry.'

'Of course you haven't,' he assured her.

She bridled at once. 'Oh? I suppose you'll tell me next that I behave like this all the time!'

He stared out of the window; young and inexperienced as he was, he could already recognize the sort of exchange no man could win.

Spirits brightened as they set off, movement bringing an illusion of progress. They were quite a gay party as they rattled down Grafton Street and into College Green. There, however, they came to a juddering halt as they joined the tail end of a line of carriages stretching the full half mile of Dame Street to the Castle Gate. 'Oh dear, oh dear!' Aunt Bill exclaimed in her vexation. 'I felt sure we'd at least reach South Georges Street before joining the tail. It must be a very large Drawing Room this year.'

Since only four carriages were allowed in the Castle Yard at any one time, including those who, like the McIvers, had wangled a private entrée, progress from this point on would be glacially slow. In fact, it took a full forty minutes for them even to reach Aunt Bill's hoped-for starting point of South Georges Street. There Rick had to get out and stretch his legs while the blinds were drawn for Judith and Henrietta to use the chamber pot. He strolled down to Callaghan's, where he was well known, and used their facilities, finding himself one of half a dozen masculine exiles from the waiting line. What heroic struggles engaged the women could be inferred from the fact that he had to wait a full ten minutes before the trap in the floor was opened and the pot emptied on to the street below. He gave them another minute before he rejoined the party within.

This lower end of Dame Street, being closest to the rookery of the Dublin Liberties, was always a terrible gauntlet for visitors to the Castle on grand social occasions. Inevitably the traffic became choked and the carriages had to stand in lines, and equally inevitably this frozen parade of wealth and quality drew forth from tenement and warren a ragged regiment of females of all ages – little totties in patched skirts, doxies in battered bonnets, and shawlies with clay pipes and few teeth to hold them. If all they did was gawp, it would have been bad enough, but they kept up a running stream of banter among themselves, most of it highly uncomplimentary.

'Would ye ever look at the snoot on tha' oul' wan!'

'And the poor wee girl beside her'll be the same before she's much older.'

'Jaysus, Mary, and Joseph! Wouldn't Ma Riordan's bonnet, the one she t'rew out last week, put *that* oul' t'ing in the halfpenny place!'

'Mother of God, Carmel! Come and look at this! Wouldn't she put ye in mind of a turkey wit' dem skinny frills on her neck, so!'

And the unfortunate ladies who were the subjects of

this badinage had no choice but to sit with frozen expressions among the frozen traffic, pretending they were not its objects as well.

'I always think of the zoo at this moment,' Aunt Bill murmured. 'Except that I suddenly feel a great deal more sympathy for the animals than usual.'

But at last they reached the end of the glacier and broke sedately from the face of it to enter the Castle Yard. The horses crossed to the entrance at a well-bred walk, which allowed the ladies time to repuff the powder on their faces and suck a little blood back into their lips.

Now, however, the ordeal proper was only just beginning, for they at once joined a sluggish line of people on the red-carpeted staircase. It was a common misconception in the newspapers that only debutantes were presented on such occasions; in fact, ladies were presented at every important 'change of ownership', as Henrietta expressed it – on coming out, on their engagement, and yet again on their marriage. Thus, for every hundred debutantes Dublin might muster there were, in theory at least – and in practice, too, to judge by the females now waiting upon the stair – two hundred in the ranks of 'the roped and the branded'. White with *poudre de ris*, they rose in muslin tier upon muslin tier to the anteroom above.

It was supposed to be a fairly solemn occasion, so there was a great deal of solemn bowing among those who recognized one another; but every now and then delight would get the better of someone and there'd be a cry of, 'Maude! Haven't seen you since the Lough Derg Regatta!' And then others, encouraged into their natural conviviality, would join in, too – until Lord Vigo, the State Steward, was forced to come out from the anteroom and shush them back into what, in Ireland, would count as peace.

Rick curled his nose at the acrid stink of evaporating

perfumes, any one of which might have been pleasant enough on its own. 'There's at least a dozen people here I recognize,' he murmured, using his scrutiny to mask his guiltily eager search for Sally, who was nowhere in sight. 'And all of them, to my certain knowledge, would call this a kind of torture. Why do we do it at all?'

'Because it's always been done this way and always will be done this way,' his aunt told him wearily. 'A hundred years ago there were debutantes standing on this staircase – and they'll still be doing it a hundred years from now. And there will still be callow youths standing at their sides asking what it's all in aid of.'

'But what *does* it achieve? D'you suppose Lord Londonderry remembers one out of a hundred of us?'

Judith took his arm affectionately but used the gesture as a mask to pinch him quite hard, just above the elbow. 'Grow up!' she said under her breath, smiling around as if she were saying something light and pleasant. He smouldered with resentment, not least because he knew she was right. He felt a perverse impulse to be even more callow now.

'If you think this is stuffy and formal,' Henrietta told him, 'you should see the carryings-on at Buckingham Palace! When I went to a Drawing Room there after my marriage to Harold, Lord Carrington was in front of me, and honestly, you'd have thought he was going to be enthroned as archbishop or something. Talk about solemn! Yet everyone knew that only a month earlier he'd galloped his carriage down Piccadilly, pelting everyone with cabbages – just for a dare. This is nice and informal compared with London, I can promise you.'

Three steps above them a girl asked her mother how Dublin Castle compared with the Czarist Court at St Petersburg; but her mother recognized it for what it was – a gauche attempt to get level with the young lady three steps behind them who was claiming such knowing familiarity with the ways of Buckingham Palace. She smiled but did not deign to reply.

And so at last they gained the anteroom where, if previous years were anything to go by, they now had a mere five minutes to wait before their names were called out. Rick went at once to Lord Vigo, who knew Aunt Bill and had therefore already ticked off their names.

Even so, his opening words were: 'All right, young Billington. Pricked you off already. What's the shootin' been like at Castle Moore this season?'

'Bellingham, actually,' Rick told him. 'Pretty good. Has Miss McIver . . .'

'Bellingham, of course. Do forgive me.' Vigo was famous for never getting *anyone's* name right. He had only taken the State Steward's post for the sake of the house in the Castle – a good address from which to marry two rather *difficult* sisters. 'We drew a covert or two at Stepaside this morning,' he added. 'Found twice but they both got clean away. Wouldn't mind going back for them. Good sportsmen, both.'

All the while he spoke he was looking Rick up and down, as he looked every eligible bachelor up and down these days.

Rick again opened his mouth to ask about Sally and again was interrupted by Vigo: 'Tell that pretty young gel in your party to keep her eye skinned for Londonderry's younger bro. Looks just like him. He's standing just before the throne and bagging a lot of extra kisses from the unwary.' He cleared his throat diffidently. 'Wouldn't care to come to dinner next Tuesday, I suppose?' he asked. 'My sister Letty is a great admirer of yours, you know.'

'Really? I didn't even know she knew me.'

'Lord yes! The winner of the half-mile swim at the Lough Cool Regatta, last year? She's something of a swimmer, too, you know. She couldn't stop talking about you for weeks. Do say you'll come.'

'Ah . . .' Rick trod water desperately, not wishing to offend someone who could make or mar this week for Judith. 'The thing is, you see . . .'

'You're a chum of young McIver, aren't you?' Vigo put in. 'Fergal McIver? He's coming. Or his sister is, anyway.'

Through all the long, empty corridors of his mind Rick could hear the sound of doors being slammed upon any room where the beast called Conscience might be found lurking. 'The reason I hesitated,' he said, 'is that I am, in fact, engaged at my aunt's that evening. But – in the circumstances – I'm sure she'll quite understand if I break it.'

Henrietta was the first to wake up the following morning – and it was early, too, considering the anxieties and stresses of the previous day. She thought she might as well acquire a little merit to offset the tens of thousands of years she must by now have earned in purgatory, so she rose and attended to her ablutions, meaning to dress at once and take early communion at St Anne's in Dawson Street. She towelled her face dry and was just about to slip off her nightgown when the sight of the bed, and especially of Judith lying there, fast asleep still, all cuddled up and warm, was too much to bear. She abandoned her good intentions – or, rather, postponed them – and slipped back into bed.

Judith burst out laughing and, throwing aside the sheets, stepped out into the cold.

'Botheration!' she cried.

'Why so?' Henrietta asked.

'Because I'd promised myself that if you went to church, I'd get up and race after you. And everyone would see how utterly virtuous we are.'

Henrietta snuggled deeper into the mattress and said,

'I blame Aunt Bill, for borrowing this house. Or her cousin Catherine for having such sinfully luxurious feather mattresses. Anyway, something as serene as this cannot possibly be wrong.'

'Oh, oh, oh!' Judith cried rapturously when she, too, returned to her own nest in the mattress. There she pulled the eiderdown up over her head until just her eyes were peeping out. Her muffled voice said, 'If I were as rich as Lady Ardilaun, I'd have the servants come in and light my bedroom fire at five every morning – in winter, anyway.'

'Mmm!' Henrietta agreed. 'Only with me, winter would end in mid-June and begin again in September.'

They contemplated this glimpse of paradise awhile in silence.

'We ought to get up and go to church, really,' Judith said. 'We'd still be in time for first communion.'

'Mmm.'

After a further silence, Judith said, 'Shall we?'

'In a minute. I'm sure I need this time to recover from the ravages of yesterday.'

'Oh, wasn't it ghastly! I'm glad it's over – at least until I get engaged. Poor Rick! I wasn't very nice to him, was I?'

Henrietta uncovered her face so that Judith could see she was teasing. 'Not until he started talking with Sally McIver at the buffet afterwards. I thought you were *extremely* pleasant to him then!'

Judith squirmed at the memory. 'Yes, I deserved it,' she admitted ruefully. 'He was only taking his revenge, though, wasn't he? Although I don't know. Fenella Bell-Stuart told me Rick sailed back on the *Pride of Hibernia* with the McIvers. She saw him and Sally on deck – and I didn't much care for the way she said it, either – all sort of smarmy-smiling.'

'Go on,' Henrietta assured her. 'Fenella's jealous of you. She's got her eye on Rick herself – or her mother has. She'd just love to turn you against him.'

Judith said nothing and her eyes were blankly unreadable.

'Don't you think?' Henrietta prompted.

'Aargh!' Judith let out a muffled cry of frustration and then drew the eiderdown off her face. 'I do *hate* all this,' she exclaimed.

'Hate all what?'

'Mothers and daughters cruising around the country like . . . like . . . I don't know what. Like buzzards! Hovering, circling, ready to pounce – scouring the landscape for our prey. I hate it.'

'Oh, I think it's more like being a good fly-fisherman, actually. Buzzards just strike and devour. But we have to play our catch with infinite skill and cunning.'

'Buzzard or fly-fisher, that's not the point. The point is we should be *doing* something with our lives – not just carting them around like an ornamental coat, waiting to drape them gracefully over some obliging masculine shoulders.'

'Oh dear!' Henrietta pulled a face. 'Who have *you* been talking to? Lord Vigo's sisters?'

'No one,' Judith protested. 'Well Rick and Fergal, actually, but a long time ago. Last September.'

'Really? Surely neither of them thinks women should be out and about, catching the world by the ears!'

Judith ceased to look at her and instead stared sulkily out through the gap in the curtains. It framed a servant girl, who was combing her hair out of the window of a back attic in Harcourt Street; Judith's own scalp felt suddenly itchy.

'Sorry,' Henrietta said. 'I didn't mean to mock, but your talk about carrying our lives around like ornamental coats stung rather. Too near the bone! What did Rick and Fergal say?'

'Oh . . .' Judith's sigh hinted it wasn't all that important anyway. 'Rick made some joke about tragedies in real life and tragedies on the stage – saying the stage ones were better because you could always shout "Author!" and pelt him with rotten eggs if you didn't approve.'

She was unwilling to say more, for fear that her own elaboration of that casual remark might sound too highfalutin. But, miraculously, Henrietta saw it at once. She said, 'We can't call for the author of *life's* tragedies, I suppose – because we're already on the stage!' She laughed.

But Judith wanted her to see the serious point, too. 'That's the sort of *doing* I was talking about,' she said. 'Not . . . women's suffrage and doing men's jobs . . . things like that. I mean doing things in *life*. Controlling the lives we've actually got, here and now. That's all. That's why I didn't like all that talk about . . . what were we saying, anyway? Oh yes – buzzards and fly-fishers.'

'Even when we have him hooked, he's not ours,' Henrietta pointed out morosely.

'Witness me and Rick!' Judith responded. 'You're right, of course. But I hate that even more. I often think I'd rather stay a spinster than play that stupid game. We make such fools of ourselves – mothers and daughters. I don't know what's gone wrong with Rick and me. There was a time last autumn when we were like that!' Briefly she poked out a hand with fingers crossed. 'I'd have said nothing could ever have come between us. And now . . . I don't know. He's as nice as pie and as attentive as ever – except when I'm beastly. But . . . I don't know. There's a feeling of estrangement all the same, and I can't seem to find the way back to where we were.'

'Don't I know that feeling!' Henrietta murmured. 'It's like being sure there's a certain room in a particular house – and you've actually been in it, so you absolutely *know* it's there. And yet you just cannot find it again. D'you ever have that dream? You scour the house from attic to cellar and it's simply not there – this room which you know so well. Or, as you say, you can't find the way to it.'

'I'm sorry!' Judith reached across and gave Henrietta's arm a sympathetic squeeze. 'Here's me chattering on about Rick and quite forgetting you have troubles of your own. I haven't liked to ask lately in case I was just opening the wound, but . . . you know?'

'Percy O'Farrelly?'

'Who else. Are you getting over it now?'

Henrietta laughed.

Judith stared at her in surprise. 'That's a merry-sounding shteam outa you, colleen!' she said accusingly.

'Have I appeared to be "getting over it"?' Henrietta asked.

'Admirably.'

'Good.'

After a pause Judith asked in frustration, 'Well? Are you or aren't you?'

Henrietta eyed her speculatively. 'Promise you'll never breathe a word?'

'Oh Lord!'

'Promise?'

'I suppose so.'

'Then I'll tell you – Percy O'Farrelly and I meet at every opportunity we can snatch – which, in practical terms, means every opportunity *I* can snatch, since our society is more designed for locking away daughters than sons.'

'But you haven't had *any* opportunity.'

Henrietta smirked. 'Remember I used to pretend to call over to the Old Glebe to see you?'

'That's what I mean. You stopped doing that before Christmas.'

Henrietta shook her head. 'I realized I couldn't use you as an excuse for ever. Now I just say I'm popping over to see Sally McIver.'

Judith gaped at her. 'And you still go to Parsonstown instead?'

The other nodded.

'But see here,' Judith objected, 'you must at least *call on* the McIvers, otherwise – this most recent time for instance – how did you know Sally and her mama had gone to London?'

'Don't remind me!' Henrietta's smile did not waver. 'I nearly came unstuck there, but, thank heavens, Aunt Bill didn't raise the matter that evening. It was the day you took tea with Madeleine Lyndon-Fury, remember? And then, just before I went in to breakfast the following morning, dear King most fortuitously let slip the fact that the McIvers were over the water.'

'Fortuitously?' Judith repeated the word with some scepticism.

'Yes, I wondered about that, myself,' Henrietta admitted. 'But he gave no sign that he knew he was helping me.'

'Lucky you, then!' Judith exclaimed, but tiny bells of caution were already ringing in her mind. 'When you and Percy meet . . .' she went on.

'Yes?' Henrietta's eyes danced merrily.

'What do you . . . you know . . . do?'

'Everything.'

Judith swallowed heavily and for some reason her heart started to thump. 'Golly!'

Henrietta was serious now. 'And nor do I feel the least bit ashamed, let me tell you.'

'Honestly?' She suddenly realized she very much wished to hear Henrietta's reasons for her lack of shame.

'Honestly! I never *chose* Harold as my husband. True, I allowed myself to be talked into imagining I loved him for a time – though in my own defence I'd say I was still in some kind of bewilderment after the Murders. Anyway, *they* chose him for me, so now they must accept the consequences if I suddenly wake up out of my dream and find I'd have made a quite different choice if they'd only left me to it.'

'What consequences?'

'The consequences of the fact that I've met a man – the only man in the world – for whom I would lie, cheat, steal, commit . . . any crime you care to name.'

Judith realized she had been about to say 'commit murder'.

Henrietta continued, 'A man for whom I'd gladly die, in fact. They never gave me the chance to meet him before they encumbered me with Harold, so now they must just put up with it. That's what I mean by consequences. What else?'

'What if you have a baby? That's what *I* thought you meant by it. I mean, with Harold away in India, you couldn't possibly pretend . . .'

'Percy's a gentleman, you know. In any case, there's absolutely no need for a girl who knows what she's doing to get herself in that predicament. Not nowadays.'

Judith swallowed heavily once more but did not even murmur this time.

Henrietta smiled impishly. 'Curious?'

'No!' Her tone was frightened. But then she smiled. 'Yes, of course I am. But I think it would be best if I didn't know, all the same.'

'I'm not the only married lady with a lover, you know,' Henrietta pointed out gently. 'I'm a bit younger than most, that's all. If you dare take your eyes off Rick this week, you just watch the matrons in their thirties and forties. See whose eyes they catch and meet across the ballroom floor. Who do they talk with in the most casual way – except that they do it rather too often for all that nonchalance. A woman can always tell these things once she knows what she's looking out for. You'll be amazed.'

'Shall we get up and go to church? We might still be in time for the first service?'

'Or we could leave it another half hour and certainly be in time for the second,' Henrietta suggested. When Judith raised no objection she went on, 'Were you surprised? You sounded surprised just now when I said King told me by chance about the McIvers and London.'

All at once Judith's mind began racing. The little alarms that had rung earlier now clanged louder still. She could not get it out of her mind that Henrietta had almost said – and certainly intended saying – that she would commit murder for Percy. Nor could she get it out of her mind that King was in a powerful position to assist or prevent her clandestine meetings with that same young man. And suddenly she knew that never again would she be able to trust her, Henrietta, her closest, dearest friend! From now on she would have to guard every word she said. And she did mean from *now* on, for she had been on the point of telling her everything she had learned that afternoon at Kitty Rohane's, and the solemn oath she had sworn there.

'Well?' Henrietta prompted.

Love! She was beginning to hate it now. It soured all relationships it did not bless – there was no neutral near it. 'I was a bit surprised,' she admitted. 'But you know my views of *that* man!'

'Me, too,' Henrietta assured her, 'I told you how suspicious I was at the time.'

Ah, but had that been the truth? Did Henrietta even realize she was no longer a free agent? She probably knew she was an abject slave of her addiction to Percy, but did she realize that that slavery cast a pall of suspicion over everything else she might do?

What if King had not simply let slip this valuable little nugget of information and then gone about his business? What if he had proceeded to point out how useful he could be to Henrietta in her desire to 'do everything', as she put it, with her darling man? What if he said something like, 'I'll arrange for you and the young fellow to meet as often as you want, if you'll just help me a little bit, too'? And what if his quid-pro-quo had been that she would keep an eye on Miss Judith and the oul' wan for him?

It shocked her to think that she could even suspect Henrietta of such duplicity – until she remembered the glint in her eye when she had tried to convey the strength and depth of her love for Percy.

Henrietta gave a little laugh. 'Funny. When Aunt Bill first announced she was going to stay on at Castle Moore, giving as her reason the necessity to keep an eye on me – I thought that was all bluff. I thought her real reason was to get at the bottom of all that business about the Murders and whether they caught the right men and whether King was mixed up in it and so on.'

'And now?' Judith asked, as if she couldn't see her drift.

'Well, she hasn't done much about it, has she – if that *was* her purpose. She doesn't go out of her way to watch King, does she? Nor call for the books . . . nothing like that.'

'I suppose not,' Judith admitted.

'And you, too, if I may say so, darling. Last September you were all fired up to roast him alive if you could.'

'If I could!' Judith laughed as if she now had difficulty in imagining she had ever been so artless. 'It would be so easy, wouldn't it, if King were dipping his fingers in the till, so to speak. Feathering his own nest – or doing it in ways that could be traced through the books. But he's not. Oh, I've no doubt he pockets *something* every now and then – what servant doesn't!'

On any other day she would have gone on to say she now realized that wasn't King's game at all. Power, not money, was what King was filching from the Bellinghams. The 'humble butler', the man who knew his place and never presumed upon the family's gratitude to him, now held their estate in the palm of his hand! Its money was worthless to him. What could he do with money? He'd turn into another pretentious nouveau riche at whom the world would laugh behind his back. No, it suited him very well to blow this golden chaff off the palm of his hand and let the Bellinghams scrabble for it once a year. It allowed him to retain the part he really wanted.

On any other day she would have tried to express these notions to Henrietta. Now she knew she never could.

'You think you may have misjudged him, then?' Henrietta asked.

Judith nodded. 'It begins to look that way, doesn't it?'

After Matins they strolled down Dawson Street, where they faced a choice between crossing the road to the south gate of Trinity, for a promenade in the college grounds, or continuing their stroll around the quarter. Judith suggested Trinity. Rick said why not go on up to Merrion Square? Henrietta said because everyone would be there and they'd had quite enough of everyone yesterday. They turned to Aunt Bill to adjudicate. She, fearing that Henrietta might have some far-fetched scheme involving Percy O'Farrelly up her sleeve and had nobbled Judith to fall in with it, plumped for whatever the two young women *hadn't* suggested. So Merrion Square it was.

They sauntered up Nassau Street. To their right stood the ranks of elegant town houses – the Kildare Street

Club among them, halfway up; across the street were the open playing fields and gardens of Trinity, secure and aloof behind their high wrought-iron railings.

'After a while in England,' Rick said, 'you start noticing little things, little differences. Just look at the height of those railings, for instance – wouldn't you just know it's a Protestant place behind them! And I'll tell you another thing. You know bits of Castle Moore are supposed to be patterned after Castle Bellingham in Norfolk? Well, you can see the likeness easily enough, especially inside the rooms, but I noticed straight away that the window sills are at least six inches lower over there. And when I mentioned it to Uncle Hereward, d'you know what he said?'

Three pairs of eyes hung on his answer.

'He said, "Ah yes, but we'd never need to use them as rifle parapets here, would we!" Makes one think, what? Protestant railings . . . Protestant window sills . . .'

There was a brief silence while they digested the remark. Then Henrietta said, 'But that's all history. The country's pacified now, surely? At the time of the Murders *everyone* was talking as if we were plunging headlong into revolution. And how long did the Land Wars last? Two years later you'd get a bigger crowd to watch a man fall off a bicycle than to organize a rent strike. Surely that was the last gasp of the Spirit of 'Ninety-eight?'

'You miss my point, sister dear,' Rick replied. 'Whichever of our illustrious ancestors commissioned that wing in the likeness of Castle Bellingham . . .'

'It was Richard,' Aunt Bill said.

'Yes, it must have been, of course.'

'But your point?' Henrietta insisted.

'Yes. I'll bet Richard felt as Irish as any of us. I'll bet he took the same deep breath of satisfaction when he stepped off the Kingstown ferry. But it didn't stop him from adding six inches to the sill heights, did it!'

'I don't believe that's got anything to do with being Irish or English,' Judith put in. 'It's about being rich or poor. I'll bet if Castle Bellingham had been built a hundred years earlier, it too would have had sills for . . . I don't know – blunderbuss parapets, or whatever they had then. And a hundred years from now, when the differences between rich and poor will be only very slight, I don't suppose there'll even be locks on doors.' Her eye caught Rick's and she added, 'Why are you grinning like that? Don't you believe me?'

'Of course I do. I was just thinking how amazing it is – I mean the way our minds run along almost identical lines.'

Henrietta gave a theatrical sigh and seized Aunt Bill's arm. 'Oh dear! Here it comes! Wake us up when he's finished.'

Rick shot her a withering glance and continued, 'I mean, that was the next thing I thought, too – that it was really just a matter of rich versus poor.'

'Don't you think the poor are getting less poor with each generation?' Judith tried to recruit Aunt Bill's agreement. 'And, what with education and all that, the differences are bound to vanish sooner or later?'

'The poor ye have with you always,' she quoted, to avoid taking sides.

'Actually, *I* think it's going to make the differences seem greater in Ireland than over the water,' Rick went on. 'As the differences between rich and poor diminish over there, the old "two-nations" England will become more united. But I don't think that'll happen here. The two-nations Ireland will become even more separated. At the moment the two Irish nations are only masquerading as rich and poor. When those differences vanish, we'll see them for what they really are.'

Judith wished he had said nothing about the similarity

between their minds for she now found herself in complete unison of thought with him; every word he spoke seemed to fall into a ready-prepared slot in her head – and she hated the notion that she was so predictable. To escape, she made a huge leap ahead, still on the same mental track, but so far ahead of him, she hoped, that he wouldn't see the connection. 'Worse than that,' she said. 'We'll probably be forced to choose between them!'

He stabbed a finger at her and laughed. 'Precisely!' he said. 'God send it doesn't come in our lifetime! Sure I don't know which I'd choose.'

She gave up and took his arm – just as they reached the corner of Clare Street at its junction with Merrion Square. A moment later she was rather glad of it, for who should be walking toward them, past the National Gallery, but Sally and Fergal McIver.

'Yoo-hoo!' Fergal called out, taking off his topper and waving it.

Sally shook him crossly and snatched the hat back on to his head. 'Do forgive him,' she said wearily as soon as they were within talking distance. 'You know what these culchies are – straight off the bog. Mrs Montgomery, how very nice to see you here. Are you enjoying the Season? We've just been to see the stuffed animals. Aren't they wonderful?'

The exchange of pleasantries continued until she had gone the round. It crossed Judith's mind that, just as the two Irish nations could pretend to be united almost all the time, so could the deadliest of rivals counterfeit the jolliest of friendships when occasion demanded.

As one happy family they crossed the road and entered the gardens, a five-acre oasis of green at the heart of the square. Mahonia was in full flower and so were some of the hardier viburnums. One daffodil had burst its bud that morning and there were dozens more on the point of doing so; but most of the shrubs were reduced to bare, brown twigs and the ornamental beds were naked earth, showing not a trace of last summer's brilliant geometrical displays.

'We were talking about the differences between being Irish and being Irish,' Rick told the newcomers.

Henrietta groaned and Judith said, 'No, we weren't. We'd talked that particular subject to death.'

Sally took hold of Rick's free arm. Fergal, seeing the path was not wide enough for four to walk in comfort, let her go and fell back a pace or two.

'That's nice,' Henrietta said, grasping his arm at once. Then she glanced apologetically over her shoulder at Aunt Bill, who smiled back and said, 'Don't worry about me!'

As if to add weight to her words, she stooped to read a plant label and make a note in her little book.

'She's terrible in the spring,' Henrietta murmured to Fergal.

'What do you mean?'

'One simply disowns her and walks away. Her bootlaces come undone at every other shrub and when she stands up again, three or four little green slips drop neatly in her handbag. The gardens at Castle Moore owe something to almost every other garden in Ireland, I should think.'

Fergal chuckled. 'Not a bad wheeze, though. Did you enjoy the Drawing Room yesterday – Mrs Austin Bellingham?'

'I'll kill Lord Vigo one of these days. Why did he take the post if he can't remember people's names – or even read them off a list?'

'To marry off his sisters, they say. The State Steward's Lodge is a pretty good address.'

'Yes!' Henrietta chuckled. 'He even has hopes of Rick! He's invited him to dine there this Tuesday.' She felt his arm twitch and quizzed him with her eyes.

'He's invited Sally and Mama, too,' Fergal explained. 'That was a mistake, eh! Still, if you can't even remember people's names properly, you can hardly be expected to remember . . . other interesting things about them.'

Ahead of them Rick made some remark and the girl on each arm laughed. Fergal said, 'If that isn't the very picture of an eligible bachelor, I don't know what is!'

'Ah g'wan!' Henrietta shook his arm playfully. 'You're not exactly beyond the pale yourself.'

After a short pause he said, 'Poor Judith, she'll be quite alone on Tuesday night.'

'If you count *my* company as a kind of loneliness,' Henrietta replied frostily and then laughed. 'Or were you about to say more?'

'I was about to suggest that – as I, too, will be in that same woeful condition – we might cure our sorrows together. I can get tickets for the theatre. They're doing *Leah the Forsaken*, a dreadful melodrama but quite affecting. And we could go on for a bite of supper after. I could get three tickets, because, of course, we shall need a respectably married lady to chaperone us.'

Henrietta held her breath, her mind whizzing with possible and impossible notions.

Fergal cut across them all when he said, 'I could get *four* tickets, indeed.'

She thought he meant the fourth for Aunt Bill until he added, 'And I could send a wire to Parsonstown as soon as the telegraph office opens tomorrow.'

Suddenly there was no such thing as an impossible notion. She was so happy she wanted to burst out with something amusing. 'After the play,' she said, 'we could call for the author and pelt him with rotten eggs.'

He frowned in bewilderment.

'According to Judith,' she explained, 'you said something like that last year – about tragedies in real life and on the stage. You or Rick.'

'Ah!' He remembered then. 'It was Rick, actually.'

Her brother, hearing his name, turned round and asked what awful things she was saying about him. The five youngsters became one group again while Henrietta explained. 'But as I said to Judith this morning,' she added, 'we'd be too ashamed to call for the author after one of life's real tragedies, we who write our own life stories.'

Rick was the youngest eligible bachelor there; most of them were in their late twenties or early thirties and attached either to the army or to one of the professions. It was a matter of simple mathematics. Assuming that parents lived, on average, to the biblical age of three score years and ten, a fellow who married at twenty and borrowed on his expectations would have spent most of the inheritance in interest by the time it actually fell to him. He therefore needed a profession to tide him over until he had a proper income of his own. Alas, what were known variously as 'emoluments, stipends, honorariums, refreshers, fees . . .' and so forth – never (ghastly word) 'salary' – were notoriously slow to pick up at the outset. Twenty-eight was really the earliest at which even the smartest bachelor with the most eminent prospects could seriously think of diamond rings, much less those made of gold. So a youth who would come of age in five days' time and who was already legatee-in-trust of a substantial patrimony in both land and shares was a fine catch indeed. Naturally, he was placed between Guinevere and Lætitia, Vigo's *difficult* sisters. Sally, to her chagrin, was placed directly opposite. And the table was five feet wide.

Rick had heard so much about 'Gwinny and Letty' that he expected a pair of old maids in their thirties. He was therefore agreeably surprised to find they were no more than twenty-five and twenty-three respectively. Nor were they as plain as the word *difficult* had led him to assume. Gwinny, dark-haired and statuesque, had a longish nose and yet it was not at all unattractive; her lips were generous and full – though they inclined toward a supercilious smile every now and then; and her eyes, though deep and full of mystery, were disconcertingly penetrating at times. Letty was shorter and generously curvaceous, though none could call her fat. Her movements were precise and she executed them with a curious air of finality; she moved the objects of her immediate world – at the moment it was cutlery, wine glasses, and so on – as if she expected them to stay where she put them, or they'd better have a jolly good reason for not doing so. Her gaze, like her sister's, was . . . Rick felt that the word 'penetrating' did not quite do her justice. He hunted for a moment before he decided that the proper adjective was 'intelligent' – and that went for both of them.

Indeed, they were so very intelligent that within two minutes of seating himself between them he felt distinctly challenged – but not unpleasantly so. And he realized, too, that the word 'difficult', as applied to nubile spinsters, was capable of many meanings.

Their knowledge of history was prodigious; so, too, of botany and zoology, Erse, the story of Sèvres porcelain, the works of Raphael, distempers of the horse, plant-hunting expeditions in China . . . and just about every other subject Rick dredged from the murk called 'education' that a succession of enthusiastic tutors had left in his mind. When he mentioned that a friend of his had trapped a Chalkhill Blue at Castle Moore last summer, Letty said it was *slightly* surprising since its only known haunt in Ireland was the Burren, over forty miles away – and was he sure it hadn't been a Blue Fritillary? Rick, no longer sure it had even been a butterfly, gave up.

In desperation, he trotted out his only intellectual

achievement of recent months – his notion that, whereas the 'two nations' of England were merely divided by class, which was notoriously inconstant – in that families could go from clogs to riches and back to clogs again in just a few generations – the 'two nations' of Ireland were divided by much deeper and more lasting forces.

Even as he spoke he was aware that a subtle alteration was overtaking the two sisters. They exchanged glances and their expressions lost a certain hauteur, which they had shown until then. 'Go on,' Gwinny urged when he had said his piece.

As he hadn't, in fact, 'gone on' much from there in his own thoughts, he said, 'I think it's something that nobody's really faced as yet.'

'And how long have you been facing it?' Letty asked.

They were both obviously struck by his idea – 'On to it like two terriers on to a rat,' as he said later. He felt flattered, especially as he had been scraping the bottom of the barrel when he trotted it out.

'Only a day or so, actually,' he admitted with some reluctance.

There was a glimmer of unfeigned admiration in Gwinny's voice at this. 'And what put the notion into your head?' she asked.

'The height of the railings around Trinity, of course,' he said, with an Irishman's desire to see confusion and fascination mingle in his audience's eyes. He went on to explain.

When he had finished, Letty looked at her sister and said, 'Shall we?'

'I think so,' she replied.

'What now?' he asked.

It was Gwinny who answered. 'My sister and I, Mr Bellingham, have only one aim in life – and it has nothing whatever to do with my brother's absurd matrimonial ambitions for us. No doubt you're fully aware of them – and fully aware, too, of the reason you have been placed between us tonight.'

'I say!' Rick cleared his throat and ran his finger round inside his collar.

'Don't be alarmed,' Letty added, with a merry sparkle in her eye. 'You were never in the slightest danger from either of us, I do assure you.'

His response was not so much alarm as annoyance. Her suggestion was plainly that, no matter how attracted he might have felt toward them, they would have remained unmoved. It was on the tip of his tongue to assure them that the sentiment was mutual when he remembered what Gwinny had said about their having only one aim in life.

He leaned back in his chair and wiped his lips on his napkin. The gesture took no more than a couple of seconds but it was long enough for the atmosphere between them to change subtly – long enough for him to realize what a splendid thing they had done. By removing the very reason for his being there, seated between them that evening, they had liberated not only him but themselves as well. Suddenly they could say things, anything that took their fancy, and no one would look for that *other* purpose behind it; the elaborate nuptial gavotte was over and they were free to dance whatever steps they liked. His spirit swelled and blossomed.

'D'you know,' he said, eyeing first one then the other with an oddly speculative glance, 'I'm just beginning to feel sorry to hear you say that. D'you mean to tell me I'd have been *utterly* wasting my time?' And he dared to fix Gwinny with the sort of uncompromising stare she had trained on him most of the meal so far.

It caught her so completely unawares that she tried to make three replies at once and ended up stammering none of them. And she *almost* blushed.

He glanced swiftly at Letty, just in time to include

her in the question, too. She was staring at her sister in amazement. Then she turned to him, her eyes alight with a rare old warmth, and said, 'Well, well, well!'

He spared Gwinny the ordeal of salvaging a coherent reply and reminded her of the 'one aim in life' she had mentioned.

'Ah yes!' She stepped gladly back on to firmer ground. 'Letty and I, you see, want to edit and publish a monthly magazine. Something like *Blackwood's*, if you know it – I'm sure you do.'

'Yes, in fact, I do.' He was slightly amazed to find himself level with them on any topic whatever. 'My Uncle Hereward takes it in Norfolk, and I shall open my own subscription when I return to Keelity.' Just in time he added, 'And one to *your* magazine, too, of course. What are you going to call it?'

'We're looking for . . .' Letty began, but was silenced by an urgent glance from her sister, who went on: '. . . looking for contributors – articles, poems, you know. We've assembled quite a few already, in fact . . .'

'Anyone I might know?' Rick now felt bold enough to ask.

'Well, ah, Trollope's estate has promised us some previously unpublished notes toward a memoir of his time in Ireland,' Gwinny replied.

'It's to have an Irish emphasis,' Letty put in, 'but no more so than *Blackwood's* is Scottish. We're thinking of calling it *New Hibernian Quarterly*. It will draw its themes from the entire literary and artistic endeavour of Europe, but every issue will carry something especially Irish, you see.'

'Not parochially Irish,' Gwinny warned.

'Not all Celtic and mystical.'

'Which is why the idea you've just mentioned is of such interest to us, you see.' Gwinny smiled. 'It has such breadth, such a universal feel.'

And now there was no trace of superciliousness there at all. And he thought how odd it was that when she smiled like that her long nose and discomfitingly intelligent eyes acquired a completely different context and she became – well, rather strikingly good-looking, in fact.

'D'you think you might work it up into an article for us?' she asked.

'Four to five thousand words,' Letty slipped in even as he mumbled that he'd have a shot at it.

And as he heard the words escape his lips, another part of his brain was already asking if he hadn't gone out of his mind? One of his tutors had once locked him in the schoolroom for eighteen hours on nothing but bread and water before he had produced a mere five hundred words on the Thirty Years' War. And that had been one of his better essays! *And* he'd had a complete set of the *Encylopædia Britannica* in there with him.

And yet, somehow, his triumph in taking these two haughty, self-sufficient, intellectual young ladies and reducing them to a condition in which they had genuine smiles on their lips, genuine laughter in their eyes, and were evincing a genuine appreciation of the quality of his own mind, made his rash promise seem very small beer indeed.

'Your sister's here for the Season, too, isn't she?' Gwinny asked. 'What is she doing this evening?'

'Oh, she's at the theatre with . . . friends. *Leah the Forsaken*, I believe.'

'Such a *shallow* tragedy,' Letty remarked.

The two words threw a lever in Rick's mind, releasing the brake and setting him off on a downhill run that was truly inspired. Ideas flashed into his brain out of nowhere, swirling in the wake of his headlong rush of thought. 'Ah, yes,' he said sagely. 'But isn't that true of even the finest stage tragedy? How shallow they all are compared with the tragedies of real life? Defects of character that should require an entire lifetime to mature are frittered away within hours upon the stage. They arrest us, engage us, and release us once again. "Three cheers!" we cry in our relief, and, "Author! Author!" But in real life those same defects grant us no release. That is the true horror of it all. On the stage, tragedy happens *to* a character. In real life it *becomes* him. It is a final curtain without a call to follow. No time to slip off the mask and wave to friends – "See you in the green room, darlings!" Eh?' He looked from one sister to the other and found them hanging on his every word. 'And,' he concluded in tones borrowed from McLysaght, 'we are too ashamed, we self-made ones, to cry, "Author! Author!" '

He sat in a little pool of dumbfounded silence – himself as dumbfounded as the two sisters. None of the ideas he had just uttered was new to him, of course; but whence had come the skill to put them together in such a ringing fashion?

'Is that something you've written?' Letty asked reverentially.

He shook his head.

'You mean it just occurred to you on the spur of the moment?' Gwinny asked.

He smiled apologetically. 'Got a touch carried away.' The smile became gallant. 'Actually, it was pure inspiration – the two of you must have inspired me.'

'Well!' Gwinny exclaimed. 'Let's hope it's the first of many, many times.'

'Yes, indeed!' Letty cleared her throat and frowned to show that she hadn't forgotten more mundane and practical matters. 'We're also, as it happens, looking for backing, you know.'

'Financial backing.' Gwinny recovered her aplomb quickly, too. 'Of course, it's out of the question to talk about filthy lucre here and now.' She smiled at him again and, once more, he felt quite flushed with his success. 'Something to look forward to on a less formal occasion, eh?' she concluded.

'Unless . . .' Letty added dubiously.

'No, he's not,' Gwinny assured her. 'You're not, are you!' she said to Rick.

'Not what?' He was prepared to be not-anything to keep her smiling like that.

'Not one of those dreadful, stuffy young men who simply won't discuss filthy lucre with the *weaker* sex.'

'Good Lord, no!' he assured her – assured them both.

And across the table Sally, who was only half-listening to her neighbour telling her rather more about the differences between ketches, yawls, and pinnaces than she ever wished to know, seethed with fury that the table in the State Steward's household was five feet wide.

It meant that, even though Rick was directly opposite her, she couldn't kick him back into his senses.

Leah the Forsaken, by Augustin Daly, was a perfect choice for the Dublin Season. It was a sentimental melodrama about the persecution of the Jews in some vaguely Balkan region of Europe, comfortably remote from its audience's everyday habitats. It thus enabled them to feel charitable without obliging them to go out and prove it in their own backyards – or three-thousand-acre estates, as the case may be.

For Judith, Henrietta, and Fergal, it had the additional merit of allowing them to feel immeasurably superior to those gullible patrons who were so taken in by the story that they left the theatre with sodden handkerchiefs spreading great damp patches in their pockets and sleeves. The youngsters, by contrast, wandered up Dame Street on gales of laughter, trying to decide which bit had been funniest.

Henrietta said, 'I loved that speech where Nathan

pretended to be on the same side as the persecutors and yet felt he had to keep reassuring us he wasn't really turning traitor.'

'Yes!' Fergal exclaimed. 'The way he kept trying to speak out of alternate sides of his mouth!' He paused, drew breath, and took up a dramatic posture. ' "Oh I shall breathe easier when these accursed Jews are gone!" *Aside!* "Fear not – I shall see them safe into Bohemia yet!" '

'What I like best,' Judith said when they had got over their laughter, 'is the way they can hustle things along when it suits them. I mean, if you go to *Hamlet*, he can spend fifteen minutes saying, "I wonder if I should kill myself? It wouldn't take long, but, on the other hand, what about the afterlife? Let's not be hasty. Too late now, anyway – here comes Ophelia." Fifteen minutes! But in *this* play, d'you remember that scene where she's waiting for Rudolf? "He is not here! This is the appointed spot, our trysting place, yet he cometh not. He will not come. Guilty thoughts! See how the lightning flashes! Art angry with me, heaven? Terror drives me back! How I tremble! Shall I knock?" – something like that, wasn't it? Shakespeare could make a whole *act* out of that, if not an entire play.'

They were almost at College Green by now, having guffawed themselves out of breath. Gradually the laughing turned to sighs, and the sighs to a wistful kind of half-seriousness. 'And yet,' Fergal said, 'through all its awfulness there shines a kind of innocent . . . I don't know – a kind of pure *goodness*. Remember that bit where Leah wonders whether to abandon old Abraham and all the others who depend on her, because she's in love with Rudolf?'

'Yes,' Judith cut in. 'Where the blind old man tells her, "From the points of thy fingers stream floods of light. When you are by me the stars rise in my firmament. My feet stumble not when you are near." Or words to that effect. That was good.'

'And yet she still knows she's going to desert them. "No longer have I strength and will. I must go! I am the seal upon my Rudolf's heart, though the way lead but to death. I have no choice. I *love!*" '

His voice trembled and broke on the two final words; he discovered what many a would-be sophisticate has learned to his, or her, cost: the power of trashy sentiment to penetrate the stoutest armour and wound the heart – most especially when that heart is already in a somewhat vulnerable condition.

Judith and Henrietta stared at him in dismay; the change in him had been so abrupt, it left them stranded, still on the shores of laughter, unable to reach him.

'Yes!' Henrietta giggled awkwardly and, trying to re-establish their former amused detachment, went on, 'And then she says, "Love! Strong as death and firm as the very hell, thyself a heavenly flame! Thou rulest every power on earth!" ' Her voice, too, began to tremble as she realized she was not going to be able to sustain her mockery. Desperately she continued, 'And then: "Search my heart, oh heaven! And yet I depart and leave them. I love! I love! Beloved, take me to thy arms!" Wasn't that too utterly . . .'

She turned away from them, pretending a sudden interest in the tobacconist's window on the corner of Grafton Street. A discreet yard or two away Judith and Fergal waited for her to collect herself once more. Judith stared at him in the dim gaslight, not dim enough to mask the shamefaced sorrow in his eyes; and she was not yet experienced enough to know that kindness, in such circumstances, is no more than the most refined cruelty. She reached across the small space between them and squeezed his arm. 'Oh, Fergal!' she murmured.

He laughed bravely. 'Sorry! A little adjustment needed

here.' He wanted to compare his behaviour to Henrietta's in the dumb crambo last autumn – so that Judith would know the cause was the same, and that his feeling was just as intense. But Henrietta was within earshot. 'Actually, we laugh at Leah because her passion is too uncomfortably close to our own. D'you think those who cried at her cried because they realized that the days are dead and gone when they themselves could feel such passion?'

She nimbly avoided a direct answer. 'What of those who both laughed *and* cried?'

He stared at the blank windows above the shop façades, as if the answer might be hidden there, cryptically, among all the golden names. In fact, he was remembering with poignant relish the way she had murmured his name and squeezed his arm just now – and he tried to think what he might say to make her do it again. 'We have a foot in both camps, obviously,' he replied. 'We long for the day when this burden of . . . mere sentiment is lifted from us.'

'Ah!' A sudden lump in her throat prevented any real answer; she wondered where all that gaiety and laughter had gone so suddenly. They both turned and fixed their attention upon Henrietta.

'Let's hurry on. I say, Hen, it'll be a lot warmer upstairs at O'Dwyer's – especially for you!' Fergal said.

'Yes, yes!' She bustled towards them, sniffing glutinously and blinking rapidly. 'Sorry, I should know myself better by now – after last September's exhibition! Heigh-ho!' She took Judith's arm. 'D'you know what he's talking about?'

'I'd be a bit of an idiot if I didn't!'

'And you don't mind? You don't think I'm utterly wicked?'

'Yes and no.' Judith chuckled.

Fergal took her other arm but she shook him off and

took his instead. 'Otherwise people will think I've had a drop too much and you're both carrying me,' she explained.

Henrietta laughed immoderately and, when Judith told her it wasn't *that* funny, she said, 'No, I was thinking of something Netty O'Farrelly told me. She said the nuns told all the girls never to walk arm in arm in the street because it only gives the boys the chance they're all waiting for – to take the free arm of one of them.'

Judith grinned at Fergal. 'D'you see, you rascal – you've been found out!'

'It's no more than I deserve.'

His lugubrious solemnity made them laugh again. Judith gave his arm an extra-friendly squeeze to show him she appreciated his effort.

'I wonder how Rick's getting on with Vigo's sisters?' Henrietta mused. 'I'll bet he's placed the poor boy between them.'

It amazed Judith that she herself had not considered that; all she had been able to think of was that Sally was there, too. 'What are they like?' she asked. 'I've never met them.'

'I wonder if Vigo's still awake,' Fergal put in, not wanting to dwell on Rick at all, in case he should blurt out what he had recently heard from Sally's maid. 'He could hardly keep his eyes open at the Drawing Room.'

'It's no wonder. He's up hunting at five every day,' Henrietta explained.

'They're a bit long in the tooth, I suppose?' Judith mused. 'What are their names again?' She added that to show how unconcerned she was.

'Guinevere and Lætitia – though I'm sure they've already permitted him to call them Gwinny and Letty.' Henrietta felt Judith's arm stiffen. She laughed. 'Actually, I think the reason they're both on the shelf is that they're very happy to be there. Poor Vigo just hasn't woken up to the fact at all. Rick's in no danger there. Probably the safest place at that table is slap-bang between the pair of them.'

As they turned into Nassau Street a passing tram drawn by a tired old nag made conversation impossible for a while. Fergal used the enforced silence for a further battle with his conscience; after all, Rick was still, in many ways, his best friend. For the past year Fergal had been enjoying a mild flirtation with Sally's maid, Sheelagh – chiefly as a way of preventing their mutual attraction from getting out of hand. He would say things like, 'Fly with me to far Cathay, my jewel!' which was a way to avoid saying: 'Come to Galway with me for a couple of days, my dear.' But in between such flights of hyperbole they did enjoy the occasional serious conversation; and only last Saturday, Sheelagh had said a thing or two about the crossing from Holyhead on the *Pride of Hibernia* – things that Judith really ought to be told. But not, his sense of honour told him, by Fergal McIver.

Perhaps he could tell Henrietta and leave it to her?

The noise of the tram died away. 'You asked something,' Henrietta said. 'Oh yes, I remember. How old? They're in their early twenties. Gwinny's twenty-four, twenty-five? And Letty's a bit younger. I hope Rick doesn't try showing off any of his knowledge. They're a couple of walking encyclopædias, those two. They'll wipe the floor with him.'

They arrived at the door to O'Dwyer's; the man himself held it open and welcomed them in. 'Was it a good show, then?' he asked amiably.

'Powerful and moving,' Fergal assured him. 'You'd need a heart of stone not to die laughing. McIver's the name. You have a supper room for us, I hope.'

'Indeed, I have, sir. One of your party's already there. The fellow with the toothache. It's the first door to your left above except the door to the broom closet.' He ushered them up ahead of him as he spoke. 'I have to put that in because some people get highly pedantical if I don't. But sure you can't blame them. I'd be the same meself if I opened a door and got buried under a shower of brushes and pans. Will I bring you a plate of loose tongue? It's all that's left at this hour except a pound or two of ham.'

They told him either would do very nicely and he left them to walk the last few yards on their own. 'Loose tongue!' Judith said.

'One commodity that's never short here!' Fergal replied.

'What did he mean about toothache?' Henrietta asked.

Her question was answered at that moment for Percy drew open the door and welcomed them with a mock fanfare: 'Didda-dee dadda-dah!' Round his jaw he was wearing a navvy's kerchief, red with white spots; also a black eyepatch.

'What have you done?' Henrietta asked, half laughing at his behaviour, half distressed at his appearance.

'Disguise!' He whipped them off and flung them on the dumb-waiter.

Judith and Fergal exchanged glances and laughed. Then they helped each other off with their coats while they pretended not to notice the other two embracing. 'Actually, old chap,' Fergal said, with his back to Percy, 'the whole point of disguise is to enable one to pass *unobtrusively* among the populace. I'll bet there's five hundred people somewhere out there who remember seeing you between Kingsbridge Station and O'Dwyer's.'

'You'll have to write that down, I'm afraid,' was the reply. 'It's a bit over my head. Good to see you, Judith. Are you enjoying the Season? I am, suddenly!' He grinned at Henrietta. 'Was the play enjoyable?'

They all answered him at once – and stopped in unison, too. 'We had a rare oul' time,' Fergal said simply.

'We were musing on the way back about the power of sentimental rubbish like that to move one's feelings nonetheless,' Henrietta said. She looked to the others to chip in but they felt they'd had enough of it by then. Their silence left her isolated. What would Percy make of her remark? she wondered. He must be asking himself why, out of all the emotions the play must have aroused in her, she had singled that one out as the most important to share with him. Did she mean it as an oblique comment on their own affair? Desperately she racked her brain for some way of scotching any such notion.

The waiter arrived with their 'loose meat', which proved to be both tongue and ham; also some vegetables, cooked to perfection about an hour earlier. O'Dwyer had a shrewd understanding of his clientèle and knew that those who took supper rooms were only vaguely interested in the actual food. The four ate heartily, drank liberally, laughed immoderately, and almost managed to forget that such a night must have its end like any other.

Fergal finished with a marmite of sardines on toast; the others had fruit. 'Well,' he said, wiping the oil from his lips, 'shall we go down and sip a liqueur in the restaurant, and listen to the band?'

'Oh yes,' Judith said eagerly. It was not a 'band' but a piano and two violins. 'They've been getting tipsier and more inventive by the minute. If we don't go soon, I'm sure they'll pass out entirely.'

All four rose but as they reached the door, Henrietta said to Judith, 'I shan't be a jiffy. You two go on. I just want a brief word with Percy.'

Judith was halfway down the stairs before she realized what was actually happening; Henrietta had sounded so convincing. It made her angry, though whether at herself for being taken in, or at Henrietta for being so devious, or at the world in general, whose rules made such stratagems necessary, she could not have said.

Fergal was quick to sense it in her, though. 'I hate it too,' he said.

The feeling deserted her as swiftly as it had come. 'Don't let's be too hard on them,' she cautioned. 'The real sin was committed by those who pressed her into a loveless marriage.'

The room was long, though not particularly narrow; it was, in fact, three rooms knocked into one – hence the three bright fires and the inviting alcoves beside each. One was empty and they took it without even consulting each other. The trio was trying to force the ample curves of a Viennese waltz into the corset of an Irish jig. 'Oh, isn't it cosy!' Judith exclaimed. 'We should have eaten down here and left them to it.'

When she spoke she did not intend that word *it* to have the precise and graphic reference it immediately assumed. Fergal, in the act of seating himself, froze momentarily and stared at the tablecloth; he went on staring at it after he had sat down. Desperately she racked her brains for some way of showing him she hadn't meant *that* – without revealing that she was now aware that he *had* thought she meant *that*!

Of course, it was impossible. So should she now go on as if she *had* meant it? A little imp of mischief whispered 'Why not?' in her ear. 'I never know whether to feel sorry for those two,' she said, 'or envious. I don't know about Percy – one never knows with men – but this *affaire* has consumed Henrietta's whole life. She lives in a whirl of clandestine messages, plots, subterfuges, connivances . . . To me it seems dreadful, and yet she says she feels alive for the first time in her life.'

He wondered if she understood what Henrietta and Percy were actually doing up there – Lord, it must be immediately overhead, in fact! One never knew with women. 'What d'you mean?' he asked. ' "One never knows with men"?'

'Maybe men do,' she replied. 'Know how other men are thinking and feeling – though I sometimes doubt it. D'you know how Percy really feels towards Hen? Would he talk to you about it?'

'Does she talk to you about it?'

'Yes, but I'd know how she feels even if she didn't. Could you say the same about Percy?'

He shrugged awkwardly. 'We're not brought up like that, are we? We're taught to hide all those soft feelings. God, who ever called them *soft*!'

' "Man's love is of man's life a thing apart",' she quoted. 'Is that Byron?'

'It's not true, whoever wrote it.'

'Not true of Percy, you mean.'

'Of any man. Of me.'

The waiter interrupted at that moment. Fergal ordered a whiskey, Judith a crème de menthe, which she had never tasted before; someone at the Drawing Room had recommended it as being very 'in'.

This intrusion of the everyday world released enough of the tension between them to enable him to go on in a voice that was almost matter-of-fact: 'We were talking about hiding our feelings and all that. Well, I think it's wrong. Why should I go on hiding the fact that I think you're the most wonderful girl who ever lived?'

She closed her eyes and held her breath.

'Why should I go on hiding the fact that you are more to me than all the world? "From the points of thy fingers stream floods of light. When you are by me the stars rise in my firmament." ' He laughed unconvincingly. 'Or words to that effect!'

She reached across the table and squeezed his arm. 'Oh, Fergal!'

* * *

Fergal returned to his studies. Rick found he was having such a good time at the Dublin Season he talked Aunt Bill into persuading Uncle Hereward to let him stay on a further three weeks, at least until after the St Patrick's Ball. Lord Vigo, who was already pleased at the friendship which seemed to have sprung up between his difficult sisters and the young inheritor of Castle Moore, was so delighted at this extension that he pulled every string within his considerable reach to get Rick invited to the more exclusive dances and suppers in the Throne Room at the Castle. Tickets to the State Ball and the St Patrick's Ball were fairly easy to come by, but invitations to events in the Throne Room were like gold. Only the very cream of society was invited – a mere two or three hundred at most. They said you could wash every gurrier in Dublin clean in the tears that were shed behind closed curtains in Merrion Square after the mounted orderlies with the invitations had passed the house by.

Much to Judith's dismay, the McIvers, pulling their quite different strings, managed to get Sally in as well.

Aunt Bill knew her duty, which was to keep an eye upon Rick on behalf of all the family. Unfortunately, it was also her duty to keep her other eye on Henrietta – a feat that became impossible when one of her charges was at Dublin Castle and the other in St Stephen's Green. Her son Arthur, the octogenarian Irish Guards major of thirty who had ruined Rick's week in London, came to the rescue. He recommended a friend of his, one Justin O'Donovan, a somewhat older captain in the Royal Dublin Fusiliers, who seemed to be at a loose end most evenings. This worthy officer was induced to squire Judith, chaperoned by Henrietta, to one or other of the numerous private parties and dances that people gave on such occasions, to explain why they had regretfully been obliged to turn down the invitation from the Castle.

After twenty minutes in Captain O'Donovan's presence,

Henrietta and Judith knew exactly why he 'seemed to be at a loose end most evenings'. Despite the fact that he had had forty-six years to observe the world and its ways, the very idea of fun seemed quite beyond his grasp. The only thing he positively enjoyed was his duty, and he enjoyed it with an enthusiasm that put the lotus eaters of the Dublin Season to shame. Aunt Bill twigged the fact at once, of course, and persuaded him it was his duty, as her son's friend, to look after *her* friend Judith Carty; after that, the Atlantic Ocean itself couldn't stop him.

Even Aunt Bill, however, had to allow that his punctilio was rather tedious. For instance, when he was to escort Judith to the first dance, at the de Veres' in Aylesbury Road, he required at least four days' notice so that he could call and leave cards and have them properly returned. Then on the afternoon of the affair he took Aunt Bill's carriage and coachman over the route, timing it with his stopwatch to make sure they would arrive at the precise moment on the invitation. He drew to a halt outside the house and inspected the approach through his field glasses, counting the number of steps up to the front door and making a careful note of any puddles that might not be so apparent in the dark.

He looked as dashing in his uniform – and was, indeed, as handsome – as any young debutante had a right to expect of any military man; yet there was nothing behind that façade. It was as if he had consulted all the best authorities on how a young(ish) army officer ought to appear and had then obliged them by turning into that paradigm. He danced divinely, but without any passion whatever. 'He might have been made by Doctor Coppelius,' someone commented to Judith. His conversation was polished but all on the surface; there was no depth to his glosses on the world. What the man himself was like, no one had the faintest idea. As Henrietta said, 'There's simply no way into him. There's no chink in his devotion to etiquette. He wears it like a seamless armour.'

'I wonder . . .' Judith mused.

And after the first excruciating evening in his company, trying to match her behaviour to his expectations, she realized she had nothing to lose and so started testing Henrietta's verdict.

'Why d'you bother sending cards, Captain O'Donovan?' she asked on their way to their second dance, which was at the Talbots' in Malahide Castle. 'Sure most people just use them for bookmarks.'

He laughed – seven hees and a haw – not thinking she could possibly be serious; she could almost hear the click of the mental stopwatch that brought it to an end. 'Oh, Miss Carty. What a tease you are!' he chided.

After several further attempts in that vein, she realized that simple iconoclasm would get her nowhere. It occurred to her then that she must burden him with a real problem, something for which no book on etiquette could possibly have prepared him. She picked her moment with care.

Supper was served in the form of a buffet. He found her a place away from the draught – which was not easy at Malahide – and consulted her wishes minutely on the choice of what he called 'viands', which he brought to her with the maximum of expedition and the minimum of fuss. And then he stayed at her side, ready to bring her second helpings or new viands, as she wished. He had done the same at the de Veres'; and, if he continued to follow the pattern of that first evening, he would now keep up a flawless patter concerning the weather, the Season, the concerts, the orchestra, and the weather – never mind that he had run them into the ground at the previous dance. And when these palled there would no doubt be safe excursions into the history of the Talbots and the Royal Dublin Fusiliers.

Judith's spirit rebelled at last. She seized the initiative and told him how truly grateful she was for the kindly and considerate way he had consented to escort her, not just to the de Veres' but to Malahide, as well. He, of course, replied that the privilege was entirely his.

'And there you show your kindness again,' she continued, adding, with an enigmatic smile, 'But perhaps I am a *little* more adult than you suppose.'

Alarm flashed briefly behind his eyes. 'Ah!' he said.

'For instance,' she pressed on, 'I am well aware that an important and busy person like yourself – a man of the world with, I'm sure, a wide circle of friends – such a man, I say, does not leap for joy at the prospect of taking an ignorant young female with no experience of life to the millionth ball of his otherwise rich and interesting career. Be honest now, dear Captain – we have surely broken the ice with each other far enough for that?'

He was relieved that by 'adult' she hadn't meant what he had, to his shame, supposed; but he was still a little nervous of this new line. She seemed to be fishing for something – but what? 'Forgive me if I seem to differ with you, Miss Carty,' he responded. 'But a military man can have too much of the bluff and hearty company of his comrades. I find the prospect of escorting a pretty and vivacious young lady (for such you are, let me add) to an occasion like this is one of unalloyed . . . oh, what's the word?'

'Bliss?' she offered in disbelief.

'Contentment! Yes. Never think otherwise.'

'All the same, you must have such a vast wealth of experience, such a deep understanding of people by now . . . I'm sure I must constantly be voicing what seem to you to be immature and shallow thoughts.'

She *was* fishing for something; the shape of it was beginning to loom in his mind. 'Such a notion has never once occurred to me, Miss Carty,' he assured her eagerly. 'In fact – I speak now with some diffidence – but I have been struck by the remarkable maturity of some of the things you have said. Your seriousness of mind is beyond question.'

She smiled at him as if he had brought a reprieve from some awful judgement. 'D'you truly think so?'

'Truly.'

'From anyone else I would think it mere flattery, Captain O'Donovan. But I know you are as incapable of that as . . . well, as I thought *I* was incapable of uttering a single remark of any consequence. When I contemplate the wealth of experience that lies behind your opinion, I simply quail. How did you come by it?' She lowered her voice and asked sympathetically, 'Was it bought with a great deal of pain?'

'Pain!' he echoed, alarmed again.

'Yes. I see it was,' she continued. 'You need not hide it from me, dear Captain O'Donovan. I find I am no stranger to pain, either.'

'Really?' He eased a finger round his collar.

'And I think I see in you a fellow sufferer. Am I not right?'

Looking into her amazing eyes, so limpid, so all-seeing, he told himself she could not possibly mean what she appeared to mean. Not even his closest comrade knew of it, so how could she? 'Really?' he repeated in even greater alarm.

'Indeed,' she assured him. 'You claim to see in me a vivacious young lady. Let me tell you – my heart is almost breaking even as we speak.' And now the floodgates were open. She told him of Rick and how he had adored her since childhood, of the feelings she had more recently come to have for him, of Sally McIver . . . 'Why, even at this minute he may be holding her in his arms, whirling her around the Throne Room, gazing into each other's eyes as you are gazing into mine – or, rather, *not* as you are gazing into mine – *not* with the wisdom of your years, *not* with the compassion I see my commonplace little tale has stirred in you.'

'The brat deserves a flogging!' he said sternly. In some distant corridor of mind he heard another O'Donovan coughing with disapproval, but he was so caught up in the poor girl's predicament he paid the fellow no heed.

'Oh no!' Judith hid her exultation that she had succeeded in rattling him so far out of his shell.

'Oh, yes!' he asserted. 'Believe me, Miss Carty, were I in that young whipper-snapper's shoes, no crusty old military bachelor in his dotage would be permitted to escort you across the road – let alone to a glittering occasion like this. And I would tear up invitations to the Throne Room, to Buckingham Palace, the Kaiserhof, the Winter Palace, and every other royal establishment in the world for that privilege.'

'*Dear* Captain O'Donovan!' she murmured, leaning across the small gap that now separated them to kiss him warmly on the cheek. 'You know exactly what to say to cheer up a silly little girl like me. Come! Dance with me the rest of the evening. While you are here, I shall not even *think* of Rick.'

Aunt Bill was especially pensive at breakfast the following morning. The moment Judith and Henrietta appeared she pounced: 'That Captain O'Donovan seemed in rather an ebullient mood last night?' Her rising tone made it a question they could not ignore.

'Justin?' Judith replied offhandedly. 'Did he? Oh dear – kedgeree *and* devilled kidneys. May I take half of each? I can't possibly be expected to choose between them.'

'Justin?' Rick echoed in an irritable tone.

'I was about to say the same,' Aunt Bill put in. 'What has been going on?'

Judith and Henrietta burst out laughing; they had spent a happy hour before going to sleep last night simply relishing their triumph. Now Judith let Henrietta explain; it would carry more weight with Rick than if she blew her own coals. But when Henrietta had finished, Judith claimed the last word: 'We simply couldn't *bear* his stuffiness a minute longer. One of us had to do something. And actually, d'you know, he's really quite an interesting person once you get beneath the crust. I think there's a broken heart somewhere there in his past. I wouldn't be surprised.'

Rick turned to his aunt, expecting to share a smile at this giddy romanticism; to his surprise she was grim of face. After breakfast she called Henrietta into the morning room. 'Now tell me straight, dear,' she said, 'no prevarication – what has been going on?'

'Nothing's been "going on", if you mean *that*,' Henrietta replied.

'Something must have happened. Crusty old bachelors don't permit pretty young debutantes to take a liberty with their names for no reason. Good heavens, I never called your Uncle Wonky by his Christian name until we were married! *Uncle* Justin I could just about accept. I suppose he calls her plain Judith now!'

Henrietta smiled. 'I don't think he calls her *plain* anything, Aunt Bill. Between you and me, I believe he's slightly smitten.'

Her aunt drew a sharp breath. 'Oh dear! And I thought there was absolutely no fear of that. I mean, the whole point of choosing him – I most particularly requested Arthur to pick me the dullest, driest, correctest gentleman he knew. And Captain O'Donovan seemed perfect for the part.'

'Too perfect. That was the trouble.'

'I simply don't understand what . . .'

'Well, when he opined – and, believe me, nobody in

the whole world can *opine* better – when he opined for the ninety-tenth time that he thought this spell of settled weather would break soon, we decided that nobody could possibly have so much surface and lack any interior. The rest followed, as I explained at breakfast just now.'

Aunt Bill pinched the bridge of her nose in irritation. 'Well, it'll just have to stop. No more Captain O'Donovan. He's a broken reed.'

Henrietta was about to protest when she saw doubt and hesitation creep into the other's eyes; she knew her aunt intimately enough by now to leave well alone. In fact, Aunt Bill was recalling that she might still require further favours of her son – at least while Rick was over the water, potentially exposed to the gambling hells and fleshpots of London. He might be less than cooperative if she were to treat one of his brother officers so brusquely. Henrietta guessed something of the sort when Aunt Bill concluded her brief reverie with the outburst: 'Oh, this wretched necessity to conduct the business of the world through *men*!' Then, not unexpectedly, she turned on her niece: 'And as for you, you're supposed to keep an eye out for that sort of thing. That's what you're there *for*!'

'That's not fair, Aunt,' Henrietta protested. 'How can I, an utter nobody, stop a gentleman twice my age and with quite a position in society from flirting with his dance partner? And that's all it is – a bit of mild flirtation.'

'You do it by force of character!' Aunt Bill snapped.

'But I have no "character" left, dear Aunt.' Henrietta smiled acidly. 'You have seen to that.'

'You ungrateful . . .' Aunt Bill reined in her anger. 'Don't you realize that what small shreds of character you may have retained are *entirely* due to my intervention? If you and the O'Farrelly youth had been permitted to continue with your wretched *affaire*, you would now be living in exile in some grubby little French pensionat. You wouldn't even be able to show your face in *Ireland*.'

Henrietta turned from her and stared out of the window. Every sensible part of her mind was advising her to let it go – her aunt and Society would always win an open confrontation. But the love of her life had been called 'a wretched *affaire*' and now her dander was up. 'Have a care, Aunt,' she murmured.

'*I* have a care!'

'Yes. You do not know how close I am to . . .' Caution withheld the obvious conclusion to her threat.

Caution must have been on the very air, for Aunt Bill drew breath for an angry reply – and then withheld it, too. 'You can have no idea how foolish that would be,' she said evenly.

The surprising lack of menace in this remark deflated Henrietta's anger a little; she replied, in equally bald tones, 'Oh yes I have.' She turned and faced her aunt, to show her how truly serious she was. 'My head is ringing with voices telling me what an utter fool I am. My conscience holds up pictures of myself making solemn vows before God at the altar . . . of little Yolande. And my pleasure-loving self reminds me of my fine house in Belgravia, of my generous allowance . . . et cetera and et cetera. My head is one long bombardment of common sense, morality, and self-interest. But it does no good. The moment there's a lull, I find myself just standing there with this great emptiness in front of me. An emptiness called Percy. A space where he ought to be, but isn't. How d'you bombard an empty space, eh? D'you know of a magic bullet that kills off nothingness?'

Aunt Bill had been thinking rapidly all during this extraordinary speech. She saw clearly that the usual threats and clichés simply would not wash. There was nothing for it but the truth. She took her courage in both hands and delivered it as succinctly as she could. 'My poor darling!' She laid a gentle finger on Henrietta's sleeve and pressed her to sit in the window seat. She herself did likewise, facing her. 'Harold's a man of the world . . .'

But Henrietta, sensing she was about to be cudgelled with kindness, flared up again. 'You mean he goes with ladies of the town!'

Aunt Bill's face was unreadable. For five very long seconds she made no response. Then she said quietly, 'Does he!' Her tone was dismissive, as if Henrietta had announced that the man breathed, or consumed three meals a day. 'Well, that doesn't entitle *you* to start behaving like one of them, too. No, no, *listen*! I know you don't think you're behaving like one of them. And in my heart of hearts, perhaps I don't think so either. But I'm not here to tell you my own private thoughts.' She laughed weakly. 'Good heavens! If Society was run according to our *private* thoughts, we should be worse than Ancient Rome at the very height of its decadence. I'm sure half the married women in England would privately applaud and envy you.'

'Three-quarters.'

'All right, three-quarters. But publicly – *collectively* – they'd all clamour to cast the first stone.'

'But that's hypocrisy!'

'Oh dear, oh dear, Henrietta! Where did I go wrong with you? You're supposed to have made *that* startling discovery at Judith's age. By the time you're twenty-three . . .'

'Not quite.'

'By the time you're twenty-*two* then, you're supposed to have discovered how to cope with it. I mean, how to use what you call "hypocrisy" to your advantage. Why not call it "magic" instead? They say you can't have your cake and eat it. But you can, you know – if you use a little magic.'

Henrietta shifted uncomfortably. 'Why did you start saying that Harold is a man of the world?'

'Because he knows how the world works. If you were to give him two good, undoubted heirs, he'd give you no trouble, in return. Daughters are all very well in their way, but you give him two sons – and not a shadow of a doubt about who fathered them – and he'll be a different man.'

It was such a bleak, sensible – and unlikely – prospect that Henrietta almost burst into tears.

Aunt Bill, suspecting something of that sort, concluded gently, 'Remember Penelope waiting for Ulysses? A woman's greatest weapon has always been her patience, her power of endurance. In the end we always win. It is only those who go for the quick kill, the easy triumph, who fall by the wayside.'

Henrietta fished around for something to say and found all avenues covered. She yielded with a hopeless shrug. 'I suppose so. But how desolate!'

'Oh?' Her aunt's eyebrows arched in surprise. 'Is it supposed to be otherwise? I never yet met a woman of the world who thought so.' She smiled. 'And now we really have to return to the problem of Judith and the Captain. You are quite, quite sure it is nothing more than a mild flirtation?'

'What else could it be? Look at the difference in their ages! And a military man like that, too – a man who's successfully repelled every advance for the past twenty-odd years! He isn't seriously going to fall in love now. Not even with a beauty like Judith.'

'Ho, ho! I have known stranger things than that!' Aunt Bill was not at all reassured. 'I have known men of *sixty* to fall in love – as they imagine – and with women of sixty, too, never mind your giddy young gels – and start behaving in ways that would have filled them with shame at sixteen. No, my dear, I think I shall forgo the pleasures of dining at the Castle – or, rather, the pleasures of letting the fact drop here and there afterwards – and accompany you to the next private dance.'

When Aunt Bill collared Henrietta and dragged her off to the morning room, Rick raised an eyebrow at Judith and asked what she thought it was all about. Her only answer was a shrug, implying that she had no idea – a lie she did not wish to commit to actual words. He suggested a walk around Stephen's Green. 'Let's make the most of this settled weather while it lasts,' he added.

She closed her eyes and clenched her fists, as if struggling to suppress a quiet scream.

'What now?' he asked. 'What did I say?'

'You were beginning to sound like Captain O'Donovan.'

'Captain who?' His eyes were full of mock innocence. 'Oh, you mean Justin!'

'Ha ha! Sarcasm is the lowest form of wit, Rick. I'll be down here waiting in ten minutes. Try and mend your humour meanwhile.'

She almost wished she hadn't said it for, when she returned, he was so forcibly jocular it was even more painful than his sarcasm. However, he was like one of the new lifeboats – you could rock him this way or that as hard as you liked and he'd very soon get back on an even keel. 'I'm not really annoyed,' he said, taking her arm as they crossed the road to the Green. 'Though it's a bit of a facer, hearing you call an old crock like that by his Christian name. I suppose he calls you Judith, too?'

'I'm surprised you remember it yourself, Rick. I was beginning to feel quite the stranger with you.'

He laughed and squeezed her arm. 'What was it somebody once said about sarcasm? Oh, just look at the daffodils! It's twice as many as yesterday. We'll pick some on the way back.'

'We will not!' She glanced sidelong and caught him grinning at the grass. Her annoyance with him evaporated – or, rather, transferred partly to herself. 'Oh, Rick,' she said, 'why do we snipe at each other like this?'

'I don't know.'

'It makes me so afraid.'

'Afraid?' The word seemed to surprise him.

'Yes. Of the future – our future. Is that what we're going to descend to? I'd hate that. I'd almost rather not . . .' She hesitated to round off the thought.

'I know,' he said.

'Do you?'

'It grows out of a sort of . . . anger. It comes over me every now and then.'

'Against me?' The day was suddenly disjointed for her; she seemed to be listening to herself and him as if she were no more than an eavesdropper.

He stopped and pulled her to face him. He raised her hand to his lips and kissed it, as if he wanted to give her that reassurance before he continued. 'Not against you – but against us, perhaps. I know, we both know, that you and I are . . . I mean, there can be no one else for me. And you feel the same about me, don't you?'

She nodded and watched him, hardly daring to blink.

'And yet sometimes I feel a terrible sort of . . . anger's the only word – or it's half anger and half impatience. Is there a single word for that?' He chuckled. 'Gwinny would know!'

'Gwinny!' she said angrily. 'Gwinny and Letty! Letty and Gwinny! That's all we hear nowadays!'

'Actually, they're rather nice. You'll like them when you get to know them.'

She gave an ironic laugh. 'Since I'm the very last

person their brother would invite to dinner, that's hardly likely, is it!'

'Well . . .' He hesitated. 'Darn it, we should have brought some bread for the ducks.' He half-turned to go back to the house but she grasped his arm and propelled him along their original line. 'What were you going to say?' she asked.

'Too late,' he told her. 'They've spotted us. Talk of the devil – that's why I suggested going back home.' He raised his voice and called, 'Hallo! What a pleasant surprise.'

Two young ladies were walking towards them, one on the tall side, the other slightly plump and jolly. Their faces, being red and blue with the cold, added a further touch of colour to the spring morning. 'Hallo, Rick,' cried one of them. 'I said you lived at this end. Gwinny was sure it was the other.'

'I don't believe you've met Miss Carty,' he said. And to Judith, 'Miss Dalton and Miss Lætitia Dalton.'

Brittle smiles bared teeth all round.

She said, 'Lord Vigo's sisters. I'm so pleased we meet at last. We've heard so much about you. In fact, I was saying as much to Rick not two minutes ago. I expect your ears were burning? They look as if they were.'

'I'm not sure my ears haven't dropped off,' Gwinny replied. 'I hope you've heard nothing to our discredit, Miss Carty.'

'Quite the contrary, Miss Dalton. In fact, Rick was hunting for a particular word and he said you'd know it like a flash.'

'Ah!' Letty put in. 'Then Rick's ears were surely burning, too, for we were discussing him. We were hoping he was looking for rather more than *one* word.'

She glanced at Gwinny, who added, 'Yes, about five thousand of them, in fact. How is it coming along, Rick?'

He stared miserably across the grass. 'Do let's pick

some of those daffodils,' he said. 'They're only going to waste there.'

'Has he not told you?' Letty asked Judith. 'We're launching a new Irish quarterly and Rick has agreed to back us with lots of filthy lucre and also to write the main article for our first number.'

'Oh, that!' Judith said, as if he had mumbled something about it over breakfast.

'We were on our way to Hely's to get . . . paper and ink and things, you know,' Rick told them earnestly.

'What was the word?' Gwinny asked.

It was a moment before Judith realized what she meant. 'Oh, a sort of halfway stage between anger and impatience.'

'Querulousness,' Gwinny replied at once.

'Peevishness,' Letty offered.

Despite her annoyance, Judith laughed. Besides, the chance was too good to miss. 'Petulance!' she exclaimed.

'Perfect!' Gwinny told her.

'*Le mot juste*!' Letty conceded.

They all laughed and turned to Rick.

'Hely's,' he said. 'Le mot even-more-*juste*!'

Gwinny continued: 'And after you've got your – what was it? – paper and ink and things – though, speaking personally, I'd recommend pencil and an indiarubber – let's walk up Grafton Street and pretend our maga is a huge success and we've got all the money in the world so we don't have to avert our gaze as we stroll past those sumptuous shop windows!'

'Yes,' Letty agreed, 'and then we'll try that new coffee house everyone's talking about in South Anne Street.'

Their jollity was so infectious, and Judith had been so starved of that commodity for weeks now, that she felt all her resistance and prejudices melting away. 'It sounds splendid,' she replied, moving between them and linking arms.

They fell into step as they set off on the diagonal path

across the Green, leaving Rick to follow. When, after a couple of dozen paces, he had made no comment, Judith looked back at him over her shoulder.

'Amn't I after telling you!' he called out happily.

The man in Hely's was plainly reluctant to deliver so pitiful an order, and Rick was certainly not going to let himself be seen carrying a parcel in Dublin during the Season; he said he'd send a maid for it later. Gwinny stayed behind and had a word with him, however, and when she rejoined them in Nassau Street she said it was all right, they would deliver after all.

'What did you tell him?' Judith asked.

'I told him I was the editrix of the *New Hibernian Quarterly* – though he plainly hadn't heard of us – and that in my opinion Rick would soon be in the very forefront of Irish writers. Also that, like any other Irishman, he has a long memory and any little favour done now would not be forgotten. Or the opposite.'

Judith laughed as loud as the rest, but it did just cross her mind that Lord Vigo's sisters were rather taking over Rick's life.

Five minutes later, however, she had revised this opinion yet again. She remembered what Henrietta had told her about these two females – that they were quite happy to be on the shelf and that Rick was safer with them (from her, Judith's, point of view) than with any other female in Dublin. At the same time she had taken it for the sort of comfort one doles out almost without thinking to a friend in distress; now she decided it was probably true, in fact.

It brought her comfort in one way, and discomfort in another – comfort in the thought that, formidable as they might be, they were not rivals with her for Rick – discomfort in the logical conclusion that theirs was the natural behaviour of women who were *not* baiting any hooks, *not* trimming their sails to the wind. They were women confidently stepping out along their own chosen path through life. They were, in fact, the living embodiment of that woman-portrait she had been trying to paint for Henrietta the other morning.

The differences were subtle. It did not make them strident and opinionated, for instance; yet they always had an opinion ready – on this dress, that piece of silver, or whatever was on display in the shop window before them – and they always voiced it with confidence. Mentally they spent almost two hundred pounds before they reached the turning into South Anne Street, and all without crossing the threshold of a single shop. With some chagrin Judith realized that, if she had been given two hundred pounds – and a week to make up her mind – she could hardly have returned with a better set of trophies. She began to pray that Henrietta had been right, for she would rather face competition from a dozen pretty little Sally McIvers, all throwing themselves at Rick's feet, than this formidable pair, who simply treated him as a friendly equal.

The influence they could exercise over him if they set their minds to it became apparent when, as they seated themselves in the new coffeehouse, Letty announced that, as she had been the one to suggest this refreshment, she would pay for it, too; they were to consider themselves her guests.

This went so against the grain for Rick that Judith expected him to walk out in protest. Yet within a couple of minutes they had persuaded him that his ideas of chivalry had been around in the days before the Ark – and should never have come back out of it when it returned to dry land . . . that if he insisted on paying he would be a bitter disappointment to them and was No Fit Person to be writing in an advanced-thinking maga like the *New Hibernian Quarterly*. And to Judith's amazement he yielded with hardly a murmur and did not even twitch when Letty took out her purse and paid for the lot – an outrageous bill of a shilling, just for four coffees and four sticky buns.

Slightly against her will she felt herself being drawn to these two strange sisters and their advanced ideas. What she liked most of all was the fact that, despite their superior knowledge about almost everything, they never gave themselves airs. They treated her as one of them – or, in fact, they treated themselves as two of *her*. And before they rose from the table they were, naturally, Gwinny and Letty and Judith.

As they returned to the street Rick offered to escort them home to the Castle. Gwinny declined very demurely but the look in her eyes left him in no doubt that that sort of behaviour, too, should have stayed in the Ark. They walked as far as Grafton Street together, a matter of a hundred yards or so. Just before they parted, Gwinny said, 'So you will have this article finished by the time we come down to Keelity, Rick? We'll bring everything else with us and we want to lay it all out before we go back.'

He assured them fervently that he would.

Letty, watching Judith's response to this, said, 'Didn't you know?'

'I was about to tell her, in fact,' he cut in. Then, to Judith, 'I've decided to put my foot down a bit about being bundled off to England the moment the St Pat's Ball is over. I don't mind the odd month or two over there – even four or five months well spread out. But Castle Moore can't be left to the likes of McGrath.'

'And King,' she said.

'Just so. There'll be battle royal with Aunt Bill, but I intend to win.'

Judith was, of course, overjoyed to hear it. But even then, though she was too happy to speak, she was aware that he would not have been so positive if he and she had been walking alone about the Green; he was assisted to it by his audience – especially by this particular audience.

She was both grateful to them and resentful of the need to be so.

Letty cut in across her reverie. 'There is only one little puzzle left to clear up,' she said.

They turned to her. 'What?'

'Which of you was impatient and which was angry!'

The St Patrick's Ball of 1888 actually fell on St Patrick's Day – the third Saturday in March. By another happy coincidence it marked not only the formal culmination of the Dublin Season but also the true high-water-mark of its gaiety. Like all the State Balls it was held in St Patrick's Hall, the longest, widest, loftiest, and in every way the most magnificent of the state apartments at the Castle. The party from St Stephen's Green had taken the precaution of visiting it on one of the open days so that they would not be tempted on the night to gawk and utter vulgar exclamations of delight. Even so, when the moment duly arrived and they saw those walls of white and gold, bathed in the brilliance of over ten thousand candles, it still managed to take the breath away.

All down one side the windows alternated with the crossed banners of the Order of St Patrick and other forms of heraldic achievement; their rich, sombre colours made a vivid contrast with the brilliant throng on the floor below – the men resplendent in their uniforms or ornate court dress and the women in their festive gowns and glittering jewellery. On the facing side, vast mirrors in gilded frames took the place of the windows. The divisions between them were marked by richly moulded Corinthian pilasters. Though three times as tall as a man, they barely rose above half the height of the chamber for they supported tier upon tier of inward-curving cornices, entablatures, and cavettos, which, taken as a whole, formed a mighty frame to three colossal ceiling paintings – St Patrick converting the Druids; Henry II receiving the submission of the Irish Chiefs; and George III being supported by Liberty and Justice – and incidentally giving the lie to those damned republicans who held that neither quality was to be found in the whole length and breadth of Ireland.

The opening cotillion of any other State Ball was usually rather formal and stuffy. The area of the floor nearest the throne was cordoned off behind a silken rope, inside which Their Excellencies and a few other moguls danced the State Quadrille while the rest of the world looked on. Only when the last curtsy had answered the final bow was the rope taken away and the floor opened for the Viennese waltzes, the one-steps, the gavottes, the lancers, the polkas, the reels, and the Sir Roger de Coverleys for the enjoyment of which some fifteen hundred guests were willing to put up with the discomforts, the snubs, and the ruinous expense of the entire Season. The Queen herself had said that you could comb the length and breadth of her empire and you'd not find an affair that was both gayer *and* more regal than an Irish State Ball.

But the opening of the St Pat's was the best of all – a truly Irish occasion. Without sacrificing any of the pomp and magnificence of such an affair, it was nonetheless infused with all the sparkle and good humour that only an Irish crowd can furnish. In place of the State Quadrille, Liddell's Orchestra played a brisk Country Dance full of old Irish jigs and reels – a prelude to a night-long ferment of laughter and light, of animated talk and infectious music, of stamping feet and swishing muslin.

Simply everyone was there, of course. If you were not bankrupt, ill, convalescing, dying, or in your dotage – or, like Aunt Bill's cousin Catherine, a fanatical gardener –

you had to be at the St Pat's Ball. It was where you heard enough new gossip to carry you through the London Season, which, for many of those present, began the following week. It was where successful Dianas showed off their new diamond rings while their unsuccessful sisters aimed whatever arrows were left in Cupid's quiver at whichever targets came within range. It was where ambitious but poor young gentlemen discreetly swopped data about dowries and even more discreetly perused each bearer of such bounty, wondering if they could face bed and breakfast with her for the next half-century or more. It was where desperate and difficult young ladies, up for their third Season running, blinded themselves with belladonna and smiled till their teeth and their hearts ached, only to watch Time walk off arm-in-arm with Hope when, yet again, the dance was done. It was, in short, the promoter of aspiration, the impresario of anticipation, and the gravedigger of expectation – all in one.

For the two unmarried Dalton sisters it was yet another chance to kill a couple of birds with one stone – to find contributors and backers for their 'maga' and to *fail* to find suitors for their hands. For Sally McIver it was the first chance of the Season to test Rick's feelings for her when Judith was no longer an absent spectre at their feast. For her brother Fergal it was the first chance of the Season to test Judith's feelings for him when Rick was no longer an absent spectre at *their* feast. For Rick it was yet another chance to enjoy his outstanding discovery of the Season: the fact that dancing no longer embarrassed him. Indeed, he adored everything about it – the gay music, the inane chatter, the perfume, the swirl of bodies, the rustle of silks and muslin, the soft embrace of candlelight on bare shoulders and décolletage.

Judith filled her programme before the end of the first set, except that she kept one dance in each section free for Rick. But, as he pointed out when he asked for no more than the last waltz, there'd be dozens of dances down in Keelity where they'd be together all evening; this was their one great opportunity to mingle with people they'd never otherwise meet. She couldn't deny the truth of his words but she regretted the relish with which he spoke them. And it was the sight of him gliding so gracefully round the floor with Sally, both of them laughing their heads off at some trivial witticism that probably wasn't at all funny, which must have induced her to let Fergal claim most of those now vacant dances. He just happened to be there at the time and he just happened to ask.

Three were still unclaimed at the start of the next set, when Rick led Letty Dalton on to the floor. It was all very well for those two girls to give themselves airs and behave as if they would run a thousand miles from an altar – it didn't prevent them from flirting with anything in uniform or court pantaloons. Indeed, they seemed to think that their unproclaimed vows of celibacy gave them carte blanche to behave in the most intimate way with every man in the room. Had it not been for the sight of Letty dancing with Rick, however, she would never have given all three remaining dances to Captain O'Donovan, who happened to ask for them at that moment.

Fergal claimed her for the first of the seven dances to which she had now committed herself with him. The congestion of the crowd required all their attention for a while.

'Penny for 'em,' Fergal said when they were out of the ruck again.

'I was thinking about why we set so much store by mere appearances.'

The ease with which the lie tripped off her tongue amazed her. A younger Judith would have told him the truth – that she had been thinking of all the crosscurrents between her and him, her and Rick, him and Rick . . . Was it a mark of her growing maturity – to lie so fluently? Did truly grown-up people *never* tell the truth, perhaps, but only come out with what suited their own interests?

She thought at once of Aunt Bill. It sent a shiver down her spine to imagine that everything the older women had ever said to her might have been either a lie or, at best, a variety of self-serving half-truth.

Her own mother, too – had she done the same?

Perhaps even Henrietta?

She felt suddenly alone, shorn of friends in an alien world, a world filled with people who wished only to manipulate and use her. She heard herself chatting away with Fergal about the 'skin-deepness' of beauty – giving out dogmas that could have been culled from ancient sermons, ladies' magazines, or old classroom homilies – and marvelled at the animation of her voice and the firmness of 'her' opinions.

Why did she feel so alone all of a sudden? Why, in the midst of this glittering crowd, gossiping so amiably, dancing with such pleasure, did she feel so isolated?

Rick, now partnered by Gwinny, swirled past at that moment; his eye caught hers across the crowded floor and he winked. Her intimation of loncliness lifted as suddenly as it had fallen upon her; but a snatch of Gwinny's conversation lingered in her mind's ear: '. . . and we have a quotation for the typesetting from . . .' The rest was drowned by Liddell's violins.

Of itself it meant nothing, but in Judith's ear it fell like seed on fertile ground – and never had the ground been more fertile than at this particular moment. She saw in the starkest contrast the one great difference between herself and a woman like the Hon. Guinevere Dalton – why it was possible for her to feel she was nothing but a pawn of others' machinations and to doubt that such a feeling ever crossed the outer threshold of Gwinny's mind. For Gwinny had a genuine purpose in life, a goal outside herself, something real out there in the real world. If she achieved it, the result would be engraved in the public record. A century from now, students at Trinity would be able to take out some fading back-numbers of the *New Hibernian Quarterly* and see her name; she'd be mentioned in books – the memoirs of great writers, volumes of *belles lettres*, and so forth.

As Fergal thanked her for the dance and returned her to Aunt Bill he wondered why he had never before noticed that her mind was really quite commonplace – at least, on certain topics. Or was it that, being so very beautiful herself, she had not needed to reflect too deeply on the subject and so had merely filled that particular space in her mind with the shallowest of received opinions? Charitably he decided on the latter explanation, for it kept his love for her unspotted by criticism.

Two or three cotillions later Judith found herself taking the floor on the arm of Captain O'Donovan. 'You're not dancing much with young Bellingham,' he commented. 'You two haven't fallen out, I hope?'

She chuckled at his bluntness, knowing it was part of a character *she* had forced him to adopt. Then she passed on Rick's explanation for his seeming neglect.

'Oh dear,' he replied. 'It's the sort of reasoning a husband might give after five years of marriage. Rather ominous, don't you think?'

She knew he was really only teasing, and yet there was a serious point behind his comment. Also, harking back to her earlier train of thought that growing up meant knowing when not to speak your mind, she now realized that its corollary was also true: growing up also meant knowing precisely when you *ought* to speak out – seeing the opportunity and grasping it. Her reasoning whirred too quickly for her to follow it step by step but the conclusion was plain – there was no better sounding board for her innermost thoughts than Justin O'Donovan and no better time to employ him than now.

'There is a peculiar bond between Rick Bellingham and me,' she said. 'To do with the Castle Moore Murders, if you recall?'

'Ah, yes . . .' His step faltered briefly – most unusually for him.

'I was there that evening, too,' she added.

He stared at her in horror. 'The little girl . . . the bullet in the chest . . . was that you?'

'Mmm-hmm.'

'I had no idea – believe me.'

'My mention of the Murders gave you a start, though?' Her rising tone turned the statement into a question.

He laughed ruefully. 'Can't hide anything from you, eh! The fact is, when the RIC went to arrest one of the fellows in Irishtown, they requested the militia in support of the civil power.'

'And that was you!' Judith guessed.

''Fraid so. Kieran O'Sullivan was the wretch's name. Lord, I'd have handled him differently if I'd known *you* were almost murdered that night, too.'

'What did he say?' she asked eagerly. 'At the actual moment of the arrest – when the police told him what it was all about. Or even before then. I mean, did he look as if he *knew* why you'd come?'

They almost collided with another couple. Again, it was most unlike O'Donovan to lead her in such a slipshod way. 'Butter wouldn't melt in his mouth, of course,' he began. But the implication behind her questioning must then have struck some chord within him, for he immediately followed his remark with: 'Why d'you ask? Was this O'Sullivan fellow particularly on your mind?'

'Oh, Justin!' She sighed as if she hadn't intended their conversation to become anything like so serious. 'I don't know if I ought to tell you this – but *none* of the men they hanged for the Murders was on my mind at all. I mean, I didn't recognize *one* of them.'

He was silent for almost half a circuit of the chamber; she avoided his eye but she couldn't avoid seeing the way he chewed at his lip. 'Am I wrong to mention it to you?' she asked.

'Wrong?' He bridled at the word.

'Yes. I mean – if you had a hand in the arrest of one of them . . . well, it's not the kindest thing to tell you, is it!'

Again he was silent for several more steps, then he said, 'Would you mind if we sat the rest of this dance out? Perhaps you'd welcome some viands?'

They were near the door to the antechamber that housed the buffet; as they walked out there he added, 'Who's your partner for the next dance? D'you think you could cry off?'

It was Fergal; she was sure she could.

She chose a blackberry sorbet. He took her to a fairly deserted spot near a potted palm and said, 'The thing is I've done a fair few of these support-of-the-civil-power jobs. They mostly take place at night, you see, and . . . well, they give a chap something to do. After a while you develop a sort of nose for the genuine criminal. They all protest their innocence, of course, but usually they crumble after a bit – you may see it wearing thin at the fringes. But I've never forgotten O'Sullivan, you know. The look of shock in his face when the sergeant said it was for the Castle Moore Murders. The fellow was a criminal all right – chatted most disarmingly about all the petty thieving he'd done. But he was absolutely adamant he'd never committed a murder, and certainly had nothing to do with the Castle Moore Murders.'

'That's right.' Judith nodded; mechanically her hand carried one spoonful of sorbet after another to her mouth.

'But . . . how dreadful,' O'Donovan said. Then, remembering how they had come upon the topic in the first place, he added, 'And d'you mean to say young Bellingham shares your opinion? Does he think they got the wrong man, too?'

'Men,' she corrected. 'The wrong men. All four of them.'

He turned pale as chalk. But his voice remained calm and decisive. 'Enough! This is no conversation for such a . . .' His voice trailed off and he bit his lip once again. 'And yet it's too important to . . . When do you leave Dublin?'

'Nine-twelve from Kingsbridge on Monday morning.'

'Hah! And I'm acting ADC to General Boyle all tomorrow. Wouldn't it just happen!' As if he were suddenly aware what a breach of etiquette it was to have allowed their intercourse to take so solemn a turn, he now tried to make a joke of it: 'Ah!' he exclaimed. ' "What further woe conspires against mine age?" '

Judith laughed. 'Is that from Shakespeare?'

He shrugged. 'I don't know. We had a teacher at school called the Tartar. He always said it. Why did you laugh in that particular tone?'

'It would take too long to explain now. Next time we meet. How *are* we going to meet? I could probably find some reason to come up to Dublin in early April. The Spring Show or something.'

He shook his head. 'Too long. Could you get your people to invite me down, perhaps?'

She pulled a dubious face. 'It would look far too suspicious.' Then she brightened. 'Aunt Bill – Mrs Montgomery – you're a friend of her son Arthur, I believe? What more natural than that she should invite you down to Castle Moore?'

'Capital!' he chortled. 'Could you . . . ah . . . ?'

'I think I could talk her into it.'

'Oh, come! I wouldn't put it like that.'

She took his arm and laughed again as she led him away. 'I know you wouldn't, Justin my dear. It's what makes you so special.'

Some moments later a triumphant Sally emerged from behind the potted palm. She had seen the couple wander off in search of some underpopulated nook of the anteroom and had subsequently worked her way round through two other rooms and a corridor to get safely behind that potted palm. She had missed most of their conversation but what she heard was quite enough; indeed, she had heard every word from his urgent – one could even say ardent – inquiry, 'When d'you leave Dublin?' onward.

Enough to make Rick finish with Judith for ever, she hoped.

Josie Rohane, Kitty's younger sister, was soon declared to be 'a treasure'. The widely discussed servant problem in England was that they were scarce and finicky; they demanded days off and the run of their teeth and beer allowances and Lord knows what – and if you didn't give in to them, they went to someone who would. Ireland had a servant problem, too, but it was different. Large families, which extended as far as second cousins and beyond, ensured a plentiful supply of mortal illnesses and funerals – which took care of the days off; they got the run of their teeth anyway, no matter where they went; and porter and poteen weren't exactly scant. The servant problem in Ireland centred on the vexed question of trainability. House girl or carpenter, it made no odds – you could explain yourself blue in the face: 'Look, this is the way I want it done . . .' – you could draw diagrams – you could actually *do* the task yourself the first time, just to make it absolutely clear. And they'd listen intently, nod wisely, take every bit of it in . . . and then go and do it the way God intended.

So when Josie actually cleaned a room the way Thelma Carty told her to and made up a bed the way Norman Carty liked it, she soon established herself as that rare one-in-a-thousand who was fit to be dubbed 'a treasure'. And so permission for her sister to call was readily granted. It was arranged for the first Wednesday in April, when Thelma was to visit friends in Simonstown and so would not need Josie's services, anyway. Judith sent word to Aunt Bill, who 'cried in' in the passing and, being disappointed to find the lady of the house absent, took a cup of tea in the hand with her daughter instead. The chance that word of these comings and goings would arouse suspicion or cause untoward comment was remote. But . . . one never knew.

The female servants at the Old Glebe were lodged above the coach house, though the only access was by way of a stair leading off the scullery passage. When Mrs Devery, the cook, saw Miss Judith take a grand lady like Mrs Montgomery up for a word with that Kitty Rohane, she knew precisely what was in the air. 'Sure hasn't she heard what satisfaction that Josie's after giving here,' she explained to Philomena Dobbs, the scullery maid. 'There'll be another Rohane at Castle Moore before long, mark my words.'

Time being short, the ladies wasted little of it on preliminaries. Aunt Bill merely asked if Josie knew what was in it and could she be trusted.

'With my life,' Kitty assured her.

'It may yet come to that,' Aunt Bill told her grimly. 'The man we're up against is ruthless enough. But you hardly need me to tell you that!' She kept a flinty eye on the younger Rohane throughout this brief speech and was reassured to see she did not flinch.

'May I be so bold as to ask what ye intend doing in this business at all, ma'am?' Kitty began.

'Discover the truth, first of all.'

'And then?'

'That rather depends on what sort of truth we discover. If the real culprits have all emigrated to America, I don't suppose there's much we can do at all. But if they're still here . . .' She left the conclusion hanging.

'But about King, ma'am?' Kitty persisted. 'Have ye an opinion on him, at all?'

By 'ye' she meant to include both ladies; it was Aunt Bill who answered: 'He's the top and bottom of it.'

'Ah . . . well now . . .' Judith ventured more cautiously.

'Of course he is!' the older woman asserted. 'His name has gone to his head – thinks he's the king of the whole county.'

''Tis a marvel to me, ma'am,' Kitty put in, 'that he's still at Castle Moore, and you thinking as you do.'

'If it was left to me, Miss Rohane,' Aunt Bill assured her, 'he'd be found drowned in Robertsons' millrace and enough spirit in his belly to explain it away.'

'Sure there'd be no place in Ireland more fitting!'

'You never spoke truer. But, you see, it's not up to me. And those who have appointed him master of Castle Moore continue to believe he is the shining star of the western sky. Believe me when I say we shall need something as big and solid as the Rock of Cashel to shake them out of that opinion. I may as well warn you now.'

Kitty nodded soberly, then, turning to Judith, asked, 'And what of young Mister Bellingham, miss? Does he be having the same opinion as ye?'

'He does,' Judith assured her, but there was enough hesitation in her voice to make Kitty continue the question with her gaze. 'He's not as single-mindedly determined on action as the two of us,' she conceded. She thought of adding that Rick was kept pretty busy with so many other preoccupations, but she realized that no cause would sufficiently explain his behaviour to the satisfaction of one who did not know Castle Moore nor understand what grasp King held on everything that happened there. 'He's not as *certain* as we are,' she added. 'He's halfway between us and the rest of the family, if you will.'

'*Have* they emigrated?' Aunt Bill asked bluntly.

'They might and they mightn't,' Kitty answered warily. 'I know I never set eyes on one of them since before the trial.'

'Then you can put names to faces?'

For reply Kitty drew forth a slip of paper on which was written 'Mick O'Leary of Streamstown. Terence Kelly of Templebreedy. Sean Jackson of Carrowbeg. Piper O'Toole of Carrowbeg.'

The name of Mick O'Leary had three lines drawn under it. Aunt Bill tapped the paper. 'The leader?' she asked.

'The one with the ginger beard?' Judith added.

'I'd doubt he has it now, but he's the quare fella of that crowd. Or was. And the hair on him the colour to shame a carrot.'

'And which Streamstown is that? There must be a dozen townlands of that name.'

'The one nearest the castle,' Kitty replied.

'Down by the Robertsons' mill?' Judith asked.

Kitty nodded. 'Sure they own most of it – Tony and Francy. What they didn't inherit they bought. And what they didn't buy they stole by legal trickery from the Deasys.'

'Ah!' Aunt Bill let out a great sigh of satisfied comprehension. 'Now that's the bit of a link I was missing.'

'You've heard of Peter Deasy, of course?' Kitty went on. 'Not my Peter but his grandfather, the great Peter

Deasy who escaped execution at Kingsbridge after the rebellion of 'Ninety-eight?'

'What, Tip-toe Deasy – the Shadow?'

'The very one, ma'am. The peelers held his name those long years. And when the old Peter Deasy gave them the slip, didn't they bide their time for eighty years and then take the young one in revenge?'

Aunt Bill's face creased in puzzlement. 'But it was King's word hanged him. What spleen is there between the Kings and the Deasys that he should do that?'

Josie gave the answer: 'Sure he did it for the Robertsons. They're his people.'

'*His* people?' Judith echoed. 'What d'you mean?'

'The Robertsons were always Castle Moore people, miss. They came over in the same plantation after Cromwell. But when the Seymour-Kanes took the water for the lake and deprived the mill . . .'

'Deprived the mill!' Aunt Bill was all scorn. 'There are three other streams run through Streamstown. Why else does it have the name!'

'Perhaps the water off Mount Argus is the most reliable?' Judith suggested.

'They always thought 'twas theirs,' Kitty put in. 'And 'twas filched off them by the Seymour-Kanes. They could have the Shannon itself flowing through Streamstown and they'd still consider the water off Mount Argus was theirs. They'd hanker after that. 'Tis in their blood, so it is.' She meant Protestant blood, of course – not-yield-an-inch blood.

At last they had an explanation that fitted all the criteria of reason and local character. Kitty's next words only tapped home the nails: 'And King does be letting them take back their own water since he was made cock of the walk at Castle Moore. Now that's what I mean when I say they're *his* people. He's the one to look after them. Had we a parliament still in Dublin, they'd vote for him and he'd put the favours in their path, so he would. And that's why he threw the name Peter Deasy into the ring. 'Twasn't only that he knew the peelers would be on to it like a travelling rat. 'Twas to gladden the heart of the Robertson boys.'

Judith named the other three who had been hanged at Mountjoy on that dreadful day: Kinch Davitt, Michael Tweedy, and Kieran O'Sullivan. 'Have they no families to avenge them?' she asked. 'I'm amazed King can put his nose out of doors at all.'

Kitty's smile was twisted and bitter. 'Did you ever write for clemency, miss? And get a printed letter back, with just the names filled in in ink, to deny the plea?'

Judith shook her head. 'I did not.'

The other was relentless, though. 'And you knowing you'd catch your death of fusiliers if King got so much as the scratch of a bullet where 'twould never blind him?'

Josie put in her penn'orth. 'And every son and daughter in the house dependent on old daycency for a crust of bread and the lend of some work? And the very roof above your head at their discretion? Begging your pardon, miss, but ye did ask.'

'I did ask,' Judith agreed ruefully. 'But why those three other fellows in particular? I mean, they didn't even *look* like the ruffians I saw firing into the summer house that evening.'

'Who may say?' Kitty replied. 'Of one thing you may be sure – they've all crossed King's people one way or another. Like my Peter – or like his family, who were no match for the Robertsons when it came to legalized theft.'

Aunt Bill, who had more experience of feuds *within* single families than Judith, asked, 'And which of them may we trust, Miss Rohane? Would you advise us to approach any of them, or shall we communicate only with you?'

Kitty fretted with her lower lip a while before replying. 'Would you leave it with me, ma'am? Let me be the first to speak with them.'

And so it was left for the moment. Future communication from Castle Moore or the Old Glebe would be by post, in envelopes written in Josie's hand; replies would be sent via Josie, too. Kitty was smiling as they left. ''Tis the first day I could say the scald had gone off my heart since they took my Peter from me,' she said. 'May the saints preserve me now till I see that man with his neck in instalments!'

After their parting with the Rohane sisters Aunt Bill invited Judith to dine en famille at Castle Moore and to bring her overnight things. As they rode off in the carriage the older woman clenched her fists and beat her thighs in frustration. 'To think I must go on being affable to that dreadful man for . . . God alone knows how much longer! If only he were embezzling money from us! But, of course, he's far too fly for that. O-e-u-r-gh!' She gave a harsh laugh. 'Money is nothing compared to power, is it! You don't realize how important power is until someone usurps it like this. But to think that he's going round, acting the old Irish chieftain, using *our* land, *our* water, *our* position in society . . . it makes me seethe!'

Judith let her continue in this vein for some time, until she had vented her dangerous head of steam and become somewhat calmer. She herself doubted that King was the grand master of the whole plot; she didn't underestimate the threat he now posed, but she didn't see him as the arch conspirator behind it all. However, she saw no reason to fall out with Aunt Bill on the matter. Instead, she took the opportunity to ask whether an invitation had gone out to Captain O'Donovan yet.

'Oh yes!' Aunt Bill was rather glad to have a change of subject. 'He's coming down for a Fri-to-Mon next week.'

'The thirteenth.'

'Goodness!' I never thought of that – Friday the thirteenth! I hope he's not superstitious. Military people so often are. D'you really think he can be of any assistance to us?'

'I do. King is so wary of us. I don't think he suspects anything's afoot, but he's like a gamekeeper's dog who can hear a twig snap at half a mile. He always has an ear cocked for anything that's a little out of the way. And you know what Justin's like! You could cock your ear a hundred years and not hear a single word out of place. He'll be impeccable.'

Aunt Bill stared out of the window, trapping the corner of her lip between her teeth and slowly pulling it free. At length she turned to Judith and said, 'You don't suppose he's just a teeny bit enamoured of you, do you, dear?'

Judith grinned naughtily. 'A teeny bit, perhaps. But it's only sentimental. He knows I belong heart and soul to Rick, so he's quite safe. He'd run like a startled rabbit if he thought there was the slightest *real* chance I'd start taking his gallantry seriously.'

Aunt Bill tilted her head dubiously. 'I hope you're right, dear.'

As they turned in at the Castle Moore gate the carriage drew to a halt.

'What now?' Aunt Bill asked crossly, thinking the lodge keeper might have fallen asleep again.

But it was the McIvers' coach, just leaving, that had blocked their path. As it drew level it halted. The window dropped and Sally poked her head out. 'Sorry to have missed you,' she said gaily. 'I had hoped for a good chinwag over tea. You'll find Rick in a foul mood, I'm afraid.'

'Why?'

'I beat him at billiards.' And off she drove.

Rick did not seem in a particularly foul mood, as it happened – at least, not until they told him about Captain O'Donovan. Then he became as prickly as a porcupine in thistles.

Spring begins in Ireland on the first day of February; the weather to match the official promise comes along five or six weeks later. By the second Saturday in April, the first full day of Justin O'Donovan's visit to Castle Moore, no one could doubt its arrival. The sun was splitting the sod. Norman Carty had already taken down his daughter's bicycle, cleaned it up, and given it a good oiling; so, shortly after the earliest possible breakfast, she went flying down the drive of the Old Glebe on the best-lubricated bearings in Keelity.

Judith loved cycling. When they had moved to Dublin, those first two years, she had learned no more of the city than the few streets around their home in Drumcondra and whatever you could see from the tram or bus into the centre; the rest was a great, smoky sprawl, which she had viewed in its entirety only once, from the Hill of Howth. Then came her first bicycle, and with it liberation whose joy could only be appreciated by one who had suffered a similar imprisonment on paving slab or omnibus seat. Places with magical, faraway names like Sandymount and Swords, Strawberry Beds and Dolphin's Barn, were suddenly within reach and soon became as familiar as the Botanic Gardens and Sackville Street. Now that spring had arrived she hoped to do the same with County Keelity, too.

Justin O'Donovan rose early and washed and shaved before any servant might come in and surprise him; he was sensitive about the bruises on his lower back, which, though they would have been easy enough to explain in a schoolboy, were rather harder to account for in a man of forty-six. His first thought as he faced the new morning was of Judith – on that as on every other day. But today was special because today they would meet again. He was not in love with her, of course; he knew that. He had long ago decided that the brand of affection he needed from a woman precluded any sort of alliance with a true lady. His heart was as susceptible as any man's but his self-discipline was more than a match for its softer urgings.

And yet . . . and yet. He could not help recalling that deep, almost supernatural look of sympathy in her gaze when she had spoken to him of *pain*; it had somehow bored its way through the stout armour of his soul, forged over two decades of resistance to the havoc a beautiful pair of eyes can wreak in a man, and touched his most vulnerable sensibilities. How could that be? Something within her, far below the level of her everyday awareness, had been able to peer into his innermost self – and then had spoken to it directly in terms that meant so much to him while they remained quite innocent to her. Naturally, he would do nothing to disturb that divine innocence; but the bond between them was now a fact. Washed, shaved, and dressed, he hummed his regimental march-past as he set out on a brisk constitutional to work up an appetite for breakfast.

Rick, who had suspected the Captain was a constitutional-before-brekker sort of fellow, went trotting up the drive after him. He wanted to know more about this enigmatic man.

When Justin heard his approach he turned round and cried, 'Hark, I hear footprints! Who goes there?'

'Friend,' Rick answered, slightly breathless, as he caught up.

'You're badly out of condition, young Bellingham,' Justin commented with jocular severity. 'A man should be able to trot half a mile, spouting Ovid all the way, and not get out of breath. What have they been doing with you over the water?' He set off again at a stiff walk.

'I had one tutor who made me run to the top of Mount Argus and back every morning,' Rick answered, not exactly to the point.

Justin, in his response to this, strayed even further: 'I see all these ex-Leander types at my London club – the minute they stop rowing . . . bang!' His hands sculpted a beer belly in the air before him. 'You want to take care. I'll bet they kept you fit at St Columba's, eh?'

Rick laughed, a little uneasily. 'As a matter of fact, sir, I didn't go away to school at all. I had tutors, here at the castle. When my parents were killed like that, the family saw it as a sort of gesture, you see – to keep me here and show the flag, as it were.'

'Private tutors, eh? Did they swish you a lot? Very good for the character, you know. You must show me the old schoolroom after brekker. Bend over! Whack-whack, eh! Nothing like it.'

Rick promised he would show him the place.

'Gad, but you're a lucky young chap to come into all this,' the Captain went on. 'Rotten way to do it, I grant you, but even so – the responsibilities of property . . . also very good for the character, you know. Are they applying the Land Acts very strictly down here?'

Rick wondered if that, too, was going to turn out to be very good for the character. 'On the whole, sir, we're really rather glad to be rid of some of the farms. A tenant who becomes an owner is a different class of neighbour altogether. He suddenly starts seeing things our way.'

The Captain paused a moment and stared at him appreciatively. 'Gad,' he said, setting out again, 'but you take a long-term view, I must say. Still, if anyone can afford to, it's a young fellow your age. By the time you're forty you'll be crying enough's enough! There's such a thing as too much progress in my humble opinion.'

Woodsmoke from the gate lodge chimney came curling among the trees, diffusing into a sweet-smelling mist. Rick sniffed at it and said, 'Apple. We cut down the old orchard last autumn.'

'So it is.' Justin sniffed the breeze and gave out an 'Ah!' of satisfaction. 'When I was a boy we had two bogs near by. Easkybeg and Easkymor – little fish and big fish. Or little water and big water. Anything Irish always has two meanings – that's a firm rule, eh? Anyway, I could walk past the tenants' cottages and tell you from which of those two bogs each household drew its turf – but I couldn't do it now to save my life.'

They reached the main gate and, in languid-military style, like a pair of officers waiting at the edge of a parade ground for the order to fall in, turned about and headed for home. 'Had you much land?' Rick asked. 'Where was that?'

'A fair few acres,' O'Donovan admitted. 'Between Recess and Clifden in Connemara. My elder bro has them now, of course.'

'Oh, well!' Rick was pleasantly surprised. 'You weren't a million miles from my aunt, Mrs Montgomery. She was an O'Hara from Letterfrack, just beyond Clifden from you.'

'Oh, I know Letterfrack well. My father used to go sea fishing in Killary Harbour with a Major O'Hara there. Would he be . . . ?'

'Beany O'Hara.'

'Egad!'

Rick glanced at him and was surprised to see the man had turned a little pale. 'Is anything the matter, sir?' he asked.

'To think I've known young Arthur Montgomery all these years and never once realized he's little Billie O'Hara's son! Nor that your aunt is *that* same Miss O'Hara! Well, well!'

'Was she called Bill even then?'

'Always. She used to row their boat. Lord, how awkward!' He halted and swallowed hard before he said, 'Look, Bellingham, old chap, be an out-and-out sport and don't breathe a word of this to your Aunt Bill, eh? Let me break it to her.'

'Of course, sir – if you ask it.'

'I do. I do. It's a long time ago. Perhaps she won't even remember. She was fourteen and I was five or six – dash it, I suppose that's a trifle ungallant. Forget I said it.' He cleared his throat. 'Much obliged.'

From behind came the tinkle of a bicycle bell. They turned – and sprang apart just in time as Judith came whizzing between them, eyes bright, skin aglow, laughing like a monkey. 'Slugabeds!' she cried. 'I'll bet you haven't even had breakfast yet! See you for coffee!'

As they watched her dwindle, stirring the brown and yellow leaves that the new shoots had pushed off the young beeches, Justin said, 'If that father of hers really put his mind to it, I'm sure he could devise some means by which a lady could ride a bicycle side-saddle. Never think it looks *decorous*, do you – to see 'em riding astride like that?'

It is only amazing what can be discovered during a good root-around in a sprawling place like Castle Moore; somehow O'Brien and his stable boys found a bicycle for all four members of the outing. Even more remarkable, they were all of the appropriate style and gender: solid, sit-up-and-beg contraptions, with and without crossbars, for the Captain and Aunt Bill, and younger, more low-slung machines for Henrietta and Rick. They creaked a little and all their tyres were flat, but liberal application of the oilcan and air pump soon showed they were serviceable and free of punctures; even so, Rick packed tyre levers and a repair outfit, just in case.

With the wind in the east they decided the most sheltered spot for a picnic lunch would be down on the lakeshore, by the mouth of the Flaxmills River – almost opposite Turk Island, in fact. Turk Island was a slightly larger twin of the island opposite Castle Moore, some four miles to the north, where Aunt Bill and the youngsters had picnicked last autumn. O'Brien and one of the lads could bring the basket out in the dogcart and carry it to the spot; the river was navigable to barges as far as the town, so there was a good towpath all the way along its northern bank.

They set off, the two men and the three ladies, amid much laughter and playful teasing, shortly after ten. The Captain, for all that it distressed him to see ladies riding astride, nonetheless made the motto of his etiquette 'ladies first'! There was, in any case, no holding Judith back and, in a straight race on a crooked road, she proved herself more than a match for Rick on his admittedly rusty old machine. After that he hung back and let O'Donovan expose himself to an equal humiliation. The Captain, eager not to be left alone with Aunt Bill, now that he knew who she was, spurted ahead, heedless of the risk to his self-esteem.

After a while Aunt Bill began to flag. When they all dismounted to walk up a rise, she was the last to get back in the saddle. 'Don't delay yourselves for me,' she called out to the others, 'Rick'll keep me company and we'll catch you up on the next downhill.'

When the others had pedalled beyond earshot, she stopped panting and said, 'Good! I want to beg a favour of you, young man, and I don't wish the Captain to overhear us.'

'Anything you ask, Aunt dear,' he replied.

'I know it's a subject most unlikely to crop up, but, all the same, I'd be obliged if you'd refrain from mentioning Letterfrack and . . . well, Connemara in general, if you wouldn't mind. Particularly Recess and Clifden.'

'Certainly, Aunt Bill.' He thought he did a pretty good job of sounding mystified. 'That's no very irksome restriction. Is one permitted to ask why?'

'It wouldn't mean a thing, even if I did explain – which I choose not to. But I seem to remember that when we had our picnic on the island last autumn, you said something to Judith about how I used to row my father around Killary Harbour. So it's just possible *she* might say something, too. Try and steer her off the topic, if you see her edging towards it, eh?'

'I'll do my best, dear Aunt, of course.' He wondered if he wasn't overdoing the mystification a bit. 'Can I ask a different question, then? May I ask *why* you've invited the man down?'

She bridled. 'Why shouldn't I? He's a close friend of Arthur's, after all.'

'I mean . . . well, it wasn't Ju who put you up to it, was it? He behaves as if she's his hostess rather than you. And another thing – I've never known her arrive at the castle so early as she did this morning.'

Aunt Bill smiled bitter-sweetly. 'Perhaps she was afraid Sally McIver might arrive even earlier!' She was pleased to see he had the grace to colour slightly.

'Sally?' he echoed, as if he had no idea what she was talking about.

'Fergal's sister – surely you remember her? From the *Pride of Hibernia* if nowhere else!'

He swallowed hard and stared at her. 'I haven't the haziest notion what you're referring to.'

Staring into his frank blue eyes she could almost believe him. 'It seems that Fenella Bell-Stuart observed . . . certain events that occurred on the deck of that redoubtable vessel as she steamed out of Holyhead. When she conveyed her observations to Judith, as we women are prone to do, the dear, sweet gel pooh-poohed them as mere tittle-tattle, of course. What a treasure she is, Rick! And, to my pleasant surprise, Henrietta's response was the same – until Fergal told her what Sally's maid – Sheelagh . . . something-or-other – told him about the same . . . shenanigans, to give them their proper name.'

'Fergal?' Rick echoed angrily. 'How dare he talk to Henrietta about such things!'

'Shenanigans *is* the proper name, isn't it, Rick?' Her voice acquired a harder edge. 'It's nothing more serious than that?'

He looked away from her, over the hedge. 'How dare he?' he muttered.

'Who should he have told, then? Judith herself, perhaps?'

'He's supposed to be a friend – my best friend.'

'And what are *you* supposed to be to Judith, may I ask?'

He shrugged awkwardly. 'That's different.'

'Because she's a woman? Or because you're a cad?'

He swung his gaze upon her, wide-eyed with shock. 'Me?' he asked in amazement. 'A cad?'

'What else do you call a supposed gentleman who divides all women into two classes – those whom he deceives and those he dallies with? Of course, you don't *call* it deceit. You call it *protecting* them! Are you hoping the McIver gel is going to lift her skirts for you before the summer's out?'

'Aunt Bill!' he gasped. 'I really must ask you . . .'

'You must do no such thing,' she insisted angrily; the bit was well between her teeth by now. 'I'll tell you what you must do, young man – if you don't wish to end up the masculine equivalent of a tart like Henrietta – you listen to me now!'

She had gone much farther than she had intended. Without even thinking it out, she had realized that her best defence against any awkward questions about Letterfrack and Connemara was to attack him instead – but she had not meant it to go anything like so far as this. However there was no turning back now. 'What you must do,' she went on, 'is make your mind up which it is to be: Judith or the McIver. And then you must finish with the discarded one as gently and as honourably as you can.'

'Well, it's Judith, of course,' he said testily, struggling to control the angry tremor in his voice.

'And the McIver gel?'

'She just . . . well, it's not the thing a gentleman says of a lady – but then one lady does not call another a tart, either.'

'She may inside the family. Grow up!'

'On that understanding, then, I'll tell you that Sally McIver took me completely by surprise that day – flung her arms round me, smothered me with kisses. What's a fellow to do? I mean, I did nothing to provoke it.'

'Oh, Rick!' Her petulant tone implied he was being deliberately perverse. 'I thought Uncle Hereward took you to London to get your barnacles scraped!'

He almost choked.

'Well, *that's* what you do!' She spoke as if to a dim four year old. 'You gracefully disentangle yourself from Miss McIver's embrace – tactfully reminding her by your gentlemanly bearing and tone that she is supposed to be a lady – and then, if her propinquity has roused you to incandescence, you go and find another pretty little barnacle scraper to take care of it. And stop behaving as if this comes as a total shock and surprise to you.'

'It's a shocking surprise to hear it from a lady,' he grumbled.

'I heartily agree with you there. But needs must when the divil drives – and there's a divil driving *you*, my lad – to your destruction, if you don't watch out. It should be your father to tell you such things. The fact that he's not here to do so is hardly my fault! Nor does it absolve me from the responsibility when it's staring me in the face.' And now, at last, she allowed her tone to soften. 'Rick, my dear nephew! You're dearer to me than any of my sons – as well you know. If Judith Carty really is your choice, and you're quite, quite sure about it, do the honourable thing – go down on your knees to her and slip a ring over her finger. Put the McIver gel out of her misery – and the Dalton sisters, too.'

He laughed. 'Gwinny and Letty? They'd guffaw like geese if I proposed to either of them.'

'Well, don't ever put it to the test is my advice to you!'

'You can ask them yourself,' he added offhandedly. 'I've invited them to stay.'

'*You've* invited them!' She flared up once again.

'It seems to be the order of the day,' he answered calmly. 'Judith invites Captain O'Donovan – or you do – or you manage it between you. Castle Moore is *my* home, in case you've forgotten. I am now legally of age. I suppose I may invite down whom I like?'

'And you *like* those two bluestockings?'

'Very much. They say I have a fine mind.'

'Hah!' She stopped and begged the very hedges and ditches to share her amusement. 'You have a fine *mine*, they mean. A goldmine! And two better prospectors were never seen this side of Eldorado! Oh, it's a great temptation to wash my hands of you, Rick. You are *such* a fool!'

He relapsed into surly silence.

'When are they coming, anyway?' she asked.

'I don't know. Next week? The week after, perhaps. They don't like being tied down to such mundane details.'

'Oh, Rick!' Despite her annoyance she had to laugh – at him and with him. 'I don't know! I really don't know!

Poor old Wonky hardly ever says a word that makes sense but he did once tell me, when I was worried stiff about Claude and the wife of a vicar who rather flung herself at him . . . he said boys are like boats, you build 'em to float on their own. But once they're launched on the sea of life, there's nothing more you can do about 'em.'

'Except,' Rick dared to point out the obvious, 'get their barnacles scraped!'

'Yes, yes.' She laughed. 'One to you, I suppose. Well, don't be scraping yours with the Dalton gels, either – even if they are beyond the pale.' She broke off and stared all about them. 'D'you realize we've been walking downhill for the best part of half a mile!'

They mounted again and, using their brakes liberally, glided slowly to the foot of the slope, where another, much briefer, walk awaited them.

'To revert to an earlier topic,' Aunt Bill said as they dismounted once more, 'or two earlier topics, actually – the question of making Judith's unofficial status official and the matter of your father's absence – you realize the two are connected?'

He shot her a puzzled glance.

'Oh yes you do,' she insisted. 'That girl will neither rest nor settle to anything while the real murderers are still free. I'm sure she wonders what your attitude is.'

He shrugged hesitantly. 'I'm as concerned as she is, of course – and you. I haven't forgotten the day you and I walked by the lake, immediately after the Murders – the things you said to me then.'

'But . . . ?' she prompted.

'What d'you mean?'

'I never heard a more deafeningly unspoken *but* in my life.'

'Well . . . life hasn't stood still since then, has it? It's all very well for Judith. She's a woman. She's got nothing else to do. It's that or water colours or amateur dramatics or . . .'

'. . . writing articles for nonexistent literary journals!'

No longer willing to argue – on that front, anyway – he smiled coldly and said, 'One to you, I suppose. What I'm saying is – I have an estate to manage, or shall have before too long. Not to mention some fairly sizeable family investments.'

'I don't see what that has to do with it. You're a man – you're supposed to be able to do a thousand wonderful things before breakfast and amaze us poor females. Are you saying you simply don't have time?'

'Not at all.' At last he seemed to have mastered the trick of *not* rising to her goadings. 'What I'm saying is that if there was once a beautiful building on a certain plot of ground, and some blackguards came along and tore it down, well, naturally one wants to catch them and make them pay for their crime. But meanwhile, the world goes on. New buildings rise on the spot, serving new purposes, creating new dependencies . . . how else can I put it? Life goes on.'

Aunt Bill smiled thinly. 'What worries Judith – and me, too, to be utterly candid with you, my dear – is that this new building of yours has the same old caretaker. The one who is widely suspected of having furnished the plans and the duplicate keys to the blackguards you mentioned just now.'

'If it can be proved, of course,' he replied, and his hand mimed the aiming and firing of an imaginary pistol.

His aunt stared at him a long, uncomfortable while before she said, 'Well, Rick, I'm glad we had this little talk.'

Fergal and Sally were waiting at Flaxmills bridge. They had ridden over to the castle only to learn that everyone had gone on a picnic; then they had doubled across the fields, overtaking the cyclists in the hope of making it seem they had been abroad for hours already.

'Good evening!' Fergal called out jovially. 'Taking a picnic? Not much daylight left.'

'You must have been out and about early,' Judith told him, 'for your wit to be so tired already. There's daylight under that girth.'

He dismounted carefully and checked.

'Ha ha!' Henrietta crowed.

He looked wearily at Judith. 'What time were you out and about, then?' he asked.

She laughed. 'Had to get you down off that high horse to do this.' She gave him a quick kiss on the cheek.

'I'll try to forgive you, then,' he murmured.

'Where's Rick?' Sally asked when the introductions were done.

'Eating a plateful of cold tongue, I rather imagine,' Henrietta replied.

'He's with Aunt Bill, bringing up the cow's tail,' Judith explained. 'We'll wait for them here.'

The row of cottages where the Rohanes lived was hard by. Kitty herself came out at that moment, in bonnet and shawl, with a basket on her arm, off for her messages. She greeted Judith as she passed.

Sally, who watched the exchange closely, asked in rather a surprised tone, 'D'you know her?'

'Kitty Rohane,' Judith answered evenly. 'Her younger sister Josie works for us.'

'Oh.'

Sally seemed vaguely disappointed. Judith wondered if she knew Kitty's story and had hoped to put two and two together. Sally had always been irked by the bond that the Murders had forged between her and Rick; she had never been able to leave the subject alone.

Judith turned to say something to Fergal and found

him staring intently at Justin, who, for his part, seemed to be counting the cottages in the row, as if committing them to memory. A sense of isolation filled her suddenly; people were so unknowable. What *were* the two men thinking? Fergal was probably wondering about the captain . . . his precise association with her . . . her attitude to him; but nothing of it showed in his expression. And what about Justin, himself? Was his military eye seeking out nooks where a sniper might lie in ambush? Did he go about Ireland automatically committing every bridge and crossroads to memory, ready for use some dark night?

And poor Henrietta, standing there, staring down into the foam-mottled waters of the river – no need to ask what she was thinking! The bubbles would form themselves into Percy's face; the lanes between them would be maps of the myriad clandestine routes in time and space between their meetings. It was all she lived for now. If the Bellingham family had had any sense, they'd have repaired the old tower at the castle and locked the lovers away in it. One of them would have murdered the other by now.

'Here they come,' Fergal said, touching his horse's flank and trotting forward to meet them.

Sally took it as a kind of licence to go, too.

'Come on,' Judith urged. 'We can start along the towpath now.'

'What's the point of hurrying?' Henrietta asked, though she mounted her bicycle readily enough. 'What do we *do* when we get there?'

'We gather driftwood for Justin to rub together and show us how the natives make a fire. When O'Brien brings the rest of our paraphernalia we spread the blankets and put up parasols. We gather flowers to press in our herbariums, or is it herbari-aaa? And we talk, I suppose. A woman's work is never done.'

'Talk about what?' Justin asked, feeling a little left out.

'The disgraceful idleness of the labouring classes?' Judith suggested. 'They're *always* going on picnics.'

He laughed, not too comfortably; it was as if, having lost his very formal personality he had found nothing suitable to replace it. 'I hope there are more *pressing* topics than that,' he replied.

Judith decided that the moment was as good as any. 'You saw that woman who greeted me by the bridge?' she asked. 'She was the sweetheart of Peter Deasy.'

The effect on the other two was electrifying.

'*That* Peter Deasy?' Henrietta asked.

Judith nodded.

'And did you know it when your mother took on the younger sister?'

'Of course. That was the whole point.'

Justin cleared his throat. 'Is this the conversation we began at the Saint Pat's Ball?' he asked.

'It is.'

Henrietta stared at her in amazement. 'Are you after telling him, too?'

'I don't know what you mean by *too*. I've told no one else – but yes, I have told Justin.'

'Why?' Henrietta turned and smiled apologetically at him. 'I'm sorry, Captain O'Donovan, I don't mean to be rude.'

'It's perfectly all right, Mrs Austin,' he assured her. 'I have wondered the same thing myself.'

'Captain O'Donovan helped arrest Kieran O'Sullivan,' Judith said.

He corrected her: 'Was present at the arrest.'

'From the man's behaviour at the time, and subsequently, he had doubts as to his real guilt.'

'Misgivings,' he put in.

'Ah.' Henrietta's alarm had turned to thoughtfulness.

Justin saw his opportunity. 'May I ask you, Mrs

Austin, whether you share Miss Carty's misgivings about the justice of the affair?'

Henrietta, gathering herself from her reverie, said, 'Is *that* why you've come down on this visit?'

'A visit to your family home is a pleasure I have long anticipated, Mrs Austin.'

She shook her head. 'No, I mean are you here officially? Is the Castle taking an official interest in the matter?'

He smiled to reassure her. 'I give you my word they are not. I have spoken to no one on the matter – and nor shall I unless the evidence of a miscarriage of justice is so plain it becomes my duty to do so.' His smile broadened further when he saw she was still not mollified. 'I hope that will set your mind at rest, Mrs Austin?'

She smiled back, then, and said it had. At that point the towpath deviated round a turning circle. When they reached its farther side and the mouth of the river came into view, she said, 'I hope you will not think me rude if I ask for a few minutes alone with Miss Carty as soon as we arrive, Captain O'Donovan? It would be better before the others join us.'

He dipped his head in acknowledgement. 'I was going to ask in whose presence we may – and may not – discuss this business. Not McIver and his sister, I take it?'

'No!' They spoke in chorus.

'Pity,' he commented. 'Then you had better want some rare orchid for your herbaria – something that will carry us far afield, eh?'

When they arrived at the river mouth they left their bicycles leaning against a ditch. Justin pointedly set off along the lakeshore, seeking driftwood for their fire; Henrietta took Judith by the arm and started walking her back along the towpath.

'Have you taken leave of your senses?' she asked as soon as they were out of earshot.

'Why?' Judith was nonplussed by Henrietta's vehemence.

'He's a Castle man. Can't you see it? What *ever* possessed you to breathe a word to him?'

Judith felt the stomach fall out of her; the possibility had not even crossed her mind. 'Aunt Bill saw nothing wrong with it,' she said defensively. 'Anyway, he's not a Castle man, as you call it. He's a rather lonely little nobody. If he weren't in the army I don't know what he'd do – he wouldn't even exist, probably.'

'Why was he present at Kieran O'Sullivan's arrest? They don't pick *those* officers' names out of a hat, you know.'

'He said it gave him something to do of an evening.'

'You mean he's done a lot of it?'

She nodded uncomfortably. 'I gather so.'

'Oh Judith, darling Judith!' Henrietta hugged her angrily. 'They're always little nonentities. They're always the last people you'd suspect. How did he get to hear of our suspicions? How did it come up in the first place? I'll bet he asked you. *He* brought it up.'

Judith breathed more easily, being now on firmer ground. 'No, in fact. It was the other way round. We were talking about Rick and you. And I told him there was a special sort of closeness between us because we'd all survived the Murders. And I felt him twitch at the mention of it. Only *then* did he tell me about the night they took O'Sullivan . . . and how the man's behaviour raised doubts in his mind . . .'

'Straight away?'

'Yes.'

But Judith now remembered it had not been straight away. Justin had asked to sit the dance out, had brought her sorbet, had suggested crying off the next dance – all before he even mentioned his doubts concerning O'Sullivan's guilt. She was not brave enough to admit it now, though. Instead, she added, 'In any case, I would have thought the Castle would be as interested in overturning a miscarriage of justice as we are. I mean, if they hanged the wrong people, and they know it, and they do nothing about it . . . well, that's a dreadful stain on British justice, surely?'

'Too dreadful to contemplate!' Henrietta replied darkly.

'What d'you mean?'

'I mean they'd never let it come out.'

'But their consciences! Their honour as gentlemen! Never mind Judgement Day . . .'

'Yes,' Henrietta laughed. 'Never mind it! Listen, I'll perform a little experiment while we're scoffing our sandwiches. We'll bait the gallant captain in his lair. I never told you why Harold was sent to India, did I? Perhaps it's time you all learned.'

'What's today?' Henrietta asked when they gathered round the fire to eat their luncheon. 'The actual date, I mean?'

'The fourteenth, I think,' Fergal told her.

'Then there should be a letter from Harold waiting for me when I get home. Always on the fourteenth and again on the last day of every month . . . you could set the calendar by Harold. Intelligence from India.'

She watched Captain O'Donovan when she said the word, but – if it had any special significance for him at all – he was well trained; not a muscle on him twitched. She tried again. 'Funny word, when you think of it,' she prattled on. 'Intelligence. Why do they call it that? They say, "We have intelligence from Naples that the enemy's fleet is massing in the bay." But you couldn't say, "We have *brains* from Naples . . . we have *genius* from Naples . . ." Why intelligence? Do you know, Captain O'Donovan?'

'Intelligence is any information of military value,' he told her.

'Yes, but why? It also means cleverness – and they're often not at all clever, are they – the actual officers who deal with intelligence.'

He pulled a dubious face. 'Bit over my head, I'm afraid, Mrs Austin. I don't have the honour to serve at those exalted levels.' He smiled at Aunt Bill, suggesting that she, at least, would understand. 'They took one look at my school reports, I expect, and marked me down for dull old regimental duties until I drop.'

Judith, seeing Henrietta's 'experiment' collapse before it had even got underway, offered some help. 'Why d'you say they're often not at all clever, Hen?'

'Yes, I was going to ask the same,' Fergal put in quite spontaneously – and was mystified to receive a grateful glance from Judith.

'Bate your breath, everyone!' Rick added sarcastically, still smarting from Aunt Bill's reprimand, earlier that morning.

'Well,' his sister replied, 'if they really were so jolly intelligent, Harold would never have been sent to India, and you wouldn't be saddled with me!'

She glanced about and saw she had their undivided attention at last – even that of Captain O'Donovan. 'Well, apparently, there's this rather stupid officer whose job is to gather *intelligence* along the Afghan frontier. There are dozens of them, of course, but this particular one did something awful. I think he was caught sneaking into the harem. Or out of it, perhaps, which would be even worse. Anyway, whatever it was, it offended some local prince or maharajah whose support we need to keep down the tribesmen. Without him we lose control of the Khyber Pass, you see. And without the Pass we lose control of the whole of Afghanistan. And then the Ruskies will walk in and use it as a base on which to build an entire empire in the Orient. One casual act of folly – and the whole course of world history is changed! So there's a lot at stake, you see.'

'But where does Harold come into it?' Rick asked. 'Surely they haven't sent him all the way out there just to lecture this intelligence chappie and get him to apologize?'

'No. That's the awful part. Really the fellow ought to be court-martialled and cashiered. But he can't be. Because officially he doesn't exist. He's not there. The Indian Army doesn't employ such creatures as "intelligence officers"! They're an unknown species. Therefore he can't possibly be court-martialled. What poor Harold has to do is find some officer who *can*. And since the maharajah's dignity has been so deeply offended, he's made it clear that nothing less than a full colonel will do.'

'Gad!' O'Donovan exclaimed. 'But that's . . .' He hesitated over the precise word.

'Quite.' Henrietta agreed. 'Harold has already found the right man, in fact – the only officer who'll do. Now he has to persuade him to do it. He's actually the colonel in command of the regiment where the so-called intelligence office was stationed. A very distinguished soldier . . . belongs to a cadet branch of Lord Scudamore's family . . . Military Medal . . . Star of India and so forth. And all Harold has to do is to persuade this gallant gentleman to accept court-martial, plead guilty, be cashiered and sent home, resign all his clubs, return his decorations, sell up his estate, and retire to France or Italy to live out his life in disgrace – all for the good of his country.'

A stunned silence greeted this revelation. O'Donovan's face was quite drained of blood. 'Gad!' he breathed. 'What a . . . what a . . .' Again the word escaped him.

'How would you set about it, Captain O'Donovan?'

Henrietta asked. 'If you were in poor Austin's shoes?'

He shook his head, but it remained unclear whether he was indicating that he would not, or simply that he was dazed.

She felt she had to press him. 'Not if it were put to you as an order?'

He recovered himself somewhat at the word. 'I would cease to hold in honour any man who presumed to issue such an order, Mrs Austin.'

'But, you see, it is not the honour of a man that is at stake here – in the giving of the order, I mean. It is the honour of the Empire.'

O'Donovan now recovered himself completely. 'I would rather lose the Empire than see its honour compromised in such a fashion,' he said. 'Besides, there must be some other way of dealing with this upstart maharajah. We can't give in to them like this. What's he going to demand next time? A whole regiment to be cashiered and disbanded?'

'How would you deal with the fellow, Captain O'Donovan?' Aunt Bill asked.

His eloquent shrug suggested there must be half a dozen effective ways; as an example he chose: 'Take his three favourite sons for a ride over the palace in a balloon – tip them out from a couple of hundred feet. He'd come to heel soon enough. It's a language those fuzzy-wuzzies understand.'

He looked around, seeing one horrified expression after another, and suddenly realized what he had said. Then, of course, he was horrified, too. 'Do forgive me!' he spluttered. 'What possessed me to say that? I was so caught up in the poor colonel's fate, I simply didn't think.'

Aunt Bill saw that only some heroic response would save the man from his own remorse. She forced herself to laugh and, setting the tone for the others, said, 'Dear

Captain O'Donovan! I admit I was rendered speechless just now – but not with horror at your proposal, rather it was with amazement that you should make it so frankly. I think it is an excellent idea, quite capable of adaptation to our own trouble with the Land Leaguers here. Do take the rest of that beer, there's a good fellow.' She turned to Judith. 'Your father might turn his ingenuity upon the actual mechanism for detaching them from the basket of the balloon?'

Judith followed her lead and laughed, too, and soon they had buried poor Justin's quite serious suggestion in a farrago of embellishments.

'Well?' Judith murmured to Henrietta.

She conceded her defeat with a shrug and, turning to Justin, said, 'You mentioned some rare orchid that grows in these parts, Captain O'Donovan. D'you think you could be terribly kind and help us find a specimen or two?'

He smiled delightedly, not knowing he had passed a test, thinking merely that two charming and guileless young ladies were doing their best to assist him over his discomfiture.

When Fergal volunteered to help in the orchid search, too, Judith took him aside and explained that she and Henrietta were trying to worm something out of the old boy, and he'd shut up like a clam if anyone else came along. Though not entirely convinced by her story, he had no choice but to let her go. As he stood there, watching them set off along the lakeshore, Rick took up station at his side.

'It can't be anything serious, can it?' he asked.

Fergal, who desperately needed that reassurance himself, nonetheless rounded on his old friend and said contemptuously, 'Perhaps Judith's asking the same questions about you and my sister.'

He spoke a mite too loud, however, for Sally overheard and came at once to join them. 'What's that?' she asked Fergal belligerently. 'I heard you, you know.'

The two young men looked at her, each wishing the other would answer.

'And you're pretty limp, I must say,' she went on, still addressing Fergal. 'Just letting them go off like that. What are you thinking of?'

Still neither of them replied.

'Who invited him down, anyway?' she said.

'Aunt Bill,' Rick said at last.

'Yes, dear?' The lady herself came to join them.

He turned and saw the two stable lads carrying away the hamper and all the things that wouldn't fit on their bicycles. 'I was just telling Sally it was you who invited the Captain down here.'

'At Judith's suggestion,' Aunt Bill added sweetly.

'Well, I'm sure you don't meekly carry out her every whim, Aunt dear. *You* must have wished it, too.'

'Well of course I did, Nephew dear. He's a nice old buffer . . . friend of Arthur's . . . a bit lonely.' The sweet smile returned. 'And Judith seems quite fond of his company. You gave her enough chances to cultivate it during the Season, so you can hardly complain now, can you!' She returned to the picnic place, threw some more wood on the fire, spread her cycling cape in the sandy loam of the foreshore, and opened her book to read.

Rick stared all about them in a rage that had no object, outside of himself. About a hundred yards up the shore was a small, ramshackle jetty. To it was tied a battered little rowing boat. 'I'm going for a spin round Turk Island,' he said. 'You two care to come with me?'

Reluctantly they agreed but before they reached the jetty Fergal cried off, saying that, dammit, he was going to join the others, come what may; in fact, he hoped that the sight of Rick and his sister alone on the lake would anger Judith into making some complementary gesture –

with him, he hoped, rather than with the dreadful O'Donovan.

A few dozen vigorous pulls took the edge off Rick's anger. Sally stared at him wide-eyed and asked did he want to get up enough speed to fly. Grinning and panting he flopped over the oars and said, 'No. It's just so annoying. So petty and so annoying – that's all.'

'What is?' she risked asking.

'Well, it's so transparent. There aren't any rare orchids on the shores of Lough Cool, are there! Have you ever heard of one?'

She warded off his words with both hands. 'I'm staying well clear of this, Rick. I'm sure you know *my* feelings.'

He started rowing at a more natural pace and strength. 'The one I really don't understand at all,' he said, 'is Aunt Bill. What possessed her to invite the fellow down?'

'Well . . .' Sally drawled reluctantly. Then she pursed her lips and stared unhappily at the horizon.

'What?' he prompted.

'Oh look!' she replied. 'There's a woman riding across those fields there with four great elkhounds at her heels. What an extraordinary sight!'

He did not take the bait. 'What *were* you about to say?' he persisted.

'My dear!' She smiled wanly. 'Wild elkhounds wouldn't drag it from me.'

He stared at the bilge between her riding boots; a small pool of water was slopping around there – but no more than had been in the boat to start with. 'I thought you were supposed to be my friend,' he challenged.

He could see her ankles – shapely swellings to which the shiny leather of her boots had grown comfortable. He could see the lacy frills of her petticoats, too. In his mind's eye he could see even more than that.

He wished Aunt Bill had not made that disgraceful remark about Sally lifting her skirts; it had supplied the most graphic image to clothe a notion that, until now, had been unthinkable. Almost.

'You're making it very hard for me,' she said morosely.

He mastered his urge to laugh. 'You do know something, then?' he asked.

She stared at him miserably. What a ruthless monster love could be, she thought. Where were her scruples, her sense of fair play? 'I . . . overheard something at the Saint Pat's Ball. The tail end of a conversation. It might have referred to something quite . . .' She was going to say 'different' but sharpened it to 'innocent'.

'About Ju?' He was on tenterhooks.

'Not *about* her. I wouldn't pass on mere tittle-tattle, Rick. I hope you think better of me than that!'

'Yes, yes, of course. I mean no, I don't imagine you would.' After a pause he said hesitantly, 'You mean you actually overheard . . . herself?'

'Not by choice. I could hardly avoid it. I was hiding from that odious Monty Falkender, behind one of those palms. And who should come and and stand just the other side of it but . . . well, both of them, actually. Judith and Captain O'Donovan.'

There was an even longer pause before he said, 'You might as well tell me now.'

She sighed. 'I suppose so. Oh dear, I only hope I'm doing the right thing. After all, it *might* have been completely innocent. Anyway, as far as I can recall now, it went like this. They'd been talking for some time so I don't know what went before, but the first words I heard him say were, "When d'you leave Dublin?" And she told him they were leaving from Kingsbridge the following morning – which irritated him because he was on duty all day. Then she said she could probably find some pretext to get up to Dublin for the Spring Show.'

'Pretext?'

'That was her word for it. Anyway, he said he couldn't possibly wait so long and couldn't her people invite him down here to Keelity?' Sally closed her eyes and shook her head. 'I should never have started this.'

'Well, you can't leave it there now,' he exclaimed, giving a couple of angry jabs with his right oar to bring them parallel with the lakeshore, for they were now on the far side of the island.

Sally drew a deep – and deeply reluctant – breath. 'Judith replied, "No, that would look far too suspicious." And then she said she'd talk Aunt Bill into inviting him. "After all," she said, "you're a great friend of her son's. It's very natural that she should invite you." And he said that would be capital.'

'And that was it?'

She eyed him warily as her tongue passed slowly over her lower lip, but she volunteered nothing further.

'There was more,' he insisted.

'Her parting words were, "Justin, my dear, you are very special to me." Something like that, anyway.'

His face was unreadable; she would have thought him quite calm if she had not noticed the muscle at his temple twitching with anger.

He rested the oars and then thumped them hard with the sides of his clenched fists, unhousing one from its rowlock. 'I can't go back ashore,' he said vehemently. 'Not like this.'

'I knew I should have kept my mouth shut,' she said bitterly.

'No no!' He made an obvious effort to control his ill-humour. 'You did absolutely the right thing – what any friend would feel obliged to do. It can't have been easy.' He smiled wanly. 'And I really do appreciate it.'

'Pull into the island,' she suggested. 'We could walk

around a bit while you calm down.'

'What a splendid idea!' His deliberate cultivation of a better spirit was taking effect; he actually did feel almost half as cheerful as he outwardly seemed. In a curious way, although Judith's treachery (to give it its proper name) hurt him deeply, there was a kind of relish in having his doubts resolved at last. His uncertainty over her true feelings – toward him and toward the absurd Captain O'Donovan – was resolved at last. His feelings toward her were now quite numb. No doubt there would be a time to grieve at her loss, but for the moment all he could feel was that a great weight of uncertainty had been lifted from him.

He leaped from the boat and took Sally's arm to lift her ashore. 'Shall I carry you?' he asked jokingly.

She laughed. 'Why not!' And, before he could say it was only a joke, she transferred enough of her weight to him to force him into it.

When they were safely ashore he tilted her preparatory to setting her down but she clung tighter to his neck and, playfully mimicking a little girl, murmured, 'No-o-o! Ickle Sally doesn't want to walk. Ickle Sally like big Rick's strong, manly arms to hold her.'

'Oh, Sal!' He leaned over and gave her a swift, impulsive peck on the cheek. 'You're such good *fun!*'

'Am I, Rick?' She abandoned the ickle-girl and stared up at him sadly. 'Nothing more than that? Just good fun?'

'Well . . .' He laughed awkwardly.

She gave the screw a further turn. 'Have I compromised my honour with you just to be called "good fun"?'

'Compromised your honour?' he echoed in surprise.

'I should never have eavesdropped so long on Judith and O'Donovan. I should have – I don't know – stopped my ears or made my presence known or forgotten I ever heard such words. But, even having heard them, I should still never have repeated them to you.'

He had carried her up the shore to the edge of the pine grove by now. The exertion, and the hot sun on his back, brought on a slight sweat. He set her down, because it was quite impossible to hold a serious conversation while he was carrying her like a baby; she did not resist him this time. 'I think a lot more highly of you than that,' he said.

She plucked a handkerchief from her sleeve and dabbed his brow. It smelled not of some bottled perfume but of her – a warm, dusky aroma, faintly redolent of cinnamon. It assailed his enfeebled senses. His body went hollow with a sudden craving for her.

'Spread your coat,' she said gently. 'Let's sit down and talk awhile.'

But the moment his coat was spread, she did not so much sit as sprawl, lying back on her elbows. She tossed off her riding hat and shook free her lustrous, strawberry-blonde hair. He, lounging on one elbow at her side, stared at her with new eyes. Her attention, however, seemed far away, fixed somewhere on the farther shore of the lake.

What wonderful creatures women are! he thought. Surely the very pinnacle of Creation. He wished he were an artist, that he could ask her to stay just as she was; he longed for some means to compel her stillness while he gazed . . . and marvelled . . . and adored.

Yes – adored!

She was all curves. The curve of her cheek, in three-quarter profile, nestling among a sweet disorder of curls in her hair . . . the firm curve of her chin . . . the swan-like elegance of her neck, planted so gracefully among the navy-blue chiffon of her riding stock . . . the strong, jutting curves of her shoulders, thrust forward like that by the slender buttresses of her arms. And, yes, it was a pose that stretched the fine grey worsted of her riding habit over those most darling curves of all, the perfect line and volume of her bosom . . .

'What are you thinking, Rick? I'll bet in your heart of hearts you despise me for speaking out.'

'I do not!'

His tone was full of pain. He reached out an impulsive hand to touch her, to underline his reassurance. But the moment his fingertips met her arm she collapsed on her back and covered her eyes. Her smile was effaced in an upside-down grin of anguish. 'Well, *I* do,' she insisted. 'I'm so ashamed of myself. I can't imagine what possessed me.'

'Oh please, Sal – *dear* Sal!' He rolled on to his front, propping himself on his elbows, bringing his head close to hers. 'The very fact that you are now prey to such barbs of conscience shows how fine your scruples are. But you are *over*-scrupulous, my darling. Also' – his tone became provocative – 'shall I tell you something else?'

'What?' She still kept her hands over her eyes.

He moved nearer her. 'You have *the* most kissable lips.'

She jerked her hand away and stared at him in utter amazement. It was plain to him that the very idea of kissing was a million miles from her mind – whereas he, or the sinful Old Adam within, was already about twenty mental steps beyond that preliminary brush of lip on lip. It was true, then, what Dr Greerly wrote about Pure Women: physical thoughts, carnal thoughts, never even flit across their minds from one year's end to the next. It was beautiful!

'Oh, Rick!' she murmured. She was beautiful.

Also: the gentleman who chooses to woo a Pure Woman elects himself the Incorruptible Guardian of her Purity.

It was a beautiful arrangement.

Gently he lowered his lips to hers and luxuriated in their sweet warmth and softness. Her arms stole up to enfold his head, clutching him tight, and crushing him ever harder to her. She began to move her head slightly, this way and that, moaning softly, breaking contact every now and then to gasp for breath – but always seeking that soft touch of him again, urgently, desperately, hungering for him.

His elbow was in an awkward position, rather painful to him. He withdrew to rearrange himself but she murmured, 'No!', and while he was off balance, pulled him closer to her. On to her, in fact – or after a moment of panic, *half* on to her.

'A-a-ah!' She let out a sigh of ecstasy and, as if to say that her muscles had lost all power to resist, allowed her arms to drop away from him and lie on his coat just where they fell.

He began to explore the rest of her face with his lips, brushing them across her cheeks, down to her chin, up to the fine curves of her nostrils, along the adorable ridge of her nose . . . to the bridge of her nose, which was so ticklish she wrinkled it and giggled.

Funnily enough Tricia had done the same. He remembered something else Tricia had taught him and grazed his lips down over Sally's eyelids . . . her cheekbone . . . coming to rest at the portals of her ear. There he extruded the very tip of his tongue and made it flutter at the rim of her earhole. She gave out a startled little 'Oh!' of wonder, as if she had never suspected such a novel thrill might have been lurking there all these years, waiting to ambush her.

Tricia had done that, too.

What was this perverse and devilish brute within him that insisted on finding parallels between the two girls? They could hardly be more different. He set his mind resolutely to avoid any such comparison in future.

'Mmm?' she whimpered, reaching her damp ear to him and begging for more.

After a while her breath began to come in short, explosive exhalations, with little moans of 'oh' and 'ah' in a lost, straying sort of voice he hardly recognized as hers.

'Rick?' she begged. There was a strange, almost reproachful edge to her tone.

'Yes?'

'I don't know.' She sounded on the verge of tears now.

And then, as if ashamed of the daylight, she turned on her side and pressed herself tight against him, shivering almost uncontrollably. 'Oh, Rick! I want . . . I want . . . I don't know. Hold me. Tight! Don't let me go.'

She strained herself hard against him. Their bodies were in touch from head to food, shivering, trembling, shuddering, in the grip of forces too cosmic to fathom. Against his will – in fact, almost concealed from his will – the fingers he had been running through her hair crept round to her cheek, to the line of her jaw, to the taut and delicate skin of her neck, to her stock . . . underneath her stock, easing it out of the neck of her habit, opening a magical chink through which he could *just* squeeze the tips of his fingers. They came to rest on the firm plate of her breastbone. Alarmed at his own boldness, he forced them toward safer territory, along the graceful curl of her collarbone.

Breastbone. Collarbone. His fingertips explored bone for a while, as if that were their only purpose. But then some small, accidental movement on her part deflected them to the softer flesh immediately adjacent.

He held his breath. One rib. Two ribs. Three . . . they became more and more difficult to discern through the increasing softness and plumpness of . . . he swallowed hard and then held his breath. His exploring fingertip now rested on the very edge of her nipple. Dare he?

While he hesitated she pulled away from him and

stretched out luxuriously on the flat of her back, giving a yawning sort of a gasp and reaching her arms toward the sun. 'Oh, Rick!' she smiled seraphically up at him. 'You are such a wonderful man. You make me feel so *safe*.'

She tucked the stock delicately but firmly back into her neck.

Rick and O'Donovan stood on the front steps of Castle Moore. They had one eye on the rainclouds that had been gathering in the western sky for the past hour and which were now almost upon them, and the other on Judith, who was, at that moment, cycling off down the drive. 'She should just about make it home before that lot comes down,' Rick said.

'In my younger day,' O'Donovan replied, 'there were no bicycles. Or nothing like these modern contraptions – nothing a lady could even consider mounting.'

Rick wondered what thoughts lay behind this remark. It was probably some obscure reprimand, aimed at him for not volunteering to escort Judith home. To be honest, he himself felt a little guilty about that, and Judith had seemed surprised. But, on the other hand, it would underline his displeasure at her thoughtless flirtation with this ass of a captain.

'Care for a cigar, Bellingham?' O'Donovan asked, profferring his case.

'Thanks.' They were such damnably good cigars he couldn't resist one.

'We might get in a little stroll down to the lake and back before it rains? What d'you think?'

'Indeed, sir.' Rick took the first step. 'In any case, it's only water, and we're about to change out of these togs.'

'Capital!'

Rick thought so, too; it would be a chance to find out what the fellow's true intentions and feelings were. He was quite sure he could worm it out of him without the chap even realizing it. He puffed his cigar to life and then began: 'I expect you think it rather odd that I didn't volunteer to accompany Miss Carty home, Captain?'

'Well,' he said indulgently, 'you've known each other a long time – or so I gather.'

Again, the intention behind the remark was obscure. Rick tried another approach. 'I don't believe I ever told you, in so many words, how very grateful I was for your support of Miss Carty during the Dublin Season. It was hugely good of you, sir.' He puffed out a luxurious cloud, which the squally wind snatched away from him before he could relish its aroma; all he had was the bitter after-taste in his mouth. He decided that, on the whole, he preferred to smoke cigars at second hand, on the breeze, as it were.

'Haven't enjoyed myself so much for years,' O'Donovan replied jovially. 'Fellow gets to be a dreadful stick-in-the-mud, don't you know – regimental duties, mess nights, spot of reading, polo, huntin' and that. Easy to forget the . . . ah . . . distaff . . . ah . . . God bless 'em. You're a lucky fellow. Or shouldn't I be saying that?'

A most uneasy feeling was creeping over Rick by now. On the surface the Captain was as crass an old bore as one could possibly wish to avoid; yet his questions seemed to carry a point that was somehow menacing. He remembered a game of Hare and Hounds when he was a boy; he had been the hare. The hounds, instead of rushing after him in a great, yelping pack, had stalked him like jungle cats. It was terrifying, because the woods were so thick he couldn't see a soul. And even the sounds he heard – the occasional crackle of a twig, the rustle of a dried leaf, the suppressed giggle – could just as easily have been his imagination. In the corner of his eye he'd see a movement, but when he'd turn to watch the spot, all was peace; not a leaf trembled.

It was like that now with O'Donovan's question and remarks – peaceful, innocent-sounding, even vapid, they nonetheless surrounded him with that undefined sense of menace.

'I don't see why you should say it, sir,' he replied.

'Before a public announcement, I mean. I gather you and she intend to tie the knot one day?'

Rick felt confused. If Judith had said as much, it was an extraordinary thing for a girl to tell a man she was flirting with. He pondered its implications so long that O'Donovan, with a dry little chuckle, remarked, 'Nuff said, eh! A disinterested old bachelor like me gets to see a lot and hear a lot. A bit like a priest except that people don't come running to us – trying to use us for their own ends.'

'I'm sure, sir,' Rick said, wishing he hadn't made that remark about its being 'only water'. He could see the first stray drops of it shivering the rippled surface of the lake. It would have made a grand excuse to cut and run.

'Of all the marriages I know anything about,' O'Donovan went on ruthlessly, 'the happiest are between those who've known each other since childhood.'

It occurred to Rick to point out that he had known Sally since childhood, too – but then he realized the man might actually be fishing for some such opening. 'I wonder why?' he replied, in a tone that betrayed no interest in the answer.

'To do with the old one-eyed monster,' the Captain assured him. 'A fellow should be able to look at his wife and recall a time with her before that fiery sword descended and the gates of Eden closed behind them for ever.'

They had reached the foot of the path and were now standing on the stone-walled lakeshore. Large, warm spots of rain were falling in a desultory fashion all about them. O'Donovan paid no heed to it; he stared across the lake at the pavilion and murmured, 'So that's where it happened, eh?'

There was a hiss as a drop landed on the glowing tip of Rick's cigar; he puffed the remnant back to full vigour. Wet, it tasted even more acrid. 'Yes,' he observed.

'And Miss Carty was here that evening, too.'

He nodded, 'She, Henrietta, and I were the only survivors – apart from King and the other servants, of course.'

'Yes . . . King, of course. He was quite the hero, I gather?'

The rain was falling in earnest now but still he paid it no regard.

'He shielded me and Miss Carty. He refused to expose us to their fire. It was only the gamekeepers coming down with the dogs that ended the impasse. They dropped one of them there and then. Ciaran Darcy of Killeen.'

'So I remember. As a matter of fact, young man, I'm slightly more involved with the events of that night than you may imagine. I was present at the arrest of Kieran O'Sullivan, you see.'

Rick was stung into facing him at last – the first time their eyes had met since they had started their walk. He saw nothing to suggest that this was anything other than a chance conversation, prompted by the fact that the site of the Murders happened to be facing them.

'You didn't know that?' the Captain added, more as an aside to himself than as a genuine question.

Rick answered it nonetheless with a shake of his head. Then a thought struck him. 'Does Miss Carty know it?' he asked.

The man's nod seemed to confirm it, but then he clouded his answer by saying, 'I mentioned it to Mrs Montgomery. She seems to have some doubt that O'Sullivan was rightly convicted and hanged.'

His use of 'she' was somehow ambiguous, even though

it immediately followed his mention of Aunt Bill.

'He confessed,' Rick pointed out. 'They all did.'

O'Donovan made no response to that. 'Your aunt is still unhappy about the business, though,' he insisted.

Rick felt an almost unbearable tension growing within him. Why did the Captain keep talking about Aunt Bill . . . Aunt Bill's suspicions . . . Aunt Bill's unhappiness? 'What do *you* think, sir, if I may ask?' he countered. 'You saw the fellow at the moment of his arrest, after all.'

He was surprised to see a flicker of admiration in the other's eyes; he had apparently asked an intelligent question. 'I've attended several such arrests in my time, Bellingham – military in support of the civil power, don't you know. Several dozen, in fact. It's not an uncommon occurrence in this troublous country, sad to say. But that's the one which sticks out in my memory.'

'Because you share my aunt's doubts? Or would you rather not say? I mean, I'd quite understand, sir. Duty is duty, after all.'

'Damn, it's gone out!' O'Donovan flicked his half-consumed cigar far into the lake. 'I suppose we'd best turn about.' After a few paces he added, 'Duty, eh? That seems to be today's great question from the Bellinghams – first your sister with her tales from the Khyber Pass, now you.' He chuckled.

The silence was like a hand, O'Donovan's hand, nudging Rick forward, making him respond. 'I wonder if it's different for a soldier, sir?' he asked. 'I mean, esprit de corps and all that sort of thing. And a different corps, at that.'

'What d'you mean – a different corps?'

'Well, if a mistake was made, it wasn't by you and your men. It was the RIC. The civil power. There are two duties, aren't there? A narrow one to the civil power, and a broad one to Justice and Liberty.' The words reminded him of the great painting on the ceiling at Dublin Castle . . . and thus of the St Pat's Ball . . . and thus of what Sally had overheard that night. He still hadn't discovered anything of substance about this fellow.

'Beg leave to differ, old man,' O'Donovan replied. 'It's the same answer I gave your sister. The broad duty sheds light on the narrow. No man of honour could support the civil power in the suppression of justice.' He smiled as he added, 'I hope that settles your doubts, too.' He hunched his shoulders and turned up his collar against the rain. 'And, talking of doubts, may I ask about yours – if you have any, that is – concerning the men they hanged for the Murders?'

Rick's cigar was now down to a length he could discard without causing offence; he turned and cast it toward the lake, but a squall caught it and carried it in a wide arc into one of the shrubberies.

'It'll kill the greenfly,' O'Donovan murmured, allowing the silence to press his question.

'I do, sir,' Rick confessed unhappily. 'From the moment I saw their pictures in the *Illustrated London News*, I felt sure they had the wrong men.'

The Captain's tone was sympathetic now. 'Dashed hard thing for a boy of . . . what were you? Fourteen . . . fifteen? Dashed hard to kick against the pricks. Did you convey your doubts to anyone at the time? King, for instance?'

'No. He was so certain, you see.'

'No one else in the neighbourhood?'

Even at the time it seemed an odd question to ask – or an odd one to put at that particular moment. Perhaps O'Donovan realized it, too, for he immediately added, 'Your Aunt Bill, for instance? Or had she returned to England by then?'

'She'd returned to England. But I hardly needed to tell her.'

'Oh?' He picked up a stick, then a stone, which he tossed in the air and batted expertly away with the stick. 'Snatch a quick single off that,' he commented with a grin. 'Sorry. You were saying?'

'She was here within a day or two of the Murders, you see, sir. And I was in such a state – I couldn't stop talking about them. I used to take people down and give them . . . "guided tours", Aunt Bill used to call them. I had to keep going over and over the same ground. I don't know why, but it helped. Anyway, I'd made such a point of describing the leader – a wild-looking red-headed man.'

O'Donovan nodded but said nothing that might stem Rick's flow.

'You recall the four defendants, the men they hanged?' Rick went on.

'Indeed. Divil a touch of ginger about them.'

'My sister said the same. I mean, she told Aunt Bill about the same man – the same fiery red hair – before they arrested anyone. Except Ciaran Darcy, of course, the man they winged on the day itself. He was half-dead when they hanged him.'

'Yes.' O'Donovan drew the word out as he sank into his own thoughts. They walked in silence a fair way before he added, 'What it boils down to is this: the adults who were present at the Murders and who survived – the servants, in other words – have no doubts about the four who were hanged. But . . .'

'They have *expressed* no doubts about them.'

'Ah!' His tone implied that the distinction had not crossed his mind until then. 'D'you mean publicly? Or at all?'

'Not at all, as far as I know.'

'Yet you still suspect . . . I mean, why did you qualify my remark?'

'I don't really know.' Rick laughed awkwardly. 'Because this is rural Ireland, I suppose. People take sides more according to what side their grandfather took in his day than to what's right and wrong *now*. They consider who's here, who's emigrated, who they've got to go on living with . . . who's going to butter their bread tomorrow, who their uncle's working for . . . where their sister's got a good place she doesn't want to lose. *You* know.'

'Yes,' he replied thoughtfully, 'there's a lot in what you say. And it applies to us, too, you realize? I've got to go on living with the civil power. You've got to go on living with . . . Castle Moore, your tenants, the whole neighbourhood.' Suddenly he stared askance at Rick. 'Gad, but you're a healthy young man,' he exclaimed. 'You're positively steaming!'

Rick laughed. 'I do rather feel as if I've wandered into a Turkish bath, sir.'

'Let's run and get out of these clothes before we catch our deaths.'

As they trotted across the broad expanse of the carriage sweep, Rick wondered if O'Donovan had deliberately not completed his comparison between the grown-ups' apparent acceptance of the trial and executions and the youngsters' unease at them.

Indoors, they parted at the stairhead, for their rooms lay in opposite directions. Henrietta, who had watched them returning through the rain, waylaid the Captain at the crook of the next flight of stairs on his way up to his room. 'Well?' she asked.

He tilted his head to one side and looked guardedly at her.

'It's all right,' she assured him. 'You may talk to me as to Judith. She and I are united in this business –

but we're unsure about Rick.'

'He doesn't trust me,' he said. 'And I can't blame him. Nobody down here's going to – except you and Judith. And Mrs Montgomery, perhaps. But I can't do anything down here.'

'Meaning you can up in Dublin?'

He nodded. 'The sooner the better, I think.'

'And what do *we* do down here meanwhile?'

'Does Darcy's family still live hereabouts? Killeen, is it?'

'They've moved to Flaxmills.'

'Start there,' he advised. 'If you're right, and they hanged the wrong men, it was his evidence put them there.'

'Or what the RIC sergeant claimed was his evidence.'

'That is what I find so unthinkable.'

At that moment King came along the corridor, leading a small procession of footmen and maids, each bearing a pail or ewer of hot water. 'Your bath, Captain O'Donovan, sir,' he said 'Or does your honour be taking it cold?'

Captain O'Donovan returned to Dublin the following afternoon. He protested he needed no one to accompany him to Parsonstown station – until he met Judith after Matins and she volunteered to see him off. Henrietta said she'd have to go along, too, of course. Then Aunt Bill took Rick aside and told him to spoil any plans his sister might have formed about meeting the O'Farrelly boy; so the man who needed no company at all ended up with a surfeit of three.

The rain had passed over before morning service but it remained showery, so they took the phæton rather than the open landau. They parted on the station platform with expressions of gratitude, protestations of almost life-long devotion, and promises to return soon. O'Donovan did a manful job of not staring at Judith more than half the time. The moment the train pulled away he sank into his seat, closed his eyes, and conjured up her image, promising himself all kinds of dire punishment if he allowed it to fade in any way.

His faculty of reason tried to challenge him, asking what in Hades' name he thought he was doing – apart from playing with fire, risking his career, overturning a lifelong vow of misogyny (or, at least, of the avoidance of pure women), and a few other minor matters in that vein. But words were powerless against the bright image of Judith . . .

Judith!

Surely the most beautiful name in all the world! The name of that legendary woman of Bethulia who saved her city from the armies of Nebuchadnezzar by getting their general, Holofernes, drunk and cutting off his head . . . If that earliest heroine had looked anything like her modern namesake, and had possessed only half her determination, then he could well understand how she managed it. He recalled a novel he had read in his youth by some German scribbler who had suggested she did it by lying with the general and putting him into a stupor – but that just showed the mentality of the Hun. Judith Carty would have got the fellow to sharpen the axe, roll back his shirt-collar, and oblige by laying his head on the block – all with a smile and a crook of her little finger.

He wasn't in love with her, of course – at least, not in the sense that he had hopes of marrying her or anything so asinine as that. She was more like a daughter to him, really – in his own mind, in his feeling toward her. Or a childhood playmate re-encountered after many years apart. The absurd disparity in their ages did nothing to tarnish that happy image. Or a ward? Yes, of all the imaginary relationships he might conjure up between them, he liked that one best.

He saw himself with her in Italy – guardian and ward, arm in arm – doing some kind of latter-day version of the Grand Tour, strolling through the Uffizi, Baedeker in hand. He would draw her attention to the finer points of Raphael and Michelangelo and she would listen with a solemn expression, her eyes filled with unbounded admiration for his kindness and learning.

And his greatest kindness would, of course, be the magnanimous way he permitted her to fly from the nest and marry young Bellingham. He would raise no objection, place no obstacle in her path – and thus ensure her deathless gratitude. Never a day would pass but she would think of him in some kindly and solicitous fashion.

Reason fired the last shot in its locker. You are forty-six years old, it reminded him.

But I am not! his soul protested. I am eighteen again! I am made over anew!

They stood on the platform at Parsonstown, waving until they felt foolish, for Captain O'Donovan didn't even poke his head out of the window, much less wave back. 'So much for him, then,' Rick commented.

'What d'you mean by that?' Judith asked.

'Just what I said. "So much for him!" Plain English, I'd have thought.' He tried it on a porter standing nearby. 'So much for him!' he cried, jerking his head toward the departing train.

'Indade, your honour.' The man nodded sagely. 'And him not worth the half of it.' He rose and lumbered toward a pile of mail sacks that had been unloaded on to the platform twenty minutes earlier. 'Sure I'd not give him the shteam off me porridge.'

Rick chuckled after the man had gone. 'See!' he said.

'Oh, you think you're so clever,' she sneered. 'He had no idea who you were talking about. Still,' she added as if to herself, 'there's justice in that, I'm sure, for you had no idea *what* you were talking about, either. So a good pair you made together.'

'Now who's being clever!' He took her arm with a kind of placatory gentleness but she shook herself free. 'What's that for?' he asked.

'I still haven't forgotten yesterday.'

'What about yesterday?'

'Oh, Rick! This parade of wounded innocence is just so *stupid!*'

'Keep your voice down, for heaven's sake.' He made a determined effort to speak gently, glancing all around with an apologetic smile in case anyone had overheard her. Then he realized they were, indeed, alone in one important sense. 'Hey, where's Hen vanished to?' he asked.

'I'll give you one guess,' she said coldly as she set off toward the way out. To herself she added, 'The Bellingham game, you could call it.'

'And meanwhile what are we supposed to do?' He trotted and caught her up. 'Don't walk so fast. It's unladylike.'

She stopped and turned on him. 'Oh, and I suppose vanishing on Turk Island like that with Sally McIver *was* ladylike – not to mention gentlemanly!'

'Ah! Now we have it,' he exclaimed, as if she had at last said the words he had been waiting for. 'I knew that was it. So your jealousy has finally overcome your good sense, has it!'

'Good sense? Where, may I ask, does good sense come into . . .'

'Until now it's the one thing that's stopped you from being so stupid as to come out with a remark like that.' Again he glanced apprehensively about them. 'Look, we can't hold this discussion in such a public place.'

She agreed with him there, at least. 'We could stroll up

to Crinkle Barracks,' she suggested. 'Or out to Riverstown and back?'

'Not Crinkle,' he said darkly. 'I've had enough of the military for a while.'

'Oh, ha ha! Wait till I split me sides.'

Again he tried to take her arm and again she shook herself free at the first touch. 'Yes,' he said, as if the conversation had not been broken, 'it was your good sense, up until now, that prevented you from saying stupid things like that – hinting that something untoward took place between . . .'

'*Un*toward!' she exclaimed. 'I think it was very toward!' They turned off along the lane to Riverstown. 'About as *toward* as any two people can get!'

He stared at her aghast.

'Oh, butter wouldn't melt in that mouth!' she sneered.

'I wish you'd speak plainly. All this hinting isn't terribly clever. Nor helpful, I may add.'

'Helpful is it!' she said vehemently. 'Well, it's helpful *you* should have been to Miss Sally McIver before you stood up again on that island yesterday! There are times when a girl needs a good looking glass, and that was one of them.'

His face blanched, she noticed. So her guess was somewhere near the mark. She decided to push a little further.

'What *are* you blathering about?' he asked pugnaciously.

'Buttons!' she exclaimed, grinning like a card player laying down the ace. 'The little ones all down the bodice of Miss McIver's riding habit. When we first saw her yesterday, they were all in their proper holes, one for one. But when it was time to say goodbye – *after* your little tête-à-tête on the island – lo and behold, there was a loose button at the bottom and a loose hole at the top! "Loose" *is* the right word for it, wouldn't you say?'

'It's the right word for your imagination, sure enough,'

he replied stoutly, secure in the knowledge that, whatever about those buttons, *he* hadn't undone a single one of them. 'Lord, did you think *that's* what we were at!'

'And her smiling like a cat on a trestle!'

'Cats, is it!' he came back at once. 'Well, if cats are in it, I know a better home for the name than Sally McIver.'

'Oh, I suppose you and she sat there staring at the sky, talking of the Celtic Revival and your next great article for the *New Hibernian Quarterly* – and six foot of solid oak between you, the way you couldn't see Miss McIver undoing her bodice and doing it up again all wrong? I don't think!'

'Would you ever hark at yourself!' he sneered, adding under his breath: 'Lord, if you knew what we *did* talk about!'

'D'you deny you kissed her?' Judith challenged, hoping to wrong-foot him – for he would be sure his 'aside' would provoke her to ask quite a different question.

'I do,' he said. But it was not too convincing and he looked away. 'Anyway, even if I did, what's a kiss?'

'A kiss with Bridey Dolan on the backstairs at Castle Moore would be nothing, but . . .'

'I have *never* snatched a kiss with Bridey Dolan, or any other maidservant, at Castle Moore,' he said vehemently.

She grinned at him and pointed a finger at his mouth. 'Now that's something more like an honest denial!' she crowed. 'Practise it if you're going to make a habit of deceit and treachery.' She turned from him and added under her breath, as he had done, 'Though why I should bother to train you, I'm sure I don't know. It won't be *me* you'll practise it on.'

'We'd better stop well short of the bridge,' he said, 'or you'd be in danger of slipping over the parapet and joining all the other eels beneath it! If you really want to know what Sally and I were talking about . . .'

'Did I say I did? I'm sure I haven't an ounce of curiosity about me on the matter.'

'Oh, you will when I tell you,' he promised savagely. 'You see, when you and the egregious Captain O'Donovan sat out a dance together – or stood it out, rather, beside that potted palm – you didn't know there was someone just the other side of it.'

She had to think back to the occasion; but when the full memory of her conversation with Justin returned to her, she felt the blood drain from her face. 'Who?' she asked urgently. 'Sally?'

'Ha! Now you *are* curious. Not to say worried. Not to say aghast!'

'Of course I'm aghast, Rick. You have no idea what that conversation was about.'

'On the contrary, Miss Carty. I think I have a very good idea.' He began to parody it, speaking like lovers in a melodrama.

'How may we meet, my angel?

- I can shlip away to Dublin in the Spring Show, my love.

- Too long, too long! I would pine away. Invite me down to the country.

- I have it – I'll get Mrs Montgomery to invite you down.

- Indeed, my angel – what could be more natural!

- Oh Justin, my dear, you are so special!' He concluded with a mocking bow. 'She heard it all, you see.'

To his amazement, Judith seemed relieved. 'You mean that's all she heard?' she asked. Then, as the implications became clearer to her, she brightened still further. 'It must be! And so she jumped to conclusions. Hah!' She gave a triumphant laugh. 'Of course she did. If she'd overheard what we were *really* talking about, she wouldn't have breathed a word of it to you. Oh, thank God!'

Rick, realizing that his words had put Sally in an invidious position, tried to recover a little ground for her. 'Actually, it wasn't Sally who overheard,' he told Judith. 'It was a friend of hers, who then passed it on.'

'Friend?' Judith echoed scornfully. 'What friend? She hasn't got any – unless it's the one who told me about you and her on the ferry from Holyhead! And anyway, what does that make you! A passer-on of third-hand gossip! For shame, Rick!'

' "Methinks the lady doth protest too much," ' he replied, wondering how he had managed to squander what had looked like a handful of trumps.

'*Hamlet*,' she told him. 'And anyway it's the other way round: "The lady doth protest too much methinks".'

'You and Mad McLysaght!' he said bitterly.

'Yes! Well at least you're getting warmer.'

They had reached the bridge by now, the line between King's County and County Keelity; they paused uncertainly and stared into the swift-flowing water for want of anything better to do. 'Eels,' he said. Then the implications of her comment struck him. 'McLysaght,' he echoed. 'Is that what you and O'Donovan . . . ?'

'We were talking about you, actually, Rick.' And she went on to explain how the subject of the Murders had come up and how O'Donovan had volunteered the fact that he had seen Kieran O'Sullivan arrested. 'And then he said he'd like to see where it happened. Not out of ghoulish curiosity but because he's unhappy about . . . the arrests and the trial and so on. And *that's* when dear Sally must have slipped behind the palm – sorry, Sally's *friend*, of course – slipped behind the potted palm and eavesdropped on the conversation. Because that's when I suggested asking Aunt Bill to invite him down.' She smiled acidly. 'And now, Rick, I think you've had quite enough time to dream up a convincing explanation for Miss McIver's wandering bodice buttons, don't you? I managed to answer you on the spur of the moment. Not a second's pause for thought, if you notice! But then, I have the advantage of telling the plain truth.'

He stared at her like some wild animal at bay. Then he said, 'What did you mean – back at the station – "The Bellingham game"?'

'I didn't think you heard.'

'Well, I did.'

'Yes. Well, in that case, I also think you know exactly what I meant by it.'

He turned from her angrily and stared out across the fields.

She went on coldly: 'And I think you also know your sporting days are over, Rick – at least as far as I'm concerned. You've played the Bellingham game against me for the last time. You may now go and play it against Sally McIver as much as you like. Indeed, I should advise you to do so while you still can. Once she's got you where she wants you, I'll bet she won't let you out of her sight!'

'Sally McIver is a great deal more . . . more . . .' he couldn't think of the word but settled for '. . . *feminine* than you.'

'Feminine is it? Rick, that stuff is fourpence a jar down at the medical hall. Her maid fetches a gallon of it every week! And it'll be every *day* before she's forty.'

He stalked angrily past her, stepping back toward Parsonstown. 'You just twist everything I say. I'm not going to utter another word.'

She stood her ground, watching him depart, wondering why she felt so numb.

After he had gone fifty yards or so he cooled enough to realize that for him to leave her there would become the talk of the town – the very fate they had taken this stroll to avoid. She knew it, too, of course, which was why she just stood there, waiting for him to come back and at least make a public show of unity. He stopped, turned, and called out, 'Well, come on, then!'

She remained by the bridge, staring at him.

Angrily he returned and took her arm. This time she did not shrug him away. So he let go instead – just to show her that he could be independent, too. 'I'm not going to say a word,' he warned her.

'Very understandable, Rick,' she murmured. 'Everything you've said so far has been a misstatement of one kind or another, either of your own devising or – if I'm to believe you in just *one* respect – third hand!'

'God, you are relentless,' he complained.

'In the pursuit of the truth, yes.'

It was the last Wednesday in April but the buds of may blossom were already blushing white, and the pink hawthorn by the tennis court was a blaze of colour – just in time to take over from the flowering cherries, whose fallen petals now carpeted every path and walk.

Henrietta stood at her window, trying to think of Percy, trying to lose herself in that seething whirl of emotion which usually possessed her at the very mention of his name. But today it wasn't working. Her thoughts kept returning to the business that had been arranged for that afternoon – an encounter with Ciaran Darcy's sister in Flaxmills.

It might have been easier to set up a secret meeting between the Pope and the Archbishop of Canterbury; at least those two dignitaries had more in common than the Castle Moore people and the Darcys. And, as Aunt Bill liked to say, Keelity is a small county, populated entirely by eyes, ears, and tongues. Once, in Westport, over a hundred miles from Castle Moore, she had bought a copy of the *Freeman's Journal* – a rag she would not be seen dead with in the normal way. Two weeks later a friend of hers in Simonstown commented on the fact and she had to explain that it had contained an obituary she wanted to cut out and send to a friend in Italy. But had she been a closet Home Ruler, who travelled far over bog, moor, river, and mountain to buy her seditious *Journal*, she would have been unmasked on the spot.

So Henrietta and Judith could not simply breeze into the Darcys' house in Flaxmills and hope that the world would take no notice. Instead, it was all arranged through Kitty Rohane. The plan was that Violet Darcy, the sister, and now chief support of her family, should call on Kitty to pay for some laundering, and that Judith, chaperoned by Henrietta, would happen to drop by with some money and a letter from Josie.

Shortly after luncheon Henrietta cycled off down the drive. Now that the moment of what might yet prove a fateful encounter was almost upon her, she was, much to her surprise, in sparkling mood. Just after the first bend she came upon King, out for his daily constitutional.

'That's a grand oul' machine you have there, Mrs Henrietta,' he remarked as she drew near.

She slowed down and pedalled at his walking pace for a while. 'It's a dreadful oul' machine, King,' she replied. 'The worst sort of a boneshaker, altogether.'

He dipped his head in judicious acknowledgement of that fact. 'It would depend, I imagine, on the distance you intend to cover.'

'Five or six miles,' she told him. 'And that's enough, believe me.'

'Ah, you'd want feathers to cushion you for a longer ride, that's certain. To Parsonstown, for instance.'

She laughed, for his fishing was not usually so blatant. 'Sure I'd want feathers sprouting from my shoulderblades to carry me there.'

'An angel, is it!' His eyes twinkled with a knowing kind of innocence. 'And wouldn't it cramp your style to arrive an angel?'

'Now now, King,' she warned jocularly. 'That's bordering on impertinence.'

'Sure I mean no harm, Mrs Henrietta,' he replied, not a whit abashed. 'Just to say, if ever you're in need of assistance – I'm your man. You know yourself now, I'd see you all right. Haven't I always?'

Though she was a little shocked at his directness, she laughed again as she cycled away. 'I'll bear it in mind,' she called back over her shoulder.

'I'm sure you will,' he murmured to himself; he watched her all the way to the lodge, where, he now noticed, the Carty girl was waiting.

Judith Carty seemed to have fallen out with the young master lately. King was still pondering whether this turn of events suited his books or not. On the whole, he thought it did. The McIver girl got very impatient whenever the Murders were mentioned. And why wouldn't she, seeing how the memory of that day had brought Rick and the other one together again, despite all those years apart. It would suit him well to have Rick spliced with a woman who'd make plain her displeasure every time the event was mentioned. On the other hand, there was a selfish streak in her that promised many a battle of wills if she ever became mistress of Castle Moore. And then again, a Judith Carty who was liberated from the constraints of that same exalted position could be a far greater nuisance than if she had to consider every action in the light of it – whose toes she would be treading on, whose quills she might ruffle . . .

No, he decided gloomily, on that particular question the jury was still out.

Henrietta, speeding away from him, thought briefly of the irony of their meeting. There they were, smiling away, joking with each other, pledging a kind of loyalty, even – and herself on her way to a meeting that might break the man! It would almost make you wonder who you could trust in this world.

She skidded to a halt in the gravelled half-circle of the entrance, shouting 'Hoa-back!' at her bicycle. 'You are a ninny,' she told Judith. 'You could at least come up to the castle and be formally polite to Rick. That would be far more effective than this sort of *mustardy* silence.'

'Effective?' Judith echoed as they set off for Flaxmills, taking the same road as they had ten days ago. 'That begs the question as to what effect I wish to have.'

'You wish him to come crawling back like a whipped cur!' Henrietta said dramatically.

'God forbid!' was the fervent response. 'This quarrel with Rick has been brewing a long time, Hen. Perhaps almost since the day my father brought us back to the Old Glebe . . . I don't know. A long time, anyway. And I've dreaded it because I was afraid of the strong feelings that would all come bubbling to the surface when it happened.'

'And did they?' asked Henrietta, forced to be serious now.

'No.' Judith's tone suggested she was still surprised at the fact. 'I just felt . . . sort of numb. And Rick – poor boy – I think he was rather . . . astonished.'

'It's his own fault for being so blind. All men are blind. At least, they are once they're sure they've got you where they want you. They don't see any reason to go on bothering.'

They passed an old woman carrying a basket of eggs and driving a goat. They got well beyond earshot before Judith replied, 'No, I don't mean to say Rick's astonished in that way. I mean, I'm sure he wonders why I'm being so severe over something so trivial. A snatched kiss with Sally McIver – that's all *he* thinks it's about, I'm sure.'

'If Percy kissed another girl, I'd kill him,' Henrietta said vehemently.

It occurred to Judith to reply that a woman who said

such things couldn't be very sure of herself – but then it struck her that certitude was the one quality that eluded her, too, these days.

And it occurred to Henrietta that Judith's silence might mean she was pondering the threat all too seriously, taking it as actual advice. Perhaps even now she was wondering whether arsenic or a shotgun would be best? 'I don't mean literally,' she added.

'I hope it *was* just a snatched kiss,' Judith replied.

'You mean on the ferry from Holyhead? What Fenella Bell-Stuart said she saw?'

'No. On Turk Island, while we were gathering orchids.'

They passed two labourers with shovels, clearing the shores; again they had to wait until they were out of earshot. 'The thing is, you see,' Judith went on, 'I asked Rick if he could explain why the buttons on Sally's bodice were buttoned up wrong when they came back off the island.'

'Were they?' Henrietta asked with interest. 'I didn't notice.'

'Actually, they weren't.' Judith made a face of mock contrition. 'I just wanted to see what he said.'

'You minx! Did he admit anything?'

'With his eyes, yes. Whole volumes! I was so . . . shattered. And then just numb. As I say – just numb.'

'It didn't make you want to go running to Fergal! Out of revenge if nothing else.'

'No.' She shook her head pensively.

'That's the most hesitant denial I ever heard from you.'

'Well, it didn't make me want to go *running* to anyone. But it did make me wonder if I wouldn't be a lot happier with Fergal. I even wondered about Captain O'Donovan! Not very seriously.'

'He's very serious about you, you know.'

But Judith refused to believe that. 'Only because he

knows it's safe. His bid will never be called. If I let him understand I'd finished with Rick and wanted to see a lot more of him, he'd say that was wonderful but unfortunately he'd just been given a staff posting to Rangoon or somewhere. And then he'd move heaven and earth to make jolly sure he wasn't lying.'

'And does it cut both ways?' Henrietta asked slyly.

'How?'

'Can you indulge in little romantic imaginings about him – just because *you* know it's safe and *your* bid will never be called.'

The flush that rose to Judith's cheek and her reluctant smile answered for her.

'But Fergal would be a more serious possibility,' Henrietta went on, becoming serious herself once more.

'Almost too serious,' Judith admitted. 'I mean, I care so much for him – even just as a friend – that I'd never . . . I mean, I can't turn to him now.'

'I hate to say it, but he'd be a much better husband than Rick. They should have sent Rick away to school, but it's too late to civilize him now.'

Judith looked at her in surprise. 'He seems quite civilized to me.'

'Oh!' Henrietta's tone was dismissive. 'He's picked up the veneer all right – opens doors for ladies . . . stands up when they come into the room . . . that sort of thing. But all the deeper marks of civilization are missing. Haven't you noticed? He's completely bound up in his own feelings . . .'

'God! Aren't you very hard on him!' Judith suspected that Henrietta was only saying these things to see whether she leaped to Rick's defence.

'I don't mean he does it selfishly or deliberately,' Henrietta went on. 'It's just that he's never been forced to consider other people's feelings. It's not his fault. But it'd make him a difficult man to live with – especially in the indissoluble bond of matrimony. Ask one who knows!'

'Well . . .' Judith shook her head sadly. 'Warnings like that aren't much good, I'm afraid. One doesn't calculate things out in that neat fashion. Love's not like a bit of double-entry bookkeeping.'

Henrietta's tone was sad, too. 'That's the usual argument for letting the grown ups arrange these things for us – and look where it got me!'

'Why d'you say he'd be better, anyway?' Judith asked, meaning she wanted to be told all Fergal's good points.

Instead, Henrietta spoke of her brother: 'The other thing is that he's still far too much under the thumb of King.' She stared quizzically at Judith. 'Can I ask you something? What do *you* think ought to happen to that man?'

'He should be out on his ear.'

'And that would be enough to satisfy you?'

She dipped her head reluctantly. 'Probably. I just want him gone. Never to be seen again. In an ideal world, of course, he'd be brought to justice, but I'll leave that to Judgement Day. Or' – she chuckled savagely – 'to Aunt Bill! She'd gladly dismember that man with her bare hands, I'm sure.'

'Really?'

'Oh, she can't abide him. But it's nothing to do with justice and fair play. It's pure hatred. It's the O'Hara in her, all dark and brooding.' A new thought struck her. 'I wonder if Rick would understand that, too?'

'Why wouldn't he?' The connection, or lack of it, puzzled Henrietta.

'Well, you say he's incapable of considering the feelings of others – those are feelings, too. Feelings "with a vengeance", to coin a phrase! I think what little boys learn when they go away to school is how to cope with the anger and selfishness of the big boys – how to be cunning and sly and get their own way by stealth and duplicity. That's one way of "taking other people's feelings into consideration" – you can't deny! But if your theory about Rick is right, he's incapable of being cunning and sly and two-faced, either. So there's good and bad to it, you see!'

Henrietta smiled. 'You're a champion defender, Ju.'

They reached the foot of the first steep hill – and the limit of their muscles, hampered as they were by long dresses. 'D'you think Rick is *totally* under King's thumb?' Judith panted as they both dismounted.

Henrietta considered the question a moment. 'No,' she said slowly. 'But he has to consider the situation *as it is*, not some ideal of justice. He has to worry about the estate . . . all the tenants . . . all the . . . I mean, it's like a spider's web.'

'Yes. And we all know who's the spider!'

'True. But that doesn't alter the fact that the whole place is caught up in the web. It's a *fact*. You and I can ignore it. And so can Aunt Bill and Captain O'Donovan. But Rick can't. That web is what's holding the estate together at the moment. All the intrigues and favours and . . . oh, *you* know – all the *Irish* connections and undercurrents and . . . God, there isn't even a word for it! Isn't that typical? *You* know what I mean and *I* know what I mean, but there's no actual word for it. It's all just nods and winks and "I'm yer man" and "I'll see ye all right, boys!" That's the web *this* spider has spun. Get rid of him and who'll repair it? I think Rick worries about that a lot.'

A spirit of gloom descended on Judith. Henrietta's words made her feel they were meddling in affairs they did not even half-understand. 'He's never said a word about it,' she complained.

'But he wouldn't, would he? I'm not even sure he could put it in so many words – the way I have. He'd say something much vaguer like, "Life goes on!" Or,

"Things change." But *that's* what he'd mean by it.'

They had come to the top of the hill. Judith stopped and drew several deep breaths. 'D'you think we ought to go on with this meeting in Flaxmills?' she asked bleakly.

'I'm sure of it. But I think we ought to be clear about one thing in our minds.'

'What?'

'All we're doing is trying to find out the truth – or as much of it as has survived. That's all. What we decide to do when we think we've found it is quite another thing. It's a decision for another day.'

'And we might even decide to do nothing?' Judith asked.

'I'm afraid so, darling.'

Most of the Darcys in Ireland were Roman Catholics of twelfth-century Norman lineage, but the particular branch to which Violet and her late brother belonged were Normandy Huguenots who fled to Ireland during the massacres of Protestants at the end of the sixteenth century; in short, they were relative newcomers. There had been quite a large plantation of Huguenots in North Keelity, for weaving was one of their most prominent trades. In the eighteenth century, however, growing prosperity had drawn them to Dublin, where they expanded into banking and various wholesale trades. The Darcys of Flaxmills were among the few survivors of that plantation in the county.

They owned a small printing shop in Simonstown and published a weekly newssheet, the *Vox Populi*, known simply as the *Vox*. Like many non-landed Protestants they were ardent Home Rulers, so the paper had a small but unswerving readership. (Ten years earlier many landed Protestants had been equally keen on the idea of lording it over their own island without Liberal interference from over the water, but the Land Wars had driven them smartly into the Unionist camp.) Coupled with the print shop was a stationery emporium, where you could also buy the most elegant hats and the finest cabbages in town – the hats because Violet's mother made them, and the cabbages because her grandfather was a keen gardener with a fair few acres. Since her brother's death she had become the manageress of both halves of the business, riding the five miles between Flaxmills and Simonstown every day.

Miss Darcy was a tall angular woman in her mid-thirties. Her usual demeanor was watchful and reserved – and never more so than on that particular afternoon when Judith and Henrietta, half-blinded by the sun, came falteringly into the dark parlour of the Rohanes' little cottage. After the introductions and the usual exchange of pleasantries were over, an awkward silence descended. Judith, her eyes only just becoming accustomed to the gloom, glanced at Henrietta, who nodded the ball swiftly back into her court.

'Ye have something to communicate, I believe?' Miss Darcy prompted.

'Yes.' Judith drew a deep breath, which the frantic beat of her heart cut into three jerky sighs. 'Both of us, Miss Bellingham and I, that is, have come reluctantly but increasingly to believe that Miss Rohane's brother and the other three who were hanged with him were innocent of that crime. And . . . er . . .'

'You want my help in getting the right ones!' Miss Darcy sneered.

'No,' Henrietta replied firmly. 'We know who did it – and we imagine they're beyond reach of the law, anyway. And we're not seeking a private evening-up of the scores, either. But there is an account to settle with . . . how may I put it?'

'With certain parties who remain,' Judith suggested. 'Parties who, even if they had no hand in the Murders themselves, certainly turned the occasion to their own advantage in the days and months that followed. Do I make our meaning plain?'

'I see.' Violet Darcy stood and took an aimless pace or two. The room was too small to allow her to walk off her agitation so she crossed to the window and stared out at the garden, at a couple of rooks fighting over a twig. At length she returned to her seat. 'I must confess,' she said, 'that when Miss Rohane first proposed this meeting, I had the fiercest doubts as to whether I should attend. I assumed – wrongly, as you now assure me – that you wished to hear from my lips the confession the polis would never have wrung from my brother's.'

'And he would surely never have named four *innocent* men, either,' Henrietta added.

'One of whom worked for him,' Kitty pointed out. 'My fella.'

'Oh, did he?' Judith asked.

Miss Darcy nodded. 'Peter Deasy used to set up the type for the handbills and generally keep the shop in order. But we're straying from my main point, which is that my brother would never have informed on the others, whoever they were. Those words were put into his mouth after his death by Sergeant Nairn . . .'

'Or by someone at Dublin Castle who ordered Sergeant Nairn to say those things,' Kitty said.

'Or,' Judith added, 'by some local crony to whom the sergeant owed a favour.'

'Well, every man who was named in that list wanted to see the backs of the English bloodsuckers,' Miss Darcy concluded. 'There's no gainsaying that. So it would've been an aisy enough favour to grant.'

'But they wanted to see a *clean* back to them,' Kitty pointed out bitterly. 'Not one riddled with gunshot.'

Henrietta seized the chance to ask the one question that really mattered to her and Judith. 'Yes, Miss Darcy,' she said. 'Whatever about the four they hanged, there can be no doubt that your brother *was* one of the men in the ambush that evening. I was there, too. I watched them standing in a half-circle round the summer house, calmly and methodically emptying their guns into my parents, my two brothers, and my older sister. He was one of them. I saw him run and I saw him fall. May I ask you what *your* feelings are now about such an outrage?'

The woman's lips trembled; she blinked rapidly, several times. When she drew breath to speak it shivered. 'My feelings are the same now as they were then, Mrs Austin. You don't own a dog and bark yourself. You don't own a newspaper and go abroad with a gun. I loved my brother but I detested what he and his "brotherhood" did. And I detest it still – even more strongly, if that were possible. Does that answer you?'

'I had to know,' Henrietta pointed out.

A curt nod of the head conceded the point. 'What now, then?'

Judith began: 'Your brother was tried and hanged by the military . . .'

'They were afraid he'd die first and cheat them!' she crowed.

'I'm sure that's true. But what I'm saying is that he died before there was even a mention of a confession.'

'Better than that,' Miss Darcy said vehemently. 'He died crowing that they never broke him, that he never uttered a syllable about his own part or that of any other man there. I know because I was there to the end – the night before they butchered him.'

'That's what we wished to know. Did anyone else hear him make that claim? Anyone outside your family?'

'Sergeant Nairn did.'

Judith sighed. 'That's no help.'

'And the constables sent in to watch him. They'd turned him over to the polis by then. The fellow couldn't lift his own hand off the bedsheet and they had him shackled by both feet! And two great louts in blue to watch!'

'And d'you know their names? Are they still in the force?'

Two simple questions – but they marked the point where Miss Darcy realized that these young ladies from the 'enemy' camp were no mere dilettantes in their pursuit of the truth. It was a passion she recognized, though from the opposite side of the fence. 'I do,' she said. 'And indeed they are. Constable Jones and Constable Hendry. Both living in Simonstown still.' She took out a notebook and wrote down their names and addresses, tearing out the page and handing it to Judith with a wary smile – the first. 'I doubt you'll get any story out of them but the one that supports Sergeant Nairn.'

'Well, we certainly shan't *start* with them! People like that go with the tide. So it's the tide itself we must attend to first.'

'I wish you luck!' Miss Darcy had the first inkling that she was dealing with two women who were perhaps not entirely rational – at least on this particular topic.

'We were rather hoping,' Judith said, 'that we would all be wishing *each other* luck.'

Miss Darcy shook her head. 'I don't see how I may help. I can hardly support you openly – that would surely be the kiss of death! And I don't see how we can continue to meet like this, without attracting comment.'

Henrietta smiled like a conjuror approaching the climax of a trick. 'I have an idea or two as to that,' she said. 'Tell me, do you know *Blackwood's Magazine*, published in Edinburgh?'

Miss Darcy nodded. 'I've seen it, of course, but I don't subscribe.'

'But could you cope with the printing of a similar

magazine – in size and thickness, I mean – here in Ireland?'

'Every month?' Her tone was both pleased and alarmed at the prospect.

'Every quarter.'

'Ah!' Now she was relieved. 'Yes, I'm sure we could manage that – as long as all the copy didn't descend on my desk in the last four days.' Her mind switched back into its more everyday grooves and began working rapidly. 'Also, someone would have to come to the works and edit it on the stone – to make it fit, you know. And would there be advertising? Who is to canvass that?'

'Hoa back!' Henrietta laughed. 'The two young ladies who propose to bring out this magazine have probably never heard of Darcys of Simonstown. Still less – or *a fortiori*, as they would probably express it – do they realize that you are going to be its printer. But they are visiting my brother early next month and I shall find some tactful way of informing them of the fact. Then, you see, we shall have every reason in the world to meet. And quite openly. And whenever we like!'

Judith stared at Henrietta in an odd mixture of dismay and pity. It had only just occurred to her *why* the poor woman was so keen to maintain this newly established connection with Miss Darcy, who, on the face of it, could be of little further assistance to them now.

Lord Vigo drove his sisters over to Castle Moore in person. The distance from Moonduff House, his seat in County Westmeath, was some forty miles, over roads battered by winter and scoured by spring, so Gwinny and Letty were not in the best of humour when they arrived. Gwinny took Rick aside at once and said, 'By the way, Vigo thinks this article you've written . . . you *have* written it, I hope?'

He crossed his fingers behind his back and nodded. 'Pretty well. Needs a better final par.'

'Par?' she echoed.

'Yes.' He chuckled glad to be one-up on her in their common profession. 'It's what we writer chappies call a paragraph, don't you know. Fellow on the local rag told me that. He gets paid so much a par.'

'Ah . . . yes.' At the mention of pay she went all vague. 'Anyway, the thing is, Vigo imagines your article is just a bit of a decoy.'

'For what?' Rick asked anxiously.

'What d'you think!'

'Lord, no! Then one of us must disabuse him before he leaves.'

'You'll do no such thing!' she said peremptorily. 'These last couple of months have been heaven for Letty and me. He's practically stopped bringing around all those odious young men for us to simper at and otherwise frighten off.' Her brother found them at that moment. 'Ah, Vigo,' she said, changing tone brightly, 'I was just telling Rick what utter heaven these last few months have been for Letty and me.'

'Good, good!' Vigo beamed and soaped his hands. 'Aren't they angels, Bellingham! Never a cross word between them, rivals though they are.'

Gwinny cleared her throat ominously but he persisted. 'Pity anyone has to choose between them, what! Pity to separate 'em. They're better matched than any carriage pair you ever saw.'

'I know, I know,' Rick sighed. 'I was thinking of turning Mussulman, actually.'

'Oh, Rick!' Gwinny exclaimed edgily. 'He's such a tease!'

Vigo stayed to dinner and then – having found the port, a Taylor's '45, very much to his liking – was obliged to stay overnight. While he was in the house nobody mentioned Rick's article, or even the *New Hibernian Quarterly*.

Rick stayed up till dawn, writing it – all five thousand words – and then snatched three hours' sleep, waking fresh as a dairymaid at his usual hour of eight. As the sisters finished breakfast he said, 'Oh, by the way . . .' and tossed his sheaf of paper nonchalantly between them.

When they cornered him in the morning room an hour later, their attitude had undergone a subtle change. 'It really is a most *excellent* piece,' Gwinny told him – stressing the word as if it were the last thing she had ever expected to be able to say about his work.

'You must have sweated blood!' Letty produced the unladylike phrase with a professionally pugnacious air.

Rick dithered between agreeing and saying he had just dashed it off. 'It wasn't all that hard,' he said finally. 'Of course, I thought about it for ages before I set pen to paper. I think that's the secret.'

'I must make a note of that.' Gwinny took out a small exercise book and, selecting a clean page, wrote: '*Think before you write!*' She stared at it, slightly dismayed, aware that it was rather a trite sort of exhortation. 'It's always the most obvious things one overlooks,' she said defensively.

Henrietta found them at that moment and, overhearing the last remark, entered, saying, 'Such as – who is going to set it up in type . . . and print it, for instance?'

'Ah, Mrs Austin!' They were not pleased at her interruption.

'Actually,' Letty said, 'we've talked to one or two printers in Athlone already.'

'Oh?' Henrietta's tone suggested that was a most surprising thing to have done. 'In Athlone?'

'They are nearest to us,' Gwinny pointed out patiently.

'And nearest to Vigo, as well,' Henrietta shot back.

'But you must have thought of that. You must be very confident that your influence will be greater than his.'

It was quite plain they had not thought of it; the looks of consternation they exchanged made it impossible to deny.

'Perhaps we should look farther afield?' Letty suggested. Then, turning to Henrietta, 'Do you by any chance know of a good local printer down here in Keelity, Mrs Austin?'

'Oh, do call me Henrietta please. We're all of an age here.' She glanced at her brother and added, 'More or less.' Then, back to the other two: 'It so happens I do.'

'Protestant?' Gwinny asked.

Henrietta's smile said: Of course. 'And what's more, they're Home Rulers.'

The Dalton sisters were aghast. 'Is that a good thing?'

'Of course!' Henrietta laughed at their simplicity. 'It means that Vigo will never exercise the slightest influence or control over them – don't you see? He'd only have to say, "Do this!" to ensure they went and did the other thing, instead.' She smiled at them indulgently. 'My dear Gwinny, my dear Letty – I'm sure you have the finest nose in Ireland for a bit of good writing. I'm sure that a hanging subordinate clause wouldn't get past you in mid-Atlantic on a moonless night. But it does strike me you need a business manager to take some of the lesser worries off your shoulders. No?'

She turned to Rick, who was staring at her in amazement. 'The *Vox?*' he asked in what was almost a whisper. 'That Darcy rag?'

'RC?' Gwinny echoed. 'I thought you said . . .'

'Darcy! Darcy!' he told her. 'Frenchies like yourselves.' Then, back to his sister, 'You cannot mean this as a serious proposal.'

'Why not?'

'You know very well why not.'

'I'm glad someone does,' Gwinny muttered.

'Ciaran Darcy was one of the Castle Moore Murderers,' he explained.

'And the very week he died,' Henrietta added in her implacable way, 'his sister Violet had the courage to write an editorial in the *Vox*, denouncing all forms of violent political agitation and outrage. She reserved her bitterest venom for those who sought to use random murder as a form of political coercion. She was reviled for it at the time, even by *our* friends, who thought that families ought to stand by one another, no matter what. But everyone respects her for it now. I think we owe it her.'

'We?' Rick echoed uneasily.

'Yes.' She smiled innocently. 'Didn't I understand it was part of the arrangement that you'd be helping to launch this new maga? Aren't you putting some money behind it?'

Gwinny and Letty stopped breathing. It was the single most important question they had come to Keelity intending to ask, though they had not the first idea how to work around to it.

Hetty let Rick stumble on for a sentence of two – explaining how jolly difficult it was for him . . . family money all tied up in trusts . . . need to satisfy trustees – all as old as Methuselah . . .

Then she said, 'Actually, my dears, I thought there might be something of that sort to hinder the project. I know he's keen as mustard *in spirit*, but there are these awkward hurdles to overcome. Fortunately, however, I have money of my own whose disbursement not even my dear husband can direct. What were you thinking of, as working capital – just to start with?'

The sisters clenched their fists tight under the table to prevent themselves from shivering. 'A hundred pounds?' Gwinny volunteered.

Henrietta made a glum face and shook her head.

They slumped in disappointment until she added, 'I believe you'll need more like four hundred. Or may I now start saying *we?*'

It was a fine calculation Lord Vigo had to make. Two nubile spinsters could stay as guests in the house, or in this case the castle, of an eligible bachelor for perhaps a week without exciting comment of an adverse nature. Perhaps even ten days . . . but that, he decided, was the limit – unless, to be sure, he could make a formal announcement of a more permanent liaison. When the ten days were up, he drove over from Moonduff to ask his sisters whether any such announcement was in the offing. He was afraid to ask Rick himself in case they hadn't quite got him cornered and he could still bolt on them.

It put the sisters in a quandary, of course. Not only were they having a splendid time, they had also put together a jolly good first issue of *New Hibernian Quarterly* – for they had brought down a number of contributions from people they had badgered during the Season. An outright no would bring it all to an end.

On the other hand, they could hardly give Vigo the yes he was hoping to hear. So they shilly-shallied a day or two, trusting he'd simply tire of it and go away, leaving them to get on with planning their second number. Naturally, it would be ten times better than the first because people would now be able to see they were serious about it. During that time Vigo watched them closely and came to the conclusion that, though all might not be lost, nothing was to be won by leaving Gwinny and Letty in young Bellingham's company; in fact, what was needed, he thought, was a good dose of *absence* – that well-known kind which makes the heart grow fonder. The following day he announced that they were off to London for the last few weeks of the season there.

What he didn't know was that, on that very morning, a letter had come for Aunt Bill from Uncle Hereward; the old boy had put his foot down at last and was insisting that Rick be returned forthwith to Norfolk. Gwinny and Letty heard of it only minutes before their brother made his grim announcement, trembling a little in anticipation of the storm he felt sure was about to break. To his surprise they flung their arms around his neck, kissed him haphazardly about the head, and told him he was the most wonderful brother they ever had.

Judith, now a stranger at the castle, heard nothing of it until they had all departed. In fact, she had swallowed her annoyance and, for the first time since their quarrel five weeks ago, called to see Rick and try to patch things up. To her surprise she was met at the door by Henrietta, dressed for a drive. 'Well timed,' was her greeting. 'You'll have to leave your bicycle in the stables.'

'But I came to see Rick.'

Henrietta told her what happened. 'I'm taking the last of the copy for the maga to Parsonstown,' Henrietta concluded. 'Surely you got my note?'

'No, I was out with Mama all morning and then I came directly here.'

They ambled round the back to the stables as they talked.

'Without luncheon?' Henrietta asked.

Judith made a wry grimace. 'I felt too nervous to eat.'

'Good heavens – you!'

'I thought it might be quite unpleasant. I mean, I *was* rather severe with poor Rick that Sunday. Heavens, is it only five weeks ago?'

'Five weeks and two days.'

Judith looked at her askance for this pedantry until she realized it was the last time she had seen Percy O'Farrelly, too. She smiled wearily. 'I stand corrected!'

'Henrietta said. 'It's interesting, isn't it – I count the hours but you don't! Food for thought, what?'

Judith said nothing.

'Anyway, you'll come, won't you? Aunt Bill won't let me go unless you do. And I had to promise on my honour I wouldn't see you-know-who.'

Judith turned to her in surprise. 'You promised that?'

Henrietta smiled tolerantly. 'I have no intention of keeping my word, of course. All's fair in love and war. In love, anyway. Put your bicycle in there – that loose box was mucked out this morning.'

When they were in the gig Henrietta returned to the parallel she had drawn earlier, saying, 'You didn't seem too crestfallen when I said Rick had gone back over the water, darling?'

After a pause Judith replied, 'Perhaps another bout of Norfolk is just what he wants. Or needs.'

'Absence makes the heart grow fonder, eh?' The cliché reminded her of something and she laughed. 'Poor Vigo! That's what he said to me – thinking of his sisters and Rick. He took them to London in the fond hope that would jerk Rick back into his senses. The poor chap simply cannot understand that those two women are never going to marry anyone.'

Judith sighed. 'Lucky creatures!'

They turned left out of the front gate and set off at a spanking trot on the Parsonstown road. 'D'you really think so?' Henrietta responded. 'That just means you're not in love yourself. It proves it, in fact.'

'Perhaps,' Judith conceded wanly. 'But that's not what I meant. I meant the possibility of *choosing* not to marry. We're not brought up to think of it as a choice, are we? It's not a choice. It's a fate.' She closed her eyes to help marshal her thoughts. 'I know I enjoyed the Dublin Season at the time, but when I look back on it, I shudder. All those desperate young butterflies in muslin –

some of them not so young any longer – and their even more desperate mamas. And all those beady-eyed bachelors . . . It suddenly struck me the other day. I couldn't think where I'd seen that glint in the eye before. And then it came to me. I've seen it in Parsonstown mart, of course – round the auction ring when they parade a new heifer. Doesn't it make *you* shudder, Hen? That's what I meant when I said the Dalton sisters are lucky. They can trot round the ring looking all the bidders in the eye' – she laughed as an image struck her – 'and then do what cows are famous for!'

'Ju! So agricultural!' Henrietta was shocked.

So was Judith, in fact; it had just tumbled out of her. 'Well,' she said, 'it sometimes makes me feel like that. It's back to my gingerbread cottage in the middle of the forest, isn't it? Except that now I have my memories of the Season to help me understand why it seems even more attractive.'

Henrietta transferred the reins to one hand and gave her a brief hug with the other. 'It'll all be over one day, darling,' she assured her.

'I'll bet *you* thought that the day you married Harold.'

Henrietta made none of her usual responses to the mention of her husband's name. She merely repeated that it would all be over one day.

She passed the rest of the journey describing the first issue of *New Hibernian Quarterly*, saying how, to everyone's surprise – and not least that of the Dalton sisters – it had actually turned out rather well. The biggest surprise of all, she thought, had been Rick's contribution.

'I never thought of him as scholarly at all,' commented Judith, who had not yet had the chance to read it.

'Oh, it's not in the least bit scholarly,' Henrietta assured her. 'Just the opposite. That's what I thought he'd write, too, mind you – something rather jejune. Whenever his tutors set him an essay, he just used to creep into the library and chiz something out of *Rees's Cyclopædia* or *Britannica*. His borrowings, as Sheridan said, "lay like lumps of marl upon a barren moor, encumbering what they could not fertilize". But . . .'

'I wonder when we'll see McLysaght again?' Judith mused.

'But this wasn't like that at all,' Henrietta insisted. 'It wasn't anything learned and profound, of course; but it wasn't all froth, either. And so *easy* to read, I couldn't believe it. It simply trips along, saying just enough to hold your attention, throwing out little squibs and paradoxes and the occasional bit of bony thought to chew on and . . .'

'Not to mention a liberal dose of mixed metaphor!'

'All right! I'm sorry. It must be tedious to hear me going on if you haven't read it. However' – she brightened – 'you'll have an hour or two to rectify that, won't you? While I'm, ah, otherwise *occupied* in Parsonstown.' She pulled a face and added under her breath, 'Now who's being agricultural!'

Violet Darcy had a cubbyhole, grandly labelled 'Editorial Office' where she scribbled copy, corrected galleys, pasted up proofs, and, when she got around to it, wrote out the bills and stuffed them in envelopes. It was also where she kept turpentine, lampblack, and boiled linseed oil for the ink; boxwood fonts for posters; humbugs and halfpennies for errand boys; and chocolate-covered marzipans for herself – and, on this particular afternoon, for Judith, too. Neither made any comment about Henrietta's absence – which was proof enough to each that the other knew all about it.

Violet, pretending to do a little bookkeeping, was actually watching Judith with the aid of a cracked looking glass propped at the end of her desk; it normally allowed her to keep an eye on the print shop without craning her neck. She knew no more than local gossip had told her – which covered the entire ground between the merest suggestion that Judith Carty and Rick Bellingham might have done a bit of a line once upon a time to the copper-bottomed guarantee that they were already secretly married. Watching her now, seeing her eyes calmly devour the pages of Rick's galley proofs, you'd never know which was nearer the truth. The girl ate her marzipans with more obvious relish than she read the pages before her.

You'd never know how serious she was, either, about unmasking the ones who were guilty of the deaths of four innocent men. The very thought of those times made Violet as uncomfortable now as it had then. She could not help wondering how it would have been if her own brother Ciaran had lived. Would he have let those men hang for a crime he knew they didn't commit? The rest of them had done so – his four cronies, Mick O'Leary and the other three who'd escaped. What must it feel like, she wondered, to know that four guiltless men died for a crime *you* committed? It was the one question she had never asked Mick O'Leary, though he had stood out there in the print shop ever since that day, a month after the Murders, when he'd suddenly shown up, beard shaved off, hair cropped short and dyed black – and him calling himself 'Jack Egan' and a Dublin accent on him thick enough to mulch rhubarb. God, if she even called him 'Mick' now he'd jump out of his skin!

How does it feel, Mick O'Leary, to sup porter and enjoy a pipe of baccy on a warm summer's eve – and maybe go out and take a salmon or three when it's dark – and to know the lime has eaten the flesh off the bones of four fine men, lying where you should lie, as you now stand on a soil that should be theirs? Oh, Mick O'Leary, was it for that you saw the flag unfurl?

God but he'd kill her!

And how does it feel, Violet Darcy, to put twenty silver shillings a week into the hands of such a creature, knowing what you do, and believing with all your heart – or so you protest – that he and what he stood for at that time is the very incarnation of all that is wrong with this wretched island of ours? My land will you ever arise!

God but she ought to do the job for him!

'Amazing,' Judith murmured, half to herself, as she set the galley down. 'I can recognize him in every line and yet I still cannot believe he wrote it. D'you want me to put a little mark or two? I noticed a couple of misprints.'

Violet pushed a pencil toward her and the almost empty box of marzipans. 'Please. This is the one place in the world where you need neither piety nor wit to cancel half a line.'

Judith smiled as she took a comfit with one hand and, with the other, lightly circled the two mistakes she had spotted. 'Nor tears to wash out a word of it,' she said, rounding off the quotation and popping the delicacy into her mouth.

'Just a blacklead pencil.' Violet took the galleys, glanced at what Judith had marked, and added, 'Yes, indeed. You have a good eye, Miss Carty. But I'll not say a word to Mrs Austin in case she'd exploit you.'

'Why not? She's doing so at this moment, in fact.'

'Ah ha!' Violet inserted the correct proof-reader's marks. 'Mr Egan, would you ever come in here?'

The man laid aside his broom and entered the office, wiping his hands on his ink-stained apron; he glanced incuriously at Judith and then just stood there, eyes downcast, waiting for orders. There was an oddly mechanical air about all his actions.

'Miss Carty's after finding two little ones, which you might as well take care of now. I'm sure that's the last.' As Violet gathered up the proofs she turned to Judith and said, 'Wouldn't it be wonderful if we could read back through our lives and revise them just as easily!'

Judith wondered if the woman truly did not wish to discuss Henrietta's behaviour; had she called in the man Egan to prevent it? She decided to give it one more go. 'To pencil a ring around a whole marriage, for example,' she murmured. 'And write *delete* or whatever the appropriate term is in the margin. There's many a man or woman would love that!'

'And what would *you* delete, Miss Carty?' She still did not pass the sheaf of papers over to the waiting Mr Egan.

Judith thought briefly and said, with a small laugh of surprise. 'Nothing! If you mean mistakes *I've* made. I mean, I once called Lady Jane Kennedy "Lady Kennedy" instead of "Lady Jane", and things like that, which make you curl with embarrassment afterwards. But it's not worth going back and undoing such things, is it?' Then, serious again, she added, 'However, if you mean things that have happened in my life, well, naturally, I'd put a ring around the Castle Moore Murders. And the mark I'd score in the margin would leave its dent through ten pages.'

Violet was watching Jack Egan throughout the latter part of this speech. Not a muscle twitched, not a sinew stiffened. 'Miss Carty was one of the lucky three who escaped that night,' she explained. 'Though she did get a bullet in the chest.'

He nodded curtly. 'That was a sorry affair, so it was.'

'Why, Mr Egan,' his employer chided. 'You're becoming quite the Midlander at last. "A sorry affee-ar", eh!' She mimicked his pronunciation, which – unusually for him – had slipped on that one word.

He held forth his hand and grinned, the Dublin jackeen consciously imitating the Midland bogtrotter. 'Is i' a lo' to do, Miss Daaarcy?'

She released the galleys to him and he left. 'He was a

wild man in his youth,' she said to his departing back.

It struck Judith that a man and a woman of similar ages, forced by their profession to work side by side, would be more or less compelled to develop a sort of joking antagonism – like a lightning conductor. Even in the brief time she had been on the premises she could not help noticing there was plenty of 'lightning' between these two, a kind of smouldering tension you could almost touch. She wondered what being 'a wild man' entailed in the particular case of Mr Egan – and how Miss Darcy knew of it.

Once again she became aware that, just beneath the placid surface of civilized life, there were undercurrents of anxiety, passion, and stress – enough to destroy most people, you'd think. The image of her safe little haven, deep in the forest, rose in her mind's eye for the second time that day. But it no longer seemed as appealing as it once had done; at least, she no longer yearned for it. Her feeling about it was now more sentimental than anything; it had joined that lumber of childhood toys and fancies – things you got out to play with every once in a while, but only for nostalgia's sake. She already knew it held nothing for her, not even as an ideal, an image of one kind of attainable perfection.

Briefly she wondered when she had crossed that watershed.

'I hope Mrs Austin won't be too long,' she said.

'Why? Have you other messages in town? I'll be here a good while yet, if you wanted to slip out now.'

'No, I need to go round by Robertsons' mill on the way home. I have an order for oats.'

Miss Darcy's eyes dwelled on hers awhile; she had twigged that was only half the story. 'Mr Egan,' she called out, 'you may leave that till the morning.'

'I have it done already,' came the reply. 'Wasn't the type standing here on the table.' A moment later he popped his head back into the office. 'I'm away so,' he told them cheerily.

This time Judith looked at him more closely. With Miss Darcy's assurance as to his former character, she studied his eyes in particular and saw a hint, a remnant, of some wildness there. Also they were green, which was most unusual in a black-haired man.

'Would he put you in mind of someone?' Miss Darcy asked when the outer door had closed behind him.

'No, I was just thinking – I never saw anyone else, man or woman, with black hair and green eyes like him. It's very unusual. What part of Dublin is he from? I used to be quite good at telling that but I couldn't place him when he was talking to you earlier – a bit of Northside and a bit of Southside.'

'Ask him,' Miss Darcy replied. 'He never goes back there. D'you get all your feed at Robertsons'? I heard it wasn't too clean sometimes.'

Judith doodled with the pencil as she replied. 'I want to talk with them about Mr King – the butler at the castle.'

'King of the Castle!'

'Just so. I want to try and discover their attitude to him.' She looked up suddenly. 'Have you ever been to the seaside, Miss Darcy?'

'I have of course. Why?'

'And did you ever walk along the rocks between the tides and see all the limpets and barnacles and things – all airing their pink petticoats? And you say to yourself, "Sure I could lift those off – aisy as you'd like!" And then you try it, and they hug themselves down on the rock, tighter than a hungry leech, the way you'd hardly prise them off with a lump hammer and a mason's chisel. Did you ever notice that?'

Miss Darcy laughed, for she knew what Judith was really talking about. 'It's even worse with humans, Miss

Carty,' she replied. 'For they can cling to their rocks of faith and certainty harder than any limpet. *And* they go on airing their pink petticoats – with a twinkle in their eye and a smile on their lips that'd make you think you were the star in their sky. Are you beginning to lose heart so soon, then?'

Judith shook her head. 'No. It's just healthy to remind myself every so often that it's not going to be easy. When we came back to Keelity last summer and I talked it over with Rick Bellingham and Henrietta – and I found we all agreed that they'd got the wrong men – I thought it was going to be so easy. We'd just swear affidavits and then place the whole affair in the hands of the proper authorities. Hah!' She gave a single, bitter laugh at her own naïvety.

Miss Darcy rose and closed the door. 'One never knows,' she commented as she returned to her seat. 'May I ask what are the attitudes of Mr Bellingham and his sister now? Have they changed since last summer?'

Judith sighed. 'As to Henrietta . . . well, there's no point in beating about the bush, is there? She's so . . . oh dear, what's a kindly word for *besotted?*'

'Possessed? Infatuated? D'you think she *is* infatuated?' She cleared her throat delicately. 'No point in beating about the bush, as you say.'

'I think besotted is actually the *kindliest* word for it. She's going to destroy her marriage, lose her child, and ruin her life – and she knows it. Even worse, she thinks it'll be worth it, too. Anyway, to get back to your earlier question, *her* attitude will be entirely dictated by that affair. Or *affaire*, perhaps. If the pursuit of truth and justice even looks like interfering with' – a nod of her head in the direction of Lumley's Tea Rooms, just down the street, supplied her meaning – 'then truth and justice can go and jump in the bog.'

Miss Darcy nodded. 'I had already concluded as much.

And her brother? Or would you rather not say?'

Judith lifted both hands briefly in a resigned sort of gesture. 'He and I have fallen out lately . . .'

'Oh, I don't wish to pry into that.'

'No, but it may have some bearing on your question. On the face of it, it's the ordinary sort of sweethearts' tiff. But deep down I suspect it's because he's ceased caring about the rights and wrongs of the affair. Henrietta says I'd be just as reluctant to open old wounds if I had to manage the estate. I, too, would have to think of all the feathers it would ruffle, all the useful connections it would sever, all the bitterness . . . disruption, and so on. And for what? It wouldn't restore the dead to life. Perhaps he's the wisest among us, after all.'

'And their aunty? Mrs Montgomery?'

The question told Judith that this woman either knew or had taken the trouble to discover rather more about the *active* members of the Bellingham family than would be common knowledge. 'She's the key to it all,' she said simply.

'In what way?'

Judith recalled how scornful – and alarmed – Henrietta had been when she first heard that she, Judith, had roped in Captain O'Donovan; that, as it turned out, had been no blunder, but she wondered if this was the same. Nonetheless, she drew a deep breath and took the plunge. 'You know what Rick says in his article – about how the Anglo-Irish think of themselves as pretty *Anglo* in Ireland, but the minute they cross the water and find themselves among the *real* sassenachs, they suddenly wake up to how deeply ingrained their Irishness is. Remember that?'

Miss Darcy smiled. 'Yes. I thought to myself, Well, he's surely kissed the Blarney Stone!'

'No, but it's true. And Mrs Montgomery is the walking proof of it. You look at her and you'd think she's the living soul of an English matron. Her husband's a huntin-shootin-fishin' lunatic. She has one son a colonel in the Guards, another is a London barrister, and the third is chaplain to the royal household. Yet when she came back to Castle Moore, immediately after the Murders – and she hardly waited to pack, even – the first thing she did was take Rick down to the island, where it all happened, and make him swear on the bones of his ancestors . . . I mean to say, if she'd had a sword by her, she'd have opened a vein and made him swear on the living blood! It's not the pursuit of truth and justice moves her. It's pure revenge. It's a Celtic feud for her. D'you follow me, now? Blood and clan and so forth.'

'And has the blood of four innocent men appeased her? Does she know they were innocent?'

'She does now. She was always uneasy, mind. But the Englishwoman in her wasn't able to stomach the thought that the RIC might have played dirty, d'you see? But she was always uneasy.'

'Why?'

'Because immediately after the Murders, Rick told her about the leader, and so did Henrietta, and so did I. We all told her about the red-bearded divil with the piercing eyes – the wild-looking man.'

'Ah!' It was a curiously satisfied sigh she gave out, as if Judith's litany had reached some expected dénouement. 'Mick O'Leary.'

'Did you know him?'

'I did.' Miss Darcy proffered the marzipans again but Judith shook her head. 'He was a spoiled priest,' she continued. 'He went for the priesthood but his passions were too strong. All of them. He couldn't sup a ball of malt but he'd drain the bottle and pass the night under a ditch. He couldn't chastise a body for a venial sin but he'd half-murder them. Moderation was on the far side of the mountain the night he was born.'

'And I suppose he couldn't kiss a girl at all!' Judith risked saying.

A faraway smile touched the other's face. 'Indeed, he could,' she murmured fondly. Then brisk again, 'But you can see he wasn't patroned for the priesthood!'

'It's a long way from that to the office of cowardly murderer,' Judith pointed out.

'Cowardly?' Miss Darcy appeared to demur.

'I was there, not ten paces from him. If I close my eyes, I can see him now, yelling at King to stand aside and let him finish off Rick as well. A fierce strong man with a gun smoking in his hand – facing a petrified little boy of fourteen. And when he wasn't let do that, didn't he turn and fire one off at me! Maybe you're right – *coward* is too weak. There should be a word ten thousand times stronger.'

'Ah, you could be right. Tell me, do you think King was part of that conspiracy – or did he just make use of it once it happened? You'd never know with that man.'

Miss Darcy's reluctance to agree that Mick O'Leary's behaviour that night had been sheer cowardice rang a little warning bell in Judith's mind. The woman might protest her total opposition to all that her brother and his cronies had done and believed in, yet some innermost part of her was tenacious to that cause still – at least where Mick O'Leary was concerned. Judith had been on the point of saying yes, she did believe King was party to the conspiracy – and that Mad McLysaght had hinted as much, too – but the words died in her throat.

'As you say,' she replied, 'you'd never know with that fellow.'

The detour to Streamstown and Robertsons' mill went by way of Baliver. About a mile before the gates Henrietta slyly suggested they should cry in on the McIvers, 'Just to keep an eye on the enemy.' Judith scorned so strong a word: 'opponent' was the farthest she'd go. And anyway, with Rick back in England the whole issue was once again on the long finger.

'On top of which,' she said, 'I don't see what else I can do. Short of bribing the Baliver servants to steam open their letters to each other – assuming he *does* write letters to her – though if she's expecting him to write daily she's in for a disappointment . . .' The disjointed thoughts petered out.

'Perhaps now he's all set to become a noted essayist – a regular contributor to *New Hibernian Quarterly* and so forth – he might improve as a private correspondent,' Henrietta mused.

'A *regular* contributor?'

Henrietta chuckled. 'You don't imagine Gwinny and Letty are going to sheathe their claws and let him off with just the one piece, do you? What did you think of it, by the way?'

'Oh, I said to Miss Darcy – anyone who knows him can recognize him in every line. Yet it still amazes me he actually sat down and wrote it.'

'Not alone that. He wrote it all in about six hours, between midnight and dawn, the night the two girls came down to the castle . . . tossed it over to them casually at breakfast as if it had been gathering dust for weeks. Don't ever tell them that, by the way. They think he's utterly dedicated and dependable.'

Judith said nothing.

'You've gone very quiet all of a sudden,' Henrietta prompted.

'I was just thinking – Rick's terribly chummy with those two, especially Gwinny. Yet I don't feel any sort of rivalry between me and them at all. Envy, yes, but not rivalry. No jealousy.'

'Why envy?'

'Because I'd love . . .' She faltered as the full meaning

of what she was about to say struck her. 'Lord!' she exclaimed.

'What?'

'I was going to say I'd love to have an easy, jolly friendship like that with Rick.'

'Instead of?'

'Instead of wanting to *improve* him somehow every time I see him. D'you think if we *did* get married, I'd turn into a scold? I can hear it in my voice sometimes. I want to take him in both hands and shake him into *doing* something.'

'He won't, you know. He'll only ever do what *he* wants – in the nicest possible way. Oh, hark at who's talking!' She slapped her own wrist playfully. 'It must be a family trait.'

They came round a bend and saw a carriage a little way ahead of them, going at a mere walk.

'Isn't that the McIvers?' Henrietta asked. 'That's surely Mick Brennan driving?'

'Yes. But judging by the speed, they're not inside it.' Judith shook out the reins and they soon caught up.

The coach was, indeed, empty. 'Hallo, Mr Brennan,' Judith called out. 'Is Miss Sally at home, d'you know? We were thinking of calling.'

'If she is, she's grown wings,' he replied, 'for I'm after setting her and her mother and six great trunks of dresses down at Banagher station to catch the two-fifteen not two hours since.'

'And Mister Fergal?' Judith asked at once – causing Henrietta to shoot her a quizzical glance.

'Sure he's carried the tale of it to Castle Moore, if I know him. 'Tis amazed I am ye didn't meet.'

'We went out for a drive,' Henrietta explained.

They reached the gates of Baliver and he left them with a cheery wave, whipping his horses into a trot now that he could be observed from the house.

'What d'you make of that, then?' Henrietta commented.

'The Banagher train? Why did they go so far? Obviously they didn't wish to be noticed – and if they were, they'd want it thought they were off to Galway . . .'

'What amazes me even more,' Henrietta cut in, 'is that we asked that fella two straight questions and got two straight answers – which hasn't happened since the Flood hereabouts. You'd almost think he *wanted* us to know.'

'Another grey day!' Judith commented.

Since the sun was still doing its late-afternoon best to scorch the trees, Henrietta raised an eyebrow at her.

'I mean *everything's* grey,' Judith complained. 'I don't know if I should pursue this business with the Robertsons at all at all. Why am *I* so concerned to see justice done? Why not Rick? Why does Aunt Bill insist on sending him away to England? And why . . .'

'Perhaps because she's more patient than you?' Henrietta suggested. 'First she has to wean him away from the whole Castle Moore . . . spirit – what's the word? Ambience! That's grey enough, I grant you.'

Judith gave an exasperated sigh. 'I didn't really mean grey. I mean *muddied*. Everything's muddied, isn't it? Who would ever have thought that we'd find ourselves in cahoots with the sister of one of the murderers!'

'And the lover of their leader!'

Judith looked at her askance. 'Was she?'

Henrietta nodded. 'That's what people say. Violet Darcy and Mick O'Leary of Streamstown were doing a line once.'

'Whew!' Judith fanned her face. 'And if she knew where he was now . . .' she hesitated.

'She'd what?'

'Well, she wants the truth to come out, doesn't she.'

Henrietta's lips made a dismissive pout. 'Yes and no.

As long as he's safe in America – or wherever he fled to – she's all for it. But if he ever came back here to Ireland, she wouldn't give you the peel off an orange.'

'Muddier and muddier!' Judith sighed. 'Look, I'm *not* going to the Robertsons'. I've changed my mind. I'll just wash my hands of the whole thing.' She recalled the solemn oath she had sworn before Kitty Rohane and cringed, knowing it was futile now to think of turning back.

Henrietta began to laugh. Judith, a little miffed at it, asked why. 'Because, dear thing,' was the reply, 'when we left Parsonstown this afternoon, the last thing on earth that I wanted to do was go and see those two brothers in Streamstown. I told myself life has moved on since the Murders – my life especially. It's a shocking thing to say, I know – in this country of all countries – but the Murders have vanished into history. Like a sheep sucked into the bog. Someone'll dig it up four hundred years from now and it'll be as fresh as the day it drowned – they'll even know what it ate for breakfast. But as far as I'm concerned, the white turf has grown back over it all. At least, that's what I thought when we left Parsonstown.'

'And now?'

She laughed again, a brief echo of the one before. 'The things you said just now – about wanting to shake Rick into *doing* something – you very kindly didn't mention *me*, but . . . a nod's as good as a wink, eh?'

Judith laughed, too, but with a humourless, almost hopeless edge to it. 'I honestly didn't mean to include you, Hen. But I suppose in this muddied world anyone can take any remark any way they like.'

'Whether you meant it or not, it's too late now. My conscience is pricked. My sinews are stiffened. I have summoned up the action of a tiger and all that.'

Judith now felt compelled to make a joke of it. 'Lord save us! You'll cry, "God for England, Harry, and St George!" next.'

But Henrietta was no longer to be diverted. 'Why not?' she replied robustly. 'Isn't England's honour as much besmirched as the Bellinghams' by what happened?' She took the handle beside her and hauled lightly on the brake as they had reached the top of the hill above Streamstown.

'Oh, very well,' Judith sighed, as if there were actually any choice in the matter. She stared down at the village, at the fine miller's house and the little cluster of cottages around it. With the turf smoke curling lazily up in the slanting sunlight, and the green fields and the densely wooded covert all around, it was the very picture of a rural idyll. It smiled up at her, inviting her to imagine the life of honest toil that people led down there, and the just rewards they reaped for it – the potatoes that were even now being set to simmer in the kettle, the rashers on the plate, the butter in the churn. And she smiled back at it, undeceived, remembering what furies dwelled beside those hearths, what rages mortared man to woman, clan to clan.

And she shivered as they went down into the sunlit valley, knowing what darkness awaited her there.

After Ascot Week at the beginning of June, there was a bit of a lull before the next highlight of the London Season: the Duchess of Devonshire's Ball. For some there was the Eton–Harrow or the Oxford–Cambridge cricket matches; for others, the naval review at Portsmouth; there were even a few fanatics who decamped to the suburbs to watch lawn tennis tournaments – the one in the village of Wimbledon being the latest fad. But there was no single event at which simply everybody had to be seen. It was most aggravating. It happened every year, of course; and every year worried matrons tut-tutted at it and said the devil makes work for idle hands and next year somebody ought to Do Something. But next year remained next year and the devil went on finding work for idle hands, and minds, and bodies.

In that particular June of 1888 the idleness was Rick's. When Hereward sent him up to London, the purpose was twofold – first to attend the private view at the Academy and broaden his appreciation of modern art; and second, to dine at the Guards Club with his cousin Arthur, so as to broaden his appreciation of . . . well, of all those other evenings of the year when he did *not* have to dine at the Guards with his cousin Arthur. The devil stepped in with an agenda of his own, however.

It was devilish hot at Liverpool Street, even under cover of the station awning; Lord alone knew what it was going to be like at Burlington House. He had read the review in the *Morning Post* on the train up and thought he might scrape through any subsequent inquisition after no more than a brisk fifteen-minute trot around the galleries. He'd already picked out half a dozen paintings that, or so he'd claim, had caught his eye; so now all he needed was to know where the bally things were hanging and what sort of colour the artist had used. Then he'd duck out and take a cab to Lords – not that he wanted to watch the cricket particularly . . . though Grace, who'd made 285 for Surrey a week or two back, was playing so it was a bit of a temptation. However, the house where Uncle Hereward had taken him to see Tricia was only a couple of streets away – and she, on a day like this, was more than a *bit* of a temptation. He was sure he could find the house again, even blindfold. And anyway, hadn't Aunt Bill more or less favoured such a visit with her blessing?

To save money he took an omnibus to Piccadilly – one of the new kind with what the jokers had dubbed 'garden seats' on top. The upper deck was empty except for an elderly maritime-looking rough smoking a vile pipe at the back and two young ladies, side by side at the front. He went forward as far as he dared, thinking he'd settle into the 'garden seat' behind them and try to catch their perfume and eavesdrop on their conversation; but the horses started off at that moment and he had to reach forward and steady himself by the back of their seat. The one nearer the aisle looked up, saw a devilishly handsome young man, and moved a token half-inch nearer her companion – an invitation it would have been churlish to refuse.

As he sat down beside her she neatly spiked any suspicion that she had been forward by glancing behind them and exclaiming, 'Oh, I thought it was full. What must you think of me, sir!'

And he replied, 'Ah, but I knew it wasn't! So what must you think of me, Miss . . . er?'

'I think you'll do nicely, sir,' she said.

'Mavis!' Her companion nudged her anxiously.

'I only meant he'd do nicely to stop any old bloke with a pipe sitting there.' She smiled at Rick and said, 'Mavis Dillon.'

'Rick Bellingham.' He shook her hand; her grip was very firm. 'Irish?' he asked.

She grinned. 'A long way back. Nothing to do with this lad who's making all the trouble in Parliament these days. This is Miss Cordelia Weldon, by the way. She's a siffleuse. I'm still in the chorus at the opera.'

'Still!' Miss Weldon echoed scornfully, then explained to Rick: 'She only joined it three weeks ago when they started this run of *Figaro*. Have you seen it, Mr Bellingham?'

Curiously enough, he had just travelled up on the train with one of the world's bores – a young fellow who *had* seen it. Though he was only a year or two older than

Rick, he thought himself no end of a superior swell and had dwelled crudely and at length on the shapely black-stockinged legs of the girls in the chorus, saying you could see right up above their knees. 'But not their figures,' he added glumly, 'more's the pity. In fact, that's why they call it *Not see de figure – oh!* Get it? Haw-haw!'

Rick wondered whether to repeat the 'joke' now and decided not to. 'And where do you . . . *siffle*, or whatever the word is, Miss Weldon?' he asked.

They were both in summery dresses, loose and frilly, and with very few layers between them and the scorching world; their nearness made him feel hollow.

'Whistle.' Mavis answered for her friend. 'You should hear her do "He's all right when you know him but you've got to know him fust". She brings the house down.'

'Mavis!' Cordelia – if that was indeed her name – coloured prettily and nudged her friend again.

'And what do you do, Mr Bellingham?' Mavis asked. 'You're Irish, aren't you? I can hear it when you speak.'

And so the conversation got on to land and farming and Norfolk – and Mavis said her people had a small farm in Norfolk (and Cordelia said, 'Mavis!' again) . . . and Rick didn't really care what they talked about as long as he was dizzyingly near them and could glimpse peach flesh through pink gauze and relish their laughter and perfume. When they alighted at the Strand, leaving him to go on alone, his senses were drowsy with a hunger he was now even more determined to satisfy.

He turned to watch the two girls go off down the aisle and saw that Mavis was coming back to him. She handed him her card and said, 'If ever you wanted to see me again, Rick, this lady is very discreet and can arrange all. She knows how to get in touch with me and keeps rooms by the hour and everything.' She pouted her adorable lips and blew two kisses at him before tripping gaily back to join Cardelia, who was flirting with the conductor to hold the bus for them.

Rick glanced at the card and saw it was not Mavis's. It announced that a Mrs Drummond was the proprietress of a discreet and respectable accommodation house in Meard Street, Soho. He felt no end of a superior swell as he tucked it into his pocket – a bit of arcane knowledge no man of the world should lack, he thought. Perhaps he would go and watch Grace bat at Lords, after all, and chance on slipping away early after dinner with Arthur, and go hell-for-leather to the Opera House to wait outside the stage door. Whistling under his breath, 'He ain't bad when you know him but you've got to know him fust', he alighted and walked across Piccadilly to Burlington House.

Judith and Holofernes – he'd have to notice that one, of course – was in Room V over the door. Personally, he wouldn't have hung it in the servants' attic, unless he wanted to drive them all away. Muttering, 'Room vee over door, room vee over door . . .' he went in search of, *Morning – Dublin from Mount Venus*, which was in 'room ex-eye-eye, facing door'. And so his hunt continued through, *Jacob wrestling with the Angel, The Rape of the Sabine Women, Stout Cortez*, and *Still Life XXIII*, which was in Room XXII. A tricky one, that; but if he got it right, it'd prove he'd been there.

He turned to make his escape from this tasteless feast of smug paint and wilting humanity. So keen was he that he almost knocked over Sally McIver and her mother, who had spotted him only moments earlier. When the apologies and dusting-down were over, Betty McIver asked if he was free to dine with them *en famille* that evening. His answer disappointed her but she was secretly glad his prior engagement was so thoroughly masculine. She inquired about the following evening.

He explained he was returning to Norfolk in the morning.

She said that was absurd. June was the very best part of the Season, full of chance arrangements and intimate little dinners – and Wimbledon. He couldn't possibly miss it. She'd send a wire to his Uncle Hereward and he wasn't to think of going back – nor of sleeping at that stuffy old club. 'Stay with us tonight and you'll be on hand when your uncle's reply comes – whichever way he decides.'

And so it was agreed. Then she saw an old friend and, saying she'd only be a mo', told them not to move away.

'Well!' Sally grinned at him.

'Yes!' he agreed. 'D'you think you could slip away later?' He turned Mrs Drummond's card over in his pocket – knowing it was an utterly caddish suggestion and yet not caring a hoot.

She shook her head sadly, and then brightened. 'But if you're staying with us in St James's, you'll hardly want me to slip *away!*'

They wanted him to stay with them for the rest of the afternoon, of course, but he invented a friend who was even at that minute waiting for him at Lords. In his present mood he felt that the odd snatched kiss with Sally in a darkened doorway – which was surely the most she had in mind, at least under her own roof – would not scrape off many barnacles.

They decided they'd had enough of the private view, anyway. Sally's eyes gleamed as she suggested to her mother, 'Wimbledon?' And Betty's eyes gleamed back as she agreed, 'Yes!' He accompanied them as far as the street, where they parted. He mentioned his friend at Lords again and said he really must dash.

On his way through Burlington Arcade, however, he realized that the idiot in the cloakroom had given him the wrong cane and he had to return to Burlington House. He was just leaving for the second time when he was stopped by a feminine cry of 'Yoo-hoo, Rick!'

It was Gwinny and Letty Dalton, apparently unaccompanied. 'Just the man!' Gwinny said, without any preliminaries or padding. And she drew from her rather capacious and unfashionable bag a set of galleys. 'Apparently Judith Carty has already cast her infallible eye over them,' she added as she thrust them into his hand. 'I can't see a single error but perhaps you can do better.'

'Gwinny!' Letty murmured, nudging her sister and looking apologetically around.

It was so like Cordelia's behaviour with Mavis that Rick had to suppress a laugh. He returned his hat and cane to the attendant and said, 'What am I supposed to do with galley proofs here? I can hardly carry them about with me. People will think I'm a reporter.'

'Excellent!' Gwinny riposted, quite unabashed. 'People will talk to an anonymous reporter when they'd need about eight introductions before they'd even nod at Rick Bellingham – or Guinivere Dalton, let me add. You could do a nice, sharp little piece about the Academy Private View, don't you think? Pretend to be the man in that painting up there. Look at his eyes! They've seen everything, wouldn't you say? They have "supped full with horrors". Yes – full with horrors, just like these galleries. What's *he* thinking about us all as he looks down from those Elysian heights? That would make a superb little piece – no more than fifteen hundred words. And *you* could do it superbly, Rick.'

All at once he felt ashamed of his earlier feelings – the urges that had driven him to think of Tricia in St John's Wood, of Mavis at the stage door, of Sally at Mrs Drummond's. It was not that his carnal hunger was in any way diminished – indeed, with Gwinny's rather fine face and her large, admiring eyes filling nine-tenths of his view, it was greater than ever; what shamed him was the thought that he had reduced those other girls to mere automata – when here was Gwinny to show him he had discarded, or blinded himself to, the best part of them: the meeting of mind as well as of body, the joining of simple friendship to that more primitive dance.

'Perhaps I will,' he replied, making a roll of the galleys and carrying it like a wand of office.

And so, together, they wandered from room to room, now looking not at the paintings but at the people looking at the paintings. Gwinny pointed out their little idiosyncrasies and invented outrageous biographies that he might care to use, until in the end he wondered why she didn't write it herself. He didn't ask her, though, in case she agreed.

At last she said, 'You ought to go somewhere at once and sketch out the first notes while it's still white hot. D'you know anywhere you can do that?'

To show himself off as the man about town, to shock her as she had been trying to shock him for the past half hour – and generally because he felt that a fellow of twenty-two (almost) had to stand up to a woman of twenty-five – he drew out Mrs Drummond's card and said, 'I don't suppose *she* minds if one just sits and scribbles there.'

Gwinny took the card, scanned it, grasped his meaning, and laid it against her lips with a soft, pensive gesture. 'Why, Rick!' she murmured, and handed it to her sister.

'Oh, I say,' he gasped. 'I didn't mean . . . I mean . . . not . . . Lord!'

She laughed and took his arm. 'I'm only teasing, darling boy! Actually, I have a much better idea and it won't cost us a penny. I'll bet Mrs Drummond insists on her pound of flesh.' She grinned. 'What an apt metaphor!'

'Where?' asked the more practical Letty.

'Cousin Freddy's in St James's, of course. It's only five minutes away.'

'But he's in Paris.'

'Quite.'

'Aren't you here with someone?' Rick asked, not liking the idea of going anywhere near St James's with these two.

'Aunt Carrie. She's snoozing by the door to Room I.' She turned to her sister. 'Pop down and tell her we're going to see Cousin Freddy and if he's out, we'll go straight home.'

'And if she insists on accompanying us?'

'She won't,' Gwinny replied confidently. 'She'd much rather be at Wimbledon and this will give her time.' She smiled triumphantly at Rick and pulled him to a vantage point where they could watch the aunt pass from a state of somnolence to one of extreme bustle and vigour.

'Can you understand this new craze for lawn tennis?' Rick asked. 'I mean for just sitting and watching it?'

'I can understand the passion for the tournament at Wimbledon,' Gwinny replied. 'They have the good sense not to start until teatime, so the players and spectators aren't victimized by the broiling noonday sun – and they do serve the most delicious teas, you know. If it's fine tomorrow, you may take Letty and me. But let's not decide just yet.'

Rick agreed most heartily with that! He also hoped Sally McIver and her mother hadn't decided to pop home to St James's to change.

As they left Burlington House he reminded her that she still had Mrs Drummond's card. 'You won't need it now,' she told him, managing somehow to imply the word 'ever', as well.

When they reached the quieter streets to the south of Piccadilly, she suddenly said, 'Tell me, Rick, would you call yourself a prude?'

'Good heavens, no!' he hastened to assure her.

'Good. I can't tell you how pleased that makes us.' She grinned at him. 'You sly old dog! You're a lot smarter than you like to pretend. This card, for instance.' She tantalized him with it briefly before putting it back in her bag. 'You didn't produce that by accident, did you? That was no spur-of-the-minute *jeu d'esprit*.'

More warily he allowed that she might be right.

'So,' she said crisply, 'let us take up your invitation, subtle and gentlemanly as it was, and talk about it in a frank and open manner.'

'Really?' he asked, trying to sound more enthusiastic than nervous.

'Unless you'd rather not,' she fired back at once. 'Letty and I often talk about it between ourselves. We find it is quite possible to be as mature and reasonable on that subject as on – say – the emotions we feel when reading a beautiful poem or the pleasures of wolfing down strawberries and cream at Wimbledon. We most decidedly shall go there tomorrow, by the way.' She allowed a brief silence before she added, 'How mature are you feeling today then, Rick?'

In for a penny, he thought, and giving a nonchalant sort of chuckle, replied, 'Oh . . . pretty much, don't you know.'

'Wonderful!' she said.

They turned into St James's, which was as sparsely peopled as he could wish – enough to reveal at a glance that neither Sally nor her mother were in sight. Which was their house, though? he wondered. She had told him the number but he'd forgotten it already.

'Were you thinking of taking a room at Mrs Drummond's for an hour or so later this evening?' Gwinny went on, just as calmly as if she were asking about taking a box at the opera.

'It did sort of cross the old mind,' he admitted.

'Yes, it does, doesn't it?' she said. 'Cousin Freddy – such a pity he's away, you and he'd get on so well – knows dozens of places like Mrs Drummond's, far better ones, too, I'm sure. Anyway, he told us once that he thinks about that sort of thing at least once an hour, *every day!* And even more often on hot days like this. I wonder is he abnormal? But it's not the sort of question one can spring on any old Tom, Dick, or Harry. But what about Rick? Do *you* think he's abnormal.'

He cleared his throat. 'Not really.'

'No, I didn't think so, either.' Gwinny laughed. 'Because it's the same with us, you see. I must say, Freddy was very surprised to hear that!'

'Lord!' Rick exclaimed, taking off his hat and wiping around inside the band. He wondered how far down the street Cousin Freddy lived; it was like running the gauntlet, where every window possibly concealed Sally and her mother.

To his relief Gwinny stopped at that moment, pulled out a key, held it up for him to see, and put it to her lips, saying, 'Ssh!' Then she tripped up the steps to their left and applied it to its intended purpose in a large, imposing door. 'Nobody knows Freddy's given us this,' she explained. 'Nor this.' It was obviously the key to their cousin's apartment inside.

The hall and stairway were cool, yet somehow airless, too. The stairs were broad and they went up three abreast. Gwinny resumed her earlier conversation. 'You see, darling Rick, Letty and I have reached the conclusion that Society perpetrates a monstrous fraud on people of our age. It diverts the flow of our most beautiful instincts into channels they were never intended to fill. Society doesn't care a hoot for our feelings, even at the most elementary level – or it would never torture Letty and me with these excruciating corsets nor try and sever your wise young head from your godlike body with that absurdly starched collar.'

Though delighted to hear her opinion of his mind and body, he rather wished she weren't piping it so loudly in this large, echoing space.

But on she went: 'Society uses our natural feelings as an engineer uses steam – to impel a vehicle of *its* devising to a destination of *its* choice. It allows you males a safety valve of sorts and it assures us females we don't need one of *any* sort. And the result, all too often, is a disastrous union like your poor, dear sister's. You don't mind my picking an example so close to home, do you? I could give you several dozen others. Not to mention the looming tragedy with the O'Farrelly boy.'

Rick winced. 'Do keep your voice down, Gwinny,' he begged.

'Oh, don't worry!' she assured him. 'They're all young bachelors – and all out at Mrs Drummond's. Or similar. We know, don't we, Letty? It's amazing what you start to observe once you've decided that Society's game is not for you.'

Mercifully they appeared to have reached Cousin Freddy's door at last. She inserted the key and turned it. 'Well oiled, eh?' She grinned and, pushing wide the door, wafted him in.

'What d'you mean precisely,' he asked, 'when you say you're not going to play Society's game?'

'Oh, Rick!' She gave him a quick peck on the cheek. 'Such a tease! I mean we get out of these corsets as soon as we can!' And she turned and offered him the run of her buttons. 'Then I'll help you with the starched collar,' she added. 'Come on, Letty, you too!'

Across the street Betty McIver said, 'Yes, here it is.' And, bearing an opened copy of *Kelly's Street Directory* in her hands, she came to her daughter, who was still glued to the window. 'There's an Honourable Frederick

Dalton on the third floor. We must look him up in *Debrett* – a cousin, most likely.'

'Perhaps that's the one Rick was going to meet at Lords,' Sally said hopefully.

'But he told us the fellow was already waiting for him there.'

'Perhaps the Dalton sisters went to tell him the Honourable Freddy hadn't gone. Sick or something. There could be a dozen innocent explanations, Mama.'

Betty McIver's heart softened at her daughter's distress, yet she still felt she had to do her duty. Wrapping her arms round her from behind she murmured, 'This is the hard lesson that every woman has to learn, my darling. Men are the most fickle, devious, faithless creatures on earth. The more charming they are, the more treacherous they become – because they snare our hearts and blind us to the truth about them. And the woman who does not learn this lesson will end her days in bitterness and woe. Therefore all means to trap them and hold them are sanctified and proper to us. We are the weaker vessel, so let us use what strength we have. Adam could have stayed in Eden if he had agreed to the expulsion of Eve. God, from what we know of him, would have agreed to such a bargain – of that I have no doubt. I sometimes think He hates us.'

'Mama!' Sally was dry-mouthed with shock.

'You are old enough to consider such matters, my precious,' she replied. 'And if you are not, you'd jolly well better try to be. Those two Dalton girls are playing some very underhand game with young Bellingham, and you've got to use every weapon in your armoury to beat them off. Think of Eve. She made sure poor old Adam never even *thought* of that bargain with the Almighty.'

On the day that Rick busied himself with private views of various kinds, Judith was at the offices of the *Vox*. This time she was on her father's business, unaccompanied by Henrietta, whom she had not even informed of the visit. Norman Carty had lately patented a machine for inserting cigarette cards in the packets, and he wanted a printed circular to advertise the fact to the world – or, at least, to that part of it which bought machines for the tobacco trade.

'Don't you miss Dublin sometimes, Mr Egan?' she asked the printer as he worked away.

'I do not, Miss Carty,' he replied solemnly. 'Sure I'd not go back there if you were to put a free ticket in my hand this minute and tell me every colleen between Chapelizod and the Pigeon House was on her knees, praying for the sight of me. That's how much I miss Dublin.'

While he spoke his hand flashed between the cases of type and his composing stick. She marvelled at the way he could be firming in one letter with the thumb of his left hand while his right was again reaching unerringly for the next. Or sometimes it would select the boxwood wedge that made a temporary space between two words. When he'd reached the measure bar at the end of a line, he'd push all the wedges down evenly, ensuring that the gaps were even, too. Then he'd gauge the spaces with a practised eye and select precisely the right slugs to fill them. He said the big newspapers had machines to do it, but she couldn't imagine any machine working much faster than Jack Egan.

'I sometimes miss Drumcondra,' she said. 'We were very convenient to the Botanic Gardens.'

'And the North Strand,' he put in.

She frowned a little at that notion. 'You must be fond of walking! Which part of Dublin in particular are you from, if I may ask?' She was craning over his neck, trying to read the type backward and upside down. She could make out the heading – *Carty's Patent Card Incorporator*

– easily enough, but the rest still defeated her; she was practising at home by holding ordinary print up to the mirror.

'I was born in Cabra,' he replied. 'But we moved to the Southside when I was ten, to the Coombe. From sea to sea, as my father used to say. He worked for Jervis the printer there.'

The man hadn't shaved that morning, or not very well. In fact, he hadn't shaved too expertly those past couple of days for there was quite a growth at the angle of his jaw, just beneath his ear. Bachelors! Her father would be just the same if her mother didn't nag him every now and then, sending him back to shave again: 'And properly, this time!' Like her father, too, Mr Egan had a reddish tinge to his beard, though his hair was dark. The hairs in his ears were almost carroty red.

'I suppose you learned your trade from him?' she asked.

'Dade I did,' he asserted with the kind of relish people employ when speaking of years spent in some kind of purgatory. He suddenly thrust the stick before her. 'Can you see an error in the second line, now? I just noticed it meself.'

She peered at it, reading the metal syllables like a child, letter by letter: '. . . begs to announce . . .'

He chuckled. 'I'm not serious, colleen. But that's the sort of thing my father used to do. And if 'twas me in your boots, now – Lord, but I'd be only quaking in them.'

'The two ens in "announce" – are they supposed to be the same?' she asked. She knew that two efs side by side were different in all *good* typesetting.

'Bedad!' he exclaimed as he slackened off the measure bar and picked up his tweezers. 'Now how did that fellow get there?' He plucked out one of the ens and, holding it as if it were tainted, carried it to the case marked

'Bembo'; the one he was presently using was labelled 'Caslon'. From it he drew a replacement, inserted it, and retightened the bar. 'Same measure, thanks be to God,' he said. 'And good girl yourself that you saw it. You have eyes like a travelling rat, so you have.'

'One of them just seemed to be more open at the bottom,' she remarked diffidently. 'Or the top, the way you hold it.'

He chuckled. 'We still call it the bottom, though it *is* the top. 'Tis a topsy-bottomsy world we live in, and no mistake.' He eyed her shrewdly. 'Would you have a crack at it yourself, Miss Carty? Will I give you a shtick for your hand and you set the caption to the diagram? That'll be italic, so you may work away beside me there, the way we wouldn't be crossing hands all the time.' He pulled the italic case from the rack and set it where she could conveniently reach.

It was too tempting an offer for her to refuse; ever since she'd seen him at work her fingers had been itching to try it, too. 'I'll make an awful hames of it, I know,' she said as she took the stick from him. 'It's hardly woman's work, I suppose.'

''Tis right enough you are there, Miss Carty,' he agreed. 'The union would cut the head out of me.'

There was an explosive snort from the passageway that linked the printing room to the shop. Violet Darcy stood in the doorway, her lip curled in scorn. 'And what do you call Sampson and Daughter, then?' she asked. 'In Benburb Street? Hasn't he seven women, all compositors? Pay no heed to that blatherskite, Miss Carty. He'd go round the world seven times a second but he couldn't tell you a thing he saw on the way.'

'He's permitting me to set the italic caption.' Judith held forth the stick like a kind of peace offering, suggesting that Miss Darcy could confiscate it if she disapproved.

'So, it's true, then,' she responded as she went into her

office. 'The divil truly does find work for idle hands.' She spoke the words humorously enough but there was an edge to them nonetheless and Judith was left feeling that any deeper companionship between herself and Mr Egan would not be welcome.

He put matters right, though, by pulling a naughty-boy face and setting the next few characters like a demon, panting to underline his exertions.

It took Judith almost half an hour to set four short lines; but at the end of it her hand could go unerringly to the compartments that held the more commonly used letters and she could see that, if she spent a week at it, she might become almost as quick as her mentor – who composed the whole of the second page while she fumbled at her measly four lines.

He surveyed it critically and told her the word spaces in the first line were too wide. She pulled a face but said nothing.

'I know what's in your mind, colleen,' he said. 'You're thinking 'tis no bigger space than I'm after using here. But italic's a lighter face, d'you see. A wide gap is the more noticeable.'

'But then I'll have to reset all four lines,' she grumbled.

He glanced guiltily over his shoulder, as if he were about to make a naughty suggestion; then, lowering his voice, he added, 'Just shlip a hair space between each letter in that first line. Sure no one'll ever notice. Lord save us!' His eyes raked the ceiling. 'And I giving away all the tricks of the trade to you on the very first day!'

The suggestion that there might be many other days delighted her; she began to do as he suggested. He returned to the roman case to start on page three. 'Is that right, Miss Carty,' he asked casually, 'what Miss Darcy's after saying – that you were one of those who escaped the Castle Moore Murders? You can't have been more than a wee shlip of a girl then.'

'I was fifteen,' she replied. 'It was my birthday, in fact. I share the same birthday – or birth date – as Mrs Austin. That's how I happened to be there. It was our sort of joint party.'

He sucked at a tooth. 'Shockin'! And were you very close?'

She nodded. 'Both to her and Rick Bellingham. I'm only six months older than him.'

'Ah – I meant close to the Murders. Were you in the room itself?'

'But it happened out of doors, Mr Egan. Down by the lake. On the island opposite the lake.'

'Jaysus, I never knew that.' He stared at her in amazement.

She thought of asking him where he'd been, for every newspaper in these islands had been full of sketches, maps, and artists' impressions – most of them showing considerable artist's licence. But she held her tongue, remembering that working men might easily be 'out of circulation' for brief periods – and she had an odd feeling about Jack Egan, anyway. There was some secret in his past that hung a cloud over him still. His aversion to Dublin, for instance – that had something to do with it. Perhaps he was a reformed drunkard? Or even a criminal – 'rehabilitated', as they called it.

She described the scene briefly, unemotionally, even when it came to her own shooting.

He seemed more interested in old McLysaght than in the grisly events themselves. 'Would that be the lad they call Mad McLysaght?' he asked.

'He's no more mad than you and me,' she assured him.

'Well now,' Miss Darcy said ominously from her doorway, '*that* begs a very big question. What in the name of God do you want to be stirring up memories like that for in the poor girl's brain? Have you no heart, man?'

'Oh, I don't mind,' Judith assured her.

'Well I *do!*' she fired back.

Judith was mortified. In the excitement of getting her hands on a composing stick at last, and in sorting out Mr Egan's confusion about the events of that evening, she had quite forgotten Miss Darcy's interest in the matter. 'Lord, but I'm sorry!' she exclaimed. 'What sort of an eejit mustn't you think me!'

'Not you, dear.' The woman was all smiles now. 'It's that spalpeen there I'm thinking of.'

He paid her no need; but, since he was only two paces from her, she flew them and, poking him viciously in the small of the back, said, 'Someone has to!' She almost shouted the words.

He grinned, without turning round, so that only Judith could see it.

'Eh?' Miss Darcy dug him in the back once more, even harder.

'Yes-ma'am-no-ma'am-three-bags-full-ma'am,' he intoned.

Miss Darcy smiled an exasperated smile at Judith. 'One day that man will wake up dead,' she promised. 'And you may tell the polis they can come looking for me.'

Someone called her from the shop and she reluctantly left them alone again.

'You tease her dreadfully,' Judith scolded. 'Can't you tell she's quite fond of you underneath all that?'

'I'll offer it up,' he said easily.

She looked at him in surprise – having assumed he was a Protestant. The words slipped out before she meant them: 'Are you a Roman Catholic, then?'

He laughed, while she struggled to apologize.

'I'm nothing!' he assured her. 'Or I'll tell you what I am. I'm a Roman *Italic!* And that's the God's truth!' His laugh grew wilder still. 'An Italian Roman from Stree . . . from the streets of Dublin.'

' "Perdition catch my soul but I do love thee!" ' The cry came from the shadows of the great beech tree at the head of the drive – shadows made darker still by the brilliance of the sun beyond.

'Mr McLysaght!' Judith called out. She reined in from the trot and a moment later the gig drew abreast of him. Making no direct reply, he took the cheek strap of the bridle in his hand and started leading the pony toward the castle. 'Aren't you awfully early this year?' she remarked.

Without looking at her he replied, ' "I am thus early come to know what service it is your pleasure to command me in." '

' "Oh Eglamour, thou art a gentleman!" ' she exclaimed.

He turned and stared at her in surprise; not often were his quotations recognized, much less capped like that.

She laughed. 'Oh, I've read a little in my time, you know! The last occasion on which you played Othello – and called down perdition on your soul, and declared your love like that – it was for Miss Henrietta, as she was then. D'you remember the day that was in it?'

' "Sweet pangs of it remember me," ' he intoned.

They were almost at the castle door by now. Henrietta, who had seen the pair of them as soon as they emerged from the shade, came out in welcome. 'You're early this year,' she said to McLysaght.

' "Betwixt too early and too late," ' he responded, turning to Judith and raising an inquiring eyebrow.

'No. You have me bet there,' she conceded.

He smiled happily but did not enlighten her; his teaching days, he claimed, were done. 'Will I take the poor beast around to the stables, Miss Carty?' he asked.

'Poor beast?' she scoffed. 'He's done nothing but gorge on new grass those two weeks past. But I'll thank you anyway.'

'Aren't we going to Parsonstown?' Henrietta asked. 'I felt sure that's why you'd come.'

'No, I'm after being there all day. Hadn't I to go over at eight this morning.' Judith laid it on a bit thick. 'I mean I had to *be* there at eight – because Papa wants these leaflets all put in envelopes tonight. All four hundred of them! But just look at this! I simply had to come and show you – my own bit of typesetting! Mr Egan allowed me to do one of the captions. It's all in italic.' She opened her pocketbook and unfolded a spill of paper.

'Egan?' McLysaght asked. 'Did you say Egan, Miss Carty?'

'You're not supposed to be listening to other people's conversations,' Henrietta told him, furious at being cheated, as she saw it, out of a visit to Parsonstown.

'Don't be such a scold,' Judith told her. 'There'll be other days. Quite soon, too. Mr Egan says I can go back and help him anytime I like. See! I did those four lines – under the drawing.' She eyed them proudly for the hundredth time.

McLysaght, completely unabashed by Henrietta's reprimand, let go of the reins and came to see what all her excitement was about. In rich, Shakespearean tones he declaimed: ' "Carty's patent card incorporator has the advantage that a completely random selection of cigarette cards is guaranteed to be inserted into the boxes that are bundled into any given carton . . ." ' He broke off. 'And what, be all the holy, is a cigarette *card*, may I ask?'

'Haven't you seen them?' Henrietta replied. 'Sure they're all the rage these days. People buy cigarettes just to get the cards. Even people who don't smoke.'

'They're coloured picture cards,' Judith put in. 'Flags of all nations. Wonders of the world. It's an American idea.'

'Enough, enough, my lady!' He held up his hand and passed her back the leaflet. 'Is it printing such cards you are in Parsonstown with Mr Jackeen?'

'No, just the leaflet about my father's machine. It's Jack Egan, anyway.'

'Is it?' He laughed. 'Jack Egan the jackeen. Well, I wasn't far off now, was I?' He returned to the pony's head and started to lead him off.

'I'm glad you're back,' Judith called after him. 'I always feel summer has come at last when I see you about the place.'

He waved acknowledgement. 'Me and the cuckoo.'

'How *could* you go to Parsonstown without letting me know?' Henrietta asked the moment he was beyond earshot.

Judith took her by the arm and started walking her round to the terrace on the sunny side of the house. 'I passed your gates at a quarter past six this morning,' she said. 'Wouldn't you have been the happy one to join me at *that* hour! Would they ever bring us a pot of tea and some scones, d'you think – outdoors, I mean? I'm only famished.'

Henrietta reluctantly agreed that six-fifteen would, indeed, have been a dash early. They sat in the shade of the wistaria, from under whose bole she plucked a handbell and rang for whatever maid was on call that afternoon.

'Anyway,' Judith repeated, 'there'll be lots of other times. As I said, old Egan has promised I can come in and help him whenever I want.' She pulled out the leaflet and marvelled at her four-line handiwork all over again.

'I can't believe I actually did that, can you?'

'Frame it and send it to the Hibernian Academy,' Henrietta suggested.

Judith laughed. 'Jack Egan. Jackeen. That's a good one. I must remember to tell him.'

'Oh?' Henrietta raised an eyebrow. 'You must be on good terms.'

'Ah, he's a darlin' man. I think there's some tragedy in his past, you know.'

'Unrequited love?' Henrietta started to show an interest.

'No, I don't think it's that. It's just a feeling I get sometimes – something he's ashamed of. Perhaps he was a drunkard once. Perhaps he did something terrible while under the influence – knocked someone down and killed them. Maybe he's been in prison. There's a camphorated reek to that one somewhere. There's a bit of him that's dead, poor man.'

'Lord save us! You'll marry him out of pity next!'

'Nothing like that,' Judith assured her.

The maid appeared with a tray of buttered scones and a pot of fresh tea.

'By the way,' Henrietta said when she'd gone, 'Fergal cried in today. Thought he might find you here. Said he had something to tell you.'

'News from Sally, I expect. Poor Fergal, he knows it doesn't help his case to pour the poison in my ear, but he's still compelled to do it.'

'Of course he is.'

'Why "of course"?'

'Because love is like that. It destroys the psyche – even when the psyche knows it's being destroyed. It's ruthless and uncaring. You know it yourself, now.'

Judith stared at the side of the house, an imposing, ivy-clad façade. The thought that she might one day be mistress of that vast mansion occurred to her but aroused neither joy nor apprehension. 'I don't know *what* I know any longer,' she sighed.

'The one good thing in the entire situation,' Henrietta reassured her, 'is that the Dalton sisters are over there, too. If anyone can keep Sally McIver at arm's length, it'll be those lasses – and the dear boy will be as safe as houses with them.'

'Mmm.' Judith agreed vaguely. 'I wonder what Fergal wanted? Maybe I malign him. It could be something important.'

Henrietta leaned forward and stared at her, both accusing and amused. 'And news of Sally's doings *wouldn't* be important?' she said.

Judith took a large bite of scone, to avoid the necessity of replying.

Henrietta settled back in her cane seat and returned to their earlier conversation. 'You quite make me want to meet your Mr Jack Egan,' she said. 'Properly, I mean. Not just to say hello-goodbye.'

'He's an RC, I think.'

'How d'you know? Are you sure? The Darcys are certainly Protestants.'

'The things he says – "Thanks be to God" . . . "My father, Lord rest him" . . . things like that.'

'Did you ask him?'

Judith laughed. 'He just said he wasn't a Roman anything – unless it was a Roman Italic.' She put her nose in the air and said grandly, 'A private, printer's joke, you know.'

'Oh, I know the terms,' Henrietta assured her. 'I know all about roman and italic – so don't be giving yourself airs, you bold girl! Bold! That's another one. I was in and out of printers' shops before you were born!'

'Where?' Judith asked scornfully.

'You wouldn't remember the one there used to be in Flaxmills, I suppose? Just below the parochial school.'

Another memory dawned on her. 'Egan was that man's name, too! Now there's a quare thing. Mick Egan.'

'There must be a hundred Egans hereabouts,' Judith pointed out.

'That's true.'

They sipped their tea and relished the tang of it, the cooling stimulus on a warm afternoon.

But Henrietta remained pensive. 'Another quare thing,' she said at last. 'Mick Egan's daughter married Sean O'Leary, the father of the red-headed leader of . . .'

'Mick O'Leary!' Judith said.

'Mick O'Leary was named after that Mick Egan, his grandfather.'

Fergal at last caught up with Judith on the following Saturday. The intervening days had been madly filled with the writing and cramming of envelopes, the collection of yet more leaflets as her father's chaotic desk and filing cabinets revealed yet more potential customers, and countless dashes ferrying letters to and stamps from the post office. 'If I taste gum tragacanth ever again in my life,' Judith said as she, Henrietta, and Fergal climbed aboard the gig, 'I'm sure I'll be ill on the spot.'

Henrietta took the reins; Fergal did not demur. 'You shouldn't lick them,' he told her as they set off for Parsonstown. 'It's not gum trag, it's hoof-and-horn glue and it can give you anthrax.'

She took his arm briefly and squeezed it. 'Dear Fergal! You'd care for all the world if it'd let you.'

He could not tell whether this was a compliment or a mild, if veiled, rebuke. 'Well, you'll remember my words when you die in horrible agony,' he assured her jovially.

'Yes,' she sighed. 'And I'll think of all the other things you've said, which I should have heeded and never did. I know, I know.' Then, laying aside her humour: 'What news of your sister and mother?'

'Hah!' He rubbed his hands with great promise. 'Had a letter this morning. Apparently they ran across Rick at Burlington House. He was sent up for the private view – told them he had to return to Norfolk the following day. Of course, they tried to arrange with the old boy, your Uncle Hereward' – he nodded toward Henrietta – 'for Rick to stay on longer and to lodge at our house in St James's.'

He paused until Judith was forced to say, 'And?'

'Well, he's lodging in St James's all right, but not chez McIver; he's putting up with Freddy Dalton, of all people!'

'Is he a brother to Gwinny and . . . no, he couldn't be. A cousin?' Henrietta asked.

'Why d'you say "of all people"?' Judith added.

'Well, he's an utter tripehound, a howling cad. He's their cousin, in fact. And between you and me' – he lowered his voice though there was not a soul in sight – 'Algy Scott told me there were some very scurrilous stories doing the rounds of the younger swells, concerning Freddy and those two ladies.'

'Men!' Henrietta exploded in disgust. 'Those poor sisters! They've only got to announce to the world that they're not interested in marriage, and at once they become fair game – a target of any malodorous and improper fancy you men care to devise. Young swells? Swollen up with their own vainglory, if you ask me! They can't bear the thought that there are two gifted and good-looking young ladies somewhere who couldn't give a hoot about them!'

Fergal tapped her on the arm. 'It's only me,' he said.

'I know.' She exaggerated her aggressiveness, to show him it was half-humorous. 'I'm surprised at you even remembering such tittle-tattle, much less passing it on.'

'More to the point . . .' Judith had been waiting patiently for a chance to speak. 'How comes it that Rick knows this Freddy Dalton?'

'Ah!' Fergal returned to his original line with relief. 'That's the burning question – *does* he, in fact, know Freddy at all?'

'But if he's staying with him . . .'

'He's lodging in Freddy's apartment. But the only people who are ever seen going in and out are Gwinny and Letty – and Rick, of course. He took up lodging on the day of the private view – last Wednesday. And the following afternoon he took them to watch a tennis match somewhere in the suburbs. More than that I can't tell you because Sally wrote the letter that same evening. She and Mama went to the match, too, and Rick was *very* discomfited to see them, because, as I said, he'd told them he was going back to Norfolk. So naturally they asked him where he was staying and he replied he was putting up at the Guards, courtesy of his cousin . . . Alfred, is it?'

'Arthur,' Henrietta said.

'What the poor fellow didn't realize is that our place is directly opposite the house where Freddy Dalton has his set of chambers. You can imagine my sister and mother – hollow-eyed from pressing the opera glasses to their cheeks!'

'Lord!' Judith shivered.

'What?' he asked. It was not the response he had expected.

'It's like carrying a little bit of Ireland across the water and dropping it in the middle of London. All our intrigues, spying, lying . . . leading double lives . . . meeting and smiling and being ever-so-charming. Everyone's trying to get someone else to behave the way *they'd* like – but they won't just come out and say it directly.'

'Do *you?*' Henrietta asked. Her conscience applied

Judith's strictures to herself even more than to the situation surrounding Rick.

'No.' Judith sighed again. 'I'm as bad as the rest. Will we ever be free?'

'I think people in every country are like that,' Fergal objected.

'Ah, but we're the virtuosi!' she countered. 'And look at the futility of it! All that conniving and lying going on there in London – and two days later, here we are, four hundred miles away in the middle of Ireland, talking our heads off about it! What's the point? Does she say what she's going to *do* about it?'

He shook his head. 'Not a word.'

'What sort of tone has she?' Henrietta tried. 'I mean, is she despairing? Angry? Resigned? Does she sound as if she's going to do anything about it at all?'

'Knowing Sally, she'll do something,' he assured her.

Judith wanted to ask what, but decided to await a better moment.

That moment came when they dropped Henrietta off at Lumley's Tea Rooms. Judith took the reins and drove on down the main street.

'Aren't you going in there?' Fergal asked as they passed the offices of the *Vox*. 'I thought that was the purpose?'

She smiled sweetly at him and nodded over her shoulder toward the Tea Rooms. '*That* was our purpose.'

'Ah. So we just drive around for an hour or so?'

'Or walk? We could leave the gig behind the Greyhound Bar and walk out to Riverstown and back. That should be just about right. D'you think it's going to rain?'

He scanned the sky. 'We'll keep an eye on that cloud.'

They parked the gig, gave the horse his nosebag, and set off up the hill that divides the valley of the Camcor from that of the Brosna – the two rivers that meet in Parsonstown, in the gardens of the castle there.

'So what d'you think Sally will do?' Judith asked as

soon as they were out in the road again.

He was a little while framing his answer, and even then he did not give it at once. 'When you talked about all the duplicity and so on,' he said, 'I thought for a moment you were talking about me.'

She gave a mirthless laugh. 'And Hen thought I really meant her!'

'And who did you mean?'

'That crowd in London – oh, all of us, I suppose!'

'And d'you want to lay all your cards on the table now? Or me? D'you want me to start?'

Did she? She drew a deep breath and tried to think.

But no thoughts came, just a series of disjointed words and half-glimpsed images. She started to speak as if she were framing an essay in the schoolroom – rationally, setting personal feelings aside: 'If I ask you to do that, I can hardly keep my own cards concealed . . .' But even that thought petered out.

Wisely he let the silence grow, until it impelled her to say more. Now she spoke without forethought – whatever came to mind: 'I have no cards. I'm concealing nothing except my own bewilderment. I don't know which way to turn.'

In her agitation she was waving her arms rather wildly. He offered her the crook of his elbow to steady herself. She slipped her hand through it gratefully and hugged herself tight against him, shoulder to shoulder. 'Thanks,' she murmured.

He gave her gloved hand a brief squeeze between his upper and lower arm; she felt the muscles ripple beneath the cloth. It called up a sudden image of him playing tennis last summer, with his sleeves rolled up and his forearm beautifully anatomized by the golden sun. It was an image of comfort in all her confusion and she dwelled on it while he spoke.

'Here we go then,' he said. 'I believe my sister is so desperate to see a diamond from Rick gleaming on her finger that there's nothing she would not do to achieve it. I know that's a caddish thing for a brother to say, but I trust we're beyond polite considerations like that?'

She nodded. 'I think that's what "putting one's cards on the table" means.'

'Well – in for a penn'orth of caddishness, in for a pound! I think she would even . . .' He swallowed heavily. 'Lord, it's so easy to think it, so hard to say it! When I say she'd do anything, I mean *anything*. D'you understand?'

'Yes. You mean like Henrietta and Percy – at this very moment, probably.'

'Quite.' He cleared his throat. 'I wondered – ever since that night in O'Dwyer's Restaurant in Dublin – if you realized that?'

She laughed and shook his arm. 'Oh Fergal, dear! I've been ferrying her here and telling lies for her those months that went past. What d'you *think* I imagined might be going on?'

'Well . . .' He tilted his head awkwardly. 'One never knows. It's tiger country, isn't it?'

'The implication of what you're saying about Sally is that you think Rick would fall for it. He'd let her use him like that.'

'That's a cruel way of putting it, Ju. But if that's the way you . . .'

'How would you put it then?'

'I think he's just so good-hearted. I mean, look how he let the Dalton girls talk him into doing that article . . .'

'It's a jolly good article. We'll call in and get a proof on the way back. You'll see.'

'Good or bad, that's not my point – even if it's the best thing anybody's written this century. The point is, Rick's the last person you'd think of if you were starting a new literary quarterly and wanted two thousand words, or whatever.'

'Five thousand.'

'Whatever. I think Letty and Gwinny Dalton were as amazed as anybody when he actually delivered what he invoiced.'

'Why else did they ask him then? That doesn't make sense, Fergal.'

They reached the top of the ridge and paused a moment to stare down into the valley of the Brosna, at Riverstown, half a mile distant and at the moment enduring a heavy shower.

'That's going to catch us,' he warned. 'Let's try and reach the tall bit of the ditch there.'

It was no more than forty or fifty paces; an easy trot brought them to it just in time. It was a thorn tree, heavily infested with traveller's joy. Last year's growth made a dense thatch that justified the name. The air turned chill and the day darkened all about them. The world beyond a hundred-yard circle vanished behind curtains of silvery wetness.

'Judith?' he said, grasping her gently by the arm.

She looked up at him and the next moment his lips were on hers. She was at first too surprised to protest. Then the very thought of breaking away died within her. His kiss, tentative to start with, became more assured; his arms slipped round her, hugging her tight against him, forming a warm haven for all her perplexity.

When at last he broke contact he placed his lips against her ear and whispered, 'Thank you!'

'Why d'you say that?' she asked.

'Because I'm not seeking to do the same to you as Sally is to Rick.'

She drew away from him sharply and stared into his eyes with amused bewilderment.

'No!' he exclaimed, impatient at his own ambiguity. 'I'm not talking about *that*! I meant I'm not trying to . . . I don't assume any sort of promise goes along with that kiss. It was just a kiss.' He kissed her again. 'And so was that.' And again. 'And that. Nothing exists outside this moment – and we just happen to be in it. You're still free.'

'Free!' she echoed glumly.

The day brightened again as the shower passed on toward Crinkle.

'And now it's passed,' he said, putting a foot outside the dry patch where they stood. He offered her the crook of his arm again. 'You're free as far as I'm concerned,' he repeated.

'Oh, Fergal!' She took his arm and they set off again in brilliant sunshine. 'If only you knew the half of it!' Their earlier conversation came back to her. 'You were going to tell me why the Dalton girls have sunk their talons into poor Rick.'

'Because he's a most wonderful sanctuary from their brother – from the remorseless way he keeps shoving them back in the auction ring long after they've scared off every bidder in sight. It's just become a battle of wills between them. So while they can say, "Oh, but Vigo, dear, we're machinating like mad on little Rick Bellingham!" he'll give them a bit of peace.'

'Like mad?' Judith asked. 'Or like Machiavelli? You don't think they might be the cunningest of all?'

He did not answer.

'Well?' she urged.

He cleared his throat. 'Would you lay one little card on the table, Ju? Or a big one, actually.' They had reached the junction with the road that led to the station; he looked left and right. 'I've not been here since I was a child.'

'I was here only six or seven weeks ago,' she told him.

'This is where Rick and I quarrelled. Before he went back to Norfolk.'

'Hah! Then there's no better place for me to ask it – the card on the table. You want to know if I think the Dalton girls aren't playing a very clever game. And I want to know how much the answer matters to you. Not *my* answer – because I could be quite wrong. But suppose I'm . . . I don't know – the Recording Angel. Suppose I know precisely what's in the minds of those two harpies. D'you really want me to tell you?'

What a question! Of course she did! She tried to play his game – making herself believe he could tell her the absolute truth. She waited for the upwelling of eagerness within her, desperate to hear his yes or no. But nothing came of it. The veins of feeling were choked. Or overloaded. Or . . . something. Anyway, they weren't delivering. 'Yes, of course I do,' she said nonetheless.

He halted and closed his eyes for a moment. Suddenly she realized why the answer was so desperately important to him. Her own selfishness shamed her. 'At least it would round it off,' she added.

The words took her by surprise; they seemed to have come from nowhere.

It put a little heart back into him. 'I think the short answer is no,' he replied. 'I don't think they're weaving the most cunning web of all around Rick.'

'And what's the long answer?' she asked.

He chuckled. 'I don't wish to sound cynical, but it's said that every man – and woman – has a price. There's a goal, a reward, an ambition, a longing . . . *something* out there for which we'd cast aside all judgement and finer feeling if we could only secure it.'

'Henrietta and Percy again,' she said.

'Pretty obviously. With other people it's more subtle, but we all have that breaking point – or so 'tis said. For Gwinny and Letty Dalton, it's to be left in peace to get on with their own lives. They don't want . . . social position, land, family, heirs, heirlooms, succession – all the bric-à-brac that well-brought-up young ladies of their class are supposed to want. I can see them, twenty years from now, running a small, not very successful art gallery in Tuscany somewhere – Florence or Pisa, say – still unmarried and happy as larks.'

'And Rick?' she asked.

'Rick's just . . .' He turned and glanced briefly behind them, back up the hill. He laughed. 'To them, Rick's just a bit of traveller's joy along the wayside!'

'I wonder if it's still under there?' Fergal mused. They were standing on the hump-back bridge at Riverstown, leaning against the parapet on the upstream side, casting bits of bulrush stem into the water and watching them vanish beneath their feet.

'Wonder if what's still there?' Judith asked.

'Last time I was here we did this with bits of twig, Sal and I. And then we'd run across the road and watch them come out on the other side. And I threw one beauty in – a real *Great Eastern* of a twig – and it never came out.' After a pause he added, 'Early training for life.'

She butted his arm playfully and watched him trying not to smile. He'd be a very easy companion, she thought.

'Just now . . .' He hesitated.

'Yes?'

'You said if only I knew the half of it.'

'Ah!'

After a silence he said, 'Well?'

She sighed. 'It's easy enough to *seek* advice, Fergal. The trouble comes when you don't act on it. Then the people who gave it feel hurt.'

'In that case I won't offer you any,' he said.

'Promise?'

'Word of honour. I'll simply tell you what *I* would do in the same circumstances.'

This time she punched his arm. 'Come on. Let's start back. I'll tell you on the way.'

She said nothing until they'd put the last of the cottages behind them. Then she began: 'D'you remember last August, the day we came back to the Old Glebe?'

'Was it only last August?'

'I know! Sometimes I can't believe it, either. Anyway – d'you remember one of the first things I said to Rick? I think you were there.'

'About the men my father defended? You said you thought they'd hanged the wrong ones.'

'Yes. The thing is, you see . . . oh dear.'

'You've changed your mind?'

'No! Quite the reverse. I'm even more convinced of it.'

Haltingly, and with many a detour and qualification, she told him of McLysaght's Lament, the one he'd composed for Kitty Rohane . . . of her meeting with Kitty and the oath she had so rashly sworn . . . of Captain O'Donovan and his present involvement . . . of her doubts about Rick and Henrietta, about their strength of purpose . . .

And so she came to her doubts about Aunt Bill, too – not of her strength of purpose but of her motives. 'I think for her it's something very dark and vengeful, Fergal. It's a blood feud which she dresses up as a quest for truth and justice. But it's really just blood, blood, blood, and she concentrates it all on King, who I don't think was the principal in the affair at all.'

'He's the principal beneficiary, though,' Fergal pointed out.

'Perhaps. But let me finish telling you about Aunt Bill – where she and I differ. I want to see it resolved properly, and as soon as possible. She wants to make it last the rest of her life – it's the most exciting thing that ever happened to her. The Irish side of her wants to pass it on through generations. But then the English side asserts itself, and she shies away from all that . . .'

'And so she wavers, too, in effect.'

'But in a different way from Hen and Rick. She wavers between two hot extremes: the Grand Old Englishwoman – and you know there's nothing on earth more implacable than that – unless it's an Irish mother out for blood, which is the other extreme.'

'I can't believe it of her,' he said – but his tone suggested he was beginning to.

'It's true. She planted that idea about blood in Rick's mind the very week it all happened. The day she arrived.'

'It'd never set down root there,' he assured her, mistaking the cause of her distress. 'You know Rick.'

'I know Rick! It *would* take root but it'd never thrive. *That's* the problem with him. It's just standing there in one corner of his mind – a sickly growth with poison berries. And it won't let anything else flourish in its shade. So you can talk to him of justice and truth and things like that, but there in the corner of his eye is that ugly, stunted tree she planted all those years ago. And he says, "I must do something about that one day." But meanwhile there's the whole business of estate management to learn, and . . . articles to write, and . . .'

'Sally to fend off.'

'Or not, as the case may be!'

'He made a pretty good job of it at Burlington House – turned down an invitation to stay under the same roof as her.' He chuckled. 'I don't know why on earth I'm defending him!'

'Anyway, my point is that I *am* interested in seeing justice done.'

'You're the only one, it seems.'

'No. There's Justin O'Donovan, too.'

He glanced sidelong at her. 'D'you believe he's *purely* interested in justice?'

She considered her reply. 'He may have other interests, but they wouldn't cloud his pursuit of justice. That's what I mean.'

'You're sure?'

'No.' She shook her head. 'I'm no longer even sure about *me*, Fergal. That's the horrifying thing. You know I felt dreadfully guilty for years after the Murders.'

'Guilty?' he echoed in astonishment.

'Of course. Guilty for having survived. I used to have a daydream to help me cope with it. I imagined that their leader – the red-bearded fellow called Mick O'Leary . . .'

'You know his name?'

'I know the names of all of them. And what they look like – or looked like then . . . where they were born . . . everything.'

'Good Lord! I think you should come and tell all this to my father.'

'Wait. Hear me out – as I say, you don't know the half of it.'

'Did Miss Darcy give you their names?'

'You're thinking like a lawyer, Fergal. Put off that thinking cap altogether. My difficulties do not lie in that direction. She didn't, as it happens. I knew their names before ever I met her. She wouldn't even confirm them. But did you know that she and Mick O'Leary were doing a line at that time?'

'No. But I'm sorry – I interrupted. You were telling me about feeling guilty, and your daydream?'

'Oh, yes. I was about to say – when the gamekeepers come running down toward them, Mick O'Leary tries to shoot me again. To finish me off. But the gun won't work. So he throws it at me. But it goes wide. And I pick it up from where it falls and aim it at them. And this time it works! So I shoot them all.'

'That would certainly assuage your guilt!'

'The reason I'm telling you, Fergal, is that I'd have done it *then* – without any hesitation. But seven years have gone by. We've all grown up. There's hardly anything left of us as we were then, is there?'

'Well . . .' he said hesitantly.

'D'you feel much kinship with Fergal McIver, aged fourteen?'

'I wasn't thinking about that. I was thinking that things like truth and justice never change. Seven years makes no difference to them.'

'But it does, it does!'

He put up his hands as if to warm them at the heat of her outburst. 'I'll take your word for it!'

She calmed down and said sadly, 'But you don't really. Let me finish the tale – as far as it's got, anyway. As part of the quest after the truth, Hen and I met Violet Darcy at Kitty Rohane's cottage. Kitty, you remember, was Peter Deasy's sweetheart.'

'Yes. Gosh, that must have been a pretty fraught meeting!'

'Not once we'd broken the ice. She's remarkably quick on the uptake. She saw we were more interested in establishing the innocence of the four they hanged than in hunting down the real murderers.'

'It would amount to the same thing,' he pointed out.

Judith held up a finger. 'Not to her way of thinking. She's a great deal more sceptical than Hen and me. She has a stepmother's eye on the world. She thought we'd still be at it forty years from now. She thinks the English would rather let *ten* real murderers go free than admit they hanged a single man in error.'

'She's probably right.'

'Of course she's right! That was why she agreed. We'd

be forty years getting nowhere – forty years a thorn in the side of the English. That's all she wanted. No wonder she agreed to help us. She must have gone home singing!'

He whistled. 'I see what you mean. It would be wonderful, of course – from their point of view – if the three survivors all swore the wrong men were hanged. Three Protestant eyewitnesses . . . landowners . . . Ascendancy people all. Especially as the real villains got safely out of the country years ago. Or so I assume?'

She did not answer.

He stopped and stared at her, doubt growing behind his eyes. 'No?' he asked.

She inhaled deeply and said, 'I believe one of them is not a mile from us at this moment. I *believe* it. I can't be sure. I think I could quite easily make sure. But do I want to? That's the . . . the crossroads where I'm standing at this moment, Fergal. You see, I thought they were all safely overseas, too. I thought there wouldn't be *that* complication.'

'Are you going to tell me who it is?'

'You remember I said Violet Darcy was doing a line with Mick O'Leary of Streamstown? I think she now employs him. I think he now calls himself Jack Egan and speaks with a Dublin accent.'

He frowned. 'You mean the printer fellow?'

They had reached the thorn bush that was infested with traveller's joy. He paused and looked at her with a hopeful smile. She smiled back but shook her head. 'We don't need a special place, Fergal.'

'Oh?' He bucked up hugely. 'D'you mean I may – to put it formally – start paying my court?'

'No promises, mind.'

He nodded. 'Agreed. Oh, Judith . . .'

'Come on!' She grasped his arm and propelled him forward. 'You spoke as if you know Jack Egan.'

'He printed my card.' He cleared his throat, mocking

his own self-importance. 'I carry my own card now, you know.' Then he frowned. 'But I thought Mick O'Leary had red hair – brilliantly red hair?'

'So does Jack Egan – where he forgets to shave properly for several days.'

Fergal shook his head. 'Most men's beards are redder than their hair – men who shave, anyway.'

'And in their ears? The hair in Jack Egan's ears is as red as a carrot. And look at his eyes – pale green. D'you know any other man with such jet-black hair and such pale green eyes? And you look inside his hat next time you get some printing done. How many dark-haired men do you know whose hair colouring stains the inside of their hatband! And will I tell you another thing?'

'What?'

'Mick O'Leary's grandfather was called Mick *Egan*! And Mick Egan was a *printer*! He lived in Flaxmills, as a matter of fact. Henrietta remembers him there when she was a little girl.'

Fergal gave a sigh and a shake of the head, conceding she was building up a formidable case. 'But it's all circumstantial,' he pointed out. 'My father's seen the most amazing coincidences of circumstantial evidence – I mean, things you'd never *imagine* would have an innocent explanation – he's seen them crumble to nothing. How many Egans are there in Ireland? Tens of thousands, surely. And the people who make black hair dye, they don't bank on having just Mick O'Leary for a customer. Jack Egan could be a bigamist. He could be a vain man going grey. He could be running from his creditors . . . Sorry, I don't mean to go on. After all, you were the first to point out you weren't sure.'

'Yes, but so far, Fergal, I've only told you the things that pointed me in that direction. I haven't told you the one thing that almost has me convinced.'

'Ah. What would that be?'

She laughed grimly. 'Something that would stand up even less to the sort of cross-examination your father would give it, but to me it's the most convincing thing of all. It's the way Violet Darcy and Jack Egan behave when they're together. At first I put it down to working side by side all the time. I mean, a man and a woman who have no sort of romantic attachment but who are in each other's company most of the waking day – they're bound to develop ways of keeping their distance, aren't they? Mostly joking ways. They swap joke-insults. They stand on their dignity, but jokingly.'

He nodded. 'I know the sort of thing. Is that how they behave?'

'No. You remember how Percy and Hen used to behave before Aunt Bill twigged what was going on between them? That's how Miss Darcy and Mr Egan behave. It's almost the same – I mean the same sort of jokes – but there's a . . . oh, what's the word?' She tensed all her muscles and played an imaginary tug of war with an invisible rope between her hands. 'You said it just now. Fraught! It's fraught between them, all the time, like a thunderstorm just about to break.'

He was pensive a while. 'The other way of looking at it, Ju, is to accept it as true and try to pick holes in it from the other side. If ebon-haired Jack Egan really is red-haired Mick O'Leary, why does he let you come within a thousand yards of him? If Violet Darcy loves him still, why does she permit it?'

'It's the way he laughs,' she replied.

'Eh?'

'I can't really explain it, but you'd understand at once if you heard him laugh.'

'I've never even seen the man smile!'

'Quite. That's his reputation. But from the moment he knew who Hen and I were – I mean, that we are survivors of the Murders – he's behaved differently toward me. Out of character.'

'How did he find out?'

'Miss Darcy warned him! Right in front of us. She called him into the office and then got Hen and me talking about it. She wanted him to understand exactly who we were. And the gleam in his eyes! I'll never forget it.'

'Judith!' He clutched her arm to him suddenly. 'You don't mean you're in danger from him?'

'No, I don't think so. But danger *is* the thing, you see. You said everyone has a dream or an ambition for which they'll sacrifice everything else. For Mick O'Leary I think it's danger. He's walking along the edge of a precipice with me – and it makes him feel alive! For the first time in years, probably.'

He dipped his head to acknowledge that possibility. 'It still doesn't explain why Violet Darcy permits it – unless she has this same addiction.'

'But I think it does!' she insisted. 'For the first time in years, too, she's got back the Mick O'Leary she first fell in love with – the croppy boy himself – a wild, bold, wayward . . . hero! There's no other word for it. He's her hero. And I've given him a new lease of life, d'you see.'

'Lord save us!' He closed his eyes and shook his head. 'It's a cauldron!'

'Isn't it just!'

He turned and faced her solemnly. 'I think you should simply turn your back on it all. Walk away from it. It's playing with fire.'

She wagged a finger at him. 'No advice. You promised.'

He shrugged. 'I mean that's what I'd do in your shoes.'

'I don't believe you.' She laughed. 'And yet I'll admit

I'd say exactly the same to you if our positions were reversed.'

'But why?' he protested. 'If you can put yourself in my shoes and see the sensible thing to do . . . why . . .'

'Sauce for the goose is sauce for the gander,' she said. 'Put yourself in *my* shoes. Think of the fascination of it!'

'Fascination?' He laughed in shock, not humour, at what seemed to him the least appropriate word of all.

'Yes!' she insisted. 'Don't think I'm blowing my own coals, but I believe that if we hadn't returned to Keelity – or if I hadn't said that to Rick about undoing the injustice of it – then nothing would have happened. I don't mean I'm some sort of demon who's goaded them on. I mean that somehow my words took the brake off each of them . . .'

'And now they're all running out of control downhill!'

'Yes, but each in their own direction. Hen wouldn't have bothered, except that *this* intrigue gives her the chance to mask her own private intrigue with Percy, which is all she's really interested in. Rick has actually run off in the opposite direction – I think it's because he can't admit how strong a hold King has over him.'

'Oh, yes. I was going to ask about King. You say he wasn't the principal, but I can't believe he had absolutely no hand in all this.'

She lifted her arms in a brief gesture of resignation. 'Shall we ever know the truth? I used to think he was behind everything. He planned it. He carried it out. He was the general. Aunt Bill still believes it.'

'And what changed your mind?'

'A conversation I'm after having with Francy Robertson – you know? The brothers who have the mill at Streamstown.'

'He's the younger one?'

'Yes. He was a close friend of Peter Deasy – Kitty Rohane's sweetheart. He *hates* King. He loathes that man with a fire . . . well, you could raise steam off him.'

'Because it was King's evidence, mainly, that hanged Peter Deasy?'

'No!' She laughed, but with a despairing kind of humour. 'Because King is some jumped up Roman Catholic pipsqueak who's gone around like the Lord of Lower Egypt ever since the Murders. And the Robertsons are one of the oldest Protestant families in Keelity, so it really sticks in his gullet. The older brother, Tony, is more philosophical – because, naturally, King has taken very good care of them. Tony likes his bread well buttered and he knows who's doing the buttering. Francy is more like Aunt Bill. She thinks King is the double-dyed villain of the western world. When she says she wants to see justice done, she has a picture of King pegged out alive on the lawn with the jackdaws helping themselves to his eyes.'

'God! Did I say cauldron?' Fergal exhaled sharply, as if winded by a blow.

'But even hating King as he does, Francy wouldn't agree he'd planned it all. He says King knew nothing about the Murders until just before they happened. When he realized he couldn't stop them, he decided to make sure he came out on top.'

'But even so, he's responsible for the hanging of four innocent men.'

'So is Mick O'Leary. So is Violet Darcy. And the Robertsons. And all those other people who were only too glad to see those poor men at the end of a rope. You've no idea, Fergal, of the ancient scores that were settled in delivering up those four innocent men to the English! You'd never believe the feuds and the curses that choke the air of all those peaceful-looking townlands around Streamstown and Flaxmills! The English and their so-called *justice* are an irrelevance; they're just an uncomprehending machine over there at the edge of the stage. The feuding clans simply *use* them. People say the days of the faction fights are over. They're not! It's merely that the English have reduced it to a kind of factory system. If they hadn't hanged those four, all neat and clean and official, then Peter Deasy, Kieran O'Sullivan, Michael Tweedy, and Kinch Davitt would have had their brains knocked out with a shillelagh up some booreen one dark night. That's the only difference. And what sort of an eejit am I that goes wandering across that field of war with a placard round me neck saying: All I want is Truth and Justice!'

Captain O'Donovan's wire to Judith had asked her to meet him at Parsonstown station. Simonstown would have been more convenient for her, but he was determined to put up at an officers' mess and the detatchment at Simonstown was too small to support one; at Crinkle Barracks, on the other hand, the mess was one of the grandest in Ireland, outside Dublin. And Wednesday was, as it happened, a good day for such a meeting, for officers – even guest officers – could invite ladies to tea in the anteroom. Judith was looking forward to it. She had visited Crinkle only once before, at a ball around Christmas, so she had never seen the barracks by day.

She almost missed Justin as he stepped off the train for he was dressed in mufti; of course, he had not been in uniform during his last visit, but, as he was going to stay at the barracks, she had expected him to wear blues.

'Justin!' she said as his moustache pecked her cheek. 'I wasn't expecting you out of uniform.'

'Yes,' he replied with an odd kind of sigh. 'It may be a sight we'll all have to grow accustomed to.'

He said no more until the porter had put his cases into the trap. Judith offered him the reins but he waved them aside. The first half mile was a long, straight lane, bordered by a few trees but otherwise open to the brilliant July sun.

'That was an odd remark,' she commented as they crossed the Roscrea road and set off up the lane.

He grunted. 'I don't mind telling you, Judith, when I started on this business I more than half-expected it to turn out a wild goose chase. After all, a man's discomfort and a woman's intuition aren't much to pit against the measured gravity and care of the legal process, are they. But now I'm convinced of it.'

'Oh, good!' Judith tried to sound enthusiastic, though her more recent thoughts on the matter, coupled with his rather sombre humour, made it difficult.

'I can't believe it!' he exclaimed with a sudden rush of feeling.

'What?'

'I imagined, you see – I'm almost tempted to say, "In my innocence, I imagined . . ." That is, I thought . . .' He relapsed into silence.

This time she did not press him.

He began again on a different tack. 'I was brought up to feel an absolute and unbounded respect for the law, you know. My grandfather was a QC and later a high-court judge. I remember him telling me the law is slow but sure. Laymen may call it ponderous as it carefully sifts every particle of evidence, filters it through the accumulated wisdom of the centuries – which we call the Common Law. But it finally arrives at a conclusion that is as infallibly correct as human judgement can be. That's been my creed, Judith. I've practically lived by it.'

'I know.' She said as little as possible, understanding what difficulty he was in.

'It's been my *life*,' he said; he was hardly addressing her now. 'When you first laid your doubts alongside mine, my first response, you know, was shame! Yes, I was ashamed that I, believing in the supremacy of British justice as I do, had kept my misgivings to myself so long. Ashamed, too, that it needed the additional force of you three youngsters, who were mere children at the time, to spur me to action. But I imagined my brother officers, my superiors – the powers that be – I imagined they would at least share my concern once I expressed it.'

'And they don't?' Judith managed to sound surprised.

'I didn't . . . I never once . . . I mean, I have not offered the slightest suggestion that I *believe* a miscarriage of justice has occurred – though I now firmly do believe it to have been so. I merely stated that some such *possibility* had come to light. My whole attitude has been that we, as men of honour, have a duty to investigate that possibility. No more than that. That's all I said.'

'And what? The floodgates opened?'

'Oh no!' He laughed bitterly. 'Outwardly they agree, pat you on the back, tut tut, most grave business, must be looked into most thoroughly, thank you so much, Captain O'Donovan. Now you can go back and play with your soldiers. Leave the rest to us.' He broke off and collected himself, breathing stertorously several times. 'And when I ask if I may be kept informed, they're as vague as a June breeze. When I say we're willing to swear an affidavit, the four of us, they tell me much has to be done before we reach that stage in the proceedings. When I ask to be allowed to see the papers in the case – even papers I myself wrote or signed at the time of the arrest – *bang*! You never saw the portcullises fall faster!'

'Perhaps it does take rather a long time, Justin?' she suggested.

'I haven't finished yet, my dear. Feeling rather fed up with all this prevarication, I requested a personal interview with General Stuart, the GOC, don't you know.'

'And what did he say?'

'He wouldn't see me! His youngest bro and I were at

school together, but he wouldn't even see me! And then . . . dear God, then!'

'What?' She began to grow anxious for she could feel him shivering at her side and his voice seemed to be straying beyond his control.

'I hardly dare tell you, my dear. I hardly dare whisper it even. Whispering! Yes – that's what it is. They've started whispering behind my back! Tubby Moreton, great friend of mine, we mess together, take leave together, went on a walking tour of Connemara last year together, known him for years – suddenly he'd hardly speak to me. Asked him what was up. Grunts. Mutters. Force it out of him at last. It turns out he's heard the most scurrilous tale about me from someone up at HQ! And he's not the only one. I got some very funny looks at the Sheridan, the day before yesterday. But forewarned is forearmed. Went directly up to one of the fellows. Asked him straight. "Have you been hearing funny tales about me?" More hemming and hawing but I thrashed it out of them at last. More tales from people close to the Castle. I couldn't believe it! They're setting out to ruin me, Judith. They're destroying everything I ever believed in.'

'Oh, Justin!' She reined the pony to a halt and stared at him in anguish. 'It's the last thing I wanted to happen!'

Her concern put new heart in him. 'Worry not, young lady!' He gave her arm a confident squeeze. 'They picked on the wrong man if they suppose they can curb me that way!'

'Oh no, Justin – please no. This has gone altogether too far. I want you to drop the whole thing . . .'

'Not a chance!' He chuckled and took the reins from her. 'We've hardly begun. I know you're only thinking of me. My career. My life in the army. You're not that sort of faintheart. But the army that can behave in this despicable manner has ceased to command my respect and must therefore forfeit my allegiance.'

She tried to argue with him all the way to the barrack gates, where they were interrupted by the sentry's challenge.

'Captain O'Donovan, Royal Dublin Fusiliers,' Justin announced, lifting his hat in response to the sentry's salute.

They were ten yards into the barracks when the staff sergeant in charge of the guard came running after them, calling out Justin's name.

Again the trap came to a halt. 'What is it, staff?' he asked.

'Colonel Hamilton's compliments, sir, but he regrets that the guest accommodation at the officers' mess is being refurbished. He recommends the King's County Arms instead.'

Justin drew three deep breaths before he composed himself for a reply. 'That's all right, staff,' he said. 'Your adjutant here – still Captain Nolan, is it?'

'Sir.'

'Old friend of mine. I'll bunk down with him.'

For a moment the man was nonplussed. The trap covered a further half-dozen paces before he called out, 'Captain Nolan's on a one-week detatchment to Simonstown, sir.'

Justin stared him levelly in the eye. 'You're sure, staff?'

'Quite sure, sir!' the man fired back, as if it were a mere formality.

'I think I understand you,' Justin said quietly as he turned the trap about and began to retrace their steps back toward the town.

'You're not staying at the County Arms,' Judith assured him as soon as they were out in the lane again. 'You'll stay with us at the Old Glebe – and for as long as you like, too. What an utter disgrace!'

'But you see what I mean?'

'I do. Oh, Justin, I'm so sorry. I feel it's all my fault.'

He ignored the accusation. 'You see, too, the difference between me and that sergeant back there. To me, truth is a duty. To him – and now, I discover, to most of my brother officers, as well – duty is a truth. *The* truth, in fact. Honour may go hang her head in shame as far as they're concerned. Well, we'll teach her she may hold it high again, eh!'

He shook the reins and cracked the pony into a trot.

In the end it was thought more appropriate – that is, Aunt Bill thought it more appropriate – for Justin O'Donovan to stay at Castle Moore. It almost broke his heart that he would not breathe the same air nor sleep beneath the same roof as his angel, Judith; but his good sense welcomed the arrangement, knowing what a torment the other would have been. The more distance he could keep between him and her, the more easily could he accept and live with his own profound unworthiness. Last time he had stayed at the castle he had watched Henrietta lungeing a young horse, cracking her whip an expert inch or two short of its flank. For weeks after, in Dublin, he had shamefacedly fought off a daydream in which *he* was in harness and Judith held the whip. He still felt corrupted by it and the thought that he might have lain in his bed in the Old Glebe, staling the very air with the whiff of such degeneracy, made him cringe with shame. No, it was a far, far better thing that he did – to lodge at Castle Moore instead.

Besides, from one or two things Judith had said, he gathered that the butler, King, was not quite the hero the world had painted him. This would be a good opportunity to cast an eye over the fellow.

On the Saturday morning after his arrival – the first Saturday in July – there was a commotion on the carriage sweep. The day was already so warm that the large french windows in the breakfast room were wide open, so they all heard it plainly. Aunt Bill and Justin, napkins in hand, merely needed to step outside and take a few paces up the path to find themselves at the front of the house.

'Rick!' she called out, not entirely bowled over with delight. 'Why did you not send a wire? And what are you doing home, anyway?'

At that precise moment what Rick was doing was thanking Liam Clancy, one of the Castle Moore tenants, who had found him walking and had offered him the ride. Rick took the horse's head and helped turn the cart before peeling off on a line that brought him to his aunt and Justin O'Donovan. 'It's a long story,' he said ruefully. 'Is there any breakfast left? I'm famished.'

'You go and wash that dust off you and I'll get something made fresh,' Aunt Bill replied.

He greeted O'Donovan and turned toward the front door.

'Your trunks?' his aunt called after him.

'Still in London – in a probably vain attempt to convince . . . people . . . that I intend to return.' He lowered his voice and looked almost fearfully up at the castle façade. 'The Dalton girls – they haven't turned up here yet by any chance?'

'Oh dear,' his aunt replied heavily. 'D'you mean we may still have that pleasure in store?'

He grew brighter at once. 'So they didn't . . . I mean they haven't! Thank God! And what about Sally McIver and her mother?'

Aunt Bill, who had half-turned to go back to the breakfast room, whirled round again and went to take his arm. 'What *has* been happening?' she asked.

He pulled a face, shook his head, and withdrew toward the front door. 'Let me wash and eat first. I need my strength.'

Ten minutes later, with the most obvious marks of travel removed, he was wolfing down a great platter of eggs, kidneys, rashers, and fried bread. Justin, who considered himself a pretty hearty eater, watched in awe. 'When did you last break bread, young fellow?' he asked.

'When did I last sleep?' Rick replied. 'Or read a paper. Or ride in the park. Or . . . *breathe*! Or do anything normal?'

They heard the sharp scrinch of a metal tyre on the gravel of the drive. 'Oh lor'!' Rick started up at once. 'That's them, I'll bet!'

'Steady the buffs!' Justin told him. 'That's Miss Carty's trap or I'll eat my head.'

'Oh!' The news did not please him as much as his earlier alarm suggested it should. 'In that case, I'll save my story until later. Where's Hen?'

'Behind you.' Henrietta entered the room as he spoke. 'Welcome home, brother dear. What an *unexpected* surprise.' She pushed down on his shoulders to prevent him from rising and kissed him on the brow. 'All alone?'

'By the skin of my teeth.' He frowned. 'Why? What have you heard?'

'Don't be so jumpy.' She broke into a slow grin. 'What should I have heard?'

The room brightened as the sun sparkled off Judith's crisp white summer frock. She caught sight of Rick, said 'Oh!' and disappeared again – but only for a second or so. Moments later she reappeared, this time with Fergal on her arm. 'Hello, Rick,' she said amiably. 'I hadn't heard you were back. How is London? Unbearable in this weather, I imagine.'

Fergal, distinctly uncomfortable at the parade Judith was making of him, merely nodded at his old friend.

'Rick?' his aunt prompted.

'Not now, Aunt Bill,' he begged.

'If we are to air two more beds – or twenty-two, for all

I know – I need as much warning as possible.'

'Beds?' Henrietta echoed. 'For whom?' She still regarded the running of Castle Moore as falling within her domain rather than Aunt Bill's.

'Half the female population of London, it would appear,' the older woman replied.

'Please, Aunt Bill?' Rick begged.

'What *have* you been doing, Rick?' Judith asked with jocular disapproval.

He soaked the last of the egg yolk into the fried bread, popped it into his mouth, and, gulping it down, said, 'Oh, all right! Might as well tell you, I suppose. The thing is . . . oh dear!' He glanced about him like a drowning man. 'I seem to have sort of half-promised to rent the old castle tower to . . . to rent it out.'

A stunned silence greeted the news.

'Yes, to rent it out,' he repeated more firmly.

'We heard you,' Aunt Bill assured him.

'To any lunatic in particular?' Henrietta asked. 'Or was it just a general sort of promise?'

'Any toast?' he asked.

From north and south they pushed half-empty toast racks toward him; butter, marmalade, honey, and Gentleman's Relish followed swiftly – cutting off a quartet of further handy delays. 'Good-oh,' he said despondently.

'Well?' Henrietta pressed as he started to make a year's work of spreading his first slice.

'The thing is, I don't believe I actually *promised* them. I know we talked it over and said, "Oh, wouldn't it be fine" and . . . and all that. But I don't remember actually promising to go through with it.'

'Promising whom?' Aunt Bill asked.

Five pairs of eyes pressed the question hard.

He almost whispered the reply. 'The Dalton sisters. You see, I agreed when they said it would be very convenient to be so close to the printer's – and with Hen being here, and managing the business side of the maga. You know how one talks about these things – never actually meaning them, or not absolutely literally.'

'No, Rick.' His aunt leaned across the table and peered intently into his eyes. 'I can't even begin to imagine how one talks about such things without meaning them. Nor why one talks about such things without meaning them. Nor where. Nor when.'

He spread honey on his first slice and bit off a chunk. 'About three o'clock in the morning, actually,' he replied, munching with gusto.

'It sounds like it.'

'Sitting in the fountains in Trafalgar Square?' Henrietta guessed.

'Well, we'll soon scotch that,' Aunt Bill said firmly. 'Set the rent at a hundred a year! That'll wipe the smiles off their faces.'

Rick shook his head. 'They'd pay it gladly, Aunt.'

'If they had it!' she mocked. 'They haven't two guineas to rub together.'

Rick was still shaking his head. 'That's all changed, I'm afraid. They now have an income of over ten thou' a year – *each*! Or will have after probate. It was in *The Times* yesterday. Old Countess Tesla – the one who married the Polish Margrave, or whatever he was – she died and left them everything. They've got a castle in Poland and a whole forest that's theirs and a house on one of those side canals off the Grand Canal in Venice . . .'

'And an unsuccessful art gallery in Tuscany?' Judith suggested, giving Fergal's arm a surreptitious squeeze.

'How did you know?' Rick asked in amazement. Then he laughed. 'No, nothing in Tuscany as far as I'm aware. Not yet.'

'So!' Aunt Bill was relieved. 'Our two wayward little paupers have turned into substantial heiresses! Well, that's quite different. They'll both be married within the year – mark my words! And in that case I see no harm in letting off the old tower to them. But get the whole year's rent in advance – non-returnable! And do stop shaking your head like that, Rick!'

'They know jolly well they'll be under siege, Aunt Bill. That's why . . .' He closed his eyes and tapped his skull. 'Oh yes, it's all coming back to me now. That's what we were talking about – how beastly it was to inherit all those responsibilities, just when they'd planned the whole of their life out on the happy assumption they'd be too poor to interest anyone and could therefore do as they jolly well liked. And I said they'd be under siege as soon as word got about. And they said . . .'

'They?' Judith asked.

'Gwinny, actually. She said if one is going to be under siege, the place to be is a castle – and what a shame that Castle Vigo had been quarried for its stone when they built Moonduff. And so I just mentioned that we still have the old place more or less intact.'

'Golly!' Judith said. 'I'll just bet that came as *the* most enormous surprise to her!'

He frowned. 'Of course it didn't. I took them over it when they were down here in May.'

'Well-well-well,' she responded.

'Anyway,' he went on, 'they seemed to think that my mere mention of the place was a sort of actual *offer*. I mean, they just said how kind I was and immediately fell to talking about redoing the roof and what colours they were going to paint this room and that. I must say – they had a better memory for the rooms and the layout than I have. And . . .' He licked his lips and looked about him.

Aunt Bill put her head in her hands. 'There's yet more,' she told the table. 'I don't think I can bear it.'

'Out with it, Rick,' his sister urged. 'If they're on the

next ferry behind yours, there's no point trying to keep it to yourself.'

'Well, they started talking about drainage and putting in bathrooms and water closets – and that heating system Peter Connellan has at Coolmore. And I could just see the value of the place going up and up. So' – he swallowed – 'when they suggested quite a long lease, I, sort of, said . . . how wonderful.'

'Did you put anything in writing?' Fergal asked.

'Not a jot or a comma.'

'Did you shake hands on it?'

Rick became uncomfortable again. 'We'd all had a fair bit to drink by then.'

'All?' Aunt Bill pressed. 'There were witnesses to this folly?'

'All three of us.'

'Only three!' She turned hopefully to Fergal, who answered with a resigned sort of shrug. 'I don't know, Mrs Montgomery,' he replied. 'It's not the sort of thing one wants to let go as far as an actual court case. The *mud* that would stick!'

There was the sound of a four-wheeler coming up the drive.

'They must have been on the same ferry as you,' Henrietta told him.

'The one that left Holyhead just behind me,' he admitted glumly. 'I bribed and talked my way on to the cargo ferry.'

They all drifted out again toward the drive, arriving just in time to see Gwinny and Letty Dalton arrive in grand style in an open landau driven by a fine pair of matched greys. 'Hallo!' they cried out gaily.

'A welcoming committee!' Gwinny added ecstatically. 'I always wanted to be met by one of those. Rick has obviously told you our news. Isn't it simply splendid!'

* * *

Immediately after that rather momentous breakfast, Aunt Bill wrote to her barrister son, Bernard, commanding him to use all the resources of the law – plus whatever aid he could muster along the fringes of the law, and indeed anything he might garner from the darkness beyond those fringes – to discover the truth about Countess Tesla's legacy to the Dalton sisters. He was to ascertain first its actual size; she had known too many bequests of 'a fair few acres' that turned out to be vast tracts of bog or callows that earned nothing but an ironical tip of the hat from the peasantry. Then he was to learn what conditions might attach to it; did it cease upon their marriage, or turn into a trust the husband couldn't touch, or a trust for the children? Or did it stipulate they should never marry? She knew Countess Tesla, by reputation at least, and it was a reputation well equal to any such tricks. And finally he was to determine how long probate might take. Were there other claimants? Was the will to be disputed? What legalistic uncertainties in general surrounded it? She desired a reply by return of post.

And meanwhile she permitted the two lucky young maidens themselves to be accommodated in the east wing at Castle Moore. She also determined to be as charming to them as possible – certainly as charming as any aunt with her nephew's best interests at heart could wish to be. But there would be limits. She would encourage them to visit the old castle tower as often as they liked, there to daydream the hours away; she would gently but firmly demur if they sought leave to bring an architect in to start turning those daydreams into something more substantial. As to the possible existence of a verbal contract on which hands might or might not have been shaken – she hoped that might be tactfully avoided for the time being.

By the afternoon of their arrival the heat had become so oppressive that all the youngsters could think of was lying prostrate in the shade or going for a swim. Aunt Bill left them to choose while she took Justin for a drive.

The lake was still cold, however, and nobody stayed in for long. Rick, who was first to dress, went across to the boathouse to see about getting the steamer out for the maiden cruise of the year. Henrietta, who had a bone to pick, went after him.

She wasted no time. The moment they were out of earshot she said, 'Why are you being such a bloody fool?'

'I beg your pardon?' He slowed for a step or two and then resumed his former pace, angry now.

'You know very well what I mean. Messing about with these two trollops. Judith's worth ten of them – and you're throwing away what small chance you still have with her. All because of this tomfoolery.'

'Oh really?' he responded coldly. 'And what about you and Percy? You don't call that tomfoolery, I suppose!'

'That's my business.'

'Snap!'

'Anyway, there's no similarity whatever between our two cases.'

Some of his belligerence evaporated at that. In an altogether gentler tone he said, 'On the contrary, Hen. They are precisely similar in almost every respect – except that there are two of them for me and only one of Percy for you.'

She stopped dead in her tracks, though they were only yards from the boathouse door by now. 'You mean you and they . . .' She could not phrase the question. 'Both of them?'

'Yes! Now perhaps you understand.'

She shook her head. 'Not at all, Rick. I understand even less than I thought I did.' Her face creased in bewilderment as she repeated her question: '*Both* of them?'

He nodded. 'That's the only difference. They are not trollops. They are extremely clear-sighted and advanced thinkers, especially Gwinny.'

She touched his arm and pointed to the boathouse door. 'Tell me when we're inside.'

He reached into the thatch, took down the key, and, after some difficulty, persuaded the padlock to open. The hinges protested as he pushed the door ajar. 'Gwinny says that Society perverts our natural desires by suppressing them. That, in turn, builds up a head of steam, which impels us into marriage – which is the most unnatural state of all.' He smiled at her, not in a challenging way but with some attempt to recruit her agreement. 'I'd have thought you of all people would agree with her there!'

She gave a reluctant shrug. 'And?'

'She says I'm rich enough and independent enough – well, all three of us are now, of course – we're rich enough not to need to bother.'

'So you're now going to flout every convention and cock a snook at . . .'

'No! That's the whole point. Gwinny says we're not out to start a revolution. We don't want to change anyone else's mind for them. We don't want to start any rival movements, we just wish to cancel our subscriptions to the one that currently prevails. That's all.'

'God! I can hear her voice in every word!'

He opened the coal bunker. 'Empty!' he said bitterly. 'Things are getting altogether too slack here.' He untied the painter on one of the rowing boats. 'We could go for a turn or two in this, I suppose.' He held out a hand to assist her into it.

When she had grasped the tiller ropes he pushed off into the daylight and shipped the oars in the rowlocks. 'I don't see why you're complaining,' he went on. 'It's exactly what you and Percy are doing.' He pulled the bows round to face her down the lake.

She almost tugged the ropes off the tiller in her frustration. 'It is exactly the *opposite* of what Percy and I are doing. If you weren't such a . . . such a – oh, you're just a bit of driftwood in Gwinny's stream of thought. Don't you see?'

He pulled vigorously on the oars. 'Well, no doubt you can invent some highfalutin' motive for what you and Percy are doing – the result's the same, though. You go somewhere private. You take off your clothes . . .'

'Yes, yes – all right. If you think that's all that matters, then I pity you. Percy and I love each other. What we *do* grows out of that love. If we did it without love, we would . . . we'd just disgust each other. How *can* you, Rick? You don't love them. They don't love you. You're just . . . like animals.'

'If you think that's a bad thing to be like, then I'm sorry for you.'

'You think it's good?' she asked in amazement.

'I think it's the next step in the advance of civilization. We've denied our animal natures too long, Hen. I'm just amazed you of all people can't see it.'

'Stop saying me of all people. I detest these . . .'

'But don't you see? The Society that forced you to marry Harold Austin was, in effect, saying to you, "My dear, you may or may not have animal desires and needs, but frankly they don't matter. If you don't have them – go to the top of the class. Consider yourself the higher and nobler type of woman, the type to whom all ladies should aspire. And so, being already half an angel, you may sacrifice your life in selfless devotion to your dear, wayward husband and your darling little chickabiddies. But if, alas, you *do* possess those base lusts and needs, then strive, strive, strive – thou polluted daughter of Eve!" And just look at the misery we see all around us, Hen!'

His eyes dwelled in hers and she read there a passionate conviction that was truly his own. It may have begun life as some bit of clever persiflage from Gwinny, but it was now his creed; his soul possessed it.

Also, she had to admit, he was not so wide of the mark when he said 'you of all people . . .' There was, indeed, a seductive message for her in what he said. 'But still there's no love in your scheme of things,' she pointed out. 'You can't say love is something that Society has simply foisted on us. It's older than all the myriads of societies that ever were.'

It was his turn to yield a point without saying it in so many words. 'There's too much clutter in the landscape,' was all he'd admit. 'The way things are, if love can find a home among us, it's just by accident. We say to it, "Now you're here you might as well stay – but just sit quietly over there and don't make a nuisance of yourself." We never invite it in. We don't give it a true home. It's a nomad.' He laughed. 'Its other name is McLysaght!'

She chuckled, too, glad to have some common perch between them. 'That's exactly what I was thinking when you spoke.' She looked him up and down appraisingly. 'You've changed, Rick.'

'Not really,' he replied. 'I know you think I've fallen under Gwinny's spell – and perhaps I did for a while. But everything she said to me rang a bell that was already there. She didn't just find an empty page and scribble her own ideas all over it. And I can see it's the same with you. Just in the few words I said a moment ago – I could see in your eyes that you, too, were hearing the answering bells. And it's not because we're especially depraved, you and me. Those bells are in everyone, just waiting to be rung. The world has ignored them for too long. We're all just beginning to awaken from our slumber. Can't you feel it? You and Percy – you may think it's utterly different from me and the Dalton girls, but it's just a different tune on the same old bells.'

'Oh . . . you!' She stared at him through eyes narrowed to mere slits.

'What?' he asked jovially.

'I hear the voice of the Serpent in Eden.'

'Yes!' he said enthusiastically. 'And not before time!'

The others came down to the jetty and called to them not to hog the boat to themselves. King stood a little apart from the group, having diverted his afternoon constitutional so as to inquire what arrangements they would like made for their tea. He addressed the question to Henrietta as they landed, but it was Rick who answered. He said they would take it in the summer pavilion. 'Oh and King,' he added, 'you'd oblige me greatly by arranging for the coal bunker in the boathouse to be refilled.'

King raised an eyebrow at this odd form of command, but he accepted it with a dip of his head.

'That was a strange way to put it,' Henrietta remarked after the butler had gone.

'Strange?' he echoed. 'By whose lights?'

'Compared with the way you'd have expressed it in the past.'

'Ah,' he said with an enigmatic smile. 'The past!'

Sally arrived at Castle Moore about half an hour before tea was carried down to the summer pavilion. She had brought her bathing suit and was disappointed to learn they had already had their dip. The two Dalton sisters, however, were already wilting again in the heat, so they volunteered to accompany her. Fergal said he'd join them, too – partly out of chivalry and partly because he was aware that Judith was using him to taunt Rick, as she had done from the moment of their arrival that morning. Even so, he would never willingly have left those two more or less alone together had not Henrietta taken him aside and advised it. He still wasn't sure whose side Henrietta was on – apart from Henrietta's, of course – but he decided to trust her this once.

However, Sally and the other two dithered so long in

the shallows, advancing an inch at a time and screaming at each fresh bite of the cold water, that he gave up in disgust and, diving off the end of the jetty, started on a solo circuit of the lake. His bravery caused Letty to shun the slow torture, too, and a moment later she set off in pursuit of him. She cut across the narrow portion at the head of the lake to intercept him on the downstream leg.

'You don't have to work on Saturdays?' was her opening remark.

'Some I do, some I don't,' he replied. 'I work in my father's chambers but he's pretty understanding about the need for maintaining a social life, too, don't you know. As long as I burn the midnight oil to catch up.'

'He's McIver the great barrister?'

Fergal laughed diffidently. 'It's kind of you to put it that way, Miss Dalton.'

'Oh, Letty, please. And I hope I may call you Fergal?'

'I'd consider myself honoured.'

She splashed at him. 'Oh, you are going to be pompous – unless someone deflates you!'

Something in him snapped. It wasn't anger. It wasn't frustration, even – at the enforced sight of Rick and Judith, lying a careful yard apart in the grass before the pavilion, talking about Lord knows what. It was a nameless tension of some kind that had been building inside him all day, ever since he saw that Rick had returned. 'I'll show you pompous!' he promised and sank beneath the water.

The lake was only six or seven feet deep at that point. His heels soon sank in the soft, muddy bed. He coiled himself like a spring and then leaped for the sky with all the force he could muster. He gave out a mighty roar as he broke the surface, reaching for her with both hands, and falling back upon her head in a cascade of green and silver.

With a scream and a gurgle she went under, but she

slipped away from him at once. He prodded this way and that with his feet, finding nothing but empty water. He scanned the surface for bubbles that would reveal her course, but there were none.

'Letty?' he called softly.

'Letty?' That was louder – and more worried.

A moment later she erupted behind him and fell on him with such force that she bore him right down to the mud. There she coiled her feet beneath her and launched herself back to the surface, using him as a base. When he regained the air, about ten seconds later, he was a sorry spectacle of green weed and black mud. 'Pax!' he gasped. 'You have me bet!' He dipped himself again and washed most of it off.

'Now you know what's going to happen if you say one more pompous thing,' she warned, bringing herself to his side in three powerful strokes.

'Have you your own gymnasium at Moonduff or what?' he asked.

'A misspent youth,' she assured him. 'Gwinny and I used to wrestle the gardener's boys and we always won.'

'So,' he went on after a couple of strokes, 'the two of you are going to rent the old castle off the young master?'

'Ho ho!' She turned on her back and propelled herself with trudgen strokes of her legs alone. 'You don't sound too approving, Fergal. I should have thought it would suit you down to the ground. Down to the moat, in this case. I wonder, could we dig it out and get it refilled with water? D'you know there's no castle left in Ireland with a moat, except for Drimnagh. And that's just a farm now.'

'Why should it suit me?' he asked.

She laughed. 'You know fine why it would suit you. You needn't worry, Fergal. Gwinny and I fully intend to keep Rick all to ourselves.'

'What d'you mean?' It was more an outburst of surprise than a request for clarification.

'Oh, don't keep asking obvious questions or I'll have to duck you again. I mean we have no intention of sharing him with anyone as lovely and as sharp-witted as Judith Carty.' She gave three more kicks and added, 'The same goes for your sister if you want to pass on the warning.'

'I can't believe my ears,' he said in bewilderment.

'I know.' Her voice was immensely sympathetic. 'It takes a little time. Gwinny and I know exactly what we want, you see. We always have done, somehow. And we go directly for it. People aren't used to women doing that. Most women go to Dublin by way of Belfast and Cork. You know that gardener I was telling you about – the one whose sons we used to wrestle? He had one leg shot off at Sebastopol. He said he watched the cannonball come bouncing toward him all the way from the cannon's mouth. I didn't know they moved slow enough to see, did you? But apparently they do. And he watched this one every inch of the way – simply not believing it was going to hit him. And then it did! He said Gwinny and I are just like that cannonball.' She laughed with pleasure at what she still took to be a compliment. 'Everyone said how immensely brave he was. Apparently if you saw a cannonball coming at you and jumped aside, you were considered a coward in those days. A real man just stood there, hurling defiance as it neatly cut him in half! Isn't it astonishing the things people used to believe?'

He had to agree that it was; but he could not say much because he was using half his energy in simply keeping up with her trudgen and the other half in making it appear effortless.

'I wonder what – out of all the things we now believe – what are our children and grandchildren going to find equally astonishing? What d'you think, Fergal?'

'The notion that women are the weaker sex,' he panted. 'D'you think you could go just a *bit* slower?'

'Sorry!' Her contrition seemed genuine enough. 'Actually,' she went on, 'it's not so much the idea that we're the weaker sex. It's the idea that we're the *fair* sex. But then, perhaps, not many believe it even now. Mmm?'

Aunt Bill thought they might drive out to the top of Knockmullin Hill, overlooking Streamstown; the prospect down the valley and across Lough Cool into County Clare was said to be one of the finest in Keelity. Captain O'Donovan said that nothing could please him more – though he could think of half a dozen things without any difficulty, including a cooling dip in the lake with the youngsters. The fear that she might recognize him as the little O'Donovan boy she knew as a girl had long since receded.

The contrast between the youngsters' world and his had never seemed starker than at this time. His world was filled with treachery, hypocrisy, backstabbing, and dishonour of every kind. Theirs, by contrast, was joyous, clean-limbed, open, frank, and loving. One only had to watch them, chattering and laughing away as they set off down the path to the lake, bathing suits clutched happily under their arms, to be aware of it. Never had he felt the loss of his own innocence as keenly as at that moment.

'How well did you get to know my nephew during the Season?' Aunt Bill asked him as their gig plunged into the dark shade of the driveway. 'D'you notice any change in him, I wonder?'

Justin confessed he had not known the lad at all well – but he saw no marked change in him, for all that.

'No,' Aunt Bill agreed pensively. 'That's the disturbing thing in a way. No change. You witnessed that extraordinary performance at breakfast, of course.'

He cleared his throat uneasily and said that indeed he had.

'Tell me frankly,' she begged, 'what did you think of it? Forget he's a relation of mine, if you can. Forget you're a guest under his roof. This is entirely for his own good, I hope. Tell me quite candidly what opinion you formed. I truly would welcome it.'

'Truly?'

She nodded. 'No matter what.'

'Well, not to mince words, I thought the boy a blithering idiot.'

'Yes.' Her tone was thoughtful again. 'So did I. And yet I know he's not, you see. That was a performance of some kind. I can't imagine what his true purpose was. Yet perhaps that *is* it: to leave me floundering in the dark.'

'I'm a simple soldier, Mrs Montgomery. It beats me, too. What other purpose might he have had?'

'Well, when he started telling us about this remarkable arrangement over the old castle tower, I assumed he was trying to provoke *me* into putting my foot down, saying that in no circumstances would those Dalton girls be permitted to rent the place.'

'Reasonable enough,' Justin commented.

'I thought he'd allowed his heart to run off with his head while he was in London and was now trying to provoke me into saving his bacon.'

He chuckled and agreed it had certainly been a most provocative performance.

'But then,' she went on, 'he casually let slip that little nugget of information about their legacy – and he must have *known* that it alters absolutely everything. He knows as well as you or I how the world works. But he tosses it out almost as an aside – just in answer to my suggestion that we should set the rent at a hundred a year to frighten them off. Did he also know I'd suggest that?

Did he actually lead me into saying it, just so that he could let it slip in that seemingly idiotic way?'

Justin – a simple soldier, as he said – was unused to the Bellingham labyrinths. 'Lord!' he murmured, hoping he wouldn't be pushed to any more profound contribution.

'Quite!' Aunt Bill replied. 'You see it at a glance, of course. The trouble was that he never went away to school. Boys who go away to school develop a common style of furtiveness and deceit. They are quite pathetically transparent. One has no difficulty in "getting their number", I think the saying goes. But boys schooled by tutors develop a solitary style of deceit that is far more cunning. And as if that weren't bad enough, Rick has had to pit his wits against King, who is cunning raised to the power of ten.'

'Ah yes, Mrs Montgomery – what about King?'

She turned to him with open admiration in her eyes. 'Nothing misses you, does it, Captain O'Donovan! Two brief sojourns under our roof and all is plain as a pikestaff to you. That man – as you've realized – is at the heart of everything. He sees himself as some kind of Celtic chieftain, you know. Or even king. The name has given him delusions of grandeur, perhaps. He treats the Castle Moore estate as his private fiefdom.'

'Yet he's deferential enough,' Justin objected.

'Of course he is. That's his cunning. Is it the Japanese or the Chinese who tell their emperors they're gods and so cannot sully their hands with mortal business? It's one of them, I know. Which is very nice, thank you, for the very *un*godly politicians – who do all the ruling for them, in their name. That's Mr Tomás King for you.'

'I gather he's an RC?'

'Yes! There's another thing. We were the first Protestant family in Keelity – probably the first outside Dublin – to dish out the senior household positions to Roman Catholics. And there's our thanks!'

'And yet fair dues to him,' Justin said, 'he identified those four blackguards who murdered your family. No hesitation or divided loyalties there!'

She was about to explode at this when she caught the look in his eye, which was more sardonic and knowing than his words implied. 'What do you know about them?' she asked sharply.

'I think,' he said, 'it is time I laid my cards on the table.'

Henrietta said she'd just slip away and pick a few daisies for a daisy chain, if they didn't mind. Judith smiled at her gratefully; Rick said nothing. He went on staring at Sally and Gwinny, dithering about at the water's edge, and at Letty, racing to cut Fergal off at the head of the lake. Lord, but she was a powerful swimmer! It struck him that he couldn't imagine the Dalton sisters doing anything unless they did it well.

As soon as they were alone Judith said, 'I hope you don't imagine Aunt Bill was the slightest bit deceived by that ridiculous performance of yours this morning? What on earth were you trying to do?'

He rolled on his back and stared at the sky. 'I was going to ask what Captain O'Donovan is doing down here,' he said.

'Ask your aunt, then. It was her invitation.'

His eyes swivelled in her direction and he smiled. 'And do you imagine I am the slightest bit deceived by that?'

She tossed her head, a little uncomfortably. 'I don't know what you mean.'

'What I mean, darling, is that everybody makes use of everybody else. You never met my old French tutor, did you – Monsieur Beruchet. He made an exercise in grammar out of it. The Grammar of Life, he called it. It's very easy. There are only four rules: the men use the women; the women use the men; the men use the men; the women use the women.' He plucked a seed head of grass, the kind they call shivery shakers, and tickled the tip of her nose with it. '*Les hommes utilisent les femmes.* I don't think that's the *first* Rule of Life, though, do you?'

'Oh, Rick!' She wrinkled her nose and turned her face away in vexation. 'Talking with you is like trying to catch soap underwater.'

'Are you serious about Fergal?' he asked suddenly.

She let the phrase re-echo in her mind as she searched it for some clue as to his own feelings, but there were none. 'Are you serious about the Dalton sisters?' she countered.

'I'm serious about taking rent off them.'

'You're not! I mean, you're not being serious at all. I don't know why I bother even to talk to you.'

'All right.' He threw away the grass stalk and raised himself on one elbow. 'I'm serious about being their ally, though not about forming any *alliance* with either of them. I hope I'm being clear?'

'Ally in what?'

'Ju?' He put a lightweight fingertip to her forearm and massaged a gentle circle. 'Just relax yourself and smooth all those hackles down, eh? There's honestly nothing to get all prickly about.'

She made an effort to soften her mood. She even managed to smile at him.

'That's more like it,' he said. 'Well, to put it as simply as possible, I am their ally in their attempts to remain free. I realize you only know them slightly – hardly at all – but I'm sure you understand why Gwinny has never found a husband despite her pedigree and despite being put through the torment of several Dublin seasons.'

Judith gave a mirthless laugh. 'I can understand that without the slightest difficulty, Rick. And the same goes for Letty, too.'

He smiled. 'I know you think you're being sarcastic, but actually you're paying them a compliment. They'd take it as a compliment, anyway. The point is that Gwinny's now been through half a dozen seasons. She's able to see what happened to those lucky, lucky debutantes who flashed their diamond rings so ecstatically at her first Season, and her second, and her third. In those days she'd have given her right arm to be among that happy band. Now she wouldn't part with the parings of one fingernail.' He checked over his shoulder to see that his sister was not eavesdropping. 'To tell you the truth, poor Hen's marriage is probably among the brighter examples of the Blessed State. The Dalton girls want no part of it. And if renting them their castle in the clouds will help them stay clear of it, I'm only too happy to oblige. Besides, they're good company . . .'

He broke off and stared out over the water. 'I say, what are Letty and Fergal playing at?'

Judith, who had spotted them several moments earlier, smiled and replied, 'They're practising their grammar, I believe.'

'Ha ha!' He continued to watch them keenly.

Judith, who suspected Fergal was only behaving in that way to provoke her, took refuge in Rick's annoyance. 'You were saying?' she prompted. 'Something about their being very good company?'

Far off up the facing hill two maids and a footman took the first steps down the path to the lake, bearing hampers of linen, cutlery, and food, as well as a spirit stove, kettle, and all the other paraphernalia of a simple alfresco tea.

'You didn't answer my question about Fergal,' he pointed out.

'No, darling,' she said evenly. 'I don't think you've established your right to ask it, either.'

'I see.' He lay on his back again but now the relaxation

was gone out of him; he was deliberately cutting out the sight of the two swimmers at their horseplay. 'That's your last word on the subject, is it?'

'Until you do as I suggest, yes.'

'What's that?'

'Establish your right to ask it.'

He gave a baffled laugh. 'How do I do that?'

'You could kiss me, for instance.'

His eyes came wide open. 'Here?'

'And now. In front of Sally. And Gwinny. And Letty – if she can take her eyes off Fergal for a moment. If not, then two out of three will have to suffice.'

He swallowed heavily. 'I couldn't do that. Anyway, here come the servants with our tea.'

'Yes, they'll be here in five minutes, too.'

'You're not being fair,' he complained.

'Fair!' she cried. 'You keep adding more and more conditions, Rick. If I'd known I was expected to play fair as well, I wouldn't even have started this round.'

'Well!' He sat up yet again and dusted his hands restlessly. 'That's that, then. It's pretty clear to me that . . .'

'No it's not, Rick,' she interrupted, angry at last. 'Nothing is clear to you. Your eyes are full of glitter and your mind is in pawn to those . . . butterflies.'

'Oh, and you have a bird's-eye view of the whole world, I suppose!'

She rose and brushed down her dress. 'At least I can see clearly what has to be done next,' she said as she sauntered off to join Henrietta.

'Judith?' he called after her.

She paid him no heed.

To everyone's surprise – not least to that of the two Dalton sisters – the first number of *New Hibernian Quarterly* was something of a success. It had a light-hearted way of dealing with serious topics that exactly caught the mood of the times – but not of *The Times*, which thundered the opinion that there was a fine line to be drawn between deft conciseness and frivolous brevity, and the *New Hibernian Quarterly* stayed resolutely on the wrong side of it.

'Just wait until they see Rick's next piece!' Gwinny said gleefully. 'The moment some good-natured friend informed me that the Old Thunderer had come out against us, I knew we had got it right.'

Indeed, they got it so right that, on the Tuesday following their sudden appearance at Castle Moore, they had to drive into Parsonstown to order a reprint of a further five hundred copies, to be at the binder's in Dublin by Friday. They also brought with them some copy for the second number, whose issue date was still many weeks away. It included Rick's second piece.

Rick did not accompany them. He had decided to pay a number of surprise visits to the premises of the Castle Moore tenants. He postponed the announcement of this decision until well after breakfast – indeed, until that moment, which came most mornings, when everybody met in the hall, saying, 'What shall we do today?'

His announcement certainly took King by surprise, for he vanished into the kitchen like a shot off a shovel. There he dispatched his kinsman Tommy, the footman, on errands of mercy among the populace. Rick, already dressed for riding, mounted his horse at once and caught up with Tommy, pedalling down the drive like a demon. He sent him back and, having concealed himself in the bushes near the front gate, sent him back again ten minutes later.

The party for Parsonstown left shortly after that in the open landau. There were four of them – the two Daltons, Judith, and Justin O'Donovan, who took the reins.

'Can you read despite the jolting?' Letty asked Judith, handing her the final draft of Rick's contribution.

She tried and found she could. '*Richard* Bellingham,' she said. 'It just doesn't sound like Rick, does it?'

'It sounds wonderfully literary, though. I'll bet half the dons at Oxford would give a year's stipend to be called Richard Bellingham – and to be able to write like him, too.'

'Shall I read it aloud to you, Justin?' she asked, clambering up into the driving seat beside him.

He didn't say as much but she could have read Lloyd's shipping list if it meant she'd sit beside him. However, he was soon as immersed in the article as Judith. It was a witty piece in which he stood the usual process of art criticism on its head – that is, instead of having real people stand in front of pictures making judgements on them, he imagined himself in the minds of various subjects in the portraits exhibited at Burlington House that year, looking down at the modish public and passing critical judgement on them. And from between the lines emerged a scathing satire on modern academic art, fashion, and the contemporary imbalance between wealth and taste. Even Justin laughed aloud at several points.

'How *does* he get his ideas?' Judith asked Letty as she handed the manuscript back. They were almost at Parsonstown by then.

'They seem to just pop into his head from nowhere,' Gwinny told her.

Justin had brought them in by the Riverstown road. When they reached the junction where the choice lay between straight on for Crinkle or left for the town, he handed her the reins and said he had a little business to transact at the barracks. Remembering the sort of welcome he had received there last week, Judith admired his persistence. 'Take the landau,' she told him. 'We can walk from here.'

At first he would not hear of it, but they made such a

parade of their stiffness and their burning desire to stretch their limbs, if only for half a mile, that eventually he accepted the offer, saying he'd come to the printer's in about an hour. Privately Judith hoped it would be an Irish hour rather than an English one; she would need every minute of it to carry out what she had come here today with the intention of doing.

The three young women set off up the rise. Looking ahead Judith saw the thorn tree that had sheltered her and Fergal last time she had come this way, just a month ago.

'I'm so glad we have this opportunity to talk to you alone, Ju,' Gwinny said. 'There is one subject on which Letty and I would welcome your opinion above all others.'

'Rick!' Judith said drily.

'How did you guess!' Gwinny laughed. 'Though actually it's more *Richard* we'd like to talk about than Rick. We were thinking of asking him to write something a little more serious next time – more like the thing he wrote in our first number – perhaps even more serious than that.'

'And what would this be on?' Judith asked. 'Is that the way you collaborate – you suggest the theme and he sits down and writes it? Is that how the Royal Academy piece was born?'

'Oh, it's sort of half and half,' she replied vaguely. 'Anyway, we were thinking of suggesting a piece on the use of force as a political weapon. He mustn't develop a reputation, you see, for writing only light-hearted things, no matter how good he is at it. Don't you agree?'

They had reached the thorn tree. Judith paused a moment in its shade and closed her eyes. Suddenly Fergal seemed very near. 'I'm sorry to say I feel quite indifferent to whatever reputation Richard Bellingham may acquire,' she said, opening her eyes and giving them both a dazzling smile.

It answered one or two questions they had not liked to ask but it still failed to address the particular point they had in mind at that moment.

Gwinny continued: 'What I'd really like to know is, do you think it would be in the worst possible taste to suggest it to him? Or would he laugh at me for even supposing it would be – in bad taste, I mean? You see, the attitude of people who have actually experienced the use of violent force is often quite different from what we imagine it to be, we who have only ever stood at the edge of that arena.'

Judith sighed. If she ever wanted lessons in persistence, she'd know where to apply. 'I can't answer for him,' she replied, 'but I'm sure he wouldn't take the request amiss. He'd just say yes or no and that would be that.'

Somehow she could not imagine Rick saying no.

'It would be marvellous to have Richard, of all people, to write it,' Letty said. 'Everyone would know the terrible story of the Murders. They'd know he'd have every reason to hate those men, and, in time, teach his children to hate their children – and so begin that process we know only too well on this side of the Irish Sea. But I'm quite sure he would take an altogether different stand on the matter. And the fact that he, of all people, turned his back on the age-old cry for blood and revenge would be so telling.'

'And it would add fresh point to the *New* in our title – *New Hibernian Quarterly*,' Gwinny concluded.

'Yes,' Judith agreed. 'It would have a meaning for so many people, too.'

In fact, it would have so much meaning for one particular couple – the man who would set it in type, scorching letter by scorching letter, and the woman who would send it out in several thousand copies to the world – that she almost decided to abandon her own plans for that day. But when the moment came it felt more like cowardice than patience simply to do nothing and wait for Rick's article to drop like a bomb in this printing shop. She had to bring it to a head now, if only to spare Justin further humiliation.

Jack Egan saw at once that the priority was to print the extra order; the setting of the new copy, urgent though it was, would have to wait. Judith seized her chance. 'There's one little thing I could set up, Mr Egan,' she told him earnestly. 'It's a poem, so I can use fixed spaces. And it's italic, so I won't be messing up the case you're working away with there.'

'Ah, g'wan wit' ye, colleen,' he said indulgently. 'You'll give me no rest if I say no.'

And so, for the next hour or so, watched occasionally, and with some envy, by the two sisters, she set up her poem. At one point Gwinny came and peered over her shoulder, reading it painfully, letter by letter; when she drew breath to say she remembered no such poem among their copy, Judith murmured, 'Don't say a word now. This isn't for you.'

Fortunately the printer was too busy setting up the first imposition on the platen press to bother with the fact that she was using the flat-bed proofing press for the first time, and without supervision. He just watched her out of the corner of his eye and, every now and then, chuckled as he gave out some such remark as, 'Jaysus, colleen, but ye'll have me out of my place here yet, so you will!'

She locked the type in its chase, inked it with a hand roller, laid a sheet of proofing paper over it, pushed the bed beneath the press, spun the weighted handle and ducked, staying down until she heard it thud against the type, and then stood up to catch it on the rebound and assist it back to the top of its thread. Her heart was hammering in her throat as she pulled the bed back out again.

'I'll give that a drop of oil for you in a sec,' Jack Egan promised. 'Lift the paper, then! It'll not get blacker for lying there.'

She knew he was desperate to see how many mistakes she'd made, but he was determined to pretend he had no interest in the matter at all.

Gingerly she peeled off the proof and read, with some pride:

Kitty Rohane's Lament

'Twas seven years ago in the woods of Coolnahinch
My love appeared to me by a weeping tree
And all the birds flew up
They were flying, they were flying
And I knew my love was dying
On the gallows tree

Seven long years ago by the waters of Lough Cool
Death appeared to me by the setting sun
And the little birds fell silent
They were crying, they were crying
As their honour lay a-dying
By the setting sun

Seven long years have rolled by the waters of Lough Cool
And Death still stalks that sward with his smoking gun
But the birds have lost their dread
They are near, they are near
The birds have lost their fear
Of the setting son

'Not a single typo!' she said proudly.

'One!' Jack Egan's finger made a stab toward the final word.

It gave her quite a start for he had crept up silently.

She squared herself to face him and said, without a tremor, 'Sure you'll know what to do about that, Mr . . . Egan.'

'Indade I will,' he replied, in a voice that sent a chill right through her.

And that was that. There could be no turning back now.

When the Castle Moore people had left, Jack Egan pulled another proof of *Kitty Rohane's Lament* and carried it into the office. There he laid it on the desk where his mistress would see it. She was in town somewhere, rustling up more paper, for the first printing had almost exhausted their stock and the new delivery was still 'on its way'. She returned, successful, about half an hour later.

'They've gone, then,' she said.

'They have.'

His abruptness startled her. She hung up her bonnet and came to him, gazing up into his eyes. 'Mick?' she murmured.

'Whisht!' He looked over his shoulder.

'Has something happened?'

He nodded. "Tis on your desk.'

Within thirty seconds she was back in the print shop, clutching the proof in her hand, which was shaking; she was shaking all over. 'I warned you,' she told him.

'So you did.'

'And that's all you've got to say for yourself? You'll have to leave. I'm surprised you're still here.'

Stolidly he continued applying small patches of make-ready to the printing bed.

She gave an exasperated sigh and stared at the proof again. 'What in the name of God did she mean by it?' she asked. 'Is she warning you to go? Why would she do that?'

'It's not me she's after,' he told her.

'What then? She must be.'

''Tis my conscience. *You* could have written that – every word of it.'

'Will you stop that fiddling and talk to me!' she cried.

He paid her no heed. 'Honour lay a-dying!' he quoted. 'You could have written that.'

'And so it did!' Violet snapped. 'But don't be giving yourself airs, now. 'Twasn't *your* honour died that evening. 'Twas all Ireland's.'

He stared at her in surprise. 'You never said that before.'

'I did, but you never listened. Perhaps she's crowing over you, Jack. They could be on their way to take you up now! She's gloating, that's what.'

'Sure anything's possible.' He dabbed fresh ink on the reservoir plate and spread it evenly with a little hand roller before he took another pull. 'In my view 'tis neither warning nor gloating.' He carried the pull to the daylight by the window. 'God, I put too much there.'

'I suppose you'll tell me what it is, then?' She clenched her fists and mentally counted to ten.

'A challenge,' he replied simply as he returned to the press and, lifting the type, removed one or two bits of makeready. 'Now,' he said.

'Lord save us!' Her tone was both mocking and despairing, mostly despairing. 'A linnet would only need to sing for the joy of life and you'd put up your fists and say 'twas a challenge. What possesses you at times? And what is she challenging you to do, may I ask?'

'What has to be done.' He locked the chase again and

worked the treadle for another pull. 'What my conscience tells me has to be done.'

'And that is?'

He laughed harshly. 'Not what *she's* after thinking, anyway – let me be the first to tell you that.' He carried the new pull to the window and grunted with satisfaction. 'Put that in your other hand, now,' he said, thrusting it at her. 'That's what has to be taken care of.'

She glanced at it unwillingly. It was the first page of Rick's article of the Irishness of the Anglo-Irish. 'What in God's name are you talking about?' she asked; the dreadful sinking feeling in the pit of her stomach had more to do with his tone than with a dawning understanding of his words.

'The English are no enemy,' he said. 'They're a disease, an infection. They are microbes. One day they'll be gone. The peelers, the fusiliers, the grand juries, the viceroy, the castle crowd – they'll all be gone. And then we'll be left with *them*!' His trembling finger stabbed at the proof of Rick's article. 'The *Irish* Anglos, they should be called. The foreigners we've helped feel at home – even as they help themselves to our homes.'

'Would you listen to yourself!' she shouted angrily. '*Our* homes! D'you think we had these acres from the day the Almighty put them into the hands of Adam and Eve? Adam O'Leary and Eve Darcy was it! 'Tis a strange Bible you've been reading! Oh Lord, do Thou save us from all who would rewrite Thy Word! And *you*!' She thrust her face close to his. 'Isn't it the lucky man you are that the sons and daughters of Adam aren't cowering behind the wall beyond, waiting to put a bullet through *your* brain, the last foreign usurper but one!'

She almost tore the straw of her bonnet in ramming it back on her head.

'You'll not do anything foolish now,' he snapped.

'No more than I've done these seven long years,' she

replied dolefully. Then, with a return of spirit, 'And I could ask the same of you.'

'I'd set forth and do it this minute but for one thing.'

'Well, it can't be your good sense.'

He ignored the jibe. 'The fella who came to collect them – *Mister* O'Donovan he called himself. A military man if ever I saw one. And the word on *her* lips, Miss Judith Carty's, was captain or major, I'm sure. But in he steps and cuts her short – *Mister* O'Donovan, says he, and pleased to make my acquaintance! That's the one to watch.'

'God send you eyes in the back of your head, so,' she said wearily. 'I'm past caring.'

Justin O'Donovan waited until they had put Riverstown at their back and had nothing but miles of open country before them. Then he asked Judith what that bit of paper was.

'Just a poem,' she replied, making light of it. 'A lament. Mad McLysaght wrote one for Kitty Rohane and he told it to Mrs Montgomery. But I never heard beyond the first verse, so I thought I'd write a couple of my own.'

'How charming.' He turned to the Dalton sisters. 'And what do our two daughters of Mæcenas think of it? Are they minded to accept it as a contribution to their esteemed journal?'

'It's rather bitter,' Letty replied guardedly.

'As a lament,' he pointed out, 'it could hardly be comic or pastoral.' He turned to Judith. 'I wonder if I might . . .'

She was already offering it to him.

He read slowly. She watched him keenly but his expression yielded nothing. He read it twice and she knew he was committing it to memory. 'It is bitter,' he said at length, handing it back to her with an air that suggested his interest in it was already waning. 'But affecting. Elegiac, one might say.' He smiled at Letty, who smiled uncertainly back, aware that something was going on to which she and her sister were not party.

'Kitty Rohane's sweetheart was one of the Castle Moore murderers – the one who died of his wounds,' Judith told him. He plainly did not wish the sisters to know he was at all concerned in that business.

'Ah!' he exclaimed, as if the poem suddenly made ten times more sense. 'The fella who "did a rat", as the police say.' He smiled again at Letty, adding to her discomfiture. 'Does this intelligence make you more or less inclined to accept it, Miss Dalton?' he asked jovially.

'It makes me wish to have as little to do with it as possible, Captain O'Donovan,' she replied.

'I can't tell you how glad I am to hear it,' he said.

They spoke of indifferent matters all the way home, but Judith, who knew him fairly well by now, was aware that her rash action did not please him in the least.

She planned to slip away while he drove the landau round to the stables, but when they arrived he handed the reins to one of the groundsmen and told him to take it round the back; then he turned to her and suggested a little promenade before luncheon. Vainly she protested she was expected at home; he simply took her arm and muttered, 'No you are not, young miss!' It was a Captain O'Donovan she had not seen before.

He led her to the path that ran down to the lake. 'And what on earth do you imagine you're doing?' he asked angrily as soon as they were alone.

'Paying a debt,' she replied.

'Indeed! I may tell you I'm finding it very hard to remain civil to you. You have no idea what . . . what *folly* you have committed.'

He paused for her to reply but she said nothing.

'I hope you're starting to feel ashamed,' he added.

'No,' she said.

'Well, you jolly well ought to.'

'I don't agree.'

'Oh well, we could go on saying 'tis-'tisn't for ever. *Why* did you do it?'

'I'd tell you if I thought you really wanted to know, Justin.'

'But I do.'

'You don't. You only want me to say something you can demolish. I could give you the best reason in the world – indeed, I *have* the best reason in the world – and you'll simply try to bury it.'

'Well,' he said bitterly, 'let's hope that's all I'd have to bury!'

After a silence he added, 'I'm sorry. I shouldn't have said that. Forgive me – but you have brought such dismal possibilities nearer to . . .'

'I'll tell you,' she said suddenly. 'I did it because I'm afraid for *you*. There now!'

'Afraid for me!' It stopped him in his tracks. 'My dear girl!'

She pointed a finger at him. 'Exactly,' she said. 'Listen, Justin, when I saw the insolence in that staff-sergeant's behaviour toward you at Crinkle last week, I wanted to die. To think that *I* had been the cause of that.'

'You?' He raised his hand to his forehead, as if he would crush it between his fingers. 'Aiee! You had nothing to do with that.'

'But I did, Justin. I know you're only trying to protect me. I know you'd protect me with your life . . .'

'I'd protect any woman with my life.'

She put herself in front of him, making him stop. She grasped his arm and said, 'Now tell me I'm *any* woman!'

He took her free hand and cradled it between his. 'You know I can't do that,' he said.

'Just so. That's why I did what I did. I know you'd go

to any lengths – no matter how dangerous, no matter how absurd – any lengths to avoid even the slightest whisper of harm to me. And I couldn't let that happen.'

'Oh, Judith!' He let go of her and walked the last three steps down to the lake shore. And there he stood awhile, staring across the water toward the summer pavilion.

After a bit she approached him again. 'I couldn't have lived with myself,' she said, 'if you'd come to harm through some silly . . . chivalrous . . . wonderful gesture – trying to protect me.'

'Oh dear!' He closed his eyes and shook his head. 'And it all looked so cut-and-dried to start with!'

'What did?' She frowned and took a short step back.

He answered her with another question: 'What do you imagine Mick O'Leary, alias Jack Egan, is going to do now?'

'Vanish, of course,' she replied. 'Both of him.'

'He won't do that!' Justin replied vehemently. 'Neither of him.'

'I think he will. Oh, he'll splutter and make vain boasts for Violet Darcy's benefit, but the wild Mick O'Leary who let the drab Jack Egan devour him for seven years won't go back to his old ways.'

Her confidence began to dent his. 'What makes you so certain?' he asked. For the first time his tone suggested he might actually accept her answer.

She tapped her forehead and smiled. 'Because he's had to become a thinking man, Justin. The name of Kitty Rohane is now burning in letters of fire in his brain. I'll bet it's making him think very hard about me. He probably knows the oath I swore to Kitty. He certainly knows the things I said to Violet Darcy before I realized she was still harbouring him. He knows Kitty's sister Josie works at the Old Glebe. He knows there's twenty of Peter Deasy's kinsmen would like to cut the head out of him if only they knew where he was – not to mention the Davitts and Tweedys and O'Sullivans. And he must know – he surely *must* know – that what I did today was like giving him one last chance to disappear.'

He threw up his hands in amazement. 'You mean you actually want him to get off scot free?'

The luncheon gong ran out through the grounds.

'The sound of summer!' she said. 'Come on! I'm famished, aren't you?'

He took her arm to slow her down. 'Answer me,' he said. 'D'you really want him to go free?'

'If you call it freedom!'

'Compared to swinging at the end of a rope, the darkest cell in Dublin would be freedom.'

'He'll be free to sing that lament, every day of his life, however many days that may be.'

'And you believe he will?' Justin asked sceptically.

She sighed. Her smile was tinged with sadness. 'I've given him the chance. That's all I can do.'

'You've given him more than that.'

'What else?' she asked.

'Your contempt. You didn't even think him worth denouncing! That's the way he'll see it.'

'But it's not true!' she protested. 'It's just that I don't want to start a new round of killing. All I want is to help clear the names of four innocent men.'

They walked in silence almost to the top of the path. As they approached the carriage sweep some of his usual ebullience returned. 'Ah well,' he said, rubbing his hands, 'perhaps you have the right of it after all. You know the man and I don't. As a matter of fact, I think I have to return to Dublin this afternoon.'

'Oh? Must you?' she asked sadly. 'Stay at least until Friday, can't you?'

'I'd love to,' he assured her. 'But duty calls. I'll tell you what I would like, though – if you don't think it would be too much of a bore? I'd like you to invite me down again for your birthday. Are you going to have a party, or perhaps you're getting a bit long in the tooth for that?'

She dug him sharply with her elbow and laughed. 'It's Henrietta's birthday, too,' she replied. 'We'll probably do something. And of course you have a standing invitation, Justin. You don't need the excuse of a special occasion.'

He drew out a large handkerchief and blew his nose rather violently.

After luncheon Aunt Bill drove him back to Parsonstown again, this time to catch the train. He told her what Judith had done that morning, which made her want to turn about at once and go back to throttle the girl. But he calmed her down again and said, 'One can't help admiring such courage. If I had a platoon of men with hearts like that, I'd cheerfully take on a regiment.'

'But she could have ruined everything, Justin! Perhaps she has? I don't see why you're so cheerful.'

'She may, unwittingly, have given us the best chance yet at O'Leary – the last of the gang. Believe me, I know these romantic Gaels. They can't resist an anniversary. He'll see it as a memorial tribute to Ciaran Darcy. But don't worry – he'll not get within a mile of Castle Moore.'

After she had seen him on to his train she went to Darcy's to get the cards for the birthday invitations printed. There was no need to ask after 'the nice Mr Egan, who is being so kind to Miss Carty'. His cap and coat were not hanging in their usual place and the press was silent. And Miss Darcy's eyes were red as rust.

When she arrived back at Castle Moore, Aunt Bill went up to her room to change; but first she did something she had not done during the daytime for as long as she could remember: she went down on her knees and prayed.

* * *

Justin was almost too late for the banquet. Aunt Bill had decreed it should be a full dress affair, so they were all waiting around, feeling rather stiff and uncomfortable, on the terrace: the two Dalton sisters; three McIvers – Sally, Fergal, and their mother (their father being at a circuit court in Kerry); Judith and her parents; Percy and Netty O'Farrelly (but not their parents); and, of course, Aunt Bill, Henrietta, and Rick. Percy O'Farrelly had been excluded until Mrs King pointed out that it would mean seating thirteen at table. To hold such a banquet at all was to cock a snook at fate; to seat thirteen might prove an intolerable provocation to that fickle spirit – to say nothing of the provocation to their nerves. So Percy was invited after all.

And there they stood, 'like butterflies and penguins', as Rick put it, waiting for Captain O'Donovan to make up the fourteen. They were just beginning to wonder whether they shouldn't start without him, and hang the superstition, when his carriage came helter-skelter up the drive, dragging a lazy cloud of dust behind it. Their cheers doubled when they saw he was already in mess kit, or what the army quaintly calls 'full dress undress'. The phrase 'dressed to kill' occurred to Gwinny but she managed not to say it. O'Donovan was profuse in his apologies though he offered no actual explanation.

They began a slow drift across the carriage sweep, making for the path down to the lake. They went wide to avoid the dust, which was settling where it hung on the breezeless air. King sidled up to Justin and, pointing to a band of dark cloud far off over southern County Clare, wondered if it wouldn't be better to hold the banquet indoors after all.

Justin stared into the butler's eyes, looking for signs of regret or uneasiness. 'I'm sure it'd be a great relief to those who have to carry the victuals down and bring back the dirties,' he commented.

'Oh, I don't think that's what would worry them, sir,' King said. 'It's the day itself that's in it. The memories. And to be holding another banquet out there, too.'

Justin made no comment on that. 'Tell me,' he went on, 'the servants who were there that night – are any of them still in service here?'

King nodded. 'Every man-jack of them – and woman-jill, too, sir – if I may so express it. There's been little else talked of for days, I can tell you. And none of them with much stomach for it, either.'

Aunt Bill joined them at that moment. 'What's the fevered discussion?' she asked.

'King thinks we should call it off. Eat in the house instead. It looks like rain over there.'

'Nonsense!' Aunt Bill snorted. 'You may start the preparations for serving the first course now, King.'

The butler bowed and withdrew.

'What was all that about?' Justin asked thoughtfully. 'And why make the suggestion to me instead of to you?'

'Because he wants you to remember it afterwards, of course. Something *is* afoot, you see – and he's party to it. But afterwards he wants you to remember he suggested calling the banquet off. Or moving it to the house. Sly old devil!' She rubbed her hands gleefully. 'But we'll see who has the last laugh before this night is out. He's not the only one who can box clever like that!'

Her behaviour amazed him. The thought that 'something was afoot' and that it might involve not one but several violent deaths, including her own, did not seem to trouble her in the least. He had seen such excitement take possession of men before a battle, but it had never occurred to him that a woman might feel it, too.

'Are all your fellows in place?' she asked eagerly.

He glanced cautiously about them before assuring her they were. 'That's what kept me.'

'I thought as much.'

Their casual saunter down the path brought them close behind Judith. She glanced back, saw them, and paused until they caught up. 'Aunt Bill,' she teased, 'you mustn't keep the most eligible bachelor in Keelity all to yourself. There are four unbetrothed females languishing in the company tonight.'

Aunt Bill's laugh was heartier than her mood. 'You're welcome to him, dear,' she said as she in turn fell back to join Sally and her mother. 'I think he's proof against the lot of you.'

'I'm a waste of powder,' he confirmed jovially as he allowed Judith to take his arm.

'Did you have anything to do with those policemen who searched the grounds this morning?' she asked when she had him more or less to herself.

He shook his head. 'I've just this minute got off the Dublin train, my dear.'

'What were you saying to King just now – or he to you?'

'Oh, we were talking about the weather, don't you know.'

Her eyes dwelled in his for a moment. 'I see,' she said at last.

'Anything else?' he prompted.

'Have you sniffed hide or hair of our friend with the inky fingers?'

He shrugged and conceded ruefully that he had not.

'Then hadn't I the right of it?' she insisted. 'He's done a bolt.'

Justin nodded again. 'It rather begins to look like it. We'll know for sure soon enough.' He dipped a hand into his pocket. 'By the way,' he added. 'Brought you a little present.'

He drew forth what looked like a small change purse, which he pressed into her hand. 'Don't show everyone.'

She, feeling the weight of it and thinking it was money,

was shocked and embarrassed – until her fingers explored it more closely and made out the unmistakable shape of a small pistol. 'Don't want to alarm you, my dear,' he added when her eyes told him she had made the discovery. 'But better to be safe than sorry, eh? The slide by your thumb is the safety catch. Forward for off.'

'Justin?' She looked around swiftly and gave him a hasty peck on the cheek.

'What's that for?' he asked with an embarrassed laugh, favouring the spot with his gloved fingertips.

'For being so cautious and . . . sound.'

'I say!' He scratched the back of his head and turned bright pink. Then, in desperation to change the subject, he said, 'I see the Dalton girls are still here?'

'More than ever!' She laughed and her eyes promised a feast of gossip later. 'Their architect practically lives here nowadays and he keeps turning out ever more exotic plans for the restoration of the old castle keep. It's going to be terribly quattrocento now – very heavy with wood. There won't be a single oak left standing in Ireland by the time he's finished.'

'Oh? So the legacy story was genuine after all.'

'Didn't you think it was?'

'Not for one moment.'

'Well, apparently it is. Bernard Montgomery made all sorts of inquiries in Admiralty, Probate, and Divorce – why do they lump those three together? I wonder. I must ask Gwinny. She can get Rick to do an article about it. That's the way they work, you know. He's a writing machine. She gives him a prod and out pops an article. Anyway, it seems that the rumoured ten thou' a year *each* was, if anything, an underestimate. And what's more, the will is not going to be contested. Lucky them, eh?'

He squeezed her arm. 'It's going to be all right, my

dear, I promise you. The countryside is only *alive* with police and soldiers.'

She drew a deep breath and let it out in a rush. 'Sorry. Am I gabbling too much?'

'Don't worry. Now what were you saying? Lucky sisters?' He pulled a dubious face. 'Poor Rick, more like it.'

She chuckled. 'That's what I try to think, too – though I'm sure *he* doesn't see himself in that light at all.'

They had reached the lake shore, where gardeners and grooms were waiting to row them over.

The moment they reached the farther jetty, McLysaght, proud of the smudge fire he had kindled, bowed low and waved his hat with a courtly flourish, crying, 'Salutation and greeting to you all!'

'As you like it,' Letty called out to him – or that was what most people thought she called.

He dipped his head in special acknowledgement to her.

'That's more comforting than last time,' Judith told Justin O'Donovan. 'On the night of the Murders he said something about loud applause and aves vehement. And also "*Ave et valete*"!'

'Did he, by George?' Justin's eyes narrowed. 'No one told me that.'

Gwinny, who had overheard the exchange, said, 'Actually, Ju, I don't think comforting's quite the word. D'you happen to know the little speech that comes before "Salutation and greeting to you all"?'

'No. How does it go?'

'Not word for word now,' she told them, 'but something like, "Surely this is the Second Flood and these are couples coming to the Ark! See, here are two very strange creatures, which in all tongues are called fools." Something to that effect.' She looked around and gave out a tinkling laugh. 'Which couple does he have in mind, d'you think? It could be almost any of us, eh?'

She drifted away. Judith turned to see how Justin responded.

'There are powerful arguments in favour of female education,' he murmured. 'But also, one is bound at times to concede, *against* it.'

They were nearing the summer pavilion. Aunt Bill rejoined them and grasped Justin's arm in a proprietorial fashion. 'You've had your chance, child,' she told Judith. 'Now into the dickey seat!'

Judith laughed and let them go on while she waited for Fergal to catch up; he had stopped to exchange a word with McLysaght. 'I told him to break off a branch with plenty of leaves and waft the smoke round a bit,' he remarked. 'It's doing no earthly good going straight up like that. Did you ever know such an airless night in Ireland?'

'Sit by me?' she said.

'I'd love to, but I'm sure you and Hen ought to sit on either side of the host.'

'Let's see.' Her eyes met Rick's at that moment.

He, as host, was already at the centre of the table with Sally and Gwinny hovering near.

He lifted an eyebrow. Judith shook her head, almost imperceptibly.

He grinned and, raising his voice, called out, 'With apologies to both McLysaght and that obscure poet he keeps quoting: "Stand not upon the order of your sitting, but sit!" In other words – wherever you think yourself, now.'

He waved a lordly hand across the wide expanse of the marble table, which once again glittered with silver and crystal, set off to perfection by damask and fine porcelain. Sally and Gwinny snapped up the chairs to his left and right. Judith took her place between Fergal and Percy. Henrietta was seated just beyond Percy – much to her aunt's annoyance, for in *her* seating plan, which Rick had just destroyed at a stroke, the two lovers had been placed at nor'-nor'east and sou'-sou'-west of the table. The older generation, with Letty marooned among them, formed a claque of their own at the southern end, nearest whatever stray breeze might eventually decide to blow. Liveried footmen and maids in starched pinafores began at once to pour the wines and serve the iced consommé.

Judith's fingers explored beneath her place mat. 'Look!' She furled back the cloth and nudged Fergal; her fingertip lay in a rough groove scored in the marble.

'How gruesome,' he said.

She let the mat fall back to cover it.

'Didn't they ever have it repaired?' Percy asked.

'Rick wouldn't let them,' Henrietta explained. 'He said we'd wear our scars with pride.'

There was a sudden commotion in the bushes, about thirty paces away. Justin sprang to his feet and his hand dived into his pocket. Judith popped the button on the purse he had given her. Fergal pushed back his chair and swivelled round. They all laughed when they saw it was only McLysaght, doing as Fergal had suggested and carrying a small uprooted birch sapling with plenty of leaves. He looked at them in astonishment, laughed, and said, 'From the smoke into the smother!'

They relaxed and, a little sheepishly, resettled themselves around the table.

'It's obviously his night for *As You Like It*,' Letty Dalton told Justin, at her left. She felt that to parade her cleverness to the entire company a second time would be vulgar, but she wanted someone, anyone, to know she had recognized the line nonetheless.

'And what precedes or follows it?' he asked laconically.

'Something about "I go from tyrant king to tyrant brother." It's the idea of "off the bakestone and on to the griddle", d'you see.'

'I do indeed,' Justin mused. 'I think I must have a talk with that man before the evening's out.'

Judith was rather shocked to feel Fergal's hand suddenly exploring in her lap – and even more shocked when her first, unthinking, response was to bring her own hand down to caress his there. But her surprise turned to mortification when she realized what his actual purpose was, for at that moment he found her 'purse'.

When his fingers had traced the unmistakable outline of the pistol it contained, he withdrew his hand and stared at her in horror.

Then he saw she was blushing.

Then he realized why – and that it had nothing to do with her possession of a gun.

Then he remembered how her hand had caressed his, rather than shoo it away, and he blushed, too.

And thus they sat, in stunned silence, side by side, desperately relishing their soup – which was, in fact, extremely relishable – and wondering what to say next.

Judith was the first to see the humour of the situation. 'Well now!' She glanced sidelong at him.

He glanced sidelong at her and smiled, as if slightly against his will. 'Well now!' he echoed. 'Is it loaded?'

The possibility that it might not be loaded had not crossed her mind; but of course it must be, or Justin would never have given it to her. She nodded.

'Well!' he repeated.

She left a polite two spoonsful of soup untouched and rested her hands in her lap. Then some imp of mischief made her right hand sidle toward his knee, which she began to tickle with the gloved tip of her little finger. At the same time she leaned across him and engaged Netty O'Farrelly, seated to his right, in innocent smalltalk. Fergal pushed her hand away a couple of times and then paid her back in kind, clasping the whole of her knee in his left hand and massaging it while he talked the most blatant legal 'shop' with Percy, across her.

After that it became a battle of wills – or, rather, of stubbornnesses. Inch by inch she moved the maddening tickle of her little finger up the inside of his thigh, all the while continuing to tell Netty about an amusing little article she had just been reading in the *Lady's Drawing Room Companion* on how to make an income of four hundred seem like a thousand by sponging off your friends. And similarly, squeeze by seductive squeeze, he moved his hand crabwise up the top of her thigh while continuing to tell Percy all about a wonderfully elaborate excuse he'd heard in court last week when a farmer tried to explain how he came to be milking his neighbour's cow in the dark at four o'clock in the morning.

In the end, sheer anatomy defeated them; they would both have needed an extra joint halfway down the forearm to continue their exploration any further – without making it obvious to the whole company. As it was, both Percy and Netty were growing distinctly puzzled at the odd twitches and mystifying surges of intonation they were witnessing and hearing. Judith's hand found Fergal's, lifted it off her thigh, gave it a friendly clasp, and firmly returned it to his own space. Then she raised her napkin to her lips and dabbed them free of nothing in particular.

Honours even, she thought. The word 'dishonour?' – carrying its own little question mark – occurred to her, but her spirit rejected it. She could feel no taint of it in what they had just done.

As course followed course – entreé, fish, entremet, game – and the wine bottles emptied, the tension slowly but surely deserted them. If O'Leary-Egan had intended taking up the challenge Judith had so blatantly hurled in his teeth, he would surely have done it by now, they thought. The moment – the most nerve-racking of all – came when she and Henrietta had jointly cut the cake, for that of all moments would have symbolized the anniversary. And symbols and anniversaries were meat and drink to the likes of that man.

The handful of people around the table who knew of his existence, or rather of his double existence, had almost forgotten him by the time the ices and sorbets were brought down from the house. Whatever threat he might have posed in their mind had dwindled to vanishing.

Rick thanked McLysaght for his attentions to the fire and asked would he ever carry a shovelful of the embers down to the boathouse and light the boiler in the steam launch.

Justin O'Donovan rose and said he had a word or two to deliver while he could still get his feet under him – though Judith, who had kept an eye on him, had noticed that he refused every offer of a refill of his wineglass. He then gave a brief but amusing speech in praise of the 'two birthday girls'. The wine he sipped in the toast that concluded it had been in his glass from the beginning of the evening.

To everyone's surprise Aunt Bill then stood up and added the name of Tomás King to the toast – 'Without whose courage and quick thinking, neither girl would be here tonight to celebrate her birthday.' Looking at her frank blue eyes, listening to her clear, sincere voice, it was impossible to believe that, in fact, she loathed the man beyond all power of measurement. And King's two-sentence reply was incoherent with embarrassment. The servants were given small glasses of mock champagne – Sillery from soda syphons – and the whole company sang, 'For they are jolly good fellows.'

Only when it was over did Judith realize she had been sitting there all the time, smiling at the compliments, but with her hand in her purse and her finger on the trigger and her thumb toying with the safety catch.

Some part of her, it seemed, knew it was *not* yet over.

McLysaght had set several snares for rabbits in the tree plantation between the pavilion and Lough Cool. He was busy examining them when Justin O'Donovan came in search of him. Never for one moment did the Captain imagine that the youngsters would operate the lock and take the steam launch out on to Lough Cool. At last he found the old fellow, washing blood and fur off the toecap of his boot down by the shore of the lough. But the greeting died in his throat as he saw the launch heading out toward the Clare shore; it seemed to be floating in an unreal sort of space between earth and sky, for there was not a ripple on the water, apart from the bow and stern waves of the boat itself. Boyish guffaws and girlish shrieks of laughter carried faintly to them, attenuated by the warm, humid air.

'Damnation!' Justin muttered. 'The one thing! The *one* thing I overlooked!'

McLysaght, who had been watching the boat, too, spun round and saw him. 'Your honour!' he called out in greeting.

Justin waved and then turned and gave a low whistle. A nightjar – rather early – called from the woodland fringe nearby. He sauntered that way, kicking a stone. When he drew near he stooped, picked it up, and hurled it idly into the water. Then, standing with his back to the trees, he asked the empty air how long it had been watching the island.

The bush behind him replied: 'Since six o'clock this evening, sir.'

'No sign of life? No activity?'

'None at all, sir.'

It only partly satisfied him. He had searched the island himself that morning at eleven – and Turk Island, too, three or four miles to the south. Both had been devoid of human life though someone – picnickers, probably – had lit a fire recently on Turk Island. The gap between eleven and six was worrying, though. 'McLysaght!' He turned to the old fellow. 'Tell me about the boats in the boathouse up there on the lake. Is there one light enough for us to drag through the trees and launch down here?'

'Indade there are, your honour, sir. Three of them – or there were until yesterday. There was only two this evening, though.'

Justin ran for the boathouse, casting off his sword and cap as he went.

Out on the lough Rick, who had sunk the best part of two wine bottles at the banquet, was being dissuaded from stripping off to prove he could swim faster than the launch – 'Any distance!' he claimed belligerently. 'Any distance you like.'

'Sure he's North Keelity champion for the three-inch sprint,' Henrietta assured the others. 'Now would you ever sit down and stop rocking this boat. You're making *me* feel sick, let alone poor Gwinny. Just look at her and have some pity.'

Her chiding had the desired effect; he sat down and became calmer. Then he gave an ironic chuckle. 'Gwinny's always being sick. Every blessed day. It's normal for her.'

Henrietta looked at her sharply and raised an eyebrow.

'I'm afraid it's true,' she confirmed with a sigh. 'I think it's the Keelity water. It's quite different from the water we drink at Moonduff. I'll get used to it, I expect.'

'Have you seen a doctor?'

She shook her head. 'I don't really believe in doctors. Anyway, it doesn't last very long ever – and actually it's better this week than last.' She brightened. 'So perhaps I'm getting used to the water already!'

'Let's hope that's it,' Henrietta said.

Rick, now rather green about the gills himself, stumbled toward the door of the rather cramped cabin. 'I wish you hadn't started talking about being sick,' he muttered.

Outside, in what little fresh air there was that evening, he felt better. He noticed that they were coming up to the island. In fact, they were coming up very close to the island. He turned to Fergal at the helm and called out, 'Starboard your tiller, man, you'll run us aground.'

'It's all right,' Fergal assured him. 'I know the channel.' He brought the bow round several degrees nearer the island, which lay on their right.

'Channel?' Rick echoed. 'Are you making for the jetty? That's the only channel.'

'Never mind,' Fergal replied irritably. 'Don't pester.'

'But we don't wish to go ashore. We've only just come aboard.' He lumbered to the stern, intending to take over the tiller.

'Rick!' Judith said wearily. 'Just drop it. I'm terribly sorry and it's all very mortifying but I simply have to go ashore for a . . . for a brief while. You can steam a wide circle and come back in about ten minutes' time. All right? As I say, I'm very sorry.'

A moment later she leaped nimbly down on to the end of the crude stone jetty and gave the launch a push, heading her prow back toward the deeper water. 'Ten minutes!' she repeated as they glided off toward the lowering sun, a coal-black speck on the oily gold of the water.

She crossed the narrow girth of the island, skirting the pine grove and putting it between her and the boat; she squatted down where a rocky outcrop would shelter her from prying eyes on the shore – and tonight, she was quite certain, there must be at least a dozen of them within a mile of this spot.

The setting sun cast her shadow against the warm limestone of the upthrust slab that shielded her. Purpose accomplished, she adjusted her dress and squatted down again to pass the time by making shadow-creatures on the rock. The butterfly soon bored her. Then a rabbit emerged shyly from round the rough edge of the boulder, where pictures were impossible; he had a wicked eye. Next an ostrich darted and shied across the uneven planes of the stone; he turned into a . . . something – a serpent, perhaps. A serpent in Eden. He had the wickedest eye of all, a luxurious golden-ochre that turned nacreous where it fell on the silvered path of a snail.

The utter lack of breeze combined with the mellow light to give her the feeling of being indoors; the entire world had dwindled to one room. A vast room whose walls and ceiling were impossibly remote – but a room nonetheless, a home, a place where she felt at home.

Then a shadow, not of her making, obscured the serpent's eye. She knew it was Mick O'Leary even before she turned and saw him rising to a low crouch, there in the undergrowth between her and the pines.

For a long moment their eyes dwelled, each in the other's. 'I didn't think you would,' she said at last. As she spoke she rose and stood on tiptoe, gazing anxiously among the pine boles, hoping for a sight of the launch. But the rise in the land was too great. All she could see were some hilltops on the Clare shore, which had already half-devoured the great red ball of the setting sun.

'Nor did Miss Darcy.' He chuckled. 'You may rest aisy, colleen, it's not yourself I'm after.'

'This time.' Now her heart caught up with what was happening and began to pound like a hammermill.

'Nor last time either,' he replied. 'But for your own folly.' He brought his gun into view – a standard army rifle that had seen better days.

'Who *are* you after?' she asked, starting to edge diagonally away from him, toward the northern end of the island.

'Stay where I can see you. Stay there,' he snapped.

Her mind was racing. If she made a dash to the crest of the rise and cried out to the launch to stay away . . . no, that would only make them return in double-quick time. And in five minutes, they'd be back here anyway. Somehow, in the next five minutes, she had to get that gun off him. Then his words penetrated her thoughts. He wanted her to stay between him and the shore because they would not fire on him while she was in between. But they wouldn't from the shore anyway; it was much too far off.

Therefore . . .

Casually she turned and scanned that distant band of green. To her surprise she saw a rowing boat about a quarter of a mile offshore and making for them as fast as its two occupants could row. It must have been there, only a little farther away, when she first crouched down behind that rock. She hadn't noticed it because she hadn't expected to notice it.

The two rowers were an even greater surprise: Justin O'Donovan, unmistakable in his mess dress, even with the tunic opened and flapping free, and old McLysaght, equally unmistakable with his leonine mane, actor's soft hat, and noble rags. Both had their backs to the island, bending and straightening with furious gusto. They were just close enough now for her to hear the hammering of the oars in the rowlocks at the end of each pull.

'Stay away!' she shouted at them, jumping up and down to attract their attention. The skin of her back crawled in anticipation of the bullet she felt sure must follow.

O'Leary chuckled. 'That's my girl! He'll come to me now.'

She turned and stared 'Him! You're after him!'

'Indade I am,' he replied grimly. 'Hasn't he hunted down the four of us who outlived that night. Haven't I three deaths to avenge this day.'

'Captain O'Donovan?' she asked incredulously. 'Oh

man, man, man! If only you knew how wrong you are. He had no connection with the Bellinghams or Castle Moore or any of us . . . I mean he knew nothing of this until he met me at a ball in Dublin last spring.'

O'Leary said nothing to that. In his eyes was a mixture of contempt and pity.

Judith's desperation increased still further. She turned her little handbag over and over, feeling the pistol Justin had given her. Would she dare? It had been so easy in her daydreams, but would she dare? 'What will you *achieve*?' she asked. 'They'll get you anyway. That shore is alive with them.

'I'll get him first – the turkey in all his pride.'

'I won't let you,' she said.

He laughed. 'You haven't that choice, Miss Carty.'

'But I have, you see.' Suddenly the pistol was in her hands, pointing at him. She had caught him off guard, with the rifle on the ground while he eased himself into a better position for firing, lying rather than crouching.

He just stared at the weapon; his face betrayed no emotion whatever.

'I will use this,' she warned him.

'Kitty Rohane,' he murmured. 'Your oath to her.'

The words did not immediately register with Judith; she was still somewhat shocked at what she had done . . . was, indeed, doing, and promising to do. Then she grasped his meaning: he thought she would shoot him because she had sworn as much to Kitty Rohane.

Nothing else could have revealed to her how stark and barren a gulf divided the two of them. He inhabited a world where oaths could tower above flesh and blood, where blood itself was of no account – though all accounts were settled in blood.

And his words now reached out and dragged her down into it. She felt herself beginning to drown in the rising tide of his zealotry.

'You'd better do it so, colleen,' he told her. 'For I have an oath of my own to keep.'

She took her finger off the trigger and massaged the pistol until it lay in the palm of her hand. She let him see what she was doing, making each gesture plain. Then she tossed it lightly upon the ground before him, well within his reach. 'It must stop somewhere,' she said.

She turned her back on him and walked down the slope to the shore. Now the skin of her back no longer prickled with fear.

When she reached the water's edge she did not stop. The warm ooze, too warm to be thought of as water, filled her boots at once. The sodden hems of her ballgown and petticoats clung about her calves, making it feel as if she were wading through pondweed. By the time the lake rose above her knees she was soaked to the waist; the material billowed out again and fluttered, white through green, in her wake.

'Judith!'

The rowing boat was almost upon her now, steering off to her right to come about beside her.

'Judith? What is the matter? Are you unwell?'

Why did O'Leary not shoot? He had a good clear line, surely? She was no longer between him and his prize.

Then it was too late. The boat was alongside and Justin had his hands beneath her arms, trying to lift her in. 'Has something happened to you?' he asked in anguish. 'Is there someone on that island?'

She shook her head feebly, knowing that if she were too vehement, he would not believe her. 'Something I ate, I think. It must be. Oh, I have such a *pain* in here. Ow!' She collapsed in his grip. 'Take me home.'

'Appendix!' he exclaimed. 'Oh God, let it not be!' He leaped into the water and, lifting her up in his arms, raised her over the gunwhale while McLysaght deftly whipped the brass rowlock out of her way.

She – having taken an earlier hint from his question: 'Are you unwell?' – now took a second from his suggestion about appendicitis and groaned horribly at every forced movement of her midriff.

The launch drew near at that moment. The mass of the island had prevented Fergal from spotting the rowing boat until after he started the return leg of the promised great circle. Now they were all crowding the forward deck, the roof of the cabin. They were laughing – until they saw Judith in the water; then the laughter turned to anxious shouts, demanding to know what was wrong.

Justin wriggled aboard the rowing boat and, lifting Judith in his arms again, raised her level with the deck of the launch. 'Careful!' he cried as half a dozen pairs of hands claimed her. 'She has a bad stomachache – something she ate, she says.'

Groaning and shivering, Judith let them lift her securely on to the deck. 'Not below,' she murmured faintly, looking up and finding Fergal's eyes, inches from hers. 'Let me just lie here where I can stretch.'

She meant where she could keep an eye on Justin and McLysaght.

And well for her that she did, too, for she saw him kneeling irresolutely in the rowing boat, staring at the island.

'Justin?' she murmured feebly.

He turned to her.

'Come back with me?'

'But . . .' He gestured vaguely at the island.

'No,' she said simply. 'Please come back with me.'

His eyes narrowed. He stood up on the rowing seat and, clutching one of the launch's low brass rails in his left hand, reached the other toward her belly. He pressed hard where a doctor would test for an appendicitis. 'Does that hurt?' he asked sharply.

She considered lying and then thought better of it. 'No,' she said.

He glanced back at the island.

'No,' she repeated.

He drew a deep breath and held it. His gaze flickered rapidly from her to the island and back again, never resting. She could only guess at what titanic struggle was going on behind those eyes.

'Very well,' he said at last. Turning to McLysaght he said, 'Can you row this boat back on your own?'

'Sure I'll drive it with my sighs if I can't, your honour,' he replied.

Fergal and Rick helped haul Justin aboard. The three of them stood over Judith, each unwilling to leave her with the other two. Percy, now at the tiller, opened the steam valve and the deck began to throb beneath her. She solved the men's dilemma by patting the deck at her side and saying, 'Justin?'

He sat where she indicated; the two younger men went to coax a little more steam out of the boiler.

'Does it hurt?' Justin asked sarcastically.

She smiled weakly up at him. 'I was going to ask the same of you.'

He lifted his eyes and stared back toward the island. Then he, too, smiled. 'Funnily enough . . . no. Or not as much as I thought.'

She fished with her hand until she found his. Giving it a happy squeeze, she said, 'That's a good start.'

ENVOI

APES IN HELL

27 August 1928

'Stop here, darling,' Judith said. 'Let's get out and walk the rest of the way.'

He pulled in to the side of the road, just before the main gate. 'Getting cold feet already?' he asked.

She nodded and gave a small, rueful smile.

'Bit late to call if off,' he pointed out.

'Oh, I don't want to call it off. But' – she shrugged – 'all those years when we could have stayed in touch. You know.'

'I know.' He put his hand on her thigh and squeezed.

'And there's no real reason why we didn't. That's what's so . . .'

'I know.'

'Stop saying you know like that.'

He patted her thigh and then reached on the back seat for his cap. 'It'll be all right, darling.' He got out of the car and went round to open her door.

'Have you got the photographs?' she asked as she stepped out.

'They're in your handbag.' He pulled his sleeves straight – a nervous tic with him – and stood awhile staring down the lane toward the lake. 'Coolnahinch,' he murmured.

She opened her bag to check yet again that the photographs were there – a nervous tic with her. Then catching sight of herself in the mirror inside the flap, she said, 'I put on too much lipstick. Why didn't you tell me?'

He went on looking at the lake while she sat half in the car, feet on the road, and worked away with tissue paper, dividing her attention between the mirror and him.

He said nothing. She wondered what he was really thinking – whether he was truly as calm about this reunion as he seemed.

'You can just see the island,' he said as they made for the front gate.

'That was a Monday, too,' she replied. 'Lord, would you look at that! There's a shock!'

They stopped at the gateway and stared in silence at the now derelict lodge. 'I know I'm going to cry when I see Castle Moore,' she murmured.

They started up the drive. 'That's why I haven't ever wanted to come back,' she went on. 'Quite apart from what happened to the Old Glebe.'

They had to pick their way around puddles and potholes. She took his arm. 'D'you remember?' she asked. 'There used always to be two men out here with rakes? No departing visitor ever saw the marks of their arrival. It would break their hearts to see it now.'

'D'you think so? I don't suppose they care one way or the other. Look how they all swore that Tomás King was the greatest man since Brian Boru. Half the county came to his funeral – and a week later you wouldn't hear a good word said of him. Especially not from that mousey little wife of his.'

She shivered theatrically. 'Don't talk about any of those things – especially with Rick. That's what I'm nervous about, you see – I don't know how he feels about . . . all that. We never talked about it after I married you. And now . . . I don't know how he feels about anything.'

'You read all his novels – for which, let me say, you have earned my undying admiration. That's all he'll care about.'

'They don't tell you anything.'

He laughed. 'Say that to him!'

'I mean about how he feels. I still wonder if King really did drown accidentally. I'll bet Rick knows, too.'

From the way he drew breath to speak she knew he was going to run for cover, so she quickly added, 'And don't just say it's what the coroner concluded!'

'Why bring all that up now?' he asked instead. 'We couldn't be sure at the time, so what hope have we now?'

'Well . . .' She made three awkward skips round a large puddle. 'Coming back here – it brings it all back, doesn't it? I almost expect old McLysaght to spring out at us. He must be dead these many years.' She peered into the now impenetrable woodland on either side of the drive. 'God knows there's concealment enough for an army there. Aunt Bill never satisfactorily accounted for those three "missing" hours did she? The night King drowned.'

'Nor did Henrietta. Nor Mrs King. Nor the gallant . . .'

'Exactly! And look how Aunt Bill condoned everything she did with Percy O'Farrelly after that night. Buying her silence – that's what that was!' She grasped his arm and shook it hard. 'Don't say any of this to Rick. Don't even hint at it.'

He laughed at her intensity. 'I hadn't the faintest intention of doing any such thing.'

But she was not reassured. 'I wish I knew what *is* going to happen. I wish it was over and done with, actually. I wish we were on our way to Limerick *now*.'

The driveway had improved to the point where they could walk easily, side by side again. He took her arm and said, 'I'll tell you what's going to happen: nothing! Absolutely nothing. We're all going to look at each other and pretend not to be shocked at what we see. We're going to say how sad it is to see the castle like that – and thank God they saved the old tower at least. We're going to have tea and cake and then wipe our fingers and show them our photographs – and, God help us, be shown theirs! And we're going to talk mostly about Damien and Celia and Crispin and . . . whatever their children are called . . .'

Judith chuckled. 'Well, they're all called Bellingham – we know *that*!'

He gave her arm a little shake. 'Now you're not to pry. It's their affair and nobody else's.'

'Go on!' She dug him lightly with her elbow. 'You're still as curious as me to know which are Letty's and which are Gwinny's. Especially after the care Rick took to conceal it all. I hope he does show us their photos because his face will give him away. If Gwinny shows them we shan't learn a thing. You try and distract her if she starts.'

After a few paces in silence he said, 'I never really knew whether you liked her or not.'

She stopped and stared at him in surprise. 'But I adored her! She made it possible to break with Rick without any . . . you know.'

'Regrets?'

'Oh no. Of course there were regrets. But without any rancour.'

They walked on. After a pause she said, 'Gwinny was so clever. From the moment she met Rick she decided to capture him. But look how she went about it! I'll bet, when it came to it, *she* proposed to him. And I'll bet she said it was just a matter of convenience – a sop to the scandalmongers. I wonder what he'd have been if she hadn't taken him under her wing? Oh!'

She stopped abruptly and lowered her head.

'What?' he asked, concerned.

'I just caught a glimpse of the house. I don't want to see it bit by bit. Take my hand and tell me when we're under the two big trees before the carriage sweep. Are they still there?'

A moment later he told her they were, indeed, still there. 'And there are goats all over the front lawn,' he added. 'If you can still call it a lawn.'

'What is it about certain kinds of upper-crust women and goats?' she asked.

When they reached the trees he said, 'Now!'

She raised her head, opened her eyes, and exclaimed 'Oh!' in a tone of pleasant surprise.

Just for a moment it was possible to believe that the house had emerged from 'the troubles' unscathed. From this precise position the ridge of Mount Argus ran exactly where the missing roofline would have been – a fact that, of course, had been apparent to no one before the roof fell in. As a result, the general shape of the house against the sky was that of an intact dwelling. Also the thick cladding of ivy and mile-a-minute provided a startling continuity between the Castle Moore she still treasured in her mind's eye and the house now before them. 'Well, it's not nearly as bad as I thought,' she said, taking the first eager step since they had got out of the car. 'Let's go and look inside before we let them know we're here.'

She skipped two paces and then turned to him with a laugh. 'Mama always told me I'd be mistress of that house one day. What would she think if she could see it now!'

'*Sic transit gloria mundi*,' he suggested.

She laughed again and said, 'I was gloriously sick in the train last Monday – that's what my father always said it meant.'

Now that the house loomed larger, blotting out the ridge of the mountain, the roofless walls were starkly obvious and some of her light humour deserted her. 'Think of all the nights Hen and I slept together in that room there!' she said. 'All those whisperings and secrets!

And all the whisperings and secrets in all the other rooms, too! Where have they all gone? What purpose did they all serve?' She took a hesitant stride up the front steps. 'D'you think it's safe.'

He cleared his throat. 'Depends what you mean, old girl.' He went past her and peered in through the now doorless entrance. 'The old hall is safe enough,' he said. 'There's nothing left to fall.'

They went inside, picking their way over the rubble of brick, stone, rotting timber, and broken slates. She peeped into the ballroom, made dark by the brambles and ivy that choked the unglazed windows.

'I wouldn't risk that,' he said.

'D'you remember the night Hen burst into tears, doing that charade? Were you here that evening?'

'We called them dumb crambos then.'

'Don't talk about Rick's latest novel!' she said suddenly.

He laughed. 'I have no intention of talking about *any* of Rick's novels. Quite apart from any other consideration, I've never been able to finish a single one of them! Why d'you say that suddenly?'

'Oh, because of Hen breaking down like that. He used it in *Apes in Hell*. What a silly title!'

'Is that the one which begins with a young man meeting two chorus girls on top of a bus – and they hand him a card?'

'Yes. And it gets even more unreal from then on.'

'Oh, I don't know.' He cleared his throat. 'I actually thought that one was quite good. Bits of it.'

'Yes, and we all know which bits! Just don't talk about it, that's all.'

'Come on.' He took her arm and plucked her back toward the entrance. 'We ought to go and make ourselves known. This is very rude.'

When they emerged on to the front steps again they

saw a portly, bearded, balding gentleman walking toward them with a bit of a stoop, beaming broadly. 'Here at last!' he cried. 'Many happy returns of the day that's in it!'

'Rick?' she replied – not meaning to put quite so much of a question into her tone.

'I know!' He burst into laughter. 'But I'd have recognized you anywhere, Ju.' He paused briefly and raised both hands, as if he had just unveiled her as an exhibit. 'Same figure. Same face. Same complexion even! How do you manage it!' He kissed her on both cheeks; she recognized his ears at least.

'And you, Fergal!' he went on, giving him a hearty handshake. 'You've hardly changed, either.' He took a pace back and stared at them quizzically. 'This is most suspicious. Are you devotees of Monsieur Coué? Or is it a daily injection of monkey glands? Or I have it! There's a Dorian Gray sort of portrait festering away in your attic. Come and meet Gwinny and Letty – they're in such a state over the prospect of seeing you again!'

Judith took his arm as they walked back round the ruined house, across what had once been the terrace, to the old castle keep. 'I adored your latest,' she said. '*Apes in Hell*. What a wonderful title!'

A waft of the hand invoiced the compliment onward. 'Old McLysaght, of course – who else! *The Taming of the Shrew* – your favourite play, he once said, if you recall. He's still alive, you know?'

'No! Heavens, he must be nearly a hundred.'

'Ninety-two. He's in a home in Parsonstown now. Or Birr, as we must call it. Still making trouble.'

She laughed. 'Why d'you say that?'

'Oh, he was a dreadful trouble-maker, Ju. Always hinting at dark deeds done by others. He's just the same now. He's in there with five old ladies and he has them at each other's throats any time he likes. Letty has to go in and read the riot act when it gets too bad. He's frightened of her.' He laughed and squeezed her arm. 'Oh, it's just like old times, isn't it? Why did we lose touch? Just bloody laziness, wasn't it? When you first went overseas.' He linked his other arm in Fergal's. 'And you, you rotter – I blame you as much as I blame myself.'

Fergal laughed awkwardly. 'We're all to blame, I'm sure. What for?'

'Oh, for going away to Paris, and Locarno, and Geneva, and generally being so *useful* to the world. I've often wondered what it must be like to be useful to the world.'

'Judith! And Fergal!' A lean, bronzed woman with fine-wrinkled skin and lively eyes – immediately recognizable as Gwinny – came sweeping out from the keep, arms aloft in benediction. Vague, silky, billowy, chiffony material trailed on the air behind her. 'Isn't it marvellous you've found us while we're still compos mentis!'

They hugged and kissed.

'I was just saying to Rick – thirty years! But it's as if it had never been.'

Letty emerged at that moment, bearing a token teapot; behind her two maids carried lavish trays of sandwiches and cakes. Their greetings and surprise were renewed yet again.

'I thought we'd eat in the little courtyard,' Letty said. 'It's cooler there. You're looking very summery. Where's your car? Didn't want to shame us, eh?'

Fergal started to explain but Judith cut him short. 'Quite right, Letty. You're as perceptive as ever.'

'The Bishop of Down has preached a sermon against *Apes in Hell*,' Rick announced. 'I feel like a real writer at last.'

'Yes, dear,' Gwinny said and, taking Judith delicately by the arm, led her round to the courtyard. 'Actually,' she said archly, 'it hasn't been thirty years in my case. I saw you in Grafton Street about five years ago. I recognized you at once. You were coming out of Bewley's.'

'Oh, but why didn't you speak to me?'

'Well . . .' She gave an embarrassed little laugh. 'You were with Sally, actually. So I didn't . . . you know.' She leaned forward and asked Fergal, 'How is your sister these days, by the way?'

'She's still with the medical missionaries out in Bombay,' he told her. 'That must have been the last time she was home – though she claims India's her real home now.'

'Good,' Gwinny said vaguely. 'And talking of which – little Netty O'Farrelly, Percy's sister – remember her? She's mother superior at the convent school in Athlone now. Fat as a barrel. Worse than this fellow!' She turned swiftly and pulled a punch on Rick's stomach.

'Who put it there?' he asked, staring at his paunch in an aggrieved fashion. 'Every ounce!'

They had arrived in the little courtyard, where tea was set on elegant but faded wrought-iron garden furniture, rescued from the big house and looking very recently cleaned.

'Stand not upon the order of your sitting . . .' Letty wafted them generally toward the chairs.

'Actually,' Gwinny said as they took their places, 'one woman goes off to be a medical missionary, another becomes a nun . . .' She turned to Rick. 'There's a novel in that.'

'It'd be banned,' he warned. 'I hope. How dare they ban Joyce and Shaw and even Sean and not *me*!'

They sat and talked, and ate the most delicious cake, and. drank lapsang souchong. Then they went over the old castle and admired every room – some quite wholeheartedly – and looked at each other's photographs, and went back to the courtyard, and sipped sherry, and laughed . . . until the sun was well down in the afternoon sky. Then Fergal glanced at his watch and said they must be thinking of pushing onward.

'There's just one more thing I have to do,' Judith said. 'D'you mind? We have time surely. I just want to go down to the lake and look at the summer pavilion.'

'It's a ruin, too,' Rick warned. 'The pillars are there but the roof's fallen in.'

'I don't want to go across to it. Just to look *at* it. D'you mind?' she asked Fergal again.

'Of course not. I'll go and get the car and bring it up here – now we know the drive is just about drivable!'

'I'll go with you, Ju,' Rick said as she set off. He did not ask either Gwinny or Letty if they minded.

'Isn't it odd?' Judith said as they walked back across the old terrace. 'I had no idea how this meeting was going to turn out, and yet each minute, as it's unfolded, I've said to myself, "Yes, of course, I should have guessed he'd say that . . . or do that." You actually haven't changed all that much, Rick.'

He put a rueful hand to his midriff.

'Oh, I'm not talking about trivial things like that. For example, I was saying to Fergal on the way up the drive that I wondered if you'd admit that some of your offspring are by Letty and some by Gwinny.' She laughed. 'I should have known.'

'I've never made any secret of it.'

She decided it wasn't worth arguing, though it was a barefaced lie. 'As I say – I should have known,' she repeated.

'We spun a coin to see which of them I'd officially marry,' he added. 'Don't ever tell them I told you that.'

'Which of them would be more hurt?'

He laughed and scratched his head. 'I couldn't honestly say.'

She put a finger to the tip of his nose and pushed gently. 'As Gwinny would say – there's a novel in *that*!'

His head was framed by the ruined house, which caught her attention for the moment. 'Which side did it?' she asked, nodding at the old place.

'Sinn Fein,' he replied without turning round. 'But only because they got to it first. They fired the Old Glebe, too, didn't they?'

'No, that was Papa's partner, that wretched little man called Noakes. We only discovered about it last year, though. Don't tell anyone about that, either – it'll only complicate the insurance.'

'Careful,' he warned. 'The brick path has gone here. It's easier to walk on the grass.'

'The goats keep it nice and short, I must say.'

'The best gardeners we ever had!'

'D'you miss it, Rick?' she asked. 'I mean the way it was in the old days?'

'I've missed *you*, Ju. You've often been in my thoughts.'

'No, be serious.'

'Funnily enough, I was being. Do I miss the old Castle Moore?' He paused briefly and stared back at the place. 'I find it hard to remember a time when it wasn't like that, you know. I mean, after the estate was broken up by the Land Commission, there was no point in it. I moved out in the 'nineties.'

'The Naughty 'Nineties.'

He chuckled and scratched his bald scalp. 'They were! They were! Then the big house stood empty until the war, when we let them use it as a convalescent home. And then – pfft! *Voilà*!' He waved a hand at it. 'I remember childhood things much more than later years. D'you see that tree over there, beyond the goat with the black patch? When that was just a sapling I chased you round and round it, remember? It was your tenth birthday party. Yours and Hen's. Good heavens! That must be . . .' He looked uncertainly at her.

She put him out of his dilemma. 'Fifty-two years ago today. I don't mind your saying it. I minded much more at forty!'

He stared again at the tree. 'Fifty-two years ago today I chased you round and round that sapling. You were so *pink*! And when I caught you, I had no idea what to do next – because I never for one moment thought I'd succeed.'

'You wouldn't have,' she assured him, 'if I hadn't let you. You kissed me – that's what you did.'

'I know. I couldn't think of anything else to do. That was the day I fell in love with you.'

He went on staring at the tree.

She touched his arm. 'Come on. We have to motor on to Limerick tonight.'

They walked side by side now, a little apart. 'Did you ever have any regrets about marrying Fergal instead of me?' he asked.

'Never for one millionth part of a second,' she told him.

'Ah.'

A brief silence followed, then she said, 'If we're both allowed to ask embarrassingly frank questions, Rick, can I have one?'

He beamed at her until she said, 'How do you *manage*? You, *and* Gwinny, *and* Letty? You know? D'you kiss one of them goodnight on the landing or what?' She laughed suddenly. 'Perhaps you spin a coin for that, too?'

'Oh . . .' He made a disappointed face. 'Well, you saw the bed in Letty's room.'

'Yes. But it didn't look terribly *used*.'

'There you are then. Anything more you want to know?'

'Oh! Now I've offended you.'

He smiled again. 'Not really. It's just that I thought

you'd want to know . . . well, something a bit more personal than that.'

She burst out laughing. 'And that's not what you call personal!'

'Not to you and me, it isn't. Anything more?'

'Yes.' She drew a deep breath. 'I might as well go for the double. Did Aunt Bill have anything to do with King's death?'

'Of course she did,' he said crossly, disappointed again. 'She stunned him and pushed him under. In the pool on Mount Argus there.' He turned round and pointed eastward. 'She and Hen together. And Francy Robertson opened the old watercourse and . . . well, the millwheel did the rest. Poetic justice, really.'

She stared at him in amazement. 'I can't believe you're as blasé about it as all that.'

They had reached the lakeshore. They stood and stared across the weed-infested water at the tumbled marble ruin. 'I wouldn't call it blasé, Ju,' he said. 'Remember, I've lived with the knowledge for forty years.' A thought struck him. '*Exactly* forty years – because it was the same night we all went out on the lake and you got appendicitis. Oh!' He hit his forehead in vexation. 'Thank God you reminded me – I'd have forgotten otherwise.' He grinned and fished something out of his pocket, wrapped in a creased silk handkerchief. 'Birthday present for you.'

Smiling in bewilderment she unwrapped it cautiously. What seemed at first to be no more than a collection of rust resolved itself into an old pistol, or what had once been a pistol.

'I found it on the island out there last summer,' he said. 'We went for a picnic and I found it.'

'How d'you know it's mine?'

'Isn't it?'

'Of course it is. But how did *you* know?'

'Justin told me he gave you one, years later. Pretty amazing find, what?'

'More than you know, Rick.' She swallowed heavily. 'I think this is the precise spot where he gave it to me that evening. He, too, pretended it was a birthday present.'

'He covered up wonderfully for Aunt Bill and Hen, you know. That's why absolutely nothing came out.' He gave a strange laugh.

'What now?' she asked, weighing the pistol, wondering for the second time in her life what to do with it. Was it still loaded? Did old bullets become unstable? She began to feel decidedly uneasy.

'Did you know he and Aunt Bill knew each other when they were children – in Connemara?'

'No!' The news intrigued her. New possibilities flashed through her mind. 'Does that mean . . . I wonder did she introduce him to me deliberately? She knew I started keeping things back from her – because everything I discovered she just used as ammunition against King, even things that couldn't possibly be laid at his door. D'you think she used him as a kind of trojan horse?'

Rick chuckled. 'If I ever use it in a novel . . .'

'You will, Rick, you will!'

'Thank you, Ju.' He smiled sourly. '*If*, I say, I ever used it in a novel, that's what I'd make happen. But, in fact, she didn't admit she knew he was *that* Justin O'Donovan until several years after King died. She could easily pretend, because she never knew him as Justin, you see. They always called him Rusty as a child, because of the way he pronounced it first.'

Judith, who had meanwhile been doing her arithmetic, said, 'But even so, they can't have been very close. There must have been all of ten years between them – which is a lot when one is six and the other sixteen.'

He shook his head. 'When she turned sixteen, he was nearly twelve. He tried to deceive me about it once, but I worked it out when I read his obit.'

'Ah. So each knew who the other was but neither of them admitted it! Oh, come on, Rick, do tell me! This is much more interesting than the way you'd put it in your novel.'

He grinned wickedly. 'I'm not sure I could use the actual truth in a novel – not *my* sort of novel, anyway. That really *would* get banned!'

Judith pretended to tear out her hair. 'I'll scream if you don't tell me. Was there something going on between them then?'

He shook his head. 'Deeper and darker than that, even. In fact, I'm not sure it's fit for your ears at all.'

'Rick, I really *will* scream.' Her eyes flashed fire at him.

'Very well.' He sighed and dipped one shoulder. 'Remember, you did force me to tell you. Apparently Aunt Bill was something of a tomboy in her childhood.'

'That's no secret! You could tell that just from the way she could row a boat.'

He held up a finger for silence. 'All her companions were boys. They were a gang and she was their leader. She used to write plays for them to perform, and they collected money for worthy causes.'

'A very literary sort of gang!'

'Not a bit. The plays were all extremely violent. Real *Grand Guignol* stuff – corpses exhumed at midnight, people having their hearts cut out, felons being flogged at the tail of a cart, Quasimodo in the pillory. Oh, a fierce lot of flogging altogether. And Aunt Bill was the one who gave it out and young Rusty O'Donovan was almost always the victim. She laughed her head off about it when it all came out into the open at last, but he *hated* it. Turned red as a boiled beetroot and became absolutely incoherent with embarrassment.' Some of Rick's humour deserted him and his tone developed a sad fall. 'I think that's why he never married, you know.'

She closed her eyes and shook her head. 'Poor Justin!' she murmured.

'Aunt Bill never realized what she'd done, of course. She went to her grave thinking it the greatest joke ever.' He smiled wanly at her. 'Even poorer Aunt Bill, perhaps? To live and die without ever understanding the richness and complexity of human love – in all its aspects.'

Judith didn't wish to think about it any further. She looked down at the pistol. The rusty pistol. Rusty's pistol! She weighed it in her open palm and then held it up before him. 'Can I do anything I like with it?' she asked.

'Of course. It is a present. I'm not pretending.'

She held it at arm's length and whirled round twice, letting it go on the second turn.

It curved in a dull red arc against the birthday sky and fell far out into the lake. The ripples began to widen.

'Excalibur!' he said.

She went on staring at the ripples, which were soon choked off in the reeds. 'Dear God,' she murmured, 'I hope not!'